W9-ACK-837

Romantic Times
hails two of the best-loved novels of *New York Times*
bestselling author

JULIE GARWOOD

GUARDIAN ANGEL
is

"A treasure. . . . A tempting, delectable read."

THE GIFT
is

"Rich in emotion. . . . You'll cherish this book."

The critics adore Julie Garwood!

"Julie Garwood has become a trusted brand name in romantic fiction."

—*People*

"Julie Garwood's stories happen in a different world, and she makes that world palpable."

—*The Kansas City Star*

"The power of Garwood's storytelling will enthrall and enchant you."

—*Rendezvous*

BOOKS BY JULIE GARWOOD

Gentle Warrior
Rebellious Desire
Honor's Splendour
The Lion's Lady
The Bride
Guardian Angel
The Gift
The Prize
The Secret
Castles
Saving Grace
Prince Charming
For the Roses
The Wedding
Come the Spring
Ransom
Heartbreaker
Mercy

The Clayborn Brides
One Pink Rose
One White Rose
One Red Rose

PUBLISHED BY POCKET BOOKS

JULIE GARWOOD

GUARDIAN ANGEL

THE GIFT

POCKET BOOKS

New York   London   Toronto   Sydney

The sale of this book without its cover is unauthorized. If you purchased this book without a cover, you should be aware that it was reported to the publisher as "unsold and destroyed." Neither the author nor the publisher has received payment for the sale of this "stripped book."

 POCKET BOOKS, a division of Simon & Schuster, Inc.
1230 Avenue of the Americas, New York, NY 10020

This book is a work of fiction. Names, characters, places and incidents are products of the author's imagination or are used fictitiously. Any resemblance to actual events or locales or persons living or dead is entirely coincidental.

Guardian Angel copyright © 1990 by Julie Garwood
The Gift copyright © 1991 by Julie Garwood

All rights reserved, including the right to reproduce this book or portions thereof in any form whatsoever. For information address Pocket Books, 1230 Avenue of the Americas, New York, NY 10020

ISBN: 1-4165-0736-1

This Pocket Books trade paperback edition January 2005

10 9 8 7 6 5 4 3 2

POCKET and colophon are registered trademarks of Simon & Schuster, Inc.

For information regarding special discounts for bulk purchases, please contact Simon & Schuster Special Sales at 1-800-456-6798 or business@simonandschuster.com.

These titles were previously published individually by Pocket Books.

Manufactured in the United States of America

Guardian Angel

This one's for you, Elizabeth.

Chapter One

London, 1815

The hunter waited patiently for his prey.

It was a dangerous deception the Marquess of Cainewood was playing. The infamous Pagan of Shallow's Wharf would certainly hear of his impersonator; he'd be forced out of hiding then, for his pride, monstrous by all whispered accounts, wouldn't allow another to take credit for his own black deeds. The pirate would certainly try to extract his own form of revenge. Caine was counting on that possibility. Once Pagan showed himself, Caine would have him.

And then the legend would be destroyed.

The Marquess had run out of choices. The spider wouldn't leave his web. Bounty hadn't worked. No, there wasn't a Judas among the seamen, which was surprising given that most ordinary men would have sold their mamas into bondage for the amount of gold he'd offered. It was a miscalculation on Caine's part, too. Each seaman voiced loyalty to the legend as his own personal reason for refusing the coins. Caine, a cynic by nature and past sour experiences, guessed fear was the real motive. Fear and superstition.

Mystery surrounded the pirate like the wall of a confessional. No one had ever actually seen Pagan. His ship, the *Emerald,* had been observed countless times skimming the water like a pebble thrown by the hand of God, or so it was reported by those who'd boasted of seeing the ship. The sight of the black beauty sparked terror in the titled gentlemen of the *ton* with fat purses, snickers of glee from the downright mean-hearted, and prayers of humble thanksgiving from the deprived, for Pagan was known to share his booty with the less fortunate.

Yet as often as the magical ship was sighted, no one could describe a single shipmate on board the vessel. This only increased the speculation, admiration, and awe about the phantom pirate.

Pagan's thievery extended beyond the ocean, however, for he was a man who obviously enjoyed variety. His land raids caused just as much consternation, perhaps even more. Pagan was discriminate in robbing only from the members of the *ton.* It was apparent the pirate didn't want anyone else taking credit for his own midnight raids on the unsuspecting. He therefore left his own personal calling card in the form of a single long-stemmed white rose. His victim usually awakened by morning light to find the flower on the pillow beside him. The mere sight of the rose was usually quite enough to send grown men into a dead faint.

Needless to say, the poor idolized the legend. They believed Pagan was a man of style and romance. The church was no less effusive in their adoration, for the pirate left trunks of gold and jewels next to the collection plates in their vestibules, topped by a white rose, of course, so the leaders would know whose soul they were supposed to pray for. The bishop was hard put to condemn the pirate. He knew better than to saint him, though, for to do so would incur the wrath of some of the most influential members of society, and therefore settled on calling Pagan rogue instead.

The nickname, it was noted, was always said with a quick grin and a slow wink.

The War Department held no such reservations. They'd set their own bounty on the pirate's head. Caine had doubled that amount. His reason for hunting down the bastard was a personal one, and he believed the end would justify whatever foul means he employed.

It was going to be an eye for an eye. He would kill the pirate.

Ironically, the two adversaries were equally matched. The Marquess was feared by ordinary men. His work for his government had earned him his own dark legend. If the circumstances had been different, if Pagan hadn't dared to prod Caine's wrath, he might have continued to leave him alone. Pagan's mortal sin changed that determination, however; changed it with a vengeance.

Night after night Caine went to the tavern called the Ne'er Do Well, situated in the heart of London's slums. The tavern was frequented by the more seasoned dock workers. Caine always took the corner table, his broad back protected by the stone wall from sneak attack, and patiently waited for Pagan to come to him.

The Marquess moved in and out of such seedy circles with the ease befitting a man with a dark past. In this section of the city, a man's title meant nothing. His survival was dependent upon his size, his ability to inflict pain while defending himself, and his indifference to the violence and crudity surrounding him.

Caine made the tavern his home in less than one night. He was a big man, with muscular shoulders and thighs. His size alone could intimidate most would-be challengers. Caine was dark haired, bronze skinned, and had eyes the color of a dark gray sky. There'd been a time when those eyes had had the power to spark a rush of flutters in the ladies of the *ton*. Now, however, those same ladies recoiled from the coldness lurking there, and the flat, emotionless expression. They whispered that the Marquess of Cainewood had been turned into stone by his hatred. Caine agreed.

Once he'd decided to play the role of Pagan, his pretense hadn't been difficult to maintain. The storytellers all agreed on the fanciful notion that Pagan was actually a titled gentleman who took to pirating as a means of keeping up with his lavish lifestyle. Caine simply used that bit of gossip to his advantage. When he first entered the tavern, he'd worn his most expensive clothing. He'd added his own personal touch by pinning a small white rose to the lapel of his dinner jacket. It was an outrageous, silently boastful addition, of course, and gained him just the right amount of notice.

Immediately, he'd had to cut a few men with his sharp knife to secure his place in their group. Caine was dressed like a gentleman, yes, but he fought without honor or dignity. The men loved him. In bare minutes, he'd earned their respect and their fear. His Herculean size and strength gained him immediate loyalty, too. One of the more fearless asked him in a stammer if the talk was true. Was he Pagan then? Caine didn't answer that question, but his quick grin told the seaman his question had pleased him. And when he remarked to the tavernkeeper that the seaman had a very cunning mind, he forced the inevitable conclusion. By week's end, the rumor of Pagan's nightly visitations to the Ne'er Do Well had spread like free gin.

Monk, the bald-headed Irishman who'd won the tavern in a crooked game of cards, usually sat beside Caine at the close of each evening. Monk was the only one who knew about the deception. He was in wholehearted agreement with Caine's plan, too, as he'd heard all about Pagan's atrocity to Caine's family. Just as significant, business had picked up considerably since the deception had begun. Everyone, it seemed, wanted to get a good look at the pirate, and Monk, a man who put profit above all other matters, charged exorbitant prices for his watered-down ale.

The tavernkeeper had lost his hair years before, but his bright orange-colored eyebrows more than made up for any lack. They were thick, curly, and crept like determined vines of ivy halfway up his freckled forehead. Monk rubbed his brow now in true frustration for the Marquess. It was almost three o'clock in the morning, an hour past time to shut down the tavern for the evening. Only two paying customers were lingering over their drinks now. When they'd belched out their sleepy farewells and taken their leave, Monk turned to Caine.

"You've got more patience than a flea waiting on a mangy dog, coming here night after night. I'm praying you don't get too discouraged," he added. He paused to pour a full goblet of brandy for the Marquess, then swallowed a hefty portion directly from the bottle. "You'll flush him out, Caine. I'm sure of it. The way I see it, he'll send a couple of his men first to try to waylay you. That's why I'm always warning you to protect your back when you leave each night."

Monk took another drink, and snickered. "Pagan's a mite protective of his reputation. Your pretense must be turning his hair gray. He'll show himself soon enough. Why, I'll wager that tomorrow will be the night."

Caine nodded agreement. Monk, his gaze piercing with promise, always ended his nightly speech with the prediction that tomorrow the prey would show himself.

"You'll pounce on him then, Caine, like a duck on a bug."

Caine swallowed a long drink, his first of the evening, then tilted his chair back so he could rest his shoulders against the wall. "I'll get him."

The harshness in Caine's tone sent a shiver down Monk's spine. He was about to give hasty agreement when the door suddenly flew open, drawing his attention. Monk half turned in his chair to call out that the tavern was closed for the night, but the sight standing in the center of the doorway so stunned him, he could only gape in astonishment. When he was finally able to regain his voice, he whispered, "Holy Mother of God, has an angel come calling on us?"

From his position against the wall, Caine faced the entrance and had a clear view. Though he didn't move or show any outward reaction, in truth, his surprise was just as great as Monk's. His heart started slamming a wild beat and he couldn't seem to catch his breath.

She did look like an angel. Caine didn't want to blink, certain his vision would vanish into the night if he closed his eyes for just a second or two.

She was an incredibly beautiful woman. Her eyes captivated him. They were the most magnificent shade of green. The green of his valley, he thought to himself, on a clear, moonlit night.

She was staring at him. Caine stared back.

Several long minutes passed while they studied each other. Then she started walking toward him. As soon as she moved, the hood of her black cape fell to her shoulders. Caine quit breathing. The muscles in his chest constricted painfully. His vision was blessed with lush, auburn-colored hair. In the candlelight, the color was as brilliant as fire.

Caine noticed the pitiful condition of her clothing when she neared the table. The quality of her cloak indicated wealth, yet the expensive material had been shredded halfway up one side. It looked as though someone had taken a knife to it. Part of the green satin lining hung in tatters around her hem. Caine's curiosity intensified. He looked back up at her face, saw the faint bruises on her right cheekbone, the small cut below her full lower lip, and the splotch of dirt marring her forehead.

If his vision was an angel, she'd just been forced to pay purgatory a visit, Caine decided. Yet even though she looked like she'd just lost the battle with Satan, she was still very appealing, too appealing in fact for his peace of mind. He grew tense as he waited for her to speak.

She stopped when she reached the other side of the round table. Her gaze was now directed on the rose pinned to his lapel.

His angel was obviously frightened. Her hands were shaking. She clutched a small white bag to her bodice and he noticed several faded scars on her fingers.

He didn't know what to make of her. Caine didn't want her to be afraid of him, though. That admission made his frown intensify.

"You're all alone?" he asked, his tone as brisk as the rising wind.

"I am."

"At this time of night, in this section of the city?"

"Yes," she answered. "Are you Pagan?"

Her voice, he noticed, was husky, whisper soft.

"Look at me when you ask your questions."

She wouldn't comply with his command but stubbornly continued to stare at the rose. "Pray, answer me, sir," she returned. "Are you Pagan? I have need to speak with the pirate. It is a terribly important matter."

"I am Pagan," Caine said.

She nodded. "It's said that you'll do any task if the price be enough. Is that true, sir?"

"It is," Caine acknowledged. "What is it you want from me?"

In answer to his question, she dropped the bag onto the center of the table. The drawstring tore open and several coins spilled out. Monk let out a low whistle.

"There are thirty pieces in all," she said, her gaze still downcast.

Caine raised an eyebrow in reaction to that statement. "Thirty pieces of silver?"

She timidly nodded. "Is that enough? It's all I have."

"Who is it you wish to betray?"

She looked startled by that assumption. "Oh, no, you misunderstand. I don't want to betray anyone. I'm not a Judas, sir."

He thought she looked insulted by his comment. "It was an honest mistake to make."

Her frown indicated she didn't agree. Caine vowed he wasn't going to let her get his temper riled. "Then what is it you ask from me?"

"I would like you to kill someone, please."

"Ah," he drawled out. His disappointment was almost painful. She looked so damned innocent, so pitifully vulnerable, yet sweetly asked him to murder someone for her.

"And who is this victim? Your husband, perchance?" The cynicism in his voice was as grating as a nail scraping down a chalkboard.

She didn't seem to mind his biting tone. "No," she answered.

"No? You're not married then?"

"Does it matter?"

"Oh, yes," he countered in a whisper to match hers. "It matters."

"No, I'm not married."

"Then who is it you want killed? Your father? Your brother?"

She shook her head again.

Caine slowly leaned forward. His patience was wearing as thin as the ale Monk watered down. "I tire of having to question you. Tell me."

He'd forced a belligerent tone, certain he'd intimidate her into blurting out her full explanation. He knew he'd failed in that endeavor, however, when he caught the mutinous expression on her face. If he hadn't been watching her so intently, he knew he would have missed the flash of anger. The frightened little kitten had a little spirit inside her, after all.

8

"I would like you to accept this task before I explain," she said.

"Task? You call hiring me to kill someone a task?" he asked, his voice incredulous.

"I do," she announced with a nod.

She still refused to look him in the eye. That fact irritated him. "All right," he lied. "I accept."

Her shoulders sagged in what Caine surmised was acute relief. "Tell me who my victim is," he instructed once again.

She slowly lifted her gaze to look at him then. The torment Caine saw in her eyes made his chest ache. The urge to reach out, to take her into his arms, to offer her comfort very nearly overwhelmed him. He suddenly felt outraged on her behalf, then had to shake his head over such a ludicrous, fanciful notion.

Hell, the woman was contracting him to murder someone.

Their gazes held a long while before Caine asked again, "Well? Who is it you want killed?"

She took a deep breath before answering.

"Me."

Chapter Two

"Holy Mother of God," Monk whispered. "You cannot be serious, dear lady."

She didn't take her gaze away from Caine when she answered the tavernkeeper. "I'm very serious, my good man. Do you think I would have ventured out into this part of town in the middle of the night if I weren't serious?"

Caine answered her question. "I think you've lost your mind."

"No," she replied. "It would be much easier if I had."

"I see," Caine said. He was trying to keep his temper controlled, but the urge to shout at her made his throat ache. "When would you like this . . . this . . ."

"Task?"

"Yes, task," Caine asked. "When would you like this task done?"

"Now."

"Now?"

"If it's convenient, mi'lord."

"If it's convenient?"

"Oh, dear, I'm so sorry," she whispered. "I didn't mean to upset you."

"Why do you think you've upset me?"

"Because you're shouting at me."

He realized she was right. He had been shouting. Caine let out a long sigh. For the first time in a good long while, his composure was completely shattered. He excused his shameful condition by telling himself that anyone with half a mind would have been caught off guard by such an outrageous request. She looked so sincere and appeared to be terribly fragile, too. Hell, the woman had freckles on the bridge of her nose, for God's sake. She should be home under lock and key with her loving family protecting her, not standing in this seedy tavern calmly discussing her own murder.

"I can see how distressed I've made you," she said. "I really do apologize, Pagan. Have you never killed a woman before?" she asked. Her voice was filled with sympathy.

She looked as if she felt sorry for him now. "No, I've never killed a woman before," he grated out. "But there's always a first time for everything, now isn't there?"

He'd meant the comment to be sarcastic. She took it to heart. "That's the spirit," she rushed out. She actually smiled at him then. "It really shouldn't be too difficult for you. I'll help, of course."

He wanted to throw his head down on the table. "You're willing to help?" he strangled out.

"Certainly."

"You have lost your mind."

"No, I haven't," she countered. "But I'm very desperate. This task must be done as soon as possible. Do you think you could hurry and finish your drink?"

"Why must it be done so soon?" he asked.

"Because they're going to come for me sometime soon, perhaps even yet tonight. I'm going to die, Pagan, by their

11

hand or yours, and I'd really rather determine my own end. Surely you can understand that."

"Then why don't you just kill yourself?" Monk blurted out. "Wouldn't that be much easier than hiring someone else?"

"For God's sake, Monk, don't encourage her."

"I'm not trying to encourage her," Monk rushed out. "I'm just trying to understand why such a pretty would want to die."

"Oh, I could never kill myself," she explained. "It would be a sin. Someone else has to do it. Don't you see?"

Caine had taken about all he could handle for one evening. He bounded to his feet, upsetting the chair in his haste, then planted the palms of his big hands on the tabletop. "No, I don't see, but I promise you I'm going to before this night is over. We're going to start at the beginning. First you'll begin by telling me your name."

"Why?"

"It's a little rule I have," he snapped. "I don't kill anyone I don't know. Now tell me your name."

"It's a stupid rule."

"Answer me."

"Jade."

"Damn it, I want your real name!" he commanded in a near roar.

"Damn it, that is my real name," she replied. She had a thoroughly disgruntled look on her face.

"You're serious, aren't you?"

"Of course, I'm serious. Jade is my name," she added with a shrug.

"Jade's an unusual name," he said. "Fitting, though. You're proving to be a rather unusual woman."

"Your opinion of me isn't at all relevant, sir. I hired you to complete an assignment and that is all. Is it customary for you to interview your victims before you do them in?"

He ignored her glare. "Tell me the rest of your name, or I may strangle you."

"No, you mustn't strangle me," she replied. "I don't want to die that way and I am the one doing the hiring, if you'll remember."

"What way did you have in mind?" he asked. "Oh, hell, never mind. I don't want to know."

"But you have to know," she argued. "How can you kill me if you don't know how I want it done?"

"Later," he interjected. "You may instruct me in the method you've chosen later. First things first, Jade. Are your parents waiting at home for you?"

"It's doubtful."

"Why?"

"They're both dead."

He closed his eyes and counted to ten. "So you're all alone?"

"No."

"No?"

It was her turn to sigh. "I have a brother. I'm not going to tell you anything more, Pagan. It's too much of a risk, you see."

"Why is it a risk, miss?" Monk asked.

"The more he knows about me, the more difficult the task will become. I believe it would be very upsetting to kill someone you liked. Don't you, sir?"

"I ain't never had to kill someone I liked," Monk admitted. "As to that, I ain't never killed anyone. Still, your theory makes sense to me."

It took all Caine had not to start bellowing. "Jade, I assure you that won't be a problem. At this moment, I don't like you at all."

She took a step back. "Well, why not?" she asked. "I haven't been half as insulting as you have. Are you just a cranky person by nature, Pagan?"

"Don't call me Pagan."

"Why not?"

"It's a danger, miss, if anyone overhears," Monk blurted out when he saw how infuriated Caine was becoming. The muscle in the side of his jaw had started flexing. Caine had a fierce temper and she was innocently shaking him into a real froth. Why if he let loose, he might very well give her her wish and frighten her to death.

"What should I call him then?" she asked the tavernkeeper.

"Caine," Monk answered with a nod. "You can call him Caine."

She let out an inelegant snort. "And he thinks I have an unusual name?"

Caine reached out and grabbed hold of her chin. He forced her to look at him again. "What is your brother's name?"

"Nathan."

"Where is Nathan now?"

"He's away on pressing business matters."

"What business?"

She slapped his hand away before answering. "Shipping business."

"When will he be back?"

Her glare could melt a lesser man. "Two weeks," she snapped. "There, I've answered all your questions. Now will you please quit pestering me and get on with your assignment?"

"Where do you live, Jade?"

"Sir, your endless questions are giving me a pounding headache. I'm not at all used to having men scream at me."

Caine glanced down at Monk and let him see his exasperation. "The daft woman wants me to kill her, yet now complains about a headache."

She suddenly reached out, grabbed hold of his chin, and nudged him back to look at her. It was a deliberate imitation of his earlier action. Caine was so surprised by her boldness, he let her have her way.

"Now it's my turn," she announced. "I'll ask you my questions and you will answer them. I'm the one giving you the silver coins, sir. First, and most important, I want to know if you're really going to kill me. Your hesitation alarms me. That and this endless inquisition."

"You're going to have to satisfy my curiosity before I decide," he told her.

"No."

"Then I won't kill you."

"You scoundrel!" she cried out. "You promised me before you knew who your victim was. You gave me your word!"

"I lied."

Her gasp of outrage nearly knocked her over. "You are a real disappointment to me. A man of honor wouldn't so easily break his word. You should be ashamed of yourself."

"Jade," he answered. "I never said I was a man of honor."

"Nay, miss, he didn't," Monk interjected.

Her eyes turned the color of green fire. She was apparently furious with him. Her hands joined his on the tabletop. She leaned forward and whispered, "I was told Pagan never, ever breaks his word."

"You were misinformed."

They were almost nose to nose now. Caine tried to concentrate on their conversation, but her wonderful scent, so clean, so fresh, so utterly feminine, kept getting in the way.

She was shaking her head at him now. Caine was literally at a loss for words. He'd never had a woman stand up to him before. No, the ladies of the *ton* usually cowered when he showed the least amount of displeasure. This one was different, however. She wasn't just standing up to him either. She was actually matching him glare for glare. He suddenly felt like laughing and didn't have the faintest idea why.

15

Her insanity was obviously the catching kind.

"You really should be hanged," she said. "You certainly had me fooled. You don't look like the sort to act so dastardly."

She tried to move away from the table but Caine's hands covered hers, trapping her. He leaned down again, until his mouth was just a scant kiss away. "I'm a pirate, madam. We're known to be dastardly."

He waited for another angry rebuttal. She burst into tears instead. Caine wasn't at all prepared for that emotional display.

While he reached for his handkerchief, Monk jumped to his feet and rushed over to comfort her. The barkeep awkwardly patted her on her shoulders. "There, there, miss, don't cry now."

"It's all his fault," she sobbed. "All I asked was a simple little favor. Just one quick task that wouldn't take him any time at all; but, no, he couldn't be bothered. I even offered to wait until he'd finished his refreshment," she continued with a wail. "I was willing to pay good coins too."

By the time she'd finished her pitiful tirade, Monk was glaring at Caine. "You've upset the pretty," he told the Marquess. "Why, you've broken her heart."

The tavernkeeper grabbed the handkerchief out of Caine's hand and began to awkwardly mop the tears away from her cheeks. "It will be all right, miss," he crooned.

"No, it won't," she argued. Her voice was muffled by the linen cloth Monk had shoved under her nose. "Do you know I've never asked anyone for anything in all my days? Yet the very first time I do ask, I'm denied my request. No one wants to make an honest living anymore. No, they'd rather steal than earn their way. It's a shame, isn't it, Monk?"

Caine was too incredulous to speak. He didn't know if he should take her into his arms and comfort her or grab her by the shoulders and shake some sense into her. One thing was certain, however. If Monk continued to frown at him, he was going to break his nose.

"Mi'lady, it really ain't honest work to take coins from a lady and kill her," Monk argued. He patted her shoulder in a bid to soften his gentle rebuke.

"Of course it's honest work," she replied. "As long as the lady wants the killing done."

Monk paused to rub his brow. "She's got a true point there, don't she?" he asked Caine.

"For the love of . . . now what are you doing?" Caine asked Jade when she began to collect her coins.

"I'm leaving," she announced. "I'm sorry I bothered you, Pagan, or Caine, or whatever your real name is," she whispered.

She tied the string into a knot, then tucked the bag in her pocket.

When she turned and started for the door, Caine called out. "Where do you think you're going?"

"That's none of your concern," she answered. "Still, I'm not half as insolent as you are and so I shall tell you I'm going to find someone more cooperative. Have no fear, sir. I won't give up. Before this black night is over, I'll find someone willing to kill me."

He caught her at the door. His hands settled on her shoulders and he slowly forced her around to look at him.

The minute he touched her, she started crying again. Caine was exasperated, unsettled too. He gave in to his overwhelming urge though, and roughly pulled her into his arms.

His bear hug seemed to be all the prodding she needed. She wept against his chest, whispering her apology for her unladylike behavior in between her loud sobs.

Caine was content to wait until she'd regained a bit of control. He couldn't possibly reason with her now. She was making so much noise she wouldn't have been able to hear a word he said anyway. And she kept blaming her current condition on him too. She was, without a doubt, the most confusing woman he'd ever encountered.

Lord, she was wonderfully soft. She fit him nicely too. He usually disliked women who cried, yet found he didn't want to let go of this one.

She was hiccupping just like a drunken peasant now, the aftermath of the quick storm.

It was high time he reasoned with her. "Jade, it can't possibly be as terrible as you now believe," he told her in a low, husky voice. "Surely, come morning, you'll be thankful I didn't give in to your request."

"I'll be dead come morning," she wailed.

"No, you won't," he replied. He gave her an affectionate squeeze. "I won't let anything happen to you. I promise. You can't really want to die just yet."

"My brother's bound to be disappointed if I die," she said.

"I would imagine so," he answered dryly.

"Still, I'm not strong enough to fight them. They're very mean-hearted men. I fear they'll use me before they kill me. I don't want to die that way. There's no dignity in it."

"Death with dignity?" he asked. "You speak like a soldier preparing for the battlefield."

"I don't want to be remembered as a coward."

"Will your brother be able to take care of your problem once he returns?"

"Oh, yes," she answered. She rested her cheek against his chest. "Nathan wouldn't let anything happen to me. Since our papa died, he's become my protector. My brother's a very strong man."

"Then I'll keep you safe until your brother returns. I give you my word."

A long, silent minute passed before she showed any reaction to that promise. Caine thought she might be too overcome with gratitude to speak. Then she moved away from him and looked up into his eyes. He realized she wasn't overcome at all. Hell, she looked downright irritated. "You've already broken your word to me, sir. You promised you'd kill me and then changed your mind."

"This is different," he argued.

"You really mean what you say?"

"Yes, I mean what I say," he answered. "You just explained that you'll be safe once your brother returns in two weeks. It is two weeks, isn't it?"

Her expression was solemn. "Perhaps even sooner. But you're a pirate. You cannot be taking such chances keeping me safe for two long weeks. There's a bounty on your head. I won't be responsible for getting you killed."

"You don't have much faith in my ability."

"I don't have *any* faith in your ability," she qualified. "Why should I? You've just admitted that the rumors about you aren't at all reliable. You probably don't even leave a white rose on your victim's pillow, do you?"

Caine was exasperated with her again. "You don't have to sound so damned disappointed in me."

"But I am disappointed!" she cried out. "You aren't even honorable. That's the real pity. Besides, you don't look at all strong enough to take on my enemies. You'd be an easy target, Caine. You're such a . . . big man. No, I'm sorry. I'm afraid you simply won't do."

He wanted to throttle her.

She turned her back on him again and tried to leave. Caine was so astonished by her attitude he almost let her get away. Almost. He caught her just as she reached the walkway outside the door.

His hold wouldn't allow her any freedom as his arm was anchored around her shoulders. He tucked her into his side with as much care as he'd give an old blanket, then turned to speak to Monk. "I don't want you telling anyone what happened here tonight. Give me your word, Monk."

"Why should he give you his word when you so freely break yours? A gentleman only asks as much as he can give in return, sir. Didn't your mama teach you any manners?" she asked.

"Ah, Jade," he said. "That's the rub." He looked down at her and slowly stroked the side of her cheek with his fingertips. "I'm not a gentleman. I'm a pirate, remember? There's a distinct difference."

She went completely still the second he touched her. Caine thought she looked quite stunned. He didn't know what to make of that odd reaction. When his hand dropped away, she came out of her stupor and shoved against him.

"Yes, there is a difference," she muttered. "Tell me this, Caine. If I make you angry enough, will you kill me in vexation?"

"The idea's beginning to have merit," he answered.

"Let go of me. You must never touch me."

"I mustn't?"

"No. I don't like to be touched."

"Then how in God's name was I suppose to kill you?"

She obviously hadn't realized he was jesting. "You were going to use a pistol," she told him. She paused to give him a suspicious look. "You do own one, don't you?"

"I do," he answered. "And where was I suppose to . . ."

"One clean shot, directly through my heart," she explained. "You'd have to be accurate, of course. I wouldn't want to linger."

"No," he agreed. "Lingering would definitely be out of the question."

"How can you find this amusing? We happen to be discussing my death!" she cried out.

"I'm not amused," he argued. "Fact is, I'm getting downright angry again. Tell me, do I get to ravage you first?"

She took a deep breath before answering. "You certainly do not."

"That's a pity," he replied, completely ignoring her outraged expression.

"Sir, do your parents happen to be first cousins? You're

acting like a complete simpleton. You're either an idiot or the most cold-hearted man I've ever met. I find your conduct disgraceful."

Her eyes were flashing with indignation. Caine had never seen such a dramatic shade of green before. It was as though the purity and the sparkle of a thousand emeralds had all been squeezed dry of their color and given to her.

"I'm not at all convinced you're in any real danger, Jade," he announced. "This could very well just be a product of your overactive imagination."

"I dislike you intensely," she whispered. "And as for your ignorant opinions, well I . . ."

"Jade, save the bluster for later. I'm not in the mood. Now, I don't want to hear another word about killing you. And if you continue to glare up at me so prettily, I swear I'm going to kiss you just to take your mind off your foolish worries."

"Kiss me?" She looked stunned. "Why in God's name would you want to kiss me?"

"I haven't the faintest idea," he admitted.

"You'd kiss someone you disliked?"

"I guess I would," he replied with a grin.

"You are arrogant, overbearing . . ."

"You're sputtering, my sweet."

She didn't have a quick comeback. Caine continued to stare down at her when he spoke to Monk again. "Well, Monk, do you give me your word?"

"I do. I won't be telling anyone about this night, Caine, but we both know your friend, Lyon, will surely find out before the sun sets again. He'll wring the truth out of me. I'm giving you warning ahead of time."

Caine nodded. The Marquess of Lyonwood was a good friend. Caine trusted him completely. The two had worked on several missions together for their government. "Yes, he will find out," he predicted. "But his new wife and son keep him occupied. Besides, when he learns what I'm up to, he'll keep it to himself. If he inquires, you may speak freely to him. No one else though, not even Rhone," Caine added, referring to Lyon's closest friend. "For all his merits, Rhone does talk too much."

Monk nodded. "I'm begging you, Caine, to let me know how it all ends up with the little lady."

"Monk?" Jade asked, drawing both men's attention. "You wouldn't happen to own a pistol, would you?"

She sounded too damned eager to him. Caine knew what she was thinking. His angel was as easy to read as a Latin text. "He doesn't and he won't," he announced.

"I don't and I won't what?" Monk asked.

"You don't own a pistol and you won't kill her," Caine answered in a clipped tone of voice.

"No, no, of course not," Monk agreed. "Caine, you aren't forgetting your trap, are you?" he asked, when he was finally able to pull his gaze away from the beautiful woman.

"No, I'm not forgetting," Caine answered. He turned to Jade and asked, "Is your carriage returning for you?"

Her exasperation was obvious. "I hired a hack," she told him. "I didn't think I'd be returning to my lodgings to-night." She pushed away from his hold and picked up the large gray satchel from the walkway. "All I own is in here. I came directly from the country," she added, almost as an afterthought.

"You left your possessions on the street for anyone to snatch?"

"It was my intention to have my things stolen," she answered. She sounded like a tutor instructing a deliberately obtuse student. "I was hoping my clothing could benefit some poor soul. I wasn't supposed to have further need once you . . ."

"Enough!" he nearly growled. "You aren't going to mention murder again. Have you got that?"

She didn't answer him quickly enough. Caine tugged on her hair. She let out a shrill cry just as he noticed the large swelling above her ear. "Good God, Jade, when did you get that?"

"Don't touch it," she demanded when he tried to prod the edges of the bump. "It still stings."

"I would think so," he said. His hand dropped back to his side. "Tell me what happened."

"I caught the heel of my boot on the carpet loop in my brother's house and tumbled down the stairs," she explained. "I hit the side of my head on the banister knob. It fairly knocked the wind out of my sails."

The wind out of her sails? Caine thought that was a rather odd remark to make, but he didn't take time to reflect upon it. "You could have killed yourself," he stated. "Are you always so awkward?"

"No, I'm never awkward," she countered. "I'm usually very ladylike. Lord, you're rude," she ended with a mutter.

"What happened after you fell?" Monk asked.

She shrugged. "I went for a walk to try to clear my head. Then they started in chasing after me, of course."

"Of course?" Monk asked.

"They?" Caine said at the very same time.

She paused to give both men a frown. "The men I saw kill the finely dressed gentleman," she explained. "For heaven's sake, do pay attention. I'm certain I mentioned that fact earlier."

Monk shook his head. "I'm just as certain you didn't, miss," he confessed. "I'm sure I would have remembered."

"You witnessed a murder? No, Jade, you sure as hell didn't mention that fact."

"Well, I meant to mention it," she muttered. She folded her arms across her chest and looked disgruntled again. "I would have explained it all to you if you hadn't turned my attention by arguing with me. So you see, this is your fault because I lost my train of thought. Yes, you're to blame."

"Did you witness the murder before or after you hit yourself in the head?" Caine asked.

"Do you suppose it was a titled gentleman she saw murdered?" Monk asked Caine.

"I did not hit myself," Jade snapped. "And it was before . . . no, it was after. At least I think it was after I fell down. Oh, I don't remember now. My head's pounding again. Do quit your questions, sir."

Caine turned back to the tavernkeeper. "Now I'm beginning to understand," he said. He looked at Jade again. "Were you wearing your cloak at the time of this mishap?"

"Yes," she answered. She looked perplexed. "But what does that . . ."

"You tore your cloak and bruised your face when you fell down, didn't you?"

His tone was a little too condescending for her liking. "Tell me exactly what it is you think you're beginning to understand."

"It's really very simple," he answered. "Your head suffered a trauma, Jade. You aren't thinking logically now, though I must admit that most women aren't ever logical. Still, with plenty of rest and care, in a few days you'll realize your mind was just playing tricks on you. You'll be worrying about what gown to wear to your next ball then."

"My mind isn't playing tricks on me," she cried out.

"You're confused."

"I am not confused!"

"Quit shouting," Caine ordered. "If you'll only think about what I'm . . ."

He gave up when she shook her head at him. "You're too addled to be reasoned with now. We'll wait until you're feeling better."

"He's right, miss," Monk whispered. "If you'd seen a titled gentleman murdered, the news would have hit this section of town right off. The men who'd done the deed would have boasted of their cunning. Listen to Caine now. He knows what's best."

"But if you believe I'm just imagining I'm in danger, then you don't need to protect me, do you?"

"Oh, yes, I do," he replied. "Only now I know who I'm protecting you against."

Before she could ask another question, he continued. "Like it or not, you're a menace until you've recovered. In all good conscience, I can't leave you on your own." His smile was gentle when he added, "I guess you could say I'm protecting you from yourself, Jade. Now give me your satchel. I'll carry it for you."

She tried to lift the bag before Caine could and ended up in a tug of war. Caine won. "What in God's name do you have in here?" he asked. "This thing weighs more than you do."

"Everything I own," she answered. "If it's too much for you, I'll be happy to carry it."

Caine shook his head. He took hold of her hand. "Come along. My carriage is waiting two blocks over. You should be home in bed."

She drew to an abrupt stop. "Whose bed, Caine?"

His sigh was loud enough to wake the drunks littering the alleys. "Your very own bed," he snapped. "Your virtue's safe. I never take virgins to my bed and I sure as certain don't want you."

He thought she would be relieved by his vehement promise not to bother her. It was only a half lie, of course. He did want to kiss her, yet he wasn't sure if it was merely out of the need to have a few minutes of blissful silence.

"Is that a little rule of yours?" she asked. "Not to bed a virgin?"

She looked highly insulted. Caine didn't know what to make of that reaction. "It is," he answered. "I also don't bed daft women I don't particularly like, sweet, so you're safe enough with me."

He dared to grin at her when he made those shameful

remarks. "I do believe I'm beginning to hate you," she muttered. "Well, you're bloody safe with me, too, Caine. I would never let you touch me, either."

"Good."

"Yes, good," she replied, determined to have the last word. "If you don't quit dragging me, I'm going to scream your name over and over again until the authorities come and take you away, Pagan."

"I'm not Pagan."

"What?"

She almost fell down. Caine grabbed her. "I said, I'm not Pagan."

"Just who in thunder are you then?"

They'd reached his carriage but she refused to let him assist her inside until he'd answered her question. She kept slapping his hands away.

Caine gave in. He tossed her satchel up to the driver, then turned back to her. "My name really is Caine. I'm the Marquess of Cainewood. Now will you get inside? This is neither the time nor the place for a lengthy discussion. When we're on our way, I'll explain everything to you."

"You promise?"

"I promise," he answered with a low growl.

She didn't look like she believed him. Jade folded her arms across her chest. "Shame on you, Caine. You've been pretending to be the noble pirate all this time . . ."

"That bastard's a lot of things, Jade, but he sure as hell isn't noble."

"How can you know if you speak truth or fancy?" she demanded. "I'll wager you never even met the man. Is your own life so unhappy that you must pretend to . . ."

The look on his face turned as stinging as his hard grip on her arm, interrupting her speech. While she watched, he tore the flower from his lapel and tossed it on the ground. He wasn't at all gentle when he half lifted, half tossed Jade inside the vehicle.

Once the carriage started moving, the interior was thrown into darkness. She couldn't see his scowl and was most relieved.

He couldn't see her smile either.

They rode in silence a short while. Jade used the time to regain her composure. Caine used the time to calm his frustration.

"Why were you pretending to be Pagan?"

"To hunt him down," Caine answered.

"But why?"

"Later," he snapped. "I'll tell you all about it later, all right?"

He was sure his hard tone of voice would discourage her from asking any more questions. He was mistaken.

"You're angry because I made you quit your hunt, aren't you?"

His sigh indicated his impatience. "You didn't make me quit my hunt. I might have failed thus far, but when we've taken care of your problem, I'll go back to my hunt. Don't worry, Jade. I won't fail."

She wasn't at all worried, but she couldn't very well tell him that. Caine hadn't failed at all. No, he'd gone into the tavern to draw Pagan out.

And that's exactly what he'd done.

She'd done her task well. Her brother was going to be pleased.

Chapter Three

The tears had been a nice touch. Jade had been almost as surprised as Caine appeared to be by the spontaneous show of emotion. It hadn't been in her plans to use such a weak ploy to get him out of the tavern. Yet once she saw how upsetting it was for him to see a woman in such a pathetic condition, she'd cried all the more, of course. Caine had looked so helpless. Jade had no idea she had such a talent. Wailing on command took concentration, however, but she quickly adapted herself to the problem, and thought she'd conquered it rather quickly, too. Why, she could probably burst into a full fit of tears before a gentleman could drop his hat if she really put her mind to it.

She didn't feel at all ashamed of her conduct. Desperate times always called for desperate measures. At least that's what Black Harry liked to say. Her adopted uncle would have a good laugh too. In all their years together, he had never seen her cry, not even when his enemy, McKindry, had used a whip on her back. The lash had hurt like fire, but she hadn't let out a single whimper. McKindry only got in one good lash before Harry tossed him over the side. Her uncle had been in such a spitting rage, he'd jumped overboard to finish the bloke. McKindry was a much stronger swimmer, however, and was last seen backstroking his way to France.

Of course, Black Harry would be in another good rage if he knew what she was up to now. He'd have her hide, he would. Yet it hadn't been possible to explain her plan to him. No, there simply hadn't been enough time to sail all the way to their island to inform him of her decision. And time was of the essence. Caine's life was at stake.

Jade knew all about the Marquess of Cainewood. He was a bit of a contradiction, too. Caine was an earthy, downright lusty man, but he was also honorable. She'd read his file through from start to finish, and every bit of it was memorized in her mind. She had the uncanny knack for recording everything in her mind the first time she read it. Although she thought that was a rather odd ability, she had to admit that the gift had certainly come in handy upon occasion.

Obtaining Caine's impressive record from the War Department had been tricky, but not impossible. The information had of course been sealed and locked away. It was a point of pride with Jade that she could undo any lock ever fashioned. She'd succeeded in getting Caine's file on her third attempt.

It was a shame that none of the information in his records mentioned the disturbing fact that he was such a handsome devil. The term "ruthless" had been sprinkled liberally throughout each account of his activities, yet never was "compelling" or "appealing" put to his name. The file didn't mention what a big man he was either.

Jade remembered how uneasy she'd felt when she read his operative name. He was called Hunter by his superiors. After reading the file in full, she understood why he'd been given that name. Caine never gave up. In one incident, when the odds had been overwhelmingly against him, he continued to stalk his adversary with the patience and the tenacity of an ancient warrior. And in the end, he had succeeded.

Caine had quit his duties the day he'd been informed of the death of his brother Colin. According to the last entry made by his senior advisor, a man by the name of Sir Michael Richards, the resignation had Caine's father's full support. The Duke of Williamshire had just lost one son to his country and wasn't about to lose another. It was also noted by Richards that until that day, Caine had had no idea his younger brother also worked for the government.

Both Colin and Caine came from a large family. Caine was their eldest child. In all there were six children: two sons and four daughters.

The children were all very protective of each other and of their parents. The one fact that kept repeating itself in his file was that Caine was a protector by nature. Whether he considered that fact a flaw or a virtue wasn't significant to Jade. She simply used it to get what she wanted.

She'd been prepared to like Caine, of course. He was Colin's brother, after all, and she was very fond of Colin, since the moment she'd fished him out of the ocean and he told her to save her own brother first. Yes, she'd been prepared to like Caine, but she hadn't been at all prepared to find herself so physically drawn to him. It was a first for her, a worry too, for she knew he could overwhelm her if she gave him the opportunity.

She protected herself by pretending to be everything she thought he disliked. When she wasn't crying like an infant, she tried to remember to complain. Most men hated ill-disciplined women, didn't they? Jade certainly hoped so. She would be forced by circumstances to stay by Caine's side for the next two weeks, and then it would be over. She'd return to her way of life and he'd probably return to his womanizing.

It was imperative for him to think he was protecting her. It was the only way she could keep him safe. His views on the inferiority of women, no doubt enhanced by four little sisters, made her plan much easier. Yet Caine was also a very perceptive man. His past training had polished his predatory instincts. For that reason, Jade had ordered her men to wait for her at Caine's country home. They were going to hide in the woods that surrounded his house. When she arrived, they would take over the task of watching Caine's backside.

The letters were at the heart of this treachery, of course, and she wished to God she'd never found the things now. What was done was done, she reminded herself. It certainly wouldn't do her any good to have regrets. It would be wasted effort and Jade never, ever wasted anything. It was all very clear-cut to her. When she'd shown her brother, Nathan, their father's letters, she'd started this mess, and she would now be the one to mop it up.

Jade forced her worries aside. She'd inadvertently just given Caine quite a little time to think. Silence, she decided, could very well be her enemy now. She had to keep Caine off guard . . . and occupied. "Caine? What do you . . ."

"Hush, sweet," Caine ordered. "Do you hear . . ."

"That odd squeak? I was just about to mention it," she replied.

"It's more like a persistent grinding noise . . . Miller," Caine shouted out the window. "Stop the carriage."

The vehicle came to an abrupt stop just as the left rear wheel snapped. Jade would have been tossed to the floor if Caine hadn't caught her in his arms. He held her tightly for a long minute, then whispered. "Damned bad timing, wouldn't you say?"

"I'd say it's probably trickery," she whispered.

Caine didn't comment on that remark. "Stay inside, Jade, while I see what can be done."

"Do be careful," she cautioned. "They could be waiting for you."

She heard his sigh when he opened the door. "I'll be careful," he promised.

As soon as he'd shut the door behind him, Jade opened it and climbed out. The driver came to stand beside his employer. "I can't fathom it, mi'lord. I'm always checking the wheels to make certain they're sound."

"I'm not faulting you, Miller," Caine returned. "We're far enough on the side of the street to leave it here for the night. Unleash the horse, Miller. I'll . . ."

Caine stopped when he noticed Jade. She was clutching a wicked-looking dagger in her hand. He almost laughed. "Put that away, Jade. You'll hurt yourself."

She slipped the knife back into the seam pocket of her gown. "We're fair targets, Caine, standing out here for anyone to grab."

"Then get back inside," he suggested.

She pretended she hadn't heard him. "Miller? Was the wheel tampered with, do you suppose?"

The driver squatted down next to the axle. "I'd say it was," he whispered. "Mi'lord, it was tampered with! Have a look here, at the cuts made in the side bar."

"What are we going to do now?" Jade asked Caine.

"We'll ride the horse," he announced.

"But what about poor Miller? They might do him in when we leave."

"I'll be all right, miss," the driver interjected. "I got me a big flask of brandy to keep me warm. I'll sit inside the carriage until Broley comes to fetch me."

"Who is Broley?" Jade asked.

"One of the tigers," Miller returned.

Jade didn't know what he was talking about. "You have a friend who is an animal?"

Caine did smile then. "Broley works for me," he explained. "I'll explain it all to you later."

"We should just hire a hack," she announced then. She folded her arms across her chest. "Then we could all ride together and I wouldn't have to worry about Miller."

"At this time of night? It's doubtful we'd find a hack."

"What about Monk's lovely tavern?" she asked. "Couldn't we go back there and wait until light?"

"No," Caine answered. "Monk has certainly locked up and gone home by now."

"We're a fair distance away from the Ne'er Do Well now, mi'lady," Miller interjected.

When the driver moved to unstrap the horse, Jade grabbed hold of Caine's hand and moved closer to his side. "Caine?" she whispered.

"Yes?"

"I think I know what happened to your fine carriage wheel. It was probably the very same men who . . ."

"Hush now," he whispered back. "It's going to be all right."

"How can you know it's going to be all right?"

She sounded so frightened. Caine wanted to comfort her. "My instincts," he boasted. "Sweet, don't let your imagination get out of hand. It's . . ."

"Too late," she countered. "Oh, Lord, my imagination's at it again."

The pistol shot rang out just as she threw herself into his side, knocking him off balance.

The shot flew past the side of his head, narrowly missing him. He could hear the whistle in his ear. Though he was certain it wasn't intentional, Jade had actually just saved his life.

Caine tightened his hold on Jade's hand, shouted a warning to Miller as he pushed her in front of him, and then started running. He forced her to stay directly in front of him so he could shield her with his broad back.

Several more pistol shots rang out. Jade could hear the thundering of men chasing them. It sounded like a herd of wild horses were about to trample them down.

Jade soon lost all track of where they were. Caine seemed to know his way around the area well enough. He pulled her through a maze of alleys and back streets, until she had a horrid stitch in her side and couldn't catch her breath. When she stumbled against him, he lifted her into his arms without breaking his stride.

He continued the grueling pace long after the sounds of pursuit had stopped. When they reached the center of the old bridge spanning the Thames, he finally paused to rest.

Caine leaned against the rickety railing, holding her close against him. "That was close. Damn, my instincts were off tonight. I never saw it coming."

He hadn't sounded a bit winded when he made that remark. She was amazed by his stamina. Why, her heart was still pounding from the exertion. "Do you do quite a lot of running through alleys, Caine?" she asked.

He thought that was an odd question. "No, why do you ask?"

"You aren't at all out of breath," she answered. "And we never once ran into a dead end," she added. "You do know your way around the city, don't you?"

"I guess I do," he answered with a shrug that almost sent her flying over the railing. She threw her arms around his neck and held on. Then she realized he was still holding her in his arms.

"You may put me down now," she announced. "I'm certain we lost them."

"I'm not," Caine drawled out.

"I've already explained that I don't like being touched, sir. Put me down." She paused to give him a hard look, then asked, "You aren't going to blame me for your instincts failing you, are you?"

"No, I'm not going to blame you. Jade, you ask the damnedest questions."

"I'm not in the mood to argue with you. Just apologize and I shall forgive you."

"Apologize?" He sounded incredulous. "What for?"

"For thinking I have an overactive imagination," she explained. "For telling me I'm confused, and most of all, for being terribly rude when you said those insulting things to me."

He didn't apologize, but he did smile at her. She noticed the wonderful dimple in the side of his left cheek then. Her heart took notice and started pounding in a wild beat again.

"We're standing on a bridge in the middle of London's most disreputable section with a band of cutthroats chasing us, and all you can think about is gaining my apology? You, sweet, really are mad."

"I always remember to apologize when I've done something wrong," she remarked.

He looked downright exasperated with her now. She couldn't help but smile at him. Lord, he was a handsome rascal. The moonlight softened his harsh features, and she barely minded his frown now.

In truth, she wanted him to smile at her again.

"Jade? Can you swim?"

She was staring intently at his mouth, thinking to herself that he had the most beautiful white teeth she'd ever seen.

He shook her. "Can you swim?" he asked. There was a little more urgency in his tone now.

"Yes," she answered with an unladylike yawn. "I can swim. Why do you ask?"

In answer to that question, he tossed her over his right shoulder and started climbing the rail.

Her long hair brushed the back of his boots. The wind was knocked out of her when he slammed her against his shoulder, but she soon recovered. "What in bloody hell are you doing?" she cried out. She clutched the back of his jacket. "Put me down."

"They've got the exits blocked, Jade. Take a deep breath, sweet. I'll be right behind you."

She only had enough time to shout her denial at him. Then she let out a bellow of outrage. The sound echoed off into the inky blackness when he threw her away from the railing.

She was suddenly flying like a disc into the biting wind. Jade kept right on screaming until her backside hit the water. She remembered to close her mouth just as the frigid water closed over her head. She came up sputtering, but immediately closed her mouth again when she got a good whiff of the stench surrounding her.

Jade vowed she wouldn't let herself drown in this filth. No, she was going to stay alive until she found her new protector and drowned him first.

Then she felt something brush against her leg. She became absolutely terrified. In her confused mind, she was certain the sharks had come for her.

Caine suddenly appeared at her side. He wrapped his arm around her waist, then let the swift current drag them under the bridge and away from the enemy stalking them.

She kept trying to climb up on his shoulders. "Hold still," he ordered.

Jade wrapped her arms around his neck. "The sharks, Caine," she whispered. "They're going to get us."

The terror in her voice and her grip told him she was close to losing all control. "There aren't any sharks," he told her. "Nothing could live in this water long enough."

"You're certain?"

"I'm certain," he returned. "Just hold on a little longer, sweet. We'll be out of this muck in no time at all."

His soothing voice did calm her a little. She was still trying to strangle him, but her grip had lessened. It was only a halfhearted attempt now.

They floated at least a good mile down the winding river before he finally pulled her out of the water and onto the grassy slope. Jade was too cold, too miserable, to blister him with her opinion of his conduct.

She couldn't even get in a decent whimper. Her teeth were chattering too much. "I smell like dead fish," she stammered out in a pitiful wail.

"Yes, you do," Caine agreed. He sounded amused.

"So do you, you . . . pretender."

"Pretender?" he repeated while he tore his jacket off and tossed it on the ground behind him. "What do you mean by that?"

Jade was trying to wring the water out of the hem of her gown. Her hair covered most of her face. She paused to toss the clumps out of her vision. "You needn't act so innocent with me," she muttered.

She gave up her task and accepted the pitiful fact that her gown now outweighed her, then wrapped her arms around her waist and tried to hug some warmth back into her bones. Her voice took on her shivers when she added, "Pretending to be the pirate, Pagan. He would never throw a gentle lady in the Thames."

"Jade, I did what I thought was best under the circumstances," he defended.

"I lost my cloak." That announcement came out in a loud gasp.

"I'll buy you another one."

"But my silver coins were in that cloak," she said. "Well?"

"Well, what?"

"Go fetch it."

"What?"

"Go fetch it," she ordered again. "I'll wait here."

"You can't be serious."

"I'm perfectly serious," she countered. "We only drifted a mile or so, Caine. It shouldn't take you any time at all."

"No."

"Please?"

"I'd never find it," he returned. "It's probably at the bottom of the river by now."

She mopped at the corners of her eyes with the backs of her hands. "Now I'm a pauper and it's all your fault."

"Don't start," he commanded. He knew she was on the verge of tears again. "Now isn't the time for hysterics or complaints, even though they seem to be the only two things you're any good at," he continued. He caught her gasp and smiled. She was getting her temper back. "Do you still have your shoes on or do I have to carry you?"

"How would I know?" she asked. "I've lost all the feeling in my feet."

"Look, damn it."

"Yes, damn it," she muttered when she'd done as he ordered. "I'm still wearing them. Well?" she added. "Are you going to apologize or not?"

"No," he answered in a clipped voice. "I'm not going to apologize. And lower your voice, Jade. Do you want every cutthroat in London after us?"

"No," she whispered. She moved close to his side. "Caine? What would you have done if I didn't know how to swim?"

"The same thing," he answered. "But we would have jumped together."

"I didn't jump," she argued. "Oh, never mind. I'm cold, Caine. What are we going to do now?"

He took hold of her hand and started up the bank. "We're

going to walk over to my friend's town house. It's closer than mine."

"Caine, you're forgetting your jacket," she reminded him.

Before he could tell her to leave it, she rushed back, lifted the jacket, rung as much of the water out of it as she could manage with her numb fingers, and then hurried back to his side. She tossed the hair out of her eyes again, just as he put his arm around her shoulders. "I look terrible, don't I?"

"You smell worse," he told her quite cheerfully.

He gave her an affectionate squeeze, then remarked, "I'd say it's more like rotten meat than dead fish though."

She started to gag. Caine slapped his hand over her mouth. "If you lose your supper, I'll become very angry with you. I have enough to contend with now. Don't you dare complicate matters by getting sick."

She bit his hand, gaining both her freedom and another blasphemy from him. "I didn't have any supper," she announced. "I wanted to die on an empty stomach."

"You still might," he muttered. "Now quit talking and let me think. Why the hell did you want to die on an empty stomach?" he couldn't help but ask.

"Some people become ill when they're frightened. I thought I might, you see, right before you . . . oh, never mind. I just didn't want to go to my Maker in a messy gown, that's all."

"I knew I shouldn't have asked," he replied. "Look, when we get to Lyon's place, you can have a hot bath. You'll feel better then."

"Is Lyon the interfering friend Monk mentioned?"

"Lyon isn't interfering."

"Monk said he'd find out what happened to you this black night," Jade replied. "Those were his very words. That certainly sounds interfering to me."

"You'll like Lyon."

"If he's your friend, I have my doubts," she returned. "Still, I will try to like him."

They lapsed into silence for several blocks. Caine was on his guard now and Jade wasn't nearly as worried as she pretended to be.

"Caine? After we've had our baths, what will we do?"

"You're going to sit down and tell me everything that happened to you."

"I've already told you what happened to me. You didn't believe me though, did you?"

"No," he admitted. "I didn't."

"Besides, your mind is already set against me, Caine. You won't believe anything else I tell you. Why should I make the effort?"

"My mind isn't set against you," he answered. His irritation was obvious in his tone.

She let out a rather inelegant snort. Caine vowed he wouldn't let her draw him into another argument. He led her through another maze of back streets. She was so exhausted by the time they'd reached the steps to the impressive, redbrick town house, she wanted to weep real tears.

A giant of a man with a rather sinister-looking scar creasing his forehead opened the door on Caine's insistent pounding. The man had obviously been asleep. He wasn't happy about being awakened, either. Jade took one look at the stranger's dark scowl, and edged closer to Caine.

The man she assumed was Lyon wore only a pair of black britches. The frightening scowl quickly turned to a look of true astonishment as soon as he saw who his visitor was. "Caine? What in God's name . . . come inside," he rushed out. He moved forward with the intent of clasping Caine's hand, then abruptly changed his mind. He'd obviously just gotten a good whiff of the two of them.

Jade was horribly embarrassed. She turned to glare at Caine, a silent message that she still believed her foul condition was all his fault, then walked into the black and white tiled foyer. She saw a beautiful woman hurrying down the winding staircase then. The woman's long, silvery blond hair flew out behind her. She was so lovely, Jade felt all the worse.

Caine made hasty introductions while Jade stared at the floor. "This is Lyon, Jade, and his wife, Christina."

"What happened to you two?" Lyon asked.

Jade whirled around, raining drops of sour water in a wide circle. She lifted her hair out of her eyes and then announced, "He threw me in the Thames."

"He what?" Lyon asked, a hint of a smile in his expression now, for he'd only just noticed what looked very like a chicken bone dangling from her hair.

"Caine threw me in the Thames," she repeated.

"He did?" Christina asked. Lyon's wife sounded astonished.

Jade turned to her. "He truly did," she announced yet again. "He didn't apologize afterward either."

After making that remark, she burst into tears. "This is all his fault," she sobbed. "First he lost his carriage wheel and then he lost his instincts. My plan was really so much better. He's just too stubborn to admit it."

"Don't start on that again," Caine warned.

"Why did you throw this poor dear in the Thames?" Christina asked again. She hurried over to Jade, her arms outstretched. "You must be chilled to the bone," she said in sympathy. Christina came to a quick stop when she got close to Jade, then backed up a space.

"It was necessary," Caine answered. He was trying to ignore Jade's glare.

"I believe I hate him," Jade told Christina. "I don't care if he's your friend or not," she added on another sob. "The man's a scoundrel."

"Yes, he can be a scoundrel," Christina agreed. "But he does have other nice qualities."

"I've yet to see them," Jade whispered.

Christina wrinkled her nose, took a deep breath, and then put her arm around Jade's waist. "Come with me, Jade. We'll have you cleaned up in no time. I think the kitchen will serve us better this night. Lyon? You best wake up the staff. We'll need help heating the water. My, you do have an unusual name," she told Jade then. "It's very pretty."

"He ridiculed my name," Jade whispered, though loud enough for Caine to overhear.

Caine closed his eyes in vexation. "I did not ridicule your name!" he shouted. "I swear to God, Lyon, that woman's done nothing but complain and weep since the moment I met her."

Jade let out a loud gasp, then allowed Christina to prod her along toward the back of the house. Both Caine and Lyon watched the pair depart.

"Do you see how insulting he is, Lady Christina?" Jade asked. "All I asked was one little favor from the man."

"And he refused?" Christina asked. "That certainly doesn't sound like Caine. He's usually very accommodating."

"I even offered to pay him silver coins," Jade announced. "I'm a pauper now. Caine threw my cloak in the Thames, too. The coins were in the pocket."

Christina shook her head. She paused at the corner to look back at Caine so he could see her displeasure. "That was terribly ungallant of him, wasn't it?"

They rounded the corner on Jade's fervent agreement.

"What was the favor she asked of you?" Lyon asked.

"Nothing much," Caine drawled out. He bent over to pull off his water-soaked boots. "She just wanted me to kill her, that's all."

Lyon let out a shout of laughter, but stopped when he realized Caine wasn't jesting.

"She wanted it done before morning," Caine said.

"She didn't."

"She was willing to let me finish my brandy first."

"That was thoughtful of her."

The two men shared a grin. "Now your wife thinks I'm an ogre because I've disappointed the woman."

Lyon laughed again. "Christina doesn't know what the favor was, friend."

Caine dropped his boots in the center of the hall, then added his socks to the pile. "I could still change my mind and accommodate the little woman, I suppose," he remarked dryly. "Damn, my favorite boots are ruined."

Lyon leaned against the archway, his arms folded across his chest, while he watched Caine pull off his shirt. "No, you couldn't kill her," he replied. His tone was mild when he added, "She wasn't really serious, was she? She seems quite timid. I can't imagine . . ."

"She witnessed a murder," Caine interjected. "Now she has several unsavory men chasing after her, obviously intent on silencing her. That's all I know, Lyon, but as soon as possible, I'm going to find out every detail. The sooner I can solve her problem, the sooner I'll be rid of her."

Since Caine was glaring so ferociously, Lyon tried to hide his smile. "She really has you rattled, doesn't she?" he asked.

"The hell she does," Caine muttered. "Why would you think a mere woman could get me rattled?"

"You just took your britches off in the middle of my foyer, Caine," he replied. "That's why I think you're rattled."

"I need some brandy," Caine countered. He grabbed his pants and started to put them back on again.

Christina strolled past him, smiled at her husband, and then continued on up the stairs. She didn't mention his near naked condition, and neither did he.

Lyon thoroughly enjoyed Caine's embarrassment. He'd never seen his friend in such a state. "Why don't you go inside the library. The brandy's on the side bar. Help yourself and I'll see about your bath. God, you do smell rank."

Caine did as Lyon suggested. The brandy warmed him a little and the fire he started in the hearth took the rest of his chills away.

Christina left Jade alone once the tub had been filled with steaming hot water. She'd already helped her wash her hair in the bucket of warm, rose-scented water.

Jade quickly stripped out of her soggy clothing. Her fingers were numb from cold, but she took the time to remove her dagger from the hidden pocket in the lining. She put the weapon on the chair beside the tub as a precautionary measure in case someone tried to sneak up behind her, then climbed into the hot water and let out a long sigh of pleasure.

She scrubbed every inch of her body twice before she felt clean again. Christina came back into the kitchen just as Jade was standing up. Since her back was to her, Christina immediately noticed the long, jagged scar along the base of her spine. She let out a gasp of surprise.

Jade grabbed the blanket from the back of the chair, wrapped it around herself, and then stepped out of the tub to face Christina. "Is something the matter?" she asked, daring her to mention the scar she knew she'd seen.

Christina shook her head. She saw the knife on the chair then and walked over to have a closer look at it. Jade could feel herself blush with embarrassment. She tried to think of a logical explanation to give her hostess as to why a gentle lady would be carrying such a weapon, but she was simply too weary to come up with a believable lie.

"Mine's much sharper."

"I beg your pardon?" Jade asked, certain she hadn't heard correctly.

"My blade is much sharper," Christina explained. "I use a special stone. Shall I fix yours for you?"

Jade nodded.

"Do you sleep with this by your side or under your pillow?" Christina asked very matter-of-factly.

"Under my pillow."

"So did I," Christina said. "It's much easier to grasp that way, isn't it?"

"Yes, but why did you . . ."

"I'll take your knife upstairs and put it under your pillow," Christina promised. "And in the morning, I'll sharpen it for you."

"That's very kind of you," Jade whispered. "I didn't realize other ladies carried knives."

"Most don't," Christina replied with a dainty shrug. She handed Jade a pristine white nightgown and matching wrapper, then helped her dress. "I don't sleep with a dagger under my pillow any longer. Lyon protects me. In time, I think you'll give up your dagger, too. Yes, I do believe you will."

"You do?" Jade asked. She was desperately trying to make sense out of the woman's remarks. "Why is that?"

"Destiny," Christina whispered. "Of course, you'll have to learn to trust Caine first."

"Impossible," Jade blurted out. "I don't trust anyone."

From Christina's wide-eyed expression, Jade assumed she'd been too vehement in her reply. "Lady Christina, I'm not at all certain I know what you're talking about. I barely know Caine. Why would I have to learn to trust him?"

"Please, you needn't call me Lady Christina," she countered. "Now come and sit by the fire while I brush the crinkles out of your hair."

She dragged the chair across the room, then gently pushed Jade down into the seat. "I don't have many friends in England."

"You don't?"

"It's my fault," Christina explained. "I don't have enough patience. The ladies are very pretentious here. You're different, though."

"How can you know that?" Jade asked.

"Because you carry a knife," Christina explained. "Will you be my friend?"

Jade hesitated a long minute before answering. "For as long as you wish me to be your friend, Christina," she whispered.

Christina stared down at the lovely woman. "You believe that once I know all about you, I'll change my inclination, don't you?"

Her new friend shrugged. Christina noticed her hands were tightly clenched in her lap.

"I haven't had time for friends," Jade blurted out.

"I noticed the scar on your back," Christina whispered. "I won't tell Caine about it, of course, but he'll notice when he takes you to his bed. You carry a mark of honor, Jade."

Jade would have bounded out of the chair if Christina hadn't grabbed her shoulders and held her down. "I meant no insult," she rushed out. "You shouldn't be ashamed of . . ."

"Caine isn't going to take me to his bed," Jade countered. "Christina, I don't even like the man."

Christina smiled. "We are friends now, aren't we?"

"Yes."

"Then you cannot lie to me. You do like Caine. I could see it in your eyes when you looked at him. Oh, you were frowning, but it was all bluster, wasn't it? At least admit that you think he's handsome. All the ladies find him very appealing."

"He is that," Jade answered with a sigh. "He's a womanizer, isn't he?"

"Lyon and I have never seen him with the same woman twice," Christina admitted. "So I do suppose you could call him a womanizer. Aren't most until they're ready to settle down?"

"I don't know," Jade replied. "I haven't had many men friends either. There just wasn't time."

Christina finally picked up the brush and began to give order to Jade's lustrous curls. "I've never seen such beautiful hair before. There are threads of red fire shining through it."

"Oh, you have beautiful hair, not me," Jade protested. "Men have a preference for golden-haired ladies, Christina."

"Destiny," Christina countered, completely changing the topic. "I have a feeling you've just met yours, Jade."

She didn't have the heart to argue with her. Christina sounded so sincere. "If you say so," she agreed.

Christina noticed the swelling on the side of her head then. Jade explained what had happened to her. She felt guilty because she was deceiving the woman, for she was telling the same lie she'd told Caine earlier, but her motives were pure, she reminded herself. The truth would only upset her new friend.

"You've had to be a warrior, haven't you, Jade?" Christina asked, her voice filled with sympathy.

"A what?"

"A warrior," Christina repeated. She was trying to braid Jade's hair, then decided it was still too damp. She put the brush down and waited for her friend to answer.

"You've been alone in this world for a long time, haven't you?" Christina asked. "That's why you don't trust anyone."

Jade lifted her shoulders in a shrug. "Perhaps," she whispered.

"We should go and find our men now."

"Lyon is your man, but Caine isn't mine," Jade protested. "I'd rather just go to bed, if you please."

Christina shook her head. "Caine will have had his bath by now and must feel refreshed again. I know both men will want to ask you some questions before they let you rest. Men can be very stubborn, Jade. It's better to let them have their way every now and again. They're so much easier to manage that way. Do trust me. I know what I'm talking about."

Jade tightened her sash on her wrapper and followed Christina. She tried to clear her mind for the inevitable sparring ahead of her. As soon as she walked into the library, she saw Caine. He was leaning against the edge of Lyon's desk, frowning at her. She frowned back.

She really wished he wasn't so handsome. He had bathed and was now dressed in clothes Lyon had given him. The fit was true, the fawn-colored britches indecently snug. A white cotton shirt covered his wide shoulders.

Jade sat down in the center of the gold-colored settee. Christina handed her a full goblet of brandy. "Drink this," she ordered. "It will warm your insides."

Jade took a few dainty sips until she became accustomed to the burning sensation, then emptied the glass.

Christina nodded with satisfaction. Jade felt immensely better, sleepy, too. She leaned back against the cushions and closed her eyes.

"Don't you dare fall asleep," Caine ordered. "I have some questions to put to you."

She didn't bother to open her eyes when she answered him. "I won't fall asleep, but when I keep my eyes closed, I don't have to see your mean frowns, Caine. It's much more peaceful this way. Why were you pretending to be Pagan?"

She'd slipped in that question so smoothly, no one reacted for a full minute.

"He was what?" Lyon finally asked.

"He was pretending to be Pagan," Jade repeated. "I don't know how many other famous people he's pretended to be in the past," she added with a nod. "Still, it seems to me that your friend has an affliction of sorts."

Caine looked as if he wanted to throttle her. Christina held her smile. "Lyon? I don't believe I've ever seen our friend this upset."

"Neither have I," Lyon returned.

Caine successfully glared him into quitting his comments. "This isn't a usual circumstance," he muttered.

"I doubt he's ever pretended to be Napoleon though," Jade interjected. "He's too tall to pull it off. Besides, everyone knows what Napoleon looks like."

"Enough," Caine bellowed. He took a deep breath, then continued in a softer tone. "I'll explain why I was pretending to be Pagan after you've told me everything that led up to this black night."

"You make it sound as though everything is my fault!" she cried out.

He closed his eyes. "I do not fault you."

"Oh, yes, you do," she argued. "You're the most exasperating man. I've been through a terrible time and you've shown me as much compassion as a jackal."

Caine had to count to ten before he could trust himself not to shout at her.

"Why don't you just start at the beginning?" Lyon suggested.

Jade didn't pay any attention to Lyon's request. Her full attention was centered on Caine. He was still a little too controlled for her liking. "If you don't start giving me a little sympathy and understanding, I'm going to start shouting."

"You're already shouting," he told her with a grin.

That statement gave her pause. She took a deep breath, then decided to take a different tack. "Those terrible men ruined everything," she announced. "My brother had just finished renovating his lovely home and they ruined it. I cannot tell you how disappointed Nathan is going to be when he finds out. Oh, quit staring at me like that, Caine. I don't care if you believe me or not."

"Now, Jade . . ."

"Don't talk to me."

"You seem to have lost control of the conversation," Lyon pointed out to Caine.

"I was never in control," Caine answered. "Jade, we're

going to have to talk to each other," he announced then. "Yes," he added when he thought she was about to interrupt. "You have been through a trying time. I'll give you that much."

He thought his tone had been filled with understanding. He wanted to appease her, yet knew he'd failed when she continued to frown at him. "You're the most galling man. Why do you have to sound so superior all the time?"

Caine turned to Lyon. "Did I sound superior?"

Lyon shrugged. Christina nodded. "If Jade thinks you sounded superior," she said. "Then perhaps you did, just a little."

"You treat me like an imbecile," Jade said. "Doesn't he, Christina?"

"Since you are my friend, I will of course agree with you," Christina answered.

"Thank you," Jade replied before turning her attention back to Caine. "I'm not a child."

"I've noticed."

His slow grin infuriated her. She could feel herself losing ground in her bid to keep him off balance. "Do you know what the very worst of it was? They actually torched my brother's beautiful carriage. Yes, they did," she added with a vehement nod.

"And that was the worst?" Caine asked.

"Sir, I happened to be inside at the time!" she cried out.

He shook his head. "You actually want me to believe you were inside the carriage when it caught fire?"

"Caught fire?" She bounded out of her seat and stood there with her hands on her hips, glaring at him. "Not bloody likely. It was torched."

She remembered her audience and whirled around to face them. Clutching the top of her wrapper against her neck, she lowered her head and said, "Pray forgive me for losing my temper, please. I don't usually sound like a shrew."

She resumed her seat then and closed her eyes. "I don't

care what he believes. I can't talk about this tonight. I'm too distraught. Caine, you're going to have to wait until morning to question me."

He gave up. The woman was certainly given to drama. She put the back of her hand up against her forehead and let out a forlorn sigh. He knew he wasn't going to be able to reason with her now.

Caine sat down on the settee beside her. He was still frowning when he put his arm around her shoulders and hauled her up against his side.

"I specifically remember telling you that I cannot abide being touched," she muttered as she snuggled up against him.

Christina turned to her husband and let him see her smile. "Destiny," she whispered. "I think we should leave them alone," she added. "Jade, your bedroom is the first on the left at the top of the steps. Caine, you're next door."

Christina tugged her reluctant husband to his feet. "Sweetheart," Lyon said, "I want to know what happened to Jade. I'll just stay down here a few more minutes."

"Tomorrow will be soon enough for you to satisfy your curiosity," Christina promised. "Dakota will be waking us in just a few more hours. You need your rest."

"Who is Dakota?" Jade asked, smiling over the affectionate way the happy couple looked at each other. There was such love in their expressions. A surge of raw envy rushed through her, but she quickly pushed the feeling away. It was pointless to wish for things she could never have.

"Dakota is our son," Lyon answered. "He's almost six months old now. You'll meet our little warrior in the morning."

The door closed softly on that promise and she and Caine were once again all alone. Jade immediately tried to move away from him. He tightened his hold.

"Jade? I never meant to sound like I was ridiculing you,"

he whispered. "I'm just trying to be logical about this situation of yours. You have to admit that tonight has been . . . difficult. I feel like I'm spinning around in circles. I'm not used to ladies asking me so sweetly if I could kill them."

She turned to smile up at him. "Was I sweet?" she asked.

He slowly nodded. Her mouth was so close, so appealing. Before he could stop himself, he leaned down. His mouth rubbed against hers in a gentle, undemanding kiss.

It was over and done with before she could gather her wits and offer a protest.

"Why did you do that?" she asked in a strained whisper.

"I felt like it," he answered. His grin made her smile. He pushed her back down on his shoulder so he wouldn't give in to the urge to kiss her again, then said, "You've been through hell, haven't you? We'll wait until tomorrow to talk. When you've had a proper rest, we'll work on this problem together."

"That is most considerate of you," she replied. She sounded acutely relieved. "Now will you please tell me why you were pretending to be Pagan? You said earlier that you wanted to draw him out, but I don't understand how . . ."

"I was trying to prick his pride," he explained. "And make him angry enough to come after me. I know that if someone was pretending to be me, I'd . . . oh, hell," he muttered. "It sounds foolish now." His fingers were slowly threading through her soft curls in an absentminded fashion. "I tried everything else. Bounty didn't work."

"But why? Did you want to meet him?"

"I want to kill him."

Her indrawn breath told him he'd stunned her with his bluntness. "And if he sent someone else in his place to challenge you, would you kill that man too?"

"I would."

"Is your work killing people then? Is that how you make your way in this world?"

She was staring into the fire but he could see the tears in her eyes. "No, I don't kill for a living."

"But you've killed before?"

She'd turned to look at him when she asked that question, letting him see her fear. "Only when it was necessary," he answered.

"I've never killed anyone."

His smile was gentle. "I never thought you had."

"Yet you really believe it's necessary to kill this pirate?"

"I do." His voice had turned hard, a deliberate choice that, for he hoped to get her to quit her questions. "I'll kill every one of his damned followers, too, if it's the only way I can get to him."

"Oh, Caine, I really wish you wouldn't kill anyone."

She was on the verge of tears again. Caine leaned back against the cushions, closed his eyes, and said, "You're a gentle lady, Jade. You can't possibly understand."

"Help me understand," she implored. "Pagan's done so many wonderful things. It seems a sin that you . . ."

"He has?" Caine interrupted.

"Surely you know that the pirate gives most of his booty to the less fortunate," she explained. "Why, our church has a new steeple, thanks to his generous donation."

"Donation?" Caine shook his head over her ludicrous choice of words. "The man is nothing but a common thief. He robs from the rich . . ."

"Well, of course he robs from the rich."

"What's that supposed to mean?"

"He takes from the rich because they have so much, they won't miss the paltry amount he steals. And it wouldn't do him any good at all to take from the poor. They don't have anything worth stealing."

"You seem to know quite a lot about this pirate."

"Everyone keeps up with Pagan's adventures. He's such a romantic figure."

"You sound as if you think he should be knighted."

"Perhaps he should," she answered. She rubbed her cheek against his shoulder. "Some say Pagan's never harmed anyone. It doesn't seem right for you to hunt him down."

"If you believe he hasn't ever killed anyone, why did you come looking for him? You wanted him to kill you, remember?"

"I remember," she answered. "If I explain my true plan, will you promise not to laugh?"

"I promise," he answered, wondering over her sudden shyness.

"I was hoping . . . that is, if he didn't want to kill me, well then, perhaps he might consider taking me away on his magical ship and keeping me safe until my brother came home."

"Heaven help you if you'd gotten that wish," Caine said. "You've obviously been listening to too many fanciful stories. You're wrong, too. That bastard pirate has killed before."

"Who has he killed?"

He didn't speak for a long minute but stared into the fire. When he finally answered her, there was ice in his voice. "Pagan killed my brother, Colin."

Chapter Four

O
h, Caine. I'm so sorry," she whispered. "You must miss him terribly. Was Colin older or younger than you?"

"Younger."

"Did he die very long ago?"

"Just a few months," Caine answered.

"Your family must be having a difficult time of it," she whispered. "Are both your parents still living?"

"Yes, though of the two, my father's having a much more difficult time accepting Colin's death. He's all but given up on life."

"I don't understand," she countered.

"Father used to be very active in politics. He was known as the champion of the poor, Jade, and he was able to force through many substantial measures that eased their burdens."

"Such as?"

She'd taken hold of his hand and was holding it against her waist. Caine didn't think she was aware of her action. It was just an instinctive attempt to give him comfort, he guessed, and he found he didn't dislike the touch or her motive.

"You were explaining how your papa helped the poor," she reminded him.

"Yes," Caine returned. "He was responsible for defeating the tax increase, for one example."

"But he quit these important duties?"

"He quit everything," Caine said. "His politics, his family, his friends, his clubs. He doesn't even read the dailies now. He just stays locked inside his study and broods. I believe, once Pagan has been punished, that my father might . . . hell, I don't know. He's such a defeated man now."

"Are you like your father? Are you also a champion of the poor? I believe you must be a protector by nature."

"Why do you say that?"

She couldn't very well tell him she'd read his file. "Because of the way you took me under your wing," she answered. "And I think you would have offered your help to any defenseless, poor person. Of course, I wasn't poor when I met you."

"Are you going to start in about the silver coins again?"

Because he was smiling at her, she knew he wasn't irritated with her. "No, I'm not going to start in, whatever that's suppose to mean. I was just reminding you. You are like your father then, aren't you?"

"I suppose we share that trait."

"Yet your father retreated from the world while you immediately went after vengeance. Your reactions were just the opposite, weren't they?"

"Yes."

"I understand why your father gave up."

"You do?"

"It's because fathers aren't supposed to lose their sons, Caine."

"No," Caine agreed. "They should die first."

"After a long, happy life, of course," she added.

She sounded so sincere, he didn't want to argue with her. "Of course."

"And you're absolutely certain it was Pagan who killed Colin?"

"I am. I have it on high authority."

"How?"

"How, what?"

"How did Pagan kill him?"

"For God's sake, Jade," he muttered. "I don't want to talk about this. I've already told you more than I intended."

"I'm sorry if I've upset you," she replied. She leaned away from him and looked into his eyes.

The worry in her expression made him feel guilty for his biting tone. "Colin was killed at sea."

"Yet someone was thoughtful enough to bring him home for burial?"

"No."

"No? Then how can you know if he's really dead? He could have washed up on a deserted island, or possibly . . ."

"Proof was sent."

"What proof? And who sent it?"

He couldn't understand her interest in this topic and determined to end the conversation. "Proof came from the War Department. Now will you quit your questions?"

"Yes, of course," she whispered. "Please accept my apology for intruding upon such a personal matter."

She let out a yawn, then begged his forgiveness for that unladylike action.

"Caine? We can't stay here long. I fear we would be putting your friends in danger."

"I agree," he answered. "We'll only stay one night."

He stared into the fire while he formulated his plans. Jade snuggled up against him and fell asleep. He told himself he was thankful for the blessed quiet. Yet he resisted the urge to go up to bed, for he liked holding the impossible woman in his arms too much to move.

He kissed her brow just for the hell of it, then kissed her once again.

Only when the fire had burned down to glowing embers and a decided chill settled in the room did he finally get up.

She came awake with a start. Jade jumped to her feet, but was so disoriented, she started walking in the wrong direction. She would have walked right into the hearth if he hadn't stopped her. He tried to lift her into his arms. She pushed his hands away. He let out a sigh, then put his arm around her shoulders and guided her up the stairs. He kept trying not to think about how lovely she looked now. Her hair was almost dry and had regained its enchanting curls. He also tried not to think about the fact that she was wearing only a thin nightgown and wrapper.

He opened the bedroom door for her, then turned to find his own.

"Caine?" she called out, her voice a sleepy whisper. "You won't leave me, will you?"

He turned back to face her. The question was insulting, yet the fearful look in her eyes softened his initial reaction. "No, I won't leave you."

She nodded, looked like she was about to say something more, and then abruptly shut the door in his face.

Christina had prepared the adjoining bedroom for Caine. The bed covers on the large bed had been turned back, and a full fire blazed in the hearth.

As inviting as the bed was, sleep still eluded Caine. He tossed and turned in the giant bed for almost an hour, all the while damning himself for his own lack of discipline. Yet no matter how valiantly he tried, he couldn't get the red-haired, green-eyed enchantress out of his mind.

He couldn't understand his own reaction to her. Hell, he wanted her with an intensity that made him burn. That didn't make any sense at all to him. He disliked bad-tempered, illogical, cry-at-the-sight-of-a-frown young ladies, didn't he?

He was simply too exhausted to think straight now. He wasn't used to being restrained either. Caine was a man who took what he wanted when he wanted it. He'd gone soft over the last few years, though. He didn't have to bother with the chase any longer. The women always came to him. They gave themselves freely. Caine took what each offered without feeling a qualm of remorse. He was always honest with his women, and he never, ever spent a full night with any of them. Mornings, he knew, would bring false hopes and foolish demands.

Yet he wanted Jade. Lord, he wasn't making any sense. Jade's sneeze echoed in the distance then. Caine immediately got out of bed. He put on his pants but didn't bother with the buttons. He now had an excuse to go into her room. She probably needed another blanket, he told himself. The night air had a chill to it. There was also the possibility of a fire, for the light coming from beneath the door indicated she'd fallen asleep with the candles burning.

He wasn't at all prepared for the sight he came upon. Jade was sleeping on her stomach. Her glorious hair was spread like a shawl on her back. Her face was turned toward him. Her eyes were closed, and her deep, even breathing indicated she was fast asleep.

His enchantress was stark naked. She'd taken off her nightgown and placed it on the chair beside the bed. She'd also kicked the covers off the bed.

The little lady had a decidedly sensual streak hidden inside her, if she preferred sleeping in the nude, as he did.

She looked like a golden goddess to him. Her legs were long, beautifully shaped. He suddenly pictured those silky legs wrapped around him and almost groaned in reaction.

He was fully aroused and aching by the time he walked over to the side of the bed. He noticed the long thin scar across her spine then. Caine immediately recognized the mark, as he had a similar one on the back of his thigh. There was only one weapon that could inflict such a jagged line. It was the thick lash from a whip.

Someone had used a whip on her. Caine was stunned, outraged too. The scar was old, by at least five years or so, judging from the faded edges, and that fact made the atrocity all the more repugnant. Jade had been a child when she'd been so mistreated.

He suddenly wanted to wake her up and demand the name of the bastard who'd done this to her.

She started moaning in her sleep. The restlessness in which she moved made him think she was in the throes of an unpleasant dream. She sneezed again, then let out another whimper of distress.

With a sigh of acute frustration, he grabbed the nightgown and turned back to the angel he'd been foolish enough to promise he'd protect. He tried to see the humor in this bleak situation. For the first time in his life, he was actually going to put a nightgown back on a woman.

Caine was just leaning over her when he saw the flash of steel out of the corner of his eye. His reaction was instinctive. He moved to block her attack with a forceful sweep of his left arm. She was already stopping herself when his arm slammed into her wrist. The dagger went flying across the room and landed with a loud clatter on the base of the hearth.

She'd turned into a hellion. Jade was on her knees now, facing him. Her breathing was harsh, her anger apparent in her dark expression. "Don't you ever sneak up on me like that again," she shouted up at him. "Good God, man, I could have killed you."

Caine was just as furious with her. "Don't you ever try to use your knife on me," he roared. "Or good God, woman, I will kill you!"

She didn't appear to be the least intimidated by that

threat. Caine decided she just didn't understand her own peril, or she certainly would have tried to act a little contrite. She'd also forgotten she wasn't wearing any clothes, either.

He hadn't forgotten. Her full, round breasts were only partially concealed by her long dark curls. Her nipples were pink, hard. Her anger made her pant, forcing her slender ribcage to rise and fall in a rhythm he found hypnotic.

He felt like a cad for noticing until she started prodding his temper again.

"You're not going to kill me," she announced. "We've already had this discussion, remember?"

He was staring down at her with the most astonished look on his face. "You aren't at all afraid of me, are you?"

She shook her head. Her long hair swayed gracefully over her shoulders.

"Why would I be afraid of you?" she asked. "You're my protector, sir."

Her irritated tone of voice was the last provocation he was going to take. Caine grabbed hold of her hands and roughly shoved her back against the mattress. He followed her down, spreading her thighs with one of his knees wedged between so she couldn't lash out at him with her legs and do real damage. He wouldn't put it past her to try to make a eunuch out of him if she had the opportunity. "I think it's high time you understood a few basic rules," he grated out.

She let out a loud gasp when his bare chest touched her breasts. Caine guessed she'd finally realized she wasn't wearing a nightgown. "Exactly," he said on a low groan.

Damn, but she was soft, wonderfully so. He wanted to bury his face in the crook of her neck and make slow, sweet love to her. He would have her, he vowed, but she'd be hot and begging for him, not muttering unladylike obscenities against his ear as she was now doing.

"Where in God's name did you learn those blasphemies?" he asked when she threatened to do him in, in the most amazing way.

"From you," she lied. "Will you get off me, you . . . wart from hell."

She was full of bravado. Yet there was a tremor of fear in her voice, too. Caine immediately reacted to it. It took extreme discipline, but he slowly moved away from her. His jaw was clenched tight and a fine sweat covered his brow. Her nipples rubbed against his chest when he moved. Caine groaned low in his throat. Her breasts were ready for him, even if the rest of her wasn't. Ready for him to take into his mouth, to kiss, to suck, to . . .

"Caine?"

He propped himself up on his elbows so he could see her expression. He immediately wished he hadn't bothered. Her intense frown was already making him angry again.

She was filled with the most conflicting emotions. She knew she should feel outraged, but the opposite was really the full truth. The dark hair on his chest, so crisp, so warm, tickled her breasts into responding. He was so warm all over, so exciting. And hard, she added to herself. The sleek bulge of muscle in his upper arms made her breath catch in her throat. She knew better than to let him know how much he was affecting her. Outrage, she remembered. I must be outraged, and frightened, too.

"Is this how you plan to protect me?" she asked, affecting just the right amount of fear in her voice.

"No, this isn't how I plan to protect you," he answered in a husky voice.

"Caine?"

"Yes?"

"You look like you want to kiss me. Do you?"

"Yes," he admitted. "I do."

She started shaking her head, but he stopped that action by cupping the sides of her face and holding her still.

"But you don't even like me much." Her voice was a breathless whisper. "You said so, remember? Have you changed your mind, then?"

He found himself smiling over the bewildered look on her face. "No," he answered, just to goad her temper.

"Then why would you want to kiss me?"

"I can't explain it," he said. "Perhaps it's because you're stark naked, and I can feel your soft skin beneath me. Perhaps . . ."

"Only once then."

He didn't understand what she meant, but the blush that covered her cheeks indicated her embarrassment. "Only once what, Jade?" he asked.

"You may kiss me, Caine," she explained. "But only once. Then you must get off me and leave my room."

"Jade? Do you want me to kiss you?"

His voice had turned so tender, she felt as though he'd just caressed her. She stared at his mouth, wondering what it would feel like to be properly kissed by him. Would his mouth be as hard as the rest of him?

Curiosity overruled caution. "Yes," she whispered. "I do want you to kiss me, Caine."

The kiss was one of absolute possession. His mouth was hard, demanding. His tongue thrust inside and rubbed against hers. She had no idea that men kissed women in such a manner, yet found she liked the stroke of his tongue very much. It was thoroughly arousing. Only when her tongue timidly imitated his bold action did he gentle the kiss. It was shameful the way he used his tongue in the erotic mating ritual, but she didn't care. She could feel his hard arousal against the junction of her thighs. He pushed against her each time his tongue slid deep into her mouth. A slow heat began to burn inside her belly.

She couldn't seem to stop touching him. His mouth made her wild. His tongue slid in and out, again and again, until she was shivering for more. Caine had wrapped her hair around his fist to hold her still, but that action wasn't really necessary. She was clinging to him now.

It was time to stop. Caine knew he was at risk of losing all control. Jade tried to bring him back to her by digging her nails into his shoulders. Caine resisted the unspoken invitation. He stared down into her eyes a long minute. He liked what he saw there, didn't even try to hide his grin of male satisfaction. "You taste like sugar and honey."

"I do?"

He brushed his mouth over hers once again. "Oh, yes, you do," he said. "Brandy too."

She moved restlessly against him. "Don't push your hips up like that," he ordered. His jaw was clenched tight against the innocent provocation.

"Caine?"

"Yes?"

"Only twice," she whispered. "All right?"

He understood. She was giving him permission to kiss her again. He couldn't resist. He kissed her again, a long, hard, wet, tongue-thrusting kiss, and when he next looked into her eyes, he was thoroughly pleased. She looked completely dazed. He'd done that to her, he knew. The passion inside her more than matched his own.

"Caine?"

"No more, Jade," he growled.

"You didn't like it?" she asked, her worry obvious in her gaze.

"I liked it all right," he replied.

"Then why . . ."

Her hands were caressing his shoulders and it was becoming an agony to maintain his discipline. "I can't promise you I'll stop if I kiss you again, Jade. Are you willing to take the risk?"

Before she could answer him, he started to ease away from her. "That wasn't a fair question to ask in your present state."

The passion began to clear her mind. "What present state?"

He let out a deep sigh. "I think I'm going to make love to

you eventually, Jade," he whispered. "But you'll make the decision before passion clouds your mind." His expression darkened when she started struggling against him. The movement reminded him of her soft breasts waiting for his touch. "If you don't quit wiggling against me like that," he grated out. "I swear it's going to happen now. I'm not made of iron, sweet."

She went completely still.

Though he was reluctant to leave her, he even assisted her in putting her nightgown back on. He refused to let her have her dagger back, even when she fervently promised him she wouldn't try to use it on him again.

"I was sound asleep," she reasoned. "And you were sneaking up on me like a thief. I had to protect myself."

Caine took hold of her hand and dragged her toward his bedroom. "You were having a nightmare, weren't you?"

"I might have been," she replied. "I don't remember now. Why are you tugging at me?"

"You're going to sleep with me. Then you won't have to worry about anyone sneaking up on you."

"Out of the boat and into the ocean, is that it?" she asked. "I really believe I'm much safer on my own, thank you."

"Can't trust yourself to keep your hands off me?" he asked.

"Yes, that's true," she admitted with a feigned sigh. "I'll have to restrain myself, though, or I'll surely be sent to the gallows. Murder's still frowned on in this part of the world, isn't it?"

Caine laughed. "You won't be thinking about murdering me when I'm touching you," he predicted.

She let out a low groan of frustration. "You really aren't going to do. A protector shouldn't be lusting after his charge."

"And what about you?" he asked. "Do you lust after your protector?"

He turned around to wait for her answer. "I don't know,"

she said. "I find you terribly appealing, Caine, yet I've never gone to bed with a man and I don't know if I want you that much. Still, this attraction is becoming too much of a distraction. You aren't going to do at all, sir. Come morning, I'm going to have to find someone else to protect me . . . someone less appealing."

She tried to pull away from him then. Caine caught her before she'd taken a step back toward her own bed. In one quick motion, he tossed her over his shoulder and carried her through the connecting doorway.

"How dare you treat me like this? I'm not a bag of feed. Put me down this minute, you bastard rake."

"Bastard rake? Sweet, you've got quite a vocabulary for a lady."

He dropped her into the center of his bed. Since he fully expected her to bounce right back out and try to escape, he was pleasantly surprised when she began to settle the blankets around herself. After she'd scooted to the far side of the bed, she fluffed the feather pillow behind her head and draped her hair over her shoulder. The alluring blaze of red curls against the pristine white nightgown looked incredibly beautiful to him. The woman who had just called him bastard was now looking like an angel again.

Caine's sigh blew out the candles.

"I am a lady," she muttered when he'd settled himself beside her. "But you've riled my temper, Caine, and that's the reason for my . . ."

"Colorful vocabulary?" he asked when she didn't finish her thought.

"Yes," she replied. She sounded forlorn when she added, "Must I apologize?"

He kept his laughter contained. "I fear you wouldn't mean it," he answered. He rolled to his side and tried to take her into his arms. When she pushed his hands away, he moved onto his back again, stacked his hands behind his head, and stared into the darkness above while he thought about the warm body next to him. She was certainly the most unusual woman he'd ever met. Why, she could have him laughing one second and shouting the next. He couldn't explain his reactions to her, for he didn't understand himself. Only one thing was certain in his mind. He knew she desired him. Her kiss had shown him that much.

"Jade?"

His husky voice sent a shiver down her arms. "Yes?"

"It's damned odd, isn't it?"

"What's damned odd?" she asked.

He could hear the smile in her voice. "You and me sharing this bed without touching each other. You do feel comfortable with me, don't you?"

"Yes," she answered. "Caine?"

"Yes?"

"Is making love painful?"

"No," he answered. "It's painful when you want to and can't."

"Oh. Then I must not want you very much, Caine, because I'm not hurting at all." She made that statement of fact in a gratingly cheerful tone of voice.

"Jade?"

"Yes?"

"Go to sleep."

She felt him turn toward her and immediately tensed in anticipation of another kiss. After waiting a long while, she realized he wasn't going to kiss her again. She was horribly disappointed.

Caine propped himself up on his elbow and stared down at her. Jade forced a serene expression in case he had cat's eyes and could see in the dark.

"Jade? How did you get that whiplash on your back?"

"From a whip," she answered. She rolled to her side and resisted the urge to scoot up against his warmth.

"Answer me."

"How do you know it was a whiplash?"

"I have an identical mark on the back of my thigh."

"You do? How did you get yours?"

"Are you going to answer my every question with a question of your own?"

"It worked quite nicely for Socrates."

"Tell me how you got your whiplash," he asked once again.

"It's a personal matter," she explained. "It's almost dawn, Caine. I've had a rather trying day."

"All right," he conceded. "You can tell me all about this personal matter in the morning."

Before she could fend him off, he threw his arm around her waist and hauled her up against him. His chin rested on the top of her head. The junction of his hard thighs was nestled against her backside.

"Are you warm enough?" he asked.

"Yes," she answered. "Are you?"

"Oh, yes."

"You will behave, won't you?" she teased.

"Probably," he replied. "Jade?" he asked, his tone much more serious now.

"Yes?"

"I would never do anything you didn't want me to do."

"But what if you thought I wanted you to . . . and I didn't really want . . ."

"Unless you gave me your approval, your wholehearted approval, I wouldn't touch you. I promise."

She thought that was the nicest promise she'd ever been given. He sounded so sincere, and she knew he really meant what he said.

"Caine? Do you know what I've just discovered? You really are a gentleman, and an honorable one at that."

He'd already fallen asleep hugging her. Jade decided to do the same. She rolled over in his arms, slipped her arms around his waist, and promptly fell asleep.

Caine woke up a bare hour later when Jade cried out in

her sleep. She muttered something he couldn't decipher, then let out a terrified scream. He shook her awake. When he brushed her hair away from her face, he felt the wetness on her cheeks. She'd been weeping in her sleep.

"Sweetheart, you're having a bad dream. It's all right now," he soothed. "You're safe with me."

He rubbed her shoulders and her back, too, until the tension eased out of her. "What were you dreaming about?" he asked, when her breathing had calmed down.

"Sharks." The word came out in a whisper filled with anguish.

"Sharks?" he asked, uncertain if he'd heard correctly.

She tucked her head under his chin. "I'm so tired," she whispered. "I don't remember the nightmare now. Hold me, Caine. I want to go back to sleep."

Her voice still trembled. Caine knew she was lying. She remembered every bit of her nightmare. He wasn't going to prod her into telling him about it, however.

He kissed the top of her head, then complied with her order and pulled her close.

Jade knew the minute he fell asleep again. She slowly eased herself away from him and moved to the side of the bed. Her heart was still slamming inside her chest. He thought she'd only had a nightmare. Was reliving an actual event the same? And would she ever be able to forget the horror?

God help her, would she ever be able to go willingly back in the water again?

She felt like crying. It took all her discipline not to give into her urge and hold on to him now. Caine was such an easy man to trust. She could get used to depending on him, she knew. Yes, he was the dependable type, but he could also break her heart.

She was thoroughly confused by her reaction to him. In her heart, she trusted him completely.

Why then didn't his own brother?

Chapter Five

Caine woke up ravenous . . . for her. Jade's nightgown was tangled up around her thighs. She had cuddled up against his side and had thrown her right leg over his thighs sometime during the short night. Her knee now covered his throbbing arousal. Out of deference to her feelings, he'd slept with his pants on. The clothing proved to be a paltry barrier against her softness, though, and Caine could feel the scorch of her body branding him with hot desire.

The side of her face rested on his bare chest. Her lips were softly parted, her breathing deep, even. She had long, black-as-night eyelashes and a healthy sprinkle of freckles across the bridge of her nose. The woman was utterly feminine. Caine continued to stare at her lovely face until he was so hard, so hurting, he was clenching his teeth.

It was a battle to move away from her. When he tried to ease her onto her back, he realized she was holding his hand. She didn't seem inclined to let go, either.

He had to pry her fingers loose. Then he remembered she'd called him a bastard rake the night before. Yet she was clinging to him now. Caine was certain she'd be wary of him once again when she was wide awake. She couldn't hide her vulnerability from him when she was sleeping, however, and that fact pleased him considerably.

A fierce wave of possessiveness consumed him. In that moment, while he stared down at his angel, he vowed he would never let anything happen to her, he would protect her with his life.

For as long as he was her guardian . . . or did he want her to stay with him much, much longer . . . Nathan would be home in two short weeks to take up the task of keeping his sister safe. Would Caine be able to let her go then?

He didn't have any ready answers; he knew only that the thought of giving her up made his heart lurch and his stomach tighten up.

It was all he was prepared to admit to himself, all he was willing to give.

It certainly wasn't possible to be logical with a half-naked beauty draped over him. Yes, he thought as he leaned down and kissed her brow, he would wait until later to sort it all out in his mind.

He washed and dressed in clothes that belonged to Lyon, then woke Jade. She tried to hit him when he nudged her awake. "It's all right, Jade," he whispered. "It's time to get up."

She was blushing by the time she'd sat up in bed. Caine watched her pull the coverlet all the way up to her chin. The act of modesty really wasn't necessary considering her state of undress the night before, but he decided against mentioning that to her now.

"Please excuse my behavior," she whispered in a husky, sleep-filled voice. "'Tis the truth I'm not at all accustomed to being awakened by a man."

"I would hope not," he replied.

She looked bewildered. "Why would you hope that?"

"You're not awake enough to play Socrates with me," he told her, his voice gentle.

Jade stared rather stupidly up at him. Caine leaned down and kissed her then, a hard, quick kiss that was over and done with before she could summon a reaction . . . or make a fist.

She had the most astonished look on her face when he pulled away from her. "Why did you do that?"

"Because I wanted to," he answered.

He started for the door, but she called out to him. "Where are you going?"

"Downstairs," he replied. "I'll meet you in the dining room. I imagine Christina left some clothes for you in the other room, sweet."

"Oh my God . . . she must think that we . . . that is . . ."

The door closed on her horrified whispers.

She could hear Caine whistling as he made his way down the corridor. Jade fell back against the pillows. The brief kiss he'd given her had left her shaken. That, and the fact that his friends now thought she was wanton.

And just what did she care what they thought? When this deception was over, she wouldn't ever see them again. Still, Christina wanted to be her friend. Jade now felt as though she'd just betrayed her in some way.

"I'll simply explain that nothing happened," she whispered to herself. She's going to understand. A true friend would, wouldn't she?

Since Jade hadn't had any true friends in the past, she couldn't be certain what rules applied.

She got out of her bed and rushed back into her own room. Caine had been correct, for Christina had left a pretty dark blue riding outfit. Dark brown boots with nary a mark on them were on the floor beside the chair. Jade prayed they were close to her size.

She couldn't quit thinking about Caine while she dressed. The man was going to be a challenge to her peace of mind. He was so dangerously attractive. The damned dimple made her want to swoon. Lyon had loaned him a pair of indecently snug deerskin-colored britches. The pants accentuated the sleek bulge of muscles in his thighs . . . and his crotch. Black Harry would throttle her if he knew she'd taken the time to notice a man's body. Caine's sexuality, so raw, so appealing, made her notice, though. She might be innocent of men, but she certainly wasn't blind.

A scant fifteen minutes later, she was ready to go downstairs. The white silk blouse was a bit too tight in the bosom, but the jacket hid that fact. The boots scrunched her toes, too, but only just a little.

She'd tried to braid her hair, but it was a disaster. She gave up the task when she saw the lopsided mess she was making. Jade had little patience and absolutely no expertise in the area of hair styling. That fact had never bothered her before, yet now it worried her. She was a gentle lady of the *ton* until this masquerade was finished, and it wasn't like her to let any little detail slip her notice.

The dining room doors were wide open. Caine was sitting at the head of a long, mahogany table. A servant was pouring dark tea into a cup from a beautiful silver pot. Caine wasn't paying any attention to the man, however. He seemed to be engrossed in the newspaper he was reading.

She wasn't certain if she was supposed to curtsy or not, then decided it really didn't matter since he wasn't paying any notice. She was mistaken in that belief, however, for as soon as she reached the chair adjacent to his, he stood up and offered her his assistance.

No one had ever held out a chair for her, not even Nathan. She couldn't make up her mind if she liked the fuss or not.

Caine continued to read his paper while she ate her breakfast. When he'd finished with what she decided was probably a daily ritual, he leaned back in his chair, folded the newspaper, and finally gave her his complete attention.

"Well?" she asked as soon as he looked at her.

"Well, what?" he asked, smiling over the eagerness in her expression.

"Was there mention of a finely dressed gentleman being murdered?" She pointed to the newspaper.

"No, there wasn't."

She let out a gasp of dismay. "I'll wager they tossed him in the Thames. Do you know, Caine, now that I reflect upon it, I did feel something slither against my legs. And you did say nothing could live for long in the Thames, didn't you? It must have been that poor . . ."

"Jade, you're letting your imagination get the better of you," he interjected. "Not only was there no mention of your finely dressed gentleman, there wasn't any mention of *anyone* being murdered."

"Then they haven't found him yet."

"If he's a member of the *ton*, someone would have noticed his disappearance by now. It's been two days, hasn't it, since you saw . . ."

"It has been two days, exactly," she interrupted.

Caine thought that if she became any more enthusiastic, she might jump out of her chair.

"Which leads me to my first question," he announced. "Exactly what did you see?"

She leaned back against her chair. "Where are Lyon and Christina, do you suppose?"

"Are you avoiding my question?"

She shook her head. "I just don't want to have to tell it twice," she explained. Even as she gave that lie her mind was racing for another plausible story.

"Lyon went out for a bit," he answered. "And Christina is tending to Dakota. Answer me, please."

Her eyes widened.

"Now what's the matter?"

"You just said please," she whispered. She sounded awestruck. "If you're not careful, you'll soon be giving me the apologies you owe me."

He knew better than to ask her why he should apologize,

guessing she had her list of his faults memorized. Besides, the smile she just gave him was so dazzling, he could barely hold his concentration.

"They pitched him from the roof."

Caine was jarred back to their topic when she made that announcement. "You were on a roof?" he asked her, trying to imagine what in God's name she'd been up to.

"Of course not," she replied. "Why would I be on a roof?"

"Jade . . ."

"Yes?" she asked, looking expectant again.

"You weren't on a roof but you saw "them" throw this man . . ."

"He was a finely dressed gentleman," she interrupted.

"All right," he began again. "You weren't on the roof but you saw several men throw this finely dressed gentleman from the roof? Is that it?"

"There were three of them."

"You're certain?"

She nodded. "I was frightened, Caine, but I could still count."

"Where were you when this happened?"

"On the ground."

"I gathered that much," he muttered. "If you weren't on the roof, I did assume . . ."

"I could have been inside another building, or perhaps riding Nathan's fine horse, or even . . ."

"Jade, stop rambling," he demanded. "Just tell me where you were and what you saw."

"What I heard is just as significant, Caine."

"Are you deliberately trying to make me angry?"

She gave him a disgruntled look. "I was just about to walk into the church when I heard all the commotion. They weren't actually on top of the church. No, they were dragging this poor man across the rectory's roof. It's a bit lower. From my position, I could see the gentleman was

75

trying to get away from them. He was struggling and shouting for help. That's how I knew, Caine. I wasn't just imagining it."

"And?" he prodded when she suddenly quit her explanation.

"They tossed him over. If I'd been just a foot to the left, well sir, you wouldn't be having to protect me now. I'd be as dead as the poor gentleman is."

"Where is this church?"

"In Nathan's parish."

"And where is that?" he asked.

"Three hours north of here," she answered.

"Am I interrupting?" Christina asked from the doorway. Jade turned to smile at her.

"Of course not," Jade answered. "Thank you for the lovely breakfast, and for loaning me your beautiful riding clothes. I shall take good care of them," she added.

Lyon came up behind his wife and put his arms around her. While Caine and Jade watched, Christina's husband nuzzled the top of his wife's head.

"Miss me?" he asked.

"Of course," Christina answered. She smiled up at her husband, then turned back to Jade. "I went into your room . . ."

"Nothing happened," Jade rushed out. "It's all his fault, really. But nothing happened, Christina. I tried to use my knife on him. That's all. He took exception, of course," she added as she waved her hand in Caine's direction. "He was so bloody furious, he dragged me into his room. Oh Lord, I'm making a muddle out of this, aren't I?"

She turned to Caine. "Will you say something, please? My new friend is going to think I'm . . ."

She quit her explanation when she noticed Caine's astonished expression. He wasn't going to be any help at all, she realized. He was back to thinking she was daft.

She could feel herself burning with embarrassment.

"I went into your room to fetch your knife," Christina explained. "You actually tried to cut him with that dull blade?"

Jade wanted to find a place to hide. "No," she answered with a sigh.

"But you just said . . ."

"At first, I did try to cut him," she explained. "He woke me up trying to put my nightgown back on . . ."

"You did?" Lyon asked Caine. His grin was downright shameful.

"Lyon, stay out of this," Caine ordered.

"Well, as soon as I realized who it was, I quit trying to stab him. He gave me a startle. I thought he was a thief."

Lyon looked like he was dying to say something more. Caine glared him into keeping silent.

"Did you find out anything?" Caine called out.

Lyon nodded. He started into the room. "Christina? Take Jade into the drawing room, would you?"

"She'll have to go in there on her own," Christina answered. "I promised to sharpen her knife for her. Jade? I couldn't find it under your pillow. That's what I've been trying to explain."

"He took it," Jade answered with a wave in Caine's direction. "I believe I saw him put it on the mantle, though I'm not absolutely certain. Would you like me to help you look for it?"

"No, I'll find it. You go and keep Dakota company. He's playing on his blanket inside. I'll join you in just a few minutes."

Jade hurriedly followed Christina out of the room. She paused at the drawing room doors when she heard Lyon's booming laughter. She smiled then, guessing Caine had just told his friend what an imbecile he thought she was.

She was feeling quite smug now. It took a certain concentration to be able to ramble on and on so convincingly, and she thought she'd pulled it off quite nicely. She had no idea

77

she was so talented. Still, she was honest enough to admit to herself that there had been a moment when she hadn't really been pretending. Jade straightened her shoulders. Pretense or not, rambling was definitely a plus when dealing with Caine.

She went inside the room then and closed the door behind her. She spotted the quilted blanket in front of the settee right away. Christina's son, however, was quite another matter. She couldn't find him anywhere.

She was about to shout an alarm when she noticed a tiny foot protruding from the back of the settee. She hurried over and knelt down, briefly thought about pulling him out by his one foot, and then decided she'd better find the rest of him first. With her backside in the air, she leaned down until the side of her face rested on the carpet.

The most magnificent blue eyes she'd ever seen were just inches away from her now. Dakota. Jade thought she might have startled him by her sudden appearance. His eyes did widen. He didn't cry, though. No, he stared at her a long, drooling moment, and then gave her a wide, toothless grin.

She thought he was the most amazing infant. Once he'd finished smiling at her, he went back to his main interest. He seemed determined to gum his way through the ornately carved wooden leg of the settee.

"Oh, that can't be at all good for you, little boy," Jade announced.

He didn't spare her a glance as he continued to chew on the wood. "Stop that now, Dakota," she commanded. "Your mama will be unhappy if she sees you eating the furniture. Come out here, please."

It was obvious that she had no experience handling children. It was also a fact that she didn't realize she had an audience watching her either.

Both Caine and Lyon leaned against opposite door frames observing the pair. They were both trying not to laugh.

"You aren't going to cooperate, are you, Dakota?" Jade asked.

The baby gurgled happily in answer to that remark.

"She's innovative, I'll give her that," Lyon whispered to Caine when Jade lifted the edge of the settee and moved it to the side.

She then sat down on the floor next to the little one. He immediately wiggled his way toward her. She wasn't at all certain how to lift a baby. She'd heard that their little necks weren't strong enough to hold their heads up until they were at least a year or so. Dakota, however, had lifted his chest off the carpet and seemed to be strong enough on his own.

He made the most delightful sounds. He was such a happy little boy. She couldn't resist touching him. She gingerly patted the top of his head, then eased her hands under his arms and slowly dragged him up onto her lap.

She wanted to cuddle him against her bosom.

He wanted something else. Dakota grabbed hold of a clump of her hair, pulled on it, hard, while he tried to find his supper.

It didn't take her any time at all to realize what he was trying to do.

"No, no, Dakota," she whispered when he arched up against her and started to fret. "Your mama's going to have to feed you. Shall we go and find her, love?"

Jade slowly gained her feet, keeping the baby close against her. His grip on her hair stung, but she didn't mind.

The baby smelled so wonderful. He was beautiful, too. He had his mother's blue eyes, but his dark curls came from his father. Jade stroked the baby's back and softly crooned to him. She was in awe of him.

She turned and noticed the men then. Jade could feel herself blush. "You have a fine son," she told Lyon in a stammer.

Caine stayed by the door while Lyon went to claim

Dakota. He had to pry his son's hands away from Jade's hair. She stared at Caine, wondering over the odd expression on his face now. There was tenderness there, but something else as well. She didn't have any idea what he was thinking.

"He's the first baby I've ever held," she told Lyon after he'd lifted his son into his arms.

"I'd say that you are a natural," Lyon replied. "Wouldn't you agree, Dakota?" he asked. He held the baby up until they were eye level. Dakota immediately grinned.

Christina breezed into the room, drawing Jade's attention. She hurried over and handed her friend the sharpened knife. The dagger was inside a soft leather carrier. "It's sharp enough now," she told Jade. "I made the pouch so you wouldn't accidentally prick yourself."

"Thank you," Jade replied.

"You aren't going to need a knife," Caine announced. He moved away from his lazy repose and walked over to Jade's side. "Let me keep it for you, sweet. You'll hurt yourself."

"I will not give it to you," she announced. "It was a gift from my uncle and I promised him I'd always have it with me."

He gave in when she backed away from him. "We have to get going," he told her then. "Lyon, you'll . . ."

"I will," Lyon returned. "Just as soon as I've . . ."

"Right," Caine interrupted.

"They seem to be speaking in a different language, don't they?" Christina said to Jade.

"They don't want me to worry," Jade explained.

"Then you understood what they were saying?"

"Of course. Lyon is suppose to start his investigation. Caine's obviously given him a few suggestions. As soon as he's found out anything of consequence, he'll get in touch with Caine."

Lyon and Caine were staring intently at her. "You deducted all that from . . ."

She interrupted Caine with a nod. Then she turned to Lyon. "You're going to try to find out if there's anyone gone missing of late, aren't you?"

"Yes," Lyon admitted.

"You'll need a description, won't you? Of course, the poor man's nose was a bit scrunched from the fall. Still, I could tell he was quite old, almost forty, I would guess. He had gray hair, bushy eyebrows, and cold brown eyes. He didn't look at all peaceful in death, either. He'd gone to fat, too, around the middle. That's yet another reason to suppose he was a member of the *ton*."

"Why is that?" Caine asked.

"Because he had more than enough to eat for one," she countered. "There weren't any callouses on his hands, either. No, he certainly wasn't a working man. I can tell you that much."

"Come and sit down," Lyon suggested. "We'd like to have descriptions of the other men as well."

"I fear there isn't much to tell," she said. "I barely saw them. I don't know if they were tall or short, fat or thin . . ." She stopped to sigh. "There were three of them and that's all I had time to notice."

She looked distressed. Caine thought she was still frightened of the ordeal she'd gone through. She had seen a man fall to his death, after all, and she was such a gentle woman, she couldn't be used to such horrors.

Jade was upset, yes, and when Caine put his arm around her shoulders, she felt all the more guilty. For the first time in her life, she actually disliked lying. She kept trying to tell herself that her motives were pure. The reminder didn't help at all, though. She was deceiving three very nice people.

"We have to leave," she blurted out. "The longer we stay, the more danger we put this family in, Caine. Yes, we must leave now."

She didn't give anyone time to argue with her but rushed over to the entrance.

"Caine? Do you have a home in the country somewhere?" she asked, knowing full well that he did.

"Yes."

"I think we should go there. You can keep me safe away from London."

"We aren't going to Harwythe, Jade."

"Harwythe?"

"The name of my country estate," he answered. "I'm taking you to my parents' home. Their property borders mine. You might not be concerned about your reputation, but I am. I'll come and see you every day to make certain you're doing all right. I'll place guards around . . . now why are you shaking your head at me?"

"You'll come and visit me? Caine, you're already breaking your word to me," she cried out. "We are not going to involve your parents in this. You promised me you'd keep me safe and by God, you aren't going to leave my side until it's over."

"She sounds determined, Caine," Lyon interjected.

"I am in wholehearted agreement with Jade," Christina interjected.

"Why?" Both Caine and Lyon asked at the same time.

Christina shrugged. "Because she's my friend. I must agree with her, mustn't I?"

Neither man had a valid argument for that explanation. Jade was pleased. "Thank you, Christina. I will always agree with you, as well," she added.

Caine shook his head. "Jade," he began, thinking to draw her back to their original topic. "I am thinking about your safety when I suggest you stay with my parents."

"No."

"Do you honestly believe you'll be safe with me?"

She took exception to his incredulous tone of voice. "I most certainly do."

"Sweet, I'm not going to be able to keep my hands off you

for two long weeks. I'm trying to be noble about this, damn it."

In the blink of an eye, her face turned crimson. "Caine," she whispered. "You shouldn't be saying such things in front of our guests."

"They aren't our guests," he countered in a near shout of obvious frustration. "We're their guests."

"The man's always using blasphemies around me," she told Christina. "He won't apologize either."

"Jade!" Caine roared. "Quit trying to change the topic."

"I don't believe you should shout at her, Caine," Christina advised.

"He can't help himself," Jade explained. "It's because of his cranky nature."

"I'm not cranky," Caine announced in a much lower tone of voice. "I'm just being honest. I don't mean to embarrass you."

"It's too late," Jade countered. "You've already embarrassed me."

Both Christina and Lyon looked absolutely mesmerized by the conversation. Caine turned to his friend. "Don't you have someplace to go?"

"No."

"Leave anyway," Caine ordered.

Lyon raised an eyebrow, then gave in. "Come along, wife. We can wait in the dining room. Caine? You're going to have to let her explain a few more facts before you leave if you want me to . . ."

"Later," Caine announced.

Christina followed her husband and son out of the room. She paused to squeeze Jade's hand on her way past her. "It's best not to fight it," she whispered. "Your fate has already been determined."

Jade didn't pay any attention to that remark. She nodded just to please Christina, then shut the door and whirled around to confront Caine again. Her hands settled on her hips. "It's absolutely ridiculous to worry about keeping your hands off me. You won't take advantage of me unless I let you. I trust you," she added with a vehement nod. Her hands flew to her bodice. "With all my heart," she added quite dramatically.

"Don't."

The harshness in his tone startled her. She quickly recovered. "Too late, Caine. I already do trust you. You'll keep me safe and I won't let you touch me. We have an easy pact, sir. Don't you try to muddy the waters now with last-minute worries. It will all work out. I promise you."

A commotion in the entryway drew their attention. Caine recognized the voice.

One of his grooms was stammering out his need to find his employer.

"That's Perry," Caine told Jade. "He's one of my grooms. You stay inside this room while I see what he wants."

She didn't obey that command, of course, but followed behind him.

When she saw Lyon's dark expression, she knew something foul had happened. Then her attention turned to the servant. The young man had wide hazel eyes and dark crinkly hair that stood up on end. He couldn't seem to catch his breath but kept making a circle with the hat he clutched in his hands.

"Everything be lost, mi'lord," Perry blurted out. "Merlin said to tell you it were a miracle the whole block wasn't set afire. The Earl of Haselet's town house was just a bit scorched. There be smoke damage we would imagine, but the outside walls are still intact."

"Perry, what are you . . ."

"Your town house caught fire, Caine," Lyon interjected. "Isn't that what you're trying to tell us, Perry?"

The servant quickly nodded. "It weren't carelessness," he

defended. "We don't know how it started, mi'lord, but there weren't any candles burning, no fire unattended in the hearths. God be my witness, it weren't carelessness."

"No one is blaming you," Caine said. He kept his voice contained, his anger hidden. What the hell else could go wrong? he wondered. "Accidents happen."

"It wasn't an accident."

Everyone in the foyer turned to look at Jade. She was staring at the floor, her hands clenched together. She seemed to be so distressed, some of Caine's anger dissipated. "It's all right, Jade," he soothed. "What I lost can easily be replaced." He turned back to Perry and asked, "No one was hurt?"

Lyon watched Jade while the servant stammered out the news that all the servants had gotten out in time.

Caine was relieved. He was about to give fresh orders to his groom when Lyon interrupted him. "Let me handle the authorities and the servants," he suggested. "You need to get Jade out of London, Caine."

"Yes," Caine answered. He was trying not to alarm Jade but he'd already guessed the fire had something to do with the men chasing after her.

"Perry, go to the kitchen and get something to drink," Lyon ordered. "There's always ale and brandy on the counter."

The servant hurried to comply with that suggestion.

Lyon and Caine both stared at Jade now, waiting for her to say something. She stared at the floor. She was wringing her hands together.

"Jade?" Caine asked when she continued to hold her silence. "Why don't you believe it was an accident?"

She let out a long sigh before answering. "Because it isn't the first fire, Caine. It's the third they've set. They do seem partial to fires."

She lifted her gaze to look at him. He could see the tears in her eyes then. "They'll try again, and again, until they finally catch you . . . and me," she hastily added. "Inside."

"Are you saying they mean to kill you by . . . ?" Lyon asked.

Jade shook her head. "They don't just mean to kill me now," she whispered. She looked at Caine and started to cry. "They mean to kill him, too."

Chapter Six

J ade wiped the tears away from her face with the backs of her hands. "They must have somehow learned your true identity," she whispered. "When I went into the tavern, I thought you were Pagan . . . but they must have known all along, Caine. Why else would they burn your town house?"

Caine went to her and put his arm around her shoulders. He led her back into the drawing room. "Monk wouldn't have told them," he announced. "I don't know how they could have . . . never mind. Jade, no more half explanations," he ordered. "I have to know everything."

"I'll tell you anything you want to know," she said.

Lyon followed the pair inside the salon. He shut the doors behind him and then took his seat across from the settee. Caine gently forced Jade to sit down beside him.

Jade looked at Lyon. "I think we lost them last night when we jumped into the Thames. Perhaps, if you told Perry to pretend to continue his search looking for Caine, whoever is watching will assume you didn't know where we were."

Lyon thought that was an excellent plan. He immediately agreed and went in search of the servant.

As soon as he left the room, Jade turned to Caine. "I can't stay with you. I understand that now. They'll kill you trying to get to me. I've tried not to like you, sir, but I've failed in that endeavor. It would upset me if you were hurt."

She tried to leave after making that explanation but Caine wouldn't let her move. He tightened his hold around her and hauled her up close to his side. "I have also tried not to like you," he whispered. He kissed the top of her head before continuing. "But I've also failed in that endeavor. We seem to be stuck with each other, sweet."

They stared at each other a long while. Jade broke the silence. "Isn't it peculiar, Caine?"

"What's that?" he countered in a whisper to match hers.

"You've just lost your town house, we're both in terrible danger now, and all I want is for you to kiss me. Isn't that peculiar?"

He shook his head. His hand moved to cup her chin. "No," he answered. "I want to kiss you, too."

"You do?" Her eyes widened. "Well, isn't that the . . ."

"Damnedest thing?" he whispered as he leaned down.

"Yes," she sighed against his mouth. "It is the damnedest thing."

His mouth took possession of hers then, ending their conversation. Jade immediately wrapped her arms around his neck. Caine nudged her mouth open by applying subtle pressure on her chin, and when she'd done as he wanted, his tongue swept inside.

He meant only to take a quick taste, but the kiss quickly got out of control. His mouth slanted over hers with hard insistence.

He couldn't get enough of her.

"For the love of . . . Caine, now isn't the time to . . ."

Lyon had made those half statements from the doorway, then strolled back over to his chair. Caine, he noticed, was reluctant to stop kissing Jade. She didn't have such reserva-

GUARDIAN ANGEL

tions, however, and shoved herself away from her partner with amazing speed.

She was beet red when she glanced over at Lyon. Since he was grinning at her, she turned her attention to her lap. She realized then that she was clutching Caine's hand against her bosom, and immediately tossed it aside.

"You forget yourself, sir," she announced.

He decided not to remind her that she'd been the one to bring up the topic of kissing in the first place.

"I think it's high time we heard her explanation," Lyon ordered. "Jade?" he asked, though in a much softer tone when he saw the startle his booming voice had caused. Lord, she was timid. "Why don't you tell us about the first fire?"

"I will try," she answered, her gaze still downcast. "But the memory still gives me the shivers. Please don't think me a weak woman." She turned to look up at Caine. "I'm really not weak at all."

Lyon nodded. "Then can we begin?" he asked.

"Jade, before you tell us about the fires, why don't you give us a little background?" Lyon asked.

"My father was the Earl of Wakerfields. Nathan, my brother, has that title now, along with numerous others, of course. Father died when I was eight years old. I remember he was on his way to London to see another man. I was in the garden when he came to say goodbye."

"If you were so young, how can you remember?" Caine asked.

"Papa was very upset," she answered. "He frightened me and I think that must be the reason I remember it all so clearly. He kept pacing back and forth along the path with his hands clasped behind his back and he kept telling me that if anything happened to him, Nathan and I were to go to his friend, Harry. He was so insistent I pay attention to what he was telling me that he grabbed me by the shoulders and shook me. I was more interested in the trinkets I wanted

89

him to bring home for me." Her voice took on a wistful quality when she added, "I was very young."

"You're still young," Caine interjected.

"I don't feel young," she admitted. She straightened her shoulders and continued. "My mother died when I was just an infant, so I don't have any memory of her."

"What happened to your father?" Caine asked.

"He died in a carriage mishap."

"He had a premonition, then?" Lyon asked.

"No, he had an enemy."

"And you believe your father's enemy is now after you? Is that the reason for your fears?" Lyon asked.

She shook her head. "No, no," she blurted out. "I saw someone murdered. The men who killed him did get a good look at me. The only reason I told you about my father was because you asked me to explain to you my . . . background. Yes, Lyon, that was your very word."

"Sorry," Lyon said again. "I didn't mean to jump to conclusions."

"What happened after your father died?" Caine asked. He was suddenly feeling immensely superior to his good friend, as Lyon now looked thoroughly confused and bewildered. It was nice to know he wasn't the only one muddled around Jade. Damned nice.

"After the burial service, Harry came to get us. When the summer was over, he sent Nathan back to school. He knew our father would have wanted my brother to finish his education. I stayed with my uncle. He isn't really my uncle, he's actually more like a father to me now. Anyway, he took me to his island where it's always warm and peaceful. Uncle Harry was very good to me. He'd never married, you see, and I was just like his very own daughter. We got along well together. Still, I missed my brother. Nathan was only able to come and visit us once in all those years."

When she paused and gave Caine such an expectant look,

he gently prodded her into continuing. "And then what happened?"

"I came back to England so I could see Nathan, of course. I also wanted to see my father's house again. Nathan had made several changes."

"And?" Lyon asked when she paused again.

"Nathan met me in London. We went directly to his country home and spent a wonderful week together catching up. Then he was called away on an important personal matter."

"Do you know what this matter was?" Caine asked.

She shook her head. "Not all of it. A messenger arrived with a letter for Nathan. My brother became very upset when he read it. He told me he had to return to London and that he would be back in two weeks. His good friend was in trouble. That's all he would tell me, Caine. Nathan's an honorable man. He would never turn his back on a friend in need, and I would never ask him to."

"So you were left alone?" Lyon asked.

"Oh, heavens no. Nathan had a complete staff in residence. Lady Briars . . . she was a good friend of my father's . . . well, she'd hired the staff and even helped Nathan with his renovation plans. She wanted to raise us, you see, and was going to petition the court for guardianship. Then Harry took us away, and she never could find us. I will have to go and see her as soon as this has been settled. I dared not go before, of course. They'll probably burn her house to the ground if they . . ."

"Jade, you're digressing," Caine interjected.

"I was?"

He nodded.

"I'm sorry. Now where was I?"

"Nathan left for London," Lyon reminded her.

"Yes," she replied. "I now realize I did do something foolish. On my island, I could come and go as I wished. I never had to worry about an escort. I'd forgotten that England isn't at all the same. Here, everyone must lock their doors. Anyway, I was in such a hurry to get outside, I wasn't looking down, you see, and the heel of my boot got caught up in the carpet loop on the way down the stairs. I took quite a tumble," she added. "And hit my head on the knob of the banister."

She paused, waiting to hear their remarks of sympathy. When both men just continued to look at her so expectantly, she decided neither was going to say anything. She gave them both a disgruntled look for being so insensitive, then continued. "About an hour later, after my head quit pounding from my fall, I set out on my own for a brisk walk. I soon forgot all about my aches and pains, and because it was such a glorious day, I forgot the time. I was just about to look inside the pretty church when I heard all the commotion, and that's when I saw the poor man being pitched to the ground."

She took a deep breath. "I shouted and went running," she explained. "I had lost my direction though, and I ended up on the rise directly above my parents' graves. That's when I saw the men again."

"The same men?" Lyon asked. He was leaning forward in his chair, his elbows braced on his knees.

"Yes, the very same men," Jade answered. She sounded bewildered. "They must have decided it wasn't worth their effort to chase after me, and they were very . . . occupied."

"What were they doing?" Caine asked.

She didn't immediately answer him. A feeling of foreboding settled around his heart. Her hands were clinging to his now. Caine doubted she was aware of that telling action.

"The digging," she finally answered.

"They were digging up the graves?" Lyon asked, his voice incredulous.

"Yes."

Caine didn't show any outward reaction. Lyon looked as though he didn't believe her. She thought it odd indeed that she could tell a lie and both men easily accepted it, yet now when she was telling them the full truth, it was quite another story.

"It's really true," she told Lyon. "I know it sounds bizarre, but I know what I saw."

"All right," Caine answered. "What happened next?"

"I started shouting again," she answered. "Oh, I realize I shouldn't have made a sound, for now I'd drawn their notice again. But I was so outraged I wasn't thinking properly. All three men turned to look up at me. The fancy dressed man held a pistol. Odd, but I couldn't seem to move until the shot rang out. I ran like lightning then. Hudson, Nathan's butler, was working inside the library. I told him what happened, but by the time he'd calmed me down and gained the full story, it was too dark to go looking for the men. We had to wait until the following morning."

"Were the authorities notified?"

She shook her head. "This is where it becomes a little confusing," she admitted. "The next morning, Hudson, with several strong men, went to find the body I'd seen pitched from the rooftop. Hudson wouldn't let me tag along. I was still very upset."

"Of course you were," Caine agreed.

"Yes," she replied with a sigh. "When Hudson and the men returned, they were trying to be as kind as you are now being, Caine, but they had to tell me the truth."

"What truth?"

"They couldn't find any body. The graves hadn't been touched either."

"So they believed you were just . . . ."

"Imagining, Lyon?" she interrupted. "Yes, I'm certain they did. Because they were in Nathan's employ, they didn't dare tell me they thought I was . . . addled, but their expressions spoke for them. I immediately went back to the grave to see for myself. The wind and rain had been fierce the night before, yet even so, it didn't look as though the ground had been touched by a shovel."

"Perhaps they'd only just begun to dig when you interrupted them," Caine suggested.

"Yes, they had only just begun," she admitted. "I'll never forget their faces."

"Tell us the rest of this," Caine suggested.

"I spent the rest of the day trying to understand what their motives were. Then I went to Hudson and told him not to bother Nathan with this problem. I lied to the butler and told him I was certain it was just the setting sun playing tricks on me. I must tell you Hudson looked very relieved. He was still worried, of course, since I'd taken that fall down the stairs and bumped my head."

"Jade, couldn't this be your . . ."

"Imagination?" Caine asked. He shook his head. "There were at least five men chasing us last night. No, it isn't her imagination."

She gave Lyon a suspicious look. "You don't believe me, do you?"

"I do now," Lyon replied. "If there were men after you, then you did see something. What happened next?"

"I refused to give up," she told him. She tried to fold her hands in her lap and only then realized she was clinging to Caine's hand again. She pushed it away. "I can be a very stubborn woman. And so, the next morning, I once again set out to find proof."

Lyon smiled at Caine. "I would have done the same," he admitted.

"What morning was this?" Caine asked.

"Yesterday morning," she explained. "I set out on horseback. I didn't make it to my parents' graves, though. They shot my horse out from under me."

"They what?" Caine asked in a near shout.

She was pleased with his stunned reaction. "They killed Nathan's fine horse," she repeated with a nod. "I cannot tell you how upset my brother's going to be when he finds out his favorite steed is dead. It's going to break his heart."

Caine reached for his linen handkerchief when he thought she was about to cry again. "And then what happened?" he asked.

"I went flying to the ground, of course. I was very fortunate because I didn't break my neck. I only sustained minor injuries. Surely you noticed the bruises on my shoulders and arms when you snuck into my bedroom last night."

She turned to look at Caine and waited for his reply. "I didn't notice," he whispered. "And I didn't sneak into your room."

"How could you not have noticed my bruises?"

"I wasn't looking at your shoulders."

She could feel herself blushing again. "Well, you should have been looking at my shoulders," she stammered. "A gentleman would have noticed my injuries right away."

Caine lost his patience. "Jade, not even a eunuch would have . . ."

"Do you want to hear the rest of this or not?"

"Yes," he answered.

"After they shot my horse, I ran all the way back to the main house. I don't know if they chased after me or not. I was very upset. This sort of thing has never happened to me before. I've led a very sheltered life."

She seemed to want agreement. "I'm sure you have," Caine supplied.

"I found Hudson again and told him what happened. I could tell right away he was having trouble believing me. The man kept trying to force a cup of tea down me. This time, however, I had proof."

"Proof?" Caine asked.

"The dead horse, man," she cried out. "Pay attention, please."

"Of course," he returned. "The dead horse. And did Hudson apologize to you when you showed him this dead horse?"

She chewed on her lower lip a long minute while she stared up at him. "Not exactly," she finally answered.

"What do you mean by not exactly?"

Lyon had asked that question. Jade turned to look at him. "I know you're going to find this difficult to believe, but when we reached the spot where the horse had gone down . . . well, he'd vanished."

"No, I don't find that difficult to believe," Lyon drawled out. He leaned back against the chair again. "Do you, Caine?"

Caine smiled. "It makes as much sense as everything else she's told us."

"Hudson insisted on returning to the stables," she continued. "He was convinced we'd find the horse had found its way back home on its own."

"And was he correct in that assumption?" Caine asked.

"No, he wasn't. The men searched the grounds for the rest of the morning but they couldn't find him. There were fresh wagon tracks along the south trail, though. Do you know what I think happened, Caine? I think they put the horse in the wagon and carried him away. What do you think of that possibility?"

She sounded so eager he was a little sorry to have to disappoint her. "You obviously don't have any idea how much a fully grown horse weighs, Jade. You can take my word it would require more than three men to lift it."

"Difficult," Lyon interjected. "But not impossible."

"Perhaps the animal only had a flesh wound and wandered off," said Caine.

"A flesh wound between his eyes? I doubt that." She let out a groan of frustration. "Nathan's going to be so upset when he finds out about his house and his carriage, too."

"His house? What the hell happened to his house?" Caine muttered. "Damn, I wish you'd tell this in sequence, Jade."

"I believe she has finally gotten to the fires," Lyon said.

"Why, it burned to the ground," Jade returned.

"When did the house burn down?" Caine asked with another weary sigh. "Before or after the horse was killed?"

"Almost directly after," she explained. "Hudson had ordered Nathan's carriage made ready for me. I had decided to return to London and find Nathan. I was good and sick of the way his servants were acting. They kept a wide berth around me, and kept giving me odd looks. I knew Nathan would help me solve this riddle."

She didn't realize she'd raised her voice until Caine patted her hand and said, "Just calm down, sweet, and finish this."

"You're looking at me the very same way Hudson . . . oh, all right then, I'll finish. I was on my way back to London when the footman shouted that Nathan's house was on fire. He could see the smoke coming over the hilltops. We immediately turned around, of course, but by the time we arrived back at the house . . . well, it was too late. I ordered the servants to go to Nathan's London town house."

"And then you set out for London again?" Caine asked. He was absentmindedly rubbing the back of her neck. It felt too good for Jade to ask him to stop.

"We stayed on the main road, but when we turned a curve, they were waiting for us. The driver was so frightened, he ran off."

"The bastard."

Lyon had made that remark. Caine nodded agreement.

"I don't fault the man," Jade defended. "He was frightened. People do . . . peculiar things when they're afraid."

"Some do," Caine allowed.

"Tell us what happened then, Jade?" Lyon asked.

"They blocked the doors and set the carriage on fire," she answered. "I was able to wiggle out through the ill-framed window. Nathan spent good coins on that vehicle, but it wasn't at all sturdy. I was able to kick the hinges away from the branches easily enough. I don't believe I'll mention that fact to my brother, though, for it would only upset him . . . unless, of course, he thinks to hire the same company."

"You're digressing yet again," Caine said.

Lyon smiled. "She reminds me of Christina," he admitted. "Jade, why don't you go and find my wife for me? She was going to pack a satchel for you to take with you."

Jade felt as though she'd just been given a reprieve. Her stomach was in a quiver of knots. She felt as though she'd just had to relive the terror.

She didn't waste any time at all leaving the room.

"Well, Caine?" Lyon asked when they were alone. "What do you think?"

"There were men chasing us last night," Caine reminded his friend.

"Do you believe her story?"

"She saw something."

"That isn't what I asked you."

Caine slowly shook his head. "Not a damned word," he admitted. "And you?"

Lyon shook his head. "It's the most illogical story I've ever heard. But damn, if she's telling the truth, we've got to help her."

"And if she's not?" Caine asked, already guessing the answer.

"You damned well better watch your back."

"Lyon, you don't think . . ."

Lyon wouldn't let him finish. "I'll tell you what I do know," he interrupted. "One, you're not being objective. I can't fault you, Caine. I reacted to Christina in much the same way you're reacting to Jade. Two, she is in danger and has put you in danger, too. Those are the only facts we can take as true."

Caine knew he was right. He leaned back against the settee. "Now tell me what your gut reaction is."

"Perhaps this has something to do with her father," Lyon suggested with a shrug. "I'll start looking into the Earl of Wakerfield's history. Richards will be able to help."

Caine started to disagree and then changed his mind. "It couldn't hurt," he said. "Still, I'm beginning to wonder if her brother might not be behind all this. Remember, Lyon. Nathan went to London to help a friend in trouble. That's when all this started."

"If we accept the story she told us."

"Yes," Caine answered.

Lyon let out a long sigh. "I only have one question to put to you, Caine." His voice was low, insistent. "Do you trust her?"

Caine stared at his friend a long minute. "If we apply logic to this bizarre situation . . ."

Lyon shook his head. "I value your instincts, friend. Answer me."

"Yes," Caine said. He grinned then. For the first time in his life, he pushed reason aside. "I trust her with my life but I couldn't give you one valid reason why. How's that for logic, Lyon?"

His friend smiled. "I trust her, too. You don't have the faintest idea why you trust her, though, do you, Caine?"

Lyon sounded downright condescending. Caine raised an eyebrow in reaction. "What are you getting at?"

"I trust her only because you do," Lyon explained. "Your instincts are never wrong. You've saved my backside more than once because I listened to you."

"You still haven't explained what your point is," Caine reminded him.

"I trusted Christina," Lyon said. "Almost from the very beginning. I swear to you it was blind faith on my part. She led me a merry chase, too. Now I must side with my wife. Christina, as you know, has some rather unusual opinions. She's on the mark this time, though."

"And how is that?" Caine asked.

"I believe, good friend, that you've just met your destiny." He let out a soft chuckle and shook his head. "God help you now, Caine, for your chase is just about to begin."

Chapter Seven

The ladies were waiting in the foyer for Caine and Lyon. A large gray and white speckled satchel was on the floor between them.

Caine tried to lift it, then shook his head. "For God's sake, Jade, no horse is going to be able to carry this load. The weight will be too much for the animal."

He knelt on one knee, flipped open the catch on the satchel and looked inside. Then he let out a low whistle. "There's a bloody arsenal in here," he told Lyon. "Who packed this thing?"

"I did," Christina answered. "There are just a few weapons I thought Jade might need to protect the two of you."

"Weapons Jade might need to protect *me?*" He looked incredulous. "Lyon, did your wife just insult me?"

Lyon smiled while he nodded. "She certainly did, Caine. You might as well apologize now and get it over with."

"Why in God's name would I apologize?"

"It will save time," Lyon explained. He was trying not to laugh. Caine looked thoroughly bewildered.

"Marriage has made you soft," Caine muttered.

"As soft as milk toast," Lyon announced with a grin.

Caine turned his attention back to stripping the unnecessary items from the bag.

While both ladies gasped in dismay, Caine tossed several long knives to the floor, two pistols, and one mean-looking link of chain. "You aren't going to need all of this, Jade. Besides, you're far too timid to use any of them."

She was already gathering up the weapons. "Leave them there, my little warrior."

"Oh, have it your way," she muttered. "And quit using endearments on me, sir. Save them for the other women in your life. I'm neither your sweetheart, nor your love, and I'm certainly not your warrior. Oh, don't look so innocently perplexed, Caine. Christina told me all about the other women."

He was still trying to make sense out of her earlier comment. "Calling you a warrior is an endearment in your befuddled mind?"

"It most certainly is, you rude man," she replied. "I won't make you apologize for calling me befuddled, but only because you're probably still cranky over the news that your town house was burned down."

Caine felt like growling in frustration. He finished stripping the bag of unnecessary weapons, then clipped the lock shut. "Thank you for going to all the trouble, Christina, but you may need your weapons to keep Lyon safe. Come along, Jade," he ordered. He took the bag in one hand and Jade's hand in the other. His grip stung.

She didn't mind. She was too pleased at how well she had told her stories—how she had at once convinced Caine and confused him. The set of Caine's jaw indicated he wasn't in a reasonable mood. She let him drag her to the back door. Lyon's groom had readied two mounts for them. Just as Jade was passing through the doorway, Christina threw her arms around her and hugged her tight. "God speed," she whispered.

Caine tied the satchel to his mount, then tossed Jade on top of the other horse. She waved farewell as she followed Caine through the back gate.

Jade glanced back again to look at Lyon and Christina. She tried to memorize Christina's smile, Lyon's frown, too, for she was certain she wouldn't ever see them again.

Christina had mentioned destiny more than once to her. She believed Caine was going to become Jade's lifelong mate. But Christina didn't understand the full situation. And when Christina learned the truth, Jade feared her new friend would never acknowledge her again.

It was too painful to think about. Jade forced herself to think only of the one reason she was there. Her duty was to protect Caine until Nathan came home.

And that was that. Her destiny had been determined years ago.

"Stay closer to me, Jade," Caine ordered from over his shoulder.

Jade immediately nudged her mount closer.

Caine certainly took a roundabout way out of London. He circled the outskirts of the city, then backtracked to make certain they weren't being followed.

He refused to take the north road until they were an hour away from the city.

The ride should have taken them approximately three hours. Yet because of his cautious nature, they were only halfway to their destination before he took to the main road.

Jade recognized the area. "If they haven't moved it, Nathan's carriage is just a little ahead of us," she told Caine.

It was further away then she remembered. Jade decided the vehicle had been dragged off when they'd ridden another half hour or so and still not spotted it.

Then they turned yet another crooked bend in the road and saw it on the side of the narrow ravine.

Caine never said a word. His expression was grim, however, when they rode past the carriage.

"Well?" she asked.

"It was gutted, all right," he answered.

She heard the anger in his voice and began to worry that he was blaming her for the destruction. "Is that all you have to say?" she asked. She nudged her mount to his side so she could see his expression. "You didn't believe me, did you? That's why you're angry."

"I believe you now," he countered.

She waited a long minute before she realized he wasn't going to say any more.

"And?" she asked, thinking to gain his apology.

"And what?"

"And haven't you anything else to say?" she demanded.

"I could say that as soon as I find the bastards who did this I'm going to kill them," he replied in a mild, thoroughly chilling voice. "And after they are dead, I'll probably want to set their bodies on fire just for the hell of it. Yes, I could say that, but it would only upset you, wouldn't it, Jade?"

Her eyes had widened during his recitation. There wasn't any doubt in her mind that he meant to do what he said. A shiver passed through her.

"Yes, Caine, it would upset me to hear such plans. You can't go around killing people, no matter how angry you are with them."

He pulled his mount to an abrupt stop next to hers. Then he reached out and grabbed the back of her neck. She was so startled, she didn't try to move away.

"I protect what is mine."

She wasn't about to give him argument. He looked as if he might throttle her if she did. Jade simply stared at him and waited for him to let go of her.

"Do you understand what I'm telling you?" he demanded.

"Yes," she answered. "You will protect what belongs to you. I understand."

Caine shook his head. The little innocent was actually

trying to placate him. He suddenly jerked her to the side of her saddle, leaned down, and kissed her. Hard. Possessively.

She was more bewildered than ever. Caine pulled back and stared into her eyes. "It's time you understood that you're going to belong to me, Jade."

She shook her head. "I'll belong to no man, Caine, and it's time you understood that."

He looked furious with her. Then, in the flash of a moment, his expression softened. Her sweet protector was back in evidence. Jade almost sighed with relief.

"It's time we left the main road again," he said, deliberately changing the topic.

"Caine, I want you to realize . . ."

"Don't argue," he interrupted.

She nodded and was about to nudge her horse down the slope when Caine took the reins from her hands and lifted her into his lap.

"Why am I riding with you?" she asked.

"You're tired."

"You could tell?"

For the first time in a long while, he smiled. "I could tell."

"I am weary," she admitted. "Caine, will Lyon's horse follow us? Your friend will be upset if his mount gets lost."

"She'll follow us," he answered.

"Good," she answered. She wrapped her arms around his waist and rested the side of her face against his chest. "You smell so nice," she whispered.

"So do you," he told her.

He sounded terribly preoccupied to her. He also seemed determined to take the most challenging route through the forest. Jade put up with the inconvenience for a good ten minutes, then finally asked, "Why are you making this journey so difficult?"

Caine blocked another low-hanging branch with his arm before answering her. "We're being followed."

That statement, given so matter-of-factly, stunned her as

105

much as a pinch in the backside would if given by a stranger. She was immediately outraged. "We're not," she cried out. "I would have noticed."

She tried to pull away from him so she could look over his shoulder to see for herself. Caine wouldn't let her move. "It's all right," he said. "They're still a distance behind us."

"How do you know?" she asked. "Have they been following us since we left London? No, of course they haven't. I really would have noticed. How many do you suppose they are? Caine? Are you absolutely certain?"

He squeezed her into quitting her questions. "I'm certain," he answered. "They've been following us for about three, maybe four miles now. More specifically, since we reached my property line. I believe their number is six or seven."

"But . . ."

"I spotted them the last time I backtracked," he patiently explained.

"I backtracked with you, if you'll remember," she countered. "And I didn't see anyone."

She sounded incensed. Caine didn't know what to make of that reaction.

"Are we very far from your house?"

"About fifteen minutes away," Caine answered.

They broke through a clearing a short while later. Jade felt as though she'd just entered a wonderland. "It's beautiful here," she whispered.

The grassy clearing was circled on two sides by a narrow stream that trailed down a lazy slope adjacent to a small cabin. Sunlight filtered through the branches bordering the paradise.

"Perhaps the gamekeeper is inside the cabin," she said. "He might be willing to help us trap the villains."

"The cabin's deserted."

"Then we'll just have to trap them on our own. Did you leave all the pistols behind?"

He didn't answer her. "Caine? Aren't we going to stop?"

"No," he said. "We're just taking a shortcut."

"Have you chosen another spot to wait for them?"

"I'm taking you home first, Jade. I'm not about to take any risks with you along. Now tuck your head and close your mouth. It's going to get rough."

Since he was back to sounding surly again, she did as he ordered. She could feel his chin on the top of her head as she squeezed her face against the base of his throat.

"Someday I want to come back to this spot," she whispered.

He didn't remark on that hope. He hadn't been exaggerating either when he said it was going to get rough. As soon as they reached the open fields, Caine pushed his mount into a full gallop. Jade felt like she was flying through the air again. It wasn't at all the same feeling as being pitched into the Thames, though, for now she had Caine to hold onto.

Whoever was behind this treachery had sent men to Caine's estate to wait for him. Jade worried about the possibility of an ambush when they neared the main grounds. She prayed her men would be there to take up the battle.

They were just about to reach the crest and the cover of the trees again when the sound of pistol shots rang out. Jade didn't know how to protect Caine's back now. She tried to twist in his arms to see where the threat was coming from, even as she instinctively splayed her hands wide up his shoulders to cover as much of him as she could.

The shots were coming from the southeast. Jade jostled herself over onto his left thigh, just as another shot echoed in the wind.

"Hold still," Caine ordered against her ear at the same second she felt a mild sting in her right side. She let out a soft gasp of surprise and tried to look at her waist. It felt as though a lion had just swatted her with his claws extended. Just as quickly, however, the ache began to dissipate. A rather irritating burning sensation radiated up her side, and Jade decided one of the branches they'd just broken through had cut into her side.

Numbness set in and she put the matter of her paltry scratch aside.

"We're almost home," Caine told her.

In her worry, she forgot to act afraid. "Watch your back when we get near the house," she ordered.

Caine didn't answer that command. He took the back road up to the stables. His men must have heard the commotion, for at least ten hands were rushing toward the forest, their weapons at the ready.

Caine shouted to the stablemaster to open the doors, then rode inside. Jade's mount galloped behind. The stablemaster grabbed the reins and had the mare slapped inside the first stall before Caine had lifted Jade to the ground.

His grip on her waist made the ache in her side start nagging again. She bit her lower lip to keep herself from shouting at him.

"Kelley!" Caine shouted.

A yellow-haired, middle-aged man with a stocky frame and a full beard rushed over. "Yes, mi'lord?"

"Stay here with Jade," he ordered. "Keep the doors closed until I get back."

Caine tried to remount his steed then, but Jade grabbed hold of the back of his jacket and gave it a fierce jerk. "Are you demented? You can't go back outside."

"Let go, sweetheart," he said. "I'll be right back."

He pulled her hands away and gently pushed her back against the stall. Jade wasn't about to give up, however. She dug into his lapels and held on.

"But Caine," she wailed while he was peeling her hands away. "They mean to kill you."

"I know, love."

"Then why . . ."

"I mean to kill them first."

He realized he shouldn't have shared that truth with her when she threw her arms around his waist and squeezed him in a grip that was surprisingly strong.

They both heard two more shots ring out while he pulled her arms away.

Caine assumed his men had taken up the fight. Jade prayed her men had already intervened and chased the villains away.

"Shut the doors after me, Kelley!" Caine shouted as he swiftly remounted and goaded his stallion around.

Another shot sounded just a minute or two after Caine had left. Jade rushed past the stablemaster and looked out the small square window. Caine's body wasn't sprawled out in a pool of blood in the field. She started breathing again.

"There's absolutely nothing to be worried about," she muttered.

"You best get away from the window," Kelley whispered from behind.

Jade ignored that suggestion until he started tugging on her arm. "Mi'lady, please wait for the Marquess in a safer spot. Come and sit over here," he continued. "The Marquess will be back soon."

She couldn't sit down. Jade couldn't stop herself from pacing or fretting, either. She prayed that both Matthew and Jimbo had taken care of the intruders. They were two of her most loyal men. Both were well trained in trickery, too, for Black Harry had personally seen to their education.

This was all Caine's fault, she decided. She certainly wouldn't be in such a state of nerves if he'd turned out to be anything like the man she'd read about in the file. He seemed to have two completely different personalities, however. Oh, she knew the file told the truth. His superiors had referred to him as a cold, methodical man when the task at hand needed his special consideration.

Yet the man she'd encountered wasn't at all cold or

unfeeling. She'd played on Caine's protector instincts, but she believed he was going to be very difficult all the same. He hadn't turned out to be difficult at all, though. He was a caring man who'd already taken her under his wing.

The problem, of course, was the contradiction. Jade didn't like inconsistencies. It made Caine unpredictable. And unpredictable meant dangerous.

The doors suddenly flew open. Caine stood there, his mount still in a lathered pant behind him.

She was so relieved to see he was safe, her knees went weak on her. Every muscle in her body began to ache. She had to sit down in the chair Kelley provided before she could speak.

"You're all right, then?" she managed to ask.

Caine thought she looked as if she were about to burst into tears. He gave her a smile to reassure her, then led his horse inside. After handing the reins to the stablemaster, and waving the men who were following him back outside, he casually leaned against the wall next to her. He was deliberately trying to make her believe nothing much out of the ordinary had happened.

"The fight was over and done with by the time I got to the forest."

"The fight was over? How could it be over?" she asked. "I don't understand."

"They must have changed their minds," he said.

"You don't have to lie to me," she cried out. "And you can quit acting as though we're discussing the crops, too. Now tell me what happened."

He let out a long sigh. "Most of the fight was over and done with by the time I got there."

"Caine, no more lies," she demanded.

"I'm not lying," he countered.

"Then make sense," she ordered. "You're supposed to be logical, remember?"

He'd never heard that tone of voice from her before. God's truth, she sounded like a commander now. Caine grinned. "It was the damnedest thing I ever saw," he admitted. "I got two of them, then turned to the area I thought hid the rest, but when I got there, they were gone."

"They ran away?"

He shook his head. "There was evidence that a fight had taken place."

"Then your men . . ."

"Were with me," he interjected.

Jade folded her hands in her lap, her gaze downcast so he wouldn't be able to see her expression. She feared she wouldn't be able to hide her relief or her pleasure. Matthew and Jimbo had done their jobs well. "No, that doesn't make any sense," she agreed.

"There was evidence of a fight," he said, watching her closely.

"Evidence?" she asked, her voice whisper soft. "Such as?"

"Footprints . . . blood on a leaf," he returned. "Other signs as well, but not a body in sight."

"Do you think they might have had an argument among themselves?"

"Without making a sound?" he asked, sounding incredulous.

"You didn't hear any noise?"

"No." Caine continued to lean against the wall. He stared at Jade.

She stared back. She thought he might be filtering through the information he'd gained over the past hours, yet the strange expression on his face worried her. She was suddenly reminded of a story Black Harry liked to tell about the wonderful, unpredictable grizzly bears who roamed the wilderness of the Americas. The animal was such a cunning breed. Harry said the bear was actually much smarter than his human trackers. Often he would deliberately lead his victims into a trap or circle back to attack. The poor unsuspecting hunter usually died before realizing he'd actually become the hunted.

Was Caine as cunning as the grizzly? That possibility was too chilling to think about. "Caine? You frighten me when you look at me that way," she whispered. "I hate it when you frown."

She underlined that lie by wringing her hands together. "You're sorry you got involved in this mess, aren't you? I can't fault you, sir," she added in a melodramatic tone of voice. "You're going to get yourself killed if you stay with me. I'm very like a cat," she continued with a nod. "I bring people terrible luck. Just leave me here in your barn and go on home. When darkness falls, I'll walk back to London."

"I believe you've just insulted me again," he drawled out. "Haven't I already explained that no one touches what belongs to me?"

"I don't happen to belong to you," she snapped, somewhat irritated he hadn't been impressed with her theatrics. The man should be trying to comfort her now, shouldn't he? "You can't just decide that I . . . oh, never mind. You're shamefully possessive, aren't you?"

He nodded. "I am possessive by nature, Jade, and you will belong to me."

He sounded downright mean now. Jade valiantly held his stare. "You're not only in error, sir, but you're horribly stubborn, too. I'd wager you never shared your toys when you were a child, did you?"

She didn't give him time to answer that allegation. "Still, I didn't mean to insult you."

Caine pulled her to her feet. He put his arm around her shoulders and started toward the doors.

"Caine?"

"Yes?"

"You can't continue to protect me."

"And why is that, love?"

"A father shouldn't have to lose two sons."

The woman certainly didn't put much store in his ability, he thought to himself. Still, she sounded so frightened, he decided not to take exception. "No, he shouldn't," he replied. "Your brother shouldn't have to lose his only sister, either. Now listen to me. I'm not sorry I got involved, and I'm not going to leave you. I'm your protector, remember?"

Her expression was solemn. "No, you're more than just my protector," she said. "You've become my guardian angel."

Before he could answer her, she leaned up on tiptoe and kissed him.

"I shouldn't have done that," she said then, feeling herself blush. "I don't usually show much affection, but when I'm with you . . . well, I find I like it when you put your arm around me or hug me. I do wonder about this sudden change in me. Do you think I might be wanton?"

He didn't laugh. She seemed too sincere and he didn't want to hurt her feelings. "I'm pleased you like it when I touch you," he said. He paused just inside the door and leaned down to kiss her. "I find I love touching you." His mouth captured hers then. The kiss was long, hard, lingering. His tongue rubbed against her soft lips until they opened for him, then slid inside with lazy insistence. When he pulled back, she had a most bemused look on her face again.

"You tried your damnedest to become my shield on that horse, didn't you, love?"

She was so surprised by that question, her mind emptied of all plausible explanations.

"What did I do?"

"You tried to become my shield," he answered. "When you realized the shots were coming from . . ."

"I didn't," she interrupted.

"And the other night, when you threw yourself into me and knocked me off center, you actually saved my life," he continued as though she hadn't interrupted him.

"I didn't mean to," she interjected. "I was afraid."

She couldn't discern from his expression what he was thinking. "If there is a next time, I promise not to get in your way," she rushed out. "Please forgive me for not being very logical, Caine. You see, I've never been chased after before, or shot at, or . . . do you know, I don't believe I feel very well now. Yes, I feel sick. I really do."

It took him a moment to make the switch in topics.

"Is it your head, sweet? We should have asked Christina for something to put on that bump."

She nodded. "It is my head and my stomach and my side, too," she told him as they walked toward the front of the main house.

She was weak with relief, for her aches and pains had waylaid his attention. Jade glanced around her, realizing for the first time how beautiful the landscape was. When they turned the corner, she came to an abrupt stop.

The drive seemed to be unending. It was lined with a multitude of trees, most at least a hundred years old by Jade's estimation. The branches arched high across the gravel drive, providing an enchanting canopy.

The redbrick house was three stories high. White pillars lined the front, adding a regal touch. Each of the oblong windows was draped in white cloth and each was identically held in place with black tiebacks. The front door had been painted black as well, and even from the drive, the attention to detail was very apparent.

"You didn't tell me you were so wealthy," she announced.

She sounded irritated to him. "I live a comfortable life," he answered, a shrug in his voice.

"Comfortable? This rivals Carlton House," she said.

She suddenly felt as out of place as a fish on the beach.

Jade pushed his arm away from her shoulders and continued on.

"I don't like wealthy men," she announced.

"Too bad," he replied, laughing.

"Why is it too bad?" she asked.

Caine was trying to get her to move again. She'd stopped at the bottom of the steps and was now staring up at the house as though it was somehow a threat to her. He could see the fear in her eyes.

"It's going to be all right, Jade," he said. "Don't be afraid."

She reacted as though he'd just defamed her family. "I'm not afraid," she stated in her most haughty tone and with a glare to match.

It had been instinctive, giving him that setdown for daring to suggest such a sin, but she soon realized her blunder. Damn, she was suppose to be afraid. And now Caine was looking at her with that unreadable expression on his face again.

She never would have made that error if she hadn't been in such sorry shape. Lord, she ached.

"You insult yourself by saying I'm afraid," she explained.

"I what?"

"Caine, if I am still afraid, then it would mean I don't have any faith in you, wouldn't it?"

Her sudden smile diverted his attention. "As to that," she continued, "I've already counted eleven men with their weapons at the ready. I assumed they were in your employ, since they aren't trying to shoot us. The fact that you'd already seen to such nice precautions set my mind to rest."

Her smile widened when she guessed he was thinking she was daft again. Then she stumbled. It wasn't another ploy to turn his attention, but a real stumble that would have felled her to the ground if he hadn't caught her.

"My knees are weak," she hastily explained. "I'm not

accustomed to riding. Do let go of my waist, Caine. It aches a bit."

"What doesn't ache, love?" he asked. His tone was filled with amusement, yet there was tenderness in his eyes.

She tried to act disgruntled. "I'm a woman, remember? And you did say all women were weak. Is that the reason you're looking so smug now, sir? Because I've just given your outrageous opinion substance?"

"When you look at me like that, I seem to forget all about how confusing you are. You have the most beautiful eyes, love. I think I know what green fire looks like now."

She knew he was trying to embarrass her. His slow, sexy wink said as much. The man could be a tease all right. When he leaned down and kissed the top of her forehead, she had to catch herself from letting out a telling sigh of pleasure. She forgot all about her aches and pains.

The front door opened then, drawing Caine's attention. With his gentle prodding, she also turned, just as a tall, elderly man appeared in the entrance.

He looked just like a gargoyle. Jade assumed the man was Caine's butler. He was dressed all in black, save for his white cravat, of course, and his austere manner more than matched his formal attire. The servant looked as though he had been dunked in a vat of starch and left out to dry.

"That's my man, Sterns," Caine explained. "Don't let him frighten you, Jade," he added when she moved a step closer to his side. "He can be as intimidating as a king when the mood comes over him."

The thread of affection in Caine's voice told her he wasn't at all intimidated. "If Sterns takes a liking to you, and I'm sure he will, then he'll defend you to the death. He's as loyal as they come."

The man under discussion advanced down the steps with a dignified stride. When he faced his employer, he made a stiff bow. Jade noticed the wings of silver hair on the sides of his temples and guessed his age to be in the middle to late fifties. Both the salt and pepper hair and his grossly unattractive face reminded her of her Uncle Harry.

She liked him already.

"Good day, mi'lord," Sterns stated before he turned to look at Jade. "Did your hunt go well?"

"I wasn't hunting," Caine answered.

"Then the pistol shots I heard were just for sport?"

The servant hadn't bothered to look at his employer when he made that remark but continued to give Jade his full scrutiny.

Caine smiled. He was vastly amused by Sterns' behavior. His man wasn't one to rattle easily. He was certainly rattled now, and Caine knew he was fighting quite a battle to maintain his rigid composure.

"I was after men, not game," Caine explained.

"And were you successful?" Sterns inquired in a voice that suggested he wasn't the least interested.

"No," Caine answered. He let out a sigh over his butler's lack of attention. Still, he couldn't very well fault the man for falling under Jade's spell. He'd already done the same. "Yes, Sterns, she is very beautiful, isn't she?"

The butler gave an abrupt nod, then forced himself to turn back to his lord.

"That she is, mi'lord," he agreed. "Her character, however, is still to be discerned." He clasped his hands behind his back and gave his lord a quick nod.

"You'll find that her character is just as beautiful," Caine replied.

"You've never brought a lady home before, mi'lord."

"No, I haven't."

"And she is our guest?"

"She is," Caine answered.

"Am I making more of this than I should, perchance?"

Caine shook his head. "No, you're not, Sterns."

The butler raised an eyebrow, then nodded again. "It's about time, mi'lord," Sterns said. "Do you require one of the guest chambers made ready or will the lady be occupying your rooms?"

Because the sinful question had been asked in such a matter-of-fact fashion, and because she was still stinging from their rudeness in talking about her as though she wasn't even there, she was a little slow to take insult. Only when the fullness of what Sterns was suggesting settled in her mind did she react. She moved away from Caine's side and took a step toward the butler. "This lady will require a room of her own, my good man. A room with a sturdy lock on the door. Do I make myself clear?"

Sterns straightened himself to his full height. "I understand perfectly well, mi'lady," he announced. Although the man's tone was dignified, there was a noticeable sparkle in his brown eyes. It was a look only Caine had been privy to before. "I shall check the bolt myself," he added with a meaningful glance in his employer's direction.

"Thank you so much, Sterns," Jade replied. "I have many enemies chasing after me, you see, and I won't rest properly if I have to worry about certain gentlemen sneaking into my room at night to put my nightgown back on me. You can understand that, can't you?"

"Jade, don't start . . ." Caine began.

"Caine suggested I stay with his mama and papa, but I couldn't do that, Sterns," she continued, ignoring Caine's rude interruption. "I don't want to drag his dear parents into this sorry affair. When one is being hunted down like a mad dog, one simply doesn't have time to worry about one's reputation. Don't you agree, sir?"

Sterns had blinked several times during Jade's explanation, then nodded when she gave him such a sweet, expectant look.

A clap of thunder echoed in the distance. "We're going to get soaked if we stand out here much longer," Caine said.

"Sterns, I want you to send Parks for the physician before the storm breaks."

"Caine, is that really necessary?" Jade asked.

"It is."

"You're ill, mi'lord?" Sterns inquired, his concern apparent in his gaze.

"No," Caine answered. "I want Winters to have a look at Jade. She's been in a mishap."

"A mishap?" Sterns asked, turning back to Jade.

"He threw me in the Thames," she explained.

Sterns raised an eyebrow in reaction to that statement. Jade nodded, pleased with his obvious interest.

"That isn't the mishap I was referring to," Caine muttered. "Jade has a rather nasty bump on her head. It's made her a little light-headed."

"Oh, that," Jade countered. "It doesn't sting nearly as much as the stitch in my side," she added. "I don't want your physician prodding at me. I won't have it."

"You will have it," Caine replied. "I promise you that he won't prod. I won't let him."

"I'm afraid it isn't possible to fetch Winters for your lady," Sterns interjected. "He's gone missing."

"Winters is missing?"

"Over a month now," Sterns explained. "Should I send for another physician? Your mother turned to Sir Harwick when she couldn't locate Winters. I understand she was pleased with his services."

"Who required Sir Harwick's attention?" Caine asked.

"Your father, though he protested most vehemently," Sterns said. "His loss of weight has your mother and your sisters very concerned."

"He grieves for Colin," Caine said, his tone abrupt, weary, too. "I hope to God he pulls out of this soon. All right, Sterns, send Parks for Harwick."

"Do not send Parks for Harwick," Jade commanded.

"Jade, now isn't the time to be difficult."

"Mi'lady, what happened to you in this unfortunate mishap? Did someone hit you on your head?"

"No," she answered shyly. She lowered her gaze to the ground. "I fell. Please don't become upset on my behalf, Sterns," she added when she peeked up and caught his sympathetic expression. "It's only a little, insignificant bump. Would you like to see it?" she asked as she lifted her hair away from her temple.

The movement made her side start nagging her again. She couldn't quite block the pain this time.

Sterns couldn't have been more interested in her injury, or more compassionate. While Caine watched, his butler turned into a lady's maid. He stammered out all sorts of condolences, and when Jade accepted his arm and the two of them started up the steps together, Caine was left to stare after them.

"We must put you to bed immediately, dear lady," Sterns announced. "How did you take your fall, mi'lady, if I may be so bold as to inquire?"

"I lost my balance and fell down a full flight of steps," she answered. "It was very clumsy of me."

"Oh, no, I'm certain you aren't at all clumsy," Sterns rushed out.

"It is kind of you to say so, Sterns. Do you know, the pain is not nearly as awful now, but my side . . . well, sir, I don't wish to alarm you, nor do I wish you to think I'm a complainer . . . Caine believes I do nothing but complain and cry. Those were his very words, sir. Yes, they were . . ."

Caine came up behind her and grabbed hold of her shoulders. "Let's have a look at your side. Take your jacket off."

"No," she answered as she walked into the foyer. "You'll only prod at it, Caine."

A line of servants waited to greet their employer. Jade breezed past them while she held on to Sterns' arm. "Sir, is my room in the front of the house? I do hope so. I would love to have a window facing the lovely view of the drive and the forest beyond."

Because of her cheerful tone of voice, Caine decided she'd been exaggerating about her aches. "Sterns, take her upstairs and get her settled while I take care of a few matters."

He didn't wait for a reply but turned and walked out the front door again.

"Have Parks fetch the physician," Sterns called down from the top of the steps. The butler turned to Jade. "Don't argue with us, mi'lady. You look terribly pale to me. I cannot help but notice that your hands feel like ice."

Jade hastily removed her hand from his. She hadn't realized she'd held onto him as she climbed the steps. Sterns had noticed, of course. The poor dear was obviously worn out. Why, she was actually trembling.

"The sun will be setting soon. You'll have your dinner in bed," he added. "Did mi'lord really throw you in the Thames?" he asked when he thought she was about to argue with his decisions.

She smiled. "He did," she answered. "And he has yet to apologize. He threw away my satchel, too. I'm a pauper now," she added, sounding cheerful again. "Lady Christina did give me some of her lovely clothes, though, and I thank God for that."

"You don't seem very saddened by your current predicament," Sterns remarked. He opened the door to her room, then stepped back so she could pass through.

"Oh, I don't believe in being sad," she answered. "Why, Sterns, what a lovely bedroom. Gold is my very favorite color. Is the coverlet made of silk?"

"Satin," Sterns answered, smiling over the enthusiasm in her voice. "May I assist you in removing your jacket, mi'lady?"

Jade nodded. "Would you open the window first? It's a bit

stuffy in here." She walked over to look outside, judging the distance to the cover of trees. Matthew and Jimbo would be waiting for her signal come darkness. They'd be watching the windows for the lighted candle, the sign they'd decided upon, to indicate that all was well.

Jade turned when Sterns began to tug on her jacket. "I shall have this cleaned for you, mi'lady."

"Yes, please," she answered. "I believe there's a small tear in the side too, Sterns. Could you have someone patch it up, too?"

Sterns didn't answer her. Jade looked up at his face. "Have you gone ill, sir?" she asked. The servant was suddenly looking quite green in the complexion to her. "Sterns, do sit down. Don't take insult, but I believe you might be in jeopardy of a swoon."

He shook his head when she shoved him into the chair adjacent to the window. The butler finally found his voice. He shouted in a true roar for his lord to present himself.

Caine was just starting up the stairs when he heard Sterns' bellow. "Now what has she done?" he muttered to himself. He rushed through the foyer where the servants were again lined up, passed a wave in their general direction, and then raced up the staircase.

He came to an abrupt stop when he reached the doorway, for the sight he came upon did surprise him. Sterns was struggling to get out of the wingback chair. Jade held him down with one hand on his shoulder. She was fanning him with a thin book she held in her other hand.

"What in God's name . . . Sterns? Are you ill?"

"He's gone faint," Jade announced. "Help me get him to the bed, Caine."

"Her side, mi'lord," Sterns protested. "Dear lady, do quit waving that book in my face. Caine, have a look at her side."

Caine understood before Jade did. He hurried over to Jade, turned her around, and when he got a good look at the god-awful blood soaking her white blouse, he wanted to sit down, too.

"Dear God," he whispered. "Oh, sweetheart, what happened to you?"

Jade let out a loud gasp when she saw the damage. She would have staggered backward if he hadn't been holding her. "Love, didn't you know you were bleeding?"

She looked dumbfounded. "I didn't know. I thought it was a scratch from one of the branches."

Sterns stood on her other side. "She's lost a fair amount of blood, mi'lord," he whispered.

"Yes, she has," Caine answered, trying his best not to sound overly concerned. He didn't want her to become any more frightened.

His hands shook when he gently lifted the garment away from her waistband. She noticed. "It's bad, isn't it?" she whispered.

"Don't look at it, sweetheart," he said. "Does it hurt?"

"The minute I saw all the blood, it started hurting like the devil."

Jade noticed the tear in Christina's garment then. "They ruined my friend's lovely top," she cried out. "They bloody well shot right through it. Just look at that hole, Caine. It's the size of a . . . of a . . . ."

"Pistol shot?" Sterns suggested.

Caine had worked the top away and was now using his knife on her chemise.

"She's getting dotty on us," Sterns whispered. "You'd best put her on the bed before she swoons."

"I'll not swoon, Sterns, and you should apologize for thinking I would. Caine, please let go of me. It isn't decent to cut my clothes away. I'll take care of this injury by myself."

Jade was suddenly desperate to get both men out of her room. Since the moment she'd seen the injury, her stomach

123

had been in an uproar. She felt light-headed now and her knees were starting to buckle up on her.

"Well, Sterns?" she asked. "Do I get my apology or not?"

Before the butler was given a chance to answer, Jade said, "Bloody hell. I *am* going to swoon after all."

Chapter Eight

Jade came awake with a start. She was surprised to find herself in bed, for she didn't have the faintest idea how she'd gotten there. After a long moment, the truth settled in. Good God, she really had fainted.

She was trying to come to terms with this humiliation when she realized the breeze coming in through the open window was cooling her bare skin.

She opened her eyes to find Sterns leaning over her from one side of the bed and Caine bending over her from the opposite side. Their deep scowls were almost enough to send her into another faint.

"The shot went clear through," Caine muttered.

"Thank the Lord for that," Sterns whispered.

"Which one of you scoundrels removed my clothing when I wasn't looking?" she asked, her tone of voice as crisp as new frost.

Sterns visibly jumped. Caine merely smiled. "You're feeling better, mi'lady?" the butler inquired after he'd regained his composure.

"Yes, thank you. Sterns? Why are you holding my hand?" she asked.

"To keep you still, mi'lady," he answered.

"You may let go of me now. I won't interfere with Caine's task."

After he'd complied with that request, she immediately tried to push Caine's hands away from her side. "You're prodding, Caine," she whispered.

"I'm almost finished, Jade."

His voice sounded terribly surly to her, yet he was being incredibly gentle, too. It was a contradiction. "Are you angry with me, Caine?"

He didn't even bother to glance up when he gave his curt answer. "No."

"You could sound a little more convincing," she countered. "You are angry," she added with a nod. "I don't understand why . . ." She paused to let out a gasp.

Caine assumed the bandage he was applying to her injury had caused her discomfort. "Is it too tight?" he asked, his gaze filled with concern.

"You think this is all my fault, don't you?" she stammered out. "You think I deliberately . . ."

"Oh, no, mi'lady," Sterns interrupted. "The Marquess doesn't blame you. You didn't mean to get yourself shot. Mi'lord always gets a bit . . ."

"Cranky?" she supplied.

The butler nodded. "Yes, he gets cranky when he's worried."

She turned her attention back to Caine. "I'm sorry if I worried you," she said then. "Are you still worried?"

"No."

"Then the injury isn't as terrible as it looked?"

Caine nodded. He put the finishing touches on his handiwork before giving her his full attention. "A mere flesh wound, Jade," he said. "You should be up and about in no time."

He really looked as if he meant what he said. Jade was immediately relieved.

"Cover my legs, Sterns, and don't look while you're doing it," she ordered. Her voice had regained some of its bite, warming a smile out of the dour-faced man.

Jade was wearing only her chemise now. One side of the lace-bordered garment had been torn wide to expose her injury. She understood the necessity of having her clothes removed, but now that she knew she wasn't in jeopardy of dying, appearances needed to be maintained.

The butler did as she requested, then left to fetch a tray of supper for her. She and Caine were all alone. "I don't care if it's only a paltry flesh wound," she said. "I've decided I'm going to linger, Caine."

He sat down on the side of the bed, took hold of her hand, and gave her a heart-stopping smile. "Why do I get the feeling there's more to this announcement?"

"How astute of you, sir," she countered. "There is more. While I'm lingering, you're going to stay by my sick bed. This is, after all, probably all your fault," she added with a nod.

She had to bite her lower lip to keep herself from laughing. Caine looked thoroughly confused.

"Oh?" he asked when she stared at him expectantly. "How have you come to the conclusion that it's my fault?"

She shrugged. "I haven't quite figured it out yet, but I will. Now give me your word, Caine. I won't rest easy until I know you won't leave my side."

"All right, love," he answered. His wink was slow, devilish. "I won't leave your side day or night."

The significance in that statement wasn't lost on her. "You may take to your own bed at night," she replied.

"May I?" he asked dryly.

Jade decided not to goad him any further, guessing he'd get downright cranky if she persisted with her orders. Besides, she'd won this round, hadn't she?

The inconvenience of getting shot was going to be turned into a nice advantage. She now had a perfectly good reason to keep him at her side. Why, she just might linger until Nathan came to fetch her.

She hadn't realized how exhausted she was. She fell asleep right after dinner, the tray still perched on her lap, and only awakened once during the night. Twin candles were burning a soft light on the night stand. Jade remembered the signal she needed to give to Jimbo and Matthew to let them know all was well, and immediately pushed the covers away.

She spotted Caine then. He was sprawled out in the wingback chair adjacent to the bed, his bare feet propped up on the bed, his white shirt opened to the waist, and was sound asleep.

Jade didn't know how long she watched him. She told herself she was just making certain he was really sound asleep. Lord, he was so appealing to her. He had quickly become far more, however, than merely handsome. He was like a safe haven from the storm, and the urge to lean on him, to let him take care of her, nearly overwhelmed her.

Her guardian angel began to snore, pulling her out of her trance. She eased out of the bed, picked up one of the candles, and went to stand in front of the window.

Light rain cascaded down upon the landscape. Jade felt a bit guilty that her men were getting a good soaking. If she'd given her signal earlier, they could have found dry shelter sooner.

"What are you doing?"

Jade almost dropped the candle, so startled was she by Caine's booming voice.

She turned around and found him just a scant foot away. "I was just looking out the window," she whispered. "I didn't mean to wake you."

His hair was tousled and he seemed to be more asleep than awake yet. A lock of his hair had fallen on his forehead, giving him the appearance of being a bit vulnerable to her. Without a thought as to what she was doing, she brushed his hair back in place.

"You may look out the window tomorrow," he returned, his voice husky from slumber.

After making that statement, he took the candle away from her, put it back on the table, and then arrogantly motioned for her to get back in bed.

"Does your side hurt?" he asked.

She didn't think he was overly concerned about her injury because he'd yawned when he'd asked the question.

Jade started to tell him no, that it didn't pain her much at all, then reconsidered. "Yes," she said. "It stings, but only just a little," she added when he looked a bit too concerned. "Why were you sleeping in the chair?"

He pulled his shirt off before answering her. "You were taking up most of the bed," he explained. "I didn't want to move you."

"Move me? Why would you want to move me?"

Caine blew out the candles, pulled the covers back, and stretched out next to her. Then he gave her a roundabout answer. "I'll just stay with you until you fall asleep again."

"But Caine, it isn't at all proper . . ."

"Go to sleep, love. You need your rest."

She stiffened when he put his arm around her. His hand rested between her breasts. When she tried to ease it away, he captured her hand and held on.

"This really isn't at all . . ." She quit protesting in mid-sentence, realizing it was wasted effort. Caine was already snoring again and certainly wouldn't hear a word she said.

She decided there was little harm in letting him sleep with her for a short while. She had, after all, run the man ragged and he surely needed his rest. She'd already noticed how cranky he became when he was weary. Odd, but she found that flaw a bit endearing.

Jade snuggled up against him and closed her eyes. She instinctively knew he would behave himself. He was a gentleman, and he'd given her his word that he'd never take advantage of her.

She was obviously just as exhausted as he appeared to be, for she fell asleep with the most confusing thought rambling through her mind.

She was beginning to wish he wasn't such a gentleman after all.

The physician, Sir Harwick, couldn't be located for two full days and nights. Caine sent messengers to his London home and to his country estate. Harwick was finally located at the residence of Lady McWilliams, attending to a birthing. He sent a missive back to Caine explaining that as soon as his duty there was completed, he would immediately ride over to Caine's estate.

Caine ranted about that inconvenience until Jade reminded him that her condition wasn't life threatening, a fact, she added, that the messenger had related to the physician, and that she was beginning to feel much better anyway and didn't need or want anyone poking at her.

Lingering soon became torture for Jade. She couldn't stand the confinement.

The weather mimicked her mood too. Since the moment she'd arrived at Caine's home, it hadn't quit raining.

Caine's mood was just as sour as her own. He reminded her of a caged animal. Every time he came into her room to speak to her, he paced back and forth, his hands clasped behind his back, while he grilled her about her past, her brother, and all the events leading up to the murder she'd witnessed. Caine always ended each dueling session with the remark that he didn't have enough information yet to draw any substantial conclusions.

His frustration was almost visible. Jade found fencing

with him just as nerve grating. She was careful not to give him too many true facts or too many lies, either, but Lord, it was exhausting work.

They spent quite a lot of time shouting at each other. Jade accused him of being sorry he ever became involved in her problems. He was, of course, insulted by such an accusation. Still, he didn't come right out and deny it.

In her heart, she thought he didn't find her appealing any longer. Why, he didn't even try to kiss her anymore, or sleep next to her, and by the third day, he was barely speaking a civil word to her.

On the fourth night of her confinement, Jade's control snapped. She tore off the fresh bandage that Sterns had changed for her just a few hours' earlier, ordered a bath for herself, and then announced that she was fully recovered.

By the time she finished washing her hair, her frame of mind had improved considerably. Sterns helped her dry the long curls, then sat her in front of the hearth where a full fire blazed.

After Sterns directed the servants in changing the bedding and removing the tub, he nagged Jade back into bed.

As soon as darkness fell, Jade gave the signal to her men, then returned to her bed. She opened one of the books she'd borrowed from Caine's library, and settled down to read to the sound of thunder rumbling in the distance.

The storm proved to be more than just bluster, however. A giant tree, as tall as Caine's three-story house, was felled to the ground by a bolt of lightning that was so powerful, the exposed roots glowed an eerie red for a good long while. The clap of thunder shook the house, and the aftermath, a sizzling, crackling sound of wood burning, snapped and popped in the night air like meat roasting over an open fire.

All the extra hands were needed in the stables to soothe the frightened horses. The scent of fire was in their nostrils, or so Kelley, the head stablemaster, professed. Caine was called when his stallion wouldn't settle down. As soon as he entered the stables, however, his mount immediately quit his tantrum.

It was well after midnight when Caine returned to the main house. Though it was only a short distance from the stables, he was still soaked through. He left his boots, socks, jacket, and shirt in the entryway and went upstairs. Another booming clap of thunder shook the house just as Caine was about to enter his room.

Jade must be terrified, he told himself as he changed direction. He would just look in on her to make certain she was all right. If she was sound asleep, he'd leave her alone. If, however, she was still awake . . . well then, perhaps they could have another shouting debate about the ills of the world and the inferiority of women. That thought made Caine smile in anticipation. Jade was turning out to be anything but inferior. She was making a mockery out of his beliefs, too. He'd go to his grave before admitting that fact to her, though, for it was simply too much fun watching her try to cover her own reactions to his opinions.

It was actually a little stunning when he realized he really wanted to talk to her. Granted, there were several other things he wanted to do as well, but he forced himself to squelch those thoughts.

He did pause to knock on her door. He didn't, however, give her time to tell him to go away, or time either, if she was sleeping, to wake up. No, he had the door opened before she could react.

He was pleased to see she wasn't sleeping. Caine leaned against the door frame and stared at her a long minute. A warm feeling of contentment filled him. In the last few days he had begun to accept that he liked having her in his house, and even when she frowned at him, he felt he'd arrived in heaven. He really must be daft, he thought then, for he was beginning to love her disgruntled expressions. The fact that he could so easily get her riled indicated that she cared, if only just a little.

The woman bewitched him. Caine didn't like admitting that truth . . . yet she was so beautiful, so soft, so feminine. A man could only take so much before surrendering. God help him, he knew he was nearing that point.

It was becoming a torment not to touch her. His mood reflected the struggle he was going through. He felt tied up in knots inside, and every time he saw her, he wanted to take her into his arms and make wild passionate love to her.

And yet he couldn't seem to stay away from her. Hour after hour he kept coming into her room to check on her. God, he was even watching her sleep.

She couldn't possibly know the torment he was going through. She wouldn't look so damned serene if she had any idea of the fantasies he was considering.

She really was an innocent. She was sitting up in bed with her back propped up by a mound of pillows, looking so pure and virginal as she shook her head at him.

Two candles burned on the side table and she held a book in her hands. While he continued to stare at her, she slowly closed the book, her gaze directed on him all the while, and then let out a long sigh.

"I knew I should have bolted the door," she announced. "Caine, I'm simply not up to another inquisition tonight."

"All right."

"All right?"

His easy agreement obviously surprised her. She looked suspicious. "Do you mean it, sir? You won't badger me?"

"I mean it," he answered with a grin.

"You still shouldn't be here," she told him in that husky, sensual voice he found so arousing.

"Give me one good reason why I shouldn't be here."

"My reputation and your near nakedness," she answered.

"Those are two reasons," he drawled out.

133

"What can you be thinking of?" she asked when he shut the door behind him. "Your servants will know you're here."

"I thought you didn't care about your reputation, Jade. Have you changed your mind, then?"

She shook her head again. The light from the candles shimmered in her hair with the movement. He was mesmerized. "I didn't care about my reputation when I thought you were going to kill me, but now that you've given me hope for continued good health, I've changed my mind."

"Jade, Sterns knows I slept in here the first night when . . ."

"That was different," she interjected. "I was ill, injured, and you were concerned. Yes, that was definitely different. Now I've recovered. The servants will surely tell your mama, Caine."

"My mama?" He burst into laughter. "You needn't worry about the servants, Jade. They're all sleeping. Besides, my motives aren't lascivious."

She tried not to let him see her disappointment. "I know," she said with another mock sigh. "But if you're not up to mischief, why are you here at this hour?"

"Don't give me that suspicious look," he replied. "I thought you might be frightened ɒy the storm, that's all." He paused to frown at her, and then added, "Most women would be frightened. You're not, though, are you?"

"No," she answered. "I'm sorry."

"Why are you sorry?"

"Because you look so disappointed. Did you wish to comfort me?"

"That thought did cross my mind," he admitted dryly. His frown intensified when he realized she was trying not to laugh at him. He pulled away from the door and walked over to the side of her bed. Jade moved her legs out of the way just a second before he sat down.

She tried desperately not to stare at his bare chest. The

mat of dark, curly hair tapered to a line that ended in the middle of his flat stomach. She wanted to run her fingers through the crisp hair, to feel his heat against her breasts, to . . .

"Hell, Jade, most women would have been afraid."

His voice pulled her from her erotic thoughts. "I'm not most women," she replied. "You'd best understand that now, Caine."

He was having trouble understanding much of anything now. He stared at the buttons on the top of her white nightgown, thinking about the silky skin hidden beneath.

His sigh was ragged. Now that he knew she wasn't worried about the storm, he really should leave. His pants, wet from the storm, were probably soaking the covers.

He knew he should leave, but he couldn't seem to move.

"I'm not at all like most of the women you know," she announced, just to fill the sudden awkward silence. Drops of water clung to his muscular shoulders and upper arms. In the candlelight, the moisture made his bronzed skin glisten. She turned her attention to his lap. That was a mistake, she realized. The bulge between his thighs was very evident . . . and arousing. She could feel herself blush in reaction.

"You're soaking wet," she blurted out. "Have you been walking in the storm, you daft man?"

"I had to go to the stables to help quiet the horses."

"Your hair turns to curl when it's wet," she added. "You must have hated that when you were a child."

"I hated it so much I wouldn't share my toys," he drawled out.

His gaze turned to her chest. He noticed her hardened nipples brushing against the thin fabric of her gown. It took a supreme act of discipline not to touch her. His control was close to snapping, and even a simple goodnight kiss would make him forget his good intentions.

Another bolt of lightning lit up the room, followed by an ear-piercing explosion of thunder. Caine was off the bed and standing by the window before Jade had kicked the covers away.

"That surely hit something," Caine announced. "I don't think I've ever seen a storm as fierce as this one."

He peered into the darkness, looking for signs of a budding fire. Then he felt Jade take hold of his hand. He hid his concern when he turned to look down at her.

"It will wear out very soon," she promised. She nodded when he looked so surprised, squeezed his hand to reassure him, and added, "You'll see."

He couldn't believe she was actually trying to comfort him. Since she looked so sincere, he didn't dare laugh. He didn't want to hurt her tender feelings, and if she felt the need to soothe him, he'd let her.

"Uncle use to tell me the angels were brawling whenever there was a thunderstorm," she said. "He made it sound as if they were having quite a party."

"And did you believe your uncle?" he asked, a smile in his voice.

"No."

He did laugh then, a full booming sound that reminded her of thunder.

"I have grown to appreciate your honesty, Jade. I find it most appealing."

She didn't look as though she wanted to hear that opinion. She let go of his hand and shook her head again. "Everything's always black and white to you, isn't it? There's never any room for deviations, is there? I tried to believe my uncle, but I knew he was lying to soothe my fear. Sometimes, Caine, a lie is all for the good. Do you understand what I'm saying?"

He stared down at her for a long minute. "Give me another example, Jade." His voice was whisper soft. "Have you ever lied to me?"

She slowly nodded.

Several heartbeats later, Caine asked, "And what was this lie?"

She didn't answer him soon enough to please him. His hands were suddenly on her shoulders and he forcefully turned her to face him. Then he nudged her chin up, demanding she look at him. "Explain this lie!" he demanded.

The look in his eyes chilled her. She couldn't find any warmth there. The color had turned the gray of winter mornings.

"You cannot abide a lie then, no matter what the reason?"

"Tell me what the lie was," he instructed again.

"I don't really dislike you."

"What?" he asked, looking incredulous.

"I said, I don't really dislike you."

"That's it? That's the lie you . . ."

"Yes."

She could feel the tension ebb from his grasp. "Well, hell, Jade, I thought it was something serious."

"Like what?" she demanded in a raised voice.

"Like perhaps you were married," he answered in a near shout of his own. "I already know you don't dislike me," he added in a softer tone of voice.

"You're impossible," she cried out. "Unbending, too. If I had other lies, I certainly wouldn't admit them to you now. You get too cranky."

"Jade?"

"Yes?"

"What other lies?"

"I thought about telling you I was married," she said then. "But I'm not any good at fabrications and I didn't think you'd believe me."

"Why would you want me to believe you were married?"

He was rubbing her shoulders now in an absentminded fashion. "Because," she rushed out. "In the tavern, well, you were looking at me very like a tiger planning his next meal, and I thought that if you believed I was married . . . or recently widowed, then I'd gain your compassion."

"So you wanted my compassion and not my lust?"

She nodded. "You must admit that we are attracted to each other. I've never wanted a man to touch me the way I want you to . . . touch me."

"That's nice to know, my love."

"Oh, you already know it," she whispered. "Quit looking so pleased with yourself. It was bound to happen sooner or later."

"What was bound to happen?"

"I was bound to find someone I wanted to get a little closer to," she explained.

"I'm glad it happened with me," he admitted.

He wrapped his arms around her and pulled her up against him. "Jade, do you want me to touch you now?"

She struggled out of his arms and took a step back. "It doesn't matter if I want you to touch me or not, Caine. You're my protector. You have to leave me alone."

She suddenly found herself pulled back up against his chest, his thighs, his hard arousal. Her flimsy nightgown proved scanty protection against his body, his incredible heat. "It doesn't work that way, Jade."

"Why not?"

"I want you."

The huskiness in his voice was her undoing. She knew she should be appalled by her own reaction to him. Yet she actually wanted to melt in his arms. The urge to let him touch her was such a sweet torment. Lord, she was confused. She'd never, ever permitted anyone to get this close to her. She'd always protected herself against involvements of any kind, having learned early in life that loving someone caused more pain than joy. Even Nathan had deserted her. She'd become so vulnerable then. Yes, only a fool would let a man like Caine close . . . only a fool.

Thunder rumbled in the distance. Neither Jade nor Caine was aware of the weather now. They were too consumed by the heat flowing between them.

They stared into each other's eyes for what seemed an eternity.

And in the end, it was inevitable. When Caine slowly lowered his head toward her, she leaned up to meet him halfway.

His mouth took absolute possession. He was as ravenous for her as she was for him. She welcomed his tongue, rubbed against it with her own. Her whimper of longing and acceptance blended with his raw growl of need.

The kiss was openly carnal. Caine was a lusty man whose hunger wouldn't be easily appeased. He wouldn't let her retreat or give half measure. Jade didn't want to draw back. She wrapped her arms around his neck, threaded her fingers through his soft curly hair, and clung to him. She never wanted to let go.

When he finally pulled away, she felt as though he'd taken her heart. She cuddled up against him quite brazenly, resting the side of her face against his warm chest. The mat of hair tickled her nose but she liked the sensation too much to move away. His scent, so wonderfully masculine, reminded her of heather and musk. The earthy fragrance clung to his skin.

Caine's voice was ragged when he asked, "Jade? Are there other lies you want to tell me about?"

"No."

He smiled over the shyness in her voice, then said, "No, there aren't any other lies, or no, you don't want to tell me about them?"

She rubbed her cheek against his chest to try to distract him, then said, "Yes, there are other lies." She felt him tense against her, then hastily added, "But they're so insignificant I can't even remember them now. When I do, I promise to tell you."

He immediately relaxed again. Lying, she decided, was on the top of his list of atrocities.

"Jade?"

"Yes, Caine?"

"Do you want me?"

He didn't give her time to answer. "Damn it, be honest with me now. No more lies, Jade. I have to know," he grated out. "Now."

"Yes, Caine, I want you. Very much."

She sounded as though she'd just confessed a dark sin. "Jade, there should be joy in wanting each other, not despair."

"There is both," she answered. She shivered inside over the knowledge of what she was about to do. She was eager . . . and terribly uncertain. I will not fall in love with him, she promised herself, and knew the lie was a mockery when her eyes filled with tears. Caine had already found his way into her heart.

When she moved back into his arms, he felt her tremble. He tightened his hold around her. "I'll take care of you, Jade," he whispered. "Love, what are you thinking?"

"That I'll survive," she answered.

He didn't understand what she meant, but the fear in her voice made his heart ache. "We don't have to . . ."

"I want you," she interrupted. "But you have to promise me something first."

"What?" he asked.

"You mustn't fall in love with me."

The seriousness in her voice told him she wasn't jesting. Caine was immediately infuriated with her. She was such a confusion to him. He decided he'd demand an explanation for her ridiculous request, but then she started caressing his skin into a fever. She placed hot, wet kisses on his chest, and when her tongue brushed against one of his nipples, his body began to burn for her.

She teased a path up the side of his neck with her sweet mouth, urging him without words to respond. Caine's control disappeared. He'd never had a woman respond to him with such innocence, such honesty. For the first time in his life, he felt cherished . . . and loved.

A low growl escaped him even as he told himself to be gentle with her. He wanted to savor each touch, each caress, to make this night with her last forever. Yet he contradicted his own command when she began to make those erotic little whimpers in the back of her throat. She drove him wild. He roughly pulled on her hair until he'd made a fist of her silky curls, then jerked her head back so he could once again claim her mouth for another searing kiss.

His passion consumed her. His mouth ate at her lips, and his tongue . . . dear God, his tongue made her shake with raw desire. Jade's nails dug into the bulge of muscle in his upper arms. She gave herself over into his care. A deep ache began to spread like wildfire through her stomach, then lower, until it became an excruciating sweet torture.

Caine's hands moved to her buttocks. He pulled her up against his arousal. Jade instinctively cuddled his hardness between her thighs and began to rub against him.

The ache intensified.

When his mouth moved to the side of her neck, when his tongue began to flick her sensitive earlobe, she barely had enough strength left to stand up. He whispered dark, forbidden promises of all the erotic things he wanted to do to her. Some she understood, others she didn't, but she wanted to experience all of them.

"There's no turning back now, Jade," he whispered. "You're going to belong to me."

"Yes," she answered. "I want to belong to you tonight, Caine."

"No," he grated out. He kissed her long, lingeringly. "Not for just one night, love. Forever."

"Yes, Caine," she sighed, barely aware of what she was promising. "Tell me what you want me to do. I want to please you."

He answered her by taking her hand and moving it to the waistband of his pants. "Hold me, sweetheart," he instructed in a husky voice. "Touch me. Squeeze me. Hard."

His size frightened her but his reaction to her touch overrode her initial shyness. His groans of pleasure made her bolder. He made her feel powerful and weak at the same time. Jade sagged against him, smiling when she heard his whispered instructions again, for his voice actually shook. As to that, so did her hand. Her fingers brushed against his flat stomach, then slipped inside the wastband of his pants. Caine inhaled sharply, telling her without words how pleased he was with her aggression. She grew bolder then and slowly began to unbutton the opening of his trousers. She was awkward, yet determined until all the buttons were undone. She hesitated then. Caine took over the task for her. He forced her hand inside the opening. Her fingers splayed downward, into the springy hair, and then lower still, until she was touching the very heat of him. He was so incredibly hot, hard, but Jade had barely caressed him when he pulled her hand away.

"It will be over for me before we've started," he grated out when she tried to touch him again.

"Caine, I want . . ."

"I know," he groaned. He was pulling her nightgown up when he made that gruff statement. Jade was suddenly embarrassed and tried to push her gown back down over her hips. "Can't I have it on?"

"No."

"Caine, don't," she stammered. "Don't . . ."

And then he was touching her there, in her most private place. The palm of his hand cupped her boldly and then his fingers began to weave their magic. He knew just where to stroke and fondle, just how much pressure to exert.

Her nightgown was quickly discarded, his pants as well. His big hands cupped her full breasts. His thumbs rubbed her distended nipples until she was straining against him.

Another bolt of lightning lit the room. When Caine saw the passion in her eyes, he lifted her into his arms and carried her over to the bed. He followed her down on the sheets. One of his knees wedged between her thighs, forcing her to open for him, and when she complied, he pushed his arousal against her moist softness.

"Oh, God, you feel good," he whispered. He propped himself up on his elbows so he wouldn't suffocate her with his weight, then lowered his head to the valley between her breasts. He kissed her there, the undersides of her breasts next, and then slowly circled one of her nipples with the tip of his tongue.

She felt as though she'd just been hit by lightning. She moved against him restlessly. When he finally took her nipple into his mouth and began to suckle, her nails dug into his shoulders. His low grunt was one of pain and pleasure.

"Do you like that, love?" he asked before he turned to take the other nipple into his mouth.

She wanted to tell him how much she liked what he was doing to her, but desire made speech impossible. His mouth captured hers again and his hands gently moved her thighs further apart. His fingers were relentless in their quest to make her ready for him. "Put your legs around me, Jade," he suddenly ordered in a harsh voice. "I can't wait any longer, baby. I have to be inside you."

She felt the moist tip of his sex, then his hands were holding her hips, lifting them. His mouth covered hers and his tongue thrust inside just as he drove inside her. The stabbing pain broke through her sexual haze. She cried out and tried to move away. Caine felt the resistance pushing against his arousal. He hesitated for the briefest of seconds. The look in his eyes when he tilted his head back to look at her showed his determination. And then he drove into her again, until he'd broken through the maidenhead and filled her completely. Jade cried out again and squeezed her eyes shut against his invasion.

He went completely still, trying to give her time to adjust to him, trying, too, to give himself time to gain control.

"You have to stop now," she cried out. "I don't want to do this any longer."

Tears streamed down her cheeks. She opened her eyes to look at him. "Stop now," she pleaded.

His expression showed his concern. A fine sheen of perspiration covered his brow. His jaw was clenched tight. She thought he must be in as much pain as she was.

And then he shook his head at her. "I can't stop now," he grated out. "Just hold me, Jade. Don't move like that . . . it makes me want to . . ."

Caine's forehead dropped to rest on top of hers. He closed his eyes against the sweet torment. "Are you in pain, too?" she asked on a near sob.

"No, love," he whispered. "I'm not in pain."

"I'm not a virgin any longer, am I? We're done now, aren't we?"

She was overwhelmed by the confusing emotions warring inside her. The pain was insistent. She wanted Caine to leave her alone . . . and yet, she wanted him to hold her, too.

"No, baby, you aren't a virgin any longer," he finally answered. "You're mine now. And we sure as hell aren't finished."

He sounded like he'd just run a great distance. The grim expression on his face when he looked at her again actually frightened her.

It was apparent he hated this as much as she did.

She felt devastated by her failure. "I knew I wouldn't be any good at this," she cried out. "Please get off me. You're hurting me."

Caine shuddered for control. "Baby, I can't stop," he said

again. He tried to kiss her, but she turned her face away and began to struggle again.

"If you don't stop, I'm going to start crying," she pleaded. "I hate to cry," she added with a sob against his ear.

He didn't mention the fact that she was already crying. Hell, she made him feel as low as a snake. He wanted to comfort her, yet the fact that he was fully imbedded inside her tight, hot sheath made his discipline all but desert him. "Love, the pain won't last long," he promised. He hoped to God he was right.

His hands roughly cupped the sides of her face, and his mouth ended their conversation.

His tongue swept inside to mate with hers, and when he felt her resistance begin to fade, he moved his hand down, between their joined bodies, to stroke the sensitive bud into arousal again.

Jade didn't forget about the pain, but it didn't seem to matter now. The restlessness came back with building insistence. Caine forced himself to stay completely still until she'd adjusted to him. When she slowly arched up against him, he partially withdrew, then drove back into her again.

Her ragged moan forced him to stop again. "Am I still hurting you?" he asked, all the while praying he wasn't causing her more pain. His body was screaming for release, and he knew, even if she begged him, he wouldn't be able to stop now. "Is it better now?"

"A little," she answered against his neck. Her voice sounded shy, uncertain. "It's a little better."

He continued to hesitate until she bit his earlobe and pushed against him again. It was all the encouragement he needed. His body took over. Though he vowed to be gentle with her, his thrusts became more powerful, more out of control.

Her thighs clenched him tight. Her toes arched against the backs of his legs. Her nails dug into his shoulder blades.

145

Caine was relentless now in his quest to push her beyond control. He drove into her and then slowly withdrew, again and again. He knew he should withdraw before he reached his own climax, for neither of them had taken any precautions against pregnancy, but she was so hot, so tight, that noble thought became untenable. And somewhere, in the dark recesses of his mind was the honest admission that he wanted to give her his child.

The mating rhythm took over. The bed squeaked with each hard thrust. Thunder blended with their low moans of pleasure, his whispered words of love. Caine wouldn't let her give half measure. Wave after wave of intense pleasure began to spiral through her body until she was shaking with her need for fulfillment. He made her burn for completion. Jade was suddenly terrified of what was happening to her. It was as though he was trying to steal her soul. "Caine, I can't . . ."

He hushed her fear with another long, drugging kiss. "Let it happen, Jade. Hold on to me. I'll keep you safe."

Safe. He would keep her safe. Jade's instinctive trust in him pushed her fear and her vulnerability away. She let the storm capture her until she became one with the wind. And then she felt as though she was splintering through the air toward the sun. Her body squeezed him tight. She cried out his name, with joy, with release, and with love.

Caine buried his seed inside her at the very same moment. His head fell to her shoulder and he let out a low grunt of satisfaction.

His own climax made him shudder in wonder. Never had he felt such blissful surrender. He felt drained . . . and renewed.

He was never going to let her go. That sudden thought hammered through his mind with the same force of his wild heartbeat. He neither fought the truth nor tried to move.

He was content.

Jade was exhausted.

Only when her arms began to ache did she realize she was still clinging to him. She slowly released her hold, then let her arms fall to her sides. She was too astonished by what had just happened to her to speak yet. No one had ever told her it would be like this. Dear heaven, she'd completely lost control. She'd given herself to him completely, body and soul, trusting him absolutely to keep her safe.

No one had ever had such power over her. No one.

Jade closed her eyes to keep her tears hidden. Caine, she decided, was a far more cunning thief than she was. The man had dared to steal her heart. Worse, she had allowed it.

Even when he felt her tense beneath him, he couldn't find the strength or the will to move away from her.

"I think you should leave now," she whispered. Her voice trembled.

Caine sighed against her neck. He wrapped his arms around her and rolled to his side. Jade couldn't resist the urge to cuddle up against his chest for just a minute. Though she didn't understand why, she actually wanted to hear a few words of praise from him before she sent him away . . . just a few little lies about love and honor, that she could pull out and savor in the future on those cold nights when she was all alone. Yes, they would be lies, but she wanted to hear them anyway.

That, of course, didn't make any sense to her. She could feel herself becoming angry with him. This was all his fault because he'd turned her into a blithering simpleton who couldn't make up her mind if she wanted to weep or shout.

"Sweet, are you already having regrets?"

She couldn't detect a shred of regret in his tone. In truth, he sounded downright amused.

When she didn't answer his question, he tugged on her hair, forcing her to look up at him.

He was thoroughly pleased by what he saw. Her face was flushed from their lovemaking, her mouth swollen from his kisses, and her eyes were still cloudy with passion.

Caine felt as though he'd left his brand on her. A wave of raw possessiveness filled him, and he arrogantly nodded. He decided to ignore her disgruntled expression, guessing it was all bluster for his benefit.

He couldn't resist kissing her again. When he slowly leaned down to claim her mouth, she tried to turn away. Caine simply tightened his hold on her hair to keep her still.

The kiss was meant to melt away her glare. As soon as his mouth covered hers, his tongue sank inside her sweet, intoxicating heat. The erotic love play coaxed her response. It was a long, intense kiss and she was clinging to him when he finally lifted his head to look at her again.

"You wanted me as much as I wanted you, Jade," he said. "You made the choice, love, and now you're going to have to live with it."

The man was a cad. Her eyes filled with fresh tears. His attitude was as callous as a hardened blister. And did he have to smile at her after making such a painful statement?

She vowed he'd never know how much his words hurt her. "Yes, Caine, I did make the choice to give you my virginity, and I will live with the consequences of my actions. Now, if you don't mind, I'm really sleepy and I would like . . ."

"That isn't what I'm talking about," he interrupted. His voice was as ragged as lightning. "The choice you made was to belong to me, Jade. We're going to get married, sweet."

"What?"

"You heard me," he replied, his voice softer now. "Don't look so appalled, my love. It isn't as bad as all that."

"Caine, I never made any such choice," she stammered out.

He wasn't in the mood to listen to her denial. He wanted her acceptance. By God, he wasn't going to leave her bed until he had it. He rolled her onto her back, then roughly pushed her thighs apart with one of his knees. His hands held hers captive above her head. He deliberately ground his pelvis against her. "Look at me," he commanded. When she obeyed that order, he said, "What we have just shared can't be undone. You're all mine now. Accept it, Jade, and it will go a hell of a lot easier for you."

"Why should I accept?" she asked. "Caine, you don't know what you're asking."

"I'm a very possessive man," he countered. His voice had taken on a hard edge.

"I noticed," she muttered. "It's a sin, that."

"I won't share what belongs to me, Jade. Understand?"

"No, I don't understand," she whispered. The look in his eyes chilled her. "Is it because I was a virgin and you feel guilty? Is that the reason you want to marry me?"

"No, I don't feel guilty," he answered. "You are going to marry me, though. I'll speak to your brother just as soon as he returns to . . ."

"You are the most arrogant, unbending man I've ever had the displeasure to meet."

A smile tugged at the corners of his mouth. "But you like arrogant, unbending men, love. You wouldn't have let me touch you otherwise."

Odd, but she couldn't fault that argument. "Please get off me. I can't breathe."

He immediately rolled to his side. Then he propped his head up with his elbow so he could watch her expressions. Jade pulled the sheet up over the two of them, folded her hands across her breasts, and stared intently at the ceiling.

"Jade?"

"Yes?"

"Did I hurt you?"

She wouldn't look at him. Caine tugged on her hair to emphasize his impatience. "Answer me."

"Yes, you hurt me," she whispered. She could feel herself blush.

"I'm sorry, Jade."

She shivered over the tenderness in his voice, then realized she needed to get control of her emotions. She felt

149

like weeping and couldn't understand why. "No, you're not sorry," she announced. "Or you would have stopped when I asked you to."

"I couldn't stop."

"You couldn't?" She turned to look at him.

"No, I couldn't."

She was almost undone by the tenderness she could see in his eyes. There was a definite sparkle there, too, indicating his amusement. She didn't know what to make of him now. "Well, it's a good thing you don't feel guilty because you have nothing to feel guilty about."

"And why is that?" he drawled out.

"Why? Because you didn't make me do anything I didn't want to do. This was all my doing."

"Was I even here?" he asked. "I seem to remember being an active participant."

She ignored the laughter in his voice. "Yes, of course you were here. But I allowed you to be . . . active."

If she hadn't looked so damned sincere, if she hadn't been wringing her hands together, he would have shouted with laughter. Her feelings were at issue, however, and for that reason he controlled himself. "All right," he agreed. "You were more active than I was. Happy now?"

"Yes," she answered. "Thank you."

"You're most welcome," he returned. "Now tell me why you wanted me to make love to you."

She looked back up at the ceiling before she answered him. Caine was fascinated by the blush that covered her face. His little innocent was embarrassed again. She'd been wild just minutes before when they'd been making love. His shoulders still stung from her nails. Her passionate nature more than matched his own, but it had also been the first time for her, and he assumed she was still shy and confused by what had happened.

"Because I wanted to," she answered. "You see, I've always known I would never marry and I wanted to . . . Oh, you aren't going to understand. I wager that soon, after I've gone away, you won't even remember me."

She turned to judge his reaction to that statement, certain she'd made him angry.

He started laughing. "You're being very rude," she announced before returning her gaze back to the ceiling. "I do wish you'd go away."

His fingers trailed a shiver down the side of her neck. "Jade? It was inevitable."

She shook her head. "It wasn't."

He slowly pulled the sheet down until her breasts were uncovered. "It was," he whispered. "God, I wanted you for so long."

He tugged the sheet lower until her stomach was in view. "You know what, love?"

"What?" she asked. She sounded breathless.

"I want you again."

He leaned down and kissed her before she could argue with him. Jade let him have his way until his mouth became more insistent. Then she nudged him away. She rolled with him, and when they were facing each other, she kept her gaze directed on his chest. "Caine?" Her fingers toyed with the crisp hair while she tried to find the courage to ask him her question.

"Yes?" he asked, wondering why she was acting shy again.

"Was it all right then?"

He tilted her chin up with his thumb. "Oh, yes, it was all right."

"You weren't disappointed?"

He was touched by her vulnerability. "No, I wasn't disappointed."

His expression had turned so somber, she decided he was telling the truth.

"I wasn't disappointed either."

"I know," he answered with that arrogant grin back in evidence.

"How do you know?"

"By the way you reacted to my touch, the way you found your own fulfillment, the way you shouted my name then."

"Oh."

His smile melted away the rest of her worry. "It was a little shattering, wasn't it, Jade?"

She nodded. "I had no idea it would be so . . . splendid."

He kissed the top of her head. "I can smell my scent on you," he said. "I like that."

"Why?"

"It makes me hard."

"I should wash."

"I'll do it for you," he offered.

She rolled away from him and was out of the bed before he could reach for her. "You'll do no such thing," she said before she gave him her back and struggled into her robe.

Her smile was dazzling but it faded quickly when she noticed the spots of blood on the sheets.

"You made me bleed." That accusation came out in a stammer.

"Love, it was your first time."

"I know that," she returned.

"You were supposed to bleed."

She looked taken aback by that statement. "You're serious?"

He nodded.

"But only the first time, Caine? Not that there's ever going to be a second time," she rushed on. "Still, I wouldn't . . ."

"Only the first time," he answered. He decided to ignore her protest about not making love again and asked instead, "Jade? Didn't anyone ever explain these facts to you?"

"Well, of course they did," she replied, feeling like a complete fool now.

He didn't believe her. "Who? Your parents died before you were old enough to understand. Was it your brother? Did Nathan explain?"

"Nathan left me." She really hadn't meant to blurt out that truth. "I mean to say, he was away at school all the time and I rarely saw him."

Caine noticed how agitated she was becoming. She was twisting the tie of her robe into knots. "When did Nathan leave you?"

"He was away at school," she said again.

"For how long?"

"Why are you asking me these questions?" she asked. "My Uncle Harry took over my education while Nathan was away. He did a fine job, Caine."

"He obviously left out a few pertinent facts," Caine remarked.

"Uncle is a very reserved man."

"Weren't there any women around who . . ."

He quit his question when she shook her head at him. "There were women but I would never discuss such a personal matter with any of them, Caine. It wouldn't have been proper."

She moved behind the screen before he could question her further. Jade washed with the slivers of rose-scented soap and water from the basin. She only then realized how sore she was. She was thoroughly irritated with him and with herself by the time she returned to her bed.

Caine looked like he was settled in for the night. The pillows were now propped up behind his head. He looked extremely comfortable. She tightened the belt on her robe and frowned at him. "Caine, you really have to understand something," she began in a firm voice.

"What's that, sweet?" he asked.

She hated it when he smiled at her so innocently. It made her heart start pounding and her mind empty of every thought. She had to stare at the floor in order to continue. "This can't happen again. Not ever. It won't do you any good to argue with me, Caine. My mind's set. Now it's time for you to leave."

In answer to her fervent order, Caine lifted the covers and motioned her over with the crook of his finger. "Come to bed, Jade. You need your rest."

She let out a loud groan. "Are you going to be difficult?"

"I'm afraid so, love."

"Please be serious," she demanded when he winked at her.

"I am being serious," he countered. "But realistic, too."

"Realistic?" She moved closer to the side of the bed, nibbling on her lower lip while she thought about the best ploy to get him moving.

Her mistake was in getting too close, she realized a little too late. Caine easily captured her. She suddenly found herself flat on her back next to him. His warm, heavy thigh locked her legs in place and one of his hands held her high around her waist. Jade realized that even in the forceful action, he'd been careful not to touch her injury. He was such an incredibly gentle man. Arrogant, too. She was good and trapped, and he had the audacity to smile over it.

"Now then," he said. "I'm realistic because I know this has only just begun," he explained. "Jade, quit pinching me. You can't honestly believe I won't ever touch you again, can you? Married couples . . ."

"Don't you dare mention marriage to me again," she interjected.

"All right," he agreed. "Since it seems to be so upsetting to you, I'll wait awhile before bringing up that topic. Still, you agree that you'll be staying here for approximately two weeks, right?"

He was back to being logical. Jade actually found that flaw quite comforting now. "Yes, though it surely won't be two weeks now. I've already been here more than half a week."

"Fine," he returned. "Now then, do you think in all the time we have left that I'm going to live like a monk?"

"Yes."

"It isn't possible," he countered. "I'm already hurting."

"You aren't."

"I am," he muttered. "Damn it, Jade, I want you again. Now."

"Damn it, Caine, you have to behave yourself."

Her voice sounded hoarse to her, but it was all his doing, she told herself. He was deliberately provocative. He stared down into her eyes as he slowly untied the belt to her robe. Then his fingers grazed the tips of her breasts. While he continued to hold her gaze, he slowly stroked a path down her belly. His fingers moved lower into the soft curls at the junction of her thighs.

He kissed the valley between her breasts while his fingers slowly stoked the fire in her. Jade closed her eyes and instinctively moved against his hand. His tongue made her nipples hard and when he eased his fingers inside her, she let out a groan of half pleasure, half pain.

He moved upward to kiss her mouth, demanding her response. His tongue wet her lips. When he'd gained her cooperation, he leaned back. "You're already getting hot for me, aren't you, love?"

"Caine," She whispered his name as she tried to pull his hand away. He wouldn't be deterred. She could barely think. "You must stop this torment. You have to fight this attraction. Oh God, don't do that."

"I don't want to fight it," he returned. He nibbled on her earlobe. "I like the attraction, Jade."

He was incorrigible. She let out a ragged sigh, then let him kiss her senseless again. She barely protested at all when he took her robe off and settled himself between her thighs. The hair on his legs tickled her toes and she was suddenly quite overwhelmed by all the wonderful differences in their bodies. He was so hard, so firm all over. Her toes rubbed against the backs of his legs and her nipples strained for more of his touch.

"Caine? Will you promise me something?"

"Anything," he answered, his voice ragged.

"We can have this time together, but when Nathan returns, then it has to be over. We . . ."

"I won't make promises I won't keep," he interrupted.

He sounded angry. "You'll change your mind," she whispered.

"You sound damn certain. Why? What is it you're hiding from me?"

"I know you'll get bored with me," she rushed out. She wrapped her arms around him. "Kiss me, please."

There was a frantic edge to her voice. Caine responded in kind. The kiss was like wildfire, and soon completely out of control.

His full attention was centered on pleasing her. He took his time building the tension by slowly driving her mad. He kissed each and every goose bump on her breasts, suckled both nipples until she was whimpering for release.

And then he slowly moved down her body. His tongue teased her flat stomach, and when he moved lower still, her moans became gasps of raw pleasure.

His teeth deliberately scraped against the soft curls. His tongue stroked the silky petals until they were sleek with moisture. And all the while his fingers caressed her with erotic deliberation.

He couldn't get enough of her. His tongue repeatedly stabbed against her as his fingers slid in and out.

Her hands tore at the sheets. The pleasure he forced on her stunned her. She had no idea a man made love in such a way. It was obvious Caine knew what he was doing. He made her wild with her need for him.

When she felt the first rush of ecstasy, when she instinctively tightened in pleasure and agony around him, he moved up and over her. She couldn't stop the splendor from consuming her. Caine drove inside her, hard, hot, full, just as she found her own release. She squeezed him tight and clung to him in joyful surrender.

He tried to hold back, yet found himself powerless to stop.

She made him desperate for his own release. His seed poured into her in a blazing orgasm that made him forget to breathe.

Until this night, he'd never given himself so completely. A part of him had always held back. He'd always been able to maintain his own rigid control. Yet he hadn't been able to withhold anything from this special woman. Odd, but he didn't look at his acceptance as surrender. In truth, it was a victory of sorts, for in his heart he knew she hadn't been able to hold back either.

He felt cleansed in body and soul. This incredible gift they'd just shared filled him with contentment.

It took all his strength to roll to his side. He was pleased when she followed him and snuggled up against him. He wrapped his arms around her and held her tight.

"I can still taste you."

"Oh, God." She sounded mortified.

He laughed. "I like the taste of you. You're all honey and female, love. It's a sexy combination. A man could become addicted."

"He could?"

"Yes," he growled. "But I'm the only one who's ever going to taste you. Isn't that right?"

He pinched her bottom to gain his answer. "Yes, Caine," she agreed.

"Did I hurt you again?"

"A little," she answered.

"I'm not sorry."

She feigned a sigh. "I know."

"I couldn't have stopped."

She tucked her face under his chin. Long minutes elapsed before she spoke again. "I shall never, ever forget you, Caine."

She knew he hadn't heard her. His deep, even breathing indicated he'd already fallen asleep.

She knew she should wake him and demand that he go

back to his own room. Sterns was bound to be disappointed when he found them together.

He tightened his hold on her when she tried to roll away from him. Even in sleep, the man was as possessive as ever.

Jade didn't have the heart to wake him. She closed her eyes and let her thoughts scatter like the wind. She fell asleep minutes later.

He dreamed of angels.

She dreamed of sharks.

Chapter Nine

The following morning the physician, Sir Harwick, arrived to have a look at Jade. He was an elderly man with dark gray hair and blue eyes that sparkled like the ocean on a calm day. He was impeccable in both his dress and manners. Jade thought he looked like a wily raccoon, for the hair on the sides of his face had been coached into sweeping curves that ended just a scant inch or so away from the edges of his severely pointed nose.

Just as she'd predicted to Caine, Sir Harwick did poke and prod at her. Caine stood at the foot of the bed, his hands clasped behind his back, acting like a sentinel guarding his treasure. When the physician finished his examination, he decreed that rest was the best ticket for her condition. Since Jade didn't believe she was in any special condition, she ignored all his suggestions.

Caine looked as if he were memorizing every dictate. He was determined to make an invalid out of her, she decided. When Harwick suggested a cold compress for the fading bump on the side of her temple, Caine immediately went to fetch it.

Jade was thankful she had the physician all to herself. "I understand you were called upon to examine Caine's father," she began. "I was sorry to hear he wasn't feeling well. Is he better now?"

The physician shook his head. "There's little anyone can do for him," he announced. "It's a pity. He's given up on life since Colin was taken from him. Why, Colin was his favorite son, you understand, and the loss has broken him."

"Why do you say that Colin was his favorite?" she asked.

"He's the firstborn from the second wife," Harwick explained. "Caine's mother died when he was just a youngster. The boy couldn't have been more than five or six."

It was apparent that Sir Harwick enjoyed a good gossip session. He pulled up a chair next to the side of the bed, took his time settling in, and then said in an enthusiastic whisper, "The first marriage was forced, you see, and from what I understand, it was a most unhappy union. Henry certainly tried to make a go of it."

"Henry?"

"Caine's father," Harwick instructed. "Henry hadn't become the Duke of Williamshire yet as his own father was still living. For that reason, he had more time to devote to his marriage. It didn't wash, though. Caine's mother was a shrew. She made life a living hell for both her husband and her son. Why, she tried to turn him against his own father, if you can believe such blasphemy. When she died, no one mourned her long."

"Did you ever meet this woman?"

"I did," he answered. "She was attractive, but her beauty hid a black heart."

"And is the Duke's second marriage happy?"

"Oh my, yes," Harwick answered. He made a sweeping gesture with his hand. "Gweneth's a fine woman. She set the *ton* on its ear, she did, when she first started attending their functions with her husband. Why, the elite follow her lead almost as fervently as they follow Brummel's dress and manners. I must say that Gweneth has been a good wife and mother. The children are all very close to each other—the proof, you see, that she did her job well."

"Do you include Caine, Sir Harwick, when you speak of the children?"

"I do," Harwick replied. "The others look up to Caine, for he is the eldest, but he tends to separate himself from the family. Unless someone tries to harm one of his brothers or sisters, of course. Then Caine involves himself." He paused to lean forward in his chair, then whispered in a conspiratorial voice, "Some say with a vengeance." He wobbled his eyebrows to emphasize that remark.

"Why do they say with a vengeance?" she asked. Her voice sounded worried to her but Harwick didn't seem to notice. Jade didn't want him to quit the conversation just yet. She schooled her expression to show only mild interest and even managed a smile. "You've made me most curious, sir," she added.

Harwick looked pleased by her interest. "My dear, Caine's made it well known he's hunting Pagan. Why, he had his men post the reward notice all over town. The gamblers have given odds. Ten to one favor Caine, of course. He'll get the pirate," he predicted. "And when he does, God have mercy."

"Yes, God have mercy," she agreed. "But Caine's father is ill, you mentioned?" she asked again, trying to pull him back to their initial topic. "Just how ill is he?"

"Gravely so," Harwick announced.

"Is there nothing that can be done?"

Harwick shook his head. "Gweneth's nearly out of her mind worrying about Henry. The man doesn't eat or sleep. He can't go on this way. No, I fear he'll be the next one to die if he doesn't come to terms with Colin's death."

"Perhaps he needs a little assistance," Jade said.

"Who needs assistance?" Caine asked from the doorway.

"Your papa," Jade called out. She turned back to Sir

Harwick then. "What is this I heard about a friend of yours disappearing?"

"Oh, yes, poor Sir Winters," Harwick answered. "A fine physician he was, too," he added with a nod.

When he gave her such an expectant look, Jade said, "You speak as though he's dead."

"I'm certain he is," Sir Harwick stated.

Caine stood on the other side of Jade's bed, trying without much success to force the cold compress on her injury. Jade was far more interested in hearing the physician's opinions than bothering about her puny bump. She kept waving the cloth away. Caine kept pushing it back.

Harwick observed the silent struggle a long minute, trying all the while not to smile. These two were certainly a pair, all right.

Jade's next question pulled him back to their topic. "Why do you think Winters is dead?"

"Has to be," Harwick countered. "His cook was the last to see him alive," he explained. "Winters was strolling through his back gardens. He turned the corner and simply vanished."

"How long ago was this?" Caine asked.

"Near to three months now," the physician answered. "Of course we all know what happened to him."

"We do?" Jade asked, startled by the abruptness in Harwick's tone. "And what is that?"

"I shouldn't be discussing it," Harwick answered. The look on his face indicated just the opposite was really the truth. The man appeared as eager as a little boy about to open birthday gifts.

Sir Harwick leaned forward in his chair. In a dramatic whisper, he said, "White slavers."

She was certain she hadn't heard correctly. "I beg your pardon?"

"White slavers," Harwick repeated. He nodded to emphasize his announcement, then leaned back in his chair.

Jade had to bite on her lower lip to keep herself from laughing. She didn't dare look up at Caine, knowing full well that if he showed the least amount of amusement, she wouldn't be able to control herself. "I didn't realize," she whispered.

Harwick looked as though he was savoring her reaction. "Of course you didn't realize," he rushed out. "You're a gentle lady and certainly wouldn't have heard about such unsavory elements. Pagan's behind the treachery, too. He's the one who snatched Winters and sold him to the slavers."

Jade wasn't amused now. She could feel herself turning red. "Why is it that Pagan is blamed for every sin in England?" she asked before she could stop herself.

"Now, now, don't get yourself upset," Sir Harwick whispered. He patted her hand then and said, "I shouldn't have told you the current speculation."

"I'm not upset," Jade lied. "I just think it's galling the way everyone uses Pagan as a convenient scapegoat. I'm not worried about your friend either, Sir Harwick, for in my heart I know Winters will turn up safe and sound one day soon."

The physician squeezed her hand with affection. "You have such a tender heart."

"Does Caine's father have a strong heart?"

It was Caine who answered her question. "He does."

Jade was surprised by the anger in his voice. She turned to look up at him. "That is good to know," she said. "Why are you frowning? Is it because I asked about your father or is it because he does have a strong heart?"

"Neither," Caine answered. His attention turned to the physician. "My father will begin to feel better when Pagan's been taken care of. Revenge will be his healing balm."

"No, Caine," Jade answered. "Justice will be his salvation."

"In this instance, they are the same," Caine argued.

The rigid set of his jaw indicated his displeasure. His stubbornness, too.

She wanted to shout at him. She thanked him instead. "It was kind of you to bring me this compress." She slapped the cold cloth against her temple. Then she turned to Sir Harwick. "And thank you, sir, for tending to me. I feel ever so much better now."

"It was my pleasure," Sir Harwick replied. He stood, clasped her hand again, and added, "As soon as you're feeling better, you must move in with the Duke and Duchess. I'm certain Caine's parents would be more than happy to have you as their guest until you've fully recovered."

His gaze turned to Caine. "I shall, of course, keep this confidence. There won't be any unsavory gossip attached to this lovely lady."

"What secret?" Jade asked, thoroughly puzzled. Sir Harwick was giving Caine such a piercing stare. It was unsettling.

"He's concerned about your reputation," Caine said.

"Oh, that." She let out a long sigh.

"She isn't overly concerned," Caine said dryly.

Sir Harwick looked startled. "Why, my dear, it simply isn't done. You shouldn't be all alone here with an unattached man."

"Yes, I suppose it isn't done," she agreed.

"But you've been ill, my dear, and certainly haven't been able to think clearly. I don't fault you or Caine," he added with a nod toward the Marquess. "Your host has acted in good faith."

"He has?" Jade asked.

"Most certainly," Sir Harwick replied. "There's a full staff in residence here. Still, the gossipers would have a holiday with this bit of news. Too many people would be hurt by the rumors. Caine's mother . . ."

"My stepmother," Caine interjected.

"Yes, of course, your stepmother," Harwick continued. "She'd be hurt. As to that, his intended would also be quite crushed."

"His what?"

She really hadn't meant to raise her voice but Sir Harwick's casually given remark stunned her. She suddenly felt sick. The color all but drained from her face. "Did you say Caine's intended?" she asked in a scratchy whisper.

"Jade," Caine began. "I believe Sir Harwick is referring to Lady Aisely."

"I see," she replied. She forced a smile for the physician's benefit. "Now I remember. Lady Aisely, the woman you're going to marry." Her voice had risen to a near shrill by the time she'd finished.

She didn't even know this Aisely woman, but she already despised her. The longer she had to mull it over, the more infuriated she was with Caine. God's truth, she hated him, too.

"Lady Aisely wouldn't take the news of your visitation here lightly," Sir Harwick predicted.

"She isn't my intended," Caine interjected. "She's my stepmother's intention for me," he qualified. He couldn't keep the laughter out of his voice. Her reaction to hearing about Lady Aisely couldn't have been more revealing. It told him she cared.

"But your dear stepmother is . . ."

"She's hell-bent on getting Lady Aisely and me together," he interrupted. "It isn't going to happen, Harwick."

Jade could feel Caine's stare. She desperately tried to feign disinterest. She realized she was wringing the compress in her hands and immediately stopped that telling action. "Who you marry doesn't concern me," she announced.

"It should."

She shook her head. "I just wish you'd mentioned your engagement before last night."

"I'm not engaged," he snapped. "And last night would have . . ."

"Caine!" She shouted his name, then lowered her voice when she added, "We have a guest, if you'll remember."

Harwick let out a rich chuckle. He walked by Caine's side over to the door. "I have a feeling about you two. Am I right?"

"Depends upon what the feeling is," Caine answered.

"She's your intended, isn't she?"

"She is," Caine replied. "She just hasn't accepted it yet."

The two men shared a grin. "I can tell she's going to be difficult, my boy."

"Difficult or not," Caine countered, in a voice loud enough to wake the dead, "she will be my wife."

The door slammed shut on her shout of denial. Jade threw the compress across the room and collapsed against the pillows. She gritted her teeth in frustration.

Why did she care who he married? As soon as Nathan returned, she was never going to see Caine again. And why in thunder did everything have to be so complicated? Lord only knew that protecting Caine was work enough. Now she had to add Caine's father to her list.

Was Lady Aisely pretty?

Jade pushed that black thought aside. She really was going to have to do something about the Duke of Williamshire. Colin was certain to be upset when he returned home and found his papa had died from grief.

Had Caine taken Lady Aisely to bed?

I cannot think about her now, Jade decided. There are too many other problems to worry about.

She was going to have to do something about Colin's father. A note, she decided, wouldn't be good enough. She'd have to confront the man and have a firm talk with him.

Had Caine's stepmother already made the arrangements for Caine's wedding? Oh God, she hoped Caine had been telling her the truth. She hoped he didn't want Lady Aisely.

"This is ridiculous," she muttered to herself. Of course Caine would marry. And of course it would be to someone other than her. When he found out the truth about her background, he wouldn't want her anymore.

With a growl of frustration, Jade gave up trying to formulate any plans. Her emotions were like the masts on the *Emerald,* blowing strong in a high wind. It was pointless to try to concentrate now. Caine's papa would just have to despair a little longer.

She avoided Caine for most of the day. They ate a quiet dinner together. Sterns surprised Jade when he pulled out a chair and sat down with them. The butler ate his meal with them, too. He kept his attention on Caine most of the time, but when he did look at her, his expression was kind, affectionate.

She decided he hadn't found out that she slept with Caine, after all. Jade was relieved. She'd already noticed that Sterns' relationship with Caine was far more than employer and employee. They were very like family, and she didn't want a man who Caine cared about to think she was a trollop.

She kept giving Sterns fretful glances until he reached over and patted her hand.

Caine did most of the talking during the meal. The conversation centered on the problems of running such a large estate. Jade was extremely interested. Surprised as well, for Caine showed he had a true concern for the members of his parish. He actually felt responsible for their well-being.

"Do you aid those who need help?" she asked.

"Of course."

"By giving them money?"

"When it's the only answer," he explained. "Jade, a man's pride is as important as his hunger. Once the stomach's been filled, a way to better himself is the next step."

She thought about that statement a long while, then said,

"Yes, a man's self-worth is important. So is a woman's," she added.

"If you take that self-worth away, there's a good chance that he . . . or she will give up altogether. A man can't be made to feel he's been manipulated or made to feel a failure."

"There's a difference between manipulation and failure," she argued.

"Not really," Caine replied. "A man's a fool if he allows either, isn't he, Sterns?"

"He most certainly is," Sterns agreed. The butler reached for the teapot before continuing. "A man's pride is most important. It should matter above all else."

"But surely you two will agree that there are times when pride must be set aside," she interjected.

"Such as?" Caine asked.

"A man's life is one excellent example," she answered.

"But a man's life isn't as important as his self-worth," Sterns said. "Don't you agree, mi'lord?"

Caine didn't answer. He was looking at Jade with that unreadable expression on his face again. Jade didn't have any idea what he was thinking now. She smiled at him just to cover her own unease, then pleaded fatigue and returned to her bedroom.

Sterns had ordered a bath made ready for her. A fire burned in the hearth, toasting the air. Jade lingered in the tub, then went to bed. She tossed and turned for almost an hour before falling into a fitful sleep.

Caine came to her bed sometime after midnight. He stripped out of his clothes, smothered out the candles, and eased into bed beside her. She was sleeping on her side, her nightgown bunched up around her thighs. Caine slowly eased the gown high, then pulled her silky bottom up against him.

She sighed in her sleep. The sound was like a fever to him. God, she was so warm, so sweet. His hand moved beneath her gown. He stroked her skin, her breasts, rubbing her nipples into hard buds. She moved against him restlessly, moaning in her sleep.

She probably thought she was in the throes of an erotic dream, Caine thought. He nibbled on her neck, teased her earlobe with his tongue, and when her backside pushed up against him more insistently, his hand slid down into the heat between her thighs.

He stoked the fire in her until she was hot, wet, ready for him. His other arm held her around the waist. She tried to turn toward him, but he wouldn't let her move. "Open up for me, Jade," he whispered. "Let me come to you."

His knee nudged the back of her thighs until he was wedged between them.

"Tell me you want me," he demanded.

She could feel the velvet tip of his sex. She bit on her lower lip to keep herself from shouting at him to quit his torment. "Yes, I want you," she whispered. "Please, Caine. Now."

It was all the surrender he needed. He gently pushed her onto her stomach, his hand splayed wide across her pelvis, and surged inside her with one powerful thrust. Her tight sheath gloved him, squeezed him. He almost spilled his seed then and there. Caine stilled his movements and took a deep breath. "Easy love," he whispered on a groan when she pushed up against him.

Her hands were making knots out of the sheets. Caine's hands joined hers. His head fell forward to rest in the fragrant hollow between her neck and shoulder.

"Caine, I want . . ."

"I know," he answered. He was determined to go slow this time, to prolong the sweet agony, but her insistent pleas drove him beyond control. He drove into her again and again, until he was mindless of everything but finding fulfillment for both of them. When he knew he was about to pour his seed into her, his hand moved down her stomach. He stroked her into finding her own release.

169

Their climax was glorious. Caine collapsed on top of her. He was exhausted, and completely at peace. "Love, are you still breathing?" he asked when his heart quit hammering in his ears.

He was teasing her, yet when she didn't answer him, he immediately moved away from her. "Jade?"

She rolled over and looked at him. "You made me beg."

"I what?"

"You made me beg."

"Yes, I did, didn't I?" he answered with a wide grin.

"You aren't the least contrite," she announced. Her fingertips caressed his warm chest. "You're a rake, all right. I don't understand why I find you so appealing."

The dreamy, passionate look was still in her eyes. Caine kissed her forehead, the tip of her freckled nose, and then claimed her mouth for a long, wet, tongue-thrusting kiss. "Do you want more, love?"

He didn't give her time to answer. "I do," he whispered in a low growl.

A long while later, the two lovers fell asleep wrapped in each other's arms.

Chapter Ten

The following eight days were magical for Jade. Caine was such a gentle, loving man. He was so considerate of her feelings, too, and had the uncanny knack of understanding her moods quicker than she did. She liked their evenings most of all. Sterns would light a fire in the hearth in Caine's study, and the three of them would read in companionable silence.

Over the years, Sterns had actually become Caine's substitute father. Jade learned that the servant had been with Caine's family from the time of Caine's birth. When Caine established his own residence, Sterns had followed.

Sterns did let her know he was aware of the new sleeping arrangements. While she blushed with mortification, he announced that he certainly wasn't judgmental. He also added that he hadn't seen Caine so carefree in a good long while. Jade, he decreed, had lightened the Marquess's mood.

A messenger arrived from Caine's mother, requesting his aid in pulling his father out of his present dire circumstances.

Caine immediately went to visit his father, but when he

JULIE GARWOOD

returned some two hours later, he was in a foul mood. His talk with his father had come to little good.

That night, after Caine had fallen asleep, Jade met with Matthew and Jimbo to give them new orders.

Matthew was waiting for her just a few feet behind the cover of the trees. The seaman was tall, reed thin, and had skin as dark as a panther's. He had the personality to match the magnificent beast, but only when he was riled. He also had an easy smile that could be quite dazzling when he was in the mood to give it.

Matthew wasn't smiling now. He had his arms crossed in front of his chest and was scowling at her just like a man who'd found a thief rummaging through his drawers.

"Why are you frowning so, Matthew?" she asked in a bare whisper.

"I saw Him standing at the window with you the other night, girl," Matthew grumbled. "Has that dandy been touching you?"

Jade didn't want to lie, but she wasn't about to share the truth with her trusted friend, either. "I was injured," she replied. "Now don't give me that look, Matthew. I took a pistol shot in my side. It was a paltry wound. Caine was . . . concerned and he stayed in my chambers that night, watching out for me."

"Black Harry's going to feed my arse to the sharks when he hears . . ."

"Matthew, you aren't going to tell Harry anything," she interjected.

The seaman wasn't at all intimidated by her angry tone. "You got yourself a sassy mouth," he replied. "I seen the fancy man put his arm around you when you were walking to the front door that first day, and I will be telling Harry. That's a fact you can start cringing over now. Jimbo wanted to put a knife in his back. Only reason he didn't is because he knew you'd be put out with him."

"Yes, I would be put out," she answered. "No one's going to touch a hair on Caine's head or he'll answer to me. Now quit frowning, Matthew. We have an important issue to discuss."

Matthew didn't want to let go of their topic. "But is he giving you real trouble?"

"No, he isn't giving me any trouble," she replied. "Matthew, you know I can take care of myself. Please have more faith in me."

Matthew was immediately contrite. He didn't want his mistress to be disappointed in him. "Of course I know you can take care of yourself," he rushed out. "But you don't know your own appeal. You're too pretty for your own good. I'm thinking now Jimbo and Harry were right. We should have cut your face when you was a youngster."

She knew from the sparkle in his handsome brown eyes that he was jesting with her. "None of you would have dared to harm me," she countered. "We're family, Matthew, and you love me as much as I love you."

"You're nothing but a puny brat," came another deep voice. Jade turned toward the sound and watched her friend, Jimbo, silently move to stand directly in front of her. Jimbo's frown matched his giant's size. Like Matthew, he was also dressed in drab brown peasant garb, for brighter colors could easily be spotted through the branches.

In the moonlight, Jimbo's frown looked fierce. "Matthew told me the dandy touched you. I could kill him, just for that. No one's . . ."

"You're both underestimating Caine if you think he'll easily let you put your knives in him," she interjected.

"I'm betting he's as puny as Colin," Jimbo argued.

Jade let him see how exasperated she was with him. "You haven't seen Colin in quite some time and he was half out of his mind because of his injuries then. He's probably as fit as ever now. Besides, you've made a serious miscalculation if you believe either brother is weak. Remember, Jimbo, I was the one who read Caine's file. I know what I'm talking about."

"If the man's got blood, he can bleed," Matthew pronounced.

Neither seaman seemed affected by her frown. Jade let out a sigh of frustration.

She turned to Matthew and said, "I must go and have a little chat with Caine's father. You must keep Caine occupied with a diversion while I'm away."

"I don't see any need for you to talk to Caine's father," Matthew protested. "Colin and Nathan are bound to show up any time now."

"The way they're dawdling? No, I dare not wait any longer. Caine's father might very well be on his death bed now. He isn't eating or sleeping. I can't let him die."

"I can see you got your mind set," Matthew muttered. "What kind of a diversion are you thinking of?"

"I'll leave that in your capable hands," Jade countered.

"When you want it done?" Jimbo asked.

"Tomorrow," she answered. "As early as possible."

Jade finally went back to her bed, content with the knowledge that Matthew and Jimbo wouldn't let her down.

The diversion began just bare minutes before dawn the following morning.

She realized then that she should have been more specific with her instructions. And when this was over, she was going to have Matthew's hide. His capable hands, indeed. The man had set the stables on fire. Fortunately, he'd had enough sense to let the horses out first.

Caine was occupied, she'd give Matthew that much credit. The horses were running wild. Three were about ready to drop their foals, and every hand was needed to squelch the spreading fire and chase the animals down.

She pretended to be asleep until Caine left the room.

Then she dressed in quick time and slipped out the back way. Caine had posted guards around the perimeter, but in the chaos, she was easily able to sneak past.

"Jimbo just left for Shallow's Wharf," Matthew told Jade as he assisted her onto the mount he'd chosen for her. "He should be back by sunset tomorrow with word for us. If the winds are strong, don't you suppose Nathan will be here soon? And are you certain you don't want me riding along with you?"

"I'm certain I want you to keep your guard on Caine's back," she replied. "He's the one in danger. I'll be back in an hour. And Matthew? Don't set anything else on fire while I'm gone."

Matthew gave her a wide grin. "It did the trick, didn't it now?"

"Aye, Matthew," she answered, not wishing to injure his pride. "It did do the trick."

She left Matthew smiling after her and arrived at her destination a half hour later. After leaving her horse in the woods adjacent to the property line, she quickly made her way to the front door. The house was monstrous, but the lock was puny by any thief's standards. Jade had it unlatched in bare minutes. There was enough light filtering through the windows for her to make her way up the winding staircase. Sounds radiated from the back of the house, indicating that the kitchen staff was already at work.

Jade was as quiet as a cat as she looked into each of the numerous bedrooms. The Duke of Williamshire couldn't be found in any of them, however. She had assumed he'd be occupying the largest bedchamber, but that giant's room was empty. A blond-headed, rather attractive elderly woman who snored like a sailor occupied the adjacent bedchamber. Jade guessed the woman was the Duchess.

At the end of the long corridor in the south wing, she found the library. It was an out-of-the-way, unusual place to house the study. Caine's father was inside. He was sound asleep in his chair behind the mahogany desk.

After locking the door against intruders, Jade studied the handsome man for a long while. He was very distinguished looking with silver-tipped hair, high, patrician cheekbones, and an angular face very similar to Caine's. There were deep circles under his eyes. The color of his skin was sallow. Even in sleep he looked as though he was in torment.

Jade couldn't decide if she should blister him with a stern lecture or apologize for causing him such needless pain.

Her heart went out to him, though. He reminded her of Caine, of course, though the father certainly wasn't as muscular. He certainly had the height, however. When she touched his shoulder, he came awake with a start and bounded out of his chair with a quickness that surprised her.

"Please don't be alarmed, sir," she whispered. "I didn't mean to startle you."

"You didn't?" he asked, imitating her low tone of voice.

The Duke of Williamshire slowly regained his composure. He ran his fingers through his hair, then shook his head in an attempt to clear his mind.

"Who are you?" he asked.

"It doesn't matter who I am, sir," she answered. "Please sit down, for I have important information to share with you."

She patiently waited until he'd obeyed her request, then leaned against the edge of the desktop close to his side. "This grieving must stop. You've made yourself ill."

"What?"

He still looked confused to her. She noticed, too, that the color of his eyes was the exact shade of gray as Caine's. His frown was similar as well.

"I said that you must stop grieving," she stated again. "Sir Harwick thinks you might well be dying. If you don't stop this nonsense . . ."

176

"Now see here, young lady . . ."

"Do not raise your voice to me," she interjected.

"Who in God's name are you? And how did you get into . . ."

The bluster went out of him and he slowly shook his head.

Jade thought he seemed more incredulous than angry. She decided that was a good beginning.

"Sir, I simply don't have time for a lengthy discussion. First, you must give me your promise that you'll never tell anyone about our conversation. Do you give me your word?"

"You have it," he replied.

"Good. Now, I believe I must apologize to you, though in truth I'm no good at it. I hate apologizing to anyone." She shrugged, then added, "I'm sorry I didn't come to you sooner. You've been caused needless grief, and I really could have spared you. Do you forgive me?"

"I have no idea what you're talking about, but if it will make you happy, I shall forgive you. Now tell me what it is you want from me."

"Your bark, sir, is just as irritating as your son's."

"And which son is that?" he asked, a hint of a smile coming into his eyes.

"Caine."

"Is this visitation concerning Caine? Has he done something to offend you? You might as well know now that Caine's his own man. I won't interfere unless there's real cause."

"No," Jade answered. "This isn't about Caine, though I'm happy to know you have such faith in your eldest son's ability to make his own decisions. By not interfering, you show your pride in your son."

"Then who is it you wish to discuss?" he asked.

"I'm a friend of Colin's."

"You knew him?"

She nodded. "I know him, yes. You see, he's . . ."

"Dead," he interjected, his tone harsh. "Pagan killed him."

Jade reached out and put her hand on his shoulder. "Look at me, please," she commanded in a soft whisper when he turned his gaze toward the windows.

When Caine's father did as she ordered, she nodded. "What I am about to tell you will be difficult for you to believe. First, understand this. I have proof."

"Proof?"

She nodded again. "Pagan didn't kill Colin."

"He did."

"I'm sick of hearing about **Pagan's** sins," she muttered. "Colin . . ."

"Did Pagan send you to me?"

"Please lower your voice," she returned. "Pagan didn't kill your son," she repeated. "He saved him. Colin's very much alive."

A long minute elapsed before the Duke reacted. His face slowly turned a blotchy shade of red while he stared at her. His eyes turned so cold, she thought he might cause frost-bite.

Before he could shout at her again, she said, "I told you I had proof. Are you willing to listen to me or is your mind so set . . ."

"I will listen," he returned. "Though if this be some sort of cruel jest, I swear I'll hunt Pagan down myself and kill him with my bare hands."

"That is a fair exchange for such cruelty," she agreed. "Do you remember the time when Colin had climbed up a giant tree and couldn't get down? He was four or five years old then. Because he was crying and feeling very cowardly, you promised him you'd never tell anyone. You also convinced him that it was quite all right to be afraid, that fear was not a sin, that . . ."

"I remember," the Duke whispered. "I never did tell anyone. How did you . . ."

"As I just said, Colin told me that story. Many others, too."

"He could have told you these stories before he was killed," the Duke stated.

"Yes, he could have, but he didn't. Pagan fished Colin out of the ocean. Your son was in sorry shape. Do you know the physician, Sir Winters?"

"He's my personal physician," the Duke muttered.

"Don't you think it odd that he disappeared?"

The anger was slowly easing away from the elderly man's expression. "I do think that odd," he admitted.

"We took him," Jade explained. "He was needed to tend to Colin. I thought it important that your son have his family physician. He was in terrible pain, sir, and I wanted him to have as many familiar comforts as possible."

Jade nibbled on her lower lip while she contemplated another way to convince him. He still looked disbelieving to her. "Colin has a birthmark on his backside," she suddenly blurted out. "I know because I took care of him until Jimbo and Matthew could take Winters captive. There! Is that proof enough for you?"

In answer to that question, the Duke slowly leaned back in his chair. "Proof was sent of Colin's death."

"By whom?"

"The War Office."

"Exactly."

"I don't understand."

"I shall explain after Colin comes home," Jade answered. "Will you explain something to me before I continue to try and convince you?"

"What is it?" he asked, his tone weary.

"Do you happen to know why Colin would make me promise not to tell Caine he was alive? I've learned to trust

179

your eldest son, and I don't understand the reason behind this promise. Colin was half out of his mind at the time, however, and perhaps his mumbling about the Bradley brothers wasn't . . ."

Caine's father bounded out of his chair again. "Colin is alive."

"Please lower your voice," she ordered. "No one must know."

"Why? I want to shout it to the heavens. My boy is alive."

"I see I've finally convinced you," she countered with a smile. "Please sit down, sir. You look faint to me."

She waited until he'd resumed his seat, then asked, "What was it that made you realize I was telling the truth?"

"When you said that Colin didn't want Caine to know . . ." He stammered to a stop, then whispered. "Lord, the Bradley brothers. I'd forgotten that incident."

Now it was her turn to look confused. "Why?" she asked, unable to keep the worry out of her voice. "Doesn't he trust his own brother?"

"Oh, no, you misunderstand," he replied. "Colin idolized Caine. I mean to say, he idolizes him. My God, this is difficult to take in."

"But if he idolizes Caine, why would he make me promise not to tell him? You've still to explain. And who, pray tell, are the Bradley brothers?"

The Duke of Williamshire let out a deep chuckle. "When Colin was just eight or nine years old, he came running home with a bloody nose and cut lip. Caine happened to be home. He demanded to know who'd done the damage, and as soon as Colin said that the Bradley brothers were responsible, Caine went charging out the door. Colin tried to stop him, of course. He hadn't told him the number of brothers, you see. A half hour later, Caine came home as bloody as his brother."

"How many brothers were there?" Jade asked.

"Eight."

"Good heavens, do you mean to say all eight brothers attacked Colin and . . ."

"No, only one went after Colin, a boy named Samuel if I remember correctly. Anyway, Samuel must have known Caine would retaliate, and he raced home to get his own reinforcements."

"Caine could have been killed," she whispered.

"Actually, my dear, your sympathy should be for the Bradley brothers. Caine was only going to put the fear of God into the boy who'd hurt Colin, but when they came at him in force, he gave them what for! My boy gave equal measure."

Jade shook her head. She didn't find the horrid story the least bit amusing. Yet Caine's father was smiling like a proud papa.

"And so you see, my dear, it isn't out of mistrust that Colin made you give your promise. It's just that Colin knows Caine very well. Colin must be thinking to protect Caine until he can explain the full situation to him. He doesn't want him charging into another group of Bradleys again. Of the two, Colin's always been the more cautious. Caine didn't know Colin was working for our government," he added. "As to that, I didn't know either. I never would have allowed it, especially when I learned that Sir Richards wasn't his superior."

"Richards," she whispered. "Yes, he was Caine's director, wasn't he?"

Caine's father looked surprised over that statement. "You've gathered quite a bit of pertinent information, haven't you? I cannot help but wonder how you came by it. Will you tell me who gave you such secrets?"

She was a little insulted by that question. "No one gave me anything," she said. "I found out on my own. I'm most resourceful, sir. My brother, Nathan, was helping Colin sort out a rather complex problem for the government. Someone didn't want them to succeed, however. A trap was set. The only reason they're both still alive is that . . . Pagan became suspicious. The pirate was able to intervene in time."

"Does Colin know who is behind this treachery?"

She shook her head. "We only know that it's someone high up in the War Office. Nathan and Colin are safe only as long as they are believed dead. I cannot tell you anything more. When Colin returns . . ."

"Will you take me to see him?"

"He should be home in just a few more days, sir. He cannot stay here, of course, unless you've cleaned your house of the servants . . . the details will have to be worked out." She paused to smile at him. "I wonder if you'll recognize your son. His hair has grown way past his shoulders. Both he and Nathan look like true pirates now."

"That must please Pagan."

"Oh, it pleases Pagan very much."

"Were their injuries severe?" he asked.

"They had been bound and gagged, then shot and tossed into the waters. Their enemies knew they weren't dead yet."

"They left them to drown."

"No, they left them for the sharks. The waters were infested with the predators and the fresh blood . . . drew their notice."

"My God . . ."

"The sharks didn't get them, though I will admit there were several close minutes. Pagan lost a good man in the rescue."

"Pagan went into those waters with this other man?"

"Yes," she answered. "Pagan is the strongest swimmer. Besides, the pirate would never ask others what . . . he could not do himself."

Jade started for the door, but was stopped by his next question. "Are you in love with my Colin?"

"Oh, heaven's no," she answered. She unlocked the door, then turned back to her new confidant. "When we next meet, you must pretend not to know me. I'm keeping Caine occupied for the present. As you know, he's determined to track down Pagan. The hunt has put him at risk, but that soon will be resolved."

"But Pagan wouldn't . . ."

"Pagan's protecting Caine," she said. "The pirate has been blamed for killing Nathan and Colin. Your government put a price on his head. Caine, as you probably know, has doubled that amount. Now consider what would happen if Caine were able to find Pagan and talked to him before he . . ."

"Pagan might be able to convince Caine he didn't kill Colin."

"Exactly," she replied. "Do you see? Whoever is behind this treachery wants to make certain Pagan isn't found."

"Or have Caine killed before he hunts down the truth."

"Yes."

"My God, Caine is at risk. I must . . ."

"Do nothing, sir," Jade announced. "As I've explained, Pagan is watching out for Caine."

"Good Lord, Pagan isn't our enemy," the Duke whispered. "I owe the man a debt I shall never be able to repay. Dear lady, is there nothing I can do for you?"

"I must take care of Caine for now," she answered. "He's a very stubborn man, but a protector by nature. He's occupied by thinking he's taking care of my problems now. When Colin comes home, then the three of you can decide what's to be done."

"Pagan sent you to Caine then?"

"Yes," she replied with a smile.

"Caine won't give up," he interjected. "I pray Colin returns soon."

"Don't worry so," Jade said. "If you tell Caine to quit his

hunt, he'll only try harder to succeed. He's too determined to stop now."

"Then you must confide in him."

"I cannot, sir. I have given my word to Colin. Besides, we've only a few more days before the truth is revealed."

"What if your brother and Colin are delayed?"

"Then we'll have to form a new plan," she announced with a nod.

"But what specifically . . ."

"We'll have to find a way to take the prey away from the hunter. Caine will be furious, but he'll be alive. I must consider this carefully," she added as she opened the door.

"When will I see you again? You mentioned that I must pretend not to know you, but . . ."

"Oh, I'm certain you'll see me again," she answered. "And there is one little thing you could do to repay me," she added. "You did say you would do anything," she reminded him.

"Yes, anything."

"Caine is your eldest son and if there must be a favorite, then he should be the one."

The Duke was clearly astonished by her remarks. "I love all my children. I wasn't aware that I favored one above the others."

"Sir Harwick believes Colin is your favorite," she said. "He also said that Caine keeps himself separate from the family. Don't allow this to continue, sir. Caine needs your love. See that he gets it."

The door closed.

The Duke of Williamshire sat at his desk a long while before his legs felt strong enough to hold his weight. Tears of joy streamed down his cheeks. He said a prayer of thanksgiving for this miracle he'd just been given.

His Colin was alive.

Henry was suddenly ravenous. He went in search of

breakfast. It was going to be difficult, for the Duke wasn't a man given to trickery, but he would have to control his smiles. None of his staff must suspect the true reason for his recovery.

He felt reborn. It was as though someone had reached down into his lonely black abyss of despair and lifted him all the way up to the stars.

The young lady he now considered his savior had the most unusual green eyes. Pagan must have named his ship after the beautiful woman. The *Emerald*. Yes, he decided with a nod. He was also certain he now knew the pirate's true identity, but he vowed he'd go to his death before revealing that truth to anyone.

He wondered, though, what Caine would say when he found out that the woman he was sheltering was actually Pagan's little sister?

There'd be fireworks aplenty, and his only prayer now was that he'd be there to protect his savior when Caine's temper exploded.

The Duke of Williamshire was certain he had it all figured out.

He was filling his plate with a second helping of eggs and kidneys when his wife, Gweneth, came rushing into the dining room. "Cook told me you were eating," she stammered out.

The Duke turned to his wife, a soft smile on his face. Poor Gweneth looked rattled. Her short blond hair was in complete disarray and she couldn't seem to get the sash to her robe tied. "Why, Henry?" she asked, staring at him so intently.

"It's the usual custom each morning," he answered. "And I was hungry."

Her brown eyes filled with tears. "You were hungry?" she whispered.

Henry put his plate down on the side bar and walked over

to his wife. He took her into his arms and kissed the top of her head. "I've given you quite a worry lately, haven't I, love?"

"But you're feeling better now?" she asked.

"I've been advised not to languish any longer," he stated.

"By whom?"

"My conscience," he lied. "In time, Gweneth, I shall explain this sudden turnabout to you. For now, however, I can only say I'm sorry for all the worry I've caused you and the children. I've grieved long enough."

"It's a miracle," she whispered.

Yes, he thought to himself, a miracle with bewitching green eyes. "Come and have a bite to eat, my dear. You look a bit peaked to me."

"I looked peaked?" Her laughter was shaky. "You, my love, look like death."

He kissed her tenderly, then led her over to the table. "After I've cleaned up, I believe I'll ride over to Caine's place."

"He'll be stunned by your recovery," Gweneth announced. "Oh, Henry, it's so good to have you back with us."

"Would you like to ride over to see Caine with me?"

"Oh, yes, I'd like that," she answered. A determined gleam entered her eyes. "It isn't proper to have guests but I believe I'll invite Lady Aisely and her dear mother down for a long weekend. You must tell Caine we expect him to . . . why are you shaking your head at me?"

"You might as well save yourself the effort, Gweneth. Give it up. Caine won't be marrying Lady Aisely."

"It's a sound match, Henry," she argued. "Give me two good reasons why I cannot encourage this union?"

"Very well," he answered. "One, she doesn't have red hair."

"Well, of course she doesn't have red hair. She has beautiful blond hair. You know that well enough."

"And two," he continued, ignoring her befuddled look. "She doesn't have green eyes."

"Henry, you aren't feeling altogether well yet, are you?"

Henry's laughter echoed throughout the dining room. "Caine needs an enchantress. You'll have to accept it, my dear."

"Accept what?" she asked.

His slow wink left her more puzzled than ever. "I believe, Gweneth, that your breakfast will have to wait a while longer. You must go back to bed at once."

"I must?" she asked. "Why?"

The Duke leaned forward and whispered into his wife's ear. When he was finished with his explanation, his wife blushed.

"Oh, Henry," she whispered. "You really are feeling better."

Chapter Eleven

Jade returned to Caine's home a short time later. After handing the reins to Matthew, she rushed up the back steps to her bedroom. When she rounded the corner, she found Sterns standing like a centurian outside her bedroom door.

He did a double take when he spotted her. Then he folded his arms across his chest. "You're suppose to be inside your bedroom, mi'lady."

She decided to take the offensive. She'd make him do the explaining. "And what are you suppose to be doing?"

"I'm guarding the door."

"Why?"

"So you won't leave."

"But I already left," she countered with a soft smile. "Sterns, I do believe your time is too valuable to be guarding an empty room."

"But mi'lady, I didn't know it was empty," he protested.

She patted him on his arm. "You may explain this to me later, sir. Now please move out of my way. I really must change out of this riding garment and go help Caine."

She scooted past the disgruntled-looking servant and shut

the door on his protests. In little time at all, she'd changed into a dark green gown and hurried downstairs by way of the main staircase.

Sterns was now guarding the front door. The set of his jaw told her he was going to be difficult. "You may not go outside," he announced in a voice that would have chilled a polar bear.

She wasn't at all intimidated. She gave him a wide smile. "I can and I will," she answered.

"My lord is most insistent that you remain inside."

"I'm just as insistent that I go outside."

In answer to that challenge, Sterns leaned against the door and slowly shook his head.

Jade decided to turn his attention. "Sterns? How many servants are there in residence here?"

He looked surprised by her question. "We're only half staffed now," he answered. "There are five of us in all."

"Where are the others?"

"In London," he answered. "They're helping to clean the town house."

"But I thought it was destroyed in the fire," she said.

"It wasn't as bad as all that," he said. "The side's been boarded up and now there's only the smoke damage to be righted. While the workers repair the structure, the servants are cleaning the inside."

"I'm wondering, Sterns, if the servants here can be trusted."

He rose to his full height before answering. "Mi'lady, all the servants are trustworthy. They are all loyal to their employer."

"You're certain?"

He took a step away from the door. "Why are you so interested in . . ."

"You'll be having two guests in the next few days, Sterns, but no one must tell that they're here. Your staff must keep silent."

"The Marquess hasn't mentioned any guests to me," he argued, seeming mildly injured.

Jade rushed past him and threw the door wide. "Caine doesn't know about the visitors just yet," she said. "That's the reason he hasn't told you. It's going to be a surprise, you see."

She could tell from his befuddled expression that he didn't see. "I just thought you'd like to be forewarned so you could have the guest chambers made ready," she explained. She picked up her skirts and started down the steps. "Now quit frowning, Sterns. I shall tell Caine you tried to keep me inside."

"And I shall inform mi'lord that you weren't in your room," he called out.

Jade found Caine going through the remains of what had been his stables. Only smoldering embers remained. The destruction was absolute.

The horses, she noticed, were now housed in a large rectangular corral the men had just put together.

Caine's white shirt was covered with soot. "Have you collected all your horses?" she asked when she reached his side.

He slowly turned to look at her. The scowl on his face could very well start a fresh fire. His tone, however, was deceptively mild when he said, "All but the one you borrowed."

"Borrowed?" she asked, feigning innocence.

"Go and wait for me in the drawing room," he commanded.

"But Caine, I want to help."

"Help?" He almost lost his temper then and there. "You and your men have helped enough." Several deep breaths later, he said, "Go back inside. Now."

His roar accomplished his goal. Jade immediately turned around and hurried back to the house. She could feel Caine's stare on her back and wouldn't have been surprised if her gown had caught fire. The man was spitting-embers angry.

It would be pointless to try to reason with him now. She'd have to wait until his anger had dissipated just a little.

When she reached the bottom step, she turned back to him. "Caine? If you must stay outside, don't be such a bloody easy target."

Sterns rushed down the stairs, grabbed hold of her elbow, and whispered, "Do as he orders, Lady Jade. You don't want to prod his temper now. Come along inside now," he added as he assisted her up the stairs. "I don't believe I've ever seen mi'lord in such a rage."

"Yes, he is in a rage," Jade whispered, irritated by the tremor in her voice. "Sterns, do you think I might have a cup of tea? This day seems to have gone completely sour," she added. "And it's not even half done."

"Of course I shall fix you some tea," Sterns rushed out. "Mi'lady, I'm certain the Marquess didn't mean to raise his voice to you. Once he gets over his anger, I'm certain he'll apologize."

"He might not ever get over his anger," she muttered.

Sterns opened the front door for her, then followed her inside. "The stables weren't even a month old," he said.

Jade tried to pay attention to what Sterns was saying, but Caine's words kept echoing through her mind. You and your men have helped enough. Yes, those were his very words. He knew about Matthew and Jimbo. But how? she wondered, and more importantly, what else did he know?

While Sterns went to see about her tea, Jade paced the confines of the large drawing room. She opened the pair of French doors at the end of the room to let in the fresh spring air. It was a precautionary measure as well, for if Caine was bent on killing her, she'd have a possible escape.

"Nonsense," she muttered as she resumed her pacing. Caine would never raise his hand against her, no matter how angry he became. Besides, he couldn't possibly know the full truth.

The front door suddenly bounded open. It banged against the interior wall twice before it was slammed shut.

Caine had arrived.

Jade rushed over to the gold brocade settee, sat down, and folded her hands in her lap. She forced a serene smile on her face. He wasn't going to know she was shaking. No, she'd go to her grave before she'd let him know he had her worried.

The doors to the drawing room flew open next. Caine filled the entrance. Jade couldn't hold her smile once she saw his expression. He looked ready to kill. Why, he was so furious, he was actually trembling.

"Where did you go this morning?" he roared.

"Don't take that tone of voice with me, sir. You'll make me deaf."

"Answer me."

She glared at him because he'd ignored her order and had shouted once again, then said, "I went to visit your dear papa."

That announcement took a little of the bluster out of him. Then he shook his head. "I don't believe you."

"I'm telling you the truth," she stated.

Caine walked into the room and didn't stop until he towered over her. The tips of his boots touched the hem of her gown. He loomed over her like an avenging god. Jade felt trapped. In the back of her mind she knew that he wanted her to feel that way. "I'm sorry you don't believe me, Caine, but I did go to see your father. I was very concerned about him, you see. Sir Harwick mentioned he wasn't feeling well and I thought a nice chat would lighten his mood."

She stared down at her hands while she made that confession.

"When did you set the fire, Jade?"

She looked up at his face then. "I didn't set any fires," she announced.

"The hell you didn't," he roared. He turned away from her and walked over to the hearth. He was so furious, he didn't trust himself to stand close to her.

She stood up, folded her hands in front of her, and said, "I didn't set your stables on fire, Caine."

"Then you ordered one of your men to do it. Now I want to know why."

"What men?"

"The two bastards who've been hanging around here since the day we arrived," he answered.

He waited to hear her denial. She had given him nothing but lies since the moment they met. He realized that now.

"Oh, those two men," she answered. She lifted her shoulders in a delicate shrug. "You must mean Matthew and Jimbo. You've met them, have you?"

His anguish was almost unbearable now. "Yes, I've met them. They were two more lies, weren't they?"

She couldn't look at him now. God help her, she was finally seeing the man she'd read about in the file. Cold. Methodical. Deadly. The descriptive words hadn't been exaggerated after all.

"Matthew and Jimbo are fine men," she whispered.

"Then you don't deny . . ."

"I won't deny anything," she answered. "You're putting me in an impossible position. I have given my word and I can't break it. You'll just have to trust me a while longer."

"Trust you?" He roared the words like blasphemies. "I will never trust you again. You must think I'm a fool if you believe I would."

She was terrified of him now. She took a deep breath, then said, "My problem is very delicate."

"I don't give a damn how delicate your problem is," he roared. "What in God's name is your game? Why are you here?"

He was back to shouting at her. Jade shook her head at him. "I will tell you only that I'm here because of you."

"Answer me."

"Very well," she whispered. "I'm here to protect you."

She might as well have told him she'd come from the heavens for all the attention he gave that statement of fact. "I want the real reason, damn it."

"That is the real reason. I'm protecting you."

Sterns appeared at the opened doorway with a silver tray in his hands. He took one look at his employer's face and immediately turned around.

"Shut the doors behind you, Sterns," Caine ordered.

"Don't you raise your voice to Sterns," Jade demanded in a near shout of her own. "He has nothing to do with this and you shouldn't take your anger out on him."

"Sit down, Jade." His voice was much softer now, far more threatening, too. It took all Jade's determination not to do as he ordered.

"You probably kick puppies when you're in a foul mood, don't you?"

"Sit down."

She glanced over to the doorway, judging the distance to safety, but Caine's next words changed her mind. "You wouldn't make it."

Jade turned back to Caine. "You aren't going to be at all reasonable about this, are you?"

"No," he answered. "I'm not going to be reasonable."

"I was hoping that we could have a quiet discussion after you've calmed down and . . ."

"Now," he countered. "We're going to have our discussion now, Jade." He wanted to grab hold of her, shake her into answering all his questions, but he knew if he touched her, he might kill her.

His heart felt as though it had just been torn in half. "Pagan sent you, didn't he?"

"No."

"Yes," he answered. "My God, the bastard sent a woman to do his work for him. Who is he, Jade? Your brother?"

194

She shook her head and backed away from him. "Caine, please try to listen . . ."

He started after her, then forced himself to stop. "All of it . . . lies, isn't that right, Jade? You weren't in any danger."

"Not all of it lies," she answered. "But you were the primary target."

He shook his head. She knew then he wasn't going to believe anything she told him. She could see the pain, the raw agony in his eyes.

"He sent a woman," he repeated. "Your brother's a coward. He's going to die. It will be fitting justice, won't it? An eye for an eye, or in this instance, a brother for a brother."

"Caine, you must listen to me," she cried out. She wanted to weep because of the torment she was causing him. "You have to understand. In the beginning, I didn't know what kind of a man you were . . . Oh, God, I'm so sorry . . ."

"Sorry?" he asked, his voice flat, devoid of all emotion.

"Yes," she whispered. "If you'll only listen . . ."

"Do you think I'm going to believe anything you tell me now?"

Jade didn't answer him. Caine seemed to be staring through her. He didn't say anything for a long time. She could almost see the fury building inside of him.

She closed her eyes against his dark expression, his anger, his hatred.

"Did you let me make love to you because Pagan ordered you to?" he asked.

She reacted as though he'd just struck her. "That would make me a whore, Caine, and I don't whore for anyone, not even my brother."

He didn't agree with her soon enough to placate her. Her eyes filled with tears. "I am not a whore," she shouted.

The sudden roar that came from the French doors turned both Caine's and Jade's attention. The bone-chilling sound was like a battle cry.

195

Jade recognized the sound. Nathan had arrived. The deception was finally over.

"Did you just call my sister a whore?"

The walls shook from the venom in Nathan's deep voice. Jade had never seen her brother so angry.

She took a step toward her brother, but suddenly found herself hauled up against Caine's side.

"Don't get in my way," he ordered, his voice mild, horribly calm.

"In the way of what?" she asked. "You aren't going to hurt my brother, Caine. I won't let you."

"Get your hands off her," Nathan roared. "Or I'll kill you."

"Nathan," Jade cried out. "Caine doesn't understand." She tried to push Caine's hands away from her shoulders. It proved impossible. His grip was as tenacious as seaweed.

She didn't know who looked more furious. Nathan's scowl was just as ugly as Caine's was, just as threatening. They were equally matched, these two giant adversaries. They were bound to kill each other if given the chance.

Nathan looked like a pirate, too. His long, dark brown hair fell way past his broad shoulders. He was dressed in snug black britches and wore his white shirt opened almost to the waist. Nathan wasn't quite as tall as Caine was, but he was certainly just as muscular.

Yes, they would kill each other. Jade frantically tried to think of a way to ease the situation while the two men took each other's measure.

"I asked you a question, you bastard," Nathan shouted again. He took a threatening step forward. "Did you call my sister a whore?"

"He didn't call me a whore," Jade shouted when Nathan reached for the knife in his waistband. "He doesn't know about Colin. I kept my word not to tell him."

Nathan hesitated. Jade pressed her advantage. "He thinks you killed Colin. He has it all figured out, Nathan."

Nathan's hand moved back to his side, away from his dagger. Jade went weak with relief. "He has, has he?" Nathan drawled out.

Caine stared at the intruder, knowing now there couldn't be any doubt that the pirate was Jade's brother. They both had the same green eyes.

"Damn right I figured it out," Caine suddenly roared. "You're Pagan and you did kill my brother."

She pushed away from Caine and took a step toward Nathan. Caine roughly shoved Jade behind his back. "Don't try to go to him, Jade."

"Are you trying to protect me from my own brother?" she asked.

Caine didn't answer her.

"Did he touch you?" Nathan shouted the question as though it was a blasphemy.

"Nathan, will you quit that topic?" she cried out. "Now isn't the time to discuss such a personal matter."

"Be silent," Caine commanded.

Jade grabbed hold of the back of his shirt when he started forward. The action didn't waylay him. Caine kicked the ornately carved tea cart out of his path and continued toward his prey. "Damn right I touched her," he roared. "Wasn't that all part of the plan, you bastard?"

Nathan let out a roar, then rushed forward. The two men were like bulls charging at each other.

"No," Jade screamed. "Nathan, please don't hurt Caine. Caine, you mustn't hurt Nathan either . . ."

She quit her pleas when she realized they weren't paying any attention to her.

Caine got in the first toss. He literally threw Nathan up against the wall. A lovely painting depicting the Thames in earlier, cleaner times fell to the floor with a loud thud. Nathan finished the destruction of the artwork when he put his foot through it in an attempt to slam his knee into Caine's groin.

He was determined to make a eunuch out of him. Caine easily blocked the blow, however, then threw Nathan up against the wall again. Jade's brother landed the first good punch, though it was most assuredly by foul means. Caine had Nathan by his neck and was just about to smash his fist through the back of his skull when his attention was caught by the man standing in the doorway. His hold immediately slackened. Nathan pressed his advantage. He slammed his fist into Caine's jaw.

Caine shook off the blow as insignificant, then shoved Nathan against the wall again.

"Colin?"

The name came out in a strangled whisper of disbelief. His mind couldn't accept what he was seeing. His brother was alive. Colin was leaning against the door frame, grinning that lopsided grin of his that was so familiar, so boyish . . . so Colin. He looked thin, terribly thin, but very much alive.

Caine was so stunned he didn't realize he was strangling Nathan until he heard him gasping for air. As soon as he lessened his grip, Nathan tore free and hit him again. Caine ignored the blow and finally let go.

Almost as an afterthought, Caine slammed his elbow into Nathan's ribs, then took a step toward Colin.

"Honest to God, Colin, I'm going to kill your brother," Nathan shouted. "Do you know what he's done to my sister? He . . ."

"Nathan, you don't have to tell Colin," Jade cried out. "Please," she added. "For once, try to be a gentleman."

Colin slowly pulled away from the door. He used his cane to aid him as he made his way over to his brother. Caine was shaking with emotion when he wrapped his arms around his little brother. "My God, you're really here. I cannot believe it."

"I'm so damned happy to see you, Caine," Colin said. "I

know you're surprised. I'll explain everything. Try not to be too angry with me. I wouldn't let anyone tell you. I wanted to explain first. They're evil men. You would have gone charging in . . ."

Colin didn't seem to have the strength to go on. He sagged against Caine, giving him most of his weight. Caine continued to hold him close while he waited for his brother to regain his composure. "Take your time, Colin," he whispered. "Just take your time."

When Colin nodded, Caine stepped back to have another look at his brother. The dimple was back in Caine's cheek and tears had formed in his eyes. "Colin, you look like a pirate, too," he announced. "Your hair's as long as Pagan's," he added with a nod and a scowl in Nathan's direction.

Nathan scowled back. "I haven't told him anything, Colin," Nathan said. "But your astute brother has it all figured out. He knows I'm Pagan and I sent my little sister to whore for me."

Jade wished the floor would open up and swallow her whole. Her face felt like it was on fire. "Nathan, if Caine doesn't kill you, I very well might," she threatened.

Colin was staring at her. When he started laughing, she knew exactly what he was thinking. "Didn't I tell you . . ." he began.

"Colin, do sit down," she commanded. "You must get your weight off that leg. It's too soon for you to be walking."

Colin wasn't about to forget Nathan's horrid comment. "I knew you and Caine would . . ." He let out a sigh. "I did warn you, didn't I?"

"Colin, I don't want to hear another word about Caine and me," she shouted. "It's over, finished. Do you understand? Where is Winters?" she added in a rush, hoping to turn his attention. "The physician should be at our side."

"Winters was with you?" Caine asked.

"Pagan convinced him to take care of me aboard the

Emerald," Colin explained. He hobbled over to the settee and sat down. "He was a little resistant at first, but Pagan can be very persuasive. And in the end, I think Winters had the time of his life."

"Well, where is he?" Jade asked.

"We let him go home," Colin answered. "Now quit fretting. It's just going to take time for the leg to heal."

Jade pushed a pillow behind Colin's back, then propped his feet up on a large round footstool.

"I believe I will order some refreshments for you, Colin," she said. "You look too pale to me. The walk from the drive tired you out, didn't it?"

She didn't give him time to answer, but picked up her skirts and started for the drawing room doors. Caine blocked her path. "You aren't going anywhere."

She refused to look up at him as she tried to move around him. Caine took hold of her arm. The grip was stinging. "Sit down, Jade."

"Jade?"

Colin said her name in a surprised whisper.

"I have allowed Caine to call me by my given name."

"Allowed?" Nathan asked.

"What do you call her?" Caine asked his brother.

"She has several nicknames," Colin answered. "I call her Red most of the time, don't I, Jade?"

When she nodded, Colin continued on. "Nathan calls her Brat all the time. He has a particular fondness for that nickname."

His slow wink increased Jade's blush. "Black Harry calls me Dolphin," Colin went on to explain. "It's meant as an insult, too."

Nathan shook his head. "Dolphins are gentle, Colin. It wasn't meant as an insult."

Caine let out a weary sigh. "Who is Black Harry?"

It was suddenly hitting him full force, this amazing miracle. He found his strength deserting him. Caine dragged

Jade over to the wingback chair that faced the settee, sat down, and forced her with his hold to sit on the arm.

He stared at his brother all the while. "I still cannot believe you're alive," he said.

"You have Pagan to thank for that," Colin replied. "And I can't believe you're so calm. I was certain you'd go into a rage when you found out I made Jade promise not to tell you. Caine, there's so much I have to explain. First, however, I do believe Nathan's sister has something she wants to tell you."

Jade was shaking her head vehemently. "I have nothing to say to him, Colin. If you feel like enlightening him on all the facts, do so after I've left."

Caine wasn't paying any attention to her rantings. He let go of her arm, leaned forward, his elbows resting on his knees, and said, "I want you to tell me who did this to you. Give me the name, Colin. I'll do the rest."

Jade took advantage of Caine's inattention. She once again tried to leave. Caine never took his gaze away from his brother when he grabbed hold of her hand. "I believe I mentioned that you aren't going anywhere."

Nathan looked incredulous. "Why haven't you put your knife through him yet?"

She shrugged before answering. "Colin would have been upset."

"What's taking Black Harry so long?" Nathan asked Colin then. He strolled over to the settee, took his place next to Colin, and propped his feet up on the same wide stool.

"He'll be a while yet," Colin explained. "He lost his spectacles."

Both men started laughing. Jade was horrified. "Black Harry's here? In England?"

Her voice shook. Only Nathan seemed to understand the reason for her distress. "He is," he announced in a hard voice. "And when I tell him . . ."

"No, Nathan, you mustn't tell him anything," she cried

out. She tried to get out of Caine's grasp. He tightened his hold in reaction.

"Who is Black Harry?" Caine asked, ignoring Jade's struggles.

"He's the uncle," Colin answered. "He took care of Jade after her father died."

Caine was trying to filter all this information through his mind. The way Jade had reacted to the news that Harry was here indicated she was afraid of him.

"How long was she with him?" he asked Colin.

"Years," Colin answered.

Caine turned to Nathan. "Where the hell were you when she was growing up? Out robbing people blind?"

"Damn it, Colin, a man can only take so much," Nathan muttered. "If he keeps it up, I'm going to kill him, even if it means losing your friendship."

Colin was still too exhausted from the walk to take part in the conversation. He wanted to rest for just a few more minutes before he started his explanation. With a loud yawn meant to draw attention, he said, "No one's going to kill anyone until this has all been straightened out." He leaned back against the cushions and closed his eyes.

A loud commotion drew everyone's attention then. Caine looked up just in time to see a large flower pot fly past the windows to the terrace. The pot crashed against the stone wall. A sharp blasphemy followed the splintering noise.

"Harry's here," Colin drawled out.

Caine continued to stare at the entrance, thinking to himself that he was prepared for just about anything now. Nothing more could ever surprise him again.

He was, unfortunately, mistaken. The man who finally strutted across the threshold was so outrageous looking, Caine almost laughed.

Harry paused, put his big hands on his hips, and glared at his audience. He was dressed all in white, with a wide red sash tied around his pot-bellied waist. His skin was bronzed

202

by the sun, his hair was silver as clouds. Caine judged his age to be near fifty, perhaps a bit more.

This one could give children nightmares for months. He was amazingly ugly, with a bulbous nose that covered most of his face. His eyes were bare slits, due to the fact that he was squinting fiercely.

The man had flair, he'd give him that much. He literally swaggered into the drawing room. Two men rushed ahead of him, moving objects out of his way. Two more filed in behind. Caine recognized the last two. They were Matthew and Jimbo. Both of their faces were covered with fresh bruises Caine had inflicted when he'd had his little talk with them.

"It's getting damned crowded in here," Caine stated.

Jade jerked her hand away from his hold and rushed over to Black Harry. She threw herself into his arms and hugged him tightly. Caine noticed Harry's gold tooth then. When he smiled down at Jade, one of the front teeth gleamed in the light.

"Oh, Uncle Harry, I've missed you," she whispered.

"Of course you missed me," the elderly man grumbled. "I'm going to beat you good though," he added after he'd given her another hug of affection. "Have you gone completely daft, girl? I'll be hearing every spoiled morsel of this tale, and then I'm going to beat the daylights out of you."

"Now, Harry," Jade said in a voice meant to soothe. "I didn't mean to upset you."

Harry let out a loud snort. "You didn't mean for me to find out, that's what you didn't mean to do," he countered. He leaned down and kissed her loudly on the top of her head.

"That one be Caine?" he asked, squinting at the man in question.

"He is," Jade answered.

"He ain't dead."

"No."

"You done your task well then," Harry praised.

"He will be dead soon enough if I get my way," Nathan drawled out.

"What's this mutiny I'm hearing?"

"Harry?" Jade asked, tugging his attention back to her. "Yes?"

She leaned up on tiptoe and whispered into his ear. Harry frowned during the telling.

When she was finished, he nodded. "I might be telling, and then again, I might not. You trust this man?"

She couldn't lie. "I do."

"What does he mean to you, girl?"

"Nothing," she blurted out.

"Then look at me eyes," he ordered. "You're talking to the floor and that tells me something tricky's going on."

"There's nothing tricky," she whispered. "I'm just glad this deception is over."

Harry didn't look convinced. "Then why'd you bother watching out for him if he meant nothing to you?" he prodded, sensing she wasn't telling him the full truth.

"He's Colin's brother," she reminded her uncle. "That is the only reason I bothered."

Harry decided to wait until they were alone before he forced the truth out of her. "I'm still not understanding," he bellowed. He was squinting in Caine's direction now. "You should be kissing Pagan's feet to my way of thinking," he added. "Your sorry brother's alive, ain't he?"

"Now that you're here, we can sort all this out, Harry," Colin called out.

Harry grunted. He looked back down at Jade. "I'm still going to beat you bloody, girl. Do you doubt me?"

"No, Harry, I don't doubt you," she answered. With an effort, she hid her smile. In all their time together, Harry had never, ever harmed her. He was a kind, gentle man with a soul so pure, so white, God was surely smiling down at him with pride. Harry liked to threaten all sorts of horrid punishments when there was an audience listening. He was a pirate, he would often remind her, and appearances had to be kept up.

Caine had started out of his chair when Harry made his first threat, but Colin motioned to him to sit down again. "Bluster," he'd whispered to his brother.

"Get me a chair, men," Harry shouted. He continued to squint at Caine as he walked over to the hearth. Both Colin and Nathan got their feet and the stool out of his way just in the nick of time. While Jade helped resettle Colin, Harry stood in front of the hearth, his hands clasped behind his back.

"You don't look anything like Dolphin," he remarked. He grinned, displaying his lovely tooth again, then added, "You and your puny-arsed brother are both homely as sin. Only family resemblance I can see."

Caine didn't think the man could see much of anything, but he kept that opinion to himself. He looked over at Colin to see how he was responding to that insult. Though Colin's eyes were once again closed, he was smiling. Caine concluded Harry's thunder was all for his benefit.

One of his men carried a big chair over to the hearth, and when Harry was settled, Jade walked over to stand behind him. She put her hand on Harry's shoulder.

"You wear spectacles, me boy?" Harry asked Caine.

Caine shook his head. "Anyone here wear them? One of your servants perchance?"

"No," Caine answered.

"Uncle, do you know where you lost your last pair?" she asked.

"Now, lovely, you know I don't remember," he answered. "If I did, I wouldn't have lost them, now would I?"

Harry turned back to Caine then. "There be a village close by?"

Colin started laughing. Even Nathan broke into a grin. Caine didn't have the faintest idea why they were so amused.

"There is a village close by," Colin said.

"No one was asking you, you twit. Go back to sleep, Dolphin. It's all you're good for," he added with a wink.

Harry turned to his cohorts and bellowed, "Men, you know what to do."

The two unsavory-looking men lounging by the terrace doors both nodded. Just as they turned to leave, Jade prodded Harry's shoulder. "Oh, all right, girl," he muttered. "No pillaging, men," he shouted then. "We're too close to home."

"Aye, Black Harry," one of the men called out.

"Did they jump to do my bidding?" Harry asked Jade in a whisper.

"They did," she answered. "As quick as lightning."

Harry nodded. He clasped his knees with his hands and leaned forward. "Now then, I was hearing talk of mutiny when I came inside. You'd think this was a time for rejoicing, but I ain't hearing any cheering. You hearing any cheering, girl?"

"No, Harry."

"Could it be that the Dolphin's such a bother, you ain't glad to have him back?" he asked Caine. "Can't say I blame you. The boy can't even play a decent game of chess."

"I was half out of my mind when we last played," Colin reminded him.

Harry snorted. "You only got half a mind, twit."

Colin grinned. "Caine? Do you know why this sorry piece of flesh is called Black Harry?"

"I'll be telling it," Harry announced. "It's because I got me a black heart."

He made that statement as a boast, then waited a full minute for Caine to appreciate his explanation. "I gave myself that nickname. It's fitting, ain't it, girl?"

"Yes, Uncle, it's very fitting. Your heart's as black as night."

"It's good of you to say so," Harry replied. He reached up and patted her hand. "As soon as me men get back from their errand, I'm leaving for the Wharf. I could use a spot of supper to hold me over."

"I shall see to it at once," Jade said. She immediately moved toward the doors, deliberately making a wide path of Caine's chair. When she reached the entrance to the foyer, she turned back to her uncle. "Please don't let Nathan and Caine fight while I'm gone, Harry."

"I wouldn't be caring," Harry called out.

"But I would care," she returned. "Please, Harry?"

"All right then, I won't let them fight."

As soon as the door shut behind Jade, Harry whispered, "She's a piece of work, that one. I should have cut her face years ago. She's too pretty for her own safety. 'Tis the reason I had to leave her behind so many times. Couldn't trust me men when my back was turned."

"She's so pretty," Nathan snapped, "that some dishonorable men would take advantage."

"Let it go for now, Nathan," Colin interjected. He opened his eyes and looked at Caine. "My brother's an honorable man."

"Like hell," Nathan growled.

Caine wasn't paying any attention to the conversation now. He'd homed in on Harry's casually stated comment that he'd left Jade behind. Where did he leave her? Who watched over her when he was away? There sure as hell hadn't been a woman there, or she would have known a little more about the facts of life.

"What's all this talk about?" Harry demanded, drawing Caine's attention again.

"Although it isn't in your nature, I'm asking you to be patient, Harry," Colin requested. "There's been a little misunderstanding, that's all."

"Clear it up quick then," Harry ordered.

"Damn it, Colin, I know all I need to know," Nathan said. "Your brother's a bastard . . ."

"You were born out of wedlock, son?" Harry interrupted. He looked absolutely thrilled by that possibility.

Caine sighed. "No, I wasn't born out of wedlock."

Harry didn't even try to hide his disappointment, another fact that made absolutely no sense to Caine.

"Then you can't be going by that nickname," he instructed. "Only those born with the stigma can boast of it. A man's only as good as his nickname," he added with a nod.

"Or a woman," Colin interjected.

Caine looked incredulous. Colin tried not to laugh. "Harry? Tell him about Bastard Bull," he suggested.

"Colin, for God's sake," Caine began.

"In time, Caine," his brother whispered. "I need a little more time to gather my thoughts."

Caine nodded. "All right," he said. He turned to Harry then. "Tell me about Bastard Bull."

"He weren't a bastard after all," Harry stated with a scowl. "He just said he was so he could sign on with us. He knew the store I put in nicknames. When we found out he'd lied, we tossed him overboard with the garbage."

"They happened to be in the middle of the ocean at the time," Colin drawled out. "Pagan wouldn't let him drown, though."

"How very considerate of you," Caine muttered to Nathan.

"Now there was this other bloke, a good, strong man . . ."

Caine let out a long sigh. He leaned back in the chair, closed his eyes, and decided he was going to have to wait until all this ridiculous talk about nicknames was finished. Colin seemed to be enjoying the conversation and he had asked for time. His brother looked half asleep now . . . and so damned pale.

For a good ten minutes or more Harry continued with his

dissertation. When he finally finished, Nathan said, "Jade has a special nickname, too."

"I'll be telling it," Harry stated. "I'm the one who came up with the special name, after all."

Nathan nodded. "All right, Harry, you tell it."

Everyone was watching Caine now. If he'd bothered to open his eyes, he would have seen their smiles.

Caine was having difficulty holding onto his patience. "And what is her special nickname, Harry?" he finally asked, his tone weary.

"Well now, me boy," Harry drawled out. "We like to call her Pagan."

Chapter Twelve

He didn't take the news at all well. For the longest time, he simply refused to believe Jade could possibly be Pagan. Only a man could get away with such daring feats, only a man.

Colin, Harry, and Nathan were all watching him closely. When he shook his head in denial, they nodded in unison.

"I can see you're having trouble accepting this," Colin said. His expression was sympathetic. "But it is true, Caine. Harry gave her that nickname years ago because . . ."

"I'll be telling it," Harry interrupted. "It was the color of her hair, son. As red as hell's fire it was when she was a youngster."

It was apparent from the look on Caine's face that he still didn't accept. Harry thought he didn't understand the reason for her special nickname. "She was as wild as the devil back then, too," he explained. "Just like a pagan baby, she was."

Caine's expression slowly turned from disbelief to fury. Both Colin and Harry became uneasy. Only Nathan seemed to be enjoying the moment. "Would a man be apt to leave a rose behind, Caine?" he asked, hoping to rub salt in his wounds. "That's the work of a woman. It's amazing to me that no one's figured it out by now. Don't you agree, Colin?"

"Yes," Colin answered, his gaze directed on his brother. "Amazing."

It was the last remark anyone made for a long while. Harry and Nathan waited for Caine to come to terms with the truth.

Colin knew his brother far better than his friends did. He patiently waited for the explosion.

Jade was in the dining room helping Sterns set the table. As soon as the butler took one look at her face, he knew something was wrong. She looked as pale as the linen tablecloth.

She wouldn't tell him anything but explained that her uncle had arrived and that he and his four men would require supper before they left. She also insisted upon using the finest crystal. Sterns went into the kitchens to order the meal, throwing both the cook and her assistant, Bernice, into a frenzy, and then returned to the dining room.

He found Jade examining a large oval silver platter. "Uncle would like this," she remarked. "The design is quite magnificent."

Sterns nodded. "A gift from the King," he explained. "When the Marquess was knighted, Colin threw quite a bash in his honor. The King showed up and gave him that platter. If you turn it over, you'll see the inscription."

Jade shook her head. She thrust the platter into Sterns' hands. "Hide it."

"I beg your pardon?"

"Hide it, Sterns," she repeated. She looked around the room, then asked, "Are there any other special things Caine would rather keep?"

"The silver tea set on the side bar," he said. "I do believe it has special meaning to mi'lord."

"Did the King give him that, too?"

"No, the set came from his grandmother."

"Hide it as well, Sterns. Put the things under Caine's bed. They'll be safe there."

"Mi'lady?" Sterns asked. "Are you feeling ill?"

"No."

"You look ill," Sterns announced. "And you're walking around as though you're in a trance. I know something's wrong . . ."

Jade walked over to the door, then turned back to Sterns. "You have been very kind to me, sir. I will always remember that."

Sterns looked startled. Jade was about to close the door behind her when Caine's command reached her.

"Jade!"

The bellow made the crystal goblets rattle. Jade showed no reaction to the summons, but Sterns jumped a foot.

"I believe your employer has just heard some distressing news," she said. "I had hoped that my uncle would wait . . . it doesn't matter."

Sterns followed her into the entrance. When she started up the stairs, he called out to her. "I believe mi'lord would like you to go to him, Lady Jade."

She continued up the stairs. "I would be happy to stand by your side," he promised. "I know his temper can be frightening at times."

Sterns waited until she was out of sight, then rushed inside the drawing room.

The butler had difficulty maintaining his steely composure when he spotted Colin. "My God, is that you, Colin?" he stammered out.

"Hello, Sterns," Colin said. "It's good to see you again. Are you still ordering your lord around?"

Sterns was slow to recover. "I give it my best," he whispered.

"Is this one a servant, Caine?" Harry asked.

"He's a dictator, not a servant," Colin announced with a grin.

Sterns turned to the older man with the obvious poor eyesight. He tried not to gape.

"Is me supper ready yet?" Harry bellowed.

Sterns decided this one had to be Jade's uncle. The stranger sitting next to Colin was too young. "It is almost ready," he told him before finally turning to Caine. "I must speak to you at once in the foyer, mi'lord. It is a most important matter."

"Not now, Sterns," Caine said, his tone weary. "Talk to me later."

"Perhaps you didn't hear me," Sterns countered. "There is a problem that must be resolved immediately. It concerns Lady Jade."

Caine wasn't at all surprised. "What's she burning now? The kitchens?"

"Mi'lord, this isn't the time for jests," the butler snapped.

"Do I look like I'm jesting, Sterns?"

The butler folded his arms across his chest. "Lady Jade isn't burning anything at the moment," he said. "She's leaving."

That announcement got just the reaction Sterns was hoping for. He moved out of his lord's way when he bounded to his feet, and nodded with satisfaction when Caine roared, "The hell she is!"

The butler waited until his employer had left the room, then turned back to Jade's uncle. "Dinner will be served in just a moment," he announced, his haughty tone of voice fully restored.

Caine took the stairs two at a time. His heart was pounding. The thought of her leaving him was untenable. For the first time in his life, he was in a panic. He didn't like the feeling at all.

As soon as he threw the door open to her bedroom, he saw

her. The panic left in a rush. He slammed the door shut behind him and leaned against it.

He took a deep breath to try to calm himself. She was pretending he wasn't there. She stood by the side of the bed, folding a gold-colored gown. Her satchel was open and nearly filled to the top.

"You might as well quit packing," he said, amazed that his voice sounded so forceful. "You aren't going anywhere."

Jade turned to confront him. She was determined to give him a piece of her mind before taking her leave, but when she caught his expression, her heart fell to her stomach and she couldn't remember any of the words she wanted to say to him.

He was so furious, the muscle in the side of his jaw flexed. She stared at it in fascination while she tried to find her courage again.

"I'm never going to let you leave me, Jade," he said. "Never. Do you hear me?"

She thought everyone in the village was hearing him. Her ear rang from his roar. It took all her strength to stand up to him. She slowly shook her head. "You called me a whore," she whispered.

The anguish in her voice got through to him. Some of his anger eased away. "No, I did not call you a whore."

"You thought it," she countered. "You were about to shout it to the world."

"I wasn't," he returned. "Jade, we have more important issues to discuss now."

She let out a gasp. "More important than calling me a whore?"

He moved away from the door and started toward her. She immediately backed up a space. "Don't come near me. I never want you to touch me again."

"Then you're going to be damned miserable for the rest of your days, Jade. I'm going to be touching you all the time."

"You don't really want me," she shouted. "You want the

vulnerable, weak woman I pretended to be, Caine. You don't know the real me. No, you don't," she continued when he shook his head at her. "I'm really very strong, determined, too. I just pretended to need you, you daft man, so that you would feel honor bound to stay by my side. I used all the ploys a weak woman would use, too. Yes, I did! I complained at every opportunity, and I wept whenever I needed to get my way."

He grabbed hold of her and jerked her up against him. "I'm leaving," she cried out. "Can't you get that through your thick . . ."

"You're staying."

"I hate you," she whispered before she burst into tears.

He rested his chin on the top of her head. "No, you don't hate me," he whispered.

"I hate everything about you," she wailed between racking sobs. "But most of all I hate the way you contradict me."

"Jade?"

"What?"

"Are your tears a pretense now?"

She couldn't quit crying long enough to give him a clear answer. "They most certainly are," she stammered out. "I never, ever cry," she added a moment later. "Only weak women cry."

"But you're not weak, are you, love?" he asked. His smile was gentle, his voice as well, but his grip continued to be as strong as iron, even after she quit her struggle to get away from him.

He wanted to hold her in his arms for the rest of his days. "Jade?"

"What now?"

"I love you."

She didn't respond to his vow, but started trembling. He knew he was terrifying her. "You're the most confusing woman," he whispered on a sigh. "God help me, I do love you, though."

"I won't love you," she stammered out. "I don't even like you. I won't trust you either." She ended her list of what she wouldn't do with a loud hiccup.

Caine wasn't the least upset by her denials. "I love you," he said again. "Now and forever."

He was content to hold her while she wept. Lord, she did have a store of tears locked inside her.

They must have stood there a full ten minutes before she was able to regain her composure.

She wiped her cheeks on the lapels of his jacket, then pulled away from him. "You'd better go back downstairs," she whispered.

"Not without you," he countered.

"No," she replied. "Nathan and Harry would know I'd been crying. I'm staying here."

"Jade, you can't put off . . ." He stopped in midsentence, then asked, "Why does it matter if they know you've been crying or not?"

"I wouldn't be what they expect me to be if I cried," she answered.

"Try to explain what you meant by that remark?" he asked gently.

She gave him a disgruntled look. "Appearances have to be kept up, Caine."

She walked over to the bed and sat down. "I don't want to talk about this." She let out a sigh, then added, "Oh, very well. I'll meet you downstairs . . ."

He was shaking his head at her. "I'll wait for you."

"You don't trust me?"

"No."

He waited for her temper to explode. She surprised him, however, when she merely shrugged. "Good," she said. "Don't trust me, Caine. I'm going to leave at the first opportunity. I won't stay here and wait for you to leave me. I'm not a fool."

He finally understood. She couldn't hide her fear or her vulnerability from him now. "And you're absolutely certain I would leave you, aren't you, Jade?"

"Of course."

She replied with such candor that he wasn't certain how to proceed. "Even though I've just told you that I love you, you still . . ."

"Nathan and Harry love me, too," she interjected.

Caine gave up trying to reason with her now, guessing it would do his cause little good. He decided he'd have to wait and find another way around her shields.

Caine suddenly wanted to go downstairs and kill both Nathan and Harry. He sighed instead. He couldn't undo the past for her. No, he could only give her a secure, safe future.

"I would never abandon . . ." he stopped himself, then said, "Very well, Jade. You may leave me whenever you want."

Her eyes widened over that announcement. She looked like she was going to start weeping again, too. Caine felt like an ogre. "Any time you want to leave, do so."

She turned her gaze to her lap. "Thank you."

"You're welcome," he drawled out. He walked over to her, pulled her to her feet, then tilted her head up. "Just one other little detail," he added.

"Yes?"

"Every time you leave, I'm going to come after you. There isn't any place you can hide, Jade. I'll find you and drag you back here. This is where you belong."

She tried to push his hand away from her chin. "You'd never find me," she whispered.

He could hear the panic in her voice. Caine leaned down and kissed her. He missed her mouth completely when she jerked away from him, then captured her soft lips by cupping the sides of her face and holding her still.

His tongue took possession then. He growled low in his

throat when she pinched him, then deepened the kiss. Her tongue finally rubbed against his own, her resistance spent. She wrapped her arms around his waist and melted against him.

"I love you," he told her again after he'd lifted his head away from her.

She promptly burst into tears again. "Are you going to do that every damned time I tell you I love you?" he demanded.

He was more amused than exasperated with her. She shook her head. "You don't understand yet," she whispered. "It hasn't settled in, Caine."

"What don't I understand?" he asked, his voice filled with tenderness.

"You don't understand what I am," she cried.

Caine let out another sigh. He took hold of her hand and dragged her out of the room. They were halfway down the stairs to the foyer when he finally answered her. "I understand, all right. You're mine."

"I hate your possessiveness, too," she told his back.

Caine paused at the door to the drawing room, then let go of her hand. "If you try to move away from me while we're in there, I swear to God I'll embarrass the hell out of you. Got that?"

She nodded. When he started to open the door, he noticed the change that came over her. Gone was the vulnerable woman he'd just held in his arms. Jade looked quite serene. Caine was so astonished by the change in her, he had to shake his head.

"I'm ready now," she announced. "But if you tell Harry we slept together . . ."

"I won't," he interjected before she could get herself all worked up again. "Unless you leave my side, of course."

She gave him a quick glare, then forced a smile on her face and strolled into the room.

The talk stopped as soon as she and Caine entered. Jade

sat on the arm of the chair adjacent to the hearth and motioned for him to take the seat.

"Is my supper near to ready?" Harry asked her.

"In just another minute or two," Jade answered. "I insisted on the best for you, Uncle. It takes a little longer."

Harry beamed at her. "I'm the lucky one, having you to take care of me, Pagan," he crooned.

"Don't call her Pagan."

That command came out in a harsh whisper. Jade shivered over the anger in Caine's voice.

Nathan grinned while Harry squinted at Caine. "Why the hell not? That's her name," he argued.

"No, her name is Jade," Caine snapped out.

"My name is Pagan."

Her voice had turned as hard as ice. "I'm sorry you don't like it, Caine, but that's . . ."

She quit her explanation when he took hold of her hand and started squeezing.

"He still doesn't believe it," Harry said.

Jade didn't answer her uncle, but she secretly believed he was right. Caine certainly wouldn't be holding her hand if it had all settled in. "He believes all women are weak, Uncle," she whispered.

Harry snorted. He was about to launch into several of his favorite stories about his Pagan's special abilities when the men he'd sent to the village returned from their errand.

The men lumbered over to Harry's side.

"Well? What have you got for me, men?"

"Eleven pair," the shorter of the two seamen announced.

While Caine watched in growing astonishment, spectacles of every size and shape were dropped into Harry's lap. The old man tried on the first pair, squinted at Caine, then took the spectacles off and tossed them over his shoulder.

"Won't do," he muttered.

The ritual was repeated again and again, until he tried on

the eighth pair. Then he let out a happy sigh. "These do," he announced.

"Uncle, try the others on," Jade suggested. "There might be another pair that will do just as well."

Harry did as she suggested, then tucked another pair in his pocket.

"You did your task well, men. I'm proud of you."

Caine's head dropped forward. The picture of how Harry's men had come by the spectacles forced a reluctant smile.

"Half of England will be squinting before Harry goes home," Colin predicted with a deep chuckle.

"You being insulting, boy?" Harry asked.

"No, just honest," Colin answered.

Sterns opened the doors then and announced that dinner was now ready to be served.

Harry bounded out of his chair. Nathan and Colin moved out of his way just as he kicked the footstool out of his path. "Are you coming with me, girl?" Harry asked as he charged past Jade.

Caine increased his grip on her hand. "No, Uncle, I'm staying here," Jade called out. "I have a little explaining to do. Enjoy your meal with your men."

As soon as Harry left the room, Jade motioned for the men to follow. Jimbo looked like he wanted to argue with that command. His expression bordered on hostility. His target was Caine.

Jade simply stared at Jimbo. The silent message got through and the big man hurried out of the room.

"Shut the doors behind you," she called out.

"I might not be able to hear you if you call out," Jimbo argued.

"You'll hear me," Jade promised.

"You'll hear me too," Nathan drawled out. "I can take care of my sister, Jimbo."

"That's still to be proven," Jimbo muttered loud enough

220

for everyone to hear. He gave Caine one last glare, then shut the doors.

"Are you rested enough to explain this problem to Caine? I really would like to get this over with, Colin, so I can leave."

Caine gave her hand another good squeeze.

"Yes, I'm rested enough," Colin said. He turned to Nathan, received his nod, then turned his attention back to Caine. "When I was in my last year at Oxford, a man by the name of Willburn approached me. He was from the War Office and he was recruiting men to do some undercover work for England. Our country wasn't officially at war with France yet, but everyone knew it was coming. Anyway, Willburn knew you worked for Richards. I was still sworn to secrecy. I should have wondered at the time why I couldn't discuss my duties with you, Caine, but I didn't. You never talked about your work, and I figured that was the way it was supposed to be. In all honesty, I think I was enamored with this spy business." His expression became sheepish when he added, "I saw myself as England's savior for a while, anyway."

"How did you meet Nathan?" Caine asked.

"Almost a year after I'd started working for Willburn. We were paired together then. He was recruited in much the same way I was. Eventually Nathan and I became good friends." He paused to smile at his friend. "Nathan's a hard man to like."

"I've noticed," Caine said.

"Get on with it, Colin," Nathan ordered.

"It took a long time to win Nathan's trust, almost another full year working together as a matter of fact. He didn't confide in me in all that time. Then, on a trip back from France, he told me about the letters Pagan had found."

Colin shifted positions, grimacing in pain. Nathan caught the expression before anyone else did and immediately righted the stool for his friend. With a gentleness surprising

221

in such a large man, he lifted Colin's injured leg, slipped a cushion under the heel, then asked, "It's better now?"

"Yes, thank you," Colin answered. "Now where was I?"

Caine was watching Nathan. He could still see the concern in Nathan's eyes. He suddenly realized he couldn't hate the man after all.

That revelation was one hell of a disappointment. Caine wanted to hate him. The bastard had deserted his own sister, left her on her own to fend for herself. He was the reason Jade had so many shields guarding her heart, the reason she had had so much pain.

Yet Colin was alive.

"Caine?" Colin asked, drawing his brother back to the discussion. "Do you believe it's possible for a government to operate within a government?"

"Anything is possible," Caine answered.

"Have you ever heard of the Tribunal?" Colin asked. His voice had dropped to a whisper.

Both Colin and Nathan exchanged a nod. They were prepared to hear Caine's denial. Then they were going to knock the breath out of him with the facts they'd uncovered.

"Yes, I've heard of the Tribunal."

Colin was astonished. "You have?"

"When?" Nathan demanded. "How?"

"There was an investigation immediately after your father's death, Nathan. The Earl was linked to all sorts of subversive activities. His lands were confiscated, his children left in poverty . . ."

"How do you know all this?" Nathan asked.

Caine looked at Jade before answering. "When she told me who her father was, I asked Lyon to make some inquiries."

"Who is this Lyon?" Nathan asked.

"Our friend," Colin answered.

"Can he be trusted?" Nathan asked.

"He can," Colin answered before his brother could. "Caine, that was a safe bet. Lyon wouldn't ask the wrong people the way I did."

Jade's back started aching from her uncomfortable position. She eased her hand away from Caine's, somewhat surprised when he gave her her freedom. She knew better than to try to leave, though. If Caine was anything, he was reliable. He would embarrass her just as he threatened.

She moved to the chair Harry had vacated, and sat down.

"Lyon didn't ask anyone any questions," Caine explained. "He simply looked the information up in the files."

"He couldn't have," Jade interjected. "My father's file was missing."

Caine raised an eyebrow over that telling remark. "And how would you know if it was missing or not?"

She daintily shrugged. "Because I took it," she admitted.

"You what?"

"Caine, the file isn't the issue now," she rushed out, hoping to placate his rising temper.

"Then how did Lyon . . ." Nathan began.

Caine continued to frown at Jade when he answered her brother. "Richards was Lyon's director as well as mine. He had his own records. Lyon read those files."

"Was my father vindicated after the investigation?" Nathan asked.

"No," Caine answered. "He wasn't condemned either, Nathan. There wasn't enough proof."

"There is now," Jade whispered.

"Proof to vindicate your father?" Caine asked.

"No, proof to condemn him. I read Papa's letters."

The sadness in her voice tore at his heart. Caine still wanted to throttle her for deceiving him, but he also wanted to be kissing her at the same time.

"Caine, how can you be smiling now?" Colin asked. "This isn't . . ."

"Sorry," Caine answered, unaware he had been smiling. "I was sidetracked."

He stared at Jade while he made that admission. She stared at her hands.

"Continue, Colin," Caine ordered then, turning his attention back to his brother.

"Right after their father's funeral, Pagan . . . I mean, Jade, left with Black Harry. The Earl trusted Harry completely."

"That's difficult to believe," Caine interjected.

"Harry's a good man," Jade said. "He has a pure heart."

"I'm sure he does," Caine agreed. "However, you mentioned that there was another close friend, a woman by the name of Lady Briars, who would have been more than willing to take you and Nathan into her home. I just don't understand why your father would have chosen a thief over . . ."

"It was a question of trust," Nathan explained. "My father had turned his heart against England, Caine. He didn't think either one of us would be safe here. Harry was our best bet."

"Why didn't he think you'd be safe?"

"The letters," Colin answered. "The Earl kept all the ones he received from the other two. Nathan's father's operative name was Fox, and he was one of the three in the Tribunal. The other two were called Ice and Prince."

"My father was a very idealistic man," Nathan interjected. "In the beginning, I think he saved all the letters for future generations. He believed he was doing something . . . heroic for England. Things soured fast, though. Soon enough it became only for the good of the Tribunal. Anything was just, as long as it furthered the scope of their power."

"It was a slow metamorphosis," Colin said. "The first letters were signed with the closing, 'for the good of England.'

Then after the tenth, or perhaps the eleventh letter, the closing changed."

"To what?" Caine asked.

"They started using the phrase, 'for the good of the Tribunal,' " he answered. "Ice was the first to sign his letter that way, and the other two followed suit. Their corruption was complete by that time."

"They started acting independently long before that, Colin," Nathan remarked.

"The end justified their means," Colin explained to Caine. "As long as they believed that what they were doing aided their country, they could justify anything."

"Very like your attitude, Jade," Caine announced.

She was so startled by that comment, her eyes widened. "No, not at all like my attitude," she argued. "Caine, I'm nothing like my father. I don't approve of what he did. It's sinful to admit, but I don't have any feelings for him, either. He chose his path."

"Your father's lands were confiscated, his fortune taken away," Caine said.

"Yes," she agreed, wondering what he was leading up to with that remark.

"It's the reason you steal from the wealthy, Jade. I'd say you're getting even."

"I'm not!"

Her shout told him he'd rattled her with that opinion. "Power corrupts," he said. "Absolute power corrupts absolutely."

"You needn't quote Machiavelli to me, Caine. I will agree that the Tribunal was after absolute power."

"You were on the same path."

"I'm not," she cried out.

"Was, Caine?" Colin asked.

"Was," Caine announced. His voice was hard.

"Then you . . ." Colin began.

"Not now, Colin," Caine ordered.

"What are you talking about?" Jade asked. "I've never been after power."

Caine ignored her protest. "Tell me the rest of this," he ordered Nathan.

"Our father had a change of heart," Nathan said. "His conscience began to bother him when his director, a man named Hammond, was sanctioned."

"Sanctioned?" Colin scoffed. "What a pleasant word for such a foul deed."

"Hammond was director over all three," Nathan interjected. "There was Ice, Prince, and Fox. Anyway, in the beginning, they did whatever they were ordered to do. It wasn't long, though, before they started acting independently. Hammond was beginning to get wise to their doings and the three were certain he was growing in his suspicions. Ice came up with the idea that they sanction him."

"My father didn't want to kill Hammond," Jade said. "Papa was on his way to London to warn the director when he was killed. At least that's what we've been able to piece together."

"Who was killed? Your father or Hammond?" Caine asked.

"Our father," Nathan answered. "He had sent Hammond a note telling him that he had to meet with him as soon as possible, that it was an urgent, life-threatening matter."

"And how were you able to piece that together?" Caine asked.

"Hammond showed me the note at my father's funeral," Nathan replied. "He asked me if I knew anything about this urgent problem. I didn't know anything, of course. I'd been away at school. Jade was too young to understand."

"Our father confided in Harry and gave him the letters he'd saved."

"And Harry told you everything when you were older?" Caine asked Jade.

She nodded. She refused to look at him and kept her gaze directed on her lap.

"Harry wanted Nathan to go with us. Father had a ship and Harry was bent on becoming a pirate. Nathan wanted to finish school. He thought Harry was taking me to an island in the south and that I'd be safe until he could come and fetch me."

"When I started hearing about the escapades of a pirate named Pagan, I have to admit I never once considered that it might be Harry," Nathan interjected.

"Why didn't you come for Jade?" Caine asked.

"He couldn't," Jade answered before her brother could. "Harry and I were never in one place long enough. Besides, Nathan had his own problems then. Father's enemies knew he'd saved the letters. They were desperate to find them. Once Nathan's rooms had been searched, they left him alone . . . for a time anyway, until we started a fresh investigation of our own."

"The letters were with you?" Caine asked. "Or did Harry hide them somewhere safe?"

"We kept them on the *Emerald*," she answered.

"I want them," Caine demanded. "Is this vessel near enough to send one of the men? Or perhaps . . ."

He stopped his question when she shook her head. "There isn't any need to fetch them. I can tell you the contents."

"Word for word," Colin said. "Pagan need only read something once, and it's committed to memory for the rest of her life."

If Caine thought that talent odd, he didn't mention it. Jade was thankful he remained silent.

"Pagan, recite the letters for Caine," Nathan suggested.

"If you call her Pagan one more time, I'm going to beat the hell out of you."

Nathan scowled at Caine a long minute, then gave in. "All right," he snapped. "I'll call her Jade, though only because I don't want anyone hearing her nickname."

"I don't give a damn what your reasons are, just do it," Caine grated out.

"Hell, Colin, I'm trying to be accommodating, but I swear to God I'm going to knock the arrogance out of him when this is over and done with."

Jade believed a fight was imminent. She drew everyone's attention by beginning her recitation. The telling took over thirty minutes. She didn't leave a word out. And when she was finished, no one said a word for a long while. Everyone was slowly filtering through the information she'd just related.

Then Colin spoke. "All right then," he began, his voice filled with enthusiasm. "That very first letter was addressed to Thorton . . . that's Nathan and Jade's father, of course, and it was signed by a man named William."

"They hadn't been assigned their operative names yet," Jade volunteered.

"Yes," Colin agreed. "Then Thorton became Fox, and William became Prince. Ice is another matter, though. We don't have any clues as to his . . ."

"Colin, we can speculate about his identity later," Nathan interrupted.

Colin nodded. "I went to Willburn and told him all about the letters, Caine. Nathan and I decided we had to trust him. He was our director, after all, and he'd taken good care of us. To this day, I still don't believe he was involved with the Tribunal."

"You're an innocent," Nathan muttered. "Of course he was involved with the bastards."

"You'll have to prove it to me first," Colin argued. "Only then will I believe."

Nathan shook his head. He turned back to Caine. "We were sent to the south on what we now know was a setup. We were supposed to meet with two informants at the harbor. It was a trick, of course. Before we knew what was happening, we had both been bound and gagged, and tossed into the warm waters."

"You aren't going to tell all of it, are you?" Jade asked. "There isn't any need, Colin."

Neither Nathan nor Colin picked up on the fear in her voice. Caine did, and immediately glanced over to look at her.

"Get on with it, Colin," Nathan muttered.

Jade, Caine noticed, was now clenching her hands together. He decided then that she must have witnessed something that had terrified her.

"I was the first to go into the waters," Colin said, drawing Caine's attention again. "After they'd made long, shallow cuts on my legs with their knives, they tossed me off the pier. Nathan understood what they were up to, though I thank God now that I didn't understand at the time. I thought I still had a chance, you see."

Colin's expression had taken on a gray cast. Nathan looked just as grim.

"Because Shallow Wharf was close by, we spent several days with Jade and Black Harry. Colin didn't know she was Pagan then, of course, and he developed quite a crush on my little sister," Nathan continued.

"Yes, I did," Colin agreed. He turned to wink at Jade. "I'll still have you, Jade, if you'll only give me a chance."

She blushed while she shook her head at him. "You were quite impossible."

"Colin followed her around like a puppy," Nathan said. "When he realized she wasn't at all interested, he was so disappointed I had to take him drinking."

"I fell in love with two other ladies that night, Nathan," Colin remarked.

"They weren't ladies," Jade remarked.

"No, they weren't," Nathan agreed. "How can you even remember, Colin? You were sotted, man."

Colin laughed. "I remember everything," he boasted.

Caine held his patience. He could tell, from their dark expressions, that they needed to jest with each other in order to get through their memory.

Jade didn't have as much patience. "Tommy and I followed Nathan and Colin when they went to keep their appointment. They were so secretive about their plans, I became very curious. I also had this feeling that something was amiss."

"Who is Tommy?" Caine asked.

Jade literally bounded out of her chair and hurried across the room. "Nathan, you finish this story while I see to refreshments. I'm tired of talking about this."

Nathan started to call out to her but Colin stayed the action by putting his hand on his friend's arm. "It's still difficult for her," he whispered.

Nathan nodded.

"Of course it's difficult for her," Caine interjected, his tone harsh. "My God, she must have watched you . . ."

"She didn't watch," Nathan whispered. "As Colin was explaining, I knew what their plan was as soon as they cut Colin's legs. I put up a struggle when they tried to use their blades on me, ended up getting shot for my trouble. My shoulder was on fire when I went into the water."

"They cut us to draw the attention of the sharks, of course. The harbor is always full of the scavangers because of all the garbage that's thrown in. The blood did draw them, like flies to a carcass."

Colin could see that Caine's patience was wearing thin. His brother was leaning forward in his chair with a grim look on his face. "Bear with us, Caine. This isn't a pleasant memory for us."

Nathan nodded. "It was just past sunset," he began.

"I could still see their fins though," Colin interjected.

Caine was sitting on the edge of his chair. He now

understood the reason for Jade's nightmares. She dreamed about sharks. My God, the terror she must have endured made his heart pound.

"Pagan told Tommy to fetch a boat, then she took his knife and came into the waters after us. The men who'd put us there were sure we were done for and had already left. Pagan . . . I mean, Jade, got to me first. I was closer, I guess. Anyway, she pulled me toward the boat. A shark got a fair nibble out of my leg when they were hauling me in. Tommy lost his balance and fell overboard. He never resurfaced."

When Colin paused and turned to Nathan, his friend took up the telling.

"I still don't understand why, but the sharks kept away from me. They were in a frenzy and Tommy had become their target. Jade had gotten Colin into the boat by then."

"I tried to help," Colin whispered. His voice was hoarse. "But I passed out. The next time I opened my eyes, I was on the *Emerald*. The oddest-looking man I'd ever seen was trying to press me into a game of chess. Honest to God, Caine, I wasn't sure if I was in heaven or hell. Then I saw Nathan sleeping on the cot next to me. I saw his sister, too, and I suddenly remembered everything. It seemed to me that it had all just happened, but I found out I'd been ill for quite some time."

Caine leaned back in his chair in an attempt to ease the tension in his shoulders. He took several deep breaths, then noticed Colin and Nathan were doing the same thing.

"Did she know . . . when she went into the water, did she know there were sharks?"

"Oh, yes," Nathan whispered. "She knew."

"My God, the courage that must have taken . . ."

"She won't talk about it," Colin interjected.

"She dreams about it."

"What?" Nathan asked.

"She has nightmares," Caine explained.

Nathan's brother slowly nodded.

"Matthew and Jimbo wanted to go after the bastards who'd tried to kill us, of course," Colin said. "Jade wouldn't let them. She had good reason, though. She wanted the men to report back to their superior that we were both dead. Jade felt it was the only way to keep us safe. It was the right decision, I think. Nathan and I are content to stay dead for a while longer, until we find out who in hell is behind this treachery."

"Hell, Caine, we were sanctioned by our own government," Nathan muttered.

"No," Caine countered. "Your government didn't even know you worked for them. Did you ever report to Richards or his superiors? Were you ever acknowledged . . ."

"Go ahead and say it," Colin interrupted.

"All right," Caine replied. "You worked for the Tribunal."

"I knew you were going to say that," Colin whispered.

"You can't be certain," Nathan argued.

"Richards didn't know until he was informed of your deaths that you worked for the department, Nathan. He's investigating now."

"Then he'll be killed," Nathan predicted.

"He's quietly investigating," Caine qualified.

"Damn, I know I've made mistakes," Nathan muttered. "I almost got you killed, Colin. I never should have involved you in this."

Colin shook his head. "We're partners, remember?" He turned back to his brother and said, "Do you really believe Richards can be trusted?"

"I trust him with my life. Jade's going to have to give him the letters as soon as possible, or recite the contents to him."

"We can write copies," Colin suggested. "That way, the originals stay safe. No one will find the *Emerald.*"

"The ship was named for her, wasn't it?" Caine asked. There was a hint of a smile on his face now. "I should have guessed that sooner. Her eyes are the color of emeralds, especially when she's angry."

"Yes, Harry named the ship after her," Colin said. "Can you understand now why you became the target?"

Caine nodded. "Yes. I was searching for Pagan. The Tribunal couldn't take the risk of me finding the pirate and gaining the truth."

"You're still at risk, Caine," Colin reminded him.

"But not for long," Caine countered. "I have a plan."

Colin grinned at Nathan. "I told you he'd have a plan." He couldn't keep the relief out of his voice.

Jade walked back into the room. She looked much calmer now, almost serene. She wouldn't look at him, Caine noticed, didn't spare him a single glance as she made her way back over to the chair in front of the hearth and sat down.

"Sterns has ordered two rooms made ready for you and Nathan," she told Colin. "As soon as yours is ready, you must go upstairs and rest."

"Are you certain we should stay here?" Nathan asked. He nudged Colin in his side. "My country home is in a very remote area. I just finished the remodeling before our last assignment," he added with a glance in Caine's direction. "We'd be very comfortable there."

Colin grinned. "I've heard so much about this palace of yours I know each room by heart. That's all you ever talked about."

"Well, then, you have to agree with me. I have to say, Caine, that it's the most beautiful house in all of England now . . . Jade, why are you shaking your head at me? You don't think my house is grand?"

She gave him a quick smile. "Oh, yes, Nathan, your house was very grand."

Nathan looked startled. "Was, you say?"

"I'm afraid I have some disappointing news, Nathan."

JULIE GARWOOD

Her brother leaned forward. "How disappointing?" he asked.

"You see, there was this fire . . ."

"A fire?" He sounded as if he were choking on something. Colin resisted the urge to slap him on his back.

"It was a rather large fire, Nathan."

Her voice reeked with sympathy. Nathan winced. "How large, Jade?"

"Your grand house was burned to the cellars."

She turned to Caine while Nathan muttered several obscenities. "I told you he'd be disappointed."

Nathan looked a little more than just disappointed, Caine decided. Jade's brother looked as though he wanted to kill someone. Since Caine had felt much the same reaction when his new stables were destroyed, he found himself in sympathy with Nathan.

Nathan took a deep breath, then turned to Colin. He sounded as if he were whining when he said, "I'd just finished the last damned room."

"Yes, he had," Jade interjected, giving her brother her full support. "The very last damned room."

Caine closed his eyes. "Jade, I thought it was all a lie."

"What was all a lie?" Colin asked.

"I didn't lie about everything," Jade interjected at the same moment.

"Exactly what didn't you lie about?" Caine demanded.

"You needn't take that tone with me, sir," she countered. "I only lied about witnessing a murder," she added with a nod. "It was the best I could come up with on the spur of the moment. At least, I think that's all I lied about. If I think of anything else, I'll mention it, all right? Now please quit your scowling, Caine. This isn't the time to be critical."

"Will you two save your arguing for later?" Nathan demanded. "Jade? Tell me how the fire started. Was someone careless with . . ."

234

"It was deliberate, not careless," Jade explained. "Whoever set out to burn your home, well, they certainly knew what they were about. They were very thorough. Even the wine cellar was destroyed, Nathan."

"Hell, not the wine cellar!" Nathan cried.

"I believe they were trying to destroy the letters," Jade said. "Since they couldn't find them when they pillaged the house, they . . ."

"They pillaged my house?" Nathan asked. "When?"

"The day before they burned it down," she answered. "Oh, dear, I just remembered," she added with a glance in Caine's direction. "I lied about falling down the stairs, too. Yes, I . . ."

Nathan let out a sigh, drawing her attention back to him. "When this is over, I will rebuild," he said. "What about the stables, Jade? Were they left intact?"

"Oh, yes, the stables were left untouched, Nathan. You needn't worry about that."

Caine was watching Jade. The worry in her gaze was so obvious, he wondered why Nathan hadn't noticed she hadn't finished giving him his disappointments yet.

"It's too bad about your house," Colin said.

"Yes," Nathan answered. "But the stables are all right. Colin, you should see my stock. There's one horse in particular, a fine Arabian stallion I paid a fortune for, but he was well worth the money. I named him Lightning."

"Lightning?" Colin asked, grinning over the absurd name. "Sounds like Harry had a hand in choosing that name."

"He did," Nathan admitted with a grin. "Still, it's fitting for the steed. He runs as fast as the wind. Only Jade and I can seat him. Wait until you see him . . ." Nathan quit his boasting when he noticed Jade was shaking her head at him again.

"What, Jade? Are you disagreeing that Lightning isn't as fast as the wind?"

"Oh, yes, Nathan, Lightning was as fast as the wind."

Nathan looked ready to weep. "Was?"

"I'm afraid I have a little more disappointing news for you, Nathan. There was this mishap and your fine horse was shot between his lovely brown eyes."

Caine had leaned forward in his chair again. The ramifications of what she was telling her brother had just hit him full force. "You mean to say you weren't lying about that, either?"

She shook her head again.

"What the hell!" Nathan shouted. "Who shot Lightning?"

She glared at Caine. "I told you he was going to be disappointed," she muttered.

"That sure as certain isn't my fault," Caine muttered. "So you can quit glaring at me so intently."

"Did Caine shoot him?" Nathan roared.

"No," Jade rushed out. "He just didn't believe you'd be so disappointed. I hadn't even met Caine then."

Her brother fell back against the cushions and threw his hand over his eyes. "Is nothing sacred?" he bellowed.

"Apparently Lightning wasn't," Caine interjected dryly.

Nathan glared at him. "He was a damned fine horse."

"I'm sure he was," Caine said before turning back to Jade. "If you're telling me the truth about this, then it can only mean . . ."

"I really would appreciate it if you'd quit insulting me, Caine," she snapped.

"Jade always tells the truth," Nathan defended.

"Really?" Caine drawled out. "I haven't seen that side of her yet. From the moment I met her, she's done nothing but lie. Haven't you, sweet? All that's going to change now though, isn't it?"

She refused to answer him.

"Sweetheart, why don't you give Nathan the rest of the bad news?"

"The rest? My God, there's more?"

"Just a little bit more," she answered. "Do you remember your lovely new carriage?"

"Not my carriage, Jade," Nathan protested with a low groan.

She turned to Colin while Nathan went through his list of expletives again. "You should have seen it, Colin. It was splendid. The interior was so large and comfortable. Nathan had the backs of the seats done in such soft leather."

Colin was trying to look sympathetic. "Was?" he asked.

"Someone torched it," Jade announced.

"Now why would anyone want to destroy a perfectly good vehicle?"

Caine answered that question. "Your sister has left out an important detail," he stated. "She happened to be inside when it was set on fire."

Colin was the first to react to that statement. "My God, Jade. Tell us what happened."

"Caine just did tell you," she said.

"No, tell us exactly how it happened," Colin insisted. "You could have been killed."

"That was their intent," she said, her voice tinged with exasperation. "They meant to kill me. After your house was destroyed, the carriage was made ready and I set out for London. I wanted to find you, Nathan . . ."

"How many men went with you?" Caine interrupted to ask.

"Hudson sent two men with me," she answered.

Caine shook his head. "I thought you told me you'd only been back in England two weeks," he said.

"Well, actually, it was a little longer," she hedged.

"How long?"

"Two months," she admitted. "I did have to lie about that."

"You could have told me the truth."

He was getting angry. She was too irritated to care. "Oh? And would you have believed me if I'd said I was Pagan and that I had just snatched Winters, given him to Nathan, and was now trying to . . . Oh, what's the use. You wouldn't have listened to me."

"Wait a minute," Nathan interrupted. "Who is Hudson, Jade? You said Hudson sent two men with you, remember?"

"He's the butler Lady Briars hired for you."

Nathan nodded. "And then what happened?" he asked.

"We were just outside London when those same three men trapped us. They'd blocked the road with fat tree branches. I leaned out the window to see what was going on when I heard the shouting. Someone hit me then, Nathan, on the side of my head. It fairly knocked the wind out of me. I must have fainted, though I'm embarrassed to admit to that possibility." She turned to look at Caine. "It isn't at all in my nature to swoon."

"Jade, you're digressing," Caine reminded her.

She gave him a disgruntled look, then turned back to her brother. "The interior of the carriage was ripped to shreds. They'd used their knives on the fine leather. I smelled smoke and of course got right out."

"They were hunting the letters?" Colin asked.

"You just opened the door and climbed out?" Nathan asked at the very same moment.

"Yes and no," Jade answered. "Yes, I do believe they thought I might have hidden the letters behind the leather, and no, Nathan, I didn't just open the door. Both sides were blocked shut with more branches. I squeezed through the window. Thank heavens the frame wasn't as durable as you believed. Actually, Nathan, now that I have time to reflect upon it, I think you paid entirely too much for that vehicle. The hinges weren't at all sturdy and . . ."

"Jade."

"Caine, don't raise your voice to me," Jade instructed.

"That was a close call," Colin interjected.

"I was very frightened," Jade whispered. She turned to

look at Caine. "There isn't any shame in admitting I was afraid."

Caine nodded. Her tone of voice suggested she was challenging him to disagree with her. "No, there isn't any shame in being afraid."

She looked relieved. Did she need his approval, then? Caine wondered about that possibility a long minute, then remarked, "Now I know how you got those bruises on your shoulders. It was when you squeezed through that window, wasn't it?"

"How the hell do you know if she has bruises on her shoulders or not?" Nathan roared his question, for he'd only just realized the significance of Caine's remark.

"I saw them."

Nathan would have gone for Caine's throat if Colin hadn't thrown his arm in front of his chest. "Later, Nathan," he stated. "You and Caine can settle your dispute later. It looks like we're going to be guests for a long while."

Nathan looked like he'd just been told he had to swim with the sharks again.

"You'll put yourself and Colin in danger if you leave," Jade said. "It would be too dangerous."

"We have to stay together," Colin added.

Nathan reluctantly nodded agreement.

"Caine?" Colin asked. "When you went after Pagan, you put yourself in danger. The remaining members of the Tribunal couldn't risk the chance of you finding the pirate."

"There was the possibility that Pagan would be able to convince you that she didn't have anything to do with your brother's death. Yes, it was too much of a risk to take."

"And so you sent Jade to me," Caine interjected.

Nathan shook his head. "We didn't send her. It was her plan from start to finish and we were informed after she'd left. We weren't given a say in the matter."

"How are we going to get the hounds away from you?"

Colin asked. "You can't help us find the culprits as long as you're being hunted." He let out a long sigh, then muttered, "Hell, it's such a mess. How in God's name are we going to find the bastards? We have absolutely nothing to go on."

"You're wrong, Colin," Caine said. "We have quite a bit of information to start with. We know that Hammond, the Tribunal's director, was a legitimate department head. The three men he recruited were Ice, Fox, and Prince. Now only one or two are still living, correct? And one or both are Willburn's directors. Willburn, by the way, has to be leading a duel life. He must be working for our government as well as for the Tribunal."

"How do you figure that?" Nathan asked.

"When we received word of your deaths, my father and I were sent files filed with minor though heroic deeds you two had allegedly fulfilled for England. Willburn was protecting his backside, Colin, and neither file had any substantial information that could be checked out. Security was given as the reason, of course. By the way, you both were given medals for valor."

"Why did they bother?" Colin asked.

"To appease," Caine answered. "Our father's a duke, Colin. Willburn couldn't just let you disappear. Too many questions would be asked."

"What about Nathan?" Colin asked. "Why did they bother honoring him after his death? His father was already dead and there weren't any other Wakerfields with a title. Did they want Jade to be appeased?"

Caine shook his head. "You're forgetting Nathan's other numerous titles," Caine said. "He's also the Marquess of St. James, remember? The Tribunal must have considered all the ramifications if they made that barbaric faction suspicious."

"I did forget about the St. James men," Colin announced. He turned to grin at Nathan. "You don't talk much about that side of your family, Nathan."

"Would you?" Nathan replied dryly.

Colin laughed. "This isn't the time for levity," Jade muttered. "Besides, I'm certain all those stories about the St. James men are pure exaggeration. Why, underneath all that gruffness, they're really very kind men. Aren't they, Nathan?"

Now it was Nathan's turn to laugh. "In a pig's eye," he drawled out.

Jade gave him a good frown for being so honest. Then she turned her attention back to Caine. "Did you go to the ceremony honoring Colin and Nathan?" she asked. "Was it lovely? Were there flowers? Was it a sizable group . . . ?"

"No, I didn't attend the ceremony," Caine interrupted.

"Shame on you," she announced. "You missed your own brother's . . ."

"Jade, I was too angry," Caine interrupted again. "I didn't want to listen to speeches or accept any medals on Colin's behalf. I let my father have that duty. I wanted . . ."

"Revenge," Colin interjected. "Just like the time you went after the Bradley brothers."

After making that remark, Colin turned to explain the incident to Nathan. Jade grew impatient again. "I would like to get back to our original topic," she announced. "Have you come up with any solutions yet, Caine?"

He nodded. "I think I have a sound plan to take the jackals off my trail. It's worth a try, anyway, but that's only one threat. We still have to worry about Jade."

"What do you mean?" Colin asked.

"Colin, we're dealing with two separate issues here. I'm one target, yes. We must assume they know I won't give up looking for Pagan, their convenient scapegoat."

"But what does that have to do with Jade?" Colin asked. "They can't possibly know she's Pagan."

Caine let out a sigh before answering. "Let's start at the beginning. It's obvious that the other two members of the Tribunal knew Fox had saved the letters. Since they couldn't locate them, they did the next best thing. They used their man, Willburn, to recruit you, Nathan. What better way to keep an eye on Fox's son."

He didn't wait for Nathan to respond to that statement, but continued on. "I imagine your rooms at Oxford were searched more than once, weren't they?"

Nathan nodded. "They had to be pretty certain you had the letters. For a time, you were the only logical candidate. Your sister was too young, and Harry had already taken her away. Now then," he added with a nod. "No one could believe that Fox would have trusted Harry with the letters. His appearance alone would lead anyone to that decision. They couldn't know Fox had known Harry for some time either."

Jade felt like sighing with relief. Caine was being so logical now. She felt as though he'd just taken the burden away from all of them. From the look on his brother's face, she concluded that Colin was feeling much the same relief.

"And?" Nathan prodded when Caine remained silent.

"They waited," Caine answered. "They knew eventually the letters would surface. And that's exactly what happened. Harry gave the letters to Jade. She showed them to Nathan and he shared the information with you, Colin."

"We know all this," Nathan snapped.

"Hush, Nathan," Jade whispered. "Caine's being methodical now. We mustn't interfere with his concentration."

"When Colin told Willburn about the letters, he went to the Tribunal, of course."

"And so we were sanctioned," Colin said. "I trusted the wrong man."

"Yes, you trusted the wrong man."

"They're still after the letters," Nathan said.

Caine's nod was quick. "Exactly."

Colin sat up a little straighter. "Now that they think we're dead, Nathan, there can only be one other person who could have the damning evidence."

He turned to look at Jade. "They know you have them."

"They can't be certain," Jade argued. "Or they would have killed me," she added. "That's why they're still searching, why your lovely house was destroyed, Nathan, the reason your fine carriage was shredded too . . ."

"Jade, they don't have anywhere else to search. There's only one avenue open to them now," Nathan interjected.

"They'll try to take her," Colin predicted.

"Yes," Nathan agreed.

"I'm not going to let anyone near her," Caine announced then. "But I'm not convinced they're certain she has the letters. Either one of you could have hidden them before you were taken. It must be making them crazed, though, waiting for the letters to surface again. They're getting desperate, I would imagine."

"So what do we do?" Colin asked.

"First things first," Caine said. He turned to look at Jade. "Do you remember what you asked of me when you came into the tavern that night?"

She slowly nodded. "I asked you to kill me."

"You what?" Nathan roared his question.

"She asked me to kill her," Caine repeated, though he never took his gaze off Jade.

"But he declined my request," Jade explained. "I knew he would, of course. And just what does that have to do with your plan?"

The dimple was back in evidence when he grinned at her. "It's really very simple, love. I've changed my mind. I've decided to accommodate you."

Chapter Thirteen

"Pagan has to die," Caine said, his voice low, emphatic. "It's the only way." He stared at Nathan when he made that statement. Jade's brother was quick to nod agreement.

Jade bounded out of her chair. "I don't want to die," she cried out. "I won't have it, Caine."

"Now, Jade . . ." Nathan began.

"He's talking about the pirate," Colin explained. "He isn't really going to kill you, love."

Jade glared at Colin. "I know exactly what he's talking about," she snapped. "And I still won't have it. Do you have any idea how many years it's taken to build my reputation? When I think . . ."

The men were ignoring her now. Nathan and Colin were actually smiling. Jade gave up. She sat down again and turned to frown at Caine. "If you hadn't started your hunt to capture Pagan, none of this would be necessary now. This is all your fault, Caine."

"Jade, it's the only way," Nathan argued. "If Pagan dies, or rather, if the world believes the pirate is dead, then Caine would have to give up his hunt, wouldn't he? The Tribunal knows he fully believes Pagan is responsible for killing his brother, remember?"

She reluctantly nodded. "Then they'd leave Caine alone, wouldn't they? He'd be safe again?"

Nathan smiled. He turned to Caine. "This plan of yours solves more than one problem," he remarked with a telling glance in his sister's direction.

Caine nodded. "Jade, you're going to have to change a few of your ways. When Pagan dies, you aren't going to be able to . . ."

"It's my work," she cried out. "It's what I do best."

Caine closed his eyes. "Exactly what is it that you do so well?"

Nathan answered him. "Harry did the pirating," he explained. "Jade was always on board, but he was the leader back then. She took care of the land raids. She does have a special talent, Caine. There isn't a safe she can't open, a latch she can't trick loose."

"In other words, she was an adequate petty thief," Caine drawled out. He was frowning at Jade when he made that statement.

She took immediate exception to both his manner and his opinion. "I don't care what you think of me, Caine. The deception's over now and you'll never see me again, so it really doesn't matter to me . . ."

Jade stopped her tirade when Harry's bellow reached her. A woman's shrill scream came next. Jade assumed one of the servants was being terrorized. "If you'll excuse me for a moment?" she asked.

She didn't bother to wait for permission, but rushed out of the room. As soon as the door closed behind her, Caine turned to Nathan. "She'll figure it all out very soon," he announced. "But hopefully by then we will have staged Pagan's death and it will be too late."

Colin nodded. "Yes, she's bound to realize they know she's with you and that killing Pagan isn't going to make any difference now. You're both still in danger. Odd, but Jade's usually much quicker," he added. "How long do you think it will take for her to sort it all out?"

It was Nathan who answered. "She already has, Colin. Didn't you see the look of relief in her eyes. It was fleeting, but there all the same. Deep down, I think she wants it to be over."

"Wouldn't you?" Caine asked Colin. "How could any of you want to go back on the ocean again? Jade isn't capable of being very logical right now. She thinks she has to resume her former . . . duties," he whispered. "It's a way of proving herself, perhaps. Still, it doesn't matter what her motives are now. She needs someone to take the possibility away from her, to demand she quit."

"And that's you, Caine?" Colin asked.

"Yes."

Jade walked back into the salon then. Nathan turned to her. "Jade? I don't think you should leave with Jimbo and Matthew just yet. Wait until we've settled this problem."

"Do you mean wait until you've found the Tribunal?" She sounded appalled. "I can't stay here, not after . . ."

Caine glared her into forgetting her protest. Jade walked over to the side of his chair and stood there. Her hands were folded in front of her.

"What about Harry?" Caine asked Nathan. "Will he give us any problems?"

"Why would he?" Colin asked with another yawn. "He's retired now. Surely you've noticed there haven't been any ships pirated in a long while."

"I noticed," Caine returned. "Still, he might take exception to having his ship burned."

"No!"

Jade was so appalled by that suggestion, she had to sit down. She moved back to the chair and collapsed.

Nathan was sympathetic. "The *Emerald* has been home for Jade," he said. "Perhaps we could find another ship, paint it to look like the *Emerald,* and set fire to it. Harry would keep the real one safely hidden."

Caine nodded. "Can he see to this chore? There have to be witnesses to the ship's sinking, witnesses who'll testify they saw Pagan die."

"If it's all spelled out for him, yes," Nathan agreed.

"If he's wearing his spectacles," Colin interjected with a grin.

"I'll go and speak to him now," Caine announced.

Nathan stood up before Caine did. "It's time for you to get some rest, Colin."

Before Caine or his brother realized Nathan's intent, he'd lifted Colin into his arms. Nathan staggered under the weight, righted himself, and then started out of the room. Colin immediately started protesting.

"For God's sake, Nathan, put me down. I'm not an infant."

"Could have fooled me," Nathan returned.

Jade watched the two friends disappear around the corner, then whispered, "Nathan has taken good care of your brother, Caine."

Caine turned to look at Jade. She was staring at her lap. "So have you, Jade," he replied.

She didn't acknowledge that compliment. "He's very gentle, my brother. He hides behind his angry expression most of the time. His back is scarred from the beatings he's taken, Caine. He wasn't always away at school. He won't talk about that long time he was missing, won't tell me where he was. I only know that there was a woman involved in his torment. He must have loved her very much, I think, and she must have betrayed him, because now he tries to be so cold and cynical all the time. Colin was able to touch Nathan's heart, though. Your brother gives his friendship without restrictions. He saved Nathan more than once, too. My brother doesn't trust many people, but Colin is the exception."

"Does your brother trust you?"

The question startled her. "Oh, yes," she rushed out. She glanced up to look at him, saw the tenderness in his eyes, and wondered what had caused that reaction. "Colin could never have managed all those stairs. Nathan knew that. My brother didn't give him time to let his pride become dented."

"It might still be dented just a little," Caine drawled out. They could both still hear Colin shouting his objections.

Jade's smile was hesitant. She stood up, then clasped her hands behind her back while she stared at Caine. "Since I cannot leave England just yet, I believe I shall send a note to Lady Briars and request an invitation to stay with her."

"No."

"No? Why not?"

"Jade, I'm really getting tired of repeating myself. You're staying with me."

"Lady Briars would welcome me into her home. It would be much easier for you if I left."

"Why?"

"Because you're going to think this all through in that logical mind of yours and then you're going to decide you can never forgive me. That's why."

"Do you want me to forgive you?"

"Not particularly."

"You're lying again."

"Does it matter?"

"Yes, it matters. Jade, I told you I loved you. Doesn't that matter?"

"It matters," she whispered. When he took a step toward her, she moved away from the chair and started backing toward the doors. The look on Caine's face worried her. Retreat seemed the logical choice now. "Why are you looking at me like that?" she asked.

"You've deceived me, manipulated me, run me in circles, but all that's going to change now, isn't it?"

"So it's finally settling in, is it?" She backed up another space. "When you apply your logic, I'm sure you'll understand that everything I did was to protect you and your brother. First you have to get past your anger . . . and your pride."

"Is that right?"

"Caine, someday soon, I believe you'll actually thank me for this deception. Besides, it's over now, finished."

He slowly shook his head. He smiled too. Jade didn't know what to make of that reaction. Because she didn't dare take her gaze away from him, she didn't look behind her and suddenly found herself backed up against the corner of the wall. She'd misjudged the distance to the entrance by several feet.

She was trapped. His smile widened, indicating he was well aware of her predicament and was thoroughly enjoying it.

"It's done," she stammered out.

"No, it has only just begun, sweet." His hands slammed against the wall on either side of her face.

"You're referring to this hunt for the Tribunal, aren't you?"

He slowly leaned down. "No, I'm referring to you and me. Did you let me touch you because you were protecting me?"

"What a ridiculous question," she muttered.

"Answer me."

"No, of course not," she whispered. She stared at his chest while she admitted that fact.

"Was it out of guilt for deceiving me?"

"No," she cried out. She realized she sounded frightened and immediately changed her tone. "I never feel guilty about lying. I do it very well. I'm proud of my talent, not ashamed."

Caine closed his eyes and said a quick prayer for patience. "Then why did you let me touch you?" he demanded.

"You know why."

"Tell me."

"Because I wanted you to touch me," she whispered.

"Why?"

She shook her head, then tried to push his hand away. He didn't budge.

"You aren't leaving this room until you've given me the full truth. No more lies, Jade."

She stared at his chin now. "You ask too much of me."

"I ask only what I can give in return," he countered. "And we're going to stand here all day until . . ."

"Oh, all right," she replied. "I wanted you to touch me because you were such a kind, gentle man and I realized how much I . . . cared for you."

She looked up into his eyes then, for she needed to know if he was going to laugh or not. If he showed even a hint of amusement, she swore she'd use her fist on him.

He wasn't laughing. He did look pleased with her admission, arrogantly so, but she decided he was entitled to that much. "Caine, you weren't anything like the man I read about in your file. Even your director doesn't know the real you."

"You read my file?"

She decided she shouldn't have mentioned that fact when he grabbed hold of her shoulders and began to squeeze fresh bruises on her skin. "Yes, I read your file," she announced. "It took most of the night. You have quite a history."

He shook his head. He was more astonished than angry. "Jade, the file should have been sealed . . . locked away, the name wiped clean."

"Oh, it was, Caine. Yes, the security was actually quite good. No faulty latches on all the doors, sturdy locks on each cabinet . . ."

"Obviously the security wasn't good enough," he muttered. "You were able to get inside. You found and read my file. My God, I haven't even read it."

"Why would you want to read it?" she asked. "You lived

250

GUARDIAN ANGEL

each event. The file only related assignments you'd handled. There wasn't much about your personal life. Why, the incident with the Kelly brothers wasn't even mentioned."

"Caine, why are you so upset?" she asked. She thought he might be trying to crush her bones now.

"You read everything? You know everything I've done?"

She slowly nodded. "You're hurting me, Caine. Please let go."

He put his hands back on the wall, blocking her exit again. "And yet, knowing all this . . . you still came looking for me. You weren't afraid?"

"I was a little afraid," she confessed. "Your history is most . . . colorful. And I was worried, yes, but after we met, I found myself doubting the accuracy . . ."

"Don't," he interrupted. "There wasn't any exaggeration."

She shivered over the briskness in his voice. "You did what you had to do," she whispered.

Caine still wasn't absolutely certain he believed her. "What was my operative name?"

"Hunter."

"Hell."

"Caine, do try to understand my position. It was necessary for me to find out everything I could about you."

"Why was it necessary?"

"You were in danger."

"Did it not occur to you that I could take care of any threats that came my way?"

"Yes," she answered. "It occurred to me. Still, I had made a promise to your brother and I was honor bound to keep you safe."

"Your word is very important to you, isn't it, Jade?"

"Well, of course it is," she countered.

"I still don't understand why you thought you needed to read my file."

251

"I needed to find your . . . vulnerability. Don't look at me like that. Everyone has an Achilles' heel, Caine, even you."

"And what did you find? What's my flaw?"

"Like your father, you have a reputation for being a champion of the weak. That isn't necessarily a flaw, but I used that part of your character to my advantage."

"By pretending to be in danger? Jade, you were in danger. Those events did take place. You . . ."

"I could have taken care of the threat on my own," she boasted. "Once I got away from Nathan's carriage, I went to Shallow's Wharf. Jimbo and Matthew were there, waiting for me. The three of us could have taken care of the problem."

"Perhaps," Caine said.

Since he was being so agreeable, and looking so distracted, she tried to duck under his arm. Caine simply moved closer to stop her. "You believed I was weaker and you therefore became my champion, my guardian angel," she finished.

"As it turns out, you were my guardian angel, too," he said.

"Does that injure your pride?"

"No," he answered. "Being manipulated has already done quite enough damage to my pride."

"You have enough arrogance to suffer this paltry blow," she whispered, a wisp of a smile in her voice. "You would have given your life to keep me safe. I heard you whisper that promise to me when you thought I was asleep."

"Damn it, Jade, was there ever a moment when you weren't deceiving me?"

She didn't answer him.

"Jade, I gave you my protection. Do you know what you gave me?"

"Lies," she answered.

"Yes, lies, but something else as well." He could tell by her blush that she understood what he was saying. "What else did you give me?"

"Well, there was . . . that," she whispered. "I was a virgin . . ."

"You gave me your love, Jade."

She shook her head.

He nodded.

"I didn't, Caine."

"You did," he replied. "Do you remember what I told you that first night we made love?"

She remembered every word. "No," she said.

"You're lying again, Jade. You have a knack for remembering everything you read or hear."

"Just everything I've read," she whispered. She started struggling to get away from him. She was suddenly filled with panic.

Caine moved closer, until his thighs were touching hers. "Then let me remind you, my little deceiver," he whispered. "I told you that you were going to belong to me. Now and forever, Jade."

"You didn't mean it," she cried out. "I won't hold you to such a foolish promise, Caine." She closed her eyes against the memory of their lovemaking. "Now is not the time to . . . Caine, stop that," she rushed on when he leaned down and kissed her forehead. "I tricked you, lied to you. Besides," she added. "You didn't know I was Pagan. Anything you said that night must be forgotten."

"I don't want to forget," he said.

"Caine, I can't possibly stay with you. You don't even like me. I'm a thief, remember?"

"No, my love, you used to be a thief," he said. "But all that's finished. There's going to be some changes, Jade."

"Impossible. You'd never be able to make so many changes, Caine. You're too rigid."

"I was referring to you!" he shouted. "You're going to be making these changes."

"I won't."

"You will. You're giving it all up, Jade."

"Why?"

"Because I won't have it, that's why."

She didn't want to understand. "What I do is of no concern to you," she argued. "My men depend on me, Caine. I won't let them down."

"They'll have to depend upon someone else then," he bellowed. "Your thieving days are over."

Her ears were ringing, but she was suddenly too angry and too frightened to worry about that. "Once I leave here, you'll never see me again. Don't worry, I won't come back to rob you." She decided she was finished with this conversation. She shoved away from Caine, then saw Nathan and Black Harry standing in the entrance, watching her. She assumed they'd heard most of the conversation. She had been shouting, she realized, almost as loudly as Caine had. And this was all Caine's doing anyway. He'd turned her into a raving shrew.

"Why do you care what she does?" Nathan asked.

For Jade's benefit, Caine kept his expression mild, contained. "Nathan, I believe it's time you and I had our little chat. Jade, wait in the dining room with Harry. Sterns?" Caine added when the butler joined the group. "See that we aren't interrupted."

Black Harry seemed to be the only one who fully understood what was about to happen. "Just a moment, me boy," he said to Caine as he made his way past Nathan. He rushed through the drawing room, snatched the silver bowl from the top of the mantle, then hurried back to the entrance. "It would be a shame to have this ruined, now wouldn't it? I'll be taking it with me," he added when Jade started to protest. "Caine would want me to have it, girl, so quit your frowns."

Nathan had moved into the drawing room. With a

whispered nod of good luck, Sterns dragged Jade out of the room and shut the doors.

"What do they have to talk about?" Jade asked Black Harry. "They don't even know each other."

The crash cleared up her confusion. "My God, they're going to kill each other," she cried out. "Harry, do something."

Jade gave that command while she tried to push Sterns out of her way. Harry rushed over and put his arm around her shoulders. "Now, girl, they've been itching to get at each other since the moment they met. Let them alone. Come along with me back to the dining room. Cook's about to do us with dessert."

"Harry, please!"

"Come along," Harry soothed. "Me men are waiting on me."

Her uncle gave up trying to persuade her to join him when she started in shouting. The sound didn't bother him much at all, considering all the noise coming from the drawing room. "You always were a mite stubborn, girl," he muttered as he moved back to the dining room. The cherished silver bowl was tucked under his arm.

A pounding began at the front door just as the dining room doors shut behind Harry. Sterns was immediately torn between duties.

"Will mi'lady please see who's come calling," he shouted so she could hear him above the noise.

Sterns' arms were folded across his chest. His back rested against the doors. Jade moved to stand beside him, then imitated his stance. "Mi'lady will guard these doors while you go see who it is."

The butler shook his head. "You cannot trick me, Lady Jade. You're wanting to get inside with the Marquess."

"Of course I want to go inside," she argued. "Caine's fighting with my brother. One's bound to kill the other."

255

Another loud crash shook the walls. Sterns decided one of the two men had thrown the settee against the wall. He mentioned that possibility to Jade. She shook her head. "Sounds more like a body hitting the wall, Sterns. Oh, please . . ."

She didn't bother to continue pleading with him when he shook his head.

The front door suddenly opened. Both Jade and Sterns turned their attention to the two guests who just walked inside.

"It's the Duke and Duchess of Williamshire," Sterns whispered, appalled.

Jade's manner immediately changed. "Don't you dare move away from these doors, Sterns."

She rushed across the foyer and made a curtsy in front of Caine's parents. The Duke of Williamshire smiled at her. The Duchess was barely paying her any notice, for her attention was centered on the entrance to the drawing room. Another loud blasphemy radiated through the doors. Caine's stepmother let out a small gasp.

"You took her innocence, you bastard."

Nathan's bellowed accusation echoed throughout the foyer. Jade felt like screaming. She suddenly hoped Caine would kill her brother.

Then she remembered their guests. "Good day," she blurted out. She had to shout so the Duke and Duchess would hear her. She felt like a simpleton.

"What is going on here?" the Duchess demanded. "Sterns, who is this lady?"

"My name is Lady Jade," she blurted out. "My brother and I are friends of Caine's," she added.

"But what is going on inside the drawing room?" the Duchess asked.

"A little dispute," she said. "Caine and Nathan, my brother, you see, are having a rather spirited debate about . . ."

She looked over at Sterns for help while she frantically tried to think of a plausible explanation.

"Crops," Sterns shouted.

"Crops?" The Duke of Williamshire asked, looking thoroughly puzzled.

"That's ridiculous," the Duchess announced. Her short blond curls bobbed when she shook her head.

"Yes, crops," Jade stated. "Caine believes the barley and wheat should be planted only every other year. Nathan, on the other hand, doesn't believe a field should go fallow. Isn't that right, Sterns?"

"Yes, mi'lady," Sterns shouted. He grimaced when the sound of glass shattering pierced the air, then said, "My lord feels quite strongly about this issue."

"Yes," Jade agreed. "Quite strongly."

The Duke and Duchess were staring at her with incredulous expressions. They thought she was crazed. Her shoulders slumped in defeat. "Upstairs, if you please."

"I beg your pardon?" the Duchess asked.

"Please come upstairs," Jade repeated.

"You want us to go upstairs?" the Duchess asked.

"Yes," Jade answered. "There's someone waiting to see you. I believe he's in the second room on the right, though I can't be certain."

She had to shout the end of her explanation as the noise had once again risen to ear-piercing dimensions.

The Duke of Williamshire came out of his stupor. He clasped Jade's hands. "Bless you, my dear," he said. "It's so good to see you again," he added. "You kept your word. I never doubted," he added. He realized he was rambling and immediately forced himself to calm down. "Come along, Gweneth. Jade wants us to go upstairs now."

"You know this woman, Henry?"

"Oh, dear, have I given myself away?" Henry asked Jade.

She shook her head. "I've already told Caine I came to see you," she said.

Henry nodded, then turned back to his wife. "I met this lovely young lady early this morning."

"Where?" Gweneth asked, refusing to let him tug her toward the steps. "I'll hear your explanation now, Henry."

"She came to see me in my study," Henry said. "You were still sleeping. Now come along, sweet. You'll understand after you've . . ."

"Henry, she has red hair!"

"Yes, dear," Henry agreed as he prodded her up the stairs.

Gweneth started to laugh. "And green eyes, Henry," she shouted in order for her husband to hear her. "I noticed her green eyes right off, Henry."

"How very astute of you, Gweneth."

Jade stared after Caine's parents until they'd reached the hallway above the stairs. "The fat's in the fire now, isn't it, Sterns?"

"I do believe that is a most accurate evaluation, mi'lady," Sterns agreed. "But have you noticed the blessed lack of noise?"

"I have," she replied. "They've killed each other."

Sterns shook his head. "My employer would not kill your brother," he said. "I believe I shall fetch the decanter of brandy for the two gentlemen. I imagine they're quite parched by now."

"Not parched," Jade wailed. "Dead, Sterns. They're both dead."

"Now, mi'lady, one must always look on the bright side."

"That is the bright side," she muttered. "Oh, go and fetch the brandy then. I'll guard the doors."

"I trust you to keep your word," he announced.

She didn't want to go inside now. She was furious with Caine and her brother, and so humiliated because the Duke and Duchess of Williamshire had strolled right into the middle of the brawl, she wanted to weep.

And just what did she care what Caine's parents thought about her? She was leaving, and that was that. She would have gone upstairs to pack her satchel then and there but she didn't want to take the chance of running into the Duchess again.

When Sterns returned with the crystal decanter and two glasses, Jade opened the door for him. Both she and the butler stopped when they saw the destruction. The lovely room was in shambles. Jade didn't think there was a single piece of furniture left intact.

Sterns found the two men before Jade did. His initial surprise wore off much faster, too. The butler straightened his shoulders and proceeded over to the far wall, where Caine and Nathan were seated on the floor, side by side, their backs propped up by the wall.

Jade stumbled after the butler. Her hands flew to cover her mouth when she looked at the two warriors. Neither looked victorious. Caine had a jagged cut on his forehead, just above his right eyebrow. Blood trickled down the side of his face, but he seemed to be oblivious to his injury. God's truth, he was grinning like a banshee.

Nathan looked just as defeated. There was a deep cut in the corner of his mouth. He held a handkerchief against the injury, and damned if he wasn't grinning, too. The area around his left eye was already beginning to swell.

Jade was so relieved to see that neither Caine nor Nathan appeared to be near death's door, she started trembling. Then, in a flash of a second, that surge of relief turned to raw anger. She became absolutely furious.

"Have you two gentlemen resolved your dispute?" Sterns inquired.

"We have," Caine answered. He turned to look at Nathan, then slammed his fist into his jaw. "Haven't we, Nathan?"

Nathan hit him back before answering. "Yes, we have." His voice was gratingly cheerful.

"You children should be sent to your rooms," Jade snapped. Her voice shook.

Both men looked up at her, then turned to look at each

other. They obviously thought her insult was highly amusing because they both burst into laughter.

"Your brother sure hits like a child," Caine drawled out when he could control himself.

"Like hell I do," Nathan countered. "Hand me the brandy, Sterns."

The butler knelt down on one knee and handed each man a glass. He then filled each goblet with a full portion of the rich liquid.

"Sterns, are you thinking to get them drunk?" Jade asked.

"It would be a marked improvement, mi'lady," Sterns replied dryly.

The butler stood up, bowed, and then slowly scanned the ruins. "I believe I was correct, Lady Jade. It was the settee that hit the wall."

Jade stared silently at the remains of what used to be a tea cart.

"Sterns, leave the bottle," Caine instructed.

"As you wish, mi'lord. Would you like me to assist you to your feet before I leave?"

"Is he always this proper?" Nathan asked.

Caine laughed. "Proper? Never, not Sterns. If I'm a minute late for supper, he eats my portion."

"Promptness is a quality I've still to teach you, mi'lord," Sterns said.

"You'd best help him to his feet," Nathan said. "He's as weak as a . . . child."

The two men started laughing again. "You'd best assist him, Sterns," Caine said. "He suffered more blows than I did."

"You never give up, do you, Caine?" Nathan asked. "You know good and well I won this fight."

"Like hell," Caine argued, using Nathan's favorite expression. "You barely scratched me."

Jade had heard enough. She whirled around, determined to get as far away from the two imbeciles as possible. Caine reached out and grabbed the hem of her gown. "Sit down, Jade."

"Where?" she cried out. "You've destroyed every chair in this room."

"Jade, you and I are going to have a little talk. Nathan and I have come to an agreement." Caine turned to Nathan. "She's going to be difficult."

Nathan nodded. "She always was."

Caine put his goblet down on the floor, then slowly stood up. "Nathan?" he said as he stared at the woman glaring so prettily up at him. "Think you can crawl out of here and give us a few minutes' privacy?"

"Crawl, my arse," Nathan growled as he stumbled to his feet.

"I don't want to be alone with you," Jade interjected.

"Too bad," Caine countered.

"Your parents are upstairs," she said when he tried to take her into his arms.

She waited for that statement to get a proper reaction and was unhappy to see that Caine didn't seem the least bit bothered. "They heard all the noise," she said then. "Sterns told them you were disputing the issue of crops."

"The issue of crops?" Caine asked Sterns.

The butler nodded, then turned to walk out of the room with Nathan at his side. "The rotation of crops, to be more specific, mi'lord. It was the best I could think of given the circumstances."

"They didn't believe him," Jade whispered, sounding as though she were confessing a grave sin.

"I would imagine they wouldn't," Caine answered dryly. He noticed that she suddenly looked close to tears.

"And that upset you, Jade?"

"No, that doesn't upset me," she cried out. She was so angry with him she couldn't even come up with a suitable insult. "I'm going up to my room," she whispered. "I need a few minutes of privacy."

She didn't mention she was going to pack her belongings, certain Caine or Nathan would try to waylay her. She simply wasn't up to another confrontation.

Without a hint of a farewell, Jade turned and hurried out of the room. Lord, how she wanted to weep. She couldn't, of course, until after she'd had a long talk with her uncle. Harry needed to understand. She didn't want him to worry about her.

She found Harry in the dining room, carefully examining the silver collection. He tucked a fork in his sash when she called out to him, then turned to smile at her. "I'm taking all the silver with me, girl. Caine would want me to have it for my collection."

"Yes," she answered. "I'm certain he would want you to have it. Uncle? I need to speak to you alone, please."

The men immediately filed out into the hallway. Jade sat down next to her uncle, took hold of his hand, and quietly told him what she was going to do. She also told him about the last two weeks, though she deliberately left out mention of her nightmares and her intimacy with Caine. Both of those facts would only upset Harry. Besides, he couldn't do anything about either now. No, he couldn't ward off her nightmares, and he couldn't make her quit caring about Caine.

Her uncle grunted several times during her explanation, but finally agreed. He didn't have any doubts in his mind that she'd be able to take care of herself. She was his protégée, after all, and as good as the best of them.

"I'll be waiting for you at the cottage," he promised. He pulled her over to kiss her cheek, then said, "Watch your backside, girl. Vermin like to sneak up on a person. Remember McKindry."

She nodded. Harry was referring to the pirate who'd marked her back with his whip. He had been vermin and he had snuck up behind her. Her uncle liked to use that memory as a lesson. "I'll remember," she promised.

Jade left her uncle taking inventory of Caine's possessions and went upstairs to pack. She passed Colin's room on her way to her own. The door was closed, but she could hear the Duke's booming laughter interspersed with his wife's loud, inelegant sobs. Colin's mama was obviously overcome with emotion and was probably weeping all over her son.

Colin's safety wasn't her concern any longer. She'd finished her task, she told herself. It was over now, finished.

Jimbo and Matthew were waiting for her in the hallway. Jimbo handed her the farewell gift she'd asked Harry to have him fetch.

"We'll be going with you, won't we?" Matthew asked, his voice a low whisper.

Jade nodded. "I'll meet you out back."

"I'll get Caine's horses ready for the ride," Jimbo whispered.

"A man can get himself hung for stealing a horse," Matthew interjected. His wide grin indicated he thought that was quite all right.

"Caine won't tell anyone," Jimbo argued. He took hold of Jade's satchel and started after his friend. "It's a shame, that. How we ever going to keep up appearances if no one . . ."

His sentence faded away as he turned the corner. Jade immediately went to Caine's bedroom. She placed the long-stemmed white rose on his coverlet. "I am Pagan," she whispered.

It was done. She turned to leave, then spotted Caine's black robe draped over the back of a chair near the window. On impulse she folded the garment and tucked it under her arm. His scent was on the robe, faint, but there still, and she wanted something to hold during the nights ahead, during the dark nightmares, to comfort her.

It was time to leave.

Both Caine and Nathan thought Jade was resting in her room. Caine had wanted to chase after her, but Nathan convinced him that his sister needed time alone to calm her temper.

"You might not have noticed yet, Caine, but Jade isn't one to take orders easily," Nathan explained.

Since Caine had more than noticed this, he didn't bother to comment.

The talk then turned to the problems at hand. Harry was dragged away from his inventory to add his suggestions. Jade's uncle had a quick mind. Caine watched him closely and came to a remarkable conclusion. Harry was civilized. He naturally kept that discovery to himself, for he guessed Harry would take grave exception to being confronted with the truth.

Uncle Harry did grumble about the fact that he was going to have to burn a ship. "It's a waste of good timber," he muttered. "Still, it could be worse. I might have to be burning my lovely *Emerald,*" he added. "Aye, it could be worse. I'd just as soon put a stake through me heart than damage my baby's ship. The *Emerald*'s been home to Jade and me all these many years."

Before Caine could comment on Harry's remarks, the uncle surprised him by adding that he was in full agreement that his baby get out of her present line of work.

A good two hours passed before their plans were set to everyone's satisfaction. Harry strolled back into the dining room.

"He's bent on eating you out of house and home," Nathan drawled out. "He'll steal you blind, too," he added with a grin. "Harry likes to keep up appearances."

"He can have whatever he wants," Caine returned. "Jade's had quite enough time to calm her temper, Nathan. It's high time your sister and I had our talk."

"If you lecture her, you'll only . . ."

"I'm not going to lecture her," Caine replied. "I'm simply going to tell her what my expectations are."

"Sounds like a lecture to me," Nathan drawled out.

Both Nathan and Caine walked into the foyer just as the Duchess was coming down the winding staircase. Both men stopped to watch her. Caine's stepmother was smiling, but also dabbing at the corners of her eyes with her lace handkerchief. She'd obviously had quite a good cry.

Gweneth almost lost her balance when she spotted Nathan. She grasped the banister and let out a soft gasp of surprise. She quickly regained her composure, however, and continued down the steps. When she reached the foyer, she moved to Caine's side. "Is he the pirate friend of Colin's?" she whispered.

Nathan heard her. "I'm not the pirate, Pagan, madam, but I am a friend of your son's."

Nathan assumed his voice had been a little too harsh for her liking when she grabbed hold of Caine's arm and moved closer to his side. Her dark brown eyes widened, too, but she valiantly held her smile.

"You look very like a pirate," she announced. She adjusted the folds of her pink gown as she waited for his reply.

"Have you seen many, madam?" Caine asked.

"No, I've never seen a pirate," she confessed. "Though this gentleman certainly fits the picture of one in my mind. I believe it's because of the length of his hair," she explained after turning back to look at Nathan. "And the scar on your arm, of course."

"He's also covered with blood," Caine drawled out.

"That, too," his stepmother admitted.

He'd meant the remark as a jest, but her expression had become so solemn, he knew she didn't understand he was teasing her. "Pirates do like to brawl," she added with a nod.

"Madam, didn't Colin explain that . . ." Caine began.

"My son insists upon keeping Pagan's true identity a secret," she interrupted. "Still, I'm not completely obtuse," she added with a meaningful glance in Nathan's direction. "I've been around the corner once or twice. I know who Pagan is," she added with a nod. "Henry also knows."

"Henry?" Nathan asked.

"My father," Caine explained.

"Henry's never wrong, dear."

She'd made that statement to Nathan. He found himself nodding in agreement. "Then I must be Pagan," he announced with a grin. "If Henry's never wrong."

She smiled over his easy acceptance. "Do not worry, sir, for I shall guard your secret. Now where is that lovely young lady I was so horribly rude to, Caine?"

"You're never rude, madam," Caine interjected.

"I didn't properly introduce myself," she argued. "Now where is she?"

"Upstairs, resting," Nathan answered. "Why do you ask?"

"You know perfectly well why," she answered. Her exasperation was obvious.

"I do?" Nathan asked.

"I must apologize for my behavior, of course, but also I must thank her for all she's done for this family."

"Nathan is Jade's brother," Caine said.

"I knew that," she answered. "His green eyes gave him away, of course."

The Duchess walked over to the man she believed was the infamous pirate. "Lean down, dear boy. I must give you a kiss for being such a loyal friend."

Nathan was a bit disconcerted. Caine's stepmother had sounded like a commander when she gave her order. He suddenly felt as awkward as a schoolboy and didn't have the faintest idea why.

He did, however, do as she asked.

The Duchess kissed Nathan on both cheekbones. "You need to wash that blood away, my dear. Then Henry will give you a proper welcome into the family."

"Will he kiss him, too, madam?" Caine drawled out. He was thoroughly enjoying Nathan's obvious discomfort.

"Of course not," his stepmother answered.

"Why would he want to welcome me into the family?" Nathan asked.

The Duchess smiled, yet didn't bother to explain herself. She turned back to Caine. "I should have realized Lady Aisely wasn't going to do."

"Who is Lady Aisely?" Nathan asked, trying to catch the drift of this conversation.

"A ball of fluff," Caine answered.

The Duchess ignored that insult. "Henry realized right off. The green eyes, you see. And the red hair, of course." She patted her blond curls and looked over her shoulder at Nathan. "Henry's never wrong."

Nathan found himself agreeing once again with the woman. He still didn't have a clue as to what she was babbling about, but he found her loyalty to her husband quite honorable.

"Henry's infallible." Caine said what Nathan was thinking.

"My baby's terribly weak," the Duchess remarked. "And as thin as a reed." She started toward the dining room. "I'm going to find Sterns. Colin needs a good hot meal."

Because Caine was in a hurry to get to Jade, he forgot all about Harry and his men. Nathan was more astute. He thought about warning Caine, or mentioning the guests to his mother, then decided he'd just wait and see what happened. Besides, Caine was already halfway up the stairs, and the Duchess had already turned the corner.

Nathan started counting. He'd only reached the number five when a shrill scream filled the air.

The noise stopped Caine. He turned around and found Nathan lounging against the door frame again, grinning broadly.

"What the . . ." Caine began.

"Harry," Nathan drawled out.

"Hell," Caine returned as he started back down the stairs. "Harry."

The Duchess was screaming like a wild woman now. "Damn it, Nathan," Caine roared. "You could have reminded me."

"Yes," Nathan replied. "I could have."

Just as Caine reached the bottom step, his father appeared at the top. "What in God's name is going on?" he shouted. "Who is making all that noise?"

Nathan answered before Caine could. "Your wife, sir."

Caine paused to glare at Nathan, then turned to his father again. He was torn between going to his stepmother's assistance, and preventing his father from doing murder.

The chilling look in his father's eyes convinced him to handle him first. There was also the fact that even though Harry was probably scaring the Duchess out of her wits, Caine knew he wouldn't really hurt her.

Caine grabbed hold of his father's arm when he reached him. "Father, it's quite all right, really."

Henry didn't look at all convinced. "Your wife has just met Black Harry," Nathan interjected.

Caine's father pulled away from his son's grasp just as the dining room doors bounded open. Everyone turned to watch the unsavory-looking men filing past.

Black Harry was the last in the procession. He was dragging the Duchess in his wake.

Nathan started laughing. Caine shook his head. The Duke's full attention, however, was centered on the giant of a man with the gleaming gold tooth who was now swaggering toward the front door. A large silver bowl was tucked under the man's arm.

Henry let out a roar and started forward. Both Nathan and Caine blocked his path. "Father, let me take care of this, please," Caine asked.

"Then tell him to unhand my wife!" his father bellowed.

"Henry, do something," Gweneth cried out. "This . . . man believes I'm going with him."

Nathan took a step forward. "Now, Harry, you can't be taking . . ."

"Get out of my way, son," Caine's father snapped.

"Father, Harry's a friend," Caine countered. "He's Jade's uncle. You owe this man a debt for helping with Colin."

Henry paused to give his son an incredulous look. "And Gweneth is payment for this debt?"

"Let me handle this matter," Caine demanded once again.

Before his father could argue with him, Caine turned. "Harry," he called out.

Black Harry whirled around and hauled the Duchess up against his side. Caine noticed his grim expression, of course, but also the definite sparkle in his eyes. Appearances, he thought to himself. And pride. Both needed to be upheld.

"I'll be taking her with me," Harry announced to his audience. His men nodded their agreement. "Caine would want me to have her."

"No," Caine replied. "I don't want you to have her."

"You being inhospitable, boy?"

"Harry, it isn't possible for you to take her."

"It's a fair exchange," Harry stated. "You're determined to have my girl, now aren't you?"

Caine nodded. "I am."

"Then I'm taking this one," Harry countered.

"Harry, she's already taken," Caine argued. He turned to his stepmother then and said, "Madam, please quit shouting. It's difficult enough to negotiate with this stubborn pirate. Nathan? If you don't quit laughing, I'm going to bloody your nose again."

"What's this woman to you, Caine?" Harry asked. "You just called her madam. Now what the hell does that mean?"

"She's my father's wife."

"But she ain't your mama?"

"She's my stepmother," Caine qualified.

"Then it shouldn't matter to you if I take her or not."

Caine wondered what Harry's real game was. "She has been like a mother to me," he said.

Harry frowned, then turned to his pretty captive. "Do you call him son?"

The Duchess lost her outraged expression and slowly shook her head. "I didn't believe he would wish me to call him son," she answered.

"He ain't your favorite," Harry announced.

The Duke of Williamshire quit trying to get past Caine. His stance became relaxed. A hint of a smile turned his expression. He understood at last what this was all about, for he remembered Jade's instructions about loving his children equally. She must have mentioned her concern to Harry.

"I don't have a favorite child," Gweneth cried out. "I love all my children."

"But he ain't yours."

"Well, of course he's mine," she snapped.

The Duchess didn't look frightened now, only furious. "How dare you suggest . . ."

"Well now, if you'd call him son," Harry drawled out, "and if he called you mother, then I couldn't be taking you with me."

"For heaven's sake, Gweneth, call Caine son!" Henry roared, trying to pretend outrage. He was so pleased inside over this surprising development, he wanted to laugh.

"Son," Gweneth blurted out.

"Yes, Mother?" Caine answered. He was looking at Harry, waiting for his next rebuttal.

Harry let go of his hostage. His chuckle was deep as he turned and walked out the doorway.

While Gweneth threw herself into her husband's arms, Caine followed Harry outside. "All right, Harry, what was that all about?"

"My reputation," Harry drawled out after his men had taken their leave. "I'm a pirate, if you'll remember."

"What else?" Caine asked, sensing there was more to tell.

"My girl worried about Colin being the favorite," Harry finally admitted.

Caine was astonished by that statement. "Where did she get that idea?"

Harry shrugged. "Don't matter where she got it," he replied. "I don't want her worrying, no matter what the niggly reason be. You're going to have to ask me for her, you know. You'll have to do it proper, too, in front of me men. It's the only way you're going to be getting her, son." He paused to grin at Caine, then added, "Course you're going to have to find her first."

A feeling of dread settled in Caine's bones. "Hell, Harry, she isn't upstairs?"

Harry shook his head.

"Where is she?"

"No need to shout, son," Harry answered. "Can't tell you where she is either," he added. He waved his men away when they started toward him, then said, "It would be disloyal."

"My God, don't you . . ."

"I'm wondering to meself why you haven't noticed both Matthew and Jimbo are missing," he interrupted. "That's telling, ain't it?"

"She's still in danger."

"She'll do all right."

"Tell me where she is," Caine demanded.

"She's running from you, I imagine."

Caine didn't want to waste any more time arguing with Harry. He turned around and almost ripped the hinges off the door as he pulled it open.

"Where you going, boy?" Harry called out.

There was more than a thread of amusement in the old man's voice. Caine wanted to kill him. "Tracking, Harry."

"You any good at it?"

Caine didn't bother to answer that question.

"She's led you a merry chase with her little deception, now hasn't she? I'd have to say she did a fair job of impressing you," Harry called out at Caine's back.

Caine turned around. "What's the point, Harry?"

"Well now, I'm thinking to meself it's about time you did a little impressing of your own, assuming, of course, that you're up to it."

Caine took the steps to his bedroom two at a time. He was pulling his shirt over his head by the time Nathan caught up with him.

"What's happening now?" Nathan demanded.

"Jade's gone."

"Damn," Nathan muttered. "You going after her?"

"I am."

"I'll go with you."

"No."

"You could use my help."

"No," Caine snapped. "I'll find her."

Nathan reluctantly nodded. "You any good at tracking?"

Caine nodded. "I'm good."

"She left you a message."

"I saw it."

Nathan strolled over to the side of Caine's bed and lifted the long-stemmed white rose from the pillow. He inhaled the sweet fragrance, then walked over to the window to look outside.

"Is she in love with you?" Nathan asked.

"She is," Caine answered. His voice lost its brittle edge. "She just doesn't know it yet."

Nathan tossed the rose back on the bed. "I'd say Jade was telling you goodbye when she left you the rose."

"No."

"She might be reminding you who she is, Caine."

"That's part of it," Caine said. He completed his change of clothes, stomped into his boots, and started for the door.

"Then what's the rest?" Nathan asked as he trailed after him.

"Harry's right," Caine muttered.

"What?"

"She's trying to impress me."

Nathan laughed. "That, too," he agreed.

Caine bellowed for Sterns as he bounded down the stairs. The servant appeared at the doorway to the drawing room. "Lyon will find Richards for us," Caine said. "When the two arrive, make them wait until I get back, no matter how long it takes."

"What if your friend can't find Richards?" Nathan asked.

"He'll find him," Caine answered. "I probably won't be back before tomorrow morning," he said. "Take care of things while I'm gone, Sterns. You know what to do."

"Meaning the guards, mi'lord?"

Caine nodded. He started for the door, but Sterns' question stopped him.

"Where are you going, mi'lord?"

"Hunting."

The door slammed shut.

Chapter Fourteen

Matthew and Jimbo appeared to be as weary as Jade was by the time they reached their destination. It had been decided that they would spend the night in the isolated inn Harry frequented when he was on the run. Jade had insisted they take a roundabout way there, adding two more hours' travel, just as an added precaution against being followed.

The innkeeper was a friend of Black Harry's, a little on the disreputable side as well, and therefore never asked unnecessary questions. If he thought it odd a finely dressed young lady was traveling with two men who looked like they'd cut a man's throat for two pence, he certainly didn't remark upon it.

Jade was given the center bedchamber above the stairs. Jimbo and Matthew took the rooms on either side of her. Since the walls were paper-thin, neither man worried that anyone would be able to breach their temporary fortress. The steps were so old and rickety, a mouse would have made noise.

Jade soaked in a hot bath, then wrapped herself in Caine's robe. She was stiff and out of sorts by the time she went to bed. Her injury from the pistol shot was almost completely healed now, but it still itched something fierce.

Jade fell asleep saying a prayer that the nightmare would not visit her tonight, worrying she might cry out and cause Matthew and Jimbo alarm.

The air turned chilly during the night. Jade burrowed under the covers. She never felt Caine climb into the bed beside her. When he put his arm around her and gently pulled her up against his side, she let out a soft sigh and snuggled closer to his familiar warmth.

Moonlight filtered through the small window. He smiled when he saw she was wearing his robe. Then he slowly slipped the garment off her. That task completed, he removed her knife from under the pillow, then began to nibble on the side of her neck.

She was slow to wake up. "Caine?" she whispered, her voice a sleepy blur.

"Yes, love?" he whispered in her ear before his tongue swept inside to tease. She started shivering. It was just the reaction he wanted.

His hand moved down her chest, circled her navel, then trailed a hot path to one of her breasts.

She sighed again. He was so warm, smelled so wonderful, and oh, how he was making the cold disappear.

Caine continued to stroke her while he waited for her to realize where she was. He was ready to silence her if she tried to call out.

The awakening came like a bolt of lightning. The palm of his hand cut off her gasp. "Now, sweetheart, if you yell, I'll have to hurt Matthew and Jimbo when they come charging in here," he whispered. He rolled her onto her back, then covered her with his body. "You wouldn't want that, would you?"

She shook her head. Caine slowly eased his hand away from her mouth.

"You're naked."

"So are you," he whispered back. "Convenient, isn't it?"

"No."

"Yes," he answered. "And it feels good, doesn't it?"

It felt marvelous. She couldn't admit that, however. "How did you get in here?"

He kissed her chin in answer to that question. Jade prodded his shoulder. "Caine, what are you doing here?"

"Impressing you, sweetheart."

"What?"

"Keep your voice down, love," he cautioned. "You don't want to wake up the boys."

"They aren't boys," she stammered out. She sounded breathless. The hair on his chest was tickling her breasts, making her nipples hard. She didn't want him to move away from her, though, and that honest admission made her frown. Lord, she was confused. "Impressing me, Caine?" she whispered. "I don't understand what you mean."

"Of course you do, sweet," he answered. He kissed the bridge of her nose. "God, I love your freckles," he said with a low groan. He kissed her long, hard, and when he was finished, she was clinging to his shoulders.

She recovered much quicker than he did. "Have you come to say goodbye then?" she asked him in a ragged whisper.

Her question was meant to rile him. The defenses again, he thought to himself. "No, I didn't come to say goodbye," he answered, determined not to get angry. "I came to make love to you."

He grinned after making that promise. Jade's heart started pounding. It was the damned dimple, she told herself. It was too irresistible to ignore . . . and so appealingly boyish. He didn't feel like a boy, though. No, he had the body of a fit man, a warrior with sleek iron-hard muscles. She couldn't stop herself from rubbing her toes against his legs.

"Someday, my love, you're going to understand just how

much I care for you. You're my light, my warmth, my other half. I only feel alive when I'm with you. I love you."

He kissed her again, then whispered, "One day, you'll tell me you love me, too. For now I'll be content to hear you say you want me."

She shook her head. Caine could see the fear in her eyes, the confusion. His smile was filled with tenderness when he pushed her legs apart and settled himself between her silky thighs. He rubbed his hard arousal against her softness. "You do want me, love."

She closed her eyes with a telling sigh. Caine nibbled at her lips, tugging on her lower lip until she finally opened for him, then thrust his tongue inside to duel with hers.

"Caine, what are you . . ."

He silenced her with another long kiss, then whispered, "It's called pillaging, Jade."

"It isn't."

"Harry would be proud," he drawled out. His mouth was now placing wet kisses on the smooth, sensitive skin below her chin. She couldn't quit trembling.

"You're mine, Jade. The sooner you understand that, the better it will be for you."

"And then what, Caine?" she asked.

He lifted his head to stare down into her eyes. He could see the fear there, and the vulnerability. "You learn to trust me," he whispered. "And then we live happily ever after."

"No one lives happily ever after."

"We will."

She shook her head. "Get off me, Caine. You're . . ."

"Solid, love," he interrupted. "Steadfast, too. I won't leave you."

The promise was given in a fervent whisper. She pretended not to understand. "Of course you won't leave me. I'm leaving you."

"I love you, Jade."

Her eyes filled with tears. "You'll get tired of me. I won't change, not for you, not for anyone."

"All right."

Her eyes widened. "All right?"

He nodded. "If you want to stay a thief, so be it. I won't get tired of you, no matter what you do. And I'll never leave you."

"You won't be able to help it."

Caine kissed her brow, then said, "I can see it's going to take a little time for me to convince you. Will you give me at least two months?"

"Caine, I don't think . . ."

"You owe me, Jade."

"I what?" She sounded outraged. "Why would you believe I owe you anything?"

"Because you deceived me," he explained. "You caused me endless worry, too. And there I was, minding my own affairs that night in the tavern when you . . ."

"I also saved your brother," she interrupted.

"Then there's the issue of my wounded pride, of course," he drawled out. "A man shouldn't be made to feel he's been manipulated."

"Caine, for heaven's sake."

"Promise me you'll stay with me for two more months or I'm going to make so much noise when I pillage you, both Matthew and Jimbo will come running."

That odious threat got her full attention. The determined look in his eyes told her he meant what he threatened, too. "You should be ashamed of yourself."

"Promise me, Jade. Now."

His voice had risen and she clamped her hand over his mouth in retaliation. "Will you explain how you settled on two months instead of one, or three, or . . ."

He shrugged. She feigned irritation. "And during those two months you'll probably be dragging me to your bed every single night, won't you?"

"I will," he answered with a grin. "Do you know, whenever I look at you, I get hard?" He shifted positions and pressed against her. "Can you feel how much I want you? You make me ache to be inside you."

His honesty made her blush. "You shouldn't say things like that," she whispered. "And I shouldn't listen."

"You like it," Caine told her. His mouth covered hers and his tongue slid inside to taste her again. Jade didn't protest. She wanted him too much to stop now. She moved against him, then froze when the bed made such a loud, squeaky noise.

"We can't . . ." The denial came out with a groan.

"We can," he said, his voice a husky caress.

He silenced her worries with another kiss while he stoked the fire in her. Jade forgot all about Matthew and Jimbo. Caine was making her burn and all she could concentrate on was finding release from the sweet agony.

His fingers drove her wild. She was wet, hot, ready, knew she was going to die from the pressure building inside her. Her nails dug into his shoulder blades. She would have shouted for him to come to her if his mouth hadn't covered hers. Caine kept the torment up until she took him in her hands and tried to bring him inside her. He threw the coverlet off the bed, then followed it down to the floor with Jade protected in his arms. He cushioned the fall, taking most of the force on his back. Jade was sprawled on top of him. She tried to roll to her side, but Caine held her tight. "Take me inside you now, love," he whispered as he pushed her thighs apart to straddle him.

She was trembling too much to help. Caine took over. He held her by the sides of her hips and slowly eased into her. He let out a low groan of raw pleasure. She whimpered at the same moment.

When he was deep within her, he twisted her hair around his hands and pulled her down for another hot kiss.

The mating rhythm took over. Caine's discipline deserted

him. His thrusts became more powerful, more determined. "Take me to heaven again, Jade," he whispered when he was about to spill his hot seed inside her. "I'll keep you safe."

Jade found her release seconds later. She arched against Caine, squeezed him tight, biting her lip to keep herself from crying out, and then collapsed on top of him.

Her face was buried in the crook of his neck. They were both covered with a sheen of perspiration. Jade tasted his skin with the tip of her tongue while she waited for her heart to slow down. She was too exhausted, too content, to move. Caine held her close. She could feel his heart pounding against her own.

"What are you thinking, Jade?" he asked.

When she didn't answer him, he pulled on her hair. "I know you found fulfillment. Are you going to deny it now?"

"No," she whispered shyly.

Caine moved to his feet in one fluid motion with Jade in his arms. When they were both back in bed and under the covers, she tried to turn her back to him. He wouldn't allow her retreat, but forced her to face him. "Well?" he demanded.

"Well, what?" she asked, staring into those dark eyes that made her feel fainthearted.

"I'm good, aren't I?"

The dimple was back in his cheek. She couldn't help but smile. "Good at what?" she asked, pretending innocence.

"Pillaging."

She slowly nodded. "Very good," she whispered.

"And did I impress you?" he asked.

"Perhaps just a little," she answered. She let out a gasp when the palm of his hand pressed against the junction of her thighs. "What are you doing?"

"Impressing you again, sweetheart."

The man was as good as his word, Jade decided a long while later. And he had far more stamina than she did. When he finally rolled away from her, she felt like a limp rag.

She fell asleep with Caine holding her close, whispering words of love.

She didn't have any nightmares that night.

By noon, they were back at Caine's house. Matthew and Jimbo couldn't leave for Shallow's Wharf quickly enough. They were both mortified by their slip up of the night before. They'd obviously underestimated the Marquess. Matthew didn't think he'd ever live down the disgrace; though, of course, Jade promised not to tell anyone he'd been caught so unaware.

Hell, Caine had prodded him awake, and how in God's name such a big man was able to get into his room without making a sound still baffled him.

As soon as they returned to Caine's home, Jade changed her gown and then went to Caine's study to make copies of the letters for him. She listened to him explain his plan. She argued something fierce about trusting Richards, but agreed that Lyon could hold a confidence.

"When you meet Richards, you'll like him as much as you like Lyon," Caine replied. "You'll trust him as much, too."

She shook her head. "Caine, I like Lyon, yes, but that isn't the reason I trust him. No, no," she continued. "Liking and trusting are two different kettles of fish."

"Then why do you trust Lyon?" he asked, smiling over the censure in her tone.

"I read his file," she answered. "Do you know, in comparison, Caine, you've led the life of a choirboy."

Caine shook his head. "I wouldn't mention reading his file to him," he advised.

"Yes," she agreed. "He'd probably get as prickly as you did when I told you," she added. "Lyon's file is just as fat as yours, but he didn't have a special name."

Caine looked thoroughly irritated with her. "Jade, exactly how many files did you read?"

"Just a few," she replied. "Caine, I really must concentrate on these letters. Please quit interrupting me."

The library door opened then, drawing Caine's attention. Nathan walked inside. "Why hasn't anyone tried to get to you, Caine, since you've been here? It's damned isolated, and I would think . . ."

"Someone did try to get to Caine the day we arrived, Nathan," Jade said without looking up.

When Jade didn't continue, Caine filled Nathan in on the details of the failed attempt.

"Nathan, how nice you look," Jade said, completely turning the topic when she glanced up and saw his handsome shirt and pants.

"That shirt looks damned familiar," Caine drawled out.

"It's yours," Nathan answered with a grin. "Fits well, too. Colin has also borrowed a few of your things. We hadn't packed sufficiently when we were tossed into the ocean. Why hasn't anyone tried to get to you since that first day?" he added with a scowl.

Nathan started to pace the room like a tiger. Caine continued to lean against the edge of the desk. "They have."

"What?" Nathan asked. "When?"

"They have not," Jade interjected. "I would have known."

"In the past ten days, four others have tried."

"And?" Nathan asked, demanding more of an explanation.

"They failed."

"Why wasn't I informed?" Jade asked.

"I didn't want to worry you," Caine explained.

"Then you had to have known Matthew and Jimbo were here," Nathan said.

"I knew," Caine answered. "I left them alone, too, until they burned down my stables. Then I had a little talk with them. Couldn't you have come up with another plan to keep me busy while you went to see my father?"

282

He was getting all worked up again. Jade guessed he still wasn't over the fire yet. Sterns had said the stables were brand new. "I should have been more specific with Matthew," she announced. "I left the diversion up to him. Still, he was very creative, effective, too. You were busy."

"You took a needless risk going off on your own like that," he snapped. "Damn it, Jade, you could have been killed!"

He was shouting at her by the time he'd finished that statement. "I was very careful," she whispered, trying to placate him.

"The hell you were!" he roared. "You were damn lucky, that's all."

She decided she needed to turn his attention. "I'm never going to finish this task if you two don't leave me alone." She tossed her hair over her shoulder and returned to her letter writing. She could feel his glare on her. "Why don't you both go see how Colin's doing. I'm sure he'd like the company."

"Come on, Caine. We've just been dismissed."

Caine shook his head. "Promise me you won't take needless risks again," he ordered Jade. "Then I'll leave."

She immediately nodded. "I promise."

The anger seemed to drain out of him. He nodded, then leaned down to kiss her. She tried to dodge him. "Nathan's here," she whispered.

"Ignore him."

Her face was bright red when he lifted his mouth away from hers. Her hands were shaking, too. "I love you," he whispered before he straightened up and followed Nathan out of the room.

Jade stared at the desktop a long while. Was it possible? Could he really love her? She had to quit thinking about it in order to calm the trembling in her hands. Richards and his friend wouldn't be able to read the letters otherwise. Besides, it didn't matter if he loved her or not. She still had to leave him. Didn't she?

Jade had worked herself into a fine state of nerves by the time dinner hour was over. Nathan had decided to eat his supper upstairs with Colin. She and Caine, and Sterns, of course, ate at the long table. They got into a heated debate about the separation between church and state. In the beginning, when Caine stated he was in favor of the separation wholeheartedly, she took the opposite opinion. Yet when he deliberately argued the opposing view, she was just as vehement in her rebuttal.

It was a thoroughly invigorating argument. Sterns ended up acting as referee.

The debate made Caine hungry again. He reached for the last slice of mutton only to have it snatched out of his reach by Sterns.

"I wanted that, Sterns," Caine muttered.

"So did I, mi'lord," the butler answered. He picked up his utensils and proceeded to devour the food. Jade took sympathy on Caine and gave him half of her portion.

Both Sterns and Caine looked at each other when the sudden pounding on the front doors echoed through the room. Caine lost the staring contest. "I'll get it," he announced.

"As you wish, mi'lord," Sterns agreed between bites of his mutton.

"Be careful," Jade called out.

"It's all right," Caine called back. "No one could have gotten to the doors without my men noticing."

A good ten minutes elapsed before Sterns finished his second cup of tea. "I believe I shall go and see who's calling," he told Jade.

"Perhaps it's Caine's papa."

"No, mi'lady," Sterns countered. "I have ordered the Duke and Duchess to stay away. It would draw suspicion if they began to pay daily visits to their son."

"You really ordered them?" she asked.

"But of course, Lady Jade." With a formal bow, the butler left the room.

Jade drummed her fingers on the table until Sterns returned.

"Sir Richards and the Marquess of Lyonwood have arrived," he announced from the doorway. "My lord is requesting both brandy and you in the library."

"So soon?" she asked, clearly startled. She stood up, smoothed the folds of her gold-colored gown, then patted her hair. "I wasn't ready to meet anyone," she said.

Sterns smiled. "You look lovely, mi'lady," he announced. "You'll like these visitors. They're good men."

"Oh, I've already met Lyon," she replied. "And I'm certain I'll like Richards just as much."

As she started for the door, her expression turned from carefree to fearful.

"There's really nothing to be concerned about, mi'lady."

Her smile was radiant. "Oh, I'm not worried, Sterns. I'm preparing."

"I beg your pardon?" he asked. He followed after her. "What are you preparing for, mi'lady?"

"To look worried," she answered with a laugh. "And to look weak, of course."

"Of course," Sterns agreed with a sigh. "Are you ill, Lady Jade?"

She turned to look at him when she reached the library door. "Appearances, Sterns."

"Yes?"

"They must be kept up. Do the expected, don't you see?"

"No, I don't see," he answered.

She smiled again. "I'm about to give Caine his pride back," she whispered.

"I wasn't aware he'd misplaced it."

"I wasn't either, until he mentioned it to me," she replied. "Besides, they're only men, after all."

She took a deep breath, then let Sterns open the door for her. She stood just inside the entrance, her head bowed, her hands folded together in front of her.

Sterns was so surprised by the sudden change in her demeanor, his mouth dropped open.

When Caine called out to her, she visibly jumped, as if his command had the power to terrify her, then slowly walked into the study. The one called Richards bounded to his feet first. He was an elderly man with gray hair, a gentle smile, and a round belly. He had kind eyes, too. Jade acknowledged the introduction by making a perfect curtsy.

She then turned to greet Lyon. When he stood to his full height, he fairly towered over her. "It is good to see you again, Lyon," she whispered, her voice little more than a faint shiver.

Lyon raised an eyebrow in reaction. He knew she was a timid creature, but he thought that she had gotten over her initial reaction to him the first time they'd met. Now, however, she acted afraid again. The contradiction puzzled him.

Caine was sitting behind his desk. His chair was tilted back against the wall. Jade sat down on the edge of the chair adjacent to the desk, her back ramrod straight. Her hands were clenched in her lap.

Richards and Lyon both resumed their chairs across from her.

Caine was watching Jade. She appeared to be terribly frightened. He wasn't buying it for a minute. She was up to something, he decided, but he would have to wait until later to question her.

Richards cleared his throat to get everyone's attention. His gaze was centered on Jade when he said, "I cannot help but notice, my dear, how worried you seem to be. I've read the letters your father saved, but before I ask you my questions, I want to make it perfectly clear that I don't hold you in less esteem because of your father's transgressions."

She still looked like a trapped doe, but she managed a timid nod.

"Thank you, Sir Richards," she replied in a bare whisper. "It is kind of you not to blame me. I was worried that you might condemn me."

Caine rolled his eyes heavenward. Richards, a man rarely given to showing any affection, was now clasping Jade's hands. The director looked like he wanted to take her into his arms and offer her solace.

She did appear to be very vulnerable. Caine suddenly remembered that that same expression had been on her face when she'd stared at him in the tavern. She'd appeared vulnerable then, too.

What was her game?

"Neither one of us condemns you," Lyon interjected. He, too, leaned forward, bracing his elbows on his knees. "You have had a difficult time of it, Jade."

"Yes, she has," Sir Richards agreed.

Caine forced himself not to smile. Both his superior and his friend were falling under Jade's spell. He thought Lyon should have known better. After all, he'd met Jade before. Still, her manner now, added to his earlier thought that she was terribly timid, obviously convinced Lyon that she was sincere.

"Are you up to answering a few questions now?" Richards asked.

Jade nodded. "Would it not be better to have Nathan answer your questions? Men are so much more logical. I'll probably make a muddle out of it."

"Jade." Caine said her name as a warning.

She turned to give him a tremulous smile. "Yes, Caine?" she asked.

"Behave yourself."

Richards turned to frown at Caine. Then he returned his attention to Jade.

"We'll ask Nathan our questions later. If it isn't too

painful to recount, please tell us exactly what happened to you from the moment you arrived in London."

Jade nodded. "Certainly," she agreed. "You see, this all begins with the letters. My Uncle Harry was given a packet of letters by my father. Just two days later, Father was killed. Harry took me away on his ship then. He saved the letters, and when he felt the time was right, he gave them to me. I read them of course, then showed them to Nathan. My brother was working with Colin at the time, and he confided in him. Now then," she continued in a brisker tone. "As Caine has probably told you, both Colin and Nathan were . . . attacked. The villains thought they'd done them in, and . . . Pagan decided to let the hired thugs return to London to report their success."

"A sound decision," Richards interjected.

"Yes," Jade said. She turned to frown at Caine. "The plan was very simple. Pagan snatched a physician to take care of the injuries, and it had been decided that when Colin was well enough to travel, he would tell his brother, Caine, about the letters and ask his assistance."

"What happened to sour this plan?" Richards asked.

Jade frowned at Caine again. "He soured it," she announced. "Pagan had been made the scapegoat for Nathan and Colin's deaths, as you know, and Caine decided to seek vengeance. His timing couldn't have been worse. The remaining members of the Tribunal couldn't take the risk of Caine finding the pirate and having a talk with him. So Caine had inadvertently put himself in danger."

"It wasn't inadvertent," Caine interjected.

She shrugged. "Colin had made Pagan promise not to tell Caine anything. His brother knew Caine would . . . charge right in, you see, and Colin wanted to explain everything. In truth, I do believe Colin wasn't thinking the thing through, but he was in terrible pain at the time and he seemed obsessed with protecting Caine. Pagan agreed, just to placate Colin."

"And where do you fit into this scheme?" Lyon asked.

"Nathan is my brother," Jade answered. "I returned to England and went to stay at his country estate. There were several of Pagan's men with me. They took turns watching out for Caine. Several attempts were made to get him, and it was then decided that I would find a way to get Caine away from his hunt. Two days before I was supposed to leave, a series of incidents took place. On the first morning, when I was taking my usual walk, I came upon three men digging up my parents' graves. I shouted, for I was in a rage, you see, over what they were doing. I drew their notice, of course. One of the villains shot at me. I ran back to Nathan's house to get help."

"Weren't Pagan's men still guarding you?" Richards asked.

Jade shook her head. "They were all needed to keep Caine safe. Besides, I had Nathan's butler, Hudson, and the other servants to assist me."

"And then what happened?" Lyon asked.

"It was too dark for the servants to go to the graves. It was decided to wait until morning. That night, the house was pillaged," she continued. "I slept through, however, and never heard a sound. Even my bedchamber was turned upside down."

"You must have been drugged," Richards announced.

"I can't imagine how it was done if I was drugged," Jade said. "The following morning, I rode one of Nathan's mounts back to the graves to see if any evidence had been left. Nathan's butler, Hudson, was having a difficult time believing me, you see, and I wanted to convince him. As it turned out, I never made it to the graves. The villains were obviously waiting to intercept me. They killed Nathan's horse. I went flying to the ground."

"Good Lord, you could have been killed by the fall," Richards said.

"I was most fortunate, as I only sustained a few bruises,"

she explained. "I went running back to the house, told Hudson what had happened. He sent men to chase after the villains. When they returned, they told me they couldn't find any evidence of foul play. The horse had vanished. I'm not certain how that was accomplished. Caine said it would take more than three men to lift it into a wagon and cart it away."

She paused to shrug, then continued. "I decided to go to London with all possible haste and immediately ordered the carriage made ready. Yet, as soon as we'd traveled down the first hill, the coachman shouted that there was a fire. We could see the smoke. I returned to the house just in time to witness the full fire. Poor Nathan's house was gutted to the ground. I then ordered Hudson and the other servants to go to Nathan's London residence, then once again set out for my own destination."

"And where was that?" Lyon asked. "Were you also going to Nathan's town house?"

Jade smiled. "No, I was going to a tavern called the Ne'er Do Well. I had a plan, you see, to get Caine away from his hunt."

Lyon nodded.

"I don't understand," Richards interjected. "What exactly was this plan? Caine isn't one to be easily fooled, my dear."

"I'll explain it all later," Caine interjected. "Let her finish with this now."

"On the way to London, the carriage was waylaid. I was hit on the side of my head. The blow made me sleep, and when I awakened, I found that the carriage had been torn apart. I was able to squeeze through the window after I'd widened the frame with the heel of my boot."

"And then?" Richards asked.

"I walked."

"All the way to London?" Lyon asked.

"No," Jade answered. "Not all the way. I was able

to . . . borrow a horse from a way station. It was unattended. The owner was probably inside having his supper."

Jade finished her accounting a few minutes later. She never mentioned the fact that she was Pagan, and Caine assumed he would have to be the one to tell Sir Richards and Lyon.

Just what was her game? Lord, by the time she'd finished her recitation, she was dabbing at the corners of her eyes with Richards' handkerchief.

The director was obviously shaken by her explanation. He leaned back in his chair and shook his head.

"Do you know who the other members of the Tribunal are?" Jade asked him.

"No."

"But you knew Hammond, didn't you?" she asked. "I understood that the two of you started out together."

"Yes, we started out together," Richards agreed. "Yet after a number of years, my dear, we were each given a different division within the War Department. Hammond had so many young men under his direction back then. He ran his own section. I met quite a few eager young saviors, but certainly not all of them."

"We have several telling clues," Lyon interjected. "It shouldn't take us long to find out the truth."

"The first letter was signed by a man named William. They hadn't been assigned their operative names yet. Hell, that's the most common name in England," Caine added. "How many Williams work for the War Office?"

Jade answered his question. "Actually, there were only three in Hammond's files."

Everyone turned to look at her. "Pagan read the files," she whispered. She blushed, then added, "It was necessary. There's William Pryors, William Terrance, and William Clayhill. All three worked for your department, Sir Richards. Two are still alive, though retired from duty, but William Terrance died four years ago."

"You're certain of these facts?" Lyon asked.

"How did Pagan get to our files?" Richards was obviously disconcerted. "By God, no one can get through our security."

"Pagan did," Caine said. He took over the conversation then, explaining in more detail how the pirate had set out to protect him. He told them about Colin's and Nathan's near miss with the sharks, too. When he was finished, no one said a word for a long while.

Jade was gripping her hands together. It wasn't a pretense now, but the memory of the sharks that made her so agitated.

"Three eager young men, bent on saving the world," Richards whispered. "But the lust for power became more important."

Jade nodded agreement. "Did you notice, sir, that the first letters were signed with the wording, 'for the good of England,' but as time went on, and they grew more and more bold, they changed the wording?"

"I noticed," Sir Richards muttered. " 'For the good of the Tribunal' was how they signed their notes," he added. "And that does say it all, doesn't it. There can be no misinterpretation here."

"Her father was killed by the two others when he refused to go along with their plans, and then Hammond was murdered," Caine said.

Richards nodded. "We must find the other two," he muttered. "Lord, there's so much to take in." He let out a weary sigh, then said, "Well, thank God Pagan seems to be on our side. When I think of all the damage he could do with those files, my blood runs cold."

"Oh, Pagan's very honorable," Jade rushed out. "Most thieves are, sir. You mustn't worry that the information will fall into the wrong hands."

"Did that bastard read my file?" Lyon demanded.

Caine didn't answer him. He didn't think there was any reason to share the truth with his friend. It would only upset him.

"The very fact that there were sharks in those waters," Richards whispered, changing the topic. "Do you realize the courage it must have taken . . ."

"Have you finished your questions?" Jade interrupted.

The director immediately reached out and patted her hands again. "We've exhausted you, haven't we, my dear? I can tell how distressing this is for you."

"Thank you for your consideration," she whispered. She stood up and didn't protest at all when Richards embraced her.

"We'll find the culprits, I promise you," he said.

Jade hid her hands in the folds of her gown, then walked over to Lyon. He immediately stood up. She leaned against him. "Thank you, Lyon, for helping us. Please give my love to Christina. I cannot wait until I can visit with her again."

She turned back to Richards and hugged him again. "I forgot to thank you as well," she explained.

She pulled away from the director, bowed, and turned to leave the room.

"Jade?"

"Yes, Caine?"

"What was all that about?"

She turned around to smile at him. "You said a man's pride is very important, didn't you?"

"I did."

"You also said that when a man is manipulated or deceived, his pride suffers, too."

"I did say that." He leaned forward. "And?"

"Well, if others were also . . . fooled . . . friends who have earned their own legends and England's respect, then wouldn't the blow be less painful?"

He finally understood. His wink was slow, his grin arrogant. "I shall go and ask Colin and Nathan to join you now," Jade announced before she left the room. The door closed softly behind her.

"What was she talking about?" Richards asked.

"A personal matter," Caine answered. He turned to Lyon then. "Well? What do you think of her now?"

His friend refilled his goblet with more brandy before he answered. "She's still damned beautiful," he said. "But I'm once again thinking she's awfully timid. Must come from being around you."

Caine laughed. "You're back to thinking she's timid?"

"What am I missing, Caine?" Lyon asked, genuinely perplexed. "What's the jest you find so amusing?"

"Put aside this talk about women," Richards ordered. "Now, son, you must promise me something."

"Sir?" Caine asked.

"Have you actually met this Pagan fellow?"

"I have."

"When this is finished, you must find a way for me to meet him."

Caine leaned back in his chair. Jade had been right. She had just given him his pride back.

"I must meet Pagan," Sir Richards demanded again.

Caine nodded. "Sir Richards, you just did."

294

Chapter Fifteen

J ade, come back here." Caine shouted that order while his two friends were trying to absorb the news he'd just given them.

When she didn't respond to his summons, Caine called for Sterns. The butler must have been standing right outside the door, for he immediately rushed inside the library. He bowed to his employer, a courtesy he never ever extended when they were alone, and then asked, "You wished something, mi'lord?"

"Bring Jade back here," Caine ordered.

"I believe she heard your bellow, mi'lord," Sterns announced in that highbrow voice of his, "She has declined the invitation to rejoin you, however. Was there something more you wanted?"

Caine wanted to strangle Sterns, but he pushed the notion aside. "Bring her to me. Drag her in here if you have to, but bring her to me. That's what I want, Sterns."

The butler nodded, then left on his errand. Caine turned back to his friends. He lost some of his irritation when he saw Lyon's grin. His friend seemed to be taking the news of Pagan's identity much better than Sir Richards was. The director still looked quite stunned.

"Hell, Caine, I should have guessed," Lyon said. "She was so timid . . . yes, I should have known, all right. You aren't one to be attracted to . . . and Christina did say that I should look below the . . ."

"Son," Sir Richards interrupted Lyon's rambling. "This isn't the time for jests. We've a serious matter here."

Jade opened the door in the middle of Richards' protests. "I was fetching Nathan and Colin for you, Caine. What is it you wanted?"

"Give them back, Jade."

His voice had the bite of a pistol shot in it. Jade pretended innocence. "Whatever are you talking about?" she asked. She pressed her hand to her bosom in mock fear and fluttered her eyelashes at him.

He wasn't at all impressed. "You know damned good and well what I'm talking about," he roared. "Give them back."

"Caine, it isn't polite to raise your voice to me in front of visitors," she instructed. Her voice had risen an octave. "It's plain rude."

"They know who you are."

"They know?"

She marched over to the front of his desk and glared at him. Her hands were planted on her hips now. "Exactly what do they know?"

"That you're Pagan."

She let out a gasp. "Why don't you just post it in the dailies?" she shouted. "Then you wouldn't have to spend so much time . . ."

"I had to tell them," Caine interjected.

"You could have waited until after I'd left."

"Since you aren't leaving, that wasn't possible, now was it?"

"My God, it's really true?" Richards interjected in a near shout of his own.

Jade glanced over her shoulder to frown at the director. "No," she snapped. "It isn't true."

"Yes," Caine countered. "It is."

"Damn it, Caine, don't you know how to keep a secret?" She didn't give him time to answer that question but turned to leave.

"I told you to give them back, Jade."

"Why?"

"These men happen to be my friends," he answered. "That's why."

"Caine, if you can't rob from your friends, who *can* you rob?" she asked.

He didn't have a ready answer to that absurd question.

"You did say it was all right for me to continue my work," she reminded him. "Have you already gone back on your word?"

He couldn't believe she had the audacity to look so outraged. Caine didn't dare stand up, certain the urge to grab her and try to shake some sense into her would be too overwhelming to ignore.

Jade turned to look at Lyon. "When I give my word, I never break it," she stated.

Caine took a deep breath, then leaned back in his chair. He stared at Jade long and hard.

She glared back.

With the crook of his finger, he motioned her closer. When she'd reached his side, he said, "I meant what I said. You may continue with your work."

She was totally perplexed. "Then why are you making such a fuss over . . ."

"You may continue to rob," he interrupted. "But every time you take something, I'm going to give it back."

Her gasp nearly knocked her over. "You won't."

"I will."

"But that's . . . ridiculous," she stammered. "Isn't it?"

He didn't answer her. Jade looked over at Lyon for help. His grin told her she wouldn't be getting any assistance from him. Sir Richards was still looking too flabbergasted to intervene.

She was on her own, she decided, just as she'd always been. "No."

"Yes."

She looked as though she wanted to weep. "Now give them their . . ."

"I switched them," she announced. "May I leave now?"

Caine nodded. He waited until Jade had reached the door, then called out, "Jade, you may leave this room, but don't you dare try to leave this house. I'll only come after you if you do. You wouldn't want to inconvenience me again, now would you?"

She didn't answer that question. Caine knew she was furious with him, though. The door almost flew off its hinges when she slammed it shut behind her.

"She's got a bit of a temper," Caine announced. His grin suggested he didn't mind that flaw much at all. "Have you recovered yet, Richards?" he asked then.

"I have," Richards agreed.

"But you never once considered . . ."

"No, no," Richards returned.

Caine nodded with satisfaction. "It's good to know my own superior was taken in. I do believe my pride has been fully restored."

Nathan and Colin walked into the library then. Colin used his cane and Nathan's arm for assistance.

"Quit treating me like an infant," Colin muttered, as Nathan helped him ease into a chair.

"You are an infant," Nathan drawled out. He pushed a footstool in front of the chair, then propped Colin's foot on it.

Nathan stood to take his measure of the two men watching him. Caine made the introductions. He shook their hands, then sat on the arm of Colin's chair.

"Jade wants me to ask you what time it is," Nathan stated then.

The director looked puzzled by that request, then shrugged. "I'd say it was going on nine, wouldn't you, Lyon?"

Lyon was more astute than his superior. He lifted the timepiece from his waist pocket. He laughed then, a full booming sound that filled the room. "I believe this one is yours, Richards. You have mine. She did embrace both of us."

Richards was duly impressed. "I certainly misjudged her," he announced. "You saw her make the switch, didn't you, Caine. That's why you called her back."

Caine shook his head. "No, I didn't," he admitted. "But when she embraced each of you, I knew she was up to something. She doesn't usually show such affection to strangers."

"No, she doesn't," Nathan agreed.

Caine looked at Lyon. "The woman has led me in circles. She's determined to make me a madman."

"I'd say she's already accomplished that goal," Nathan drawled out.

"This sounds familiar to me," Lyon said. He smiled, remembering the bizarre circumstances leading up to his marriage. "I've been led in a few circles by Christina, too. Tell me this, Caine. What did you do while she was leading you?"

"Same thing you did," Caine answered. "I fell in love with her."

Lyon nodded. "God help you now, friend. It isn't going to get any easier after you've married her. When is the wedding, by the way?"

"Yes, Caine, when *is* the wedding?" Nathan demanded.

"There damned well will be a wedding." Colin made that statement of fact. He was frowning intently at his brother.

"Yes," Caine answered. "There will be a wedding."

"Sounds to me as if you don't have any choice, son," Sir Richards interjected. "Will you say your vows with a pistol aimed at your back?"

"If a pistol is needed, it will be aimed at Jade's back, not mine," Caine countered. "I still have to convince her that I mean what I say. Hell, I'll probably even have to get down on one knee in front of her men."

Even Nathan smiled over that picture. Colin scoffed. "Jade won't make you kneel before her," he said.

"No, but Black Harry sure as hell will," Caine replied.

"Who is Black Harry?" Richards asked.

"Nathan, you start explaining," Caine announced. "While I go after Jade."

"She's gone?" Nathan asked.

Caine stood up and started for the door. "Of course she's gone. I never make the same mistake twice, Nathan. I'll be back soon."

Since Caine was already wearing his riding britches and boots, he went directly to the corral housing the horses.

The speckled mare was missing. "How many men do you have trailing her?" he asked the stablemaster.

"Three at the back door chased after her," the servant answered.

Caine bridled his stallion but didn't bother with the saddle. He grabbed hold of the black mane and mounted the steed in one quick motion.

He trailed her to the cabin on the edge of his property. She was standing next to the creek, watering her horse.

Caine broke through the trees, then goaded his mount into a full gallop. Jade heard the sound of pounding hooves. She turned to run into the woods. Caine's stallion never broke stride as he leaned down and lifted her into his arms. He slammed her bottom down in front of him, turned direction and headed back toward home.

He didn't say a word to her, nor she to him, and he didn't slow his pace until they'd reached their destination.

Sterns was waiting at the front door. Caine dragged Jade up the steps. "Lock her in her room!" he roared. "Post two guards below her windows and two more outside the door."

He didn't let go of Jade until he'd dragged her inside the house and bolted the door behind him.

He kept his expression as ugly as he could manage until he was once again inside the library. When he was back in his chair behind his desk, he let himself smile.

"I assume you found her," Nathan said.

"I did," Caine answered. "Impressed the hell out of her, too. Now catch me up on what you've told my friends," he ordered.

The talk returned to the letters and the men didn't finish formulating their plans until well past eleven. Richards and Lyon were given chambers in the North wing. Both appeared to be reluctant to say goodnight.

Richards insisted on taking the copies of the letters to bed with him. "There's information still to be ferreted out," he announced.

No one argued with the director. Caine went directly to Jade's room. He dismissed the guards, unlocked the door, and went inside.

Jade was reading in bed. She wouldn't look at him, but kept her gaze on the book she held in her hands.

"You need more light if you're going to read," Caine announced. "The fire needs to be stoked, too. It's damned cold in here."

She didn't even look up at him. "It's ridiculous to pretend I'm not here," he told her, his exasperation obvious in his tone.

"As ridiculous as giving back everything I take?" she countered, her attention focused on her book.

Caine added two more candles to the bedside table. He went to the hearth next. "Where's Sterns?" he asked.

"Sterns has gone to bed," she answered. "You'd make a good butler, Caine. Your man has trained you well."

He didn't jump to the bait. "You're spoiling for a fight, sweetheart, but I'm not going to accommodate you."

"I'm not spoiling for a fight," she snapped. She slammed her book shut while she watched him add another fat log to the embers.

In the firelight, his skin looked as bronzed as a statue. His shirt was opened to the waist, his sleeves rolled up to his elbows. The fabric was stretched tight across the back of his shoulders, showing the splay of muscle there when he reached for the iron staff to prod the fire into a full blaze.

She thought he was the most appealing man in all the world.

Caine turned, still bent on one knee, and smiled at her. The tenderness in his gaze tugged at her heart. He was such a good man, a trusting man, a loving man.

He deserved better than the likes of her. Why didn't he realize that obvious fact?

Tears welled up in her eyes and she started trembling. It was as though the blankets had suddenly turned into snow. She was freezing . . . and terrified.

Don't ever let me leave you, she suddenly thought. Make me stay with you forever.

Oh, God, how she wanted to love him, to lean on him.

And then what would she become, she asked herself, when he left her. How in God's name would she survive?

The change in her was startling. Her face had turned the color of her white nightgown.

"Sweetheart, what's the matter?" he asked. He stood up and walked toward the bed.

"Nothing," she whispered. "Nothing's wrong. I'm just cold," she added in a stammer. And afraid, she wanted to add. "Come to bed, Caine."

She desperately needed to hold him close. Jade added to the invitation by pulling the covers back for him. Caine ignored her request. He went to the wardrobe, found another blanket on the top shelf, then draped it over the other covers on the bed.

"Is that better?" he asked.

"Yes, thank you," she answered, trying not to sound too disgruntled.

"If you aren't too tired, I want to ask you a few questions," he said.

"Ask your questions in bed, Caine," she suggested. "You'll be more comfortable."

He shook his head, then sat down in the chair and propped his feet up on the foot of the bed. "This will do," he said then, trying his damnedest not to smile.

She wanted him, perhaps even as much as he wanted her. And by God, she was going to have to tell him so.

Jade tried to hide her irritation. The man was as dense as rain. Didn't he realize she wanted to be held? She'd told him she was cold, damn it. He should have immediately taken her into his arms, then kissed her of course, and then . . .

She let out a long sigh. Caine apparently didn't realize what she needed when he started in with his questions about the stupid files again.

It took all her determination to hold onto her concentration. She had to stare at her hands so his heart-stopping smile wouldn't detract her.

"Jade?"

"Yes?" She looked startled.

"I just asked you if you read the files on our Williams," he said.

"They aren't our Williams," she replied.

She gave him an expectant smile, waiting for his next question.

Caine's smile widened. "Are you going to answer me?" he asked.

"Answer what?"

"You seem preoccupied."

"I'm not."

"Sleepy then?"

"Not at all."

"Then answer my question," he instructed again. "Did you read the files . . ."

"Yes," she interrupted. "You want to hear them, don't you?"

"Yes, I do," he answered. "Was there something else you wanted to do?" he asked.

The blush came back to her cheekbones. "No, of course not," she answered. "All right, Caine, I'll tell you . . ."

A knock sounded at the door, interrupting them. Caine turned just as Nathan peeked inside.

When Jade's brother saw Caine lounging in the chair, he frowned. "What are you doing here, Caine?"

"Talking to Jade," Caine answered. "What do you want?"

"I couldn't sleep," Nathan admitted. He strode over to the hearth and leaned against it. Nathan was barefoot and shirtless now. Caine saw the scars on Nathan's back, of course. He didn't mention them, but he wondered how Nathan could have survived such a beating.

"Here's Caine's robe, if you're cold, Nathan," Jade said. She pointed to the empty chair on the other side of the bed. "You'll catch a chill if you don't cover up."

Nathan was in an accommodating mood. He put Caine's robe on, then sprawled out in the chair.

"Go back to bed, Nathan," Caine ordered.

"I want to ask my sister a couple of questions."

Nathan had left the door opened. For that reason, Sir Richards didn't bother to knock when he reached the room. The director was dressed in a royal blue robe that reached his bare feet. He looked positively thrilled to see the gathering.

Jade pulled the covers up to her chin. She looked at Caine to see his reaction to this invasion.

He looked resigned. "Pull up a chair, Sir Richards," Caine suggested.

"Be happy to," Richards replied. He smiled at Jade then. "I couldn't sleep, you see, and so I thought I'd look in on you and . . ."

"If she was awake, you were going to question her," Caine guessed.

"This isn't at all proper," Richards said as he dragged a chair close to the bed. His chuckle indicated he didn't mind that fact at all. "Nathan?" he added then. "Would you mind fetching Lyon for us? By now he'll have a few questions of his own."

"He might be sleeping," Jade said.

"I could hear him pacing in the chamber next to mine. This Tribunal has us all rattled, my dear. It's quite a lot to take in."

Nathan returned with Lyon by his side. Jade suddenly felt ridiculous. She was in bed, after all, and dressed only in her nightgown. "Why don't we go down to the library to discuss this?" she suggested. "I'll get dressed and . . ."

"This will do," Caine announced. "Lyon, Jade's going to give us the files on the Williams."

"Do I have to repeat every word, Caine?" she asked. "It will take days."

"Start with just the pertinent facts," Richards suggested. "Lyon and I are going back to London tomorrow. We'll read the files from start to finish then."

Jade shrugged. "I'll start with Terrance then," she announced. "The dead one."

"Yes, the dead one," Lyon agreed. He leaned against the mantel and smiled encouragement.

Jade leaned back against the pillows and began her recitation.

Lyon and Richards were duly impressed. When they got over their initial astonishment, they took turns interrupting her to ask specific details on certain missions William Terrance was involved in.

She didn't finish with the file until two in the morning. She couldn't quit yawning either, a hint of the exhaustion she was feeling.

"It's time we all took to our beds," Sir Richards announced. "We'll start in again come morning."

The director was following Lyon and Nathan out of the room when Jade called out to him. "Sir Richards? What if the William you're looking for isn't one of the three in the files?"

Richards turned back to her. "It's just a starting place, my dear," he explained. "Then we begin the cross-check, read through each and every file the superiors in every department kept. It will take time, yes, but we will persevere until we get to the bottom of this."

"There couldn't be a chance they're both dead now?" Jade asked.

She looked so hopeful, Richards hated to disappoint her. "I'm afraid not," he said. "Someone wants those letters, dear. At least one of the two remaining members of the Tribunal is still very much alive."

Jade was relieved to be alone with Caine again. She was exhausted, worried, too, and all she wanted was for him to take her into his arms and hold her close. She pulled back the covers for Caine, then patted the sheet.

"Goodnight, Jade," Caine said. He walked over to the bed, leaned down, and gave her a horribly chaste kiss, then blew out the candles on his way to the door. "Pleasant dreams, sweetheart."

The door closed. She was astonished he'd left her.

He didn't want her any longer. The thought was so repugnant to her, she pushed it aside. He was just angry with her still because he'd had to chase after her again, she told herself . . . he was tired, too, she added with a nod. It had been a long, exhausting day.

Damn it, the man was suppose to be reliable.

She didn't have pleasant dreams. She was drowning in the blackness, could feel the monsters circling her as she went down, down, down . . .

Her own whimpers awakened her. She instinctively turned to Caine, knowing he'd soothe away her terror.

He wasn't there. She was wide awake by the time she'd made that determination, and shaking so much she could barely get the covers out of her way.

She couldn't stay in bed, but went to the window and stared out at the starless night while she contemplated her bleak situation.

She didn't know how long she stood there, worrying and fretting, before she finally gave in. She was going to have to go to him.

Caine woke up as soon as the door opened. Since it was dark, he didn't have to hide his smile. "I don't know how to dance, Caine," she announced.

She slammed the door shut after making that statement, then walked over to his side of the bed. "You might as well know that right off. I can't do needlework, either."

He was resting on his back with his eyes closed. Jade stared at him a long minute, then prodded his shoulder. "Well?" she demanded.

Caine answered her by pulling the covers back. Jade pulled off her nightgown and fell into bed beside him. He immediately took her into his arms.

The shivers vanished. She felt safe again. Jade fell asleep waiting for Caine to answer her.

He woke her up a little past dawn to make love to her, and when he was done having his way with her and she having her way with him, she was too sleepy to talk to him. She fell asleep listening to him tell her how much he loved her.

The next time she was nudged awake, it was almost noon.

Caine was doing the nudging. He was fully dressed and sweetly demanding she open her eyes and wake up.

She refused to open her eyes, but tried to kick the covers away and make him come back to bed. Caine insisted on holding the covers up to her chin. She didn't understand why he was being so contrary until she finally opened her eyes and saw Sterns standing at the foot of her bed.

She took over the task of shielding her nakedness then. Jade could feel her face turning crimson. It would be pointless to try to bluster her way through this embarrassment. "Oh, Sterns, now you're ashamed of me, aren't you?"

The question came out in a wail. Sterns immediately shook his head. "Of course not, mi'lady," he announced. "I'm certain my employer dragged you into his bed," he added with a nod in Caine's direction.

"By her hair, Sterns?" Caine asked dryly.

"I wouldn't put it past you, mi'lord."

"He did," Jade announced, deciding to let Caine take all the blame. "You mustn't tell anyone," she added.

Sterns' smile was gentle. "I'm afraid there isn't anyone left to tell."

"Do you mean Sir Richards and Lyon know?"

When Sterns nodded, she turned to glare up at Caine. "You told them, didn't you? Why don't you just post that in the dailies too?"

"I didn't tell," Caine countered, his exasperation obvious. "You didn't shut your door when you . . ." He paused to look at Sterns, then said, "When I dragged you in here. They noticed the empty bed on their way downstairs."

She wanted to hide under the covers for the rest of the day.

"Jade? Why is my silver under my bed?"

"Ask Sterns," she said. "He put it there."

"It seemed an appropriate place, mi'lord," Sterns announced. "One of your guests, the big man with the gold tooth, certainly would have taken a liking to the silver.

Mi'lady suggested a safe haven for the pieces once I'd explained their special meaning to you."

She thought he might thank her for saving his treasures. He laughed instead. "Come downstairs as soon as you're dressed, Jade. Richards wants to start questioning you again."

Sterns didn't leave the room with his employer. "The Duchess has sent over several gowns belonging to one of her daughters. I believe the fit will be close, mi'lady."

"Why would she . . ."

"I requested the clothing," Sterns announced. "When I was unpacking your belongings, I couldn't help but notice there were only two gowns."

She looked as though she were going to protest, but Sterns didn't give her time. "The selection is hanging in the wardrobe. Cook will act as your lady's maid. I shall go and fetch her immediately."

It wouldn't do her any good to argue with him. Sterns had turned from butler to commander. He selected the garment she'd wear, too—a deep, ivory-colored gown with lace-embroidered cuffs. The gown was so elegant looking, Jade couldn't resist.

There were undergarments as well. Though Sterns didn't make mention of them, he put the silk treasures on the foot of her bed, next to the thin-as-air stockings and matching ivory-colored shoes.

Jade was washed and dressed in the finery a scant fifteen minutes later. She sat in a straight-backed chair while Cook pulled on her hair. The elderly woman was tall and rotund. Her salt and pepper hair had been clipped into short, bobbing curls. She attacked Jade's hair as if it were a side of beef. Still, Jade would have put up with the mild discomfort for the rest of the day if it would put off having to face Lyon and Sir Richards again.

The meeting couldn't be avoided, however. "You're a looker, you are," the servant announced when she'd finished her task. She held up a hand mirror and gave it to Jade. "It's a simple braid, but those little wisps of curls along the sides of your face soften the look. I would have put it up in clusters atop your head, mi'lady, but I fear the weight would have toppled you over."

"Thank you so much," Jade replied. "You've done a splendid job."

Cook nodded, then hurried back downstairs. The meeting couldn't be avoided any longer. Caine would only come and fetch her if she stayed closeted in his room. When Jade opened the door, she was surprised and irritated to find two guards in the hallway. Both men looked a little undone by the sight of her. Then one stammered out what a fair picture she was. The other blurted out that she looked just like a queen.

Both guards followed her downstairs. The dining room doors were closed. The bigger of the two men rushed ahead to see them opened for her. Jade thanked the man for his consideration, then straightened her shoulders and walked inside.

Everyone was seated at the long table, including Sterns. And everyone, including the rascal butler, was staring at her.

All but Colin stood up when she entered the room. Jade kept her gaze on Caine. When he moved to pull out the chair adjacent to his, she slowly walked over to his side.

He leaned down and kissed her brow. Nathan broke the horrid silence. "Get your hands off her, Caine."

"My hands aren't on her, Nathan," Caine drawled out. "My mouth is." He kissed Jade again just to goad her brother. Jade fell into the chair with a sigh.

Sterns saw to her breakfast while the men continued their discussion. Sir Richards sat at one end of the long table, Caine at the other. When her plate had been taken away, Sir Richards called everyone to attention. She realized then that they had all been waiting for her.

"My dear, we've decided that you must come to London

with us," Sir Richards announced. "We'll keep the security tight," he added with a glance in Caine's direction.

Richards then pulled the pen and ink well close. "I'd like to make a few notes while I question you," he explained.

"Sir? Why must I come to London?" Jade asked.

The director looked a little sheepish now. Lyon, Jade noticed, was grinning.

"Well, now," Richards began. "We need to get in the file room. If I request the keys during working hours, my name will have to go into the entry book."

"They want to go during the night," Colin interjected. "Without keys."

"You did say you'd broken into the building once and read the files," Richards reminded her.

"Three times," Jade interjected.

Sir Richards looked as if he wanted to cry. "Is our security so puny then?" he asked Lyon.

"Apparently," Lyon returned.

"Oh, no," Jade said. "The security is very good."

"Then how . . ." Richards began.

Caine answered. "She's better than good, Richards."

Jade blushed over the compliment. "Sir Richards, I understand your need for secrecy. You don't want the Tribunal knowing you're hunting them, but I believe they probably know already. They've sent men here. Surely they saw you and Lyon arrive and reported back . . ."

"No one who was sent by the Tribunal has returned to report to anyone," Lyon explained.

"But how . . ."

"Caine took care of them."

Jade's eyes widened over Lyon's statement. He sounded so certain. She turned to look at Caine. "How did you take care of them?"

Caine shook his head at Lyon when he thought his friend might explain. "You don't need to know," he told Jade.

"You didn't kill them, did you?" she whispered.

She looked frightened.

"No."

Jade nodded, then turned to look at Lyon again. She noticed his exasperated expression but decided to ignore it. "He didn't kill them," she announced. "Caine doesn't do that sort of thing any longer. He's retired."

She seemed to want Lyon's agreement. He nodded, then knew his guess had been correct when she smiled at him.

"Jade?" Colin asked, drawing her attention. "You can stay with Christina and Lyon when you reach London. Caine will stay in his town house, of course . . ."

"No," Caine interrupted. "She stays with me."

"Think of the scandal," Colin argued.

"It's almost summer, Colin," Caine countered. "Most of the *ton* is away from London now."

"It only takes one witness," Colin muttered.

"I've said no, Colin. She stays with me."

His hard voice didn't suggest his brother continue the argument. Colin sighed, then reluctantly nodded agreement.

Jade wasn't certain she understood. "What did you mean by one witness?"

Colin explained. Jade looked appalled by the time he'd finished telling her the damage that could be done by one malicious gossiper. Sterns sat down next to Jade, patted her hand, and said, "Do look on the bright side, mi'lady. Mi'lord won't have to post it in the dailies now."

She turned to glare him into silence. Sterns couldn't be intimidated, though. He squeezed her hand. "Do not fret, dear lady. It has all been arranged."

She didn't know what he was talking about but his grin suggested he was up to something. Sterns turned her attention, however, by arrogantly motioning to his empty tea cup. She immediately went to fetch a fresh urn.

As soon as she'd left the room, Sterns turned to Caine. "Your guests should be arriving in half an hour's time."

"Guests? We can't be having any bloody guests," Colin bellowed.

Nathan nodded. "Damned right we can't. Caine, are you out of your mind to invite . . ."

Caine was staring at Sterns. "I didn't invite anyone," he said. A hint of a smile turned his expression. "Why don't you tell us who these guests are, Sterns?"

Everyone was staring at the elderly man as though he'd just grown another head. "I have taken the liberty of inviting your parents, Jade's uncle and cohorts, and one additional guest."

"What the hell for?" Nathan demanded.

Sterns turned to smile at him. "The ceremony, of course."

Everyone turned to look at Caine. His expression didn't tell them anything.

"The license, Sterns?" Caine asked in a blasé tone of voice.

"Secured the day after you signed the request," Sterns answered.

"Isn't this man your butler, Caine?" Sir Richards asked.

Caine wasn't given time to answer that question, for Nathan blurted out, "She'll argue fierce."

Colin agreed. "I don't think Jade has come to terms with her future just yet."

"I'll persuade her," Caine announced. He leaned back in his chair and smiled at his butler. "You've done well, Sterns. I commend you."

"Of course I've done well," Sterns agreed. "I've seen to everything," he boasted.

"Oh?" Nathan asked. "Then tell us how Caine's going to convince Jade?"

In answer to that question, Sterns removed the empty pistol he'd concealed in his waistband. He dropped the weapon in the center of the table.

Everyone stared at the pistol until Sterns broke the silence again. He addressed his remarks to Richards. "I believe I overheard you suggesting the pistol be aimed at Lady Jade's shoulders, or was I mistaken?"

The laughter was deafening. Jade stood at the door, the urn in her hands while she waited for the men to calm down.

She then poured Sterns his tea, put the urn on the sideboard, and returned to her seat. She noticed the pistol in the center of the table, but when she asked what it was doing there, she couldn't get a decent answer. The men had all started laughing again.

No one would explain. Jade guessed someone had told a bawdy jest and they were too embarrassed to share it with her.

Jade was ready to return to their plans. Caine surprised her by suggesting she return to her room.

"Why?" she asked. "I thought we were going . . ."

"You need to pack your things," Caine said.

Jade nodded. "You just want to tell more of your jests," she announced before she took her leave.

They were all smiling at her like happy thieves looking over their booty. She didn't know what to make of that. The two guards were waiting for her in the foyer. They helped her carry the gowns Sterns had placed in Caine's wardrobe down to her chambers, then waited outside in the hall while she packed.

When she was finished with her task, she sat down by the window and began reading the book she'd only half finished two nights ago.

A short time later, there was a timid knock on the door. Jade closed her book and stood up just as Black Harry came into the room.

She was clearly astonished to see him. Her uncle was carrying a dozen long-stemmed white roses. "These are for you, girl," he announced as he shoved the bouquet into her arms.

"Thank you, Uncle," she replied. "But what are you doing here? I thought you were going to wait for me at the cottage?"

Harry kissed her on the top of her head. "You look fit,

Pagan," he muttered, completely ignoring her question. "Caine should be wearing my clothes this proud day."

"Why should Caine wear your clothes?" she asked, thoroughly confused now. She'd never seen her uncle act so nervous. He looked terribly worried, too.

"Because my shirt is the very color of your pretty gown," Harry explained.

"But what does . . ."

"I'll be telling it in my own good time," Harry blurted out. He hugged her close, squishing the flowers in the process, then stepped back. "Caine asked me if he could wed you, girl."

Harry took another precautionary step back after making his announcement, fully expecting an explosion. He got a dainty shrug instead. He noticed, though, that she was gripping the flowers tightly. "Watch for thorns, girl," he ordered.

"What did you tell him, Uncle?" she asked.

"He asked me real proper," Harry rushed out. "I could have had him down on one knee," he added with a nod. "He said he would, if it be needed to win my permission. He said it loud and clear right in front of me men, he did."

"But what did you tell him?" she asked again.

"I said yes."

He took another hasty step back after telling her that. She shrugged again, then walked over to the side of the bed and sat down. She put the bouquet of roses on the coverlet beside her.

"Why aren't you getting your temper up, girl?" Harry asked. He rubbed his jaw while he studied her. "Caine said you might be resistant to the notion. Ain't you angry?"

"No."

"Then what is it?" he demanded. He clasped his hands behind his back while he tried to guess her reasons. "You care for this man, don't you?"

"I do."

315

"Well then?" he prodded.

"I'm afraid, Uncle."

Her voice had been a bare whisper. Harry heard her but was so astonished by her admission, he didn't know what to say. "You're not," he stammered.

"I am."

He shook his head. "You ain't never been afraid of anything before." His voice was gruff with affection. He went to the bed, sat down beside her on top of the flowers, and awkwardly put his arm around her shoulders. "What's different now?"

Oh, yes, she wanted to shout, I've been afraid before . . . so many times, so many near mishaps, she'd lost count. She couldn't tell him, of course, for if she did, he'd think he'd failed her.

"It's different because I'll have to give up my work," she said instead.

"You know it's time, what with me retiring and all," he countered. "I've hid it from me men, girl, but my eyes, well, I ain't seeing as proper as I used to. They'll balk at following a blind pirate."

"Then who will they follow?" she asked.

"Nathan."

"Nathan?"

"He wants the *Emerald*. It belonged to his father, after all, and he has that little business to take care of. He'll make a fine pirate, girl. He's learned how to be real mean."

"Yes, he would make a good pirate," she admitted. "But Uncle Harry, I can't be the kind of woman Caine wants."

"You are the woman he wants."

"I'll make so many mistakes," she whispered. She was on the verge of tears and was valiantly trying to keep her emotions controlled for Harry's sake. "I don't know how to do all the things a proper wife should know how to do. I'm no good with a needle, Harry."

"Aye, you're not," Harry admitted bleakly, remembering the time she tried to mend his sock and stitched it to her gown.

"I can't dance," she added. She looked so forlorn when she'd made that confession, Harry threw his arm around her shoulder and hugged her. "All the fine ladies of the *ton* know how to dance," she ended on a wail.

"You'll learn," Harry predicted. "If you want to learn."

"Oh, yes," she admitted in a rush. "I've always wanted . . ."

Now she sounded wistful. Harry didn't know what was going on inside her mind. "What?" he asked. "What have you always wanted?"

"To belong."

The look on his face indicated he didn't understand what she was talking about.

"Are you wishing now I'd given you to Lady Briars? She would have taken you, girl. Why, she fought me something fierce for you, too. She's the reason we snuck off real quiet-like right after your father's funeral. I guessed she'd come back with the authorities and try and steal you away from me. I weren't your legal guardian, if you'll remember. Still, your papa wanted you to get away from England."

"You kept your word to my father," she interjected. "You were very honorable."

"But are you wishing now I wasn't so honorable back then?"

She shook her head. For the first time in all their days together, she was seeing Harry's vulnerability. "I cannot imagine my life without you, Harry. I would never wish that things had been different. You loved me as though I were your very own daughter."

Harry's arm dropped to his side. He looked dejected. She put her arm around his shoulders, trying now to comfort him. "Uncle, Lady Briars would have taught me all the rules, yes, but she couldn't have loved me the way you did. Besides, you taught me far more important rules. You taught me how to survive."

Harry was quick to perk up. "I did," he admitted with a grin. "You had the makings though. I've never seen such a natural thief or a born liar in all my days. I'm right proud of you, girl."

"Thank you, Uncle," she replied, blushing over his praise. Harry wasn't one to give idle compliments and she knew he spoke from his heart.

His expression soured, however, when he returned to her initial remark. "Yet you didn't think you belonged? You did say you wanted to belong, girl."

"I meant to be a proper wife," she lied. "That's what I meant by belonging now."

"You weren't speaking plain enough, girl," Harry announced. He looked relieved. "As for me, I've always wanted to be a grandpapa."

She started to blush. "I don't know how to have babies either," she wailed.

Harry had meant to lighten her mood. He realized he'd taken the wrong approach. "Hell, no woman knows how until the time comes, girl. Tell me this. Do you love Caine? He says you do."

She skirted his question. "What if he gets tired of me? He'll leave me then, Harry," she whispered. "I know he will."

"He won't."

"He needs time to realize . . ." She paused in midsentence. "That's it, Harry. If the courtship is long enough, perhaps he'll realize he's made a mistake." She smiled then. "And during that time, in case he isn't making a mistake, I could try to learn all that would be required of me. Yes, Uncle, that's it. Caine's being very honorable now, trying to do the right thing . . ."

"Well, now, girl," Harry interrupted. "About this lengthy courtship plan . . ."

"Oh, Harry, that is the only answer," she interrupted. "I'll insist on a year. I'll wager he'll agree right off."

She was so pleased with her decision, she rushed out of the room. Harry adjusted his ill-fitting spectacles on the bridge of his nose, grabbed the bouquet and tucked it under his arm, and chased after her.

"Wait up," he bellowed.

"I must talk to Caine at once," she called over her shoulder. "I'm certain he's going to agree."

"I'm just as certain he ain't going to agree," Harry muttered. "Girl, hold fast. There's still a bit of the telling I have to do."

She'd already reached the foyer by the time Harry reached the landing above. "They're in the drawing room," her uncle shouted as he lumbered down the stairs.

Jade came to an abrupt stop when she opened the doors and saw the gathering. Harry caught up with her and forced her hand on his arm. "We're doing this proper, girl," he whispered.

"Why are all these people here?" she asked. She looked at the group, recognized everyone but the short, partially bald-headed man standing by the French doors. He held a book in his hand and was in deep conversation with the Duke and Duchess of Williamshire.

Caine was standing by the hearth, talking to Lyon. He must have sensed her presence, for he suddenly turned in midsentence and looked at her.

His expression was solemn.

He knew at once by her puzzled expression she didn't understand what was going on. Caine braced himself for the fireworks he was sure were about to erupt, then walked over to face Jade.

"I ain't had time to finish explaining," Harry said.

"I can see you haven't," Caine interjected. "Jade, sweet, we're going . . ."

"I'll be telling it," Harry insisted.

He clasped Jade's hand flat on his arm so her nails wouldn't do injury, then said, "There ain't going to be a year's courtship, girl."

She continued to stare up at him with that innocent, angelic gaze. Harry tightened his hold on her hand. "But there's going to be a wedding."

She was beginning to understand, Harry guessed, when he noticed her eyes were turning the color of emeralds again.

She was trying to tug her hand away. Harry held tight. "When is this wedding?" she asked in a hoarse whisper.

Harry grimaced before answering. "Now."

She opened her mouth to shout her denial, but Caine moved closer, blocking her view from the audience. "We can do this the easy way, Jade, or the hard way. You call it."

She shut her mouth and glared up at him. Caine could see how frightened she was. She was in a near panic. She was actually shaking. "The easy way is for you to walk over to the minister and recite your vows."

"And the hard way?" Jade asked.

"I drag you over there by your hair," Caine told her. He made sure he looked as if he were up to that task, too. "Either way, I win. We are getting married."

"Caine . . ."

The fear in her voice tore at his heart. "Decide," he ordered, his voice hard. "Easy or hard?"

"I won't let you leave me," she whispered. "I won't! I'll leave you first."

"What are you stammering about, girl?" Harry asked.

"Jade? Which is it?" Caine demanded again, ignoring both her protest and Harry's interference.

Her shoulders sagged. "Easy."

He nodded.

"I'll be walking her over to the preacher man," Harry announced. "Nathan," he called out. "You can trail behind."

"In just a minute," Caine ordered.

While Jade stood there trembling with panic and Harry stood there giving the Duchess downright lecherous looks, Caine went over to the minister and spoke to him. When he was finished, he handed a piece of paper to the man.

All was finally ready. Colin stood up at his brother's side, supported by Caine's arm. Jade stood beside Caine. Harry had to support her.

Jade repeated her vows first, a breach from tradition Caine had insisted upon. He stared at his bride while he repeated each of his vows. He let her keep her gaze downcast until he reached the end of the litany. Then he tilted her chin up and forced her to look at him.

She looked so scared, so vulnerable. Her eyes glistened with tears. He loved her so much. He wanted to give her the world. But first he had to gain her trust in him.

The minister closed his book, opened the sheet of paper in his hand, and began to read. "Do you promise to stay with your wife for as long as you shall live? Do you give your word before God and these witnesses that you will never leave her until death do you part?"

Her eyes had widened during the minister's questions. She turned and saw the paper he was holding.

"I do," Caine whispered when Jade turned back to him. "And now the last," Caine directed the minister.

"This is highly irregular," the minister whispered. He turned to address Jade. "And do you promise to tell your husband you love him before this day is out?"

Her smile was radiant. "I do," she promised.

"You may kiss the bride," the minister announced.

Caine happily obliged. When he lifted his head, he said, "You're mine now."

He pulled her into his arms and hugged her tight. "I never make the same mistake twice, sweetheart," he whispered.

"I don't understand, Caine," she replied. She was still on the verge of tears and was desperately trying to maintain her composure. "Then why didn't you have the minister make me promise not to leave you? Don't you believe I'd honor my vows?"

"Once you give your word, I know you won't break it," he answered her. "But you have to give it freely. When you're ready, you'll tell me."

He wasn't given any more time to talk to her, for the crowd of well-wishers moved in on them to offer their congratulations.

Harry stood in the corner with his men, dabbing at his eyes with the edge of his sash. Caine's mother seemed genuinely happy to have Jade in the family. Of course she didn't know her new daughter-in-law was a common thief, Jade reminded herself.

"Will your uncle be visiting you often?" Gweneth asked after giving Harry a quick glance.

"He lives a fair distance from England," Jade explained. "He'll probably come just once a year."

Caine heard the last of Jade's explanation, saw his mother's quick relief, and started to laugh. "My mother's a little nervous around your uncle," he said.

"Oh, you shouldn't be," Jade countered. "Harry is really a very kind man. Perhaps if you got to know him better . . ."

Caine's mother looked absolutely appalled by that suggestion. Jade didn't know what to make of that. "That was Harry's idea a while back," Caine explained. "He wanted to get to know my mother a whole lot better."

Since Jade hadn't witnessed Harry trying to drag the Duchess out the front door, she didn't understand why his mother was looking so horrified. She didn't understand Caine's amusement, either.

"Now, son, this isn't the time . . ."

"You called him son," Jade blurted out. "And you called her mother, didn't you?"

"He is my son," Gweneth announced. "What else would I call him, dear? I have his permission."

Jade was so pleased, she couldn't quit smiling. "Oh, I misunderstood," she whispered. "I thought he only called you madam, and that you never, ever called him son. I wanted him to belong . . . yes, I was mistaken."

Neither Caine nor his mother set her straight. They smiled at each other.

"Where's Henry?" Gweneth suddenly asked. "Harry's coming over here."

The Duchess picked up her skirts and went running toward her husband before Caine or Jade could stop her.

"You were worried I didn't belong?" he whispered.

She looked embarrassed. "Everyone should belong to someone, Caine, even you."

Harry shoved the bouquet of roses in her hands. "These will be the last roses Jimbo's going to fetch for you, girl, so you might as well enjoy them." He thought his announcement might have sounded surly, so he gave her a kiss on her forehead. Then he turned to Caine. "I need to give you the telling about the fire we got planned for the ship," he said. "The painting should be done by tomorrow."

"If you'll excuse me, I want to talk to Nathan," Jade said. She noticed her brother standing all alone on the terrace.

Caine listened to Harry as he outlined his plans, but he kept his gaze directed on his bride all the while. Jade faced her brother and spoke to him a long time. Nathan nodded several times. His expression was serious. He looked startled, too, when Jade pulled one of the roses from her cluster and held it out to him.

He shook his head. She nodded.

And then he smiled at his sister, accepted the rose, and pulled her into his arms.

For the first time since Caine had met Nathan, he was seeing the real man. He was completely unguarded now. The look on his face as he held his sister close was filled with love.

Caine didn't intrude. He waited until Jade moved away from Nathan and walked back to his side.

Harry and his men were all watching Nathan now. When Jade's brother lifted the rose in the air, a resounding cheer went up. The men immediately went to Nathan. Both Jimbo and Matthew pounded him on his back.

"What is that all about?" Caine asked Jade. He put his arm around her and pulled her into his side.

"I gave Nathan a wedding present," she told him.

Her eyes sparkled with merriment. He was sidetracked by the sudden desire to kiss her. "Well?" she asked when he just stared down at her so intently. "Don't you want to know what I gave him?"

"A rose," he whispered. He leaned down and kissed her brow. "Love, let's go upstairs for a few minutes."

The urgency in his voice, added to the look on his face, left her breathless. "We can't," she whispered. "We have guests. And we have to go to London," she added with a nod.

Caine let out a long sigh. "Then quit looking at me like that."

"Like what?"

"Like you want to go upstairs, too," he growled.

She smiled. "But I do want to go upstairs."

He kissed her then, just the way he wanted to, using his tongue in erotic love play, pretending for just a moment that they were really all alone.

She was as limp as lettuce when he lifted his head back. Lord, how he loved the way she responded to him.

He remembered the promise she'd given the minister then. "Jade, wasn't there something you wanted to say to me?" he gently prodded when her glazed expression began to fade.

"Yes," she whispered. "I wanted to tell you I gave Nathan a white rose."

She looked so sincere, he knew she wasn't jesting with him. He decided then he'd have to wait until they were alone before nagging her into admitting she loved him. Damn, he needed to hear her say the words.

"Do you understand the significance, Caine?"

He shook his head. "I gave him my name," she explained.

He still didn't understand. "He's going to look damned silly answering to your name, sweetheart."

"Pagan."

"What?"

She nodded when he looked as if he wanted to argue with her. "Nathan's going to be Pagan now. It was my gift to him."

She looked so pleased with herself, he felt guilty for arguing. "Jade, Pagan has to die, remember?"

"Just for a little while," she replied. "The men have a new leader, Caine, Nathan wants the *Emerald*. He has business to take care of."

"What business?"

"He has to fetch his bride."

That statement did get a reaction. Caine was stunned. "Nathan's married?"

"Since he was fourteen," she returned. "By the King's command."

"Where's his wife?" Caine asked.

She laughed, delighted by his astonishment. "That's the business he has to attend to, Caine."

He started to laugh. "Do you mean to tell me Nathan lost his wife?"

"Not exactly," she answered. "She ran away from him. Now can you understand why he's so cranky?"

Caine nodded. "Sweetheart, how many other secrets have you still to share with me?"

She wasn't given time to mull that question over. Sir Richards interrupted with the reminder that it was time they left for London.

"Jade, you'd better change into your riding garments," Caine instructed. "We won't be taking the carriage."

She nodded, quickly said her farewells, and went upstairs to change. Sterns carried her satchel downstairs to give to the stablemaster so he could secure it on the back of her horse.

Caine was just putting his jacket on when she walked into his room. He'd already changed into snug-fitting fawn-colored britches and dark brown Hessian boots. He wore the same white shirt but had removed the cravat.

"I'm ready," she called out from the doorway to get his attention.

"It's a hell of a way to begin our marriage," Caine muttered.

"We could have waited," she replied.

He shook his head. "No, we couldn't have waited."

"Caine? Why couldn't we have taken the carriage?"

"We're taking the back way, through the woods, starting out in the opposite direction, of course, and then circling. We're going to sneak up on London, sweet."

She smiled. "Just like McKindry," she announced.

Caine slipped the long knife into one boot, his attention turned to his task, and asked, "Who's McKindry?"

"The man who used the whip on me," Jade answered. "Don't forget your pistol, Caine."

"I won't," he answered. He turned to look at her. "McKindry's the bastard who marked you?" he demanded.

"Don't look so angry, Caine, it was a long time ago."

"How long ago?"

"Oh, I was eight, perhaps nine years old at the time. Harry took care of McKindry. And it was a very good lesson for me," she added when his expression turned murderous.

"What lesson?"

"McKindry sneaked up behind me," she explained. "After that, every time Harry left me, his very last words were, always, remember McKindry. It was a reminder, you see, that I must always be on my guard."

What the hell kind of a childhood was that? he asked himself. Caine kept his anger hidden. "And how often did Harry leave you?" he asked, his tone mild. He even turned toward the wardrobe so she wouldn't see his expression.

"Oh, all the time," she answered. "Until I was old enough to help, of course. Then I went with him. Caine, you'd really better hurry. Sir Richards will be pacing. I'll go downstairs . . ."

"Come here, Jade."

His voice was a hoarse whisper, his expression solemn. Jade was thoroughly confused by his behavior. She walked over to stand in front of him.

"Yes, Caine?" she asked.

"I want you to remember something else besides McKindry," he said.

"What?"

"I love you."

"I could never forget you love me." She reached up and gently brushed her fingertips down his cheek.

She tried to kiss him then, but he shook his head. "I also want you to remember something else," he whispered. "Remember your promise to me that you're never, ever going on the ocean again."

Her eyes widened. "But I didn't promise you . . ."

"Promise me now, then," he ordered.

"I promise."

She was looking quite stunned. Caine was satisfied by that reaction. "I'll tell Harry he'll have to come to England if he wants to see you. We won't be going to him. I'll also tell him I made you promise me. He won't argue over that."

"How long have you known, Caine?" she asked.

"That you're afraid of the water?"

She timidly nodded. "Since the first nightmare," he explained. He took her back into his arms. "You've been worried, haven't you?"

"A little," she whispered. Then she shook her head. "No, Caine, I wasn't just a little worried. I was terrified. Harry wouldn't understand."

A long ponderous moment passed before she whispered, "Caine, do you think me a coward for being afraid of the water?"

"Do you have to ask me that question?" he replied. "Don't you already know the answer, Jade?"

She smiled then. "No, you don't believe I'm a coward. I'm sorry for insulting you by asking. I'm just not use to admitting . . ."

"Sweetheart, Poseidon wouldn't go back in the water if he'd been through your terror."

She started to laugh and cry at the same time. She was so relieved he'd just taken her burden away, she felt positively light-headed. "Nathan's stronger than I am," she said then. "He's going on the waters again."

"Nathan isn't human, love, so he doesn't count," Caine replied.

"Oh, he's human, all right. If I tell you a secret, will you keep it? You won't torment my brother with . . ."

"I promise."

"Nathan gets seasick."

Caine laughed. "He's going to make a hell of a pirate then," he drawled out.

"I love you."

She'd blurted out her confession, her face hidden in the lapels of his jacket.

He quit laughing. "Did you say something?" he asked, pretending he hadn't heard her. He nudged her chin up and stared down into her eyes.

It took her a long time to get the words out again, and every ounce of courage she possessed. Her throat tightened up, her heart hammered a wild beat, and her stomach felt like it was tying itself in knots.

She wouldn't have been able to tell him if he hadn't helped. The look on his face was so filled with love, it made some of the panic ebb away. The dimple did the rest. "I love you."

He felt relieved, until she burst into tears again. "Was that so difficult? To tell me you loved me?"

"It was," she whispered while he kissed her tears away. "I'm not at all used to telling what's in my heart. I don't believe I like it at all."

He would have laughed if she hadn't sounded so damned vulnerable. He kissed her instead.

"You didn't like making love the first time, either," he reminded her before kissing her sweet mouth once again.

Both of them were shaking when they drew apart. He would have dragged her over to the bed if Sir Richards' bellow hadn't interrupted them.

They sighed in unison. "Come along, sweetheart. It's time to go."

He started out the doorway, tugging her by her hand.

Lyons and Richards were waiting for them in the foyer. The time for gaiety was quickly put aside. They walked in silence through the backwoods where Matthew and Jimbo waited with their horses.

Caine took the lead. Jade was next in line, with Lyon responsible for protecting her back. Sir Richards trailed last.

Caine was cautious to the point of fanaticism. The only

time they stopped to rest was when he backtracked on his own to make certain they weren't being followed. Still, Jade didn't mind the inconvenience. She was comforted by his precautions.

Each time Caine left, Lyon stayed by her side. And every time he talked to her, the topic was always about his file. It was apparent he was concerned about someone else getting hold of it.

She suggested he steal his own file so that he could gain peace of mind. Lyon shook his head. He tried not to smile as he explained it wouldn't be ethical. There might also come a time, he added, when someone would question one of his missions. The file couldn't be destroyed or stolen, for the truth was his protection.

Jade didn't argue with him, but she decided the file would be much better protected in his home than in the War Office. She made the decision to take care of that little chore on her own.

By the time they reached the outskirts of London proper, the sun was setting. Jade was exhausted from the long ride. She didn't protest when Caine took her into his lap. She rode the rest of the distance with his arms wrapped around her.

And all the while she kept thinking to herself that Caine was such a solid, reliable man. A woman could depend on him.

She was just drifting off to sleep when they reached his town house. Caine went inside first, curtly dismissed his servants for the night, then took Jade into the library. The scent of smoke was still in the air, and most of the walls were still blackened from the fire, but the servants had done a good job righting the damage. The town house was sound enough to live in.

When Lyon and Richards joined Jade and Caine, Richards said, "We'll leave as soon as it goes completely dark."

"It would be safer if we waited until midnight," Jade interjected. "There are two guards until then."

"And what happens at midnight?" Sir Richards asked.

"Only one guard stays during the blackest hours of the night," she explained. "His name is Peter Kently and he's always half-sotted by the time he takes over the watch. Now, if we wait until half past, he'll have finished the last of his bottle, and he should be fast asleep."

Sir Richards was staring at her with his mouth gaping wide. "How did you . . . ?"

"Sir, one must always be prepared for any eventuality if one is going to be successful," she instructed.

While Sir Richards sputtered about the lack of morals in government workers, Lyon asked Jade about the locks. "The back door is a piece of work," she announced. Her eyes sparkled with merriment, for she was obviously warming to her topic.

"A piece of work?" Caine asked, smiling over her enthusiasm.

"Difficult," she qualified.

Sir Richards perked up considerably. "Well, thank God something's up to snuff."

She gave him a sympathetic look. "Difficult, Sir Richards, but not impossible. I did get inside, if you'll remember."

He looked so crestfallen, she hastened to add, "It took quite a long while that first time. Double locks are rather tricky."

"But not impossible," Lyon interjected. "Jade? Just how long did it take you that first time?"

"Oh, five . . . perhaps as many as six minutes."

Richards hid his face in his hands. Jade tried to comfort him. "There, there, Sir Richards. It isn't as bad as all that. Why, it took me almost an hour to get inside the inner sanctuary where the sealed files are kept."

The director didn't look as if he wanted to be comforted

now. Jade left the men to their plans and went to the kitchens to find something to eat. She returned to the library with an assortment of food. They shared apples, cheese, cold mutton, day-old bread, and dark brown ale. Jade took her boots off, tucked her feet up under her, and fell asleep in the chair.

The men kept their voices low while they talked about the Tribunal. When Jade awakened several hours later, she saw Caine was rereading the letters she'd copied.

He had a puzzled look on his face, his concentration absolute, and when he suddenly smiled and leaned back in his chair, she thought he might have sorted through whatever problem he'd been contemplating.

"Have you come to any conclusions, Caine?" she asked.

"I'm getting there," Caine answered, sounding positively cheerful.

"You're being logical and methodical, aren't you?" she asked.

"Yes," he answered. "We take this one step at a time, Jade."

"He's a very logical man," she told Lyon and Sir Richards. Caine thought she sounded like she was making an excuse for a sorry flaw. "He cannot help himself," she added. "He's very trusting, too."

"Trusting?" Lyon snorted with laughter. "You can't be serious, Jade. Caine is one of the most cynical men in England."

"A trait I developed by running with you," Caine drawled out.

Jade was amazed by Lyon's comments. He sounded so certain. Sir Richards was nodding too. She turned to smile at Caine, then said, "I'm honored then that you trust me."

"Just as much as you trust me, sweetheart," he answered.

She frowned at him. "And just what is that supposed to mean?" she asked. "Are you being insulting?"

He grinned. Jade turned to Lyon. "Do you have any idea how maddening it is to be married to someone who's so damned logical all the time?"

Caine answered her. "I haven't the faintest idea."

She decided to quit the topic. She eased her feet to the floor, grimacing over the discomfort that movement caused her backside. If she'd been all alone, she would have let out a loud, unladylike groan. "I'm not at all accustomed to riding for such long hours," she admitted.

"You did well today," Lyon praised. He turned to look at Caine. "When this is finished, Christina and I will give a reception for the two of you."

"That would be fine," Caine interjected. "You know, Lyon, Jade and Christina are really quite alike."

"Is she a thief then?" Jade asked before she could stop herself. Her voice was filled with enthusiasm. "We got along quite well right from the start. No wonder . . ."

"Sorry to disappoint you, love, but Christina isn't a thief," Caine said.

She looked crestfallen. Lyon laughed. "Christina isn't very logical either, Jade. She comes from a rather unusual family. She could teach you all sorts of things."

"God help us," Caine interjected, for he was very familiar with Lady Christina's unusual background. Lyon's wife had been raised in the wilderness of the Americas by one of the Dakota tribes.

Jade misunderstood Caine's reaction. "I'm certain I'm a quick study, Caine. If I apply myself, I could learn everything Christina would like to teach me."

She didn't give him time to argue with her. "I'm going to change my clothes. We must leave soon."

Caine, she noticed, was glaring at Lyon when she took her leave. Jade quickly changed into her black gown. She carried a cloak with her. The hood would shield her brightly colored hair in the lamplight.

333

They walked most of the way to the War Office. The building was across town, but they used the hired hack for only half the distance. When they reached the alley behind the building, Jade moved to Caine's side. She took hold of his hand while she stared up at the top floor of the brick structure.

"Something's wrong, Caine."

"What?" Sir Richards asked from behind her back. "Your instincts, my dear, or . . ."

"There's a light in the third window on the right," she explained. "It shouldn't be showing any light."

"Perhaps the guard at the entrance . . ."

"The entrance is on the other side," Jade interrupted. "That light comes from the inner office."

Caine turned to Lyon. "If someone's in there going through the files, he'll use the back door when he leaves."

"Let him pass when he does," Sir Richards directed. "I'll follow him."

"Do you want me to go with you?" Lyon asked. "If there's more than one . . ."

Richards shook his head. "I'll see who the leader is and follow that bloke. You're needed here. We'll meet back at Caine's, no matter what the hour."

They moved to the shadows a fair distance from the back door, then patiently waited. Caine put his arm around Jade's shoulders and held her close.

"You don't want me here with you, do you, Caine?" she whispered when his grip became almost painful.

"No, I don't want you to be here," he answered. "Jade, if there's trouble inside . . ."

"Lyon will take care of it," she interjected before he could finish his thought. "If there's any killing done, God forbid, then Lyon should be the one doing it. He's used to it."

Lyon heard her announcement and raised an eyebrow in reaction. He wondered if she'd read Caine's file all the way through. It was a fact that Caine was every bit as capable as Lyon was.

Their whispers stopped as soon as the back door squeaked open. While they watched, two men scurried outside. In the moonlight, Jade could see their faces clearly. She couldn't contain her gasp. Caine clamped his hand over her mouth.

The second man out turned and locked the door. How had he secured the keys? Jade wondered. She held her silence until the men had turned the corner. Sir Richards left to follow them.

Then she turned to Caine. "The security is deplorable," she whispered.

"Yes," he agreed. "You recognized them, didn't you?"

She nodded. "They are two of the three men who waylaid Nathan's carriage. The bigger of the two is the one who hit me on the head."

The look on his face frightened her. She thought he might very well go after the two men then and there. "Caine, you must be logical now, please. You can't chase after them."

He looked exasperated with her. "I'll wait," he said. "But when this is over . . ."

He didn't finish that statement, but took hold of her hand and led her over to the door. With the special tool Harry had given her for her tenth birthday, she was able to get the lock undone in quick time. The second latch took only a few minutes longer.

Lyon went inside first. Jade followed, with Caine taking up the rear. She nudged Lyon out of the way and took the lead. They went up to the third floor by way of the back steps. Jade remembered the squeak in the fourth rail on the second staircase, motioned for both men to avoid it, then felt Lyon's arms on her waist. He lifted her over the step and put her down. She turned to smile her appreciation before continuing on.

The guard wasn't sleeping at his post behind the desk in

the outer office. He was dead. Jade saw the handle of the knife protruding from his shoulders. She took a quick step back. Caine's hand immediately covered her mouth again. He must have thought she was going to cry out.

Through the glass window of the door, they could see two shadows. Caine pulled Jade over into the corner, motioned for her to stay there, and then followed Lyon into the inner office. She was impressed by their silence. The two of them would make proper thieves, she decided.

They were taking too long, though. She stood there with her back pressed against the cold wall, wringing her hands together while she waited. If anything happened to Caine, she didn't know what she would do. Until she had to leave him, of course, she qualified in her mind . . . God help her, she needed him.

She didn't realize her eyes were squeezed shut until she felt Caine's hand on her shoulder. "Come on, we're alone now."

"What about the men inside?" she whispered. "And for heaven's sake, lower your voice. We're at work now."

He didn't answer her. Jade followed Caine inside the sanctuary, tossed her cloak on the nearest desk while Lyon added another candle to the lights.

She noticed the two men on the floor in the corner then. She couldn't contain her gasp. "Are they dead?" she asked.

She couldn't quit staring at the bodies sprawled atop each other. Caine moved to block her view. "No," he said.

Her relief was obvious. "Jade, didn't any of your men ever have to . . ."

"They most certainly did not," she interrupted. "I would have had their hides. Killing wasn't allowed. Now quit talking so much, Caine. You must hurry. If they wake up, they'll shout an alarm."

"They won't wake up for a long while," Caine said. He pulled out a chair, gently pushed her down into it. "You rest. This is going to take some time."

"Rest while I'm at work? Never." She sounded appalled by his suggestion.

"Terrance's file is missing," Lyon announced, drawing their attention. He was bent over the file drawer, smiling broadly. "Interesting, wouldn't you say?"

"The lamplighters probably think it's very interesting, too," Jade snapped. "Do keep your voice down, Lyon."

"Yes, it is interesting," Caine said quietly in answer to Lyon's remark.

"Then we can leave now?" Jade asked, glancing over at the two men on the floor once again.

"Jade, why are you so nervous?" Caine asked. "You've been in and out of this room several times before," he reminded her.

"I was working with professionals then," she announced.

Lyon and Caine shared a smile. "She's worried about us," Lyon said.

"No," Caine countered. "That would be insulting if she . . ."

She couldn't believe he was daring to tease her now. "Of course, I'm worried. You two aren't even proper apprentices. Even an imbecile would know that now isn't the time for idle chitchat. Do get on with it."

"She is insulting us," Lyon drawled out. He started to laugh, but her glare changed his mind.

The men turned serious then. They labored over certain files for two long hours. Jade didn't interrupt. She didn't dare rest, either, for she was determined to keep on her guard in case of intruders.

"All right, we're finished," Caine said as he slammed the last file shut.

Jade stood up and walked over to the drawer. She took the folder from Caine, turned, and put it back in its proper place. Her back was to the men and it didn't take her any time at all to remove both Caine's and Lyon's fat files.

She turned around, determined to have it out with them

then and there if they offered one word of protest. Luck was on her side, however, for the men had already moved to the outer office.

"Aren't you going to go through their pockets?" she called out. She pointed to the sleeping men.

"We already did," Caine answered.

Jade wrapped the files in her cloak. She blew out the candles and followed the men downstairs. Since they were all alone inside the building, she guessed they didn't need to be quiet. Each was taking a turn muttering expletives. Caine's, she noticed, were every bit as colorful as Lyon's were.

"I am never taking either one of you on another raid again," she muttered. "I wouldn't be surprised if the authorities were waiting for us outside."

Neither Caine nor Lyon paid any attention to her ramblings. She soon became too weary to lecture them anyway.

Sir Richards was waiting for them in the alley. "There's a hack waiting four blocks over," he announced before he turned and took the lead.

Jade stumbled when they rounded the corner. Lyon grabbed her, lifted her into his arms. She thought he might have felt the folders when he transferred her into Caine's arms, then decided he hadn't noticed after all when he grinned down at her and turned to take up the rear guard.

She fell asleep in the vehicle with the cloak clutched to her breasts. It was such a comfort to realize she didn't have to worry. As long as Caine was nearby, she felt safe, protected. For the first time in a good long while, she didn't have to remember McKindry. Caine would keep his guard up for both of them. He'd never make a proper thief, of course, but he certainly wouldn't let the evil McKindrys of the world sneak up behind them, either.

She found herself in Caine's bed when she woke up. He was trying to pry her cloak away from her. "Are they waiting for you downstairs?" she asked in a sleepy whisper.

"Yes, they are. Sweetheart, let me help you . . ."

"I can undress myself," she said. "Do you need me . . ."

She was going to ask him if he needed her to go downstairs with him, but he interrupted her. "I'll always need you, Jade. I love you."

He leaned down and kissed her. "Go to sleep, sweetheart. I'll join you as soon as we've finished."

"I don't want to need you."

She blurted out that confession in a voice filled with panic. Caine's smile was almost sympathetic. "I know, love, but you do need me. Now go to sleep."

She didn't understand why, yet found she was comforted by his contradiction. He was so sure of himself, so confident. It was a trait she couldn't help but admire.

Jade let out a loud sigh. She was simply too tired to think about the future now. She hid the files, took her clothes off, and fell back into bed. She thought she very well might have the horrid nightmare again, then realized she wasn't dreading it as much as before.

She fell asleep hugging the promise Caine had given her. She would never have to go near the ocean again.

Caine didn't come to bed until after seven in the morning. Jade opened her eyes just long enough to watch him pull back the covers and stretch out beside her. He hauled her up against his side, his arm wrapped tightly around her waist, and was snoring like a drunk before she got settled again.

She went downstairs around noon, introduced herself to Caine's London staff, and then went into the dining room to have breakfast.

Caine suddenly appeared at the doorway, dressed only in a pair of light-colored britches. He looked exhausted, angry, too, and when he crooked his finger at her she decided not to argue.

"Come here, Jade."

"Did you get up on the wrong side of the bed, Caine?" she

asked as she walked over to face him. "Or are you always this surly when you first wake up?"

"I thought you'd left."

Her eyes widened over that confession, but she wasn't given time to think about it too much. Caine lifted her into his arms and carried her back upstairs. She realized just how furious he was when she noticed the muscle in the side of his jaw was flexing. "Caine, I didn't leave you," she whispered, stating the obvious. She reached up to caress his cheek, smiling over the stubble there. "You need a shave, husband."

"That's right, I am your husband," he grated out. He tossed her onto the bed, took his pants off, and stretched out beside her, facedown, with his arm anchored around her waist. She was fully clothed; he was stark naked.

She would have laughed over the absurdity of her circumstances if the fullness of what he'd just implied hadn't settled in her mind. How dare he not trust her? She was furious. She would have given him a good piece of her mind, too, if he hadn't looked so damned peaceful. She didn't have the heart to wake him up.

The lecture would have to wait until later. She closed her eyes, selected a book from her memory, and reread it in her mind while she patiently waited for Caine to get the rest he needed.

He didn't move until almost two that afternoon. He was in a much better frame of mind, too. He smiled at her. She glared at him.

"Why don't you trust me?" she demanded.

Caine rolled onto his back, stacked his hands behind his head, and let out a loud yawn. "Take your clothes off, sweetheart," he whispered. "Then we'll discuss this."

Her gaze moved down his body to his obvious arousal. She blushed in reaction. "I think we should discuss it now, Caine," she stammered out.

He pulled her on top of him, kissed her passionately, and

then ordered her to take her clothes off again. Odd, but she didn't mind obeying his command now. He was such a persuasive man. Demanding, too. She climaxed twice before he finally filled her with his seed.

She could barely move when he finally moved away from her. "Now what was it you wanted to discuss?"

She couldn't remember. It took them another hour to get dressed, for they kept stopping to kiss each other. It wasn't until they were on their way downstairs that Jade remembered what it was she wanted to lecture him about.

"Haven't I proven myself to you?" she asked. "You should trust me with all your heart."

"You don't trust me," he countered. "It works both ways, Jade, or not at all. You've made it clear you'll leave me at the first opportunity. Isn't that right, love?"

He paused on the bottom step and turned around to look at her. They were eye to eye now. Hers, he noticed, were cloudy with tears.

"I don't wish to talk about this now," she announced, struggling to maintain her composure. "I'm hungry and I . . ."

"It gives you the edge, doesn't it, wife?"

"I don't understand what you mean," she returned. Her voice shook. "What edge?"

"In the back of that illogical mind of yours lurks the possibility that I'll eventually leave you," he explained. "Just like Nathan and Harry did. You're still afraid."

"I'm afraid?" she stammered out.

He nodded. "You're afraid of me."

He thought she'd argue over that statement of fact. She surprised him by nodding. "Yes, you make me very afraid," she admitted. And I can tell you, sir, I don't like that feeling one little bit. It makes me . . ."

"Vulnerable?"

She nodded again. He let out a patient sigh. "All right, then. How long do you suppose it's going to take you to become unafraid?" His voice was so gentle, his expression so serious.

"How long before you get tired of me?" she asked, her fear apparent.

"Are you deliberately misunderstanding?"

"No."

"Then in answer to your absurd question, I will never get tired of you. Now tell me how long it will take you before you trust me?" he ordered again. His voice wasn't at all gentle now. It was as hard, as determined as his expression.

"I told you I loved you," she whispered.

"Yes, you did."

"I repeated the vows before you and God." Her voice had risen an octave. He could also see her panic, her insecurity.

"Well? What more do you want from me?"

She was shouting now, wringing her hands together. Caine decided she still wasn't ready to surrender wholeheartedly.

He felt like an ogre for upsetting her. "Jade . . ."

"Caine, I don't want to leave you," she blurted out. "I do trust you. Yes, I do. I know you'll keep me safe. I know you love me, but there's a part of me that still . . ." She stopped her explanation and lowered her gaze. Her shoulders slumped in dejection. "Sometimes the feelings locked inside me since I was a little girl do get in the way of being logical," she admitted a long minute later. "I suppose you're right. I'm not at all logical about this, am I?"

He pulled her into his arms and held her close. The hug was more for his benefit than hers. In truth, he couldn't stand to see the torment in her eyes.

"I want to tell you something, sweetheart. The first time you tried to leave me . . . when Harry told me you'd left, it threw me into a panic. I've never had such a god-awful feeling before, and I sure as hell hated it. Now I'm beginning to realize that you've lived with that feeling a long time, haven't you?"

She mopped her tears away with his shirt before she answered. "Perhaps."

"And so you learned how to make it completely on your own," he continued. "You've been teaching yourself not to depend on anyone else. I'm right, aren't I?"

She shrugged against him. "I don't like talking about this," she whispered, trying to sound disgruntled and not terrified. "I love you with all my heart," she added when he squeezed her. "And I know you love me now, Caine. Yes, I'm sure of that."

Neither said a word for a long while after she'd made that statement. Jade used the time to calm her racing heart. He used the silence to think of a logical way to ease her illogical fears.

"What if we make this a short period?" he suddenly blurted out.

"What?" She pulled away from him so she could see his expression. Surely he was jesting with her.

The look on his face indicated he was quite serious. "You want to make our marriage a short union? But you just told me you loved me. How can you . . ."

"No, no," he argued. "If we just make this commitment to each other for six months' time, if you can just promise me you'll stay with me for that length of time, won't some of your panic ease away?"

He sounded so enthusiastic, looked so arrogantly pleased with himself. She realized then he was quite sincere in this absurdity. "You already said you'd never leave me. Now you're telling me six months . . ."

"I won't ever leave you," he snapped, obviously irritated she wasn't embracing his plan wholeheartedly. "But you don't believe I mean what I say. Therefore, you have only to promise to give me six months, Jade."

"And what about you, husband? Does this promise hold for you as well?"

"Of course."

She threw herself back into his arms so he couldn't see her smile. She didn't want him to think she was laughing at him. Odd, too, but she suddenly felt as though a weight had been lifted from her chest. She could breathe again. The panic was gone.

"Give me your word, wife."

The command was given in a low growl. "I give it," she replied.

"No," he muttered. "It won't work. It's too short a time," he added. "Hell, if I ever forgot, you'd be gone before I . . . I want a full year, Jade. We'll start from the day we were married. I won't ever forget our anniversary."

He squeezed her shoulders when she didn't answer him quickly enough. "Well? Do you promise not to leave me for a full year?"

"I promise."

Caine was so relieved, he wanted to shout. He'd finally come up with a way to keep her happy. He'd just given her the edge he was certain she needed. "Say the words, wife," he ordered, his voice gruff. "I don't want any misunderstandings."

The man really should have become a barrister, she decided. He was so logical, so clever, too. ' I'll stay with you for one year. Now you must promise me, husband."

"I won't leave you for one full year," he announced.

He tilted her chin up with his thumb. "You do believe me, don't you?" he asked.

"Yes, I do."

"And you're relieved, aren't you?"

She didn't answer him for a long minute. The truth wasn't at all slow in coming, either. It hit her like a warm bolt of sunshine, filling her heart and her illogical mind all at once. He would never leave her . . . and she could never leave him. The vulnerable childlike feelings hidden inside her for so many years of loneliness evaporated.

"Sweetheart? You are relieved, aren't you?"

"I trust you with all my heart," she whispered.

"You aren't in a panic now?"

She shook her head. "Caine, I want to tell . . ."

"I took the panic away, didn't I?"

Because he looked so supremely pleased with himself, she didn't want to lessen his arrogant satisfaction. A man had to have his pride intact, she remembered. "You have made me sort this all out in my mind," she whispered. "And yes, you have taken my panic away. Thank you, Caine."

They shared a long sweet kiss. Jade was shaking when Caine lifted his head away. He thought his kiss had caused that reaction.

"Do you want to go back upstairs, love?" he asked.

She nodded. "After you've fed me, Caine. I'm starving."

He took hold of her hand and started for the dining room.

"Do you know, husband, I have the oddest feeling now."

"And what is that?" he asked.

"I feel . . . free. Do you understand, Caine? It's as though I've just been let out of a locked room. That's ridiculous, of course."

Caine held out the chair at the table for her, then took his own. "Why is it ridiculous?"

She immediately looked disgruntled. "Because there isn't a locked room I can't get out of," she explained.

Caine ordered their breakfast, and when Anna, the servant, had left the room, he asked Jade to tell him about some of the adventures she'd had. "I want to know everything there is to know," he announced.

"You'll only get angry," she predicted.

"No, no," he argued. "I promise I won't get angry, no matter what you tell me."

"Well, I don't mean to boast," she began. "But I do seem to have a natural ability for getting in and out of tight spots. Uncle Harry says I'm a born thief and liar," she added.

"Now, sweetheart, I'm sure he didn't mean to criticize you," Caine replied.

"Well, of course not," she returned in exasperation. "Those were compliments, husband. Uncle's praise meant all the more to me because he doesn't usually give compliments to anyone. He says it isn't in his nature," she added with a smile. "Harry worries that others will find out the truth about him."

"And what might that truth be?" Caine asked. "That he's actually a little civilized after all?"

"How did you guess?"

"From the way you turned out," he explained. "If he was such a barbarian, you wouldn't have become such a lady."

She beamed with pleasure. "It is good of you to notice," she whispered. "Uncle is very intelligent."

"He's the one who taught you how to read, isn't he?"

She nodded. "It proved fortunate, too, for his eyes started failing him. At night I would read to him."

"From memory?"

"Only when there weren't any books available. Harry stole as many as he could get his hands on."

"The way he speaks," Caine interjected. "That's all part of his deception, too, isn't it?"

"Yes," she admitted. "Appearances, after all. He doesn't even use proper grammar when we're alone, fearing he'll slip up in front of his men, you see."

Caine rolled his eyes. "Your uncle became a bit of a fanatic about his position as leader, didn't he?"

"No," she argued. "You misunderstand. He enjoys the deception, Caine." She continued to talk about her uncle for another few minutes, then turned the topic to some of her most memorable escapades. Because he'd promised not to get angry, Caine hid his reaction. His hands were shaking, though, with the true need to wring good old Uncle Harry's neck, by the time she'd finished telling him about one particularly harrowing incident.

He decided he didn't want to know all about her past after all. "I think I'd better hear these stories one at a time."

"That's what I'm doing," she countered. She paused to smile at the servant when the woman placed a tray of crusty rolls in front of her, then turned back to Caine. "I am telling them one at a time."

Caine shook his head. "I mean I want you to tell me one every other month or so. A man can only take so much. I promise you I'll be thinking about the story you just told me a good long while. Hell, Jade, I can feel my hair turning gray. You could have been killed. You could have . . ."

"But you aren't getting angry," she interjected with a smile. "You did promise."

Caine leaned back in his chair. "I think we'd better change the subject. Tell me when you realized you love me," he commanded. "Did I force you?"

She started to laugh. "You can't force someone to love you," she said. "I believe, however, that when I read your file, I was already falling in love with you."

She smiled over the astonished look on his face. "It's true," she whispered.

"Jade, I'm not very proud of some of the things I had to do," he said. "You did read the entire file, didn't you?"

"I did," she answered. "You were determined, methodical too, but you weren't inhuman about it. In every accounting, you were always so . . . reliable. People depended upon you and you never let them down. I admired that quality, of course. And then I met you," she ended. "You were a little like McKindry, because you snuck up behind me and stole my heart before I even realized what was happening. Now you must tell me when you realized you loved me."

"It was during one of our many heated debates," he said.

It was her turn to look astonished. "We never debated," she said. "We shouted at each other. Those were arguments."

"Debates," he repeated. "Loud ones but debates all the same."

"Are you telling me you fell in love with my mind first?"

"No."

She laughed, delighted by his honesty.

"Shouldn't your man be here with us? It might look suspicious if he stays in the country, Caine."

"Sterns never comes to London with me," he explained. "Everyone knows that. Sterns hates London, says it's too cluttered."

"I miss him," she admitted. "He reminds me of you. Sterns is most opinionated—arrogant, too."

"No one understands why I put up with him," Caine said. "But if the truth were out, I don't understand why he puts up with me. He's been like a shield to me, especially when I was a lad. I did get into quite a bit of mischief. Sterns softened the telling, though. He pulled me out of certain death several times, too."

Caine told her a story about the time he almost drowned in a boating incident and how Sterns had saved him only to toss him right back in the waters to learn the proper way to swim. Both of them were laughing by the time Caine ended the tale, for the picture of the sour-faced butler in full clothing swimming alongside his small charge was quite amusing.

Jade was the first to grow somber. "Caine, did you and your friends come to any conclusions last night after I went to bed?"

"The man Richards followed home was Willburn. Do you remember Colin told us that Willburn was his director and how he confided in him?"

"Yes, I remember," she replied. "Nathan said he never trusted Willburn. Still, my brother doesn't trust anyone but Harry and Colin, and me, of course."

"Colin was wrong, Jade. Willburn did work for the Tribunal. He's now employed by the one remaining member."

Before she could interrupt him, he continued. "We're pretty certain William Terrance was the second man. Since he's dead, and your father too, that only leaves the third. Richards is convinced Terrance was called Prince. That leaves Ice unaccounted for."

"How will we ever find Ice? We really don't have much to go on. The letters were very sparse with personal information, Caine."

"Sure we do, sweetheart," he replied. "In one of the letters, there was mention that Ice didn't attend Oxford. Also, both Fox and Prince were surprised when they met Ice."

"How did you gather that bit of information?"

"From one of the remarks made by your father to Prince in the third . . . no, the fourth letter."

"I remember," she countered. "I just didn't think it significant."

"Richards believes Ice could very well be a foreigner."

"And you?" she asked.

"I'm not convinced. There are other important clues in those letters, Jade. I just need a little more time to put them all together."

She had complete faith in his ability to sort it all out. Once Caine put his mind to a problem, he would be able to solve it.

"Richards put a watch on Willburn. He thinks he might lead us to Ice. It's a start, but I'm not putting my money on it. We have other options, too. Now, sweetheart, I don't want you to leave this town house, no matter what the reason, all right?"

"You can't leave either," she returned. "Agreed?"

"Agreed."

"Whatever will we do to keep ourselves occupied?" she asked with as much innocence in her tone as she could manage.

"We could do a lot of reading, I suppose," he drawled out.

She stood up and went to stand behind his back. "Yes, we could read," she whispered as she wrapped her arms around his broad shoulders. Her fingers slipped inside the top of his shirt. "I could learn how to embroider," she added. "I've always wanted to learn that task." She leaned down and nibbled on his earlobe. "But do you know what I want to do most of all, husband?"

"I'm getting a fair idea," he answered, his voice husky with arousal.

"You know? Then you'll teach me?"

"Everything I know, sweetheart," he promised.

He stood up and took her into his arms. "What will we do for music?" she asked.

If he thought that an odd question, he didn't say so. "We'll make our own music," he promised. He dragged her by the hand into the foyer and started up the steps.

"How?" she asked, laughing.

"I'll hum every time you moan," he explained.

"Don't you think the drawing room will be better?" she asked.

"The bed would be more comfortable," he answered. "But if you're determined to . . ."

"Learn how to dance," she interjected. "That is what this discussion is all about, isn't it?"

She smiled ever so sweetly up at him after telling that lie, waiting for his reaction. She thought she'd bested him with her trickery. Caine, however, proved to be far more cunning than she was, more creative, too. He followed her into the drawing room, locked the doors behind him, and then proceeded to teach her how to dance.

It was a pity, but she was never going to be able to show off her new skill in public, for Caine and she would scandalize the *ton* with the erotic, absolutely sinful way he taught her how to dance. And though he was thoroughly logical in his explanation, she still refused to believe the ladies and gentlemen of the *ton* took their clothes off before they did the waltz.

Caine kept her entertained the rest of the day, but as soon as darkness fell, they had their first argument.

"What do you mean, you're leaving?" she cried when he put his jacket on. "We agreed that we wouldn't leave this town house . . ."

"I'll be careful," Caine interrupted. He kissed her on her forehead. "Lyon and Richards are waiting for me, sweet. I'm going to have to go out every night, I'm afraid, until we finish this. Now quit worrying and tell me you won't wait up for me."

"I will wait up for you," she stammered out.

"I know," he answered with a sigh. "But tell me you won't anyway."

She let him see her exasperation. "Caine, if anything happens to you, I'm going to be very angry."

"I'll be careful," he answered.

Jade chased after him to the back door. "You'll remember McKindry?"

He turned, his hand on the doorknob. "That's your lesson, sweetheart."

"Well, you can damned well learn from it, too," she muttered.

"All right," he answered, trying to placate her. "I'll remember McKindry." He turned and opened the door. "Jade?"

"Yes?"

"You will be here when I come home, won't you?"

She was amazed by his question, insulted, too, and she would have blistered him with a piece of her mind if he hadn't sounded so vulnerable. "Have I made you so insecure, then?" she asked instead.

"Answer me," he commanded.

"I'll be here when you come home."

Those parting words became their ritual. Each night, just as he was leaving, he would tell her he would remember

McKindry, and she would tell him she would be waiting for him.

During the dark hours of the night, while she waited for her husband to come home to her, she thought about his vulnerability. At first, she believed she was the cause. After all, she'd let him see her own insecurity often enough. But she sensed, too, that Caine's background was another reason for his own vulnerability. She couldn't imagine what his early life must have been like. Sir Harwick had called Caine's mother a shrew. She remembered he'd also said that the woman had tried to turn her son against his father. It couldn't have been a peaceful time for Caine.

The more she thought about it, the more convinced she became that Caine actually needed her just as much as she needed him.

That realization was a comfort.

Lady Briars sent several notes inviting Jade to visit. Caine wouldn't let her leave the town house, however, and sent word back that his wife was indisposed.

In the end, her father's dear friend came to see her. Jade's memory of the woman was hazy at best, but she felt horribly guilty about pretending to be ill when she saw how old and frail the woman was. She was still beautiful, though, with clear blue eyes and silvery gray hair. Her intellect appeared to be quite sharp, too.

Jade served tea in the drawing room, then took her place next to Caine on the settee. He seemed quite determined to participate in the women's conversation.

Both husband and wife listened to Lady Briars extend her condolences over Nathan's tragic death. Jade played the role of grieving sister well, but she hated the deception, for Lady Briars was so sincere in her sympathy.

"When I read about the tragedy in the papers, I was stunned," Lady Briars said. "I had no idea Nathan worked for the government doing such secretive work. Caine, I must tell you how sorry I was to hear your brother was also killed by that horrid pirate. I didn't know the lad, of course, but I'm certain he must have had a heart of gold."

"I never met Colin either," Jade interjected. "But Caine has told me all about him. He was a good man, Lady Briars, and he died for his country."

"How did Pagan become involved in this?" Lady Briars asked. "I'm still hazy on the details, child."

Caine answered her question. "From what the War Department was able to piece together, Nathan and Colin were waylaid when en route to investigate a highly secretive matter."

"Isn't it rather ironic that you two ended up together?" Lady Briars asked. There was a smile in her voice now.

"Not really," Caine answered. "Both of us missed the ceremony honoring our brothers," he explained. "Jade came to see me. She wanted to talk about Nathan and I guess I needed to talk about Colin. We were immediately drawn to each other."

He paused to wink at Jade, then continued, "I believe it was love at first sight."

"I can see why," Lady Briars said. "Jade, you've turned into a beautiful woman." She shook her head and let out a little sigh. "I never understood why your father's friend snatched you away so quickly after your father's funeral. I will admit I was going to petition the Crown for guardianship. I'd always wanted a daughter. I also believed you would have fared much better with me. Now, after visiting with you, well, I must concede that you were properly raised."

"Uncle Harry insisted we leave right away," Jade explained. "He wasn't our legal guardian and he knew you'd fight for Nathan and me."

"Yes," Lady Briars agreed. "Do you know, I feel in part responsible for Nathan's death. Yes, I do. If he'd come to live with me, I certainly wouldn't have allowed him to go off on those sea voyages. It was too dangerous."

"Nathan was a fully grown man when he made his decision to work for England," Caine interjected. "I doubt you could have kept him home, Lady Briars."

"Still," she countered. "I still don't understand why your father didn't consider me for guardianship . . ."

"I believe I understand," Jade said. "Harry told me that Father had turned his heart against England."

"I cannot imagine why," Lady Briars returned. "He seemed very content to me."

Jade shrugged. "We probably will never know his reasons. Harry believed Father was being chased by demons who lived in his head."

"Perhaps so," Lady Briars agreed. "Now enough about your father, Jade. Tell me all about your early life. We have so much catching up to do. What was it like living on this tiny island? Did you learn to read and write? How did you keep yourself occupied, child? Were there many functions to attend?"

Jade laughed. "The people on the island weren't part of society, Lady Briars. Most didn't even bother to wear shoes. I never managed to read or write because Harry couldn't find anyone who could teach me."

Jade told that lie because Caine had insisted no one know she'd conquered those skills. Every little edge would give them an added advantage, he'd explained. If everyone believed she hadn't learned how to read, then she couldn't have read the letters.

She thought that reasoning was filled with flaws, but she didn't argue with her husband. She concentrated on making up several amusing childhood stories to satisfy Lady Briars' curiosity. She ended her remarks with the admission that although it had certainly been a peaceful time, it had also been a little boring.

The topic returned to the issue of their recent marriage. Caine answered all of the woman's questions. Jade was amazed by the easy way he told his lies. He obviously had a natural talent, too.

Her father's old friend appeared to be genuinely interested. Jade thought she was a terribly sweet woman.

"Why is it you never married?" Jade asked. "I know that's a bold question, but you're such a beautiful woman, Lady Briars. I'm certain you must have set the young men scurrying around for your attention."

Lady Briars was obviously pleased by Jade's comments. She actually blushed. She paused to pat her hair before answering. Jade noticed the tremor in the elderly woman's hand then. The ravages of age, she decided as she waited for her to answer.

"I had my hopes set on your father for a long time, my dear. Thorton was such a dashing man. That special spark was missing, though. We ended up good friends, of course. I still think about him every once in a while, and I sometimes bring out some of the precious little gifts he gave me. I get quite maudlin," she admitted. "Do you have any special mementos to remember your father by, Jade?"

"No," Jade answered. "Everything that belonged to my father burned in the fire."

"Fire?"

"This is going to disappoint you, Lady Briars, but the lovely house you helped Nathan renovate caught fire. Everything was destroyed."

"Oh, my poor dear," Lady Briars whispered. "It has been a difficult time for you, hasn't it?"

Jade nodded agreement. "Caine has been a comfort, of course. I doubt I would have gotten through this last month without him at my side."

"Yes, that is fortunate," Lady Briars announced. She put her teacup down on the table. "So you say you don't have anything at all to remember your father by? Nothing at all? Not even a family bible or a time piece or a letter?"

Jade shook her head. Caine took hold of her hand and squeezed it. "Sweetheart, you're forgetting the trunk," he interjected smoothly.

She turned to look at Caine, wondering what his game was. Not a hint of her confusion appeared in her expression however. "Oh, yes, the trunk," she agreed.

"Then you do have something to remember your father by, after all," Lady Briars announced. She nodded in apparent satisfaction. "I was going to rush right home and go through my things to find something for you. A daughter must have a trinket or two from her father. Now, I remember a lovely porcelain statue your father gave me as a birthday gift when I turned sixteen . . ."

"Oh, I couldn't take that from you," she interjected.

"No, she couldn't," Caine said. "Besides, she has the trunk. Of course, we haven't had a chance to look inside yet. Jade's been so ill these past weeks with the worrisome fever."

He turned to smile at Jade. "My dear, what say we go over to Nathan's town house next week? If you're feeling up to the outing," he added. "We still have to settle her brother's affairs," he told Lady Briars.

Jade thought Caine had lost his mind. She smiled, just to cover her unease, while she waited for his next surprise.

It wasn't long in coming. "Perhaps you'd like to accompany us over to Nathan's place and have a look at the trunk with us," Caine suggested.

Lady Briars declined the invitation. She insisted that Jade come to see her soon, then took her leave. Caine assisted the frail woman into her carriage.

Jade paced the drawing room until he returned. "And just what was that all about?" she demanded as soon as he walked inside again.

He shut the doors before answering her. She noticed his grin then. Caine looked thoroughly pleased with himself.

"I didn't like lying to that dear woman one bit, Caine," she cried out. "Besides, I'm the accomplished liar in this family, not you. Why did you tell her there was a trunk, for heaven's sake? Were you thinking to make her feel better so she wouldn't have to give up any of her cherished possessions? Do you know, now that I reflect upon this, I don't like hearing you lie at all. Well?" she demanded when she needed to pause for breath. "What have you got to say for yourself?"

"The lie was necessary," Caine began.

She wouldn't let him get any further. "'No lie is ever necessary,'" she quoted from memory. "You told me that days ago. Remember?"

"Love, you're really upset because I lied?" he asked. He looked astonished.

"I most certainly am upset," she returned. "I've come to depend upon your honesty, Caine. Yet if you tell me the lie was really necessary, then I must assume you have a plan. Do you think Lady Briars might mention this imaginary trunk to someone? Is that it?"

She thought she had it all figured out. "No," he answered, smiling over the frown his denial caused.

"No? Then you should be ashamed of yourself for lying to that old woman."

"If you'll let me explain . . ."

She folded her arms across her chest. "This had better be good, sir, or I just might blister you."

He thought she sounded like her Uncle Harry now. She was certainly blustering enough to make him draw that conclusion. He laughed and took his disgruntled looking wife into his arms.

"Well?" she muttered against his jacket. "Explain, if you please, why you lied to a dear family friend."

"She isn't a dear family friend," Caine told her, his exasperation apparent in his tone of voice.

"Of course she is," Jade protested. "You heard her, husband. She has kept all the little presents my father gave her. She loved him!"

"She killed him."

Jade didn't react to that statement for a long, silent minute. Then she slowly lifted her gaze to stare into his eyes. She shook her head.

He nodded.

Her knees went weak on her. Caine had to hold her up when she slumped against him. "Are you trying to tell me," she began, her voice a mere thread. "Do you mean to say that Lady Briars is . . ."

"She's Ice."

"Ice?" She shook her head again. "She can't be Ice," she cried out. "For God's sake, Caine. She's a woman."

"And women can't be killers?"

"No," she returned. "I mean to say yes, I do suppose . . ."

He took mercy on her confused state. "All the clues fit, Jade. Now sit down and let me explain it to you," he suggested.

She was simply too stunned to move. Caine led her over to the settee, gently pushed her down on the cushions, and then settled himself next to her. "It's really very logical," he began as he put his arm around her shoulders.

A small smile tugged at the corners of her mouth. She was recovering from her initial surprise. "I knew it would be logical."

"I was suspicious when I reread the letters, of course. And I never make the same mistake twice, love, remember?"

"I remember that you like to make that boast whenever possible, husband, dear. Now explain to me what this mistake is that you didn't repeat."

"I thought Pagan was a man. I never once considered that

he could be a she. I didn't make that same error when I was hunting Ice."

"You are really convinced Lady Briars is Ice? How did you come to that conclusion?" she asked.

He wasn't about to let the topic completely turn just yet. "Jade? Did you ever consider that Ice could be a woman? Tell me the truth," he commanded in that arrogant tone she liked so much.

She let out a sigh. "You're going to gloat."

"Yes, I'm sure I will."

They shared a smile. "No, I never once considered that possibility. There, are you happy?"

"Immensely," he drawled out.

"Caine, you still have to convince me," she reminded him. "Lord, I'm still having difficulty believing this. Ice killed people and threatened to kill Nathan and me. Remember that one letter, where he told my father that if the letters weren't returned, he would kill us?"

"Not he, love," Caine replied. "She." He let out a long sigh, then added, "Jade, some women do kill."

"Oh, I know," she countered. "Still, it isn't at all ladylike."

"Do you remember in one of the earlier letters, when they were given their operative names, that Ice admitted to being furious over that name? That comment made me curious. Not too many men would care one way or the other. A woman would mind, though, wouldn't she?"

"Some might."

"There are more substantial clues, of course. Briars hired the full staff for Nathan's country home. They were her men, loyal to her. The fact that the house was pillaged told me they were searching. And guess where Hudson, Nathan's butler, turned up?"

"He's staying at Nathan's town house, isn't he? He's guarding it until we close it up."

"No, he's currently in Lady Briars' residence. I imagine we'll find that your brother's town house has been turned upside down by now."

She ignored his smile. "I never trusted Hudson," she announced. "The man kept trying to force tea down me. I'll wager it was poisoned."

"Now, Jade, don't let your imagination get the better of you. By the way, all those confusing incidents were Hudson's doing. They did dig up your father's grave on the off chance that the letters had been hidden there. They cleaned up the mess, too."

"Did Hudson shoot Nathan's fine horse?"

"No, Willburn did," Caine explained.

"I'm telling Nathan."

Caine nodded. "Hudson had the cleanup detail. You were right, by the way, a cart was used to carry the horse away. It must have taken seven strong men to lift the steed."

"How did you learn all this?"

"You're impressed with me, aren't you?"

He nudged her into answering. "Yes, Caine, I'm impressed. Now tell me the rest."

"My men have been ferreting out the facts for me so I can't take all the credit. The horse was found in a ravine almost two miles away from the main road."

"Just wait until I tell Nathan," Jade muttered again.

Caine patted her shoulder. "You can explain it all to him after this is finished, all right?"

She nodded. "Is there more to tell me, Caine?"

"Well, once I decided that Briars was certainly the most logical candidate, I looked into her background. On the surface, everything appeared to be above board, but the deeper I looked, the more the little oddities showed up."

"For instance?"

"She did a hell of a lot of traveling for a woman," he remarked. "For instance," he added before Jade could interrupt, "she went back and forth to France at least seven times that I know of, and . . ."

"And you thought that odd? Perhaps she has relatives . . ."

"No," he countered. "Besides, Jade, she did most of her traveling during war time. There were other telling clues."

"I do believe I'm married to the most intelligent man in all the world," she praised. "Caine, it's only just beginning to make sense to me. What do Sir Richards and Lyon have to say about your discovery?"

"I haven't told them yet," he answered. "I wanted to be absolutely certain. After listening to Briars' questions, I don't have any doubts left. I'll tell them tonight when I meet them at White's."

"What question did she ask that made you suspicious?"

"She asked you right away if you could read, remember? Considering the fact that most well-bred ladies in England have acquired that skill, I thought it was a telling question."

"But she knew I'd been raised on an island," Jade argued. "That's why she asked, Caine. She was trying to find out if I'd been raised properly without coming right out and . . ."

"She was also a little too interested in finding out what your father had left you," he interrupted.

Jade's shoulders slumped. "I thought she was sincere."

"We'll have to tighten the net around Nathan's town house," Caine remarked. "I only have two men guarding it now." He paused to smile at Jade. "Your poor brother will probably have his town house burned to the ground before this is over."

"You needn't look so cheerful over that possibility," she said. "Besides, Hudson has had ample time to find out there isn't any trunk." She let out a small gasp. "I have another disappointment for you, Caine. Lady Briars knows I was lying when I said I couldn't read. I believe she asked that question to find out if we might be on to her. Oh, yes, I do believe we've mucked it up this time."

Caine lost his smile. "What are you talking about? Why do you think Briars knows you were lying?"

"Hudson saw me reading almost every night," she rushed out. "After dinner, I'd go into Nathan's lovely study and read until I became sleepy. There were so many wonderful books I hadn't memorized yet. Hudson would light the fire in the hearth for me. I'm certain he told Lady Briars."

She patted his hand to soften his disappointment. "Now, what will you do?" she asked, certain he'd come up with an alternate plan of action in no time at all. Caine was simply too logical not to have covered every possibility.

"Eventually we'll be able to compare the handwriting, once we get the letters from the *Emerald.*"

"We have a sample here," Jade said. "Lady Briars sent two notes requesting I call on her. I hate to disappoint you, but the handwriting didn't look at all familiar."

"I doubt she wrote those notes," Caine returned. "She's old, Jade, but she hasn't gotten careless yet. No, she probably had one of her assistants pen the letters."

"Would you like for me to steal . . ."

"I'd like you to stay here day and night," he stated. The suggestion was given as a command. "This is going to get sticky before it's finished. Everything I've gathered is actually circumstantial evidence in a court, Jade. I've still got some work to do. Now promise me you won't leave."

"I promise," she answered. "Have a little faith in me, husband. You know that once I give my word, I'll keep it. Please tell me what you have planned."

"Lyon's been itching to put a little pressure on Willburn. I think it's time he had his way. Willburn hasn't been at all accommodating thus far. We hoped he'd lead us to Ice, but he stays hidden behind his drapes all day. Yes, it's time we had a talk with him."

. "I don't like the idea of you leaving every night, Caine. Until the ship is burned and the rumor of Pagan's death hits

London, I think you should stay home. I'll tell you this, sir, if the people in this town celebrate my death, I'm going to be very disappointed."

Caine's smile was gentle. "They would mourn," he promised. "Anyway, we'll never know. It isn't necessary to burn the ship now."

"Why?"

"Because I know who Ice is," he explained. "And she isn't going to quit coming after me, either. She knows we're on to her."

"Yes," Jade countered. "If you hadn't made me lie about not knowing how to read, she wouldn't be on to us, husband. See? That lie wasn't all for the good."

"Don't sound so smug, my love."

"Harry's going to be happy he doesn't have to burn a ship," she announced, ignoring his remark. "You will send someone to tell him, won't you?"

"Yes, I'll send someone to Shallow's Wharf," he replied. "You're going to have to tell me exactly where that is, Jade. It's an operative name for somewhere else, isn't it?"

Jade cuddled up against her husband. "You are so clever," she whispered. "You will be careful when you go out, won't you? She's on to us, all right. I don't want you turning your back on anyone, Caine. I have come to rely on you."

"And I have come to rely on you," he answered. His grin was telling. "This is sounding damned equal to me."

"It is equal," she said. "But you can pretend it isn't if it will make you feel better."

He ignored that comment and tickled the side of her neck instead. Jade shivered in reaction. "Do you feel like another dance lesson now?"

"Will I be on my knees again?"

"Didn't you like it, love? You acted like you did. Your mouth was so sweet, so . . ."

"I liked it," she admitted in a rush.

"Can we?"

"Oh, yes." Her voice was breathless.

"Upstairs or here?"

"Upstairs," she whispered. She stood up and tugged on his hand. "But this time, Caine, I want to lead."

They spent the rest of the day in each others' arms. It was a blissful time that ended all too soon. Before she knew it, she was reminding him to remember McKindry and he was demanding her promise to stay put until he returned.

Jade was so exhausted, she slept quite soundly until an hour or so before dawn. She awakened with a start, then rolled on her side to take Caine into her arms.

He wasn't there. Jade rushed downstairs to check inside the library. Caine hadn't come back to her yet. Since he'd never taken this long before, she started worrying.

She'd worked herself into a frenzy when another hour passed and he still hadn't returned.

Her instincts were screaming a warning. Something was terribly wrong. The familiar ache had settled in her stomach just like in the old days when a plan would go amiss.

She had to be ready. Jade dressed in quick time, added a dagger to her pocket, the special clip to her hair, then resumed pacing again.

Caine had left two guards for her protection. One stood in the shadows outside the front door and the other guarded the back entrance.

Jade decided to talk to Cyril, the man guarding the front entrance. Perhaps he'd know what they should do. She opened the door just in time to see a man hand Cyril a piece of paper and then run away.

Cyril bounded up the steps two at a time. "It's a letter for you," he said. "At this hour of the night," he added in a near growl. "It can't be good news, mi'lady."

"I hope it's from Caine," she blurted out. "Come inside, Cyril. Bolt the door behind you. Something's wrong," she added as she tore the seal from the envelope. "Caine has never taken this long before."

Cyril grumbled his agreement. "Aye," he said. "I feel it in my gut."

"Me, too," Jade whispered.

As soon as Jade unfolded the sheet of paper, she paled. She recognized the script immediately. The note came from Ice.

"What is it, mi'lady?" Cyril asked. He spoke in a hushed tone, an oddity, that, for Cyril was a big man with a booming voice to match.

"Caine's in trouble," Jade whispered. "I have one hour to go to a building on Lathrop Street. Do you know where that is?"

"It's a warehouse if it's on Lathrop," Cyril answered. "I don't like this," he added. "I'm sniffing a trap. What happens if we don't go?"

"They'll kill my husband."

"I'll go fetch Alden," Cyril announced. He started toward the back door but stopped when Jade called out to him.

"I'm not going."

"But . . ."

"I can't leave. I have to stay here, Cyril. This could be a trick and I gave my word to Caine. No, I have to stay here. Do you know how late White's stays open?"

"It's closed for certain by now."

"Caine might have gone to have a talk with a man named Willburn. Do you know where he lives?"

"I do," the guard answered. "He's just six, perhaps seven blocks over."

"Send Alden over there now. Lyon and Caine might be having a visitation with the infidel."

"And if they aren't?"

"While Alden goes to Willburn's house, I want you to run

over to Lyon's residence. Now then, if Lyon isn't home, then go on to Sir Richards' town house. Do you know where those two men live?"

"Yes," Cyril said. "But who will guard you while we're tracking Caine down? You'll be all alone."

"I'll bolt the doors," she promised. "Please hurry, Cyril. We need to find Caine before the hour is up. If we can't find him, then I have to assume the note wasn't trickery."

"We'll hurry," Cyril promised on his way toward the back of the house.

Jade clutched the letter in her hands and stood in the center of the foyer a long while. She then went upstairs to her bedroom. She bolted the door behind her.

The pounding started on the front door just a few minutes later. She knew it wasn't Caine. He had a key, of course. The sound of glass shattering came next.

Had she inadvertently played right into their hands? Were they so certain she'd send the guards to look for Caine? Jade found solace in that possibility, for it meant Caine hadn't been taken captive after all.

She prayed she was right, prayed, too, that God wouldn't get angry with her. She was probably going to have to kill someone, and very soon, judging from the sounds of men lumbering up the steps.

Jade grabbed the pistol from the drawer of the nightstand on Caine's side of the bed, backed herself into a corner, and took aim. She decided she would wait until they'd broken the latch, then shoot the first man who entered the room.

Her hand was steady. A deadly calm came over her, too. And then the door was kicked open. A dark form filled the entrance. And still she waited, for she wanted to be absolutely certain it was her enemy and not one of Caine's hired men arriving to save her.

"Light a candle," the voice shouted. "I can't see the bitch."

Jade squeezed the trigger. She must have caught the man somewhere in the middle, for he let out a loud scream of pain as he doubled over. He fell to the floor with a loud thud.

She won that round, she told herself, though the battle went to Ice. Jade was surrounded by three men. When the first reached for her, she cut his hand with her knife. The second villain grabbed her weapon just as the third slammed his fist into the side of her jaw. The blow felled her to the floor in a dead faint.

Jade didn't wake up again until she was being carried inside a dark, damp building. There were only a few candles lighting the area but quite enough for Jade to see the crates stacked up along the stone walls. At the end of the long corridor stood a woman dressed in white. Lady Briars was there, waiting for her.

The man carrying her dropped her when he'd reached his leader. Jade staggered to her feet. She rubbed the sting in her jaw while she stared at her adversary.

The look in those eyes was chilling. "I understand now why you were given the name Ice," she heard herself say. "You don't have a soul, do you, Lady Briars?"

Jade was rewarded by a sound slap across her face. "Where are the letters?" Briars demanded.

"Safe," Jade answered. "Do you really believe stealing the letters back is going to save you? Too many people know what you've done. Too many . . ."

"You fool!" Briars shouted. There was such strength, such cruelty in her voice that Jade suddenly felt as though she were facing the devil. She resisted the urge to cross herself. "I will have those letters, Jade. They are my proof to the world of all the glorious feats I've accomplished. No one's going to deny me now. No one. In years to come, the world will realize what my Tribunal was able to accomplish. We could have ruled England, if I had chosen to continue with my work. Oh yes, I will have the letters back. They will be kept in a safe place until the time is right to reveal my genius."

She was mad. Jade could feel the goose bumps on her arms. She tried desperately to think of a way to reason with the woman before she finally came to the conclusion that the crazed woman was beyond any kind of reason. "If I give you the letters back, will you leave Caine alone?" she asked.

Lady Briars let out a high-pitched snicker. "If? Don't you have any idea who I am? You can't possibly deny me, Jade."

"Oh, I know who you are," Jade replied. "You're the woman who killed my father. You're the woman who betrayed her country. You're the foul creature who was born from the devil. You're the demented . . ."

She quit her tirade when Briars hit her again. Jade backed up a space, then straightened her shoulders. "Let Caine go, Briars, and I will get you the letters."

In answer to that promise, Briars turned to one of her cohorts. "Lock our guest in the back room," she ordered. She turned to Jade then. "You're going to be the bait, my dear, to get Caine here. He has to die," she added in a singsong voice. "But only after he's given me the letters, of course. Then I shall kill you, too, little Jade. Your father was the true traitor, for he turned his back against me. Me! Oh, how I wished I could have been there when his son died. You will have to make up for that regret, dear, dear child, by dying slowly by my hand . . . Get her out of here!" Briars ended in a near shout.

Jade felt like weeping with relief. They hadn't taken Caine after all. He would come for her, she knew, and there was still danger . . . but he was safe for the moment.

She actually smiled to herself when they led her to her temporary prison. They believed they had her now. They mustn't tie her hands, she thought to herself. Jade started whimpering so that her captors would believe she was frightened. As soon as they opened the door, she rushed inside, then collapsed on the floor in the center of the room, and began to cry.

The door slammed shut behind her. She kept up her wailing until the sound of footsteps faded. Then she took inventory. Moonlight filtered in through the gray filmed window. The opening was a good fifteen feet up. There was only one piece of furniture, an old scarred desk with only three legs, and they certainly knew she wouldn't be able to reach the window even if she stood on top of the desk.

Yes, they thought they had secured her inside. Jade let out a little sigh of pleasure.

She pulled the special clip from her hair that she used for just such an occasion, and went to work on the lock.

Because she was in such a desperate hurry to get to Caine before Briars' men did, she wasn't as quick as she would have been under calmer circumstances. It took her a little over ten minutes to work the lock free.

It was pitch black inside the warehouse proper. Even though Jade was certain Briars had taken all her men with her, she still made her exit as quietly as possible. Jade was completely disoriented when she reached the street. She ran in one direction for two long blocks before she got her bearings and realized she'd taken the wrong way.

Jade was in absolute terror now. She knew it was going to take her another fifteen minutes to reach home. While she ran, she made several fervent promises to her Maker. She gave him her word that she would never lie or steal again, if he would only keep Caine safe. "I know you gave me those special talents, Lord, and you know that once I give my word, I won't break it. I won't follow in my father's path, either. Just let me live long enough to prove myself. Please, God? Caine needs me."

She had to stop when the stitch in her side intensified. "If you'll only give me a little added strength, Lord, I won't use blasphemies either."

Odd, but the stitch in her side faded. She was able to catch her breath, too. That last promise must have been the one her Maker was waiting to hear, she decided.

"Thank you," she whispered as she picked up her skirts again and started running.

Jade didn't stop again until she reached the street their town house was located on. She kept to the shadows as she made her way toward the steps. When she spotted three men littering her stoop, she started running again. The men weren't in any condition to waylay her. They looked restful too, in their forced slumber.

Caine had obviously come home.

Jade couldn't remember the number of men Briars had with her. She began to fret again. Should she sneak in by way of the back door or should she boldly walk into the foyer and try to confront Briars once again.

The question was answered for her when Caine's bellow reached her.

"Where is she?" Caine roared through the door.

The anguish in his voice tore at Jade's heart. She pulled the door open and rushed inside.

They were all in the drawing room. Lyon, Jade noticed, was holding Caine by the shoulders. Briars stood in front of the two men. Sir Richards stood next to her. Both Cyril and Alden stood behind the director.

"She'll die of starvation before you find her," Briars shouted. She let out a snort of amusement. "No, you'll never find her. Never."

"Oh, yes, he will."

Briars let out a screech when Jade's soft voice reached her. Caine and Lyon both whirled around.

Caine simply stood there, smiling at her. She saw the tears in his eyes, knew her own were just as misty. Lyon looked as startled as Richards. "Jade . . . how did you . . ."

She looked at Caine when she gave her answer. "They locked me in."

It took a full minute before anyone reacted. Lyon was the first to laugh. "They locked her in," he said to Caine.

Jade kept smiling until Caine walked over to her. When he reached out to touch her face with his fingertips, she burst into tears and ran up the stairs.

She went into the first bedroom, slammed the door shut behind her, and threw herself down on the bed. Caine was right behind her. He pulled her into his arms.

"My love, it's all over now," he whispered.

"I didn't leave you. I stayed right here until they came inside and dragged me away. I didn't break my word."

"Hush, Jade. I never thought . . ."

"Caine, I was so scared," she wailed against his chest.

"So was I," he whispered. He squeezed her tight, then said, "When Cyril told me . . . I thought you were . . . Oh, God, yes, I was damned scared."

She mopped her eyes on his jacket, then said, "You can't say damn anymore. We can't ever use another blasphemy, Caine. I promised God."

His smile was filled with tenderness. "I see."

"I would have promised anything to keep you safe," she whispered. "I need you so much, Caine."

"I need you, too, my love."

"We can't steal anymore, or lie, either," she told him then. "I made those promises, too."

He rolled his eyes heavenward. "And your promises are also mine?" he asked her. He hid his smile now, for she looked so sincere, and he didn't bother to mention to her that he'd never stolen anything before.

"Yes, of course my promises are also yours," she answered. "We are suppose to share everything, aren't we? Caine, we are equal partners in this marriage."

"We are equal," he agreed.

"Then my promises are also yours?"

"Yes," he answered. He suddenly pulled away from her.

The worry in his expression was obvious. "You didn't give up anything else, did you?"

He looked as though he dreaded her answer. She immediately guessed what he was thinking. "Like dancing?"

"Like making love."

She laughed, a full rich sound filled with joy. "Aren't they the same thing?"

"This isn't the time for jests, Jade."

"No, Caine, we didn't give up dancing or making love. I would never give a promise I couldn't keep," she added, quoting back his very words to her.

Caine wanted to tear her clothes off and make love to her then and there. He couldn't, of course, for there was still the mess to be cleaned up downstairs.

He wasn't able to spend much time with his bride over the next couple of days. He and Lyon were both occupied dictating their findings for their superior's records. Lady Briars was locked away in Newgate Prison. There was talk that she was going to be transferred to a nearby asylum, for the court had decreed that the woman was quite mad. Jade was in wholehearted agreement.

Caine was finally free to keep his other promise to Jade. They settled down to live a peaceful life together.

And just as he'd predicted, they did live happily ever after.

He was still terribly insecure, however. Jade did worry about that. On the morning of their first anniversary, he demanded she give him her pledge to stay for another year.

Jade thought the question was ill-timed, considering the fact that she was in the midst of an excruciating contraction. She gritted her teeth against the agony.

"Caine, we're going to have our baby," she said.

"I know, my love," he answered. He rolled to his side and gently rubbed her swollen abdomen. "I noticed quite a long time ago," he added just to tease her. He leaned down to kiss her damp brow. "Are you too warm, Jade?"

"No, I'm . . ."

"Give me your promise," he interrupted while he pulled the top cover away. "Then you can go back to sleep. You were very restless during the night. I think you stayed up too late talking with Lyon and Christina. I was glad to see them, of course, and I'm happy Christina wants to offer her services when the time comes, but I still insist that a physician be in attendance, Jade."

Jade was too exhausted to argue. She'd been having sporadic contractions during the long night. She didn't wake Caine, though. She was following her good friend's advice. Christina had suggested that it would be better if her husband weren't bothered until the very last minute. Husbands, Christina had explained, fell apart too easily.

Christina considered Jade her blood sister, ever since the night she handed her Lyon's file and told her to keep it safe. The two ladies trusted each other completely and spent hour upon hour telling each other favorite stories about their pasts.

Caine gently prodded his wife. "I want your word now."

As soon as the fresh contraction faded, she answered him. "Yes, I promise you. And, Caine, we're going to have our baby now. Go and wake Christina."

The babe Jade was certain was going to present himself at any moment didn't actually arrive for another three hours.

Through the intense labor, Caine remained as calm, as solid and dependable as Jade had expected. She thought then that Christina had been wrong. Not all men fell apart so easily.

Christina sent Caine down to the library when Jade's contractions became too unbearable for him to watch. Caine only lasted five minutes below the stairs, however, and was then back at Jade's side, clutching her hand in his and begging her forgiveness for putting her through this god-awful ordeal.

He was more hindrance than help, of course. He didn't

panic during the birthing, however, and just bare minutes later was holding his beautiful daughter in his arms.

Sterns couldn't restrain himself. As soon as he heard the lusty cries of the newborn, he bounded into the room. He immediately took the baby away from Caine, announced that she was indeed magnificent, and then proceeded to give her her first bath.

Christina took care of Jade. Caine helped her change the sheets and Jade's gown, as well, and when Christina told Caine he'd held up rather well, he actually managed a smile.

Caine was pale, his hands were shaking, his brow was drenched with sweat, he still couldn't speak a coherent word, but he had held fast.

Yet once the trauma was over, his discipline deserted him.

Christina had just left the room to give the wonderful news to her husband. Sterns was cuddling his new charge in his arms, and Jade was simply too weak to catch her husband.

"Is he all right?" Jade asked Sterns. She couldn't even find the strength to look over the edge of the bed.

"He swooned."

"I know he swooned," Jade replied. "But is he all right? He didn't hit his head on anything sharp, did he?"

"He's fine," Sterns announced. He hadn't bothered to look down at his employer when he made that pronouncement but continued to stare down at the beautiful infant. The look on his face was one of true adoration.

"Do help him up," Jade whispered. She was biting her lip to keep herself from laughing.

"He doesn't appear to be ready to get up just yet," Sterns announced. "The babe needs my full attention now. You've done very well, mi'lady, very well, indeed. I'm certain the Marquess will agree when he finishes his faint."

Jade beamed with satisfaction. Her eyes filled with tears. "You're never going to let him live this down, are you, Sterns?"

Caine groaned then, drawing her attention. "We must never tell anyone he swooned. He'd die of embarrassment."

"Don't worry, mi'lady," Sterns returned. "I certainly won't tell anyone. I promise."

She should have realized from the determined sparkle in his eyes that he wasn't going to honor his promise. Three days later, she read all about Caine's fainting spell.

The rascal butler had posted it in the dailies.

The Marquess of Cainewood took it all in stride. He didn't mind the jests from the well-wishers at all.

Nothing could rile his temper. After all, his mission had been successful. He'd hunted down the infamous pirate . . . and now she belonged to him.

The hunter was content.

The Gift

For Bryan Michael Garwood.
This one's all yours.

Prologue

England, 1802

It was only a matter of time before the wedding guests killed one another.

Baron Oliver Lawrence had taken every precaution, of course, for it was his castle King George had chosen for the ceremony. He was acting as host until the king of England arrived, a duty he embraced with as much joy as he would a three-day flogging; but the order had come from the king himself, and Lawrence, ever loyal and obedient, had immediately complied. Both the Winchester family and the St. James rebels had protested his selection most vehemently. Their noise was all for naught, however, for the king was determined to have his way. Baron Lawrence understood the reason behind the decree. Unfortunately, he was the only man in England still on speaking terms with both the bride's and the groom's families.

The baron wouldn't be able to boast about that fact much longer. He believed his time on the sweet earth could well be measured in heartbeats. Because the ceremony was to take place on neutral ground, the king actually believed the gathering would behave. Lawrence knew better.

1

The men surrounding him were in a killing mood. One word given in the wrong tone of voice, one action perceived to be the least bit threatening could well become the spark needed to ignite the bloodbath. God only knew they were itching to get at one another. The looks on their faces said as much.

The bishop, dressed in ceremonial whites, sat in a high-backed chair between the two feuding families. He looked neither to the left, where the Winchesters were sequestered, nor to the right, where the St. James warriors were stationed, but stared straight ahead. To pass the time the clergyman drummed his fingertips on the wooden arm of his chair. He looked as though he'd just eaten a fair portion of sour fish. He let out a high-pitched sigh every now and then, a sound the baron thought was remarkably like the whinny of a cranky old horse, then let the damning silence envelop the great hall again.

Lawrence shook his head in despair. He knew he wouldn't get any help from the bishop when the real trouble broke out. Both the bride and the groom waited in separate chambers above the stairs. Only after the king had arrived would they be led, or dragged, into the hall. God help the two of them then, for all hell would surely break loose.

It was a sorry day indeed. Lawrence had actually had to post his own contingent of guards betwixt the king's knights along the perimeter of the hall just as an added deterrent. Such an action at a wedding was unheard of, yet it was just as unheard of for the guests to come to the ceremony armed for battle. The Winchesters were so loaded down with weapons they could barely move about. Their insolence was shameful, their loyalty more than suspect. Still, Lawrence was hard put to condemn the men completely. It was true that even he found it a challenge to blindly obey his leader. The king was, after all, as daft as a duck.

Everyone in England knew he had lost his mind, yet no one dared speak the fact aloud. They'd lose their tongues, or worse, for daring to tell the truth. The marriage about to take place was more than ample testimony to any doubting Thomases left in the *ton* that their leader had gone around the bend. The king had told Lawrence he was determined to have everyone in his kingdom get along. The baron didn't have an easy answer to that childlike expectation.

But for all of his madness, George was their king, and damn it all, thought Lawrence, the wedding guests should show a little respect. Their outrageous conduct shouldn't be tolerated. Why, two of the seasoned Winchester uncles were blatantly fondling the hilts of their swords in obvious anticipation of the bloodletting. The St. James warriors immediately noticed and retaliated by taking a unified step forward. They didn't touch their weapons, though, and in truth most of the St. James's men weren't even armed. They smiled instead. Lawrence thought that action was just as telling.

The Winchesters outnumbered the St. James clan six to one. That didn't give them the advantage, however. The St. James men were a much meaner lot. The stories about their escapades were legendary. They were known to tear a man's eyes out just for squinting; they liked to kick an opponent in his groin for the fun of hearing him howl; and God only knew what they did to their enemies. The possibilities were simply too appalling to think about.

A commotion coming from the courtyard turned Lawrence's attention. The king's personal assistant, a dour-faced man by the name of Sir Roland Hugo, rushed up the steps. He was dressed in festive garb, but the colorful red hose and white tunic made his imposing bulk all the more rotund-looking. Lawrence thought Hugo resembled a plump rooster. Because he was his good friend, he kept that unkind opinion to himself.

The two men quickly embraced. Then Hugo took a step back. In a hushed tone he said, "I rode ahead the last league. The king will be here in just a few more minutes."

"Thank God for that," Lawrence replied, his relief visible. He mopped at the beads of sweat on his brow with his linen handkerchief.

Hugo glanced over Lawrence's shoulder, then shook his head. "It's as quiet as a tomb in your hall," he whispered. "Have you had a time of it keeping the wedding guests amused?"

Lawrence looked incredulous. "Amused? Hugo, nothing short of a human sacrifice could keep those barbarians amused."

"I can see your sense of humor has helped you through this atrocity," his friend replied.

"I'm not jesting," the baron snapped. "You'll quit your smile, too, Hugo, when you realize how volatile the situation has become. The Winchesters didn't come bearing gifts, my friend. They're armed for battle. Yes, they are," he rushed on when his friend shook his head in apparent disbelief. "I tried to persuade them to leave their arsenal outside, but they wouldn't hear of it. They aren't in an accommodating mood."

"We'll see about that," Hugo muttered. "The soldiers riding escort with our king will disarm them in little time. I'll be damned if I allow our overlord to walk into such a threatening arena. This is a wedding, not a battlefield."

Hugo proved to be as good as his threat. The Winchesters piled their weapons in the corner of the great hall when they were confronted with the order by the infuriated king's assistant. The demand was backed up by some forty loyal soldiers who'd taken up their positions in a circle around the guests. Even the St. James rascals handed over their few weapons, but only after Hugo ordered arrows put to the soldiers' bows.

If he lived to tell the tale, no one was ever going to believe him, Lawrence decided. Thankfully, King George had no idea what extreme measures had been taken to secure his protection.

When the king of England walked into the great hall the

4

soldiers immediately lowered their bows, though their arrows remained securely nocked for a quick kill if the need arose.

The bishop rallied out of the chair, bowed formally to his king, and then motioned for him to take his seat.

Two of the king's barristers, their arms laden with documents, trailed in the king's wake. Lawrence waited until his leader was seated, then hurried over to kneel before him. He spoke his pledge of loyalty in a loud, booming voice, hoping his words would shame the guests into showing like consideration.

The king leaned forward, his big hands braced on his knees. "Your patriot king is pleased with you, Baron Lawrence. I am your patriot king, champion of all the people, am I not?"

Lawrence was prepared for that question. The king had taken to calling himself by that name years before, and he liked to hear affirmation whenever possible.

"Yes, my lord, you are my patriot king, champion of all the people."

"That's a good lad," the king whispered. He reached out and patted the top of Lawrence's balding head. The baron blushed in embarrassment. The king was treating him like a young squire. Worse, the baron was beginning to feel like one.

"Stand now, Baron Lawrence, and help me oversee this important occasion," the king ordered.

Lawrence immediately did as he was told. When he got a close look at his leader he had to force himself not to show any outward reaction. He was stunned by the king's deteriorating appearance. George had been a handsome figure in his younger days. Age hadn't been kind to him. His jowls were fuller, his wrinkles deeper, and there were full bags of fatigue under his eyes. He wore a pure white wig, the ends rolled up on the sides, but the color made his complexion look all the more shallow.

The king smiled up at his vassal in innocent expectation.

Lawrence smiled back. There was such kindness, such sincerity in his leader's expression. The baron was suddenly outraged on his behalf. For so many years, before his illness had made him confused, George had been far more than just an able king. His attitude toward his subjects was that of a benevolent father watching over his children. He deserved better than he was getting.

The baron moved to the king's side, then turned to look at the group of men he thought of as infidels. His voice shook with fury when he commanded, "Kneel!"

They knelt.

Hugo was staring at Lawrence with the most amazed expression on his face. He obviously hadn't realized his friend could be so forceful. As to that, Lawrence had to admit that until that moment he hadn't known he had it in him either.

The king was pleased with the united show of loyalty, and that was all that mattered. "Baron?" he said with a glance in Lawrence's direction. "Go and fetch the bride and groom. The hour grows late, and there is much to be done."

As Lawrence was bowing in answer to that command the king turned in his chair and looked up at Sir Hugo. "Where are all the ladies? I daresay I don't see a single lady in evidence. Why is that, Hugo?"

Hugo didn't want to tell the king the truth, that the men in attendance hadn't brought their women along because they were set on war, not merriment. Such honesty would only injure his king's tender feelings.

"Yes, my patriot king," Hugo blurted out. "I have also noticed the lack of ladies."

"But why is that?" the king persisted.

Hugo's mind emptied of all plausible explanations to give for the oddity. In desperation he called out to his friend. "Why is that, Lawrence?"

The baron had just reached the entrance. He caught the edge of panic in his friend's tone and immediately turned around. "The journey here would have been too difficult for such . . . frail ladies," he explained.

He almost choked on his words. The lie was outrageous, of course, for anyone who had ever met any of the Winchester women knew they were about as frail as jackals. King George's memory wasn't up to snuff, however, because his quick nod indicated he was appeased by the explanation.

The baron paused to glare at the Winchesters. It was their conduct, after all, that had forced the lie in the first place. He then continued on his errand.

The groom was the first to answer the summons. As soon as the tall, lanky marquess of St. James entered the hall a wide path was made for him.

The groom strolled into the hall like a mighty warrior ready to inspect his subjects. If he'd been homely, Lawrence would have thought of him as a young, arrogant Genghis Khan. The marquess was anything but homely, however. He had been gifted with dark, auburn-colored hair and clear green eyes. His face was thin, angular, his nose already broken in a fight he had, of course, won. The slight bump on the bridge made his profile look less pretty and more ruggedly handsome.

Nathan, as he was called by his immediate family, was one of the youngest noblemen in the kingdom. He was just a scant day over fourteen years. His father, the powerful earl of Wakersfield, was out of the country on an important assignment for his government and therefore couldn't stand beside his son during the ceremony. In fact, the earl had no idea the marriage was taking place. The baron knew he was going to be furious when he heard the news. The earl was a most unpleasant man under usual conditions, and when provoked he could be as vindictive and evil as Satan. He was known to be as mean as all the St. James relatives put together. Lawrence supposed that was the reason they all looked up to him for guidance on important matters.

Yet while Lawrence thoroughly disliked the earl, he

couldn't help but like Nathan. He'd been in the boy's company several times, noticed on each occasion that Nathan listened to the views the others had to give, and then did what he felt was best. He was just fourteen, yes, but he had already become his own man. Lawrence respected him. He felt a little sorry for him, too, for in all their visits together Lawrence had never once seen him smile. He thought that was a pity.

The St. James clan never called the marquess by his given name, though. They referred to him simply as "boy," for in their eyes he had still to prove his worth to them. There were tests he would have to conquer first. The relatives didn't doubt the lad's eventual success. They believed he was a natural leader, knew from his size that he would be a giant of a man, and hoped, above all other considerations, that he would develop a streak as mean as their own. He was family, after all, and there were certain responsibilities that would fall on his shoulders.

The marquess kept his gaze directed on the king of England as he made his way over to stand in front of him. The baron watched him closely. He knew Nathan had been instructed by his uncles not to kneel before his king unless commanded to do so.

Nathan ignored their instructions. He knelt on one knee, bowed his head, and stated his pledge of loyalty in a firm voice. When the king asked him if he was his patriot king, a hint of a smile softened the boy's expression.

"Aye, my lord," Nathan answered. "You are my patriot king."

The baron's admiration for the marquess increased tenfold. He could see from the king's smile that he was also pleased. Nathan's relatives weren't. Their scowls were hot enough to set fires. The Winchesters couldn't have been happier. They snickered in glee.

Nathan suddenly bounded to his feet in one fluid motion. He turned to stare at the Winchesters for a long, silent moment, and the look on his face, as cold as frost, seemed to chill the insolence right out of the men. The marquess didn't turn back to the king until most of the Winchesters were intently staring at the floor. The St. James men couldn't help but grunt their approval.

The lad wasn't paying any attention to his relatives. He stood with his legs braced apart, his hands clasped behind his back, and stared straight ahead. His expression showed only boredom.

Lawrence walked directly in front of Nathan so that he could nod to him. He wanted Nathan to know how much his conduct had pleased him.

Nathan responded by giving the baron a quick nod of his own. Lawrence hid his smile. The boy's arrogance warmed his heart. He had stood up to his relatives, ignoring the dire consequences that were sure to come, and had done the right thing. Lawrence felt very like a proud father—an odd reaction to be sure, for the baron had never married and had no children to call his own.

He wondered if Nathan's mask of boredom would hold up throughout the long ceremony. With that question lurking in the back of his mind he went to fetch the bride.

He could hear her wailing when he reached the second story. The sound was interrupted by a man's angry shout. The baron knocked on the door twice before the earl of Winchester, the bride's father, pulled it open. The earl's face was as red as a sunburn.

"It's about time," the earl bellowed.

"The king was delayed," the baron answered.

The earl abruptly nodded. "Come inside, Lawrence. Help me get her down the stairs, man. She's being a mite stubborn."

There was such surprise in the earl's voice, Lawrence almost smiled. "I've heard that stubbornness can be expected of such tender-aged daughters."

"I never heard such," the earl muttered. "'Tis the truth

9

this is the first time I've ever been alone with Sara. I'm not certain she knows exactly who I am," he added. "I did tell her, of course, but you will see she isn't in the mood to listen to anything. I had no idea she could be so difficult."

Lawrence couldn't hide his astonishment over the earl's outrageous remarks. "Harold," he answered, using the earl's given name, "you have two other daughters, as I recall, and both of them older than Sara. I don't understand how you can be so—"

The earl didn't let him finish. "I haven't ever had to be with any of them before," he muttered.

Lawrence thought that confession was appalling. He shook his head and followed the earl into the chamber. He spotted the bride right away. She was sitting on the edge of the window seat, staring out the window.

She quit crying as soon as she saw him. Lawrence thought she was the most enchanting bride he'd ever seen. A mop of golden curls framed an angelic face. There was a crown of spring flowers on her head, a cluster of freckles on the bridge of her nose. Tears streamed down her cheeks, and her brown eyes were cloudy with more.

She wore a long white dress with lace borders around the hem and wrists. When she stood up the embroidered sash around her waist fell to the floor.

Her father let out a loud blasphemy.

She repeated it.

"It's time for us to go downstairs, Sara," her father ordered, his voice as sour as the taste of soap.

"No."

The earl's outraged gasp filled the room. "When I get you home I'm going to make you very sorry you've put me through this ordeal, young lady. By God, I'm going to land on you, I am. Just you wait and see."

Since the baron didn't have the faintest idea what the earl meant by that absurd threat, he doubted Sara understood any better.

She was staring up at her father with a mutinous expression on her face. Then she let out a loud yawn and sat down again.

"Harold, shouting at your daughter isn't going to accomplish anything," the baron stated.

"Then I'll give her a good smack," the earl muttered. He took a threatening step toward his daughter, his hand raised to inflict the blow.

Lawrence stopped in front of the earl. "You aren't going to strike her," he said, his voice filled with anger.

"She's my daughter," the earl shouted. "I'll damn well do whatever it takes to gain her cooperation."

"You're a guest in my home now, Harold," the baron replied. He realized he was also shouting then and immediately lowered his voice. "Let me have a try."

Lawrence turned to the bride. Sara, he noticed, didn't seem to be at all worried by her father's anger. She let out another loud yawn.

"Sara, it will all be over and done with in just a little while," the baron said. He knelt down in front of her, gave her a quick smile, and then gently forced her to stand up. While he whispered words of praise to her he retied the sash around her waist. She yawned again.

The bride was in dire need of a nap. She let the baron tug her along to the door, then suddenly pulled out of his grasp, ran back to the window seat, and gathered up an old blanket that appeared to be three times her size.

She made a wide path around her father as she hurried back to the baron and took hold of his hand again. The blanket was draped over her shoulder and fell in a heap on the ground behind her. The edge was securely clasped under her nose.

Her father tried to take the blanket away.

Sara started screaming, her father started cursing, and the baron developed a pounding headache.

"For God's sake, Harold, let her have the thing."

"I'll not," the earl shouted. "It's an eyesore. I won't allow it."

"Let her keep it until we reach the hall," the baron commanded.

The earl finally conceded defeat. He gave his daughter a good glare, then took up his position in front of the pair and led the way down the stairs.

Lawrence found himself wishing Sara was his daughter. When she looked up at him and smiled so trustingly he wanted to take her into his arms and hug her. Her disposition underwent a radical change, however, when they reached the entrance to the hall and her father once again tried to take her blanket away.

Nathan turned when he heard the noise coming from the entrance. His eyes widened in astonishment. In truth, he was having difficulty believing what he was seeing. He hadn't been interested enough to ask any pertinent questions about his bride, for he was certain his father would have the documents overturned as soon as he returned to England, and for that reason he was all the more surprised by the sight of her.

His bride was a hellion. Nathan had trouble maintaining his bored expression. The earl of Winchester was doing more shouting than his daughter was. She, however, was far more determined. She had her arms wrapped around her father's leg and was diligently trying to take a fair chunk out of his knee.

Nathan smiled. His relatives weren't as reserved. Their laughter filled the hall. The Winchesters, on the other hand, were clearly appalled. The earl, their unspoken leader, had pulled his daughter away from his leg and was now involved in a tug of war over what resembled an old horse blanket. He wasn't winning the battle, either.

Baron Lawrence lost the last shreds of his composure. He grabbed hold of the bride, lifted her into his arms, snatched the blanket away from her father, and then marched over to

Nathan. With little ceremony he shoved the bride and the blanket into the groom's arms.

It was either accept her or drop her. Nathan was in the process of making up his mind on the matter when Sara spotted her father limping toward her. She quickly threw her arms around Nathan's neck, wrapping both herself and her blanket around him.

Sara kept glancing over his shoulder to make certain her father wasn't going to grab her. When she was certain she was safe she turned her full attention to the stranger holding her. She stared at him for the longest while.

The groom stood as straight as a lance. A fine sweat broke out on his brow. He could feel her gaze on his face yet didn't dare turn to look at her. She just might decide to bite him, and he didn't know what he would do then. He made up his mind that he would just have to suffer through any embarrassment she forced on him. He was, after all, almost a man, and she was, after all, only a child.

Nathan kept his gaze directed on the king until Sara reached out to touch his cheek. He finally turned to look at her.

She had the brownest eyes he'd ever seen. "Papa's going to smack me," she announced with a grimace.

He didn't show any reaction to that statement. Sara soon tired of watching him. Her eyelids fell to half mast. He stiffened even more when she slumped against his shoulder. Her face was pressed up against the side of his neck.

"Don't let Papa smack me," she whispered.

"I won't," he answered.

He had suddenly become her protector. Nathan couldn't hold onto his bored expression any longer. He cradled his bride in his arms and relaxed his stance.

Sara, exhausted from the long ride and her strenuous tantrum, rubbed the edge of her blanket back and forth under her nose. Within bare minutes she was fast asleep.

She drooled on his neck.

The groom didn't find out her true age until the barrister began the reading of the conditions for the union.

His bride was four years old.

Chapter One

London, England, 1816

It was going to be a clean, uncomplicated kidnapping.

Ironically, the abduction would probably hold up in the courts as a completely legal undertaking, save for the niggling breaking and entering charges, of course, but that possibility wasn't the least significant. Nathanial Clayton Hawthorn Baker, the third marquess of St. James, was fully prepared to use whatever methods he deemed necessary to gain success. If luck was on his side, his victim would be sound asleep. If not, a simple gag would eliminate any sounds of protest.

One way or another, legal or nay, he would collect his bride. Nathan, as he was called by those few friends close to him, wasn't going to have to act like a gentleman—a blessing, that, considering the fact that such tender qualities were completely foreign to his nature anyway. Besides, time was running out. There were only six weeks left before he would be in true violation of the marriage contract.

Nathan hadn't seen his bride since the day the contracts were read fourteen years earlier, but the picture he'd painted in his mind wasn't fanciful. He didn't have any illusions

15

about the chit, for he'd seen enough Winchester women to know there wasn't any such thing as a pick of the litter. They were all a sorry lot in both appearance and disposition. Most were pear-shaped, with big bones, bigger derrières, and, if the stories weren't exaggerated, gigantic appetites.

Although having a wife by his side was about as appealing to him as a midnight swim with the sharks would be, Nathan was fully prepared to suffer through the ordeal. Perhaps, if he really put his mind to the problem, he could find a way to meet the conditions of the contract without having to stay with the woman day and night.

For most of his life Nathan had been on his own, refusing to receive counsel from any man. Only his trusted friend Colin was privy to his thoughts. Still, the stakes were too high for Nathan to ignore. The booty the contract afforded after one year's cohabitation with Lady Sara more than made up for any repulsion he might feel or any inconvenience he might have to endure. The coins he would collect by the crown's decree would strengthen the fledgling partnership he and Colin had formed the summer before. The Emerald Shipping Company was the first legitimate business either man had ever attempted, and they were determined to make it work. The reason was simple to understand. Both men were tired of living on the edge. They'd fallen into the business of pirating quite by accident —had done fairly well for themselves, too—yet they felt that the risks involved were no longer worth the aggrava-tion. Nathan, operating as the infamous pirate Pagan, had made quite a legend for himself. His list of enemies could carpet a good-sized ballroom. The bounty on his head had increased to such an outlandish amount that even a saint would be tempted to turn traitor for the reward. Keeping Nathan's other identity a secret was becoming more and more difficult. It was only a matter of time before he was caught, if they continued with their pirating escapades, or so Colin relentlessly nagged, until Nathan finally agreed.

Exactly one week after that momentous decision had been

made the Emerald Shipping Company was founded. The offices were located in the heart of the waterfront, the furnishings sparse. There were two desks, four chairs, and one filing cabinet, all blistered from a previous fire. The former tenant hadn't bothered to cart them away. Since coins were at a premium, new furniture was at the bottom of their list of purchases. Additional ships for their fleet came first.

Both men understood the ins and outs of the business community. They were both graduates of Oxford University, although as students neither had anything to do with the other. Colin never went anywhere without a pack of friends in attendance. Nathan was always alone. It was only when the two men were partnered as operatives in a deadly game of secret government activities that a bond formed between them. It took a long while, a year or so, before Nathan began to trust Colin. They had risked their lives for each other and for their beloved country, only to be betrayed by their own superiors. Colin had been stunned and outraged when the truth became known. Nathan hadn't been surprised at all. He always expected the worst in people and was rarely disappointed. Nathan was a cynical man by nature and a fighter by habit. He was a man who thoroughly enjoyed a good brawl, leaving Colin to clean up the mess.

Colin's older brother, Caine, was the earl of Cainewood. He'd married Nathan's younger sister, Jade, just the year before, and in so doing unknowingly strengthened the bond between the two friends. Colin and Nathan had become brothers by marriage.

Because Nathan was a marquess and Colin was the brother of a powerful earl, both men were invited to all the affairs of the *ton*. Colin mingled quite easily with the staunch upper crust and used each occasion to mix pleasure with the business of building their clientele. Nathan never attended any of the parties, which was, as Colin suggested, probably the reason he was invited. It was a fact that society didn't consider Nathan a very likable man. He certainly wasn't bothered by the *ton*'s opinion of him, though, for he much preferred the comfort of a seedy tavern on the wharf to the stiffness of a formal salon.

In appearance the two men were just as different. Colin was, as Nathan liked to remark whenever he wanted to prick his temper, the pretty one in the partnership. Colin was an attractive man with hazel eyes and a strong patrician profile. He'd taken to the unsavory habit of wearing his dark brown hair as long as his friend's, a lingering leftover from his pirating days, but that minor fashion sin didn't detract from the perfection of his unscarred face. Colin was almost as tall as Nathan was, but much leaner in build, and as arrogant as Brummell when the occasion called for it. The ladies of the *ton* thought Colin incredibly handsome. Colin had a noticeable limp due to an accident, but that even seemed to add to his appeal.

When it came to appearance, Nathan hadn't been as blessed. He looked more like a warlord from the ancient days than a modern Adonis. He never bothered to bind his auburn-colored hair in a leather thong behind his neck the way Colin usually did but left it to fall past his shoulders as was its natural inclination. Nathan was a giant of a man, muscular in both shoulders and thighs, with nary a pinch of fat on his frame. His eyes were a vivid green—an attention-getter, to be sure, if the ladies weren't in such a hurry to get away from his dark scowl.

To outsiders the two friends were complete opposites. Colin was considered the saint, Nathan the sinner. In reality, their dispositions were very much alike. Both kept their emotions locked inside. Nathan used isolation and a surly temper as his weapons against involvement. Colin used superficiality for the same reason.

In truth, Colin's grin was as much a mask as Nathan's scowl. Past betrayals had trained the two men well. Neither man believed in the fairy tale of love or the nonsense of living happily ever after. Only fops and fools believed in such fantasies.

Nathan's scowl was in full evidence when he walked into the office. He found Colin lounging in a wingback chair with his feet propped up on the window seat.

"Jimbo has two mounts ready, Colin," Nathan said, referring to their shipmate. "You two have an errand to do?"

"You know what the mounts are for, Nathan. You and I are going to ride over to the gardens and have a look at Lady Sara. There's going to be quite a crush of people in attendance this afternoon. No one will see us if we keep to the trees."

Nathan turned to look out the window before answering. "No."

"Jimbo will watch the office while we're away."

"Colin, I don't need to see her before tonight."

"Damn it all, you need to get a good look at her first."

"Why?" Nathan asked. He sounded genuinely perplexed.

Colin shook his head. "To prepare yourself."

Nathan turned around. "I don't need to prepare myself," he said. "Everything's ready. I already know which window belongs to her bedchamber. The tree outside will hold my weight; I tested it to be sure. There isn't a lock on her window to worry about, and the ship is ready to sail."

"So you've thought of everything, have you?"

Nathan nodded. "Of course."

"Oh?" Colin paused to smile. "And what if she won't fit through the window? Have you considered that possibility?"

That question got just the reaction Colin wanted. Nathan looked startled, then shook his head. "It's a large window, Colin."

"She might be larger."

If Nathan was chilled by that possibility, he didn't let it show. "Then I'll roll her down the stairs," he drawled.

Colin laughed over that picture. "Aren't you at all curious to see how she turned out?"

"No."

"Well, I am," Colin finally admitted. "Since I won't be

19

going along with you two on your honeymoon, it's only decent to satisfy my curiosity before you leave."

"It's a journey, not a honeymoon," Nathan countered. "Quit trying to bait me, Colin. She's a Winchester, for God's sake, and the only reason we're sailing is to get her away from her relatives."

"I don't know how you're going to stomach it," Colin said. His grin was gone, his concern obvious in his expression. "God, Nathan, you're going to have to bed her in order to produce an heir if you want the land, too."

Before Nathan could comment on that reminder Colin continued. "You don't have to go through with this. The company will make it with or without the funds from the contract. Besides, now that King George has officially stepped down the prince regent will surely rule to overturn the contract. The Winchesters have been waging an intense campaign to sway his mind. You could turn your back on this."

"No." His tone was emphatic. "My signature's on that contract. A St. James doesn't break his word."

Colin snorted. "You can't be serious," he replied. "The St. James men are known to break just about anything when the mood strikes them."

Nathan had to agree with that observation. "Yes," he said. "Regardless, Colin, I won't turn my back on this matter any more than you would take the money your brother offered. It's a point of honor. Hell, we've been over this before. My mind's made up."

He leaned against the window frame and let out a long, weary sigh. "You aren't going to let up unless I agree to go, are you?"

"No," Colin answered. "Besides, you'll want to count the number of Winchester uncles there so you'll know how many you have to contend with this evening."

It was a paltry argument, and they both knew it. "No one's going to get in my way, Colin."

That statement was made in a soft, chilling tone of voice.

Colin grinned in reaction. "I'm well aware of your special talents, friend. I just hope to God there isn't a bloodbath tonight."

"Why?"

"I'd hate to miss all the fun."

"Then come along."

"I can't," Colin answered. "One favor deserves another, remember? I had to promise the duchess I'd attend her daughter's recital, heaven save me, if she could find a way to get Lady Sara to attend her party this afternoon."

"She won't be there," Nathan predicted. "Her bastard father doesn't let her attend any functions."

"Sara will be there," Colin predicted. "The earl of Winchester wouldn't dare offend the duchess. She specifically requested that Lady Sara be allowed to join in the festivities."

"What reason did she give?"

"I haven't the faintest idea," Colin answered. "Time's wasting, Nathan."

"Damn." After muttering that expletive Nathan pulled away from the frame. "Let's get it done, then."

Colin was quick to take advantage of his victory. He strode out the door before his friend could change his mind.

On their way across the congested city he turned to ask Nathan, "Aren't you wondering how we'll know which one is Sara?"

"I'm sure you have it all figured out," he remarked dryly.

"That I do," Colin returned in a gratingly cheerful voice. "My sister Rebecca has promised she'll stay close to Lady Sara all afternoon. I've hedged my bets, too."

He waited a long minute for Nathan to inquire as to how he'd done that, then continued. "If Rebecca is waylaid from her duty, I've lined up my other three sisters to take turns stepping in. You know, old boy, you really could show a little more enthusiasm."

"This outing is a complete waste of my time."

Colin didn't agree, but he kept that opinion to himself.

Neither man spoke again until they'd reached the rise above the gardens and reined in their mounts. The cover of the trees shielded them well, yet they had a clear view of the guests strolling about the gardens of the duchess's estate below.

"Hell, Colin, I feel like a schoolboy."

His friend laughed. "Leave it to the duchess to go overboard," he remarked when he noticed the crowd of musicians filing toward the lower terrace. "She hired an entire orchestra."

"Ten minutes, Colin, and then I'm leaving."

"Agreed," Colin placated. He turned to look at his friend. Nathan was scowling. "You know, she might have been willing to leave with you, Nathan, if you'd—"

"Are you suggesting I send another letter?" Nathan asked. He raised an eyebrow over the absurdity of that possibility. "You do recall what happened the last time I followed your advice, don't you?"

"Of course I remember," Colin answered. "But things might have changed. There could have been a misunderstanding. Her father could have—"

"A misunderstanding?" Nathan sounded incredulous. "I sent the note on a Thursday, and I was damn specific, Colin."

"I know," Colin said. "You told them you were going to collect your bride the following Monday."

"You thought I should have given her more time to pack her belongings."

Colin grinned. "I did, didn't I? In defense of my gentlemanly behavior, I must say I never imagined she'd run away. She was quick, too, wasn't she?"

"Yes, she was," Nathan replied, a hint of a smile in his voice.

"You could have gone after her."

"Why? My men followed her. I knew where she was. I just decided to leave her alone a little longer."

"A stay of execution, perchance?"

Nathan did laugh then. "She's only a woman, Colin, but yes, I do suppose it was a reprieve of sorts."

"There was more to it than that, though, wasn't there? You knew she would be in danger as soon as you claimed her. You won't admit it, Nathan, but in your own way you've been protecting Sara by leaving her alone. I'm right, aren't I?"

"You just said I wouldn't admit it," he countered. "Why bother to ask?"

"God help the two of you. The next year is going to be hell. You'll both have the world trying to do you in."

Nathan shrugged. "I'll protect her."

"I don't doubt that."

Nathan shook his head. "The daft woman actually booked passage on one of our own ships to run away from me. That still chafes. A bit of an irony, wouldn't you say?"

"Not really," Colin answered. "She couldn't have known you owned the ship. You did insist upon remaining a silent partner in the company, remember?"

"We wouldn't have any clients otherwise. You know damn well the St. James men aren't liked by the members of the *ton*. They're still a little rough around the cuffs." His grin told his friend he found that trait appealing.

"It's still odd to me," Colin announced, switching the topic. "You had your men follow Lady Sara—watch out for her, too—yet you never bothered to ask any of them to tell you what she looked like."

"You didn't ask any of them either," Nathan countered.

Colin shrugged. He returned his attention to the crowd below. "I suppose I thought you'd decide the contract wasn't worth the sacrifice. After all, she . . ." He completely lost his train of thought when he spotted his sister strolling toward them. Another woman walked by her side. "There's Becca," he said. "If the silly chit would just move a little to the left . . ." That remark went unfinished. Colin's indrawn breath filled the air. "Sweet Jesus . . . could that be Lady Sara?"

JULIE GARWOOD

Nathan didn't answer him. In truth, he doubted he was capable of speech right then. His mind was fully consumed taking in the vision before him.

She was enchanting. Nathan had to shake his head. No, he told himself, she couldn't possibly be his bride. The gentle lady smiling so shyly at Rebecca was simply too beautiful, too feminine, and too damn thin to belong to the Winchester clan.

And yet there was a hint of a resemblance, a nagging reminder of the impossible four-year-old he'd held in his arms, something indefinable that told him she really was his Lady Sara.

Gone was the wild mop of honey-colored curls. Her hair was shoulder-length, still given to curl, but as dark as chestnuts. Her complexion looked pure to him from the distance separating them, and he wondered if she still had the sprinkle of freckles across the bridge of her nose.

She'd grown to only average height, judging by the fact that she was eye level with Colin's younger sister. There certainly wasn't anything average about her figure, however. She was rounded in all the right places.

"Look at all the young bucks moving in," Colin announced. "They're like sharks circling their prey. Your wife seems to be their target, Nathan," he added. "Hell, you'd think they would have the decency to leave a married woman alone. Still, I suppose I can't really fault them. My God, Nathan, she's magnificent."

Nathan was fully occupied watching the eager men chase after his bride. He had an almost overwhelming urge to beat the foppish grins off their faces. How dare they try to touch what belonged to him?

He shook his head over his illogical reaction to his bride.

"Here comes your charming father-in-law," Colin said. "God, I didn't realize how bowlegged he is. Look how he shadows her," he continued. "He isn't about to let his prize out of his sight."

Nathan took a deep breath. "Let's ride, Colin. I've seen enough."

Not a hint of emotion was in his voice. Colin turned to look at him. "Well?"

"Well, what?"

"Damn it, Nathan, tell me what you think."

"About what?"

"Lady Sara," Colin persisted. "What do you think of her?"

"The truth, Colin?"

His friend gave a quick nod.

Nathan's smile was slow, easy. "She'll fit through the window."

25

Chapter Two

Time was running out.

Sara was going to have to leave England. Everyone would probably think she'd run away again. They'd begin to call her coward, she supposed, and although that slander would sting, she was still determined to go through with her plans. Sara simply didn't have any other choice. She'd already sent two letters to the marquess of St. James requesting his assistance, but the man to whom she was legally wed hadn't bothered to respond. She didn't dare try to contact him again. There simply wasn't enough time left. Aunt Nora's future was at stake, and Sara was the only one who could—or, more specifically, who would—save her.

If the members of the *ton* believed she was running away from the marriage contract, so be it.

Nothing ever turned out the way Sara imagined it would. When her mother had asked her to go to Nora's island the previous spring to make certain she was all right Sara had immediately agreed. Her mother hadn't received a letter from her sister in over four months, and fear about her health was beginning to make Sara's mother ill. In truth,

Sara was just as concerned about her mother's health as she was about her aunt's. Something had to be amiss. It simply wasn't like her aunt to forget to write. No, the monthly packet of letters had always been as dependable as the inevitable rain on the annual Winchester picnics.

Sara and her mother agreed that neither one of them would confide the real reason behind her sudden departure. They settled on the lie that Sara was simply going to visit her older sister Lillian, who lived in the colonies of America with her husband and infant son.

Sara had considered telling her father the truth, then discarded the notion. Even though he was certainly the most reasonable of the brothers, he was still a Winchester through and through. He didn't like Nora any better than his brothers did, though for his wife's sake he wasn't as vocal in his opinions.

The Winchester men had turned their backs on Nora when she disgraced them by marrying beneath her station. The marriage to her groom had taken place fourteen years earlier, but the Winchesters weren't a forgiving lot. They put great store in the expression "an eye for an eye." Revenge was as sacred to them as the commandments were to most of the bishops, even when the infraction was as slight as a brief month of public embarrassment. Not only would they never forget their humiliation, they would also never, ever forgive.

Sara should have realized that fact sooner. She never would have allowed Nora to come home for a visit otherwise. Heaven help her, she'd actually believed that time had softened her uncles' attitude. The sad truth was quite the opposite. There wasn't a happy reunion allowed between the sisters. Sara's mother didn't even get to speak to Nora. As to that, no one did, for Nora had simply vanished a scant hour after she and Sara had left the ship.

Sara was nearly out of her mind with worry. The time had finally come to put her plan into action, and her nerves were at the screaming point. Her fear had become an almost tangible thing, tearing at her determination. She was accustomed to letting other people take care of her, but the shoe was on the other foot, as Nora liked to say, and Sara needed to be the one in charge. She prayed to God she was up to the challenge. Nora's life depended upon her success.

The horrendous pretense Sara had had to endure the past two weeks had become a nightmare. Each time she heard the door chime sound she was certain the authorities had come to tell her Nora's body had been found. Finally, when she thought she couldn't stand the worry another minute, her faithful servant Nicholas had found out where her uncles had hidden Aunt Nora. The gentle woman had been closeted away in the attic of her Uncle Henry's townhouse until all the arrangements could be made with the court for guardianship. Then she was going to be spirited away to the nearest asylum, with her fat inheritance divided between the other men in the family.

"The bloody leeches," Sara muttered to herself. Her hand shook when she clipped the latch shut on her satchel. She told herself it was anger and certainly not fear that made her tremble so. Every time she thought about the terror her aunt must be going through she became infuriated all over again.

She took a deep, calming breath as she carried her satchel over to the open window. She tossed the garment bag down to the ground. "That's the last of it, Nicholas. Hurry now before the family returns. Godspeed, friend."

The servant collected the last bag and rushed toward the waiting hack. Sara closed the window, doused the candle, and climbed into bed.

It was almost the midnight hour when her parents and her sister Belinda returned from their outing. When Sara heard the footsteps in the hallway she rolled onto her stomach, closed her eyes, and feigned sleep. A moment later she heard the squeak of the door as it was opened and knew her father was looking in to see that his daughter was where she was supposed to be. It seemed to Sara an eternity passed before the door was pulled shut again.

Sara waited another twenty minutes or so to let the household settle down for the night. Then she slipped out from under the covers and collected her belongings from where she'd hidden them under the bed. She needed to be inconspicuous on her journey. Since she didn't own anything black, she wore her old dark blue walking dress. The neckline was a little too revealing, but she didn't have time to worry about that problem. Besides, her cloak would conceal that flaw. She was too nervous to braid her hair and had to settle on tying it behind her neck with a ribbon so it would stay out of her way.

After she'd placed the letter she'd written to her mother on the dressing table she wrapped her parasol, white gloves, and reticule in her cloak. She tossed those possessions out the window, then climbed out on the ledge.

The branch she wanted to grasp was just two feet away but a good three to four feet below her. Sara said a quick prayer she'd make it as she wiggled closer to the edge. She sat there a long while until she could summon up enough courage to jump. Then, with a whimper of fear she couldn't contain, she pushed herself off the ledge.

Nathan couldn't believe what he was seeing. He was just about to climb up the giant tree when the window opened and various articles belonging to a woman came flying down. The parasol hit him on his shoulder. He dodged the other items and moved deeper into the shadows. The moon gave him sufficient light to see Sara when she climbed out on the ledge. He was about to shout a warning, certain she was going to break her neck, when she suddenly jumped. He raced forward to catch her.

Sara caught hold of a fat branch and held on for dear life. She said another prayer to keep herself from crying out. Then she waited until she quit swinging back and forth so violently and slowly wiggled her way toward the trunk.

"Oh, God, oh, God, oh, God." She whispered that litany all the way down the tree. Her dress got tangled up in another branch, and by the time her feet finally touched the ground the hem of her gown had worked its way up and over her head.

Sara righted her dress and let out a long, ragged sigh. "There now," she whispered. "That wasn't so horrible after all."

Lord, she thought, she was starting to lie to herself. She knelt down on the ground, gathered up her possessions, mumbling all the while, and wasted precious minutes putting on her white gloves. Dusting her cloak off took a bit longer. After she'd adjusted the garment around her shoulders she untwisted the strings of her reticule, slipped the satin cords around her wrist, tucked the parasol under her arm, and finally walked toward the front of the house.

She stopped quite suddenly, certain she heard a sound behind her. Yet when she whirled around she didn't see anything but trees and shadows. Her imagination was getting the better of her, she decided. It was probably just her own heartbeat making all the ruckus in her ears.

"Where is Nicholas?" she muttered to herself a short time later. The servant was supposed to be waiting for her in the shadows next to the front stoop. Nicholas had promised to escort her to her Uncle Henry Winchester's townhouse. Something must have happened to waylay him, she decided.

Another ten minutes passed before Sara accepted the fact that Nicholas wasn't going to return to fetch her. She didn't dare wait any longer. There was too much risk of being found out. Since her return to London two weeks before her father had taken to the habit of looking in on her during the night. There would be hell to pay when he realized she'd run away again. Sara shivered just thinking about the consequences.

She was completely on her own. That admission made her heartbeat go wild again. She straightened her shoulders and then started walking toward her destination.

Uncle Henry's townhouse was just three short blocks

away. It shouldn't take her any time at all to walk over there. Besides, it was the middle of the night, and surely the streets would be deserted. Villains needed their rest, too, didn't they? Lord, she certainly hoped so. She would fare all right, she told herself as she hurried down the street. If anyone tried to waylay her, she'd use her parasol as a weapon to defend herself. She was determined to go to any length to save her Aunt Nora from having to spend one more night under her uncle's sadistic supervision.

Sara ran like lightning the first full block. A stitch in her side forced her to slow down to a more sedate pace. She relaxed a little when she realized she was actually quite safe. There didn't seem to be anyone else on the streets that night. Sara smiled over that blessing.

Nathan followed behind. He wanted to appease his curiosity before he grabbed his bride, tossed her over his shoulder, and headed for the wharf. In the back of his mind was the irritating thought that she might be trying to run away from him again. He discarded that notion as foolish, for she couldn't possibly know about his plans to kidnap her.

Where was she going? He mulled that question over in his mind while he continued to trail her.

She did have gumption, though. He found that revelation astonishing, since she was a Winchester. Yet she'd already shown him a glimpse of real courage. He'd heard her cry out in obvious fear when she'd thrown herself off that ledge. The woman had gotten herself caught up in the branches, too, then prayed her way down to the ground in a low, fervent voice that had made him smile. He'd gotten a healthy view of her long, shapely legs while she was in such an unseemly position and had to restrain himself from laughing out loud.

It soon became evident to him that she was still blissfully oblivious to his presence. Nathan couldn't believe her naïveté. If she'd only bothered to look behind her, she certainly would have seen him.

She never bothered to look back. His bride rounded the first corner, passed a dark alley at a brisker pace, then slowed down again.

She hadn't gone unnoticed. Two burly men, their weapons at the ready, slithered out of their makeshift home like snakes. Nathan was right behind them. He made certain they heard his approach, then waited until they were turning around to confront him before he slammed their heads together.

Nathan tossed the garbage back into the alley, his gaze directed on Sara all the while. The way his bride strolled down the street should be outlawed, he thought to himself. The sway of her hips was too damn enticing. Just then he saw another movement in the shadows ahead. He rushed forward to save Sara once again. She'd just turned the second corner when his fist slammed into her would-be attacker's jaw.

He had to intervene on her behalf yet again before she finally reached her destination. He assumed she was going to call on her Uncle Henry Winchester when she paused on the bottom step of his residence and stared up at the dark windows a long while.

Of all her relatives, Nathan thought Henry was the most disreputable, and he couldn't come up with a single logical reason why Sara would want to call on the spineless bastard in the middle of the night.

She wasn't there for a visit. Nathan came to that conclusion when she crept around to the side of the townhouse. He followed her, then lounged against the side gate to keep other intruders out. He folded his arms across his chest and relaxed his stance while he watched her fight her way through the shrubs and breach the house through the window.

It was the most inept burglary he'd ever witnessed.

She spent at least ten minutes working the window all the way up. That simple accomplishment was a short victory, though. She was just about to hoist herself up onto the ledge when she tore the hem of her gown. Nathan heard her cry of distress, then watched her turn and give full attention to her gown. The window slid back down while Sara lamented over the damage.

If she had a needle and thread handy, he thought she might very well sit down next to the shrubs and repair the dress.

She finally turned back to her purpose, though. She thought she was being quite clever when she used her parasol to prop the window open. She adjusted the strings of her reticule around her wrist before she jumped up to grab hold of the ledge. It took her three tries before she made it. Getting in through a window proved to be far more difficult than getting out through one. She fairly knocked the wind out of herself before she finally made it. She wasn't at all graceful, either. When Nathan heard the loud thud he decided his bride had landed on either her head or her backside. He waited only a minute or two before he silently climbed in after her.

He adjusted to the darkness quickly. Sara didn't make the adjustment quite as swiftly, however. Nathan heard a loud crash that sounded like glass hitting stone, followed by an unladylike expletive.

Lord, she was loud. Nathan strolled into the foyer just in time to see Sara rush up the steps to the second story. The crazed woman was actually muttering to herself.

A tall, willow-thin man Nathan assumed was one of the servants drew his attention then. The man looked ridiculous. He was dressed in a white knee-length nightshirt. He carried an ornately carved candlestick in one hand and a large crust of bread in the other. The servant lifted the candlestick above his head and started up the steps after Sara. Nathan clipped him on the back of his neck, reached over his head to take the candlestick out of his hand so it wouldn't make a clatter when it hit the floor, then dragged the servant into a dark alcove adjacent to the stairs. He stood next to the crumpled form a long minute while he listened to all the racket coming from above the stairs.

Sara would never make a proper thief. He could hear the doors being slammed shut and knew it was his bride making all the noise. She was going to wake the dead if she didn't quiet down. And what in God's name was she looking for?

A shrill scream rent the air. Nathan let out a weary sigh. He started toward the stairs to save the daft woman once again, then suddenly stopped when she appeared at the landing. She wasn't alone. Nathan moved back into the alcove and waited. He understood the reason for her errand. Sara had her arm around another woman's stooped shoulders and was assisting her down the stairs. He couldn't see the other woman's face, but he could tell from her slow, hesitant walk that she was either very feeble or in terrible pain.

"Please don't cry, Nora," Sara whispered. "Everything's going to be fine now. I'm going to take good care of you."

When the pair reached the foyer Sara took off her cloak, adjusted it around the other woman's shoulders, and then leaned forward to kiss her on her forehead.

"I knew you would come for me, Sara. I never doubted. I knew in my heart that you would find a way to help me."

Nora's voice cracked with emotion. She mopped at the corners of her eyes with the backs of her hands. Nathan noticed the dark bruises on her wrists. He recognized the marks. The old woman had obviously been tied up.

Sara reached up to adjust the pins in her aunt's hair. "Of course you knew I would come for you," she whispered. "I love you, Aunt Nora. I would never let anything happen to you. There," she added in as cheerful a tone of voice as she could manage, "your hair looks lovely again."

Nora grasped Sara's hand. "Whatever would I do without you, child?"

"That's a foolish worry," Sara answered. She kept her

34

voice soothing, for she knew her aunt was in jeopardy of losing her control. Sara was actually in much the same condition. When she'd seen the bruises on her aunt's face and arms she'd wanted to weep.

"You came back to England because I asked you to," Sara reminded her. "I thought you would have a happy reunion with your sister, but I was wrong. This atrocity is all my fault, Nora. Besides, you must know you're never going to have to do without me."

"You're such a dear child," Nora answered.

Sara's hand shook when she reached for the door lock. "How did you find me?" Nora asked from behind.

"It doesn't matter now," Sara said. She worked the lock free and opened the door. "We're going to have all the time in the world to visit after we've boarded the ship. I'm taking you back home, Nora."

"Oh, I can't leave London just yet."

Sara turned around to look at her aunt. "What do you mean, you can't leave just yet? Everything's been arranged, Nora. I've booked passage with the last of my funds. Please don't shake your head at me. Now isn't the time to turn difficult. We have to leave tonight. It's too dangerous for you to stay here."

"Henry took my wedding band," Nora explained. She shook her head again. The silvery cluster of hair at the top of her head immediately sagged to one side. "I won't leave England without it. My Johnny, God rest his soul, gave me orders never to take it off the day we were wed fourteen years ago. I can't go home without my wedding band, Sara. It's too precious to me."

"Yes, we must find it," Sara agreed when her aunt started to weep again. She was alarmed by the wheeze in her aunt's voice, too. The dear woman was obviously having difficulty catching her breath. "Do you have any idea where Uncle Henry might have hidden it?"

"That's the true blasphemy," Nora answered. She leaned

against the banister in an effort to ease the ache in her chest, then said, "Henry didn't bother to hide it. He's wearing it on his little finger. Sporting it like a trophy, he is. Now, if we could determine where your uncle is drinking tonight, we could fetch the band back."

Sara nodded. Her stomach started aching at the thought of what she was going to have to do. "I know where he is," she said. "Nicholas has been following him. Now, are you up to a short walk to the corner of the block? I didn't dare order the hack to wait out front for fear Uncle Henry would come home early."

"Of course I'm up to a walk," Nora answered. She moved away from the banister. Her gait was stiff as she slowly made her way to the door. "Heavens," she whispered. "If your mother could see me now, she'd die of shame. I'm about to take a walk in the dead of night dressed in my nightgown and a borrowed cloak."

Sara smiled. "We aren't going to tell my mother, though, are we?" She let out a gasp when she saw her aunt grimace. "You're in terrible pain, aren't you?"

"Nonsense," Nora scoffed. "I'm already feeling much better. Come along now," she ordered in a brisker tone. "We mustn't linger here, child." She clutched the rail and started down the steps. "It will take more than a Winchester to do me in."

Sara started to pull the door shut behind her, then changed her mind. "I believe I shall leave this door wide open in the hope that someone will come along and help himself to Uncle Henry's possessions. I dare not get my hopes up, though," she added. "There don't seem to be any villains on the streets tonight. On my walk over here I saw nary a one."

"Good Lord, Sara, you actually walked over here?" Aunt Nora asked, clearly appalled.

"I did," Sara answered. There was a hint of a boast in her voice. "I kept my guard up, of course, so you can quit your frown. I didn't have to use my parasol once to fend off anyone with ill intentions, either. Oh, heavens, I've left my lovely parasol in the window."

"Leave it be," her aunt ordered when Sara started back up the steps. "We're pressing our luck against the devil if we stay here much longer. Now give me your arm, dear. I'll hold onto you while we make this short walk. You really walked over here, Sara?"

Sara laughed. "To tell you the full truth, I do believe I ran most of the way. I was very frightened, Nora, but I made the journey without mishap. Do you know, I believe all this talk about our streets being so unsafe is just exaggeration."

The two ladies strolled arm in arm down the dark, narrow street, Sara's laughter trailing behind them. The hack was waiting for them at the corner. Sara was assisting her aunt inside the black vehicle when a hopeful assailant came rushing toward them. Nathan intervened by simply moving forward into the moonlight. The man took one look at him, did a hasty turnaround, and blended back into the shadows again.

Nathan thought the old woman might have gotten a look at him. She had glanced back over her shoulder just when he'd moved forward, but he decided her eyesight must have dimmed with age when she turned around again without shouting a warning to her niece.

Sara certainly hadn't noticed his presence. She had a heated discussion over the fare with the driver, finally agreed to his exorbitant fee, and then joined her aunt inside the vehicle. The hack was in motion when Nathan grabbed hold of the back rail and swung himself up on the ledge. The vehicle rocked from the added weight before picking up speed again.

Sara was certainly making her own kidnapping easy work. Nathan had heard her tell her aunt that they would be leaving London by ship. He therefore assumed their destination was the wharf. Then the hack veered off onto one of the side streets near the waterfront and came to an abrupt stop in front of one of the most notorious taverns in the city.

She was going after the damn wedding band, he supposed with a growl of irritation. Nathan jumped down from the ledge and moved into the light further behind the hack. He wanted the men loitering in front of the tavern to get a good look at him. He braced his legs apart for a fight, moved his right hand to the hilt of the coiled whip hooked to his belt, and scowled at the sizable group.

They noticed him. Three of the smaller ones edged their way back inside. The other four leaned back against the stone wall. Their gazes were directed on the ground.

The driver climbed down from his perch, received fresh instructions, and hurried inside. He came back outside a scant minute later, muttered that he'd best be getting a giant bonus for all the trouble he'd had to endure, and then climbed back up to his seat.

Another few minutes elapsed before the door of the tavern opened again. A sour-faced man with a grossly distended belly came outside. He was dressed in rumpled, soiled clothing that was ripe from wear. The stranger slicked his greasy hair back from his brow in a pitiful attempt at grooming as he swaggered over to the carriage.

"My employer, Henry Winchester, is too sotted to come outside," he announced. "We come to this part of town when we don't want to be noticed," he added. "I'm here in his stead, m'lady. Your driver said there be a woman in need of something, and I'm thinking I'm just the man you're needing."

The disgusting man scratched his groin while he eagerly waited for a reply to his offer.

The stench radiating from the foul-smelling man came in through the window. Sara almost gagged in reaction. She placed her perfumed hankerchief over her nose, turned to her aunt, and whispered, "Do you know this man?"

"I most certainly do," her aunt answered. "His name's

Clifford Duggan, Sara, and he's the one who helped your uncle waylay me."

"Did he strike you?"

"Yes, dear, he did," Nora answered. "Several times, as a matter of fact."

The servant under discussion couldn't see inside the dark carriage. He leaned forward to get a better look at his prize.

Nathan walked over to the side of the carriage. His intent was to tear the man from aft to stern for daring to leer at his bride. He stopped when he saw the white-gloved fist fly through the open window and connect quite soundly with the side of the man's bulbous nose.

Clifford hadn't been prepared for the attack. He let out a howl of pain, staggered backwards, and tripped over his own feet. He landed with a thud on his knees. While he spewed one crude blasphemy after another he diligently tried to regain his feet.

Sara pressed her advantage. She threw the carriage door open, catching the villain in his midsection. The servant did a near somersault before landing in the gutter on his backside.

The men lounging against the wall hooted in appreciation of the spectacle they'd just witnessed. Sara ignored her audience as she climbed out of the carriage. She turned to hand her reticule to her aunt, took another minute to remove her gloves and pass those through the window to her aunt, too, and then finally gave her full attention to the man sprawled on the ground.

She was simply too infuriated to be afraid. She stood over her victim looking very like an avenging angel. Her voice shook with fury when she said, "If you ever mistreat a lady again, Clifford Duggan, I swear to God you'll die a slow, agonizing death."

"I ain't never mistreated a lady," Clifford whined. He was trying to catch his breath so he could pounce on her. "How would you be knowing my name?"

Nora leaned out the window. "You're a shameful liar, Clifford," she called out. "You're going to burn in hell for all your sins."

Clifford's eyes widened in astonishment. "How did you get out—"

Sara interrupted his question by giving him a sound kick. He turned his gaze back to her. His expression was insolent. "You think you got the meat to hurt me?" he sneered. He glanced back at the men leaning against the wall. In truth, the servant was more humiliated than injured by her paltry attack. The snickers echoing behind him stung far more than her little slap. "The only reason I ain't retaliating is because my employer will want to beat you good and sound afore he lets me have you."

"Do you have any idea how much trouble you're in, Clifford?" Sara asked. "My husband is going to hear about this atrocity, and he will certainly retaliate. The marquess of St. James is feared by everyone, even ignorant pigs like you, Clifford. When I tell him what you've been up to he'll give you equal measure. The marquess does whatever I tell him to do just like that." She paused to snap her fingers for effect. "Oh, I can see I've gotten your full attention with that promise," she added with a nod when Clifford's expression changed. The man looked downright terrified. He had quit trying to regain his feet and was actually scooting backward on his backside.

Sara was inordinately pleased with herself. Her bluff had worked quite well. She didn't realize that Clifford had just gotten a good look at the giant standing a scant ten feet behind her. She thought she'd just put the fear of a St. James into the servant. "A man who strikes a lady is a true coward," she announced. "My husband kills cowards as easily as he would a bothersome gnat, and if you doubt me, just remember he is a St. James through and through."

"Sara, dear," Nora called out. "Would you like me to accompany you inside?"

Sara didn't take her gaze off Clifford when she gave her aunt answer. "No, Nora. You aren't dressed for the occasion. I won't be long."

"Hurry, then," Nora called out. "You'll catch a chill, dear."

Nora continued to lean out the window, but her gaze was directed at Nathan. He returned her wide-eyed stare with a brisk nod before turning his attention back to his bride.

Nora was quick to notice how the big man was keeping the hounds at bay. His mere size was intimidating. It didn't take her any time at all to realize he was actually providing safety for Sara. Nora thought about calling a warning to her niece, then discounted the notion. Sara had enough to worry about. Nora would wait to mention the savior when she was finished with her important errand.

Nathan kept his attention on Sara. His bride was certainly full of surprises. He was having difficulty coming to terms with that fact. He'd seen what cowards the Winchesters were. The men in the family always did their dirty work under cover of darkness, or when a man's back was turned. Sara, however, wasn't acting at all like a Winchester. She was courageous in her defense of the old woman. And Lord, was she in a fury. He didn't think he would have been surprised if she'd pulled out a pistol and shot her victim between his eyes. She was definitely angry enough.

Sara skirted the servant, paused to give him a good glare, and then hurried on inside the tavern.

Nathan immediately walked over to Clifford. He grabbed him by his neck, lifted him high into the air, and then flung him against the stone wall.

His audience scattered like mice to avoid being hit. Clifford struck the wall with a loud splat, then crumpled to the ground in a dead faint.

"My good man?" Nora called out. "I do believe you'd better go inside now. My Sara's bound to need your assistance yet again."

Nathan turned to scowl at the woman who dared to issue him an order. Just then the whistles and hoots of laughter coming from inside the tavern gained his full attention. With a growl of frustration over what he considered a damned inconvenience he slowly uncoiled his whip and walked toward the door.

Sara located her uncle who was hunched over his ale at a round table in the center of the establishment. She made her way through the throng of customers to get to him. She thought she would use shame and reason to get Aunt Nora's ring back. Yet when she actually saw the silver band on his finger her mind emptied of all reasonable ploys. There was a full pitcher of dark ale on the table. Before Sara could contain herself she lifted the pitcher and emptied the contents over her uncle's balding head.

He was too far gone from drink to react swiftly. He let out a loud bellow, interrupted himself with a rank belch, and then staggered to his feet. Sara had worked the wedding band off his finger before his mind had cleared sufficiently to ward her off.

It took him a long while to focus on her properly. Sara slipped the ring on her own finger while she waited.

"My God . . . Sara? What are you doing here? Is something amiss?" Uncle Henry stammered out his questions in a bluster. The effort cost him what little strength he had left. He slumped back down in his chair and squinted up at her with bloodshot eyes. Henry noticed the empty pitcher. "Where's my ale?" he shouted to the barkeep.

Sara was thoroughly disgusted with her uncle. Even though she doubted he'd remember a single word of her lecture, she was determined to let him know what she thought about his sinful conduct.

"Is something amiss?" She repeated his question in a derisive tone. "You are despicable, Uncle Henry. If my father knew what you and his other brothers were doing to Nora, I'm certain he'd call the authorities and have you all carted off to the gallows."

"What say you?" Henry asked. He rubbed his forehead while he tried to concentrate on the conversation. "Nora? You're ranting at me because of that worthless woman?"

Before Sara could chastise him for making that shameful remark he blurted out, "Your father was in on the plan from the very beginning. Nora's too old to take care of herself. We know what's best for her. Don't try throwing a tantrum with me, girl, for I'm not going to tell you where she is."

"You do not know what's best for her," Sara shouted. "You wanted her inheritance, and that's the real reason. Everyone in London knows about your gaming debts, Uncle. You found an easy way to pay them off, didn't you? You were set to lock Nora away in an asylum, weren't you?"

Henry's gaze darted back and forth between the empty pitcher and his niece's outraged expression. It finally dawned on him that she had poured his ale over his head. He touched his collar just to be sure, and when he felt the sticky wetness there he became livid. His own anger made his head start pounding. He was in desperate need of another drink. "We are going to put the bitch away, and you can't do anything about it. Now get on home before I put my hand to your backside."

A snicker sounded behind her. Sara turned around to glare at the customer. "Drink your refreshment, sir, and stay out of this." She whirled back to her uncle only after the stranger turned his gaze to his goblet. "You're lying about my father," she stated. "He would never be a party to such cruelty. As for striking me, do so and suffer my husband's wrath. I'll tell him," she threatened with a nod.

Sara had hoped that since her empty threat about her husband's retaliatory methods had been so successful with the hired servant Clifford, the same bluff might work on her sotted relative.

It was a vain hope. Henry didn't look at all intimidated. He let out a loud snort. "You're as crazed as Nora if you believe a St. James would ever come to your defense. Why, I could beat you good, Sara, and no one would give a notice, least of all your husband."

Sara stood her ground. She was determined to gain her uncle's promise to leave Nora alone before she left the foul-smelling tavern. Her fear was that he or one of his brothers would send someone after her aunt and drag her back to England. Nora's inheritance from her father's estate was sizable enough to make the journey worth the nuisance.

She was so incensed with her uncle, she didn't notice that some of the customers were slowly edging their way toward her. Nathan noticed. One man he judged to be the leader of the pack actually licked his lips in apparent anticipation of the morsel he thought he would soon get to devour.

Sara suddenly realized the futility of her plan. "Do you know, Uncle Henry, I've been trying to find a way to get you to promise to leave Nora alone, but I now realize my own foolishness. Only a man of honor would keep his promise. You're too much of a swine to keep your word. I'm wasting my time here."

Her uncle reached up to slap her. Sara easily dodged him. She stopped backing away when she bumped into something quite solid, turned around, and found herself surrounded by several disreputable-looking men. All of them, she immediately noticed, were in desperate need of a bath.

Everyone was so mesmerized by the beautiful lady they never noticed Nathan. He thought they might be too consumed with lust to think about caution. In time they would realize that error, of course. Nathan leaned back against the closed door in the corner and waited for the first provocation.

It came with lightning speed. When the first infidel grabbed hold of Sara's arm Nathan let out a roar of outrage. The sound was deep, guttural, deafening. Effective, too. Everyone in the tavern froze—everyone but Sara. She jumped a good foot, then whirled around toward the sound.

She would have screamed if her throat hadn't closed up

on her. In truth, she was having difficulty catching her breath. Her knees buckled when she spotted the big man standing in front of the door. Sara grabbed hold of the table to keep herself from falling down. Her heart was slamming inside her chest, and she was certain she was about to die of sheer fright.

What in God's name was he? No, not what, she corrected herself, but who. She was nearly frantic. He was a man—yes, a man—but the biggest, the most dangerous-looking, the most . . . oh, God, he was staring at her.

He motioned to her with the crook of his finger.

She shook her head.

He nodded.

The room began to spin. She simply had to get hold of her wits again. She desperately tried to find something about the giant that wasn't so horribly terrifying. She realized then that someone was clutching her arm. Without taking her gaze away from the big man trying to stare her into a faint she slapped the hand away.

The giant looked as if he bathed. There was that much. His hair appeared to be clean, too. It was a dark bronze in color, as bronzed as his face and arms. Dear Lord, she thought, his upper arms and shoulders were so . . . muscular. So were his thighs. She could see the sleek bulge of steel indecently outlined by his snug britches. But they were clean britches, she told herself. Villains usually wore only crumpled, smelly garments, didn't they? Therefore, she reasoned illogically, *he* couldn't be a villain. That conclusion made her feel better. She was actually able to take a breath. All right, she thought to herself, he isn't a villain; he's just a warlord, she decided when she'd finished her thorough inspection, perhaps even a Viking warrior from the length of his hair. Yes, he was simply a barbarian who had somehow transported himself across time.

Her mind had snapped, she concluded then. The green-eyed warlord motioned to her to come to him again. She looked behind her to make certain he wasn't motioning to someone else. There wasn't anyone there.

He meant her, all right. Her stomach lurched. She blinked. He didn't disappear. She shook her head in a bid to clear her mind of the vision from hell.

He crooked his finger at her again. "Come to me."

His voice was deep, commanding, arrogant. God help her, she started walking toward him.

And then all hell broke loose. The sound of the whip cracking in the air, the scream of pain from the fool who tried to touch her as she moved past him echoed in Sara's ears. She never looked toward the commotion. Her gaze was locked on the man who was methodically destroying the tavern.

He made it look so easy. A simple flip of his wrist that didn't seem to cost him the least amount of effort made such a lasting impression on his audience.

She also noticed that the closer she got to him, the deeper his scowl became.

The warlord obviously wasn't in a good mood. She decided to humor him until she could regain her composure. Then she was going to run outside, jump into the hack with Nora, and race to the waterfront.

It was a fine plan, she told herself. The problem, of course, was getting the Viking away from the door first.

She realized she'd stopped to stare at him again when he motioned for her to move. She felt a restraining hand on her shoulder, glanced down at it, then heard the crack of the whip.

Sara was suddenly in full flight. She ran to him, determined to get there before her heart completely failed her.

She came to a swaying stop directly in front of him, tilted her head back, and stared up at those piercing green eyes until he finally looked down at her. On impulse she reached out and pinched his arm just to make certain he really wasn't a figment of her imagination.

He was real, all right. His skin felt like steel, but warm

steel. The look in those beautiful eyes saved her from insanity, though. The color was hypnotizing, intense.

Odd, but the longer she stared at him, the safer she felt. She smiled with acute relief. He raised an eyebrow in reaction. "I knew you weren't a villain, Viking."

Sara was suddenly weightless. She felt as though she were floating through a dark tunnel and on her way toward the bronzed Viking standing in the sun.

Nathan caught her before she hit the floor. His bride was in a full faint when he tossed her over his shoulder. He scanned the tavern for any leftovers he might have missed. There were bodies all over the wooden floor. That wasn't good enough, he thought. He had an almost overwhelming urge to mark the bastard uncle who was cowering under the table. He could hear the choked sobs coming from the man.

Nathan kicked the table across the room in order to see his prey. "Do you know who I am, Winchester?"

Henry was locked in fetal position. When he shook his head his jowls rubbed back and forth against the floorboards.

"Look at me, bastard."

His voice sounded like thunder. Henry looked up. "I'm the marquess of St. James. If you ever come near my wife or that old woman, I'll kill you. Do we understand each other?"

"You're . . . him?"

The bile had risen in Henry's throat, making speech nearly impossible. He started gagging. Nathan gave him a sound shove with the tip of his boot, then turned and walked out of the tavern.

The barkeep peeked out from his hiding place behind the grill and looked at the devastation around him. There wouldn't be any more ale purchased that dark night, for nary a one of his customers was in any condition to drink. They covered his floor like discarded peanut shells. It was a sight he wouldn't soon forget. He wanted to remember every single detail so he could relate the happening to his friends.

He already knew how he was going to tell the ending, too. The Winchester dandy crying like an infant would provide a good, hearty laugh for his future customers. The sound of gagging pulled the barkeep from his musings. The high and mighty Winchester was puking all over his floor.

The tavern owner's shout of anger mingled with Aunt Nora's gasp of fear. When she saw her niece draped over the stranger's shoulder her hand flew to her bosom.

"Is Sara hurt?" she cried out. Her mind was already picturing the worst.

Nathan shook his head. He opened the door of the carriage, then paused to grin at the old woman. "She fainted."

Nora was too relieved at that news to take exception to the fact that the man was amused over her niece's condition. She moved over to make room for Sara. Nathan placed his bride on the opposite seat, however. Nora gave her niece a quick once-over to make certain she was still breathing, then turned to look at their savior again. She watched him recoil the whip and hook it to his belt.

Nora hadn't expected him to join them inside the vehicle. When he did so she squeezed herself into the far corner. "Sara can sit next to me," she offered.

He didn't bother to answer her. He did, however, take up all the space across from her. Then he lifted Sara onto his lap. Nora noticed how very gentle he was when he touched her niece. His hand lingered on the side of Sara's cheek when he pressed her face into the crook of his neck. Sara let out a little sigh.

Nora didn't know what to make of the man. The carriage was in full motion before she tried to engage him in conversation.

"Young man, my name's Nora Bettleman. The dear lady you just saved is my niece. Her name is Sara Winchester."

"No," he said in a hard voice. "Her name is Lady St. James."

After making that emphatic statement he turned his gaze to the window. Nora continued to stare at him. The man had a nice, strong profile. "Why are you helping us?" she asked. "You won't convince me you're in the employ of the Winchester family," she added with a firm nod. "Could one of the St. James men have hired you?"

He didn't answer her. Nora let out a sigh before turning her attention to her niece. She wished Sara would hurry up and finish with her swoon so she could sort out the confusion.

"I've come to depend upon the child you're cradling in your arms, sir. I cannot abide the thought of anything ill happening to her."

"She isn't a child," he contradicted.

Nora smiled. "No, but I still consider her such," she admitted. "Sara's such an innocent, trusting soul. She takes after her mother's side of the family."

"You aren't a Winchester, are you?"

Nora was so pleased that he was finally conversing with her, she smiled again. "No," she answered. "I'm Sara's aunt on her mother's side. I was a Turner before I married my Johnny and took his name."

She glanced over to look at Sara again. "I don't believe she's ever fainted before. Of course, the last two weeks must have been a terrible strain on her. There are shadows under her eyes. She obviously hasn't been sleeping well. The worry about me, you see," she added with a little wheeze. "Still, she must have seen something quite frightening to make her swoon. What do you suppose . . ."

She quit her speculation when she caught his grin. The man was certainly on the peculiar side, for he smiled over the oddest remarks.

And then he explained himself. "She saw me."

Sara started to stir. She felt dizzy still, disoriented, yet wonderfully warm. She rubbed her nose against the heat, inhaled the clean, masculine scent, and let out a sigh of contentment.

"I do believe she's coming around," Nora whispered. "Thank the Lord."

Sara slowly turned her gaze to her aunt. "Coming around?" she asked with an unladylike yawn.

"You swooned, dear."

"I didn't," Sara whispered, clearly appalled. "I never faint. I . . ." She stopped her explanation when she realized she was sitting on someone's lap. Not someone, she realized. His lap. The color drained from her face. Memory was fully restored.

Nora reached over to pat her hand. "It's all right, Sara. This kind gentleman saved you."

"The one with the whip?" Sara whispered, praying she was wrong.

Nora nodded. "Yes, dear, the one with the whip. You must give him your appreciation, and for heaven's sake, Sara, don't faint again. I don't have my smelling salts with me."

Sara nodded. "I won't faint again," she said. To insure that promise she decided she'd better not look at him again. She tried to move off his lap without his noticing, but as soon as she started to scoot away he increased his grip around her waist.

She leaned forward just a little. "Who is he?" she whispered to Nora.

Her aunt lifted her shoulders in a shrug. "He hasn't told me yet," she explained. "Perhaps, dear—if you tell him how thankful you are—well, then he just might give us his name."

Sara knew it was rude to talk about the man as though he weren't even there. She braced herself before she slowly turned to look at his face. She deliberately stared at his chin when she said, "Thank you, sir, for coming to my defense inside the tavern. I shall be in your debt forever."

He nudged her chin up with his thumb. His gaze was inscrutable. "You owe me more than gratitude, Sara."

Her eyes widened in alarm. "You know who I am?"

"I told him, dear," Nora interjected.

"I don't have any coins left," Sara said then. "I used all I had to book passage for our journey. Are you taking us to the harbor?"

He nodded.

"I do have a gold chain, sir. Will that be payment enough?"

"No."

The abruptness in his answer irritated her. She gave him a disgruntled look for being so ungallant. "But I don't have anything more to offer you," she announced.

The hack came to a stop. Nathan opened the door. He moved with incredible speed for such a big man. He was outside the carriage and assisting Nora to the ground before Sara had straightened her gown. The man had all but tossed her into the corner of the hack.

His arms were suddenly around her waist again. Sara had only enough time to grab her reticule and her gloves before she was hauled out of the carriage like a sack of feed. He dared to put his arm around her shoulders and pull her up against his side. Sara immediately protested that liberty. "Sir, I happen to be a married woman. Do remove your arm. It isn't decent."

He obviously suffered from a hearing impairment, for he didn't even glance at her when she'd given that order. She was about to try again when he let out a piercing whistle. The moonlit area had been completely deserted until that moment. Within a blink of an eye she found herself completely surrounded by men.

Nathan's loyal crew stared at Sara. They acted as though they'd never seen a pretty woman before. He looked down at his bride to see how she was reacting to their stares of obvious adoration. Sara wasn't paying any attention to the men, though. She was occupied glaring up at him. Nathan almost smiled in reaction.

He gave her a quick squeeze to get her to quit her show of insolence, then turned his attention to the old woman. "Do you have any baggage?"

"Do we, Sara?" Nora asked.

Sara tried to shove herself away from her anchor before answering. "I told you I was a married woman," she muttered. "Now unhand me."

He didn't budge. She gave up. "Yes, Nora, we do have baggage. I borrowed some of my mother's things for you to wear. I'm certain she won't mind. Nicholas stored the bags at the Marshall storefront. Shall we go and claim them?"

She tried to take a step forward and found herself hauled up against the giant again.

Nathan found his man Jimbo in the back of the crowd and motioned to him. A tall, dark-skinned man walked over to stand in front of Sara. Her eyes widened at the sight of the near-giant. She stared at him a long minute, then came to the conclusion that he might have been attractive if it weren't for the odd-looking gold earring looped through his ear.

He must have felt her stare on him, for he suddenly turned his full attention on her. He folded his massive arms across his chest and gave her a good scowl.

She scowled back.

A sudden sparkle appeared in his midnight-dark eyes, and he gifted her with a full smile. She didn't know what to make of that strange behavior.

"Have two men see to the baggage, Jimbo," Nathan ordered. "We'll board the *Seahawk* at first light."

Sara couldn't help but notice that the Viking had included himself in her plans.

"My aunt and I will be perfectly safe now," she said. "These men seem to be . . . pleasant enough, sir. We've wasted enough of your valuable time."

Nathan continued to ignore her. He motioned to another man. When a thick-muscled though squat-framed older

52

man came forward, Nathan nodded toward Nora. "Take care of the old woman, Matthew."

Nora let out a gasp. Sara thought it was because they were about to be separated from each other. Yet before she could argue with their unwanted protector Nora straightened her shoulders and slowly walked over to the enormous man.

"I'm not an old woman, sir, and I take grave exception to such an insult. I'm only one year past fifty, young man, and feeling as spry as can be."

Nathan's eyebrow rose a fraction, but he kept his smile contained. A strong gust of wind would topple the old woman, so frail did she appear to him to be, yet she had the tone of voice of a commander.

"You should apologize to my aunt," Sara said.

She turned back to her aunt before he had time to react to that statement. "I'm certain he didn't mean to hurt your feelings, Nora. He's just rude."

Nathan shook his head. The conversation was ridiculous to him. "Matthew, move," he ordered in a clipped voice.

Nora turned to the man hovering by her side. "And just where do you think you're taking me?"

In answer, Matthew lifted Nora into his arms.

"Put me down, you rascal."

"It's all right, lovey," Matthew replied. "You look a might peaked to me. You don't weigh more than a feather."

Nora was about to protest again. His next question changed her mind. "Where did you get those bruises? Give me the name of the bloody infidel, and I'll be happy to cut his throat for you."

Nora smiled at the man holding her. She judged his age to be near her own and had also noticed what a fit man he appeared to be. She hadn't blushed in years, yet she knew from the sudden heat in her cheeks that she was certainly blushing at that moment. "Thank you, sir," she stammered out as she patted the bun back into place on top of her head. "That is certainly a kind offer."

Sara was astonished by her aunt's behavior. Why, she was fluttering her eyelashes and acting very like a flirt at her first ball! She watched the pair until they were out of sight, then noticed that the crowd of men had also vanished. She was suddenly all alone with her contrary savior.

"Is my Aunt Nora going to be safe with that man?" she demanded to know.

His answer was a low growl of obvious irritation. "Does one grunt mean yes or no?" she asked.

"Yes," he answered with a sigh when she poked him in his ribs.

"Please let me go."

He actually did as she asked. Sara was so surprised she nearly lost her balance. Perhaps, she decided, if she could maintain her pleasant tone of voice, she could get him to obey other commands. It was certainly worth a try.

"Am I going to be safe with you?"

He took his sweet time answering her. Sara turned until she was standing face-to-shoulders in front of him. The tips of her shoes touched the tips of his boots. "Please answer me," she whispered in a sweet, coaxing tone of voice.

He didn't seem to be impressed with her attempt to have a pleasant conversation. His exasperation, on the other hand, was evident. "Yes, Sara. You'll always be safe with me."

"But I don't want to be safe with you," she cried out. She realized how foolish that statement sounded as soon as the words were out of her mouth, and she hastily tried to correct herself. "What I mean to say is that I do always want to be safe. Everyone wants to be safe. Even villains . . ."

She stopped rambling when he grinned at her. "I want to be safe without you. You aren't planning to sail with Nora and me, are you? Why are you staring at me like that?"

He answered her first question and ignored her second one. "Yes, I'm sailing with you."

"Why?"

"I want to," he drawled. He decided to wait a little longer before giving her the particulars. Her cheeks were flushed again. Nathan couldn't decide if the cause was fear or temper.

His bride still had freckles on the bridge of her nose. He was pleased by that fact. It made him remember the little hellion he'd held in his arms. She wasn't a little girl any longer, though. She'd grown up quite nicely, too. She was, however, obviously still a bit of a hellion.

She actually nudged him in his chest to gain his attention again. "I'm sorry, sir, but you simply cannot travel with Nora and me," she announced. "You're going to have to find another boat. It wouldn't be safe for you to be on the same vessel with me."

That strange statement gained his full attention. "Oh? And why is that?"

"Because my husband won't like it," she announced. She nodded when he looked incredulous, then continued. "Have you heard of the marquess of St. James? Oh, of course you have. Everyone knows about the Marquess. He's my husband, Viking, and he's going to pitch a fit when he finds out I'm traveling with a . . . protector. No, I'm afraid it won't do. Why are you smiling?"

"Why did you call me Viking?" he asked.

She shrugged her shoulders. "Because you look like one."

"Should I call you shrew?"

"Why?"

"You're acting like one."

She felt like screaming in frustration. "Who are you? What do you want with me?"

"You still owe me, Sara."

"Oh, Lord, are you going to harp on that issue again?"

His slow nod infuriated her. He was thoroughly enjoying himself. When Sara realized that fact her bluster of indignation evaporated. She knew then that she was never going to get him to make sense. The man was daft. The sooner she got away from this barbarian, she thought, the better. First, however, she would have to find a way to placate him.

"All right," she agreed. "I owe you. There, we are in

complete agreement. Now then, please tell me exactly what it is you think I owe you, and I shall endeavor to make payment."

He moved forward so that he could catch her in the event she fainted on him again before he gave her an answer. "My name's Nathan, Sara."

"And?" she asked, wondering why he'd suddenly decided to tell her his name.

She was slow to catch on. His sigh was long, weary. "And you, Lady St. James, owe me a wedding night."

Chapter Three

She didn't faint; she screamed. Nathan didn't try to quiet her down. When he couldn't stand the grating noise another second he simply dragged her over to the Emerald Shipping Company offices. He left the hysterical woman in her aunt's capable hands. Because he believed he was capable of gentlemanly behavior upon rare occasion, he didn't start laughing until he was once again outside.

Nathan had thoroughly enjoyed her reaction to his announcement. Lady Sara wasn't at all subtle. He doubted he would ever have to worry about knowing what was on her mind. Nathan, conditioned to sneakiness all his life, found his straightforward bride refreshing. Loud, he added as an afterthought, but refreshing all the same.

After he took care of a few remaining details Nathan joined the last of the crew aboard the ship. Jimbo and Matthew were waiting on deck for him. They were both scowling, but Nathan decided to let them get away with their show of insolence. He had saddled the loyal men with the chore of getting Sara and Nora settled in their cabins.

"Did she finally quit screaming?" Nathan asked.

"When I threatened to put a gag in her mouth," Jimbo answered. The big man increased his frown and added, "She hit me then."

Nathan let his exasperation show. "I assume she isn't too frightened any longer," he replied dryly.

"I'm not so certain she ever was frightened," Matthew interjected. The older man grinned. "Didn't you notice the fire in her eyes when you dragged her into the offices? She looked bloody furious to me."

Jimbo reluctantly nodded. "After you left she kept shouting that it was all just a cruel jest. Not even her sweet-tempered aunt could calm her down. Your lady actually demanded that someone pinch her so she'd wake up and find it was all just a black nightmare."

"Aye, she did," Matthew agreed with a chuckle. "Felix took her to heart, too. For all his bulk, the boy isn't very cunning."

"Felix touched her?" Nathan was more incredulous than angry.

"No, he didn't touch her," Jimbo rushed out. "He tried to give her a little pinch, that's all. He thought he was being accommodating. You know how the boy likes to please. Your little bride turned into a wildcat as soon as he went for her. I wager Felix won't be so eager to obey next time she gives an order."

Nathan shook his head in vexation. He started to turn away. Matthew stopped him with his next remark. "Perhaps Lady Sara will do better if we put her in with her aunt."

"No."

Nathan realized how abrupt he'd sounded when both men smiled at him. "She stays in my cabin," he added in a much softer tone of voice.

Matthew paused to rub his chin. "Well now, boy, that could be a problem," he drawled. "She doesn't know it's your cabin."

Nathan wasn't at all concerned about that announcement. He frowned at Matthew, but only because the seaman had used the ridiculous nickname "boy" when he'd addressed him. Nathan knew his unspoken censure wouldn't do him any good, though. Both Matthew and Jimbo called him that insulting nickname whenever they were alone with him. They didn't think he was seasoned enough to merit the name "captain" in private. Nathan had inherited the pair when he'd taken over the vessel. The two men had quickly proven to be invaluable. They knew all the ins and outs of pirating and had shown him the way. He knew they thought of themselves as his guardians. God only knew they'd told him so often enough. Still, they'd put their lives on the line countless times in the past to save his backside. Their loyalty far outweighed their irritating habits.

Since the two men were staring at him with such expectant looks on their faces, Nathan said, "She'll find out soon enough whose cabin she's in."

"The aunt is in a poor way," Matthew said then. "I'd wager a couple of her ribs are cracked. As soon as she falls asleep I'm going to strip her raw and bind her tight around the middle."

"The Winchesters did the damage, didn't they?" Jimbo asked.

Nathan nodded. "Which bastard brother was it?" Matthew asked that question.

"It appears that Henry was behind the scheme," Nathan explained. "But I would imagine the other brothers were aware of what was going on."

"Are we going to take Nora home?" Matthew asked.

"We're charted in that direction," Nathan answered. "I don't know what the hell else to do with the woman. Is she strong enough to make the journey?" he asked Matthew. "Or are we going to have to bury her at sea?"

"She'll do all right," Matthew predicted. "There's a tough hide underneath all those bruises. Yes, if I coddle her real nice, she'll make it." He nudged Jimbo in his side, then added, "Now I'm having to nursemaid two weaklings."

Nathan knew he was being baited. He turned and walked

away. From behind Jimbo called out, "He's referring to you, boy."

Nathan raised his hand high into the air to make an obscene gesture before disappearing down the stairs. The men's hearty laughter followed him.

The next several hours were spent on chores for every hand aboard the *Seahawk*. The cargo was secured, the jib raised, the anchor weighed, and the eight cannons given a last spit and oiling before the command was given to sail.

Nathan did his part until his stomach became so queasy he was forced to stop. Jimbo took over command of the forty-two seamen when Nathan went below again.

It was a ritual getting seasick the first couple of days out. Nathan had learned to put up with the inconvenience. He was certain no one besides Matthew and Jimbo were aware of his problem, but that fact didn't ease his embarrassment at all.

From past experience he knew he had another hour or two before he was completely out of commission. Nathan decided to look in on his bride to make certain she was all right. If luck was on his side, she would be sound asleep, and the inevitable confrontation could be put off until later. God knew she should be exhausted. His bride had been awake for over twenty-four hours, and the tantrum she'd thrown when she found out that he was indeed her husband surely had worn her out. Still, if she wasn't sleeping, Nathan determined to have it out with her and get it over and done with. The sooner the rules were set down for her, the sooner she could come to terms with his expectations for their future together.

She would probably get hysterical on him again, Nathan guessed. He braced himself against the inevitable pleading and weeping and opened the door.

Sara wasn't asleep. As soon as Nathan walked into the cabin she bounded off the bed and stood there with her hands clenched at her sides, facing him.

It was apparent she wasn't quite over her fear or her anger

yet. It was damp and stuffy inside the cabin. He shut the door behind him, then walked over to the center of the large square room. He could feel her staring at him when he reached up and lifted the square trap built into the ceiling. He propped the makeshift window open with a stick wedged into the third groove.

Fresh sea air and sunlight flooded the cabin. Nathan's stomach lurched in reaction. He took a deep breath, then walked back over to the door and leaned against it. In the back of his mind lurked the possibility that his bride might just decide to take flight. He wasn't in any condition to go chasing after her, and therefore he blocked the only exit.

Sara stared at Nathan a good long while. She could feel herself shaking and knew it was only a matter of time before her fury got the upper hand. She was determined to hide her anger from him, though, no matter what the cost. Showing any emotion in front of the barbarian would certainly be a poor beginning.

The expression on Nathan's face was one of resignation. His arms were folded in front of his chest, his stance relaxed.

She thought he looked bored enough to fall asleep. That didn't sit well. His intense stare was making her toes curl, too. Sara forced herself to stare back. She wasn't about to cower in front of him, and if anyone was going to win the rude staring contest, it was going to be she.

Nathan thought his bride seemed quite desperate to hide her fear from him. She wasn't doing a very good job of it, for her eyes were already getting misty, and she was trembling.

Lord, he hoped he was up to another round of hysterics. His stomach was railing against the pitch of the ship. Nathan tried to block the feeling and concentrate on the matter at hand.

Sara was a beautiful woman. The streamers of sunlight made her hair look more golden than brown. There was a pick of the litter in the Winchester family after all, he thought to himself.

She was still dressed in the unappealing dark blue gown.

The neckline was too damned low, in his opinion. He thought about mentioning that fact to her later, after she'd gotten rid of some of her fear, but her sudden frown changed his inclination. It was imperative that she understood who was in charge.

He stood in the shadows of the door, but she could still see the long, wicked scar running the length of the side of his right arm. The white mark against such bronzed skin was noticeable. Sara stared at it a long minute while she wondered how he'd come by such a horrible injury, then she let out a soft little sigh.

He was still dressed in a pair of indecently snug fawn-colored britches. It was a miracle to her that he could even breathe. His white shirt was unbuttoned to the waist, the cuffs rolled up to his elbows, and the casualness of his attire irritated her almost as much as his sudden frown. She thought about waiting until later to tell him that one simply didn't wear such unseemly attire when one was traveling aboard such a fine vessel, but his intense frown changed her inclination. It was imperative that he understand what was expected of him now that he was married.

"You dress like a tavern wench."

It took a full minute for the insult to penetrate. At first Sara was too astonished to react. Then she let out a loud gasp.

Nathan hid his smile. Sara didn't look as if she was going to weep. In truth, she looked like she wanted to kill him. It was a nice beginning. "You're falling out of your neckline, bride."

Her hands immediately covered the top of her gown. Her face was flaming red in the space of a heartbeat. "It was the only dress that was dark enough to conceal me when I walked along . . ." She stopped her explanation as soon as she realized she was actually defending herself.

"Conceal?" Nathan drawled. "Sara, it doesn't conceal anything. In future you will not wear such revealing gowns.

The only one who sees your body will be me. Do you understand me?"

Oh, she understood all right. The man was a cad, she concluded. How easily he'd turned the tables on her, too. Sara shook her head. She wasn't about to let him put her in such a vulnerable position when he had so much accounting to do.

"You look like a barbarian," she blurted out. "Your hair's much longer than is fashionable, and you dress like a . . . villain. Guests traveling aboard such a fine boat should keep their appearances impeccable. You look like you've just carried in the crops," she added with a nod. "And your scowl is downright ugly."

Nathan decided he was finished with foolish banter and homed in on the true matter at hand.

"All right, Sara," he began. "Get it over and done with."

"Get what over and done with?"

His sigh was long, weary, absolutely infuriating to her. She desperately tried to hold onto her temper, but the urge to shout at him was making her head pound and her throat ache. Her eyes stung with tears. He had so much explaining to do before she would ever consider forgiving him, she thought, and he had damn well better get on with it before she decided his sins were too mortal ever to be forgiven at all.

"The fit of weeping and begging," Nathan explained with a shrug. "It's obvious to me that you're afraid," he continued. "You're about to start crying, aren't you? I know you must want me to take you back home, Sara. I've decided to save you the humiliation of pleading by simply explaining that no matter what you say or do, you're staying with me. I'm your husband, Sara. Get used to it."

"Will it bother you if I weep?" she asked in a voice that sounded like someone was choking her.

"Not in the least," he said. It was a lie, of course, for it would bother him to see her upset, yet he wasn't about to admit to that fact. Women generally used that kind of information against a man and burst into tears every time they wanted something.

Sara took a deep breath. She didn't dare speak another word until she'd gained control of herself. Did he actually think she would beg? By God, he was a horrid man. Intimidating, too. He didn't seem to possess an ounce of compassion.

She continued to stare at him while she gathered her courage to ask him all the painful questions she'd stored up inside her for such a long time. She doubted that he would tell her the truth, but she still wanted to hear what he had to say for himself.

He thought she looked ready to cry. Sara was apparently back to being terrified of him, he decided. Hell, he hoped she wouldn't faint again. He had little patience with the weaker sex, yet found he didn't want Sara to be too frightened of him.

In truth, he felt a little sorry for her. She couldn't possibly want to be married to him. He was a St. James, after all, and she had been raised a Winchester. She had certainly been trained to hate him. Poor Sara was just a victim in the scheme, a pawn the daft king had used to try to right the differences between the two feuding families.

Still, he couldn't undo the past for her. His signature was on that contract, and he was bound and determined to honor it.

"You might as well understand that I'm not going to walk away from this marriage," he stated in a hard voice. "Not now, not ever."

After making that statement he patiently waited for the fit of hysterics sure to come.

"What took you so long?"

She'd spoken in such a soft whisper, he wasn't certain he heard her correctly. "What did you say?"

"Why did you wait so long?" she asked him in a much stronger voice.

"Wait so long to do what?"

He looked completely bewildered to her. She took another deep breath. "To come for me," she explained. Her voice shook. She gripped her hands together in a bid to hang onto her temper, then said, "Why did you wait so long to come and get me?"

He was so surprised by her question, he didn't immediately respond. That Nathan didn't even think she merited a response was the last blow to her pride that Sara was going to take. In a near shout Sara demanded, "Do you have any idea how long I've waited for you?"

His eyes widened in surprise. His bride had just shouted at him. He stared at her in a way that made her think he thought she'd lost her mind.

And then he slowly shook his head at her. Her composure shattered. "No?" she shouted. "Was I so insignificant to you that you couldn't even be bothered getting around to the chore of coming for me?"

Nathan was stunned by her questions. He knew he shouldn't let her raise her voice to him, but her comments so astonished him, he wasn't certain what to say.

"You actually want me to believe you're angry because I didn't come for you sooner?" he asked.

Sara picked up the nearest object she could get her hands on and threw it at him. Fortunately, the chamberpot was empty. "Angry?" she asked in a roar worthy of a commander. "What makes you think I'm angry, Nathan?"

He dodged the chamberpot and the two candles that followed, then leaned back against the door. "Oh, I don't know," he drawled. "You seem troubled."

"I seem . . ." She was too incensed to stammer out another word.

Nathan's grin was in full evidence when he nodded. "Troubled," he finished for her.

"Do you own a pistol?"

"Yes."

"May I borrow it?"

He forced himself not to laugh. "Now why would you want to borrow my pistol, Sara?"

"I want to shoot you, Nathan."

He did laugh then. Sara decided she hated him. The bluster went out of her. She wanted to weep with frustration. Perhaps her relatives had been right after all. Perhaps he did despise her, maybe even as much as her parents told her he would.

She gave up the battle and sat down on the bed again. She folded her hands in her lap and kept her gaze downcast. "Please leave my cabin. If you wish to explain your sorry conduct to me, you may do so tomorrow. I'm too weary to listen to your excuses now."

He couldn't believe what he was hearing. She dared to give him orders. "That isn't how our marriage works, Sara. I give the orders, and you obey them."

His voice had been hard, angry. It was deliberate, of course, for he wanted her to understand he meant what he said. He thought he was probably frightening her again. She started wringing her hands in obvious agitation, and though he felt a bit guilty because he had to resort to such intimidating tactics, the issue was far too important to soften his approach. Nathan promised himself that no matter how pitiful she looked or sounded when she started crying, he would not back down.

Sara continued to wring her hands for a long minute, pretending that it was her husband's stubborn neck she had between her fingers. The fantasy helped to lighten her mood.

Nathan nagged her back to reality when he growled, "Did you hear me, bride?"

God, she hated the name "bride!" "Yes, I heard you," she answered. "But I don't really understand. Why is that how this marriage works?"

The tears were back in her eyes again. Nathan suddenly felt like an ogre. "Are you trying to bait me?" he asked.

She shook her head. "No," she answered. "I just supposed our marriage was going to go along in the opposite direction.

THE GIFT

Yes, I always did," she added in a rush when he frowned intently at her.

"Oh? And just how did you think this marriage was going to go along?"

He actually seemed to be interested in her opinion. Sara immediately took heart. She lifted her shoulders in a dainty shrug. "Well, I supposed that it would always be my duty to tell you what I wanted."

"And?" he prodded when she quit her explanation.

"And it would always be your duty to get it for me."

She could tell from his dark expression he didn't like hearing that opinion. She could feel herself getting riled up again. "You're supposed to cherish me, Nathan. You did promise."

"I did not promise to cherish you," he countered in a shout. "For God's sake, woman, I didn't promise you anything."

She wasn't about to let him get away with that lie. She jumped to her feet to confront him again. "Oh, yes, you did promise," she shouted back. "I read the contract, Nathan, from start to finish. In return for the land and the treasury you're supposed to keep me safe. You're also supposed to be a good husband, a kind father, and most of all, Viking, you're supposed to love and cherish me."

He was at a loss for words. He suddenly felt like laughing again. The twisted turn in the topic was exasperating. Exhilarating, too.

"You really want me to love and cherish you?"

"I most certainly do," she replied. She folded her arms across her chest. "You promised to love and cherish me, Nathan, and by God, you're going to."

She sat down on the bed again and took her time straightening the folds in her gown. The blush that covered her cheeks told of her embarrassment.

"And what are you supposed to be doing while I'm loving and cherishing you?" he asked. "What are your promises, bride?"

"I didn't promise anything," she answered. "I was only four years old, Nathan. I didn't sign the contract. You did."

He closed his eyes and counted to ten. "Then you don't believe you have to honor your father's signature? The promises he made on your behalf aren't binding?"

"I didn't say that," she whispered. She let out a loud sigh, then added, "Of course I will honor them. They were given in my name."

"And what are they?" he demanded.

She took a long time answering him. She looked thoroughly disgruntled, too. "I have to love and cherish you, too," she muttered.

He wasn't satisfied. "And?"

"And what?" she asked, pretending ignorance.

He decided then and there that his bride was trying to make him crazed. "I also read the contract through from start to finish," he snapped. "Don't try my patience."

"Oh, all right," she countered. "I have to obey you, too. There, are you happy now?"

"Yes," he returned. "We're now back where we started," he said then. "As I instructed you before, I will be the one to give the orders, and you will be the one to obey them. And don't you dare ask me why again."

"I will try to obey your orders, Nathan, when I think they're reasonable."

His tolerance was at an end. "I don't give a damn if you think they're reasonable or not," he roared. "You will do as I say."

She didn't seem at all upset that he'd raised his voice to her. Her voice was quite mild when she said, "You really shouldn't use blasphemies in a lady's presence, Nathan. It's common, and you happen to be a marquess."

The look on his face was chilling. Sara felt completely defeated. "You hate me, don't you?"

"No."

She didn't believe him. Lord, the mere sight of her was making him ill. His complexion had a gray cast to it. "Oh, yes, you do hate me," she argued. "You can't fool me. I'm a Winchester, and you hate all the Winchesters."

"I do not hate you."

"You don't have to shout at me. I'm only trying to have a decent conversation, after all, and the least you could do is control your temper." She didn't give him time to shout at her again. "I'm very weary, Nathan. I would like to rest now."

He decided to let her have her way. He opened the door to leave, then turned around again.

"Sara?"

"Yes?"

"You aren't at all afraid of me, are you?"

He looked quite astonished. It was as though the truth had just dawned on him. She shook her head. "No."

He turned around again so she wouldn't see his smile.

"Nathan?"

"What?"

"I was a little afraid of you when I first saw you," she admitted. "Does that make you feel better?"

His answer was to shut the door.

The minute she was alone again she burst into tears. Oh, what a naïve fool she'd been. All those wasted years of dreaming about her wonderful knight in golden armor coming to claim her for his bride. She'd imagined him to be a gentle, understanding, sensitive man who was thoroughly in love with her.

Her dreams mocked her. Her knight was more tarnished than golden. He had just proven to be as understanding, as compassionate, as loving as a goat.

Sara continued to feel sorry for herself until exhaustion overcame her.

Nathan looked in on her again an hour later. Sara was sound asleep. She hadn't bothered to remove her clothes but slept on top of the multicolored quilt. She rested on her stomach, her arms thrown wide.

A feeling of contentment settled inside him. It was a

strange, altogether foreign feeling, but he found he actually liked seeing her in his bed. He noticed Nora's wedding band was still on her finger. Odd, but he didn't like seeing that at all. He pulled the ring off her finger just to rid himself of his own irrational irritation and put the band in his pocket.

He turned his attention to taking Sara's clothes off. After he'd unbuttoned the long row of tiny clasps down her back he eased the gown off. Her shoes and stockings came next. He was awkward with the task, and the petticoats almost defeated him. The knot in the string was impossible to untie. Nathan used the tip of his knife to cut the string away. He kept at the chore until he'd stripped his bride of all but her silk chemise. The white garment was extremely feminine, with lace edging the scooped neckline.

He gave in to his urge and brushed the back of his hand down her back.

Sara didn't wake up. She let out a little sigh in her sleep and rolled over onto her back just as Nathan was tossing the rest of her garments on the nearby chair.

Nathan didn't have any idea how long he stood there staring at her. She looked so innocent, so trusting, so damned vulnerable when she slept. Her eyelashes were black, thick, startling against the creaminess of her skin. Her body was magnificent to him. The fullness of her breasts, only partially concealed by the flimsy chemise, aroused him. When he realized he was physically reacting to her he turned to leave the cabin.

What in God's name was he going to do with her? How could he ever maintain his distance from someone as enticing as his bride?

Nathan put those questions aside when a wave of seasickness hit him. He waited until his stomach quit lurching so violently, then lifted the blanket from the hook and covered Sara. His hand touched the side of her face, and he couldn't help but smile when she instinctively rubbed her cheek against his knuckles. She reminded him of an affectionate little kitten.

She turned, and her mouth touched his skin. Nathan abruptly pulled his hand away. He left the room and went to look in on Sara's aunt. Nora appeared to be sleeping peacefully. She looked pale, and her breathing was labored, but she didn't seem to be in much pain. Her expression was serene. Nathan remembered the ring in his pocket. He walked over to the side of the bed, lifted her hand, and slipped the band back on.

Nora opened her eyes and smiled at him. "Thank you, dear boy. I'll rest much easier now that I have my Johnny's ring back."

Nathan acknowledged her gratitude with a curt nod, then turned and walked back to the door. "You think I'm a sentimental fool, don't you?" she called out.

His smile was quick. "Aye," he answered. "I do."

His blunt honesty made her chuckle. "Have you spoken to Sara yet?" she asked.

"I have."

"Is she all right?" Nora asked. She wished he'd turn around so she could see his expression.

"She's sleeping," Nathan announced. He opened the door and started out.

"Wait," Nora called out. "Please don't leave yet."

He reacted to the tremor he heard in her voice and immediately turned around again.

"I'm very frightened," Nora whispered.

Nathan shut the door and walked back over to the old woman's side. His arms were folded across his chest. He looked relaxed, save for the frown on his face. "You needn't be afraid," he told her. His voice was soft, soothing. "You're safe now, Nora."

She shook her head. "No, you misunderstand," she explained. "I'm not afraid for myself, dear boy. My worry is for you and Sara. Do you have any idea what you're letting yourself in for? You can't possibly know what those men are capable of. Not even I understood the depths to which they would sink for greed. They'll come after you."

Nathan shrugged. "I'll be ready," he answered. "The Winchesters aren't a challenge to me."

"But dear boy, they—"

"Nora, you don't know what I'm capable of," he countered. "When I tell you I'll be able to handle any challenge, you'll just have to believe me."

"They'll use Sara to get to you," Nora whispered. "They'll hurt her if they have to," she added with a nod.

"I protect what's mine." His voice was hard, emphatic.

His arrogance actually calmed her, too. She slowly nodded. "I believe you will," she said. "But what about the Winchester women?"

"Do you mean all of them, or one specifically?"

"Sara."

"She'll do all right," he said. "She isn't a Winchester any longer. She's a St. James. You insult my capabilities when you worry about her safety. I take care of my possessions."

"Possessions?" she repeated. "I've never heard a wife referred to in quite that fashion."

"You've been away from England long years, Nora. Nothing's changed in all that while, though. A wife is still a husband's possession."

"My Sara's very tenderhearted," Nora said, turning the topic a bit. "These past years haven't been easy for her. She's been considered an outsider because of the marriage contract. Some would say she was a leper in her own family. Sara was never allowed to attend any of the functions young ladies so look forward to. The fuss was always made over her sister Belinda."

Nora paused to take a breath, then continued. "Sara's fiercely loyal to her parents and her sister, of course, though for the life of me I can't understand why she would give any of them the time of day. You'd best beware of Sara's sister, for she's as cunning as her Uncle Henry. They're cut from the same evil bolt."

"You worry too much, Nora."

"I just want you to understand . . . Sara," she whispered.

The wheeze was back in her voice, and it was obvious that she was becoming weary. "My Sara's a dreamer," she continued. "Look at her drawings, and you'll understand what I'm saying. Her head's in the clouds most of the time. She sees only the goodness in people. She doesn't want to believe her father is like his brothers. I place the blame on Sara's mother, of course. She's lied to her daughter all these years, made up excuses for each and every sin the others committed."

Nathan didn't comment.

"Dear boy," she began again.

His sudden frown stopped her. "Madam, I'll make a pact with you," Nathan said. "I'll refrain from calling you old woman if you'll quit calling me your dear boy. Are we in agreement?"

Nora smiled. She was squinting up at the giant of a man. His very presence seemed to swallow up the room. "Yes, calling you dear boy was rather foolish," she agreed with a chuckle. "Do I have your permission to call you Nathan?"

"You do," he answered. "As for your concerns about Sara, they're all ill-founded. I will not allow anyone to hurt her. She's my wife, and I will always treat her kindly. In time she'll realize her good fortune."

His hands were clasped behind his back like a general's, and he was pacing the small room.

"There is also the telling fact that you protected her from those thugs the other evening," Nora said. "I know you'll take good care of her. I only hope you'll consider her tender feelings, too, Nathan. You see, Sara's actually very shy. She keeps her thoughts bottled up inside her. It's very difficult to know what she's feeling."

Nathan raised an eyebrow over that announcement. "Are we talking about the same woman, madam?"

Nora's grin was telling. She paused to pat a stray hair back into her bun. "I happened to overhear a little of your conversation with my niece," she confessed. "I'm not in the habit of eavesdropping," she added, "but it was a rather loud discussion the two of you were having, and actually they were mostly Sara's comments I overheard. Just a snatch here and there," she added. "Tell me this, Nathan. Will you?"

"Will I what?"

"Love and cherish her?"

"You heard that particular snatch, did you?" He couldn't contain his grin when he remembered the militant way his bride had dared to challenge him.

"I do believe your entire crew overheard Sara's remarks. I must have a little chat with her about her unladylike bellowing. I've never heard her raise her voice before, yet I cannot truly fault her. You did take your time coming to claim her. She's been stewing over your . . . forgetfulness. You must believe me when I tell you it isn't at all in her nature to raise her voice to anyone."

Nathan shook his head. He turned and walked out of the cabin. He was pulling the door shut behind him when Nora called out, "You've still to answer me. Will you love and cherish her?"

"Do I have a choice, madam?"

He shut the door before she could answer him.

Sara awakened a short time later to the horrid noise of someone retching. The tortured sound made her own stomach queasy. She sat up with a start. Her first thought was for Nora. The rolling motion of the ship must have made her aunt sick.

Sara immediately tossed the cover aside and rushed to the door. She was still so sleepy, she felt completely disoriented. She didn't even realize she was only partially dressed until she tripped over one of her petticoats.

One of Nathan's maids had obviously been at work. Sara saw that her trunk had been placed next to the far wall and realized she must have slept through its delivery. She blushed over the realization that a man had come into her cabin while she'd been asleep. She hoped the maid had covered her with the blanket before the visitation had taken place.

She heard a sound in the hallway and opened the door. Nathan was just walking past when she peeked outside. He never bothered to glance her way, just reached out and pulled the door closed again when he strode by.

Sara wasn't offended by his rudeness, and she wasn't worried about her aunt any longer. When she had seen the color of Nathan's complexion she'd known immediately, of course. Her fierce Viking husband looked as green as the sea.

Could it be possible? she asked herself. Was the invincible, ill-mannered marquess of St. James afflicted with seasickness?

Sara would have laughed out loud if she hadn't been so exhausted. She went back to bed and took a long nap, getting up only briefly to eat dinner with Nora before returning yet again to her bed for more badly needed sleep.

The air inside the chamber cooled considerably during the night, and Sara woke up shivering. She tried to pull the quilt up around her shoulders, but the blanket was caught on something quite solid. When Sara finally opened her eyes she found the cause. The blanket was tangled up in Nathan's long, naked legs.

He was sleeping next to her.

She almost had heart failure. She opened her mouth to scream. He clamped his big hand over half her face.

"Don't you dare make a sound," he ordered.

She pushed his hand away. "Get out of my bed." The command came out in a furious whisper.

He let out a weary sigh before responding to that command. "Sara, you happen to be sleeping in my bed. If anyone's going to leave, it's going to be you."

He sounded sleepy to her, and mean. Sara was actually comforted by his callous attitude. She guessed he was so exhausted he only wanted to sleep, and her virtue was therefore still safe.

"Very well," she announced. "I'll go and sleep with Nora."

"No, you won't," he answered. "You aren't going to leave this cabin. If you wish to, bride, you may sleep on the floor."

"Why do you persist in calling me bride?" she demanded. "If you have to call me something other than my name, then call me wife, not bride."

"But you aren't my wife yet," he responded.

She didn't understand. "I most certainly am your wife . . . aren't I?"

"Not until I've bedded you."

A long silent minute passed before she responded to that statement.

"You may call me bride."

"I don't need your permission," he growled. He reached out to take her into his arms when she started shivering again, but she pushed his hands away.

"My God, I can't believe this is happening to me," she cried out. "You're supposed to be kind, gentle, understanding."

"What makes you think I'm not?" he couldn't resist asking.

"You're naked," she blurted out.

"And that means I'm not—"

She wanted to hit him. Her face was turned away from him, but she could hear the laughter in his voice. "You're embarrassing me," she announced. "On purpose."

His patience was at an end. "I am not deliberately trying to embarrass you," he snapped. "This is just how I sleep, bride. You'll like it, too, once—"

"Oh, God," she said on a groan.

She decided she was through with the shameful conversation. She scooted down to the bottom of the bed so that she could get out, as one side was blocked by the wall, and the other side was blocked by Nathan. It was too dark inside the cabin to find her wrapper. Nathan had kicked one of the covers off the bed, though. Sara grabbed it and wrapped it around herself.

She didn't know how long she stood there glaring at his back. His deep, even breathing indicated he was sound asleep.

She was freezing in no time. Her thin nightgown offered little protection against the chill in the room.

She was miserable. She sat down on the floor, tucked her bare feet under the blanket, and then stretched out on her side.

The floor felt as though it were covered with a layer of ice. "All married couples have separate chambers," she muttered. "I have never, ever been treated so poorly in all my days. If this is your idea of how you plan to cherish me, you're already failing, Nathan."

He heard every word of her whispered tirade. He held his smile when he said "You're a quick learner, bride."

She didn't know what he was talking about. "And what is it you think I've learned so quickly?" she asked.

"Where your place is," he drawled. "It took my dog much longer."

Her scream of outrage filled the cabin. "Your dog?" She came to her feet in one swift action, then poked him in his shoulder. "Move over, husband."

"Climb over, Sara," he ordered. "I always sleep on the outside."

"Why?" she asked before she could stop herself.

"For protection," he answered. "If the cabin is breached, the enemy will have to get through me in order to get to you. Now will you go to sleep, woman?"

"Is this an old rule or a new one?"

He didn't answer her. She poked his shoulder again. "Have there been other women in this bed, Nathan?"

"No."

She didn't know why, but she was immensely pleased with that surly denial. Her anger dissipated when she realized her husband really meant to try to protect her. He was still an ogre, but he would do his best to keep her safe. She got into bed and squeezed herself up against the wall.

The bed soon began to shake from her shivers. Nathan's tolerance was gone. He reached out and roughly pulled her into his arms. Sara was literally covered by his warmth. And his nakedness. He draped one of his heavy legs over both of hers, immediately warming the lower half of her body. His chest and arms took care of the rest of her.

She didn't protest. She couldn't. His hand was clamped over her mouth. She snuggled closer to him, tucked the top of her head under his chin, and closed her eyes.

The instant Nathan removed his hand from her mouth, she whispered, "If anyone is going to sleep on the floor, it's going to be you."

His low grunt of irritation was his only response. Sara smiled to herself. She was feeling much better. She let out a yawn, moved even closer to her husband, and let him take her shivers completely away.

She fell asleep feeling warm and safe . . . and just a little bit cherished.

It was a nice beginning.

Chapter Four

Sara felt much better when she awakened the following morning. She'd finally caught up on her rest, and she felt ready to take on the world. More directly, she felt strong enough to talk to her Viking husband again.

She had come up with a wonderful plan during the night, and she was certain that once she'd explained exactly what she wanted from her husband, he would agree. Oh, he'd probably grumble and growl, but in the end he'd see how much it meant to her, and he would give in.

There were several issues that needed to be discussed, but she decided she would get the most worrisome one over and done with first.

She wanted a courtship and a proper marriage. No matter how rude and arrogant he became when she explained her request to him, she was determined to hold onto her temper. She would simply use a sweet tone of voice and be as logical as possible.

Lord, she did dread the task ahead of her. Nathan wasn't a very easy man to talk to. Why, he acted as though it was a chore to be in the same room with her.

That realization led to a dark thought. What if he really didn't want to be married to her?

"Nonsense," she muttered to herself. "Of course he wants to be married to me."

That attempt to bolster her confidence didn't last long. She was so accustomed to thinking of Nathan as her husband that she had never once considered being married to anyone else. She'd grown up with the idea, and because she had such an easygoing, accepting nature, she never questioned her fate.

But what about Nathan? He didn't seem to be the type of man who accepted much of anything without putting up a fight.

She guessed that she would continue to fret about the situation until she'd talked to him.

She dressed with care, determined to look her best when she confronted Nathan. It took her almost an hour to unpack her possessions. The dark green walking dress was her first choice, but she couldn't shake all the wrinkles out of the skirt, so she settled on wearing her light pink gown. The neckline wasn't nearly as revealing as the one Nathan had rudely remarked upon, and she thought that fact might put him in a good mood.

Their cabin was actually quite nice. It was much larger than the one she'd visited Nora in. Why, her chamber was actually three times the size. The ceiling was much higher, too, adding to the feeling of spaciousness.

It was sparsely furnished, though. There was a twisted metal grate in the corner of the cabin. Sara assumed that was the hearth, though she admitted she didn't care for the modern design overly much. In the opposite corner of the room was a tall white screen. There were hooks on the wall behind it to hold clothing, and a washstand with a porcelain pitcher and bowl set on top. In the corner opposite the bed was her trunk. A table and two chairs took up the center of the room, and a large mahogany desk was set against the wall.

Yes, the room was sparsely furnished, she mused, but it would certainly do for the next month or two, depending upon the weather. If the sea remained calm, the journey to her aunt's island shouldn't take them too long.

Sara removed Nathan's clothes from the hooks, folded them, and put them on her trunk. She then hung up her gowns. She also removed the papers and charts from the top of his desk and put her sketch pads and charcoals there instead.

After donning the pink gown and matching shoes she brushed her hair and tied it behind her neck with a pink ribbon. She grabbed her matching pink parasol from her trunk and then went to look in on Nora. She hoped her aunt would be feeling rested enough to stroll along the upper decks. Sara wanted to go over her prepared speech with her aunt before confronting Nathan.

Nora was sound asleep, however, and Sara didn't have the heart to wake her.

When she left her aunt's cabin she noticed that the dark, narrow hallway actually widened into a large rectangular room. Sunlight filtered down the steps and made the wooden floors sparkle. The pristine area was devoid of furniture, but there were a multitude of black iron hooks protruding from the ceiling. She wondered what in heaven's name the area was used for, or if it was just wasted space. Her attention was turned when one of the crew came lumbering down the steps.

The man tucked his head under the low overhand, then came to an abrupt stop when he spotted her. Sara recognized the man from the wharf but decided to pretend that she didn't. After all, she had acted most unladylike, and that incident was best forgotten.

"Good day, sir," she announced with a curtsy. "My name is Lady Sara Winchester."

He shook his head at her. She didn't know what to make of that.

"You're Lady St. James."

She was too surprised by his boldness to correct him for contradicting her. "Yes," she agreed. "I am Lady St. James now, and I thank you for reminding me."

The big man shrugged. The gold earring in his earlobe fascinated her. So did the fact that he seemed to be a little wary of her. Perhaps the seaman just wasn't used to visiting with gentle ladies of breeding. "I'm very happy to make your acquaintance, sir," she said.

She waited for him to tell her his name. He stood staring down at her for a long minute before he finally responded. "We met last night, Lady St. James," he said. "You hit me, remember?"

She remembered. She gave him a disgruntled look for bringing up her bad behavior, then slowly nodded. "Yes, I do remember, sir, now that you mention it, and for that shame I must apologize to you. My only excuse is that I was in a bit of a startle at the time. What is your name?"

"Jimbo."

If she thought that name odd, she didn't remark upon it. She reached out and clasped his right hand in both of hers. The feel of her soft skin against his calluses startled him. Her parasol fell to the floor, but Jimbo was still too surprised by her touch to fetch it, and she was too intent on gaining his friendship to fetch it herself. "Do you forgive me, sir, for hitting you?"

Jimbo was rendered speechless. The woman he'd met two nights before was a far cry from the soft-spoken lady standing so humbly before him. Lord, she was a fair sight, too. She had the prettiest brown eyes he'd ever seen.

He got hold of his thoughts when she gave him a puzzled look. "Does it matter to you if I forgive you or not?" he muttered.

Sara gave his hand an affectionate squeeze before she let go. "Oh, my, yes, Mister Jimbo. Of course it matters. I was very rude."

He rolled his eyes heavenward. "All right, I forgive you.

You didn't do any real damage," he added in a grumble. He was feeling as awkward as a schoolboy.

Sara's smile melted his frown away. "I do thank you, sir. You have a kind heart."

Jimbo threw back his head and shouted with laughter. When he was able to regain his composure he said, "Be sure to mention my . . . kind heart to the captain. He'll appreciate hearing such high praise."

She thought that was a fine idea. "Yes, I will mention it," she promised.

Since the seaman seemed to be in such a pleasant mood, she decided to ask him a few questions. "Sir? Have you seen the maids about this morning? My bed has still to be made up, and I have several gowns that need attention."

"We don't have any maids aboard this vessel," Jimbo returned. "Fact is, you and your aunt are the only women traveling with us."

"Then who . . ." She stopped that question in midsentence. If there weren't any maids, who had taken her clothes off her? The answer came to her in a flash. Nathan.

Jimbo watched as a fine blush covered her cheeks and wondered what she was thinking about.

"I have one other question to ask you, sir, if you're patient enough to listen."

"What?" he countered abruptly.

"What is this room called? Or does it have a specific name?" She made a sweep with her hand to indicate the area around her. "I thought it was just a hallway, yet now, with the light streaming down the steps, I can see it's much larger. It would make a wonderful salon," she added. "I hadn't noticed that folding screen when I first boarded, and I . . ."

She quit her speech when Jimbo moved the screen off to the side and secured it in the buckles and straps against the wall next to the stairs. "This is the wardroom," Jimbo told her. "Or so it's called on all true frigates."

The hallway was completely gone, and once the screen

had been moved Sara could see the steps leading down to another level. "Where do those steps lead?"

"The wine and water are stored on the level below us," Jimbo answered. "Lower still is the second hold, where we keep the ammunition."

"Ammunition?" she asked. "Why would we need ammunition?"

Jimbo smiled. "You didn't chance to notice the cannons, m'lady, when you boarded?"

She shook her head. "I was a little upset at the time, sir, and I didn't pay much attention to details."

A little upset was certainly the understatement of the year, Jimbo thought. The woman had been in a rage.

"We have eight cannons in all," Jimbo announced. "That's way below the usual number for most ships, but our aim is always on target, and we don't need more. This ship is a scaled-down version of a frigate the captain took a liking to," he added. "The ammunition stores are kept below the water level in the event of an attack. They're safer from explosion that way."

"But Mister Jimbo, we aren't at war now. Why would the captain have such weapons on board? What is the need?"

Jimbo shrugged. Sara's eyes suddenly widened. "Pagan." She blurted out the name of the infamous pirate and then nodded. "Yes, of course. How cunning of our captain to be prepared for the villains who roam the seas. He thinks to defend us against all the pirates, doesn't he?"

It was a mighty effort, but Jimbo was able to hide his smile. "You've heard of Pagan, have you?"

She let him see her exasperation. "Everyone has heard of that villain."

"Villain? Then you don't like Pagan?"

She thought that had to be the oddest question ever put to her. The sparkle in his eyes puzzled her, too. He seemed to be vastly amused, and that didn't make any sense at all. They were talking about the horrid pirate, not sharing the latest jest making the rounds in London.

"I most certainly don't like the man. He's a criminal, sir. Why, there's a bounty the size of England on his head. You're obviously given to a romantic nature if you believe all those silly stories about Pagan's goodness."

The piercing sound of a whistle interrupted her lecture. "What is that noise?" she asked. "I heard it earlier when I was dressing."

"That's the boatswain piping the change," he explained. "You'll be hearing the sound every four hours, night and day. It's the notice of the change of duty."

"Mister Jimbo?" she asked when he started to turn away from her.

"Lady Sara, you don't have to call me mister," he grumbled. "Jimbo will do fine."

"Then you must quit calling me Lady Sara," she countered. "We are friends now, and you may simply call me Sara." She grabbed his arm. "May I ask you just one last question?"

He glanced over his shoulder. "Yes?"

"Last evening . . . or was it the night before? Well, I noticed that you seemed to be in my husband's employ. Is that correct?"

"Yes."

"Do you happen to know where Nathan is? I would like to have a word with him."

"He's aft."

She looked startled but was quick to recover. Then she shook her head at him. The censure in her expression gained his full attention. He turned completely around. "He's aft, I'm telling you."

"Yes, he might very well be daft, Jimbo," she began. She paused to pick up her parasol and then walked around the big man. "But you're most disloyal when you voice that thought aloud. I'm Nathan's wife now, and I won't listen to such talk. Please don't show such disrespect again."

Matthew came down the stairs just in time to hear his

friend mutter something about respect. Lady Sara smiled as she made her way past him.

"What was that all about?" Matthew asked his friend. "I thought I heard you—"

Jimbo cut him off with a glare. "You aren't going to believe this, but I just promised not ever to tell anyone Nathan was aft."

Matthew shook his head. "She's a strange one, isn't she, Jimbo? I'm wondering how such an innocent could have come from such a mean-hearted family."

"Sara isn't anything like our Jade," Jimbo announced. He was referring to Nathan's younger sister. "In all our travels together I never once saw Jade cry."

"No, she never cried." There was pride in Matthew's voice. "But this one . . . I didn't know a woman could carry on the way she did that first night."

"Screaming like a hellion, too," Jimbo interjected. "Now, Jade," he continued, "she never screamed."

"Never," Matthew agreed. His voice was emphatic.

Jimbo suddenly grinned. "The two are as different as fire and snow," he said. "Still, they do have one thing in common."

"What's that?"

"They're both damn fair in looks."

Matthew nodded.

The comparison between the two ladies was cut short when a shrill scream reached them. They both knew it was Sara making all the racket. "She's a piece of work, isn't she?" Matthew drawled out.

"A damned loud piece of work," Jimbo muttered. "Wonder what's got her all riled up this time."

Odd, but both men were eager to get back up on deck to see what was happening. They were both smiling, too.

Sara had just located Nathan. He was standing behind a spoked wheel. She was about to call out to him when he turned his back on her and pulled off his shirt.

She saw the scars on his back. Her reaction was instinctive. She let out a shout of outrage.

"Who did that to you?"

Nathan immediately reacted. He grabbed hold of his whip and turned to confront the threat. It didn't take him any time at all to realize there wasn't any enemy trying to harm his bride. Sara stood all alone.

"What is it?" he roared at her while he tried to calm his heartbeat. "I thought someone was . . ."

He stopped himself in mid-bellow, took a deep breath, and then said, "Are you in pain, madam?"

She shook her head.

"Don't you ever scream like that again," he ordered in a much softer tone of voice. "If you wish my attention, simply ask for it."

Sara's parasol fell to the deck when she walked over to her husband. She was still so stunned by what she'd seen, she wasn't even aware she'd dropped it. She stopped when she was just a scant foot away from Nathan. He saw the tears in her eyes. "Now what is it?" he demanded. "Did someone frighten you?" Damn, he didn't have the patience for this, he told himself.

"It's your back, Nathan," she whispered. "It's covered with scars."

He shook his head. No one had ever dared mention his disfigurement to him. Those who'd seen his back pretended not to notice.

"Thank you for telling me," he snapped. "I never would have known . . ."

Hell, she started to cry. His sarcasm was obviously too much for her, he decided. "Look, Sara," he muttered in true exasperation. "If the sight of my back offends you, go below."

"It doesn't offend me," she answered. "Why would you say such a mean thing?"

Nathan motioned to Jimbo to take over the wheel, then

clasped his hands behind his back so he wouldn't grab her. The urge to shake some sense into the woman fairly overwhelmed him. "All right, then, why did you scream?"

His voice was as brisk as the wind. Sara guessed he was a little sensitive about his marks. "I was very angry when I saw the scars, Nathan. Did you have an accident?"

"No."

"Then someone deliberately did this thing to you?" She didn't give him time to answer. "What monster inflicted such pain? My God, how you must have suffered."

"For God's sake, it happened a long time ago."

"Was it Pagan?" she asked.

"What?" he asked.

He looked startled. Sara thought her guess had been right after all. "It was Pagan who did that to you, wasn't it?"

Jimbo started coughing. Nathan turned to glare him into silence. "Why in God's name would you think it was Pagan?" he asked Sara.

"Because he's mean enough," she answered.

"Oh?" he asked. "And how would you know that?"

She shrugged. "I heard that he was."

"It wasn't Pagan."

"Are you absolutely certain, Nathan? No one knows what the villain looks like. Perhaps it was Pagan, and you just didn't realize it because he didn't give you his true name."

He let her see his exasperation. "I know who did it."

"Will you tell me who it was, then?"

"Why?"

"So I can hate him."

His anger vanished. Such loyalty stunned him. "No, I won't tell you who it was."

"But it wasn't Pagan."

She could drive a man to drink, Nathan thought to himself. "No," he answered once again.

"Nathan, you don't have to shout at me."

He turned his back on her in dismissal. Jimbo moved

away from the wheel. Sara waited until she and her husband were all alone and then moved closer.

He felt the touch of her fingertips on the top of his right shoulder. He didn't move. The feathery light caress down his back was incredibly gentle, and provocative, too. He couldn't ignore it, or the strange feelings her touch evoked.

"I wouldn't have poked you in your back last night if I'd known about your injury," she whispered. "But I couldn't see in the dark, and I didn't . . . know."

"For God's sake, woman, it doesn't hurt now. It happened years ago."

His abrupt tone startled her. Her hand dropped back to her side. She moved over to stand beside him. Her arm touched his. She looked up at his face and simply waited for him to look at her again. His expression could have been chiseled in stone, she thought to herself. He looked just the way she pictured a Viking. The ripple of muscles cording his shoulders and his upper arms were those of a fit warrior. His chest was covered with dark curly hair that tapered to a V at the waistband of his breeches. She didn't dare look any lower, for to do so would be brazen, and when she returned her attention to his face again she found him watching her.

She blushed. "Nathan?"

"What?"

Did he always have to sound so resigned when he talked to her? Sara forced herself to sound pleasant when she apologized. "I'm sorry if I hurt your feelings."

He didn't think that comment was worthy of a response.

"Will the captain mind?" she asked then.

"Mind what?"

"Mind that you're directing his boat for him."

His smile was heartwarming to her. "It isn't a boat, Sara. You may call the *Seahawk* a ship or a vessel, but you must never call her a boat. It's an insult, bride, and we captains take grave exception to hearing such blasphemy."

"We captains?"

He nodded.

"Oh, Nathan, I didn't realize," she blurted. "Then we're rich?"

"No."

"Well, why not?"

Hell, he thought, she looked disgruntled. Nathan quickly told her how he and his friend Colin had started the shipping company together, why they'd decided that he should remain a silent partner, and he ended his brief summary with the fact that in approximately ten months time, give or take a month or two, their company would take a turn into sure profits.

"How can you be so certain that in just a year we'll be rich?"

"The contract I signed."

"Do you mean a contract for shipping services?"

"No."

Her sigh was dramatic. "Please explain, Nathan."

He ignored her request. She nudged him. Lord, getting anything out of him was such a strain. "If you're so certain about this, I'll be happy to help you."

He actually laughed. Sara took heart. Her offer to lend a hand had obviously pleased him. Her voice was filled with enthusiasm when she said, "I could help you with the books. I'm really quite good with figures. No?" she added when he shook his head. "But I want to help."

He let go of the wheel and turned to face her. Lord, she was a fair sight today, he thought to himself as he watched her try to manage her wild curls. The wind was high, making the task impossible. She was dressed in pink. Her cheeks were flushed, adding to the lovely picture. His gaze settled on her mouth. Her lips were just as rosy as the rest of her.

He gave in to his sudden urge. Before she could back away from him he grabbed hold of her shoulders. He pulled her up against his chest, then threaded one hand through the curls behind her neck. Her hair felt like silk to him. He made a fist of the curls, then jerked her head back so her face was tilted up toward him. He told himself that it was only for his own peace of mind that he was going to kiss her, knowing full well that once he explained the special task she was going to have to undertake she'd start screaming again.

"We'll each have a special duty to perform," he told her. His mouth was getting closer to hers. "It's my duty to get you pregnant, Sara, and it will be your duty to give me a son."

His mouth settled on top of hers just in time to capture her outraged gasp.

Sara was simply too stunned to react at first. His mouth was hard, hot, incredibly demanding. He was drowning her with his warmth, his taste, his wonderful masculine scent.

Nathan wanted her response. She didn't disappoint him. When his tongue moved inside her mouth to mate with hers, her knees went weak. She put her arms around his neck and clung to him even as she tried to wiggle out of his embrace.

She didn't realize she was kissing him back, didn't know the sounds she heard belonged to her.

Only when Nathan had her full cooperation did he gentle the kiss. God, she was soft. He could feel the heat inside her, wanted to get closer, closer. His hands moved to cup her derrière, and he slowly lifted her off the ground until her pelvis was touching his own, then pulled her tight against his arousal.

His mouth slanted over hers again and again. He wanted to be inside her. Nathan knew he was close to losing all sense of discipline. His hunger was demanding to be appeased.

The whistles and hoots of laughter penetrated his mind then. His crew was obviously enjoying the spectacle he was giving them. Nathan tried to pull away from Sara.

She wouldn't let go of him. She pulled on his hair to get him to deepen the kiss again. He gave into her silent plea with a low growl. The kiss they shared was openly carnal, but when her sweet tongue rubbed against his he forced himself to stop.

They were both out of breath when they drew apart. Sara

couldn't seem to keep her balance. She fell back against the wooden ledge adjacent to the wheel. One hand rested on the swell of her bosom, and she let out a ragged little whisper. "Oh, my."

As soon as their captain had quit touching his bride the men returned to their duties. Nathan glared at several backs before he looked at Sara again. He couldn't help but feel extremely satisfied when he saw the bemused look on her face. It made him want to kiss her again.

He had to shake his head over his own lack of discipline. He decided he'd wasted enough time on his bride and turned his attention back to the wheel. He scowled when he noticed his hands were shaking. The kiss had obviously affected him a little more than he'd thought.

It took Sara much longer to recover. She was trembling from head to foot. She had no idea a kiss could be so . . . thorough.

He certainly hadn't been affected, she thought when she saw the horridly bored look on his face again.

She suddenly felt like crying and didn't understand why. Then she remembered the obscene remarks he'd made about her special duty. "I'm not a brood mare," she whispered. "And I'm not at all certain I like you touching me."

Nathan glanced back over his shoulder. "You could have fooled me," he drawled. "The way you kissed me—"

"I believe I hated it."

"Liar."

It was an insult, yes, but the way he'd said the word actually warmed her heart. He made it sound very like an endearment.

That didn't make any sense. Was she so desperate for a word of kindness from the Viking that she now responded to insults? Sara could feel herself blushing. She stared at her shoes and folded her hands demurely in front of her. "You can't kiss me again," she announced, wishing her voice had sounded a little more forceful and less breathless.

"I can't?"

His amusement was apparent. "No, you can't," she told him. "I've decided that you're going to have to court me first, Nathan, and then we must have a proper ceremony performed by a true minister before you may kiss me again."

She hadn't looked at him when she made that emphatic speech, but when she was finished she glanced up to gauge his reaction. His expression, unfortunately, didn't tell her anything. She frowned at him. "I believe our marriage could be challenged in the courts unless we say our vows to each other in front of a man of God."

He finally let her see his reaction. She wished she'd been left guessing. Lord, his scowl was as hot as the noon sun beating down on them.

But his eyes . . . the color was so vivid, so true, so mesmerizing. When he was looking directly into her eyes he made her forget to breathe. A sudden thought settled in her mind. Her Viking was actually very handsome.

Why hadn't she noticed that before? she asked herself. Good God, was she beginning to find him appealing?

Nathan pulled her from her thoughts when he said, "Are you thinking you've found a way to breach this contract?"

"No."

"Good," he countered. Almost as an afterthought he added, "As I instructed you before, I'm not about to dissolve this contract, Sara."

She disliked his arrogant tone. "I already knew that before I was so instructed."

"You did?"

"Yes, I did."

"How?"

She started to shake her head at him again, but Nathan stopped that action when he hauled her back into his arms. He firmly grabbed hold of her hair.

"Unhand me, Nathan. You make my head ache when you tug on my hair like that."

He didn't let go, but he did begin to rub the back of her neck. His touch was very soothing. Sara had to catch herself from letting out a telling little sigh.

"You realize how much I want the money and the land, don't you, Sara?" he asked. "That's why you know I won't walk away from the contract."

"No."

Nathan didn't know why he pressed her for an explanation. His curiosity was caught, however, because she was acting so damn shy. The woman didn't make any sense to him, and he was determined to understand how her mind worked.

"Then why did you know I would want to be married to you?"

"Well, why wouldn't you?" she whispered.

"Why wouldn't I?"

"Nathan, I'm everything a husband could want in a wife," she blurted out. She tried to sound as arrogant, as self-assured as he did whenever he talked to her. "Truly," she added with a vehement nod.

"Is that so?"

She could see the laughter in his eyes. Her bluster of pride immediately began to evaporate. "Yes, I am," she said.

A fine blush covered her cheeks. How could anyone sound so arrogant and look so shy at the same time? he wondered. She was such a contradiction to him. "Would you care to tell me why you think you're everything I could want?"

"Certainly," she replied. "For one, I'm pretty enough. I'm not plain," she added in a rush. "I'll admit I'm not a raving beauty, Nathan, but that shouldn't signify."

"You don't believe you're a . . . raving beauty?" he asked, amazed.

She gave him a good frown, for she was certain he was deliberately baiting her. "Of course not," she said. "You must have a cruel streak inside you to taunt me over my appearance. I'm not overly ugly, Nathan. Just because I have

94

brown hair and brown eyes doesn't necessarily mean I'm
. . . homely."

His smile was tender. "Sara, haven't you ever noticed how
men stop and stare when you pass by?"

She wished she could strike him. "If you mean to imply
that I'm that unappealing, well, sir," she muttered.

"Well, what?" he asked when she seemed to be at a loss for
words.

"You're no prize either, husband."

He shook his head. He wasn't married to a vain woman.
That fact pleased him considerably. "You're right," he
announced. "I have seen prettier women, but as you just
said, that shouldn't signify."

"Lest you think you make me feel completely inferior
with that rude remark, you're mistaken," she returned. The
blush had moved to her voice. "I'm really all a man could
want. Dare you smile at me? I mean what I say. I've been
trained to be a good wife, just as you've been trained to be a
good provider. It's the way of things," she ended with a
deliberate shrug.

The vulnerability in her expression was apparent. She had
pricked his curiosity, too. The woman said the damnedest
things. "Sara, exactly what is it that you've been trained to
do?"

"I can run a household with ease, no matter the number
of servants you employ," she began. "I can sew a straight
stitch without pricking my finger, plan a formal dinner party
for as many as two hundred," she exaggerated, "and accomplish any other duty associated with the running of a large
estate."

She was certain she'd impressed him with her list. She'd
even impressed herself. Most of what she'd just boasted of
was pure fabrication, of course, as she didn't really have the
faintest idea if she could run a large estate or not, but
Nathan couldn't possibly know about her inadequacies,
could he? Besides, just because she'd never entertained

anyone before didn't necessarily mean she couldn't organize a party for two hundred guests. She believed she could accomplish any goal if she really put her mind to the challenge. "Well?" she asked when he didn't make any comment. "What think you of my accomplishments?"

"I could hire someone to run my household," he countered. "I don't have to be married to have a comfortable home."

He almost laughed out loud, for the look of disappointment on her face was comical.

She tried not to feel defeated by his remark. "Yes, but I can also engage in intelligent conversation with your guests on any current topic. I happen to be very well-read."

His grin stopped her. His conduct, she decided, was proving just what one would expect from a man bearing his name. Nathan was turning out to be as despicable as the rest of the St. James men. He was certainly as muleheaded.

"You could not hire anyone with such a fine education," she muttered.

"And that's it?" he asked. "There isn't anything else you've been trained to do?"

Her pride was like a shredded gown pooled around her ankles. Wasn't there anything she could say that would impress the man?

"Such as?"

"Such as pleasing me in bed."

Her blush intensified. "Of course not," she stammered out. "You're supposed to teach me how . . ." She paused to step on his foot. Hard. "How dare you think I would be trained in that . . . that . . ."

She couldn't go on. The look in her eyes confused him. He couldn't decide if she was about to burst into tears or try to kill him. "A mistress could see to those duties, I suppose," he said just to goad her.

Lord, he thought, she really was a joy to tease. Her reactions were so uninhibited, so . . . raw. He knew he should quit his game. She was getting all worked up, but he was enjoying himself too much to stop just yet.

"You will not have a mistress."

She'd shouted that statement. He deliberately shrugged. She stepped on his foot again. "No matter how pretty she is, no matter how . . . talented she may be, no matter what," she said. "I won't have it."

She didn't give him time to respond to that statement but continued. "As for sleeping next to me, Nathan, well, you can just forget such notions in future. I'm going to be properly courted by you and wed before a minister first."

She waited a long minute for his agreement. "Well?" she demanded.

He shrugged again.

How could she have thought he was the least bit appealing? Lord, she wished she had enough strength to give him a sound kick in his backside. "This is a very serious matter we're discussing," she insisted. "And if you shrug at me once more, I swear I'll scream again."

He didn't think it was the time to mention the fact that she was already screaming. "Not we," he said in soft, soothing voice. "You're the one who thinks this is a serious matter," he explained. "I don't."

She took a deep breath and tried one last time. "Nathan, please try to understand my feelings," she whispered. "I've decided that it isn't decent for you to sleep with me." She was too embarrassed to continue with that particular bend in the topic. "Are you going to marry me or not?"

"I already did."

Lord, she was furious with him. Her face was as red as sunburn, and she couldn't meet his gaze. She was staring intently at his chest. The subject was obviously extremely distressing to him.

And yet she persisted. "Look," she muttered. "It's really very simple to understand, even for a St. James. I want to be properly courted, Nathan, and you aren't going to touch me until we've said our vows in front of a man of God. Do you hear me?"

"I'm certain he heard you clear, miss," came a shout from behind her. Sara shoved herself away from Nathan and turned around to find an audience of some ten men smiling at her. All had paused in their duties, she noticed, and all were nodding at her. Most were actually a fair distance away.

"Aye, I'd wager he caught every word," called another. "You ain't going to let the captain touch you until you're wed proper. Ain't that right, Haedley?"

A baldheaded, bent-shouldered man nodded. "That's what I heard," he shouted back.

Sara was mortified. Lord, she must have been screaming like a shrew.

She decided to blame Nathan. She turned around to glare at him. "Must you embarrass me?"

"You're doing a fair job on your own, bride. Go back to the cabin," he ordered. "Take that gown off."

She was immediately waylaid by that command. "Why? Don't you like it?" she asked.

"Take everything off, Sara. I'll be down in a few minutes."

Her heart almost failed her when the fullness of what he'd just said settled in her mind. She was simply too furious to try to reason with him any longer. Without a word of farewell she turned around and slowly walked away from him.

She passed Jimbo on her way toward the steps. "You were correct, Mister Jimbo," she said in a hoarse whisper. "Nathan is daft."

The seaman wasn't given time to reply, for Lady Sara was already gone.

She didn't start in running until she reached the wardroom area. Sara picked up her skirts and ran like lightning then. She didn't pause at her cabin door but continued on to the far corner, where Aunt Nora's quarters were located.

For all his bulk and age, Matthew could still be quick when the occasion called for such action, and he reached the door at the same time Sara did.

"Lady Sara, I'm hoping you won't disturb sweet Nora with a visit now," he said from behind.

She hadn't heard his approach. She let out a loud gasp and turned around. "You gave me a startle," she began. "You shouldn't sneak up on someone, sir. What is your name?"

"Matthew."

"I'm pleased to meet you," she returned. "As for my aunt, well, I just wanted to look in on her."

"I'm taking care of your aunt," Matthew interjected. "She isn't up to visitors today. She's tuckered out."

Sara immediately felt guilty. She had fully intended on pouring her heart out to her aunt so that she could gain her assistance in dealing with Nathan. Her own problems seemed paltry, however. "Nora isn't truly ill, is she?" she asked, fear obvious in her voice. "I saw the bruises, but I thought—"

"She's going to heal just fine," Matthew announced. He was pleased by her caring attitude. "Nora's needing plenty of rest, though. She shouldn't move about neither. Her ribs were cracked—"

"Oh God, I didn't know."

"Now, now, don't start in weeping," Matthew pleaded. Lady Sara's eyes were already looking misty to him. He didn't know what he'd do if she went full-blown on him. The thought of having to comfort the captain's wife made his stomach tighten up. "It ain't as bad as all that," he announced with a nod for emphasis. "I've wrapped her tight around the middle. She just needs rest is all. I don't want her fretting about anything, either," he added. He gave her a knowing look when he made that last remark.

Sara immediately concluded he'd guessed what her mission was. She bowed her head in contrition and said, "I was going to burden her with a special problem that has developed. I won't bother her, of course. I don't want to worry her. When she awakens will you please tell her that I'll come to visit her as soon as she asks for me?"

Matthew nodded. Sara took hold of his hand. The show of affection rattled him. "Thank you for helping Nora. She's such a good-hearted woman. She has suffered so, Mister Matthew, and all because of me."

Lordy, she looked like she was about to burst into tears again. "Now, now, you didn't do the damage to your aunt," Matthew said. "You aren't the one who kicked her in the ribs. I was told it was your father and his brothers behind the foul deed."

"My Uncle Henry was behind this treachery," she returned. "Still, I'm just as responsible. If I hadn't insisted that Nora come back to England with me . . ."

She didn't go on with her explanation. She gave Matthew's hand another quick squeeze, then surprised a smile out of him when she made a formal curtsy and told him how pleased she was to have him on her staff.

Matthew mopped his brow as he watched her walk back to her cabin. He grunted over the foolishness of it all, for the fact that he was actually nervous because she had almost cried was simply ludicrous. Still, he was smiling when he strolled away.

Sara continued to think about Nora until she opened the door to her cabin. As soon as she spotted the big bed the problem of Nathan became uppermost in her thoughts.

She didn't dare waste another minute. She shut the door, bolted it, and then dragged her heavy trunk over to the entrance, straining her back with the effort.

She hurried over to the table, thinking she'd put that piece of furniture up against the trunk to add to her fortress.

No matter how much grit she put to the chore, she couldn't get the table to budge. She finally located the cause. The legs had been nailed to the floor. "Now why would anyone want to do such a thing?" she muttered to herself.

She tried to move the desk and found that it had also been

nailed to the floor. The chairs, thankfully, weren't stationary. They were heavy, though. Sara dragged one over to the trunk and spent precious minutes struggling with the weight until she'd lifted the awkward piece of furniture and had it propped up on top.

She stood back to observe her work. She rubbed her lower back, trying to take the sting away. She knew that blocking the door was only a temporary measure, but she still felt she'd been very clever. It didn't take her long to discard that bit of praise, however, when she realized how childishly she was behaving. Yes, she thought to herself, her conduct was infantile, but then so was Nathan's. If he wasn't going to be reasonable, why should she? Perhaps by nightfall her Viking would come to his senses and realize her request had validity. And if the muleheaded man didn't agree, well, she was determined to stay inside the cabin until he gave in. If she starved to death, so be it.

"I like it better the other way."

Sara jumped a foot, then whirled around. She found Nathan lounging against the edge of the desk, smiling at her.

He didn't wait for her question but simply pointed up to the trapdoor. "I usually come in through the top," he explained in a soft whisper. "It's quicker."

She might have nodded, but she couldn't be sure. She leaned back against the trunk and stared at him. Oh, God, now what was she going to do?

His bride couldn't seem to find her voice. Nathan decided to give her a little more time to calm down before he pressed her. The color was completely gone from her face, and there was the real possibility that she might swoon on him again.

"I assume you were trying to change the room around?"

His voice had been pleasant, soothing. She wanted to scream. "Yes," she blurted out instead. "I like it better this way."

He shook his head. "It won't do."

"It won't?"

"You might not have noticed, but the trunk and the chair

101

are actually blocking the door. Besides, I don't think either one of us will want to sit . . . up there."

His remarks were ridiculous, of course. They both knew why the door was blocked. Sara pretended to give the matter her full attention, however, in an attempt to save her pride. "Yes, I do believe you're right," she announced. "The furniture is blocking the door. I only just noticed. Thank you so much for pointing out that fact to me." She didn't pause for breath when she added, "Why is the table nailed to the floor?"

"You tried to move that, too?"

She ignored the laughter in his voice. "I thought it would look much nicer in front of the trunk. The desk, too," she added. "But I couldn't move either one."

He stood up and took a step toward her. She immediately backed away. "When the pitch of the sea gets rough, the furniture moves," he explained. He took another step toward her. "That's the reason."

She felt as though she was being stalked. Nathan's long hair swayed about his shoulders when he moved. The muscles in his shoulders seemed to roll with his pantherlike swagger. She wanted to run away from him, and yet in the back of her mind was the honest admission that she wanted him to catch her. She thoroughly liked the way he kissed her . . . but that was all she was going to like.

From the look on Nathan's face she knew he would like a lot more from her. His intimidating tactics were making her daft. She frowned at him for confusing her.

He smiled back.

She'd made a half circle of the cabin but trapped herself at the head of his bed. Nathan stopped when he saw the fear in her eyes. He let out a long sigh.

She thought he might be having second thoughts, yet before she could grasp the joy in that possibility his big hands were on her shoulders, and he was pulling her toward him.

He tilted her chin up, forcing her to look into his eyes. His voice was actually very gentle when he said, "Sara, I know this is difficult for you. If there was more time, perhaps we could wait until you knew me a little better. I won't lie to you and tell you I could or would court you, though, for in truth I don't have the patience or the experience for such a chore. Still, I don't want you to be afraid of me." He paused to shrug, then smiled at her. "It shouldn't matter to me if you're afraid or not, but it does."

"Then . . ."

"There isn't time," he interrupted. "If you hadn't run away from me eight months ago, you'd be carrying my son now."

Her eyes widened over that announcement. Nathan thought she was reacting to his mention of a babe. She was such an innocent, and he knew she didn't have any experience in sexual matters. And Lord, that did please him.

"I didn't run away from you," she blurted out. "Whatever are you talking about?"

That denial surprised a frown out of him. "Don't you dare lie to me." He gave her shoulders a little squeeze to emphasize his words. "I will not abide it, Sara. You must always be completely honest with me."

She looked as furious as he'd sounded. "I'm not lying," she returned. "I never ran away from you, Viking. Never."

He believed her. She looked too sincere, and thoroughly outraged.

"Sara, I sent a letter to your parents informing them of my intent to come for you. I sent the messenger on a Friday. You were supposed to be ready the following Monday. I even gave the hour. You left for your aunt's island on Sunday morning, the day before. I simply put two and two together."

"I didn't know," she returned. "Nathan, my parents must not have received your letter. Neither one said a word to me. It was such a chaotic time. My mother was worried sick about my Aunt Nora, her sister. Nora always wrote at least one letter a month, but Mother hadn't received a missive in such a long time: She was making herself ill worrying about Nora. When she suggested I go to her sister and find out what was wrong, well, I immediately agreed, of course."

"Just when did your mother confide this worry in you?" he asked.

His cynicism irritated her. She knew what he was thinking and frowned in reaction. "A few days before I left," she admitted. "But she wouldn't have confided her concerns to me if I hadn't caught her crying. And she was most reluctant to burden me. Very reluctant," she added. "Do you know, now that I reflect upon it, I'm certain I was the one who suggested I go to Nora's island."

A sudden thought turned her attention. "How did you know my true destination? My family told everyone I had gone to the colonies to visit my older sister."

He didn't bother to explain that his men had been following her, and he didn't mention that she'd booked passage on one of his ships. He simply shrugged. "Why couldn't they have told the truth about the matter?"

"Because Nora was in disgrace," Sara said. "She married her groom and fled from England over fourteen years ago. I was certain everyone would have forgotten the scandal, but as it happens, no one did."

Nathan turned the topic back to the letters. "So you didn't know that Nora hadn't written to your mother until two days before you left?"

"Mother didn't want me to worry," Sara said. "I won't allow you to think that my mother had anything to do with trickery. My father or my sister might have tried to intercept your missive, Nathan, just to make you wait a little longer, but my mother would never have gone along with such deceit."

Nathan found her defense of her mother honorable. Illogical, but honorable all the same. For that reason he didn't force her to accept the truth. Her belief that her father was innocent, however, irritated the hell out of him.

And then it dawned on him that she hadn't tried to run away from him. He was so pleased over that revelation, he quit frowning.

Sara stared up at her husband while she tried to think of another way to convince him that her mother was completely innocent of any treachery. And then the truth of what he had just told her settled in her mind.

He hadn't forgotten her.

Her smile was captivating. He didn't know what to make of the sudden change in her. She threw herself against his chest, wrapped her arms around his waist, and hugged him. He grunted in reaction. He was more confused than ever by her bizarre behavior. Yet he found he liked the sudden show of affection she was showing him, liked it very much.

Sara let out a little sigh, then moved back from her husband.

"What was that all about?" he asked, grimacing inside over the hard edge in his voice.

She didn't seem to notice. She patted her hair back into place as she whispered, "You didn't forget me." She tossed a strand of curls back over her shoulder in a motion he found thoroughly feminine, then added, "Of course, I knew you hadn't. I was certain there was just a little misunderstanding of sorts, because I . . ."

When she didn't continue, he said, "Because you knew I wanted to be married to you?"

She nodded.

He laughed.

She gave him a disgruntled look, then said, "Nathan, when I couldn't find Nora I sent several notes to your residence asking for your assistance, and you never responded. I did wonder then . . ."

"Sara, I don't have a residence," Nathan announced.

"Of course you do," she argued. "You have the townhouse. I saw it once when I was out for a ride in . . . why are you shaking your head at me?"

"My townhouse was burned to the ground last year."

"No one told me!"

He shrugged.

"I should have sent the message to your country home, then," she said. "All right," she added in a mutter. "Now why are you shaking your head?"

"The country home was also destroyed by fire," he explained.

"When?"

"Last year," he answered. "About a month before my townhouse was gutted."

She looked appalled. "You have had your share of mishaps, haven't you, Nathan?"

They weren't mishaps, but he didn't tell her that. The fires had been deliberately set by his enemies. They'd been looking for incriminating letters. Nathan had been working for his government, and at the end of the investigation the bastards had been dealt with, but he hadn't had time to right the damage to his estate just yet.

"You actually wrote to me asking my assistance in locating Nora?" he asked.

She nodded. "I didn't know who else to turn to," she admitted. "I think it was your Uncle Dunnford St. James who was behind this trickery," she added.

"Which trickery?" he asked.

"He probably intercepted the missive you sent to my parents."

He let her see his exasperation. "I think it was your father who was behind that scheme."

"And just why would you think that?"

"Because Attila the Hun's been dead for years," he said. "And your father is the only other man mean enough to come up with such a vile plan."

"I won't listen to such slander against my father. Besides, I'm just as certain it was Dunnford."

"Oh? And is he the one who beat your aunt?"

Her eyes immediately filled with tears. He regretted his question at once. She turned to stare at his chest before answering. "No," she whispered. "That was the work of my Uncle Henry. He's the one you saw inside the tavern the other night. And now you know the truth about me," she ended with a pitiful wail.

Nathan lifted her chin up with the crook of his finger. His thumb rubbed her smooth skin. "What truth?"

She stared into his eyes a long minute before answering. "I come from bad stock."

She'd hoped to gain a quick denial, even a bit of praise. "Aye, you do."

The man didn't have a sympathetic bone in his body, she thought. "Well, so do you," she muttered. She pushed his hand away from her chin. "We really shouldn't have children."

"Why not?"

"Because they could end up turning out like my Uncle Henry. Worse, they could behave like your side of the family. Even you have to admit that the St. James men are all mean-looking and just as mean-hearted. They're villains," she added with a nod. "Every last one of them."

He wouldn't admit to any such thing, of course, and he made his position known at once. "For all their rough behavior, they're damned honest. You know when you've got them riled. They're very straightforward."

"Oh, they're straightforward, all right," she countered.

"What's that supposed to mean?"

She knew she was getting him riled up again, but she didn't care. "Your Uncle Dunnford was straightforward when he shot his own brother, wasn't he?"

"So you heard about that, did you?" He tried hard not to smile. Sara looked so disapproving.

"Everyone heard about it. The incident took place on the steps of his townhouse in the middle of the morning, with witnesses strolling by."

Nathan shrugged. "Dunnford had good reason," he drawled.

"To shoot his brother?" She sounded incredulous.

He nodded.

"And what was his reason?" she asked.

"His brother woke him up."

She was waylaid by his sudden grin. He was back to looking handsome to her. She found herself smiling.

"Dunnford didn't kill his brother," Nathan explained. "He just made it a little inconvenient for him to sit for a couple of weeks. When you meet him, you'll—"

"I did meet him once," Sara interrupted. She was suddenly out of breath. The way he was staring at her made her feel so strange inside. "I met his wife, too."

She was still smiling at him. There was a mischievous glint in her eyes. He took heart. She wasn't acting at all afraid of him. He tried to think of a way to bring the topic around to the most important matter in his mind: bedding her.

He was gently rubbing her shoulders in an absentminded fashion. Sara didn't think he was even aware of what he was doing, for he had a faraway look in his eyes. She thought he might be thinking about his relatives.

She wanted him to rub away the sting at the base of her back, and since he was looking so preoccupied she decided to take advantage of his inattention. She moved his right hand to her spine. "Rub there, Nathan. My back aches from moving the furniture."

He didn't argue over her request. He simply did as she asked. He wasn't very gentle until she told him to ease his touch a little. Then she moved both his hands to the base of her spine. When he began to rub there she leaned against him and closed her eyes. It felt like heaven.

"Better?" he asked after a few minutes of listening to her sighs.

"Yes, better," she agreed.

He didn't stop rubbing her back, and she didn't want him to. "When did you meet Dunnford?" he asked. His chin dropped to rest on the top of her head. He inhaled her sweet, feminine scent.

"I met him at the gardens," she answered. "Both your uncle and your aunt were there. It was a frightening experience I shall never forget."

He chuckled. "Dunnford does look like a barbarian," he said. He slowly pulled her closer to him by pressing against her spine. She didn't resist. "My uncle's a big man, muscular. He's given to bulk in his shoulders. Yes, I suppose he could be a little frightening."

"So is his wife," Sara interjected with a smile. "I couldn't tell them apart."

He pinched her backside for being so insolent. "Dunnford has a mustache."

"So does she."

He pinched her again. "The St. James women aren't as fat as the Winchester women," he countered.

"The Winchester ladies are not fat," she argued. "They're just . . . fit."

It was high time they confronted the true issue here, she decided. She took a deep breath, then said, "Nathan?"

"Yes?"

"I'm not going to take my clothes off."

That announcement got his full attention. "You're not?"

She moved back a fraction of an inch so she could see his expression. His smile was slow, easy. It gave her courage to set down the rest of her rules. "No, I'm not," she said. "If we must do this thing, I'm keeping my clothes on. Take it or leave it, Nathan."

She worried her lower lip while she waited for his reaction. Nathan thought she might be frightened again. That chafed him. "For God's sake, Sara, I'm not going to hurt you."

"Yes, you will," she whispered.

"And just how would you know?"

"Mother said it always hurts." Sara's cheeks turned scarlet.

"It doesn't always hurt," he snapped. "The first time might be a little . . . uncomfortable."

"You just contradicted yourself," she cried out.

"You don't have to act as though—"

"I'm not going to like it much either," she interrupted. "You might as well understand that right this minute. How long does it take? Minutes or hours?" she asked. "I would like to try to prepare myself."

He wasn't rubbing her backside now. He was gripping her. Hard. He looked a little startled by her question. Sara pushed her advantage. "I have only one little favor to ask of you. Couldn't you please wait until tonight to do this thing? Since you're so determined, couldn't you at least give me a few more hours to come to terms with my fate?"

Come to terms with her fate? Nathan felt like throttling her. She acted as though she was going to an execution. Hers. He frowned even as he gave in. "All right," he said. "We'll wait until tonight, but that is the only favor I'm willing to give you, Sara."

She leaned up on tiptoes and kissed him. Her lips rubbed against him for just a fleeting instant, and when she moved back she was looking damned pleased with herself.

"What the hell was that supposed to be?"

"A kiss."

"No, Sara," he growled. "This is a kiss."

He hauled her up against his chest, tilted her face up, and slammed his mouth down on hers. He wasn't at all gentle, but in truth she didn't mind at all. She melted against him and let him have his way. After all, she thought to herself, she'd just gotten her victory, and she guessed he was entitled to one, too.

Odd, but it was the last thought she could hold. The kiss became one of blatant ownership. The intensity, the raw intimacy made her weak in the knees. She clung to her husband and let out a little whimper of sheer bliss when his tongue moved inside her mouth.

He squeezed her backside and lifted her up against his pelvis. Her hips instinctively cuddled his hardness. He pulled. She pushed.

The feeling was erotic, arousing. Nathan quit trying to subdue her when he realized he had her full cooperation. Lord, she was responsive. She was tugging on his hair even as she tried to get closer to him.

He pulled back quite suddenly, then had to hold her up until she recovered from the kiss. He was arrogantly happy over that telling fact.

And damn, he wanted her. He pushed Sara down the bed and turned to leave. He had to move the chest and chair before he could get to the door.

Sara had gathered her wits by the time he'd gotten the door open. "In future, Nathan," she began, grimacing over the shiver in her voice, "I would really appreciate it if you wouldn't come into our chamber by way of the chimney. I promise I won't bolt the door again," she added when he turned around and gave her an incredulous look.

"Come in through what?" he asked, thinking he surely hadn't heard her correctly.

"The chimney," she explained. "And you still didn't answer my question. Is this thing you're so determined to do going to take minutes or hours?"

Her question turned his attention, and he was no longer interested in explaining that the trapdoor wasn't a chimney. He'd explain that fact to the ignorant woman later. "How the hell would I know how long it's going to take?" he muttered.

"Do you mean you've never done it before?"

Nathan closed his eyes. The conversation had gotten out of hand.

"Well, have you?"

"Yes." He sounded disgusted. "I've just never timed it before," he snapped.

He was pulling the door shut behind him when he suddenly turned back and smiled at her.

She was amazed by the quick change in him. "Sara?" he asked.

"Yes?"

"You aren't going to hate it."

The door closed on that promise.

Chapter Five

Sara didn't see Nathan for the remainder of the day. She kept busy by righting the cabin and sorting through the rest of her possessions. Since she didn't have a lady's maid, she made the bed herself, dusted the furniture, and even borrowed a broom to sweep the dust from the floor. She remembered the parasol she'd left up on the deck, but when she went to fetch it she couldn't find it anywhere.

By sundown her nerves were at the breaking point. She hadn't been able to come up with any suitable plan to gain another reprieve. Sara was a little ashamed of her own cowardice. She knew that the bedding would have to happen sometime, knew that she would continue to dread it until it was over and done with, but those realizations didn't ease her fear.

When the knock sounded at her door she almost screamed. She quickly regained her composure when she realized that Nathan certainly wouldn't knock. No, he'd barge right in. The cabin belonged to him, after all, and she supposed he had the right to come in unannounced.

Matthew was waiting outside her door. She curtsied to the

seaman and invited him inside. He declined her offer with a shake of his head. "Your Aunt Nora's waiting to have a visit with you now," he announced. "While you're in her cabin I'll have Frost bring in the tub. The captain thought you might be wanting a bath, so he ordered us to bring fresh water. It's a treat you won't be getting too often," he added. "You'd best enjoy it."

"That was very thoughtful of Nathan," Sara returned.

"I'll be sure to tell him you thought so," Matthew replied for lack of anything better to say. He walked by Sara's side, feeling both awkward and ridiculously shy. He blamed his condition on the fact that he wasn't used to being treated like an equal except by Nathan. He'd never had a lady curtsy to him either. There was also her enchanting smile, he admitted. His shoulders slumped forward a little. Lord, he was falling under the pretty's spell just like that ox Jimbo had.

When they reached Nora's door Matthew forced himself out of his stupor and muttered, "Don't you tire her out, all right?"

Sara nodded, then waited for Matthew to open the door for her. He was a bit slow to catch on until she motioned to show what she wanted. She thanked him after he'd thrown the door wide, then walked inside. Matthew pulled the door closed behind her.

"Matthew had the most bewildered look on his face," Nora called out.

"I didn't notice," Sara admitted. She smiled at her aunt as she hurried over to the side of the bed to kiss her. Nora was propped up by a mound of fat pillows.

"I did notice what a worrier he is, though, and all on your behalf, Aunt," Sara announced. She pulled up a chair, sat down, and brushed the crinkles out of her gown. "I believe he's become your champion."

"He's a handsome man, isn't he, Sara? He has a kind heart, too. His nature is very like my late husband's, though the two men are nothing alike in appearance."

Sara held her smile. "You're a little smitten with Matthew, aren't you, Nora?"

"Nonsense, child. I'm too old to be smitten."

Sara let the subject go. "Are you feeling better today?"

"Yes, dear," Nora answered. "And how are you feeling?"

"Fine, thank you."

Nora shook her head. "You don't look fine to me," she announced. "Sara, you're sitting on the edge of that chair, looking like you'll bolt at the first provocation. Is it Nathan worrying you?"

Sara slowly nodded. "I was also worried about you, of course," she confessed. "But now that I see you, I realize you're going to be fine."

"Don't change the topic," Nora ordered. "I want to talk about Nathan."

"I don't."

"We're going to all the same," Nora countered. The cheer in her tone took the sting out of her remark. "How are you and your husband getting along?"

Sara lifted her shoulders in a dainty shrug. "As well as can be expected, given his disposition."

Nora smiled. "Has he kissed you yet?"

"Nora, you shouldn't be asking me that question."

"Answer me. Has he?"

Sara looked at her lap when she answered. "Yes, he did kiss me."

"Good."

"If you say so."

"Now, Sara, I know Nathan isn't exactly what you imagined he would be, but if you'll only look below the gruff exterior, I believe you'll find yourself a good man."

Sara was determined to keep the conversation light. "Oh?" she teased. "And how would you know what I imagined him to be?"

"In your wildest dreams you couldn't possibly have imagined yourself married to Nathan. He's a bit overwhelming at first sight, isn't he?"

"Oh, I don't know," Sara whispered.

"Of course you do," Nora returned. "You fainted when you saw him that first time, didn't you?"

"I was exhausted," Sara argued. "Nora, he wants to . . sleep with me," she suddenly blurted out.

Nora didn't seem to be at all surprised by that announcement. Sara was acutely relieved that her aunt wasn't embarrassed. She desperately needed her advice.

"That would be his natural inclination," Nora announced. "Are you afraid, Sara?"

"A little," Sara answered. "I know what my duty is, but I don't know him very well, and I did want a courtship."

"What is it you're worried about?"

Sara shrugged.

"Do you think he's going to hurt you?"

Sara shook her head. "It's the most peculiar thing, Aunt. Nathan's such a ferocious-looking man when he's frowning at me, which is most of the time, but in my heart I know he won't hurt me. He even told me he didn't want me to be afraid of him."

"Good."

"But he won't wait until I get used to the idea," Sara explained.

Nora smiled. "I would expect that he wouldn't want to wait, Sara. You are his wife, and I could see the way he watched you that first night. He wants you."

Sara could feel herself blushing. "What if I disappoint him?"

"I don't believe you will," Nora soothed. "He'll see to it that you don't."

"We have to have a child if Nathan is going to get the second half of the treasury set aside by the king, and since he was forced to wait to come for me . . . did you know he thought I had run away from him?" Sara explained what she'd learned, and when she'd finished Nora was frowning.

"Aren't you pleased Nathan tried to come for me?"

116

"Of course. I'm frowning because I believe your parents have deceived you yet again."

"Nora, you can't believe—"

"As I told you before," Nora interrupted, "I never quit writing to your mother. I will even allow for the possibility that one or two of my letters got lost, but certainly not all six of them. No, it was all a lie, Sara, to get you out of England."

"Mother wouldn't agree to such a lie."

"Of course she would," Nora muttered. "My poor sister is afraid of her husband. She always was, and she always will be. We both know it, Sara, and it's pointless to pretend to each other. Get your head out of the clouds, child. If Winston told her to lie to you, she would. Now enough about your sorry parents," she rushed on when Sara looked as if she was about to interrupt. "I want to ask you a question."

"What is it?"

"Do you want to be married to Nathan?"

"It doesn't matter what I want."

"Do you or not?"

"I've never thought about being with anyone else," Sara answered hesitantly. "I don't really know how I feel, Nora. I dislike the notion of any other woman having him, though. Do you know I didn't realize that until he mentioned the word 'mistress' to me? I reacted most vehemently to that proposal. It's all very confusing."

"Yes, love is always confusing."

"I'm not talking about love," Sara countered. "It's just that I've been trained to think of Nathan as my husband all these years."

Nora let out an inelegant snort. "You were trained to hate the man. They thought they'd raised another one just like your sister Belinda, but they couldn't do it, could they? You don't hate Nathan at all."

"No, I don't hate anyone."

"All these years you've protected him in your heart, Sara,

just as you've protected your mother whenever you had a chance. You listened to their lies about Nathan, and then you discarded them."

"They think I hate him," Sara confessed. "I pretended to agree with everything my relatives told me about him so they would leave me alone. Uncle Henry was the worse. Now he knows the truth. When I confronted him in the tavern, when I saw your band on his fat little finger, well, I lost my temper. I boasted that Nathan would retaliate and added to that lie by telling him that Nathan and I had been on the best of terms for a long while."

"Perhaps it wasn't all a lie," Nora said. "I do believe Nathan would retaliate on my behalf in future, Sara. And do you know why?"

"Because he realizes what a dear, sweet lady you are," Sara answered.

Nora rolled her eyes heavenward. "No, dear, I don't believe he realizes that just yet. He'll watch out for me because he knows how much you love me. Nathan is the kind of man who takes care of the people close to him."

"But Nora—"

"I'm telling you he's already beginning to care for you. Sara."

"You're being fanciful."

The conversation came to an abrupt end when Matthew came into the room. He gave Nora a wide smile and a slow wink. "It's time for you to have a rest," he told her.

Sara kissed her aunt goodnight and went back to her cabin. The bath was ready for her. She took her time soaking until the water turned cold, then dressed in her white nightgown and matching wrapper. She was sitting on the side of the bed, brushing the tangles out of her hair, when Nathan came into the room.

Two younger men followed him inside. The seamen nodded at her, then lifted the tub between them and carried it out. Sara clutched the top of her robe against her neck in an attempt at modesty until the men left, then resumed brushing her hair.

Nathan shut the door and bolted it.

He didn't say a word to her. He didn't have to. The look on his face told her all she needed to know. The man was determined, all right. There wouldn't be any more favors doled out, no more hasty reprieves. She started trembling.

Nathan had had a bath, too, she realized. His hair was still wet. It was slicked back behind his neck. His unforgiving profile wasn't softened at all. He wasn't wearing a shirt either. Sara stared at him while she continued to brush her hair, wondering what in God's name she could talk about to ease the tension inside her.

Nathan stared back at her while he pulled the chair out from the table, sat down, and slowly removed his boots. The socks came off next. Then he stood up, facing her still, and began to unbutton his pants.

She closed her eyes.

He smiled over her shyness. It didn't deter him, though. He took off the rest of his clothes and tossed them on the chair.

"Sara?"

She didn't open her eyes when she answered. "Yes, Nathan?"

"Take your clothes off."

His voice was soft, tender, he thought. He was trying to ease a little of her fear away. There wasn't any doubt in his mind that she was afraid, for she was ripping that brush through her hair with such vigor that she had to be giving herself one hell of a headache. She'd knock herself senseless if she didn't calm down.

She wasn't soothed by his voice, however. "We've already had this discussion, Nathan," she announced as she slammed the brush against her temple again. "I told you I was keeping my clothes on."

She'd tried to make her voice firm, determined. The effort

didn't work. Even she could hear the tremor in her hoarse whisper. "All right?" she asked.

"All right," he agreed with a sigh.

His easy agreement calmed her. She quit brushing her hair. She still wouldn't look at him when she stood up and slowly crossed the room. She made a wide path around him, her gaze directed on the floor.

After she put her brush away she took a deep breath and turned around. She was determined to pretend his nakedness didn't bother her. She was his wife, she reminded herself, and she shouldn't be carrying on like a silly, innocent chit.

The problem, of course, was that she *was* an innocent. She'd never seen a naked man before. Lord, she was nervous. I'm a woman now, not a child, she told herself. There's absolutely no reason to be embarrassed.

Then she got a rather thorough look at her husband, and all thoughts about being worldly flew out the chimney. Nathan was in the process of closing the trap in the ceiling. He was half turned away from her, but she still saw quite enough of his physique to make her forget how to breathe.

The man was all muscle and steel. Bronzed, too. It suddenly dawned on her that his backside was almost as dark as the rest of his body. How did he get that private area bronzed?

She wasn't about to ask him that question, though. Perhaps after they'd been married some twenty or thirty years she'd feel comfortable enough to broach that topic.

Perhaps, too, one day in the future she might be able to look back on the night of agony and have herself a good laugh.

She certainly wasn't laughing at the moment. She watched Nathan light the candle. The soft glow made his skin glisten. She was grateful that he had his back turned to her when he saw to that task. Was he deliberately giving her time to get accustomed to his size?

If that was his aim, it wasn't working, she thought to

herself. The man could masquerade as a tree. He was certainly big enough.

Sara let out a little sigh when she realized how childishly she was behaving. Her only saving grace was the fact that he wasn't going to know how terrified she was. She averted her face so he couldn't see her blush, then said, "Are we going to bed now?"

She was pleased with herself. She'd sounded very nonchalant when she'd asked that question.

He thought she sounded like she'd just swallowed a spike. He knew he was going to have to find a way to deal with her fear before he bedded her.

The question, of course, was how. He let out a sigh and turned to take her into his arms. She ran to the bed. He grabbed hold of her shoulders and slowly forced her around to face him.

His bride certainly wasn't having any difficulty meeting his gaze, he thought. No, he didn't have to nudge her chin up to get her full attention. Nathan held his smile. He doubted Sara would have lowered her gaze even if he told her there was a snake slithering across her feet.

"Does my nakedness upset you?" He asked the obvious, thinking to attack the problem head on.

"Why would you think that?"

His hands moved to the sides of her neck. He could feel her pulse pounding under his thumb. He kept his touch gentle. "You like it when I kiss you, don't you, Sara?"

She seemed surprised by that question. "Do you?" he asked again when she continued to stare at him.

"Yes," she admitted. "I do like you to kiss me."

He looked arrogantly pleased.

"But I don't believe I'm going to like the other thing at all," she said, thinking to give him fair warning once again.

He didn't look offended by her honesty. He leaned down and kissed her on her forehead, then kissed the bridge of her nose. His mouth brushed against hers for a fleeting second. "I'm going to like it," he told her in a low growl.

She didn't have a ready comeback for that comment, so she was silent. She kept her mouth closed, too, when his mouth settled on hers again.

He felt as if he were kissing a statue. He wasn't deterred, though. He sighed against her mouth and slowly tightened his hold around her neck. When her skin began to sting she opened her mouth to order him to let go of her. That demand got all tangled up in her confused mind, however, when his tongue moved inside to touch hers.

Her response was nice. The ice inside her began to melt. Nathan softened his hold as soon as she opened her mouth for him. His thumbs made lazy circles along the sides of her neck. He was deliberate in his bid to overwhelm her and thought he was succeeding when she moved closer to him and put her arms around his neck.

Her sigh of pleasure mingled with his growl of need. He didn't let up on his gentle attack. The kiss was long, hard, damned thorough. His mouth slanted hungrily over hers again and again while his tongue stoked the fire inside her.

The kiss seemed endless. Because she was innocent of such new feelings it didn't take him long at all to rid her of her shyness, her resistance. He tried to contain his own hunger, but when her fingers threaded through his damp hair and he felt the sensual, feathery-light caress the flame inside him began to burn.

He wasn't very deliberate. He'd tamed her and was suddenly impatient. Sara let out a ragged moan when he pulled her arms away from his neck. His mouth continued to plunder hers, but it wasn't enough. She wanted to get close to his heat again, to wrap herself around his warmth. He wasn't cooperating. He kept blocking her arms and tugging on her at the same time. She didn't understand what he wanted from her, couldn't seem to sort it all out in her mind, for she was too occupied kissing him, and simply too overwhelmed by the strange, wonderful feelings rioting inside her.

"Now you can put your arms around me again," he

whispered when he ended the kiss. His smile was filled with tenderness. Lord, she was transparent. Her bemused expression hid nothing from him. Passion and confusion were there for him to see. Nathan had never known a woman who could respond with such openness, such abandon.

It shook him a little when he realized how very much he wanted to please her. The innocent trust she willingly gave to him made him feel as though he could conquer the world.

He was going to have to conquer her first. "Don't be afraid," he whispered in a deep, husky voice. He stroked the side of her face with the backs of his fingers, smiling anew over the way she instinctively tilted her face to the side to gain more of his caress.

"I'm trying not to be afraid," she whispered back. "It does ease my worry because I know you care about my feelings."

"And when did you come to that conclusion?"

He wondered over the sudden sparkle that came into her eyes. She seemed to be amused about something.

"When you agreed that I could keep my clothes on."

Nathan's sigh was long. He decided it wasn't the time to mention the fact that he'd just removed her robe and nightgown. He guessed she'd find out soon enough.

"I'm not a very patient man, Sara, when I want something as badly as I want you."

He put his arms around her waist and pulled her up against him. Skin touched skin. Her eyes widened in reaction, but before she could get her wits about her to decide if she liked the feeling or not, his mouth settled on top of hers again.

The man certainly knew how to kiss. She didn't make him force her mouth open—instead she quickly became the aggressor. Her tongue rubbed against his first. He grunted in reaction. She thought that sound might mean he liked her show of boldness, and she became all the more wanton.

The kiss was wild. He wanted to rekindle the passion between them. When she began to make those erotic little whimpers in the back of her throat he knew he'd accomplished his goal. She was already hot for him again. And Lord, the sound made him ache to be inside her.

Her hands gripped his shoulders. Her soft breasts rubbed against his chest. He lifted her up and pulled her tight against his arousal, then drowned out the gasp that intimacy caused with another long, hot kiss.

Sara couldn't seem to catch hold of a thought. The sensations his kiss caused were so strange, so wonderful, so consuming. She couldn't even hold onto her shyness. She knew he'd taken her clothes off, had deliberately baited him when she'd reminded him that he'd promised she could leave them on. It was trickery on her part, but her reason had made perfectly good sense to her at the time. She wanted him to slow down, to give her time to get used to his body, his heat, his touch.

She didn't have any idea how they'd gotten over to the bed, but Nathan was suddenly pulling the covers back. His mouth left hers when he lifted her up and gently placed her on her back in the center of the sheets. He didn't give her time to try to shield her nudity from him but followed her down on the bed, covering her from head to foot with his warm body.

It was too much, too soon. Sara began to feel trapped and totally at his mercy. She didn't want to be afraid, and she didn't want to disappoint him.

The haze of passion cleared in an instant. She didn't want to do this anymore.

But she didn't want him to quit kissing her either. And God, she was frightened.

He'd probably take exception if she started screaming. For that reason she kept her mouth closed in an effort to contain the shout locked in her throat.

His knee tried to nudge her legs apart. She wouldn't allow that intimacy and began to struggle against him. She slapped his shoulders, too. He immediately stopped trying. He propped himself up on his elbows to ease his weight away from her, then began to nibble on the side of her neck. She liked that. His breath was warm, sweet, teasing against her ear. She shivered in reaction. In a dark whisper he told her how much she pleased him, how much she made him want her, and even told her how beautiful he thought she was. When he was finished with his words of praise he was certain he'd coaxed her into accepting him completely.

He was mistaken. As soon as he tried to nudge her thighs apart again she went completely rigid on him. He gritted his teeth in frustration.

The feel of her soft skin made him wild with his own need to be inside her. But she wasn't ready for his invasion yet. His forehead was beaded with perspiration from the effort of holding back. Each time his hands moved to touch her breasts she tensed up on him. His frustration soon made his hunger acutely painful.

It would only be a matter of minutes before he completely lost his control. God, he didn't want to hurt her. He was feeling desperate to thrust inside her heat, but she was going to be hot for him, wet, ready, when he finally made her his.

She sure as hell wasn't ready now. She was pinching his shoulder and trying to get him to move away from her.

He decided to let her have her way for just a minute or two. Nathan rolled to his side, thinking to put a little distance between them before he completely lost his sanity, forced her thighs apart, and drove into her.

He thought he only needed a couple of minutes to regain his discipline. When his heart quit slamming inside his chest, when it didn't hurt so much to breathe, when the god-awful ache in his loins abated a little, he would try again.

Wooing a virgin was damned hard work, he thought, and since he had absolutely no expertise with either wooing or with bedding virgins, he felt completely inadequate.

Perhaps one day in the future, when he was an old, old man, he might be able to look back on this night of sweet torture and have himself a good laugh. At the moment he wasn't in the mood to laugh, though. He wanted to grab hold of his bride and shake some sense into her while he demanded at the same time that she not be afraid of him.

The contradiction in those conflicting thoughts made him shake his head.

Sara was trembling from head to foot. As soon as he moved away from her the helpless feeling of being trapped vanished. She wanted him to kiss her again.

The look on Nathan's face worried her, though. He looked like he wanted to shout at her. She took a deep breath, then rolled to her side to face him. "Nathan?"

He didn't answer her. His eyes were closed, his jaw clenched tight.

"You told me you were a patient man."

"Sometimes."

"You're upset with me, aren't you?"

"No."

She didn't believe him. "Don't frown," she whispered. She reached out to touch his chest.

He reacted as though she'd just burned him. He visibly flinched. "Don't you want to do this any longer?" she asked. "Have you quit wanting me?"

Not want her? He wanted to grab hold of her hand and force her to feel how very much he wanted her. He didn't, of course, for he was certain she'd become terrified again.

"Sara, just give me a minute," he said in a clipped voice. "I'm afraid . . ." He didn't finish that explanation, didn't tell her he was afraid he would hurt her if he touched her. That admission would only increase her fear, so he kept silent.

"You don't have to be afraid," she whispered.

He couldn't believe what he was hearing. He opened his eyes to look at her. She couldn't really think . . . and yet the tenderness in her eyes indicated she did believe he was afraid.

"For God's sake, Sara, I'm not afraid."

Her fingers slowly trailed down his chest. He caught hold

of her hand when she reached the flat of his stomach. "Stop that," he ordered.

"You've only taken experienced women to your bed, haven't you, Nathan?"

His answer was a low grunt.

She smiled. "Nathan, you like kissing me, don't you?"

He'd asked her that very question not fifteen minutes earlier, when he'd been trying to rid her of her fear. God's truth, he would have laughed if he hadn't been in so much pain. The woman was treating him as though he were the virgin.

He was about to straighten out her thinking when she edged closer to him. He suddenly realized that his bride was no longer afraid of him. "Do you?" she persisted.

"Yes, Sara, I like kissing you."

"Then kiss me again, please."

"Sara, kissing isn't the only thing I had in mind. I want to touch you. Everywhere."

He waited for her to go rigid on him again. God, he wished he had the patience for this. His nerves felt as though they were about to snap, and all he could think about was spilling his seed inside her.

He closed his eyes and growled.

And then he felt her take hold of his hand. He opened his eyes just as she placed his hand on the side of her full breast.

He didn't move for a long minute. She didn't either. They stared into each other's eyes. He waited to see what she would do next. She waited for him to get on with his duty.

Sara soon became impatient with him. He was gently stroking her breasts. The feeling made her tingle inside. It made her reckless, too. She rubbed her toes against his legs and slowly leaned up to kiss him.

"I hate the feeling of being trapped," she whispered between feathery-light kisses. "But I don't feel trapped now, Nathan. Don't give up on me yet, husband. This is a new experience for me. Truly."

He gently caressed the side of her face. "I'm not going to give up," he whispered. There was a bit of laughter in his voice when he added, "Truly."

She sighed against his mouth and kissed him just the way she wanted to. When her tongue moved inside to mate with his, Nathan's control snapped. He became the aggressor again, deepening the kiss even more with wild abandon.

He kept up the gentle assault until she rolled onto her back and tried to bring him with her. Nathan didn't give in to her demand but leaned down to kiss the fragrant valley between her breasts. His mouth teased first one and then the other nipple until they were both hard nubs. His tongue drove her wild. When she couldn't stand the sweet torment any longer she grabbed hold of his hair and began to tug on him.

She felt as if she'd been hit with hot lightning when he finally took her nipple into his mouth. She arched up, demanding more. He began to suckle.

A warm knot formed in the pit of her stomach. "Nathan, please," she moaned. She didn't have any idea what she was begging him for, only knew the incredible heat was driving her beyond reason.

He turned to her other breast even as his hand slid down between her thighs. She didn't clench against him but let out another ragged groan.

He leaned up on one elbow so he could watch her expression. She tried to hide her face in the crook of his shoulder. He reached out and caught hold of her hair.

"I like the way you respond to me," he whispered. "Do you like the way I'm touching you?"

He already knew the answer. He could feel how ready she was for him. How hot. His fingers rubbed against the nub hidden between her folds until she was slick with moisture. His finger slowly eased up inside her.

Her hands had been fisted at her sides until that minute. She came apart then. She stroked his shoulders, his back.

Her nails scraped his backside. "Nathan," she whispered. "Don't do that. It hurts. Oh, God, don't stop."

She continued to contradict herself by arching up against his hand. Nathan could barely understand what she was saying to him. He shook with raw desire to have her.

He silenced her weak protest with a kiss and moved to cover her. She didn't try to lock her legs together but moved to cuddle his hardness between her thighs.

He twisted her hair in his hand to hold her steady for his kiss. The way she rubbed her pelvis against him drove him crazy. He wasn't being gentle. She wouldn't let him. Her nails stung. He liked that. She was moaning, too. He liked that even more.

He slowly eased into her but stopped when he felt the thin shield of her resistance. He lifted his head up enough so that he could look into her eyes.

"Put your legs around me," he ordered, his voice harsh with determination.

When she did as he commanded he let out a low growl. And still he hesitated.

"Look at me, Sara."

She opened her eyes and stared into his.

"You're going to belong to me. Now and forever."

Her eyes were misty with passion. She reached up to clasp the sides of his face. "I have always belonged to you, Nathan. Always."

His mouth covered hers again. He thrust deep inside her in one swift motion, thinking to get the pain he knew she'd feel over and done with as quickly as possible.

"Hush, baby," he whispered when she cried out. He was fully embedded in her. Her tight heat surrounded him, squeezed him. "God, that feels good," he said with a groan.

"No, it doesn't feel good," she cried out. She tried to shift positions to ease the throbbing pain, but he held her hips and wouldn't let her move.

"It will feel better in a minute," he told her. His breathing was labored. He sounded out of breath to her. His face rested in the hollow of her shoulder. He nipped at her skin with his teeth, tickled her at the same time with his tongue. The sweet torture made her forget some of the pain.

"Don't push against me like that, Sara," he ordered. His voice was harsh, strained. "I'm not stopping now. I can't."

His tongue rubbed her earlobe. She quit struggling and let out a sigh of pleasure.

"The pain won't last long," he whispered then. "I promise."

She reacted more to the tenderness, the caring in his voice than to the promise he'd just given her. She hoped he was right, though. She still hurt. The throbbing was insistent, but after a minute it did begin to lessen. Yet when he started to move again the pain immediately returned.

"If you don't move, it isn't so terrible," she whispered.

His groan was harsh.

"All right, Nathan?" she pleaded.

"All right," he answered, responding to the worry in her voice. It was a lie, of course, but she was too innocent to understand how much he needed to move. "I won't move."

Her hands began to stroke his hair, the back of his neck. His fever was burning out of control, and the pain of having to hold back was demanding to be appeased.

She couldn't seem to quit touching him. "Nathan, kiss me."

"The pain's gone now?"

"Almost."

He deliberately withdrew just a little when he moved to kiss her again, then just as slowly eased back inside her.

"You moved," she cried out.

Instead of agreeing with her he kissed her. When he tried to withdraw again her nails dug into his hard thighs. She was trying to keep him still against her. He ignored her protests and sought to make her burn the way he was burning. His hand slipped down between their joined bodies, and his thumb slowly stoked the fire inside her.

Her head fell back on the pillows, and her grip on his thighs relaxed.

And then she began to move. Her hips pushed up against his. Her actions were instinctive, primal, uncontrollable.

She soon became demanding, too. He responded to her by slowly pulling back and thrusting more powerfully inside.

She squeezed him tight and arched up against him just as forcefully. The mating ritual took over. The bed creaked from the rocking motion. Their bodies glistened with perspiration in the candlelight. Her sweet moans blended with his raw growls.

They were both wild to find fulfillment. He couldn't stop his own climax, nor the near shout he gave when he spilled his hot seed inside her.

His head dropped against her shoulder in complete surrender to the blazing orgasm that overtook him.

He knew she was close to finding her own release. His thrusts continued to be just as forceful, and when he felt her tense against him, he forced her orgasm by driving hard into her again.

She screamed. His name.

His ears rang from the noise. He collapsed on top of her, giving her his full weight in an attempt to stop her trembling.

Neither one of them moved for a long, long while. Nathan was too content. She was too exhausted.

She felt a trickle of moisture near her ear, reached up to touch it, and only then realized she'd been crying. Lord, she'd really lost her composure, hadn't she? She was too pleased to worry about that, though. And too satisfied. Why hadn't anyone ever told her how wonderful making love would be?

Her husband's heartbeat pounded in unison with her own. She let out a happy sigh. She was his wife now.

"You can't call me bride anymore," she whispered against his neck. On impulse she tickled his skin with the tip of her tongue. The taste of him was salty, male, wonderful.

"Am I too heavy for you?"

He sounded weary to her. She answered him, yes, he was getting heavy, and he immediately rolled onto his back.

She didn't want him to leave her just yet. She wanted him to hold her, to tell her what a fine woman she was, to give her the words of praise and love all new wives longed to hear. She wanted him to kiss her again, too.

She didn't get anything. Nathan's eyes were closed. He looked peaceful and sleepy.

She didn't have any idea of the war Nathan was waging with himself. He was desperately trying to understand what had just happened to him. He'd never lost control so completely. She'd bewitched him. Confused him, too. He was feeling vulnerable, and damn, that feeling scared the hell out of him.

Sara rolled onto her side. "Nathan?"

"What?"

"Kiss me again."

"Go to sleep."

"Kiss me goodnight."

"No."

"Why not?"

"I'll want you again if I kiss you," he finally explained. He didn't bother to look at her but stared at the ceiling. "You're too tender."

She sat up in bed, flinching over the discomfort she felt between her thighs. He was right. She was tender. It didn't seem to matter, though. She still wanted him to kiss her.

"You're the one who made me tender," she muttered. She poked him in his shoulder. "I specifically remember telling you not to move."

"You moved first, Sara. Remember that?" he drawled.

She blushed. She took heart. He wasn't sounding too

surly. She cuddled up against him, wishing he'd put his arms around her. "Nathan, isn't the after as important as the during?"

He didn't know what she was talking about. "Go to sleep," he ordered for the second time. He jerked the covers up over the two of them, then closed his eyes again.

She threw her arm over him. She was exhausted. Frustrated, too. She told him so.

He laughed. "Sara, I know you found fulfillment."

"That isn't what I'm talking about," she whispered.

She waited for him to ask her to explain what she'd meant, then gave up when he kept silent. "Nathan?"

"Hell, what now?"

"Please don't take that mean tone with me."

"Sara . . ." he began in a warning tone of voice.

"After you took those other women to your bed, well, after . . . what did you do?"

What in God's name was she getting at? "I left," he snapped.

"Are you going to leave me?"

"Sara, this is my bed. I'm going to sleep."

Her patience was at an end. "Not before I explain proper etiquette to you," she announced. "After a man finishes . . . that, he should tell his wife what a fine woman she is. Then he should kiss her and hold her close. They fall asleep in each other's arms."

He couldn't stop himself from smiling. She said the damnedest things. Sounded like a general, too. "It's called lovemaking, Sara, and how would you know what's proper and what isn't? You were a virgin, remember?"

"I just know what's proper," she countered.

"Sara?"

"Yes?"

"Don't shout at me."

He turned to look at her. Hell, she looked as if she was going to cry. He didn't have the patience to deal with her tears. God, she was vulnerable . . . and beautiful. Her mouth was all rosy and swollen from his kisses.

He reached over and hauled her into his arms. After giving her a quick kiss on the top of her head he pushed her face down into the crook of his shoulder and muttered, "You're a fine woman. Now go to sleep."

He didn't sound like he meant what he said, but she didn't care. He was holding her close. He was stroking her back. She thought that was a little telling. She snuggled up against him and closed her eyes.

His chin rested on the top of her head. Each time the memory of their lovemaking came into his thoughts he blocked it. He wasn't ready to let his emotions get the upper hand. He was simply too disciplined to let a woman get that close.

He was just drifting off to sleep when she whispered his name again. He squeezed her to let her know he wanted her to keep quiet. She whispered his name again.

"Yes?" he answered with a deliberate yawn.

"Do you know what this holding and hugging each other is called?"

She wasn't going to let up on him until she told him what was on her mind. Nathan squeezed her again, then gave in. "No, Sara, what's it called?"

"Cherishing."

He groaned. She smiled. "It's a good start, isn't it?"

His snore was her only answer. Sara wasn't bothered that he had rudely fallen asleep in the middle of her fervent speech. She'd simply explain it all to him again the next day.

She couldn't wait for morning light. She was going to find a hundred ways to make Nathan realize his good fortune. She already knew she was the perfect mate for him. He didn't know it yet, but eventually, with patience and understanding, he'd realize how much he loved her. She was certain.

She was his wife, his love. Their marriage was true in

every sense. There was a bond between them. Marriage was a sacred institution, and Sara was determined to protect and cherish her vows.

She fell asleep holding him tight. The next day was going to be the official start of her new life as Nathan's wife. It was going to be a day in heaven.

Chapter Six

It was a day in hell.

Nathan had already left the cabin by the time she awakened. He'd opened the chimney lid for her, and the room was flooded with fresh air and sunshine. It was much warmer than the day before. After she bathed, she dressed in a lightweight royal-blue gown with white linen borders and then went to find her husband. She wanted to ask him where the fresh sheets were kept so that she could change the bedding. She also wanted him to kiss her again.

Sara had just reached the top step on the way to the main deck when she heard a man's shout. She hurried forward to see what all the commotion was about and almost tripped over the fallen man sprawled on the deck. The older seaman had obviously taken quite a fall, for he was sleeping soundly.

The parasol she hadn't been able to find the day before was twisted between his feet. Jimbo was bent on one knee over the prostrate man. He slapped the side of the man's face twice in an attempt to waken him.

In a matter of seconds a crowd gathered around their

friend. Each immediately offered a suggestion or two as to how Jimbo could bring the man around.

"What the hell happened?"

Nathan's booming voice sounded directly behind Sara. She didn't turn around when she answered his question. "I believe he tripped on something."

"It weren't something, m'lady," one of the crew announced. He pointed to the deck. "It were your parasol that caught up in his legs."

Sara was forced to accept full responsibility. "Yes, it was my parasol," she said. "His injury is my fault. Will he be all right, Jimbo? I really didn't mean to cause this mishap. I—"

Jimbo took pity on her. "No need to carry on so, Lady Sara. The men know it was just an accident."

Sara glanced up to look at the crowd. Most were nodding and smiling at her. "No need to get yourself in a dither, m'lady. Ivan will get his wits back in a minute or so."

A man with a full orange beard nodded. "Don't be fretting," he interjected. "It weren't that bad. The back of his head broke his fall."

"Murray?" Jimbo called out. "Bring me a bucket of water. That ought to bring him around."

"Will Ivan be able to cook up our meal tonight?" The man Sara remembered was named Chester asked that question. He was frowning at Sara.

She frowned back. It was apparent he blamed her for the unfortunate circumstance. "Is your stomach more important to you than your friend's health?" she asked. She didn't give him time to answer her but knelt down beside the sleeping man and gently patted his shoulder. The elderly man didn't respond. His mouth was gaping.

"My God, Jimbo, have I killed him?" she whispered.

"No, you didn't kill him," Jimbo returned. "You can see he's breathing still, Sara. He'll just have a fair head split when he wakes up, that's all."

Nathan lifted Sara to her feet and pulled her back away

from the crowd. She didn't want to leave. "I'm responsible for this accident," she said. Her gaze was fully directed upon Ivan, but she could still see the nods from the men surrounding her. She felt herself blush in reaction to their easy agreement. "It was an accident," she cried out.

No one contradicted her. That made her feel a little better. "I should take care of Ivan," she announced then. "When he opens his eyes I must tell him how sorry I am for forgetting my parasol."

"He won't be in the mood to listen," Nathan predicted.

"Aye," Lester agreed. "Ivan the Terrible isn't one to forgive a slight for a good long while. He loves a good grudge, doesn't he, Walt?"

A slightly built man with dark brown eyes nodded agreement. "This is more than a slight, Lester," he muttered. "Ivan's going to be in a rage."

"Is Ivan the only cook?" Sara asked.

"He is," Nathan told her.

She finally turned around to look at her husband. Her blush was high, and she really didn't know if the heat in her cheeks was due to the fact that this was their first encounter since their night of intimacy or because she'd caused such commotion.

"Why do they call him Ivan the Terrible?" she asked. "Is it because he has a mean temper?"

He barely spared her a glance when he answered. "They don't like his cooking," he said. He motioned for one of the men to toss the contents of the bucket in Ivan's face. The cook immediately started sputtering and groaning.

Nathan nodded, then turned and walked away from the group.

Sara couldn't believe he'd leave without a word to her first. She felt humiliated. She turned back to Ivan and stood wringing her hands while she waited for her chance to apologize. She silently vowed she would find Nathan and give him another lesson in proper etiquette.

As soon as Ivan sat up Sara knelt down beside him. "Pray

forgive me, sir, for causing you this injury. It was my parasol that caused you to trip, though if you'd only been looking where you were going, I'm certain you would have noticed it. Still, I beg your forgiveness."

Ivan was rubbing the back of his head while he glared at the pretty woman trying to give him a bit of the blame for his near brush with death. The worry in her expression kept his surly retort inside. That, and the fact that she was the captain's woman.

"It wasn't much of a hit I took," he muttered instead. "You didn't do it on purpose, now did you?"

There was a faint Scottish brogue in his voice. Sara thought he sounded quite musical. "No, of course I didn't do it on purpose, sir. Are you strong enough to stand? I'll help you to your feet."

She could tell from his wary expression that he didn't want her assistance. Jimbo pulled the cook up, but as soon as he let go Ivan began to sway. Sara was still kneeling at his side. She reached out to grab her parasol from between his feet just as another crewman reached out to steady his friend. Poor Ivan was suddenly caught in a tug-of-war of sorts, for the captain's wife was pushing against his legs. He ended up sprawled on his backside.

"Get away from me, all of you," he roared. His voice didn't sound at all musical. "You won't be getting my soup tonight, men. My head's aching, and now my arse is stinging, too. Damned if I'm not taking to my bed."

"Watch your tongue, Ivan," Jimbo ordered.

"Yes," another man called out. "We got us a lady present."

Jimbo lifted Sara's parasol and handed it to her. He turned to leave, but her next words so startled him that he turned around again.

"I'm going to prepare the soup for the men."

"No, you aren't," Jimbo told her. His hard tone of voice didn't leave room for argument. "You're the captain's woman, and you won't be doing such common work."

Because she didn't want to get into a disagreement with Jimbo in front of the rest of the men she waited until he'd left. Then she smiled at the men watching her. "I'm going to make a lovely soup for everyone. Ivan? Will it make you feel better to have the rest of the day off and rest? It's the very least I can do to repay you for this accident."

Ivan cheered up considerably. "You ever make soup before?" he asked her with a half grin, half scowl.

Since everyone was staring at her, she decided to lie. How difficult could it be to make soup? "Oh, my, yes, many times," she boasted. "I helped our cook make many wonderful dinners."

"Why would a fine lady like yourself be doing such common work?" Chester asked.

"It was very . . . boring in the country," she countered. "It gave me something to do."

They looked as if they believed that lie. "If you're strong enough to direct me to your kitchen, Ivan, I'll get started right away. A good soup needs to simmer long hours," she added, hoping she was right.

Ivan allowed her to take hold of his arm. He continued to rub the back of his head with his other hand as he directed her toward the work area. "It's called a galley, m'lady, not the kitchen," he explained. "Slow down, lass," he added in a grumble when she rushed ahead of him. "I'm still seeing two of everything."

They walked down one dark corridor after another until she was completely disoriented. Ivan knew his way, of course, and led her right to his sanctuary.

He struck two candles, secured them in glass globes, and then sat down on a stool against the wall.

There was a giant oven in the center of the room. It was surely the largest she'd ever seen. When she made that comment to Ivan he shook his head. "It isn't an oven, it's the galley stove. There's an open pit on the other side. You've got to walk around the corner to get a look at it.

That's where I cook my meat on a sturdy spit. On this side you can see the giant coppers sunk down low in the top. There are four in all, and every one of them needed to make my beef soup. There's the meat—some went bad. I've already separated the tainted half from the good beef. Most is simmering in the water I added before I went up on deck to have a word with Chester. It gets a might stifling down here, and I needed a breath of fresh sea air."

Ivan waved a hand toward the pile of bad meat he'd left on the sidebar, thinking to tell her that as soon as he was feeling a little better he'd toss the garbage overboard, but he forgot all about explaining when his head started in pounding again.

"There isn't much else to do," he muttered as he regained his feet. "Just chop up those vegetables and add the spices. Of course, you know all that. Do you want me to stay until you learn your way around my galley?"

"No," Sara answered. "I'll do just fine, Ivan. You go and have Matthew take a look at that bump. Perhaps he has some special medicine he can give you to ease your ache."

"That he does, lass," Ivan replied. "He'll be giving me a pint full of grog to ease my aches and pains, or I'll be knowing the reason why."

As soon as the cook took his leave Sara went to work. She was going to make the finest soup the men had ever eaten. She added the rest of the meat she found on the sidebar, a little of each to each copper. She then sprinkled a fair amount of the spices she found in the cubbyhole below the coppers into each vat. One bottle was filled with crushed brown leaves. The aroma was quite pungent, so she only added a little dash of that.

Sara spent the rest of the morning and part of the afternoon in the galley. She thought it a little odd that no one had come looking for her. That thought led to Nathan, of course.

"The man didn't even give me a proper greeting," she

muttered to herself. She mopped at her brow with the towel she'd tied around her waist and pushed the damp strands of hair back over her shoulders.

"Who didn't give you a proper greeting?"

The deep voice came from the doorway. Sara recognized Nathan's low growl.

She turned around and frowned at him. "You didn't give me a proper greeting," she announced.

"What are you doing here?"

"Making soup. What are you doing here?"

"Looking for you."

It was warm in the galley, and she was sure that was the reason she was suddenly feeling so lightheaded. It couldn't be a reaction to the way he was looking at her.

"Have you ever made soup before?"

She walked over to stand in front of him before giving her answer. Nathan leaned against the doorway, looking as relaxed as a panther about to spring.

"No," she said. "I didn't know how to make soup. I do now. It wasn't difficult."

"Sara . . ."

"The men were all blaming me for Ivan's mishap. I had to do something to win their loyalty. Besides, I want my staff to like me."

"Your staff?"

She nodded. "Since you don't have a house and you don't have servants, well, you *do* own this ship, and so your crew must also be my staff. When they taste my soup they'll like me again."

"Why do you care if they like you or not?" he asked.

He straightened away from the wall and moved closer to her. Hell, he thought, he was drawn to her like a drunk drawn to drink. It was all her fault for looking so damned sweet and pretty.

Her face was flushed from the heat in the galley. Strands of her curly hair were wet. He reached out and gently brushed a curl away from the side of her face. He seemed to be more surprised by the spontaneous touch than she was.

"Nathan, everyone wants to be liked."

"I don't."

She gave him a disgruntled look for disagreeing with her. He took another step toward her. His thighs touched hers. "Sara?"

"Yes?"

"Do you still hurt because of last night?"

Her blush was instantaneous. She couldn't look him in the eye when she answered him but stared intently at his collarbone. "It did hurt last night," she whispered.

He tilted her face up with his thumb. "That isn't what I asked you," he said in a soft whisper.

"It isn't?"

"No," he replied.

"Then what is it you wanted to know?"

She sounded out of breath to him. She needed some fresh air, he decided. Hell, he didn't want her fainting on him again. "I want to know if you hurt now, Sara," he said.

"No," she answered. "I don't hurt now."

They stared at each other a long, silent minute. Sara thought he might want to kiss her, but she couldn't be sure. "Nathan? You still haven't given me a proper greeting."

She put her hands on the front of his shirt, closed her eyes, and waited.

"What the hell is a proper greeting?" he asked. He knew exactly what she wanted from him, but he wanted to see what she would do next.

She opened her eyes and frowned at him. "You're supposed to kiss me."

"Why?" he asked, baiting her again.

Her exasperation was obvious. "Just do it," she commanded.

Before he could ask another aggravating question she clasped the sides of his face with her hands and pulled his head down toward her. "Oh, never mind," she whispered. "I'll do it myself."

He didn't offer any resistance. But he didn't take over the duty either. Sara placed a chaste kiss on his mouth, then leaned back. "This would feel much better if you cooperated, Nathan. You're supposed to kiss me back."

Her voice was low, sensual, as soft as her warm body pressed against his. A man could only take so much teasing. Nathan lowered his head and slowly rubbed his mouth over hers. He caught her sigh when he opened her mouth and deepened the kiss.

She was already melting in his arms. He was once again nearly undone by her easy response to his touch. His tongue dueled with hers, and he couldn't contain his low growl of pleasure.

When he finally pulled back from her she slumped against him. He couldn't stop himself from putting his arms around her and holding her tight. She smelled like roses and cinnamon.

"Who taught you how to kiss?" he demanded in a rough whisper. It was an illogical question, he supposed, given the fact that she'd been a virgin when he'd taken her to his bed, but he was compelled to ask anyway.

"You taught me how to kiss," she answered.

"You never kissed anyone before me?"

She shook her head. His anger dissipated in a flash. "If you don't like the way I kiss . . ." she began.

"I like it."

She quit protesting.

He suddenly pulled completely away from her, grabbed hold of her hand, and dragged her over to the candles. He blew both flames out and then headed for the corridor.

"Nathan, I can't leave the galley," she announced.

"You need a nap."

"I what? I never take naps."

"You do now."

"But what about my lovely soup?"

"Damn it, Sara, I don't want you cooking again."

She frowned at his broad back. Lord, he was bossy. "I already explained why I took on this duty," she muttered.

"Do you think you can win the men's loyalty with a bowl of slop?"

If he slowed down just a little, she thought, she would be able to kick him in the back of his legs. "It isn't slop," she shouted instead.

He didn't argue with her. He continued to drag her along all the way back to their cabin. She was a bit surprised when he followed her inside.

He shut the door behind him and bolted it.

"Turn around, Sara."

She gave him a good frown for being so dictatorial, then did as he commanded. He was much quicker unbuttoning the gown than he had been the last time.

"I really don't want to have a nap," she told him again.

He didn't quit prodding her until her gown fell to the floor. It still hadn't dawned on her that he really wasn't interested in forcing her to sleep. He stripped her down to her chemise, but when he tried to remove that garment she pushed his hands away.

Nathan stared at her a long minute. Her body was simply perfection to him. Her breasts were full, her waist narrow, and her legs long, shapely, exquisite.

His hot stare soon made her uncomfortable. Sara tugged on the straps of her chemise, trying without much success to conceal a little more of her breasts.

She quit feeling embarrassed when he unbuttoned his shirt. That action gained her full attention. "Are you taking a nap, too?"

"I never take naps."

He tossed his shirt aside, leaned back against the door, and began to pull his boots off. Sara backed up a space.

"You aren't just changing your clothes, are you?"

His grin was lopsided, endearing. "No."

"You don't want to . . ."

He didn't look at her when he answered. "Oh, yes, I want to," he drawled.

"No."

His reaction was immediate. He stood to his full height and walked toward her. His hands were on his hips. "No?"

She shook her head.

"Why the hell not?"

"It's daylight," she blurted out.

"Damn it, Sara, you aren't afraid again, are you? Honest to God, I don't think I can go through that ordeal again."

She was outraged. "Ordeal? You call making love to me an ordeal?"

He wasn't going to let her stray from answering his question. "Are you afraid?" he demanded.

He looked as though he dreaded her answer. Sara suddenly realized she had a way out if she wanted it, but she immediately discarded that idea. She wasn't going to lie to him.

"I wasn't afraid last night," she announced. She folded her arms across her chest and then added, "You were."

That remark wasn't worthy of a retort. "You said you didn't hurt anymore," he reminded her as he moved forward another step.

"I'm not tender now," she whispered. "But we both know I will be if you persist in getting your way, Nathan."

His smile indicated his amusement. "Will that be so unbearable?"

A warm knot was already forming in the pit of her stomach. All the man had to do was look at her in that special way of his and she came apart.

"Are you going to want to . . . move again?"

He didn't laugh. She looked so worried, and he didn't want her to think he was mocking her feelings. He wasn't going to lie, either. "Yeah," he drawled as he reached for her. "I'm going to want to move again."

"Then we aren't going to do anything but nap."

The little woman really needed to understand who was husband and who was wife, Nathan thought to himself. He decided he'd explain all about her duty to obey him later. All he wanted to do was kiss her. He threw his arm around her shoulders, dragged her over to the trap, and didn't let go of her when he reached up and pulled the wooden door shut.

The cabin was pitched into darkness. Nathan paused to kiss Sara. It was a hot, wet, lingering kiss that let her know with certainty that he was going to get his way.

Then he turned to light the candles. Her hand stayed his action. "Don't," she whispered.

"I want to see you when you . . ."

He stopped his explanation when he felt her hands on his waistband. Sara's hands were shaking, but she got the buttons to his breeches undone in little time. Her fingers brushed against his hard stomach. His indrawn breath told her he liked that. It made her bolder. She rested the side of her face against his chest, then slowly edged the waistband down. "You wanted to see me when I what, Nathan?" she whispered.

It took all he had to concentrate on what she was saying. Her fingers were slowly easing their way down toward his groin. He closed his eyes in sweet agony.

"When you find fulfillment," he said on a low groan. "God, Sara, touch me."

His body was rigid now. Sara smiled to herself. She had no idea her touch could so arouse him. She pushed his clothing down a little further. "I am touching you, Nathan."

He couldn't take the torment any longer. He took hold of her hand and placed it where he needed her touch most.

She wanted to stroke him. He wouldn't let her. His growl was deep, guttural. "Don't," he ordered. "Just hold me, squeeze me, but don't . . . oh, God, Sara, stop now."

He sounded as if he was in pain. She pulled her hand away. "Am I hurting you?" she whispered.

He kissed her again. She put her arms around his neck

and held him close. When he moved to the side of her neck and began to place wet kisses below her earlobe she tried to touch his hard arousal again.

He took hold of her hand and put it on his waist. "It's too soon for me to lose my control," he whispered. "You make it unbearable."

She kissed the base of his neck. "Then I won't touch you there, Nathan, if you promise not to move around so much when you make love to me."

He laughed. "You'll want me to move," he told her.

He pulled her back up against his chest. "You know what, Sara?" he said between fervent kisses.

"What?"

"I've decided I'm going to make you beg."

He was as good as his word. By the time the two of them were in bed and he was settled between her thighs she was begging him to end the sweet torment.

The fire of passion inside her was completely out of control. Nathan did hurt her when he finally moved inside her. She was so tight, so hot, it was blissful agony for him to slow down. He tried to be a gentle lover, knowing how tender she was, and he didn't move at all until she began to writhe underneath him.

She found her release before he did, and her tremors gave him his own orgasm. He hadn't spoken a word during the mating. She never quit talking. She rambled on and on, tender words of love. Some made sense. Others didn't.

When he finally collapsed on top of her, when he finally regained his ability to think at all, he realized she was crying.

"God, Sara, did I hurt you again?"

"Only a little," she whispered shyly.

He leaned up to look into her eyes. "Then why are you crying?"

"I don't know why," she answered. "It was so . . . amazing, and I was so . . ."

He stopped her rambling by kissing her. When he next

looked into her eyes he smiled. She looked thoroughly bemused again.

This one could get to his heart, he suddenly realized. The sound of the boatswain's whistle announcing the change of the watch was like a warning bell going off inside Nathan's mind. It was dangerous to be so attracted to his wife, foolish . . . irresponsible. To care for the woman would make him vulnerable, he knew. If he'd learned anything of consequence in his escapades, it was to protect himself at all costs.

Loving her could destroy him.

"Nathan, why are you frowning?"

He didn't answer her. He got out of bed, dressed with his back to her, and then walked out of the cabin. The door closed softly behind him.

Sara was too stunned by his behavior to react for a long minute. Her husband had literally fled the cabin. It was as though he had a demon chasing him.

Had their lovemaking meant so little to him that he couldn't wait to leave her? Sara burst into tears. She wanted, needed his words of love. God, he treated her as though she was nothing but a receptacle for his passion. Fast spent, fast forgotten. A whore was treated better than he'd just treated her, she thought to herself. Women of the night at least earned a shilling or two.

She hadn't even merited a growl of farewell.

When her tears were spent she took her frustration out on the bed. She made a fist and slammed it into the center of Nathan's pillow, taking great satisfaction in pretending it was her husband's head. Then she pulled his pillow against her bosom and held it tight. Nathan's scent clung to the pillowcase. So did hers.

It didn't take her long to realize how pitiful she was being. She tossed the pillow aside and turned her attention to righting the cabin.

She stayed in the room the remainder of the afternoon. She dressed in the same blue dress, and when the cabin was cleaned she sat down in one of the chairs and began to make a sketch of the ship using her pad and charcoals.

Sketching took her mind off Nathan. Matthew interrupted her when he knocked on the door to ask if she wanted to eat her dinner with the first or second change in the watch. She told him she would wait and share her meal with her aunt.

Sara was eager to find out what the men thought about her soup. The aroma had been quite nice when she'd finished stirring in all the spices. It should have a hearty flavor, she thought, for it had simmered long hours.

It was only a matter of time before the men came to thank her. She brushed her hair and changed her gown in preparation for their visitations.

Her staff would soon be completely loyal to her. Making the soup was a giant step in that direction, anyway. Why, by nightfall they would all think she was very, very worthy.

Chapter Seven

By nightfall they thought she was trying to kill them.

The watch turned at six that evening. The first group filed into the galley to collect their dinner just a few minutes later. The men had put in a hard day's work. The decks had been scoured, the hammocks scrubbed, netting mended, and half the cannons had been given another thorough cleaning. The seamen were weary, and their hunger was fierce. Most ate two full bowls of the heavily flavored soup before they were appeased.

They didn't start getting sick until the second watch had just eaten their share.

Sara had no idea the men were ill. She was getting impatient, though, for no one had come along to tell her what a fine job she'd done.

When a hard knock sounded at her door she rushed to answer it. Jimbo stood at the entrance, frowning at her. Her smile faltered.

"Good evening, Jimbo," she began. "Is something wrong? You look very unhappy."

"You haven't had any soup yet, have you, Lady Sara?" he asked.

His obvious concern didn't make any sense to her. She shook her head. "I was waiting to share my dinner with Nora," she explained. "Jimbo, what is that horrid sound I'm hearing?"

She looked out the door to see if she could locate the sound.

"The men."

"The men?"

Nathan suddenly appeared at Jimbo's side. The look on her husband's face made her breath catch in the back of her throat. He looked bloody furious. Sara instinctively backed up. "What's the matter, Nathan?" she asked, her alarm obvious. "Is something wrong? Is it Nora? Is she all right?"

"Nora's fine," Jimbo interjected.

Nathan motioned Jimbo out of the way, then stalked into the cabin. Sara continued to back away from him. She noticed his jaw was clenched tight. That was a bad sign.

"Are you upset about something?" she asked Nathan in a faint whisper.

He nodded.

She decided to be more specific. "Are you upset with me?"

He nodded again. Then he kicked the door shut.

"Why?" she asked, trying desperately not to let him see her fear.

"The soup." Nathan's voice was low, controlled, furious.

She was more confused by his answer than frightened. "The men didn't care for my soup?"

"It wasn't deliberate?"

Since she didn't have any idea what he meant by that question, she didn't answer. He could see the confusion in her eyes. He closed his own and counted to ten. "Then you didn't deliberately try to kill them?"

She let out a loud gasp. "Of course I didn't try to kill them. How could you think such a vile thing? The men are all part of my staff now, and I certainly wouldn't try to harm them. If they didn't like my soup, I'm sorry. I had no idea they were such persnickety eaters."

"Persnickety eaters?" He repeated those words in a roar. "Twenty of my men are now hanging over the sides of my ship. They're retching up the soup you prepared for them. Another ten are writhing in agony in their hammocks. They're not dead yet, but they sure as hell are wishing they were."

She was appalled by what he was telling her. "I don't understand," she cried out. "Do you mean to suggest that my soup wasn't any good? The men are ill because of me? Oh, God, I must go and comfort them."

He grabbed hold of her shoulders when she tried to rush past him. "Comfort them? Sara, one or two of them just might comfort you right off the ship."

"They wouldn't throw me overboard. I'm their mistress."

He felt like shouting. Then he realized he already was. He took a quick breath. "The hell they wouldn't toss you overboard," he muttered.

Nathan dragged her over to the bed and pushed her down on the quilt. "Now, wife, you're going to tell me just how you made that damned soup."

She burst into tears. It took Nathan almost twenty minutes to find the cause, and it wasn't Sara who finally gave him sufficient information. He couldn't make head or tail out of her incoherent explanation. Ivan remembered the tainted meat he'd left on the sidebar. He remembered, too, that he hadn't told Sara it was bad.

Nathan locked Sara inside the cabin so she couldn't cause any more mischief. She was furious with him because he wouldn't let her go and apologize to the men.

He didn't come to bed that night, as he and the other healthy men had to take over the next watch. Sara didn't understand that duty called and believed he was still too angry with her to want to sleep next to her.

She didn't know how she was ever going to find the

courage to face her staff again. How could she convince them that she hadn't deliberately tried to do them in? That worry turned to anger in short time. How could the men believe such a sinful thing about their mistress anyway? Why, they besmirched her character by believing she would hurt them. Sara determined that once she won their trust again she would sit them all down and have a firm talk with them about their tendency to jump to conclusions.

Nathan was slow to forgive her error, too. He came down to the cabin the following morning. He glared at her but didn't speak a word. He fell asleep on top of the covers and slept the morning away.

She couldn't stand the confinement long. She couldn't stand his snoring either. It was half past the noon hour when she slipped out of the room. She went up on deck, opened her blue parasol, and set out for a brisk walk.

It turned out to be a humiliating experience. Each man she approached turned his back on her. Most still had a gray cast to their complexions. All of them had scowls. She was in tears by the time she reached the narrow steps to the highest deck. She was scarcely aware of where she was going and only wanted to get as far away from the dark frowns as possible, if only for just a few minutes.

The highest level was filled with ropes and masts. There was barely room to walk. Sara found a corner near the tallest sail, sat down, and put her opened parasol between two fat ropes.

She didn't know how long she sat there trying to think of a plan to persuade the men to like her again. Her face and arms soon turned pink from the sun. It wasn't at all fashionable for a lady to walk around with a bronzed complexion. Sara decided she'd better go back down and look in on her Aunt Nora.

It would be nice to visit with someone who cared about her. Nora wouldn't blame her. Yes, a pleasant visit was just the thing she needed.

She stood up and tugged on her parasol only to find that

the delicate spokes had become caught up in ropes. It took her a good five minutes to loosen the knots in the ropes enough to work the parasol partially free. The wind was high again, making the task more difficult. The sound of the sails slapping against the posts was loud enough to drown out her frustrated mutters. She gave up on the task when the material of her parasol tore. She decided then to ask Matthew or Jimbo for assistance.

Sara left the parasol dangling in the ropes and made her way back down the steps.

The crash, when it came, nearly toppled her over the side of the ship. Chester caught her in the nick of time. Both of them turned to the noise on the upper deck just in time to see one of the masts slam into a larger one.

Chester took off running, shouting for assistance as he raced up the steps. Sara decided she'd better get out of the way of the sudden chaos around her. She waited until several more men had rushed past her, then made her way down to Nora's cabin. Matthew was just coming out of the room when Sara strode past him.

"Good day, Matthew," she said in greeting. She paused to curtsy, then added, "I'll only stay a few minutes. I just wanted to see how my aunt is doing today. I promise I won't wear her out."

Matthew grinned. "I believe you," he replied. "But I'm still coming back in a half hour's time to check on Nora."

The booming crash shook the vessel then. Sara grabbed hold of the door to keep herself from pitching forward to her knees. "Heavens, the wind is fierce today, isn't it, Matthew?"

The seaman was already running toward the steps. "That wasn't the wind," he shouted over his shoulder.

Sara shut the door to Nora's cabin just as Nathan came charging out of his quarters.

Her aunt was once again propped up with pillows behind her back. Sara thought she looked a little more rested and said so. "The color's back in your cheeks, Nora, and your bruises are beginning to fade to yellow now. You'll be strolling around the decks with me in no time at all."

"Yes, I do feel better," Nora announced. "How are you faring, Sara?"

"Oh, I'm just fine," she answered. She sat down on the side of the bed and took hold of her aunt's hand.

Nora frowned at her. "I heard about the soup, child. I know you aren't doing fine."

"I didn't eat any of the soup," Sara blurted out. "But I do feel terrible about the men. I didn't mean to make them ill."

"I know you didn't mean to," Nora soothed. "I told Matthew so. I took up your defense, Sara, and told him you didn't have a malicious thought in your head. Why, you'd never do such a terrible thing on purpose."

Sara's frown matched her aunt's. "I think it's horribly rude of my staff to think such evil thoughts about their mistress. Yes, I do. Why, they're as contrary as their captain, Nora."

"What about Nathan?" Nora asked. "Is he blaming you, too?"

Sara shrugged. "He was a little upset about the soup, of course, but I don't believe he thinks I poisoned the men on purpose. He's probably being a little more understanding because he didn't eat any of it. Anyway, I've decided I don't care what the man thinks of me. I'm more upset with him than he is with me. Yes, I am," she added when Nora began to smile. "He isn't treating me at all well."

She didn't give her aunt time to respond to that dramatic statement. "Oh, I never should have said that. Nathan's my husband, and I must always be loyal to him. I'm ashamed of myself for—"

"Has he harmed you?" Nora interrupted.

"No, of course not. It's just that . . ."

A long minute passed while Nora tried to guess what was the matter and Sara tried to think of a way to explain.

When Sara started blushing Nora surmised that the

problem had something to do with the intimate side of their marriage. "He wasn't gentle with you when he bedded you?"

Sara looked down at her lap before answering. "He was very gentle."

"Then?"

"But afterwards he didn't . . . that is, the second time—well, after—he just left. He didn't say a single tender word to me, Nora. In fact, he didn't say anything at all. A whore is treated with more consideration."

Nora was too relieved that Nathan had been gentle with Sara to take issue over his lack of thoughtfulness. "Did you say any tender words to him?" she asked.

"No."

"It would seem to me that Nathan might not know how to give you what you want. He might not know you need his praise."

"I don't need his praise," Sara countered in a disgruntled voice. "I would just like a little consideration. Oh, heaven help me, that's not the truth. I do need his words of praise. I don't know why I seem to need them, but I do. Nora? Do you notice how the boat is tilted to one side now? I wonder why Nathan doesn't straighten it out."

It took her aunt a minute to make the switch in topics. "Yes, it is at an angle, isn't it?" she responded. "But you did say the wind was brisk today."

"We don't seem to be clipping along either," Sara interjected. "I hope we don't topple over," she added with a sigh. "I never did learn how to swim. That shouldn't signify, though. Nathan can't let me drown."

Nora smiled. "Why can't he?"

Sara seemed surprised by that question. "Because I'm his wife," she blurted out. "He promised to protect me, Nora."

"And you have ultimate faith that he will?"

"Of course."

The vessel suddenly shifted again, pitching them even

further toward the water line. Sara saw how startled Nora was; her aunt was gripping her hand. She patted Nora and said, "Nathan is the captain of this vessel, Nora, and he wouldn't let us fall over into the ocean. He knows what he's doing. Don't worry."

A sudden roar filled the cabin. It was her name being bellowed. Sara grimaced in reaction, then turned to give Nora a thoroughly disgruntled look. "Do you see what I mean, Nora? The only time Nathan says my name, he screams it. I wonder what has him in a snit now. The man has such a sour disposition. It's a wonder I can put up with him."

"Go and see what he wants," Nora suggested. "Don't let him frighten you with his shouts. Just remember to look below the bluster."

"I know," Sara said with a sigh. She stood up and brushed the wrinkles out of her gown. "Look below the surface, and I'll find myself a good man," she added, repeating her aunt's suggestion of the day before. "I will try."

She kissed Nora and hurried out into the corridor. She almost bumped into Jimbo. The big man grabbed hold of her to steady her. "Come with me," he ordered.

He started to lead her toward the steps that led down to the lower level. She pulled back. "Nathan is calling for me, Jimbo. I must go to him. He's up on deck, isn't he?"

"I know where he is," Jimbo muttered. "But he needs a few more minutes to calm himself down, Sara. You can hide down here until he—"

"I'm not hiding from my husband," Sara interrupted.

"Damned right you're not."

Sara jumped a foot when Nathan's booming voice sounded behind her. She turned around and valiantly tried to manage a smile. After all, there was a member of her staff standing right beside her, and for that reason personal irritations should be placed aside. The scowl on her husband's face changed her inclination, though. She no longer cared that Jimbo was watching. She scowled back. "For heaven's sake, Nathan, must you sneak up on me like that? You gave me a good scare."

"Sara," Jimbo began in a whisper, "I wouldn't be . . ."

She ignored the seaman's mutterings. "And while I'm on the topic of your bad habits, I might as well point out that I'm getting mighty sick of your shouting at me all the time. If you have something you wish to say to me, kindly speak in a civil tone of voice, sir."

Jimbo moved to stand by her side. Matthew suddenly appeared out of the shadows and took up his position on her other side. In the back of Sara's mind was the astonishing fact that both men were actually trying to protect her.

"Nathan wouldn't ever hurt me," she announced. "He may want to, but he would never touch me, no matter how angry he is."

"He looks like he wants to kill you," Jimbo countered in a low drawl. He actually grinned, for he found Sara's gumption worthy. Wrongheaded, he added to himself, but worthy still.

Nathan was trying to calm down before he spoke again. He stared at Sara and took several deep breaths. He counted.

"He always looks like he wants to kill someone," Sara whispered back. She folded her arms in front of her, trying her damnedest to look irritated and not worried.

Nathan still hadn't said a word. The look in his eyes made her skin burn. In truth, he did look like he wanted to throttle her.

Look below the surface, her aunt had suggested. Sara couldn't manage that feat. She couldn't even hold Nathan's gaze for more than a heartbeat or two. "All right," she muttered when she couldn't stand his hot glare any longer. "Did someone else have some of my soup? Is that the reason you're in such a state, husband?"

The muscle flexed in the side of his jaw. She decided she

shouldn't have asked him that question after all. It only reminded him of the confusion she'd caused the day before. Then she noticed he was holding her parasol.

Nathan's right eyelid twitched. Twice. God, he was developing an affliction, he noted, thanks to his innocent wife's mischief. He still couldn't trust himself to speak to her. He took hold of her hand and pulled her into their cabin. He slammed the door, then leaned on it.

Sara walked over to the desk, turned, and leaned against it. She was trying to look nonchalant. "Nathan, I cannot help but notice that you're once again upset about something," she began. "Are you going to tell me what's bothering you, or are you going to continue to stand there and glare at me? Lord, you do strain my patience."

"I strain *your* patience?"

She didn't dare nod in answer. He'd roared that question at her, and she guessed he didn't want an answer.

"Does this look familiar?" he demanded in a rough voice. He lifted her parasol but kept his gaze fully directed on her.

She stared at the parasol and noticed right away that it had been broken in half.

"Did you break my lovely parasol?" she demanded. She looked incensed.

His eyelid twitched again. "No, I didn't break it. When the first mast let loose it broke your damned parasol. Did you untie the latchings?"

"Please quit your shouting," she protested. "I cannot think when you're yelling at me."

"Answer me."

"I might have untied a few of the fatter ropes, Nathan, but I had good reason. That's a very expensive parasol," she added with a wave of her hand toward him. "It got caught up, and I was trying to . . . Nathan, exactly what happens when the ropes become untied?"

"We lost two sails."

She didn't comprehend what he was telling her. "We what?"

"Two sails were destroyed."

"And that is why you're so upset? Husband, you have at least six others on this boat. Surely—"

"*Ship,*" he roared. "It's a ship, not a boat."

She decided to try to placate him. "I meant to say ship."

"Do you have any more of these things?"

"They're called parasols," she replied. "And yes, I do have three more."

"Give them to me. Now."

"What are you going to do with them?"

She rushed over to her trunk when he took a threatening step toward her. "I can't imagine why you would need my parasols," she whispered.

"I'm throwing them in the ocean. With any luck they'll cripple a couple of sharks."

"You cannot throw my parasols in the ocean. They match my gowns, Nathan. They were made just for . . . it would be a sin to waste . . . you can't." She ended her tirade in a near wail.

"The hell I can't."

He wasn't shouting at her any longer. She should have been happy over that minor blessing, but she wasn't. He was still being too mean-hearted to suit her. "Explain why you want to destroy my parasols," she demanded. "Then I might give them to you."

She located the third parasol in the bottom of the trunk, but when she straightened and turned to confront him again she clutched all three against her bosom.

"The parasols are a menace, that's why."

She looked incredulous. "How could they be a menace?"

She was looking at him as though she thought he'd lost his mind. He shook his head. "The first parasol crippled my men, Sara," he began.

"It only crippled Ivan," she corrected.

"Which is why you made the damn soup that crippled the rest of my crew," he countered.

He had a valid point there, she had to admit, but she

thought it was terribly unkind of him to bring up the topic of her soup again.

"The second parasol crippled my ship," he continued. "Haven't you noticed we aren't gliding across the waters now? We had to drop anchor in order to see to the repairs. We're easy prey for anyone sailing past. That's why your other damned parasols are all going into the ocean."

"Nathan, I didn't mean to cause these mishaps. You're acting as though I did everything on purpose."

"Did you?"

She reacted as though he'd just slapped her backside. "No," she cried out. "God, you're insulting."

He wanted to shake some sense into her. She started crying.

"Quit that weeping," he demanded.

Not only did she continue to cry, but she threw herself into his arms. Hell, he'd been the one to make her weep in the first place, he thought, and she certainly should have been upset with him just a little, shouldn't she?

Nathan didn't know what to make of her. Her parasols littered the floor around his feet, and she was clinging to him as she sobbed wet tears all over his shirt. He put his arms around her and held her close even as he tried to understand why in God's name he wanted to comfort her.

The woman had damn near destroyed his ship.

He kissed her.

She tucked her face in the side of his neck and quit crying. "Do the men know I broke the ship?"

"You didn't break it," he muttered. God, she sounded pitiful.

"But do the men think I—"

"Sara, we can fix the damage in a couple of days," he said. It was a lie, for it would take them close to a week to see to the repairs, but he'd softened the truth just a little to ease her worry.

He decided then that he had lost his mind. His wife had caused nothing but chaos since the moment she'd boarded his ship. He kissed the top of her head and began to rub her backside.

She leaned against him. "Nathan?"

"Yes?"

"Does my staff know I caused this mishap?"

He rolled his eyes heavenward. Her staff, indeed. "Yes, they know."

"Did you tell them?"

He closed his eyes. There had been such censure in her voice. She thought he was being disloyal to her, he surmised. "No, I didn't tell them. They saw the parasol, Sara."

"I wanted them to respect me."

"Oh, they respect you all right," he announced. His voice had lost its angry bite.

She heard the smile in his voice and felt a quick rush of hope until he added, "They're waiting for you to bring on the plague next."

She thought he was teasing her. "They don't believe that nonsense," she replied.

"Oh, yes, they do," he told her. "They're making wagers, Sara. Some think it will be boils first, then the plague. Others believe—"

She pushed away from him. "You're serious, aren't you?"

He nodded. "They think you're cursed, wife."

"How can you smile at me when you say such sinful things?"

He shrugged. "The men are superstitious, Sara."

"Is it because I'm a woman?" she asked. "I've heard that seamen think it's bad luck to have a woman on board, but I didn't credit such foolishness."

"No, it isn't because you're a woman," he answered. "They're used to having a woman on board. My sister Jade used to be mistress of this ship."

"Then why—"

"You aren't like Jade," he told her. "They were quick to notice."

She couldn't get him to elaborate. A sudden thought

163

changed her direction. "Nathan, I'll help with the repairs," she said. "Yes, that's it. The men will realize I didn't deliberately—"

"God save us all," he interrupted.

"Then how am I going to win their confidence again?"

"I don't understand this obsession with winning the men over," he returned. "It makes absolutely no sense."

"I'm their mistress. I must have their respect if I'm going to direct them."

He let out a loud sigh, then shook his head. "Direct yourself to bed, wife, and stay there until I come back."

"Why?"

"Don't question me. Just stay inside this cabin."

She nodded agreement. "I won't leave this cabin save for going to visit with Nora, all right?"

"I didn't say—"

"Please? It's going to be a long afternoon, Nathan. You might be too busy to come home for hours yet. You didn't come to bed at all last night. I tried to wait up for you, but I was very weary."

He smiled because she'd called their cabin home. Then he nodded. "You'll wait up for me tonight," he ordered. "No matter what the time."

"Are you going to want to shout at me again?"

"No."

"All right, then," she promised. "I'll wait up for you."

"Damn it, Sara," he countered. "I wasn't asking. I was telling."

He grabbed her and squeezed her shoulders. It was actually more of a caress. She pushed his hands away and wrapped her arms around his waist again.

"Nathan?" she whispered.

Her voice sounded shaky to him. His hands dropped to his sides. He thought she might be afraid he'd hurt her. He was about to explain that no matter how much she provoked him he would never, ever raise a hand against her. But Sara suddenly leaned up on tiptoes and kissed him. He was so

164

surprised by the show of affection he didn't know how to respond.

"I was very upset with you when you left the cabin so quickly after we had . . . been so intimate."

"Do you mean after we made love?" he asked, smiling over the shyness in her voice.

"Yes," she replied. "I was very upset."

"Why?"

"Because a wife likes to hear that she . . ."

"Satisfied her husband?"

"No," she returned. "Don't mock me, Nathan. Don't make what happened between us so cold and calculated either. It was too beautiful."

He was shaken by her fervent speech, knew she believed what she'd said with all her heart. He found himself inordinately pleased with her. "Yes, it was beautiful," he said. "I wasn't mocking you," he added in a rougher tone. "I was just trying to understand what it is you want from me."

"I want to hear that you . . ."

She couldn't go on.

"That you're a fine woman?"

She nodded. "I'm at fault, too," she admitted. "I should have given you a few words of praise, too."

"Why?"

He really looked bewildered to her. That did irritate her. "Because a husband needs to hear such words, too."

"I don't."

"Yes, you do."

He decided he'd wasted enough conversation on his confusing wife and bent on one knee to collect the parasols.

"May I please have those back?" she asked. "I'll destroy them myself right away. I don't want my staff to see you throw them overboard. It would be most humiliating."

He reluctantly agreed, though only because he was certain she couldn't do any real damage with the useless things as long as they stayed inside the cabin. Still, just to be on the safe side, he made her give him her promise.

"The parasols won't leave this chamber?"

"They won't."

"You will destroy them?"

"I will."

He was finally satisfied. He actually began to feel a little more peaceful. By the time he left the cabin he was convinced his wife couldn't possibly wreck anything else.

Besides, he reasoned, what more could she do?

Chapter Eight

She set his ship on fire.

She'd lulled them into a state of feeling safe again. A full eight days and nights passed without a single mishap taking place. The men were still wary of Sara, but they weren't scowling nearly as often. Some were even whistling every now and again as they saw to their daily tasks. Chester, the doubting Thomas of the crew, was the only one who continued to make the sign of the cross whenever Sara strolled past.

Lady Sara pretended she didn't notice.

Once the sails had been repaired they made good catch-up time. They were just a week or so away from Nora's island home. The weather had been accommodating, though the heat was nearly unbearable in the early afternoons. The nights continued to be just as chilly, however, and thick quilts were still needed to take the shivers away.

All and all, things were looking calm.

Nathan should have realized it wouldn't last. It was late Friday night when he finished giving directions for the watch. He interrupted Jimbo's conversation with Matthew to give them fresh orders for the drill and the firing of the cannons they would practice tomorrow.

The three of them were standing directly in front of the trapdoor that led down to Nathan's cabin. For that reason Jimbo kept his voice low when he said, "The men are beginning to forget this talk about your wife being cursed, boy." He paused to glance behind him, as if that action would assure him that Sara couldn't overhear, then added, "Chester is still telling everyone mischief trails in three. We'd best continue to keep a close watch on Sara until—"

"Jimbo, no one would dare touch the captain's wife," Matthew muttered.

"I wasn't suggesting anyone would," Jimbo countered. "I'm just saying that they could still hurt her feelings. She's a bit tenderhearted."

"Did you know she considers us all part of her staff?" Matthew remarked. He grinned, then stopped himself. "Lady Sara obviously has you in the palm of her hand, if you're so concerned about her feelings." He started to continue on that same topic when the scent of smoke caught his attention. "Am I smelling smoke?" he asked.

Nathan saw the stream of gray smoke seeping up around the edges of the trapdoor before the other two men did. He should have shouted fire to alert the others of the danger. He didn't. He bellowed Sara's name instead. The anguish in his voice was gut-wrenching.

He threw open the hatch. A thick black sheet of smoke billowed up through the opening, blinding the three men. Nathan shouted Sara's name again.

Matthew shouted, "Fire!"

Jimbo went running for the buckets, yelling his own order for seawater on the double, while Matthew tried to keep Nathan from going below by way of the trap.

"You don't know how bad it is," he shouted. "Use the steps, boy, use the—"

Matthew quit his demand when Nathan slipped down through the opening, then turned to run down the steps.

Nathan could barely see inside the cabin, for the smoke was so thick it blackened his vision. He groped his way over to the bed to find Sara.

She wasn't there. By the time he'd searched the cabin his lungs were burning. He staggered back to the trap again and used the buckets of seawater Jimbo handed down to him to flood the flames out.

The threat was over. The near miss they'd all had made the men shake. Nathan couldn't seem to control his heartbeat. His fear for his wife's safety had all but overwhelmed him. Yet she wasn't even inside the cabin. She hadn't been overcome by smoke. She wasn't dead.

Yet.

Matthew and Jimbo flanked Nathan. All three men stared at the corner of the room to gauge the damage done.

Several of the planks under the potbellied stove had fallen through the floor to the next level. There was now a gaping, glowing hole in the floorboards. Two of the four walls had been licked black all the way to the ceiling by the scorch of the fire.

The damage to the cabin wasn't what held Nathan mesmerized, though. No, his full attention was riveted on the remains of Sara's parasols. The spokes still glowed inside the two remaining metal fittings of the stove.

"Did she think this was a hearth?" Matthew whispered to Jimbo. He rubbed his jaw while he considered that possibility.

"I'm thinking she did," Jimbo answered.

"If she'd been asleep, the smoke would have killed her," Nathan said, his voice raw.

"Now, boy," Jimbo began, certain that the boy was getting himself all worked up, "Sara's all right, and that's what counts. You're sounding as black as the soot on these walls. You've only yourself to blame," he added with a crisp nod.

Nathan gave him a murderous stare. Jimbo wasn't the least intimidated. "I heard Sara call the trap a chimney. Had myself a good laugh over that comment, too. I thought you set her straight."

"I don't suppose he did," Matthew interjected.

Nathan wasn't at all calmed by Jimbo's argument. He sounded as if he was close to weeping when he bellowed, "She set my ship on fire."

"She didn't do it on purpose," Matthew defended.

Nathan wasn't listening. "She set my ship on fire," he repeated in a roar.

"We heard you plain the first time, boy," Jimbo interjected. "Now calm yourself and try to reason this little accident through."

"I'm thinking it's going to take him a few more minutes before he can think at all," Matthew said. "The boy always was a hothead, Jimbo. And Sara did set the fire. That's a fact, all right."

The two men turned to leave the cabin. They both thought Nathan needed to be alone for a spell. Nathan's shout stopped them in their tracks. "Bring her to me. Now."

Jimbo motioned for Matthew to stay where he was and then rushed out the doorway. He didn't give Sara any warning of the problem at hand when he found her in Nora's cabin but simply informed her that her husband would like to have a word with her.

Sara hurried back to her cabin. Her eyes widened when she saw all the water on the floor. A loud gasp followed after she noticed the gaping hole in the corner.

"My God, what has happened here?"

Nathan turned to look at her before answering. "Fire."

Understanding came in a flash. "Fire?" she repeated in a hoarse whisper. "Do you mean the fire in the hearth, Nathan?"

He didn't answer her for a long, long minute. Then he slowly walked over to stand directly in front of her. His hands were close enough to grab her by the neck.

He resisted that shameful temptation by clasping his hands behind his back.

She wasn't looking at him. That helped. Her gaze was still fully directed on the damage to the cabin. She worried her lower lip with her teeth, and when she began to tremble Nathan guessed she'd realized exactly what she'd done.

He was wrong. "I never should have left the hearth unattended," she whispered. "Did a spark . . ."

He shook his head.

She looked into his eyes then. Her fear was obvious.

He immediately lost some of his rage. Damn if he'd have her afraid of him. It was an illogical thought, given the circumstances, yet there it was, nagging him to ease his scowl.

"Sara?" His voice sounded quite mild.

He sounded furious to her. She forced herself to stay where she was, though the urge to back away from him was nearly overpowering. "Yes, Nathan?" she replied, her gaze directed on the floor.

"Look at me."

She looked. He saw the tears in her eyes. The sight tore the rest of his fury right out of him.

His sigh was long, ragged.

"Was there something you wanted to say to me?" she asked when he continued to stare intently at her.

"It isn't a hearth."

Nathan walked out of the cabin. Sara stared after him a long minute before turning around to look at Matthew and Jimbo.

"Did he just say that the hearth isn't a hearth?"

The two men nodded in unison.

Her shoulders slumped. "It looks like a hearth."

"Well, it isn't," Matthew announced. He nudged Jimbo in his side. "You explain it."

Jimbo nodded, then told Sara that the metal parts stacked in the corner of the cabin had been carted back from Nathan's last trip. They were to be used to repair the old stove in the Emerald Shipping Company offices. Nathan had just forgotten to take the parts off the ship when they'd docked, Jimbo continued, though he was certain the captain wouldn't be forgetting next time.

Matthew finished up the explanation by telling Sara that the trap was simply an air duct and nothing more. It wasn't a chimney.

Lady Sara's face looked as red as fire by the time the two men had given her their explanations. She then thanked them for their patience. She felt like an ignorant fool. "I could have killed everyone," she whispered.

"Aye, you could have," Matthew agreed.

She burst into tears. The two men were nearly undone by the emotional show. Jimbo glared at Matthew.

Matthew suddenly felt like a father trying to comfort his daughter. He took Sara into his arms and awkwardly patted her on her back.

"There now, Sara, it's not so bad," Jimbo said, trying to soothe her. "You couldn't have known it wasn't a hearth."

"An idiot would have known," she cried out.

The two men nodded to each other over the top of Sara's head. Then Matthew said, "I *might* have thought it was a hearth if I . . ." He couldn't go on because he couldn't think of a plausible lie.

Jimbo came to his aid. "Anyone would have thought it was a hearth if he wasn't used to sailing much."

Nathan stood in the doorway. He couldn't believe what he was seeing. Jimbo and Matthew, two of the most bloodless pirates he'd ever had the honor to work with, were now acting like nursemaids. He would have laughed if his attention hadn't wandered over to the fire damage just then. He frowned instead.

"When you're through beating bruises in my wife's back, Matthew, you might want to have some of the men clean up this mess."

Nathan turned to Jimbo next. "The planks went through the lower level, too. See to righting the damage, Jimbo. Matthew, if you don't get your hands off my wife, I'll . . ."

He didn't have to finish that threat. Matthew was halfway

out the door by the time Nathan reached Sara. "If anyone is to comfort my wife, it's going to be me."

He jerked Sara into his arms and shoved her face against his chest. Jimbo didn't dare break into a smile until he'd exited the room. He did let out a rich chuckle after he'd closed the door behind him, however.

Nathan continued to hold Sara for a few more minutes. His irritation got the better of him then. "God, wife, aren't you through crying yet?"

She mopped her face on the front of his shirt, then eased away from him. "I do try not to cry, but sometimes I can't seem to help it."

"I've noticed," he remarked.

He dragged her over to the bed, shoved her down, and then felt sufficiently calm to give her a firm lecture on the one overriding fear each and every seaman harbored. Fire. He paced the room, his big hands clasped behind his back, while he gave his speech. He was calm, logical, thorough.

He was shouting at her by the time he'd finished. She didn't dare mention that fact to him, though. The vein in the side of his temple throbbed noticeably, and she concluded her husband wasn't quite over his anger.

She watched him pace and shout and grumble, and in those minutes when he was being his surly self she realized how very much she really loved him. He was trying to be so kind to her. He didn't know he was, of course, but there he stood, blaming himself, Jimbo and Matthew, and even God for bringing on the fire because no one had bothered to explain ship life to her.

She wanted to throw herself into his arms and tell him that even though she had always loved him, the feeling had become much more . . . vivid, much more real. She felt such peace, such contentment. It was as though she'd been on a journey all those years while she waited for him and was home at last.

Nathan drew her attention by demanding she answer him. He had to repeat his question, of course, for she'd been daydreaming and had no idea what he'd asked. He only looked a little irritated by her lack of attention, and Sara guessed he was finally getting used to her. God only knew she was getting used to his flaws. The man was all bluster. Oh, his scowl, when set upon her fully, could still give her the hives, but Nora had been right after all. There really was a good, kind man behind the mask.

Nathan finally finished his lecture. When he asked her she immediately gave him her promise that she wouldn't touch anything else on his ship until they were in port.

Nathan was content. After he left the cabin Sara spent long hours scrubbing the mess. She was exhausted by the time she'd changed the bedding and had her own bath, but she was determined to wait up for her husband. She wanted to fall asleep in his arms.

Sara pulled her sketch pad from the trunk, sat down at the table, and drew a picture of her husband. The paper didn't seem big enough to accommodate his size. She smiled over that fanciful notion. He was just a man. Her man. The likeness was remarkably well done, she thought, though she refused to put a frown on his face. She'd captured his Viking stance, too, with his muscular legs braced apart and his hands settled on his hips. His hair flowed down behind his neck, and she wished she had her colors so she could show the magnificence of his auburn hair and his beautiful green eyes. Perhaps when they reached Nora's home she could buy new supplies so that she could do a proper sketch of her husband.

It was well after midnight when Nathan came back down to the cabin. Sara was sound asleep. She was curled up like a kitten in the chair. Her long curly hair hid most of her face, and she looked utterly feminine to him.

He didn't know how long he stood there staring at her. God, it felt right to have her close to him. He couldn't understand why he felt such contentment, even admitting that it was a dangerous reaction, for there wasn't any way in hell he would allow a woman to mean more to him than baggage would.

She was simply a means to an end, he told himself. And that was all.

Nathan stripped, washed, then went over to the table. He saw the sketch pad and gently pried it out of her grasp. Curiosity caught him, and he slowly thumbed through the work she'd done. There were a good ten or twelve drawings completed. They were all sketches of him.

He didn't know how to react. The drawings were amazingly well done. She'd certainly captured his size, his strength. But then her mind had taken a fanciful turn, he decided, for damn if he wasn't smiling in every last one of them.

Sara really was a hopeless romantic. The old woman had told him that Sara's head was in the clouds most of the time. He knew that comment wasn't exaggeration.

Yes, his wife was a foolish dreamer. And yet he stood there, lingering over one particular drawing for a long, long while. It was all wrong, of course, but it still held him mesmerized.

The picture showed him from the back, standing on the deck, next to the wheel, looking off into the fading sunset. It was as though she'd sneaked up behind him to catch him unawares. His hands were clasped on the wheel. He was barefoot and shirtless. Only a hint of his profile was visible, just enough to tell that he was supposed to be smiling.

There weren't any scars on his back.

Had she forgotten about them, or had she decided she didn't want to include his scars in her work? Nathan decided the issue wasn't important enough to think about any longer. He had scars, and she'd damn well better accept them. He shook his head over that ridiculous reaction, then lifted Sara into his arms and put her to bed.

Nathan left the trap open so that the cabin would be rid of the lingering smoke, and he stretched out next to her.

She immediately rolled over and cuddled up against his side. "Nathan?"

"What?"

He made his voice as harsh as possible so she'd realize that he didn't want to talk to her.

His message was lost on her. She scooted closer to him and put her hand on his chest. Her fingers toyed with the thick hair until he flattened his own hand on top of hers. "Stop that," he ordered.

She put her head down on his shoulder. "Why do you think I'm having such a difficult time adjusting to ship life?" she asked in a whisper.

He answered her with a shrug that would have sent her flying into the wall if he hadn't been holding her.

"Do you think it might be because I'm not used to running a vessel?"

He rolled his eyes heavenward. "You aren't supposed to run my ship," he answered. "I am."

"But as your wife I should—"

"Go to sleep."

"Help," she said at the very same time.

She kissed the side of his neck. "I'll do much better when we're on land, Nathan. I can run a large household, and—"

"For God's sake, Sara, you don't have to run through your list of accomplishments again."

She stiffened against him, then relaxed. She must have finally decided to obey him, he thought to himself. The woman was going to go to sleep.

"Nathan?"

He should have known better, he told himself. She wasn't going to sleep until she was good and ready.

"What is it?"

"You forgot to kiss me goodnight."

God, she was aggravating. Nathan let out a weary sigh. He knew he wouldn't get any sleep until he gave in to her. His wife could be quite singleminded. She was more nuisance than not, he told himself. At the moment he was hard pressed to think of any redeeming qualities she might possess. Why, she was as stubborn as a mule, as bossy as a mother-in-law, and those were just two of the numerous flaws he'd already noticed.

He did kiss her, though, fast and hard, just to get her to quit nagging him. Damn but she tasted good, he thought. He had to kiss her again. He used his tongue. So did she. The kiss was far more thorough, more arousing.

She squeezed herself up against him. The provocation was too much to resist. She was all soft and feminine. He had to make love to her then. He didn't even make her nag him into doing that duty. She was still a little resistant, though. When he ordered her to take her nightgown off and turned to light the candle she asked him to leave them in darkness. He told her no, that he wanted to watch her, and she turned crimson before trying to hide her body from him by pulling the covers up to her chin.

He tossed the blankets aside and set about the task of wooing the shyness out of her. In no time at all she became quite brazen. She wanted to touch him everywhere with her hands and her mouth. He let her have her way, of course, until he was so hot for her he was shaking with his desire.

Lord, she was the most incredibly giving woman he'd ever touched. There was always such honesty in her reactions, such trust. That worried him. She didn't hold anything back, that sweet temptress of his, and when he finally settled himself between her silky thighs she was wet and hot and begging him to come to her.

He wanted to take it slow and easy, to make each thrust last forever, but she made him forget his good intentions by squeezing him tightly inside her. The sting of her nails drove him wild, and the erotic little whimpers she made soon forced him to let go of his own control.

He spilled his seed into her at the moment she found her own release. He held her close, absorbing her shudders with his own.

The scent of their lovemaking clung to the air between them. The feeling of peace was there, too.

He tried to roll away from her. She wouldn't let him. Her arms were tightly wrapped around his waist. The restraint was puny, but he decided to stay for a few more minutes, until she'd calmed down just a little. Her heartbeat still sounded like a drumbeat, as did his own.

He could feel the wetness on his shoulder, knew she'd cried again. That amused him. Sara always ended up crying when she found her own release. She always screamed, too. His name. She'd excused her behavior by telling him they were tears of joy she wept because she'd never experienced such bliss.

Neither had he, he thought to himself. For the second time that night the realization worried him.

"I love you, Nathan."

That scared the hell out of him. He reacted to her whispered pledge as though he'd just been slashed with a whip. His accommodating body went from warm flesh to cold steel in the space of a heartbeat. She let go of him. He rolled over onto his side away from her. She suddenly found herself staring at his back.

She waited for him to acknowledge her words of love. Long minutes passed before she accepted the fact that he wasn't going to say anything. His snoring helped her come to that conclusion.

She felt like crying. She didn't, though, and found a small victory in that new strength. Then she concentrated on finding something else to be pleased about.

At least he hadn't left the cabin after they'd made love, she thought to herself. She supposed she should be thankful for that. But in truth, she wasn't overly thankful.

She was shivering. Sara rolled away from Nathan's heat and reached for the quilts. When she was finally settled under the blankets she and Nathan were back to back.

She felt lonely, vulnerable. And it was all his fault, she thought to herself. He was the one who was making her feel so miserable. She decided then and there that if it wasn't her sole duty to love him with all her heart, she just might hate him. Lord, he was coldhearted. Stubborn, too. He had to know how much she needed to hear his words of love and yet he refused to give them to her.

He did love her, didn't he? Sara thought about that worry a long while. Then Nathan rolled over and took her into his arms again. He grumbled in his sleep as he roughly pulled her up against his chest. Her hair was caught under his shoulder. His chin rubbed the top of her head in what she thought was an affectionate gesture, and she suddenly didn't mind that he'd forgotten to tell her he loved her.

She closed her eyes and tried to go to sleep. Nathan did love her, she told herself. His mind was just having a little difficulty accepting what his heart already knew . . . had always known, she corrected herself, from the moment they were wed to each other.

In time her husband would realize. Why, it was only because he had such a cranky disposition that it was taking him longer to accept than it would most ordinary husbands.

"I do love you, Nathan," she whispered against his neck.

His voice was gruff from sleep yet tender when he said, "I know, baby. I know."

He was snoring again before she could gather enough nerve to ask him if he'd been pleased by her fervent declaration.

She still couldn't go to sleep. She spent another hour trying to think of a way to make Nathan realize his good fortune in having her for his wife.

The way to Nathan's heart certainly wasn't through his stomach, she decided. He wasn't about to eat anything she prepared for him. The man was distrustful by nature, and her soup had soured him on her cooking skills.

She finally settled on a sound plan. She'd sneak up on her husband by way of his staff. If she could prove her value to the crew, wouldn't Nathan begin to see how wonderful she really was? It shouldn't be difficult to convince the men how goodhearted and sincere their mistress was. Yes, they were a superstitious lot to be sure, but men were only men, after all, and gentle words and kind actions would surely woo their loyalty.

Why, if she really put her mind to the problem she could certainly find a true method to win the men's loyalty in less than a week.

Chapter Nine

They were all wearing cloves of garlic around their necks by the end of the week in an attempt to ward off Lady Sara's mischief.

She'd spent the entire seven days trying to gain their confidence. When she found out why they were wearing the smelly necklaces she was so disgusted with her staff that she quit trying to win them over.

She also quit running back to her cabin whenever they glared at her. She just pretended she hadn't noticed. She wasn't about to let any of them know how upsetting their conduct was to her. She kept her composure and her tears firmly in check.

Only Nathan and Nora knew how she really felt. Sara kept both of them informed about her injured feelings. Nathan did his best to ignore the situation. Nora did her best to soothe her niece.

The problem, of course, was that each minor accident, no matter what the cause, was blamed solely on Sara's very presence. They thought the woman was cursed, and that was

181

that. The minute Chester noticed a fresh wart on his hand he blamed Sara. His hand had brushed against hers, he remembered, when they passed on deck.

How could she reason against such idiocy? Sara put that question to Nathan at least twice a day. His answers never made a lick of sense, though. He either grunted with what she interpreted as true irritation or shrugged with what she knew was total indifference to her plight. He was as sympathetic as a goat, and each time he finished giving her his oblique opinion she kissed him just to be contrary.

By the following Monday Sara didn't think her life could get any bleaker. But then, she hadn't counted on the pirates They attacked the ship on Tuesday morning.

It started out to be a nice, sunny, peaceful day. Matthew was taking Nora for a stroll along the decks. Nora's arm was linked through Matthew's, and the two of them took turns whispering to each other and laughing like children. The elderly couple had become extremely close over the past weeks. Sara thought Matthew was just as smitten as Nora appeared to be. He had taken to smiling quite a lot, and Nora seemed to be blushing just as often.

When Sara set out on her stroll Jimbo walked beside her. She was never allowed to be alone. She believed it was because her staff had turned so belligerent on her. When she made that comment to Jimbo, though, he shook his head.

"That might be a little part of it," he said, "but the full truth is that the captain doesn't want anything else broken, Sara. That's why you've got yourself a guard trailing you day and night."

"Oh, the shame of it all," Sara cried out.

Jimbo had difficulty holding back his grin. Sara was certainly given to drama. He didn't want her to think he was laughing at her, though. "Now, now, it isn't that terrible," he remarked. "You needn't sound so forlorn."

Sara was quick to rally. Her face heated up, and she let him see her irritation. "So that's how it's to be, is it?" she asked. "A few little mishaps and I'm now condemned by my

staff as a witch and condemned by my own husband as a
defiler of property? Jimbo, must I remind you that nothing
out of the ordinary has happened since the fire, and that was
over seven days ago. Surely the men will come to their
senses in time."

"Nothing out of the ordinary?" Jimbo repeated. "You
cannot be serious, Sara. Have you forgotten Dutton's little
mishap, then?"

He would have to bring up that unfortunate incident. Sara
gave him a disgruntled look. "He didn't drown, Jimbo."

Jimbo rolled his eyes heavenward. "No, he didn't
drown," he agreed. "But it was mighty close."

"And I did apologize to the man."

"Aye, you did," Jimbo said. "But what about Kently and
Taylor?"

"Which ones are they?" Sara asked, deliberately feigning
ignorance.

"The ones you knocked stupid two days ago when they
slipped on the cannon grease you spilled," he reminded her.

"You cannot place the blame for that solely on my
shoulders."

"I can't?" he asked. He was eager to hear the excuse she
would give to explain away those injuries. "You did spill the
grease, didn't you?"

"Yes," she admitted. "But I was on my way to fetch a rag
to mop up the mess when those men rushed past me. If they
hadn't been in such a hurry to get away from me, they would
have stopped, of course, and I could have warned them
about the slippery deck. So you see, Jimbo, the blame really
belongs on their superstitious shoulders."

The shouted warning of a ship in the distance stopped
their conversation. Within a blink of the eye the deck was
filled with men running to their posts.

Sara didn't understand what all the commotion was
about. Nathan bellowed her name before Jimbo could give
her a proper explanation.

"Nathan, I didn't do it," she cried out when she saw him

striding toward her. "Whatever has happened, I swear to
you that I had nothing to do with it."

That vehement speech gave Nathan pause. He actually
smiled at her before grabbing hold of her hand and dragging
her toward their cabin.

"I know you're not responsible," he told her, "though the
men will probably blame you all the same."

"What is it they're going to blame me for this time?" she
asked.

"We're about to have some unwanted guests, Sara."

"Unwanted?" she whispered.

They reached their cabin. Nathan pulled her inside but
left the door open. It was obvious he wasn't planning on
staying long. "Pirates," he explained.

The color immediately left her face.

"Don't you dare faint on me," he ordered, though he was
already reaching out to catch her in the event she decided
not to obey him.

She pushed his hands away. "I'm not going to swoon," she
announced. "I'm furious, Nathan, not frightened. Damn if
I'll let my staff think I've brought on pirates, too. Make them
go away, Nathan. I'm not up to another upset."

They were in for quite a battle, Nathan knew, but he
wasn't going to share that information with his wife. In
truth, he was worried, for he knew he should have used the
faster clipper for their journey. They would never be able to
outrun the bastards closing in on them. The *Seahawk* was
too bulky and too weighted down to accomplish that feat.

"Give me your promise that you'll be careful," Sara
demanded.

He ignored that command. "Matthew took Nora below,"
he said. "Stay here until he comes for you."

After giving her that order he turned and strode out the
doorway. Sara ran after him. He was forced to stop when she
threw her arms around his waist. It was either that or drag
her up the steps with him. Nathan turned around then,
peeling her hands away as he moved. "For God's sake,

woman, now isn't the time to demand a good-bye kiss," he roared.

She was about to tell him, no, that certainly wasn't the reason she'd stopped him, but he waylaid her intent by giving her a quick kiss.

When he pulled away she smiled at him. "Nathan, now isn't the time to be . . . romantic," she said. "You have a fight on your hands. Do see to it."

"Then why did you stop me?" he demanded to know.

"I wanted you to promise me you'd be careful."

"You're deliberately trying to make me crazy, aren't you, Sara? It's all a plot to make me lose my mind, isn't it?"

She didn't answer that ridiculous question. "Promise me, Nathan. I won't let go of your shirt until you do. I love you, and I'll worry unless you give me your word."

"Fine," he countered. "I'll be careful. Happy now?"

"Yes, thank you."

She turned and hurried back into her cabin to prepare herself for the coming battle. She rushed over to the desk drawers, intending to find as many weapons as possible. If the pirates were actually successful in breaching the ship, Sara was determined to help her husband any way that she could.

She found two loaded pistols in the bottom drawer and one wickedly sharp dagger in the center slot. Sara tucked the knife into the sleeve of her gown and put the pistols in a blue reticule. She wrapped the strings of the purse around her wrist just as Matthew came charging into the cabin. A loud booming sound echoed in the distance. "Was that one of our cannons or one of theirs?" Sara asked, her voice shivering with her worry.

Matthew shook his head. "It was one of theirs," he answered. "They missed their mark. They aren't close enough to do any damage yet. That's the reason we aren't firing our own cannons, Sara. Come with me now. I've got Nora safely tucked away below the water level. You can wait it out there with her."

Sara didn't argue, knowing full well that Nathan was behind the order, but she felt very cowardly. It didn't seem honorable to her to hide.

It was pitch black in the hull. Matthew went down the rickety steps first. He lifted her over the first rung, explaining that the wood was filled with rot and would be replaced just as soon as he had time for the chore.

When they reached the bottom and turned a sharp corner the soft glow of a single candle led the way to where Nora patiently waited.

Sara's aunt was settled on top of a wooden box. Her bright red shawl was draped around her shoulders. The older woman didn't look at all afraid. "We're about to have an adventure," she called out to her niece. "Matthew, dear, do be careful."

Matthew nodded. "It would be an adventure all right, if we didn't have such precious cargo on board," he announced.

"What precious cargo?" Sara asked.

"I believe he's referring to you and me, dear," Nora explained.

"Aye," Matthew agreed. He started back up the squeaky steps. "Now we've got to defend instead of offend," he added. "It's going to be a first for the crew."

Sara didn't know what he was talking about. It was apparent that Nora did understand, though. Her smile said as much. "What do you suppose Matthew meant by that remark, Aunt?" she asked.

Nora briefly considered telling Sara, then just as quickly discarded the notion. She decided that her niece was too innocent to understand. Sara still saw everything as good or evil. In her idealistic mind there weren't any shades of gray. In time she would come to understand that life wasn't that simple. Then she would be able to accept the fact that Nathan had led a rather colorful life. Nora hoped she would be there when Sara was told she was married to Pagan. She smiled just thinking about her niece's reaction to that news.

186

"I believe the crew would fight more vigorously if they didn't have to keep us safe," Nora said.

"That doesn't make any sense," Sara argued.

Nora agreed but changed the topic instead of saying so. "Is this where the munitions are kept?"

"I believe it is," Sara answered. "Do you suppose those kegs are filled with powder?"

"They must be," Nora said. "We must watch the candle flame. If a fire started down here—well, I needn't tell you what could happen. Don't let me forget to blow out the flame when Matthew comes to fetch us."

The ship suddenly felt as though it had just let out a giant belch. It shook from aft to stern. "Do you think they hit us with that shot?" Sara asked.

"It certainly felt as though they did," Nora answered.

"Nathan had better finish this quickly. My nerves cannot take such an upset. Nora, you and Matthew have become very close, haven't you?"

"What a time you've chosen to ask me that," Nora said with a little chuckle.

"I just wanted to take our minds off the worry at hand," Sara replied.

"Yes, that might be a good idea. And you're right, Matthew and I have become quite close. He's such a gentle, understanding man. I'd quite forgotten how comforting it is to be able to confide my thoughts and worries in someone who cares about me."

"I care about you, Aunt."

"Yes, dear, I know you do, but it isn't at all the same. You'll understand what I'm saying when you and Nathan become a little closer."

"I fear that day will never come," Sara returned. "Does Matthew confide in you as well?" she asked.

"Oh, yes, often."

"Has he talked about Nathan much?"

"Several times," Nora admitted. "Some things were given in confidence, of course, and so I cannot speak about—"

"Of course you can," Sara interrupted. "I'm your niece, after all, and anything you would tell me wouldn't go any further. You do trust me, don't you, Nora?"

Sara kept up her prodding for another ten minutes or so before Nora finally relented. "Matthew told me all about Nathan's father. Did you ever meet the Earl of Wakersfield?"

Sara shook her head. "It's said that he died when Nathan was just a boy, Nora. I couldn't have been more than a babe. I did hear that he was knighted, though."

"Yes, he was knighted. It was all a sham, though. Matthew told me that the earl actually betrayed his country while he was in service. Yes, that's true, Sara," she added when her niece let out a gasp. "It's a horrifying story, child. Nathan's father was in cahoots with two other infidels, and the three thought they could overturn the government. They called themselves the Tribunal, and as Matthew related the sequence of events to me, they almost pulled off their treacherous scheme. Nathan's father had second thoughts, though. His conscience got him killed before the truth was let out."

Sara was horrified by what she'd just learned. "Poor Nathan," she whispered. "The shame must have been unbearable."

"No, not at all," Nora returned. "You see, no one knows the full truth. It's still believed that the earl was killed in a carriage accident. There hasn't been any scandal. I warn you that if your family got wind of this, they'd use the information to get the prince to overturn your marriage contract."

"Oh, it's too late for that," Sara returned.

"You're being naïve if you believe that it's too late, Sara. The circumstances were so unusual, what with the king not feeling at all well."

"He was daft," Sara whispered.

"And you were only four years old," her aunt whispered back.

"Still, we are living as man and wife now. I don't believe the prince regent would dare overturn—"

"He can dare whatever he wants to dare," Nora argued.

"Your worry doesn't signify," Sara interjected. "I'm not going to tell anyone about Nathan's father, so my parents aren't ever going to find out. I won't even let Nathan know that I know, all right? He'll have to confide in me first."

Nora was appeased. "Do you know I also found out how Nathan's back was injured?"

"I believe someone took a whip to him," Sara returned.

"No, it wasn't a whip," Nora countered. "His back was scarred by fire, not a whip. You only have to look to realize that, child."

Sara felt sick to her stomach. "Oh, God, was it deliberate? Did someone burn him on purpose?"

"I believe so, but I can't be certain. I do know a woman was involved. Her name was Ariah. Nathan met her when he was visiting a foreign port in the east."

"How did Nathan meet this woman?"

"I wasn't given the details," Nora admitted. "I do know that this Ariah has rather loose morals. She dallied with Nathan."

Sara let out a little gasp. "Do you mean to say that Nathan was intimate with this harlot?"

Nora reached out and patted Sara's hand. "Nathan was just sowing his oats, dear, before he settled down. There's no need to get yourself all worked up."

"Do you think he loved her?"

"No, of course he didn't love her. He was already pledged to you, Sara. Nathan strikes me as being terribly sensible. He wouldn't have allowed himself to fall in love with the woman. And I'll wager you my inheritance that when Ariah was finished with him he most likely hated her. Matthew told me that the woman used Nathan to manipulate her other lover. Yes, it's true," she added in a rush when Sara looked disbelieving. "According to Matthew, Ariah was a master at her game. For that reason I do believe Nathan was tortured by her command. Thank the Lord, he was able to escape. It was during a small revolution, you see, and those sympathetic to the anarchists aided him when they released the other prisoners. Then Jimbo and Matthew took over Nathan's care."

"Nathan has certainly had a time of it, hasn't he?" Sara whispered. Her voice shook with emotion. "He must have been very young when that horrid woman betrayed him. I believe he loved her, too, Nora."

"I believe he didn't," Nora countered.

Sara let out a weary sigh. "It would be nice if it was just a dalliance," she said. "And if they did share the same bed, well, he wasn't really being unfaithful to me, because we hadn't started our married life together. You know, it's all beginning to make sense to me now."

"What is beginning to make sense?"

"I hadn't confided this to you before, but I have noticed that Nathan seems to be very concerned with protecting his feelings. Now I think I understand why. He doesn't trust women. I cannot fault him. If your fingers are burned once, you won't put your hand near the fire again, will you?"

"It was a long time ago," Nora replied. "Nathan is a grown man now, Sara, and surely he has sorted all this out in his mind."

Sara shook her head. "How else can you explain his attitude? Nathan doesn't like it at all when I tell him I love him. He stiffens up on me and goes all cold. And he's never once told me he cares for me. He just might still hate all women—except me, of course."

Nora smiled. "Except you?"

"I believe he does love me, Nora. He's just having difficulty knowing that he does."

"Give him time, dear. Men take so much longer to figure things out. It's because they're such stubborn beasts, you see."

Sara was in wholehearted agreement with that remark. "If I ever chance to meet this Ariah woman, I'll—"

"You've a good chance of meeting up with her," Nora

interjected. "She has been living in London for the past year
or so. Matthew says she's looking for yet another sponsor."

"Does Nathan know she's in England?"

"I would imagine so," Nora countered.

The noise became too loud for the two of them to
continue the discussion. While Nora fretted about the battle
Sara worried over the information her aunt had just shared
with her.

Another twenty or thirty minutes passed. Then a chilling
silence filled the ship. "If I could just see what's happening, I
wouldn't be so worried," Nora whispered.

Sara thought that was a fine idea. "I'll just sneak up to the
cabin level and see if everything is ail right."

Nora was vehemently against that suggestion. The hatch
opened in the middle of their argument and the two women
fell silent. They both began to pray that it was Matthew
coming down to collect them. Yet when no one called down
to them they drew the terrifying conclusion that the enemy
had indeed taken over the ship. Sara motioned to Nora to
squeeze herself into the corner behind a large crate, then
turned and blew out the candle. She worked her way over to
the side of the steps to wait for her chance to fell the villains.

God, she was scared. That didn't stop her, though. Her
first consideration was Nathan. If the enemy really was on
board, was her husband dead or alive? She pictured him
lying in a pool of blood, then forced herself to block the
horrid thought. She wouldn't be any help to her husband if
she let her imagination get the better of her.

A bit of light shone down when the hatch was fully
opened. It was no thicker than a straight pin, but still
enough for Sara to see two men wearing brightly colored
scarves on their heads coming down the stairs.

The first pirate missed the weak rung in the steps. The
second one didn't. He let out a low blasphemy when he fell
through the narrow opening. The man ended up wedged
between the slats. His feet dangled below him, and his arms
were pinned to his sides.

"What the hell?" the first man muttered when he turned around. "You got yourself trapped, don't you?" he added with a snicker. He was reaching out to pull the board free but came to a sudden stop when he felt a quick breeze brush his face.

The enemy was in the process of turning around again when Sara slammed the butt of her pistol into the back of his skull. She was apologizing when he crumpled to the ground.

He didn't cry out. She did. Then she noticed that he was still breathing, and she immediately calmed down, relieved to see that he wasn't dead.

Sara lifted the hem of her dress and daintily jumped over the fallen man. She hurried up the steps to confront her second victim. The ugly man was squinting up at her with the most astonished look on his face. If he hadn't been staring directly at her, she might have been able to hit him, too. She didn't have the heart for such treachery, though, for the villain was already pinned down and at her mercy, so she ended up tearing a piece of fabric from her petticoat and stuffing the thing into his mouth to keep him from crying out for help. Nora came to her assistance then and helped her tie up the man from arms to feet.

Her aunt seemed to be taking the situation quite well. Sara thought Nora just didn't understand the severity of their circumstance. If men had breached the munitions hold, then others had to be on board, too.

"Look, dear, I've found some rope. Shall I tie up the other gentleman for you?"

Sara nodded. "Yes, that would be a splendid idea. He might wake up at any moment. Do put a rag in his mouth, too. Here, use some of my petticoat. The thing's quite ruined now."

She paused to tear another long strip, then handed it to her aunt. "We wouldn't want him shouting for help, now would we, Nora?"

"We most certainly wouldn't," her aunt agreed.

Sara tried to press one of the pistols into her hands, but her aunt declined the weapon. "You might need both when you save Matthew and Nathan, dear."

"You've certainly placed a burden upon my shoulders," Sara whispered. "I'm not so certain I can save anyone."

"Go along now," Nora ordered. "You have the element of surprise on your side, Sara. I'll wait here until you've finished your task."

Sara would have hugged her aunt farewell, but she was afraid one of the pistols might discharge.

She prayed all the way up to the cabin level. The wardroom area was deserted. Sara was about to look inside her cabin when she heard the sounds of men starting down the steps. She squeezed herself into the triangular corner behind the folded screen and waited.

Jimbo came stumbling down the stairs first. Sara got a good look at her friend by peeking through the seam in the screen. Jimbo had a fair-sized cut in his forehead. Blood trickled down the side of his face. He couldn't wipe the blood away, for his hands were tied behind his back, and he was surrounded by three pirates.

The sight of the injury made Sara forget to be afraid. She was furious.

Sara saw that Jimbo was looking toward the steps. She heard additional footsteps, and then Nathan came into view. Like the shipmate, Nathan had his hands tied behind his back. Sara was so thankful he was still alive, she started shaking. The look on her husband's face made her smile a little, too. He looked downright bored.

She watched him give Jimbo a nod. It was so quick, so fleeting, she knew she would have missed it if she hadn't been watching him so closely. Then Jimbo turned his head just a little toward the screen.

She guessed then that Nathan knew she was hiding there. Sara looked down, saw that the bottom of her dress was half-protruding, and quickly pulled her skirt back.

"Take them inside the cabin," a mean voice ordered.

Nathan was being shoved forward again. He stumbled, turned in what looked like an attempt to keep himself from falling to his knees, and ended up pushing against the corner of the screen. His hands were just a foot or so away.

"Here comes Banger with the grog," another man called out. "We can have us a toast while we see to the killing. Perry, you going to let their captain die first or last?"

While that question was being asked Sara put one of the pistols into Nathan's hands. When he didn't immediately take advantage of the edge she'd given him she gave him a little nudge.

He didn't show any reaction to her prodding. She waited another minute, and when he still didn't fire she remembered his hands were tied.

She recalled the dagger in the sleeve of her gown, too, and immediately went to work cutting through the thick ropes. She accidentally pricked his skin twice. Then Nathan grabbed hold of the blade with his fingers and took over the task.

It seemed that an eternity had passed, yet she knew not even a full minute had actually gone by.

"Where the hell is the captain?" another voice shouted. "I'm wanting my grog."

So they were waiting for their leader before they began their murderous festivities, Sara concluded.

Why was Nathan waiting? His hands were free, but he was acting as though they weren't. He held the knife by the blade, probably so that he would be ready to hurl the thing when the time came. The pistol was in his other hand, pointed to the floor.

He looked ready to do battle, all right, but still he waited. He was squeezing her against the wall. Sara was surprised the hinges to the screen he pressed against hadn't already snapped from his weight.

Nathan was obviously giving her his silent message to stay put.

As if she was in the mood to go anywhere, she thought to herself. Lord, she was getting worried again. Why didn't her husband take over the advantage now? Was he waiting for the number of pirates to double from five to ten before he acted? Sara decided then to give him a little message of her own. She reached around the side of the screen and pinched him in his backside.

He didn't react. She pinched him again. She pulled her hand back when she heard the sound of another man coming down the stairs. It was obviously the leader of the pirates, for one of his men called out to him that it was high time they all had a taste of grog before getting on with their work.

One of the other villains rushed across the wardroom and opened the door to her cabin. He went inside, then came rushing back a scant second or two later. The infidel was holding one of her gowns in his hands. It was her light blue dress, her very favorite, and the filthy man had his hands all over it.

She vowed she'd never wear that gown again.

"We got us a woman on board, Captain," the foul man called out.

Their leader stood with his back to Sara so she couldn't get a proper look at his face. She was a little thankful for that reprieve. His size alone was terrifying enough. The man stood shoulder to shoulder with Nathan.

The captain let out a low, disgusting snicker that made Sara feel as though there were bugs crawling all over her skin. "Find the bitch," he ordered. "When I'm finished with her you men can each take a turn."

Sara put her hand over her mouth to keep herself from gagging.

"Ah, Captain," another man called out, "she'll be dead afore we get our chance."

A round of snickers followed that remark. Sara wanted to weep. She'd heard all she wanted to hear about their foul plans. She pinched Nathan again. Harder. She nudged him, too.

He finally gave in to her request. He moved like lightning. He turned into a blur when he rushed toward the two men standing in front of their cabin door. Yet even as he was moving he threw his knife. The blade found its mark between the eyes of a villain lounging by the steps. The shot from his pistol brought down another infidel.

Nathan slammed his shoulders into the two men blocking the door. The force of the blow sent both infidels inside. Nathan followed them. He made short work of the battle by knocking their heads together.

Jimbo used his head to fell the pirates' leader. His hands were still tied behind his back, and the hit only knocked the captain off balance. He was quick to recover. He clipped Jimbo on the side of his neck and shoved him to the floor. The captain kicked him aside. It wasn't a terribly accurate kick, though, for the leader wasn't really watching what he was doing. His full attention was centered on digging the pistol out of his pocket.

Nathan had just started out the doorway when the leader raised his pistol. There was venom in his voice when he hissed, "You're going to die slow and painfully."

Sara was too outraged to be afraid. She skirted her way around the screen and silently moved to stand directly behind the villain's back. Then she pressed the tip of her pistol against the base of his skull. "You're going to die quick and easy," she whispered.

When the leader felt the touch of cold steel he went as rigid as a day-old corpse. Sara was pleased by that reaction. So was Nathan, she noticed. He actually smiled.

She smiled back. Things weren't looking so very bleak, she thought. Still, she didn't know if she'd be able to kill the man. It was a test she didn't want to fail. Her husband's life was dependent upon her courage, after all.

"Nathan?" she called out. "Would you like me to shoot between the ears or in the neck this time?"

That bluff worked nicely. "This time?" her victim strangled out.

It wasn't good enough, though. He was still pointing his pistol at Nathan.

"Yes, this time, you stupid man," she said. She tried to make her voice sound as mean as possible, and thought she'd succeeded rather well, too.

"What's your preference?" Nathan called out. He deliberately leaned against the side of the doorway, giving the appearance of being very relaxed.

"The neck," Sara answered. "Don't you remember the mess it was cleaning up after the last one? The stains didn't come out for a week. Still, this infidel seems to have a smaller brain. Oh, you decide. I'm ever obedient."

The leader's hand fell to his side, and his pistol dropped to the floor. Sara thought victory was secure, yet before Nathan could get to the man he suddenly whirled around. The back of his fist slammed into her left cheek in an awkward move to knock the pistol out of her hand.

Sara heard Nathan's roar. She staggered backwards, tripped over Jimbo's big feet, and promptly discharged the pistol. A howl of pain followed that sound, and her enemy grabbed at his face.

It seemed to take her a long, long time to fall to the floor. Everything was in slow motion, and her last thought before she let her faint overtake her was a horrifying one. Good God, she'd shot the villain in his face.

Sara awakened a few minutes later. She found herself in bed with Matthew and Jimbo both leaning over her. Matthew held a cold cloth to the side of her face. Jimbo fanned her with one of the charts from Nathan's desk.

Her husband wasn't there. As soon as Sara realized that fact she tossed the coverlet aside and tried to stand up. Jimbo pressed her back down. "Stay put, Sara. You took quite a hit. The side of your face is already swelling up."

She ignored his instructions. "Where's Nathan?" she asked. "I want him here with me."

Before Jimbo could answer her he found himself sitting on the bed. Sara snatched the cold cloth away from Matthew and began to clean the cut in Jimbo's forehead.

"The woman's little, but she's mighty when she's riled, isn't she, Matthew?" Jimbo muttered, trying to sound surly. "Quit your fussing over me," he grumbled.

She didn't pay any attention to that dictate. "Matthew, do you think he's going to be all right? The cut doesn't look overly deep to me, but perhaps . . ."

"He'll be fine," Matthew answered.

Sara nodded. Then she turned the topic back to her other worry. "A husband should comfort his wife when she's been felled," she announced. "Anyone with an ounce of sense would know that. Matthew, go and fetch Nathan. By God, he's going to comfort me, or I'll know the reason why."

"Now, Sara," Matthew interjected, using his soothing tone of voice, "your husband happens to be the captain of this ship, and he's having to see to a few important . . . details right now. Besides, you wouldn't want his company just yet. The boy's in a killing rage."

"Because the pirates boarded his fine ship?"

"Because the bastard struck you, Sara," Jimbo muttered. "You were sleeping, Sara, after that hit, so you didn't get to see your husband's face. It was a sight I won't soon forget. I've never seen him so furious."

"That's nice to know," Sara whispered.

The two shipmates shared a look of true exasperation. Sara ignored the men, for she'd just remembered the mortal sin she'd committed. "Oh, God, I shot their leader in his face," she cried out. "I'm damned to hell now, aren't I?"

"You were saving your husband at the time," Jimbo interjected. "You won't be going to hell, Sara."

"He'll be . . . ugly for the rest of his days," she whispered.

"Nay, Sara, he already was ugly," Matthew told her.

"I wished you'd killed the bastard," Jimbo said. "As it is, you just shot his nose—"

"My God, I shot his—"

"You're getting her all worked up, Jimbo," Matthew muttered.

"Did I shoot that poor man's nose completely off his face?"

"Poor man?" Jimbo scoffed. "He's the devil's own, that one. Do you know what would have happened to you if—"

"The bastard's still got a nose," Matthew interjected. He gave his friend a dark scowl. "Quit worrying her, Jimbo," he ordered before turning back to Sara. "You just put a little hole in his nose, that's all."

"You saved the day, Sara," Jimbo told her then.

That remark did cheer her up considerably. "I did save the day, didn't I?"

Both men nodded.

"Does my staff know I . . ." She quit her question when they nodded again. "Well, then, they can't think me cursed any longer, can they?"

Before either man could answer that question she asked another. "What details did Nathan have to see about?"

"Retaliation," Jimbo announced. "It will be an eye for an eye, Sara. They were going to kill us—"

He never finished his explanation. Lady Sara let out an outraged gasp and ran out of the cabin. Both Jimbo and Matthew chased after her.

Nathan was standing by the wheel. The pirates who'd tried to take over their ship were lined up across the deck. Nathan's men surrounded them.

Sara hurried over to her husband's side. She touched his arm to gain his attention. He didn't look at her but kept his gaze directed on the leader of the pirates standing a few feet away from him.

When Sara looked at the man she instinctively took a step forward. The villain had a rag in his hands and was holding it against his nose. She wanted to tell him she was sorry she'd injured him. She also wanted to remind him that it was all his fault, for if he hadn't struck her, the pistol wouldn't have gone off.

Nathan must have guessed her intention. He grabbed her arm in a hold that stung and literally jerked her up against his side.

"Go back below," he ordered in a soft don't-you-dare-argue-with-me tone of voice.

"Not until you tell me what you're going to do to them," she announced.

Nathan might have been able to soften the truth for his gentle wife's benefit if he hadn't glanced down at her first. As soon as he saw the swelling on the side of her face his rage returned full force. "We're going to kill them."

He turned back to his crew before giving her his order again. "Go back to our cabin, Sara. It will be over in a few minutes."

She wasn't going anywhere. She folded her arms in front of her and stiffened her posture. "You will not kill them."

She'd shouted that command. She'd gained her husband's full attention, too. And his wrath. He looked like he wanted to kill her.

"The hell I won't," he countered in a low growl.

Sara heard several grunts of approval from Nathan's men. She was about to repeat her disapproval, but Nathan took the bluster right out of her when he suddenly reached out and gently touched the side of her face. He leaned down just a little and then whispered, "He hurt you, Sara. I have to kill him."

It all made perfectly good sense to him, and he thought he'd been very reasonable by taking the time to explain his determination to her. She didn't understand, though. The incredulous look on her face indicated as much.

"Do you mean to tell me that you would kill everyone who has ever struck me?" she asked.

He didn't care for the censure in her voice. "Damn right," he muttered.

"Then you're going to have to kill half my family," she blurted out.

Lord, she really shouldn't have said that, she realized. He looked bloody furious again. Yet his voice was surprisingly mild when he gave her his answer. "You give me the names, Sara, and I'll retaliate. I promise you. No one touches what belongs to me."

"Aye, m'lady," Chester bellowed. "We mean to kill every last one of these bastards. It's our right," he added.

"Chester, if you use another blasphemy in my presence, I'll wash your mouth out with vinegar."

She gave the seaman a hard glare until he nodded, then turned back in time to catch Nathan's grin. "Nathan, you're the captain," she said. "Only you can make this important decision. Since I'm your wife, I should be able to sway you, shouldn't I?"

"No."

Oh, he was a stubborn one, she thought. "I won't have it," she shouted. The urge to stomp his foot was fairly over-whelming. "If you kill them, you're no better than they are. You'll all be villains then, Nathan, and since I'm your wife, I would also be a villain."

"But m'lady, we *are* villains." Ivan the Terrible made that statement.

"We are not villains," Sara announced. "We are all law-abiding, loyal citizens of the crown."

Sara's distress finally penetrated Nathan's fury. He put his arm around her shoulders. "Now, Sara—"

"Don't you dare now-Sara me," she interrupted. "Don't use that condescending tone of voice, either. You aren't going to be able to soothe me into allowing murder."

He wasn't in the mood to soothe or discuss, but he knew he was going to have to get her to go below before he unleashed his anger full force. He thought about ordering Jimbo to drag her down the stairs, then changed his mind and settled on an alternative plan of action. "Democracy will rule in this instance," he announced. "I'll put it to the vote of my men, Sara. Will that appease you?"

He was fully prepared for an argument before she gave in and was quite surprised when she immediately nodded. "Yes, that will certainly appease me."

"Fine," he replied. He turned back to the crew. "All those in favor—"

The hands were already going up into the air when Sara interrupted. "Just one minute, if you please."

"Now what?" Nathan growled.

"I have something to say to my staff before this vote is taken."

"Hell."

"Nathan, did I or did I not save the day?"

That question caught him off guard. Sara pressed her advantage. "Jimbo said I saved the day. Now I would like to hear you admit it, too."

"I had a plan," Nathan began. "But . . . hell, Sara, yes," he added with a sigh. "You saved the day. Happy now?"

She nodded.

"Then go below," he ordered again.

"Not just yet," she replied. She turned and smiled at her staff. She couldn't help but notice how impatient the men looked. That didn't deter her, however. "You all know that I was the one who untied Nathan," she called out. She realized that statement not only sounded like a boast but also made her husband sound a bit incapable. "Though, of course, he would have . . . untied himself if I hadn't beat him to the task, you see, and he did have a plan—"

"Sara," Nathan began in a warning tone of voice.

She quit rambling, straightened her shoulders, and then said, "And I shot the leader, though I'll admit to you that I didn't mean to hurt the man. Now he'll carry a scar for the rest of his days, and that should be enough punishment for anyone."

"It was a paltry hit at best," one of the men called out. "The shot went clean through his nostrils."

"She should have blown his head off," another shouted.

"Aye, she should have blinded him at the very least," yet another called out.

My God, they were a bloodthirsty lot, she thought. Sara took a deep breath and tried again. She waved her hand toward the pirate's leader and said, "That man has suffered enough."

"Yes, Sara," Matthew interjected with a grin. "He'll be thinking of you every time he's wanting to blow his nose."

A hearty round of laughter followed that remark. Then Chester took a threatening step forward. His hands were on his hips when he bellowed, "He won't be thinking about anything much longer. None of them will. They'll all be fish bait if the vote goes the way I'm thinking it will."

The vehemence in his tone unnerved Sara. She instinctively backed away from him until she was literally leaning against her husband's chest.

Nathan couldn't see her face, but he knew she was afraid. Without a thought as to why he was doing so he put his arm across her shoulders. She rested her chin on his wrist.

His touch had taken her fear away. She glared at Chester and said, "Were you born with a sour disposition, sir?"

The seaman didn't have a ready answer for that question and shrugged in reaction.

"All right, then," Sara shouted. "Have your vote." She pushed Nathan's arm away and took a step forward. "Just remember this," she hastily added when the hands shot back up in the air. "I'm going to be very disappointed if any of you vote in favor of death. Very disappointed," she added in a dramatic tone of voice. "If, on the other hand, you vote to toss the villains overboard and let them swim back to their ship, I would be very pleased. Does everyone understand my position?"

She scanned her audience until each man had given her a nod.

"That's it?" Nathan asked. He sounded incredulous. "That's all you have to say to sway the men?"

He actually smiled at her. She smiled back. "Yes, Nathan. You may vote now. I don't think you should be allowed to vote, though."

"Why not?" he asked before he could stop himself.

"Because you aren't thinking straight now."

The look on his face told her he didn't understand. "You see, Nathan, you're still very angry because . . . your dear wife was injured."

"My dear wife?"

She gave him a disgruntled look. "Me."

God, she was exasperating. "I know who the hell my wife is," he grumbled.

"Just leave it to your crew to decide," she prodded.

He agreed just to get her to leave. Sara forced a smile when she picked up her skirt and strolled toward the steps.

"Stay inside your cabin, Sara, until this is finished," Matthew ordered.

She could feel every man's gaze on her. She knew they were all waiting until she was out of sight before going forward with their shameful intentions. Jimbo had even closed the trapdoor to her cabin, she noticed, probably so that the horrid noise wouldn't reach her.

She didn't feel at all guilty for what she was about to do. Her motives were as white as fresh snow. She couldn't let her staff murder the pirates, no matter how dastardly their behavior had been; and once her men rid themselves of their anger they'd be thankful she'd intervened.

Sara stopped when she reached the top step. She didn't turn around. Her voice was very pleasant when she called out to her husband. "Nathan? I won't be waiting in the cabin, but do send someone to tell me how the voting went. I want to know if I should be disappointed or not."

Nathan frowned over that odd request. He knew she was up to something, but he couldn't imagine what she could possibly do to sway the men's minds.

"Where will you be waiting, m'lady?" Jimbo called out.

Sara turned around so that she could see their expressions when she gave her answer. "I'll be waiting in the galley."

It didn't take most of the men any time at all to catch her meaning. They looked horrified. Nathan, she noticed, was grinning at her. She glared back. Then she addressed her staff. "I didn't want to have to resort to such tactics, men, but you've left me with no alternative. The vote had better not disappoint me."

A few of the less astute seamen still didn't understand the hidden threat. Chester fell into that group. "What would you be doing in the galley, m'lady?"

Her answer was immediate. "Making soup."

Chapter Ten

The vote was unanimous. No one wanted Sara to be disappointed. The pirates were tossed overboard and allowed to swim back to their ship.

Nathan did have the last word, however, or rather the last action. He ordered two cannons made ready and took great satisfaction in putting a large hole in the pirates' vessel. When Sara asked what the noise was he told her they were simply emptying the cannons.

The *Seahawk* had suffered damage as well. Most of the repairs that needed to be seen to at once were above the water line. The very same sails Sara had nearly destroyed with her parasol had been sliced in half by one of the enemy's cannon shots.

The crew set about righting as much of the damage as possible. They smiled as they worked—a rarity—and every one of them had tossed his necklace of garlic cloves away. They were feeling safe again, for they believed the curse had been removed.

Their mistress had saved their hides. Why, even sour-tempered Chester was singing her praises.

Sara went with Matthew to fetch Nora from the hold, and it wasn't until the hatch was opened that she remembered the captives trapped below. Nathan waited until Sara had turned to leave the deck, then slammed his fist into the midsection of each man. The loud groans caught Sara's attention, yet when she turned around and asked her husband what the awful noise was he simply shrugged at her and then graciously helped the doubled-over captives to take flight over the rail.

Sara took great delight in retelling the sequence of events to Nora. Her aunt was an appreciative audience of one. She praised her niece for her courage and her cunning.

"I cannot let you believe I was completely courageous," Sara confessed. She stood with her aunt in the middle of the wardroom area. She'd already shown Nora where she'd hidden behind the screen. "I was terrified all the while," she added with a nod.

"That doesn't signify," Nora countered. "You helped your husband. It means all the more because you were afraid and yet you didn't fail him."

"Do you know Nathan hasn't said a word of praise to me?" Sara said. "I hadn't realized that until this very minute. You would think—"

"I would think he hasn't had time to say thank you, Sara, and I doubt he will when he does have the time. He's a bit . . ."

"Stubborn?"

Nora smiled. "No, dear, not stubborn, just proud."

Sara decided he was a little of both. The rush of excitement was over, but Sara's hands started shaking. She felt sick to her stomach, too, and the side of her face was throbbing quite painfully.

She wasn't going to worry Nora, though, and so she kept her aches and pains to herself.

"I know you've heard the whispers comparing you to Nathan's sister," Nora said.

She hadn't heard any such whispers, but she pretended

she had just so that her aunt would continue. Sara nodded and said, "Jade was mistress of this vessel for a long while, and the men were very loyal to her."

"I know their comments must have hurt your feelings, child," Nora said.

"Which comments are you referring to?" Sara asked. "I've heard so many."

"Oh, that you cry all the time," Nora answered. "Jade never cried. She kept her emotions under lock and key, or so Matthew likes to boast. She was extremely courageous, too. I've heard such wonderful stories about the feats she and her men accomplished. But you've heard all that," Nora continued with a wave of her hand. "I'm not bringing up this topic to make you think the men still believe you inferior, Sara. No, quite the opposite is the case now. Why, you've won their hearts and their loyalty today. They won't be making comparisons in future, I'll wager. They've seen you're every bit as courageous as their Jade."

Sara turned to go into her cabin. "I believe I'll have a little rest, Aunt," she whispered. "The excitement has worn me out."

"You do look pale, Sara. It was quite a morning, wasn't it? I believe I'll go find Matthew and, if he isn't too busy, spend a few minutes with him. Then I'm going to have a rest, too."

Sara's light blue walking dress was on the floor of the cabin. As soon as she shut the door behind her and spotted the gown she remembered how the infidel had clutched it in his arms. She remembered all the foul words they'd said, too.

It was finally settling in. The realization of what could have happened made her stomach lurch. "I mustn't think about all the possibilities," she whispered to herself.

Nathan could have been killed.

Sara unbuttoned her gown and took the garment off. Her petticoats, shoes, and stockings came next. She was excruciatingly exact with her task. Her gaze kept returning to the gown on the floor, though, and she couldn't block the memories.

They'd really meant to kill her husband.

Sara decided she needed something to do to take her mind off her fear. She cleaned the cabin. Then she took a sponge bath. By the time she was finished with that task the trembling had eased up just a little.

Then she noticed the dark bruise on the side of her face.

The terror returned full force. How could she ever live without Nathan? What if she hadn't thought to take the pistols with her to the hold? What if she'd stayed below with Nora and hadn't . . .

"Oh, God," she whispered. "It's all a mockery. I'm such a coward."

She leaned over the washstand and stared into the mirror. "An ugly coward."

"What did you say?"

Nathan asked that question. He'd entered the room without making any noise. Sara jumped a foot, then turned to look at him. She tried to hide the right side of her face by pulling her hair forward.

She realized she was crying. She didn't want Nathan to notice, though. She bowed her head and walked toward the bed. "I believe I'll have a nap," she whispered. "I'm very weary."

Nathan blocked her path. "Let me see your face," he ordered.

His hands rested on her hips. Sara's head was still bowed, and all he could see was the top of her head. He could feel her trembling. "Does it hurt, Sara?" he asked, his voice gruff with concern.

Sara shook her head. She still wouldn't look up at him. Nathan tried to nudge her chin up. She pushed his hand away. "It doesn't hurt at all," she lied.

"Then why are you crying?"

The tenderness in his voice made her trembling increase. "I'm not crying," she whispered.

Nathan was getting worried. He wrapped his arms around her waist and pulled her close. What the hell was going on inside her mind now? he wondered. Sara had always been so transparent to him. He never had to worry about what she was thinking. She always told him. Whenever she had a problem or a worry he knew about it immediately. And as soon as she'd blurted out whatever was on her mind she demanded that he fix it.

Nathan smiled to himself. And damn if he didn't always fix it, too, he thought.

"I would like to rest now, Nathan," she whispered, turning his thoughts back to her.

"You will tell me what's bothering you first," he ordered.

She burst into loud tears.

"Are you still not crying?" he asked in exasperation.

She nodded against his chest. "Jade never cries."

"What did you say?"

She wouldn't repeat herself. She tried to move away from him then, but Nathan wouldn't let her. He was more forceful, more determined. He held her secure with one arm and pushed her chin up. His touch was gentle when he brushed the hair away from her face.

When he saw the dark swelling on her cheek his expression turned murderous. "I should have killed the bastard," he whispered.

"I'm a coward."

She blurted out that confession, then nodded vehemently when he looked incredulous. "It's true, Nathan. I didn't realize it until today, but now I know the truth about myself. I'm not at all like Jade. The men are right. I don't measure up."

He was so surprised by her fervent speech that he didn't realize he'd let go of her until she'd turned and hurried over to the bed. She sat down on the side and stared at her lap.

"I'm going to have my nap now," she whispered again.

He was never going to understand her. Nathan shook his

head and tried not to smile. It would injure his wife's feelings if she thought he was mocking her. Sara was pulling her hair over the right side of her face. It was obvious she was embarrassed about the bruise. "I'm not just a coward, Nathan. I'm an ugly one. Jade has green eyes, doesn't she? The men say her hair is as red as fire. Jimbo said she's beautiful."

"Why the hell are we talking about my sister?" Nathan asked. He regretted his gruff tone of voice immediately. He wanted to ease Sara's distress, not increase it. In a much softer voice he said, "You aren't a coward."

She looked up at him so that he could see her frown. "Then why are my hands shaking, and why do I feel like I'm going to be sick? I'm so afraid right now, and all I can think about is what could have happened to you."

"What could have happened to me?" He was stunned by her admission, humbled. "Sara, you were also at risk."

She acted as though she hadn't heard him. "They could have killed you."

"They didn't."

She started crying again. He let out a sigh. This was going to take time, he decided. Sara needed more than just a quick denial. She needed him to touch her.

And he needed to touch her as well. Nathan stripped out of all his clothes but his pants. He'd unbuttoned them and was about to pull them off, but then he decided he didn't want Sara to know what his intent was just yet. It would only turn her attention, and he wanted to address the problem first.

Sara stood up when Nathan sat down. She watched him get comfortable. He leaned against the wood behind the pillows. One leg was stretched out, the other bent at the knee. He pulled her in front of him, then settled her between his legs. Her back rested against his chest, and with prodding her head fell back against his shoulder. Nathan's arm was around her waist. She wiggled her backside against him until she was comfortable. The movement made him grit his teeth. His wife still didn't have any idea how provocative she could be. She didn't realize how quickly she could make him want her.

"Now you don't have to hide your face from me," he whispered. He gently brushed her hair away from the side of her face, leaned down, and kissed the side of her neck. Sara closed her eyes and tilted her head just a little to give him better access.

"Nathan? Did you see how quickly that man turned on me? If the pistol hadn't discharged, I couldn't have defended myself. I don't have the strength. I'm puny."

"You don't have to have strength to defend yourself," he replied.

That remark made absolutely no sense to her. "I hit Duggan, but afterwards my hand stung for the longest time. It was a paltry hit, too. Yes, one must have strength if one is going to—"

"Who's Duggan?"

"The man with Uncle Henry at the tavern the first night we met," Sara explained.

Nathan remembered. He smiled when he pictured the dainty white-gloved fist coming through the window. "You had the element of surprise on your side, but you didn't make a proper fist."

He took hold of her hand and showed her how. "Don't tuck your thumb underneath your fingers. You'll get it broken if you do. Put it here, on the outside, below your knuckles. Now squeeze tight," he ordered. "Let the force of the blow come from here," he added as he rubbed his finger back and forth across the tip of her knuckles. "Put your whole body into the action."

Sara nodded. "If you say so, Nathan."

"You need to know how to take care of yourself," he muttered. "Pay attention, Sara. I'm instructing you."

She hadn't realized she was feeling so insecure with

Nathan until that moment. "Don't you want to take care of me?" she asked.

His sigh parted her hair. "There will be times when I won't be with you," he reasoned. He was trying to be patient with her. "Now then," he added in a brisker tone of voice, "where you hit is just as important as how you hit."

"It is?"

She tried to turn around to look at him. Nathan pushed her head back on his shoulder. "Yes, it is," he said. "The most vulnerable area of a man's body is his groin."

"Nathan, you cannot believe I'd—"

He could hear the blush in her voice. He rolled his eyes heavenward in true exasperation. "It's ridiculous for you to be embarrassed. I'm your husband, and we should be able to discuss anything with each other."

"I don't think I could hit a man . . . there."

"The hell you couldn't," he countered. "Damn it, Sara, you will defend yourself because I command it. I don't want anything to happen to you."

If he hadn't sounded so irritated, she would have been pleased with his admission. Nathan hadn't sounded happy about the fact that he didn't want anything to happen to her, though. Lord, he was a complex man. He pushed and prodded her to do things she didn't know if she could do. "And if I can't hit a man there? Cowards don't defend themselves," she announced. "And I've already admitted that sin to you."

God, she sounded pitiful. Nathan tried not to laugh. "Explain to me why you consider yourself a coward," he ordered.

"I already did explain," she cried out. "My hands are still shaking, and every time I think about what could have happened I'm filled with terror. I can't even look at that gown without feeling sick to my stomach."

"What gown?" he asked.

She pointed to the blue dress on the floor. "That gown,"

she whispered. "One of those villains held it. I want you to throw it overboard," she added. "I'm never going to wear it again."

"All right, Sara," he soothed. "I'll get rid of it. Now close your eyes, and you won't have to look at it."

"You think I'm being foolish, don't you?"

He started to nuzzle the side of her neck. "I think you're experiencing aftermath," he whispered. "It's a natural reaction, that's all. It doesn't mean you're a coward."

She tried to concentrate on what he was saying to her, but he was making it very difficult. His tongue was teasing her ear, and his warm breath was making her warmer. The shivers were easing away, and she was beginning to feel drowsy.

"Do you ever have . . . aftermath?" she asked in a faint whisper.

His hand was caressing the underside of her breast. The rustling of silk against skin was arousing. "Yes," he told her.

"What do you do about it?"

"I find a way to vent my frustration," he answered. He pulled the ribbon free from the drawstring bow at the top of her chemise and then eased the straps down her shoulders.

Sara was feeling relaxed. Nathan's voice was soothing against her ear. She let out a little sigh of pleasure and closed her eyes again.

His hand rested on her thigh. When he began to caress the sensitive skin near the junction of her legs she moved against him restlessly.

His fingers slipped beneath the edge of her chemise, and he slowly began to stoke the fire in her. He knew just how much pressure to exert, just where to touch to drive her wild. She let out a ragged moan when his fingers thrust inside her.

"Easy, baby," he whispered when she tried to stop him. "Don't fight it, Sara. Let it happen."

He held her tight against him and continued his sweet

torture. His fingers were magical, demanding. Sara was soon mindless to everything but finding her release.

"I love the way you respond to me. You get so hot, so wet. It's all for me, isn't it, Sara?"

She couldn't answer him. He was becoming more forceful with his demands and she was coming unglued. She couldn't stop the climax. It happened before she realized it was going to happen. Her hands reached down to hold his hand between her thighs, and she tightened around him by drawing her knees up and squeezing him tight.

It was a shattering orgasm. Sara went limp from the wonder of it. She fell back against her husband's chest in blissful surrender.

As soon as her heartbeat slowed a little and she was able to catch a thought she became embarrassed. Her chemise was down around her waist, and Nathan was gently caressing her breasts.

"I didn't know that I could . . . that is, without you inside me, I didn't think it was possible. . . ." She couldn't go on.

"I was inside you," he whispered. "My fingers were, remember?"

He turned her around until she was on her knees facing him. God, he was sexy. Her breath caught in her throat, and she suddenly realized she wanted him again. Her gaze held his as she pushed the chemise down over her thighs.

She leaned forward until her breasts were pressed against his chest. He was already pulling his pants off. It was awkward, but in seconds they had both tossed their garments aside. Sara was once again kneeling between her husband's legs. She held his gaze as she reached down to touch him. His low groan told her he liked that boldness.

Then his hands were fisted in her hair, and he was pulling her toward him. "This, Sara, is how you get rid of the aftermath," he whispered. His mouth claimed hers, cutting off any reply she might have made. Sara didn't mind. He was, after all, instructing her, and she was his ever-attentive student.

They spent another hour together before Nathan went back to directing the repairs. Sara did a lot of sighing as she dressed. She collected her charcoals and her sketch pad and went up on deck to sit in the afternoon sun.

In little time the work had ceased, and she was surrounded by men who wanted her to draw their likenesses. Sara was happy to accommodate the men. They praised her work, and their disappointment seemed sincere when she'd used the last paper and had to quit.

Nathan was up on the spar deck, helping to strengthen one of the smaller sails that had been knocked loose when the cannon had hit. He finished that chore and then turned to go back to the wheel.

He paused when he spotted his wife. She was sitting on the wooden ledge below him. At least fifteen of his men were sitting on the deck by her feet. They seemed to be extremely interested in what she was saying to them.

Nathan moved closer. Chester's voice reached him. "Do you mean to say you were only four when you wed the captain?"

"She just explained it all to us, Chester," Kently muttered. "It were by the daft king's demand, weren't it, Lady Sara?"

"Do you wonder why the king wanted to end the feud?" Ivan asked.

"He wanted peace," Sara answered.

"What caused the rift in the first place?" another asked.

"No one can recall," Chester guessed.

"Oh, I know what caused the disagreement," Sara said. "It was the cross of gold that started the feud."

Nathan leaned against the post. He smiled even as he shook his head. So she believed that nonsense, did she? Of course she did, he thought to himself. It was a fanciful story, and Sara would certainly believe it.

"Tell us about this cross of gold," Chester asked.

"Well, it began when a Winchester baron and a St. James baron went on a crusade together. The two men were good friends. This was back in the early middle ages, of course, and everyone was out to save the world from infidels. The two barons' holdings were adjacent to each other, and the story has it that they grew up together in King John's court. I don't know if that was true or not, though. Anyway," she added with a shrug, "the two friends went to a foreign port. One of them saved the life of the ruler there, and in return he was given a gigantic cross made all of gold. Yes," she added when the men looked so impressed, "it was encrusted with large stones, too. Some were diamonds, others rubies, and it was said to be quite magnificent."

"How big was it said to be?" Matthew called out.

"As big as a full-grown man," Sara answered.

"But what happened then?" Chester asked. He was eager to hear the rest of the story and didn't like the interruptions.

"The two barons returned to England. Then the cross suddenly disappeared. The Winchester baron told everyone who would listen that he'd been given the cross and that the St. James baron had stolen it. The St. James baron gave the very same story."

"It weren't ever found, m'lady?" Kently asked.

Sara shook her head. "War broke out between the two powerful barons. Some say there never was a cross, and that it was used only as an excuse to gain the other's land. I believe the cross exists."

"Why?" Chester asked.

"Because when the St. James baron was dying he was said to have whispered, 'Look to the heavens for your treasure.'"

She nodded after making that statement. "A man doesn't lie when he's about to meet his Maker," she instructed. "Directly after saying those words he clutched his heart and dropped dead."

Her hand moved to her bosom, and she bowed her head. Some of the men started to applaud, then stopped themselves. "You aren't believing this story, are you, Lady Sara?"

"Oh, yes," she answered. "One day Nathan's going to find the cross for me."

Nathan thought his wife was a hopeless dreamer. He smiled, though, for he suddenly realized he liked that flaw in her.

"Sounds like the captain will have to go to heaven to find it," Chester said.

"Oh, no," Sara argued. "It was just a little clue the baron was giving when he said 'Look to the heavens.' He was being cunning."

The talk continued for a few more minutes. A storm was brewing, however, and the wind soon became too high to ignore. Sara went back to her cabin to put her charcoals away. She spent the remainder of the day with her Aunt Nora, but by nightfall Nora was yawning like an infant, and Sara took her leave so that her aunt could get her needed rest. The events of the long day had clearly worn her out.

In truth, Sara was just as exhausted. She started having the telltale back pains while she readied herself for bed. The pain was a sure indication that she was about to start her monthly.

An hour later the cramps came on with a vengeance. They were much worse than usual. She was in too much pain to worry that Nathan might find out about her condition. She was freezing, too. The pain did that to her, and it didn't matter at all that it was warm and humid inside the cabin. She was still chilled through to the bone.

She put on her heavy white cotton sleeping gown, then crawled into bed and covered herself with three quilts.

She couldn't get comfortable no matter what position she tried. Her lower back felt as though it had been broken in half, and the agony soon made her start whimpering.

Nathan didn't come down to the cabin until the night watch had changed. Sara usually left a candle burning for him, but the room was pitched into darkness.

He heard her groan. He quickly struck two candles and hurried over to the bed.

He still couldn't see her. She was cocooned beneath a mound of covers.

"Sara?"

His alarm was obvious in his tone of voice. When she didn't immediately answer him he jerked the covers away from her face.

Fear made him break out in a cold sweat. Her face was as white as the sheets. Sara pulled the covers back over her head.

"Sara, what in God's name is the matter?"

"Go away, Nathan," she whispered. Her voice was muffled by the quilts, but he understood her all the same. "I don't feel well."

She sounded near death. His worry intensified. "What's the matter with you?" he demanded in a rough whisper. "Does your face hurt now? Damn, I knew I should have killed that bastard."

"It isn't my face," she cried out.

"Is it fever, then?" He jerked the covers away again.

Oh, God, she couldn't explain her condition to him. It was too humiliating. She let out another low groan and rolled onto her side, away from him. Her knees were pulled up against her stomach, and she began to rock back and forth in an attempt to ease the pain in her back. "I don't want to talk about it," she said. "I just don't feel well. Please go away."

He wasn't about to do any such thing, of course. He put his hand on her forehead. It was cool, though damp, to his touch. "It isn't fever," he announced with an added grunt of relief. "God, Sara, I didn't hurt you this afternoon, did I? I know I was a little . . . rough, but—"

"You didn't hurt me," she blurted out.

He still wasn't convinced. "You're certain?"

She was warmed by his obvious worry. "I'm certain. You didn't cause this illness," she added. "I just need to be alone now."

A cramp claimed her full attention then. She let out a low moan, then added, "Let me die in peace."

"The hell I will," he muttered. Another black thought

gave him the chills. "You didn't make anything when you were in the galley, did you? You didn't eat something you prepared?"

"No. It isn't stomach upset."

"Then what the hell is it?"

"I'm not . . . clean."

He didn't know what in God's name that was supposed to mean. "You're sick because you aren't clean? Sara, that's got to be the most illogical illness I've ever heard of. Will you feel better if I order a bath made ready for you?"

She wanted to scream at him yet knew the effort would cost her more pain. "Nathan, it's a . . . woman's condition," she whispered.

"A what?"

Lord, he was going to make her spell it out for him. "I'm having my monthly," she shouted. "Oh, I hurt," she added in a whimper. "Some months are worse than others."

"You're having your monthly . . ."

"I'm not pregnant," she blurted out at the same moment. "Please go away now. If God is truly merciful, I'll die in just a few more minutes . . . if not from the pain, then from the shame of having to explain my condition to you."

He was so relieved she wasn't suffering from a life-threatening ailment, he let out a ragged sigh. Then he reached out to pat her shoulder. He pulled back before actually touching her, though. Damn, he felt awkward. Inadequate, too.

"Is there anything I can do to ease your pain?" he asked. "Do you want something?"

"I want my mother," she muttered. "But I can't have her, can I? Oh, just go away, Nathan. There isn't anything you can do."

She pulled the covers back over her face and let out another pitiful moan. Nathan must have decided to let her have her way, she decided when she heard the door shut. She burst into tears then. How dare he leave her when she was in such agony? She'd lied when she said she wanted her mother. She wanted Nathan to hold her, and the obstinate man should have been able to read her mind and know that was what she needed.

Nathan immediately went to Nora's cabin. He didn't bother to knock. As soon as he threw the door open a deep voice called out, "Who's there?"

Nathan almost smiled. He recognized Matthew's booming voice. The seaman was obviously sharing Nora's bed. "I have to talk to Nora," he announced.

Sara's aunt came awake with a start. She let out a gasp and pulled the covers up to her chin. Her blush was as high as the candle flame.

Nathan walked over to the side of the bed and stood there with his hands clasped behind his back, staring at the floor.

"Sara's ill," he announced before Nora could say a word.

Nora's embarrassment over being found in such a compromising position quickly faded in the light of that announcement.

"I must go to her," she whispered. She struggled to sit up. "Do you know what the ailment is?"

"Do you want me to have a look at her?" Matthew asked in a rush. He was already tossing the covers aside.

Nathan shook his head. He cleared his throat. "It's this . . . woman's thing."

"What woman's thing?" Matthew asked, genuinely perplexed.

Nora understood. She patted Matthew's hand but kept her gaze on Nathan's face. "Is she in much pain?"

Nathan nodded. "She's in terrible pain, madam. Now tell me what I can do to help her."

Nora thought he sounded very like a military commander, so brisk was his tone of voice. "A stiff drink of brandy sometimes helps," Nora suggested. "A gentle word wouldn't hurt either, Nathan. I remember becoming very emotional during that time of month."

"Isn't there anything else I can do for her?" Nathan muttered. "My God, Nora, she's in pain. I won't have it."

With extreme effort Nora was able to contain her smile. Nathan looked like he wanted to kill someone. "Have you asked her what might help?"

"She wanted her mother."

"How would that help?" Matthew asked.

Nora answered, "She needs her husband, dear. Nathan, she wants someone to comfort her. Try rubbing her back."

Nora had to raise her voice to give that last suggestion, for Nathan was already striding out the doorway.

As soon as the door closed behind him Nora turned to Matthew. "Do you think he'll tell Sara that you and I—"

"No, my love, he wouldn't say a word," Matthew interjected.

"I hate to deceive Sara, but she does tend to see everything in black or white. I don't think she'd understand."

"Hush now," Matthew soothed. He kissed Nora and pulled her into his arms. "Age will season her."

Nora agreed. She changed the topic then and whispered, "Nathan is beginning to care for Sara, isn't he? It won't be long before he realizes he loves her."

"He may love her, Nora, but he won't ever admit it. The boy learned a long time ago to protect himself against any true involvement."

Nora snorted over that remark. "Nonsense," she countered. "Given an ordinary woman, perhaps you would be right, Matthew, but surely you've noticed by now that my Sara isn't ordinary. She's just what Nathan needs. She thinks her husband loves her, and it won't take her long to convince him that he does. Just wait and see."

Sara didn't have any idea she was the topic of discussion. She was in the throes of self-pity.

She never heard Nathan come back into the cabin. He was suddenly touching her shoulder. "Sara, drink this. It will make you feel better."

She rolled over, saw the goblet in his hands, and immediately shook her head.

"It's brandy," he told her.

"I don't want it."

"Drink it."

"I'll throw up."

She couldn't be any blunter than that, he supposed. He hastily put the goblet on the desk and then got into bed beside her.

She tried to push him out. He ignored her struggle and her demands.

Sara rolled back onto her side again, facing the wall. She might as well pray for death, she supposed. It was an overly dramatic request she gave her Maker, and in the back of her mind she really hoped He wasn't listening, and that thought didn't make a lick of sense to her either.

She couldn't take the pain much longer. Then Nathan put his arm around her waist. He pulled her a little closer to him and began to rub her lower back. The gentle touch was heaven. The ache immediately began to lessen. Sara closed her eyes and scooted closer to her husband so that she could steal a little more of his warmth.

She barely noticed the rocking and pitching motion of the ship. Nathan noticed. His own stomach was in torment, and he wished to God he hadn't eaten anything. It was only a matter of time before he would turn completely green.

He kept rubbing her spine for fifteen minutes or so without speaking a word to her. He tried to concentrate on the woman cuddled up against him, but each time the ship rolled, so did his stomach.

"You can stop now," Sara whispered. "I'm feeling better, thank you."

Nathan did as she requested, then started to get out of bed. She waylaid that intent with her next request. "Will you hold me, Nathan? I'm so cold. It's chilly tonight, isn't it?"

It was as hot as blazes to him. His face was drenched in perspiration. He did as she asked, though. Her hands felt like ice, but in just a few minutes he'd hugged her warm again.

He thought she was finally asleep and was just easing himself out of her hold when she whispered, "Nathan? What if I'm barren?"

"Then you're barren."

"Is that all you can say? We can't have children if I'm barren."

He rolled his eyes heavenward. God, she sounded like she was going to cry again. "You can't possibly know if you're barren or not," he said. "It's too soon to jump to that conclusion."

"But if I am?" she prodded.

"Sara, what do you want me to say?" he asked. His frustration was almost visible. His stomach lurched again. Deep breaths weren't helping. He tossed the covers aside and tried to leave the bed again.

"Would you still want to be married to me?" she asked. "We won't get the land the king promised if I don't have a baby by the time—"

"I'm aware of the conditions of the contract," he snapped. "If we don't get the land, then we'll rebuild on the land my father left to me. Now quit your questions and go to sleep. I'll be back in a little while."

"You still haven't answered me," she said. "Would you still want to be married to a barren woman?"

"Oh, for God's sake—"

"You would, wouldn't you?"

He grunted. She took that sound to mean he would. She rolled over and kissed his back. He'd left the candles burning, and when she looked up at his face she saw how gray his complexion had turned.

She was quick to put two and two together. The ship was bouncing like an errant ball in the water. The goblet of brandy was pitched to the floor. Nathan closed his eyes and grimaced.

224

He was seasick. Sara was filled with sympathy for her poor husband, but that emotion was quickly squelched when he muttered, "I wouldn't be married to anyone if it wasn't for the damned contracts. Now go to sleep."

After grumbling out that remark he swung his legs over the side of the bed.

Sara was suddenly furious again. How dare he take that tone of voice with her? She was just as ill as he was, perhaps even more. She forgot all about the gentle way he'd treated her and decided to teach the man a lesson he wouldn't soon forget.

"I'm sorry I'm keeping you from whatever business you have to attend to," she began. "My back is feeling much better now, Nathan. Thank you. My stomach isn't upset either. I suppose I shouldn't have had that fish for supper. It tasted wonderful, though, especially when I put a little dab of chocolate on top. Have you ever tasted fish sweetened that way? No?" she asked when he didn't answer her.

He seemed to be in quite a hurry to get his pants back on. Sara held her smile. "I usually just put sugar on top, but I wanted to experiment tonight. By the way, the cook has promised to serve us oysters when we reach port. I love oysters, don't you? The way they sort of . . . slide down your throat . . . Nathan, aren't you going to kiss me good-bye?"

The door slammed shut before she'd finished her question. Sara smiled. She gained tremendous satisfaction from her sinful actions. It was high time her husband realized his good fortune in having her for his wife. High time indeed.

"Serves him right for being so obstinate," she muttered to herself. She pulled the covers up over her shoulders and closed her eyes. She was sound asleep in minutes.

Nathan spent most of the night hanging over the side of the ship. He'd gone to the usually deserted area, and no one paid him any attention.

The sun was easing up into the sky when he returned to the cabin. He felt as wrung out as a wet sail. He literally collapsed on the bed. Sara was bounced awake by that action. She rolled over and cuddled up against her husband's side.

He started snoring so she wouldn't start talking again. Sara leaned up and kissed the side of his cheek. In the soft candlelight she could see how pale he was. He was in dire need of a shave, too. He looked fierce with the dark shadow along his jawline. Sara reached up to touch the side of his cheek with her fingertips. "I love you," she whispered. "Even with all your flaws, Nathan, I still love you. I'm sorry I deliberately made you seasick. I'm sorry that you suffer from such an ailment."

Satisfied with her confession, especially because she knew he hadn't heard a word of what she'd just said, she rolled away from him. Her sigh was loud. "I do believe you should consider another line of work, husband. The sea doesn't seem to suit you."

He slowly opened his eyes, then turned to look at her. She appeared to be asleep again. She looked damned peaceful to him. Angelic.

He wanted to throttle her. His wife had somehow found out about his illness and had deliberately used that knowledge to get even with him. She must have taken exception to his remark about not being married at all if it weren't for the contracts.

His flash of anger dissipated in little time, and he found himself smiling. Little Sara wasn't such an innocent after all. She'd done exactly what he would have done if he'd had such a weapon at his disposal and wasn't strong enough to physically retaliate.

When he was angry he liked to use his fists. She used her head and it pleased him. Still, it was high time she understood just who was in charge of the marriage. High time indeed. She wasn't supposed to use cunning on him.

And Lord, she looked lovely. He suddenly wanted to make love to her. He couldn't, of course, because of her delicate condition, and he almost shook her awake to ask her how long this woman's thing lasted.

Exhaustion finally overcame him. Just as he was drifting off to sleep he felt Sara take hold of his hand. He didn't pull away. His last thought before falling asleep was a bit unsettling.

He needed her to hold him.

They were just two days away from Nora's home, and Nathan was once again beginning to think that the rest of the voyage might prove uneventful.

He should have known better.

It was late evening on the twenty-first of the month. There were more stars than sky above, and the breeze was every bit as pretty by a seaman's measure. The wind was gentle, yet coaxingly insistent. They were making good time—a clipping speed, in fact. The mighty ship set straight in the water and cut directly through the ocean without rocking or lurching to either side. A man could put a keg of grog on the rail without fear of losing it, so calm was the sea, and there was nary a worry to annoy a seaman's dreams.

Nathan stood next to Jimbo behind the wheel. The two men were in deep discussion over the plans to expand the Emerald Shipping Company. Jimbo was in favor of adding additional clippers to their fleet, while Nathan favored heavier, more durable ships.

Sara interrupted their conversation when she came rushing across the deck. She was dressed only in her nightgown and wrapper. Jimbo noticed that right away. Nathan's back was to his wife, however, and because she was barefoot he didn't hear her approach.

"Nathan, I must speak to you at once," she cried out. "We have a horrible problem, and you must take care of it right away."

Nathan had a resigned look on his face when he turned around, but that expression faltered as soon as he saw the pistol in his wife's hand. The weapon, he couldn't help but notice, was pointed at his groin.

Sara was in a high fit about something. She looked a sight. Her hair was in wild disarray around her shoulders, and her cheeks were bright.

Then he noticed her state of attire. "What are you doing strutting around the deck dressed in your nightclothes?" he demanded.

Her eyes widened over his rebuke. "I wasn't strutting," she began. She stopped herself with a shake of her head. "This isn't the time to lecture me about my attire. We have a serious problem, husband."

She turned her attention to Jimbo. The pistol made her curtsy awkward. "Please forgive my unladylike appearance, Jimbo, but I've had quite an upset, I can tell you, and I didn't take time to dress."

Jimbo nodded even as he dodged the pistol she was waving back and forth between Nathan and him. He didn't think she realized she was holding the weapon.

"You've had an upset?" Jimbo prodded.

"What in God's name are you doing with that pistol?" Nathan demanded at the same time.

"I might have need for it," Sara explained.

"Lady Sara," Jimbo interjected when Nathan looked as if he was at a loss for words, "calm yourself and tell us what has you so upset. Boy," he added in a growl, "get that damn pistol away from her before she shoots herself."

Nathan reached out to take the weapon from her hand. Sara backed up a space and put the pistol behind her back. "I went to see Nora," she blurted out. "I just wanted to say goodnight to her."

"And?" Nathan asked when she didn't continue.

She stared at Jimbo a long minute before deciding to include him in her explanation, then glanced over her shoulder to make certain no one else was within hearing distance. "She wasn't alone."

She'd whispered that statement and waited for her husband's reaction. He shrugged.

She wanted to shoot him. "Matthew was with her." She nodded vehemently after telling that news.

"And?" Nathan prodded.

"They were in bed together."

She waved the pistol again. "Nathan, you have to do something."

"What would you like me to do?"

He sounded very accommodating, but he was grinning. The man wasn't at all surprised by the news she'd just given him. She should have guessed he'd react that way. Nothing ever seemed to upset him . . . except her, of course. She always upset him, she admitted.

"She wants you to make Matthew leave," Jimbo interjected. "Isn't that right, Sara?"

She shook her head. "It's a little late to shut the barn door, Jimbo. The cow's already out."

"I'm not getting your meaning," Jimbo returned. "What do cows have to do with your aunt?"

"He dishonored her," she explained.

"Sara, if you don't want me to make Matthew leave Nora alone, just what do you think I should do?" Nathan asked.

"You have to make it right," Sara explained. "You're going to have to marry them. Come along with me, husband. We might as well get it done right away. Jimbo, you can serve as witness."

"You can't be serious."

"Quit your smile, husband. I'm very serious. You're captain of this vessel, so you can legally marry them."

"No."

"Lady Sara, you do come up with the most astonishing suggestions," Jimbo said.

It was obvious to her that neither man was taking her seriously. "I'm responsible for my aunt," Sara said. "Matthew has blemished her honor, and he must marry her. You know, Nathan, this will really solve another worry. My Uncle Henry won't come chasing after Nora for her inheritance once she's remarried. Yes, this could have a happy ending, to my way of thinking."

"No." Nathan's voice was emphatic.

"Sara, does Matthew want to marry Nora?"

She turned to frown at the seaman. "It doesn't matter if he wants to or not."

"Aye, it does," Jimbo argued.

She started waving the pistol around again. "Well, I can see I won't be getting any help from either of you."

Before the two men could agree with that statement Sara whirled around and started for the steps again. "I do like Matthew," she muttered. "It's a shame."

"What are you thinking to do, Lady Sara?" Jimbo called out.

She didn't turn around when she called out her answer. "He's going to marry Nora."

"And if he doesn't?" Jimbo asked, smiling over the matter-of-fact way she'd made that announcement.

"Then I'm going to shoot him. I won't like it, Jimbo, but I'll have to shoot him."

Nathan was right behind Sara. He put his arm around her waist, hauled her up against him, then reached over her shoulder and grabbed hold of the pistol. "You aren't going to shoot anyone," he told her in a low growl.

He handed the pistol to Jimbo, then dragged Sara down to their cabin. He shut the door behind him and continued on toward the bed.

"Unhand me, Nathanial."

"Don't ever call me Nathanial," he ordered.

She pushed away from him and turned to look at his face. "Why can't I call you by your given name?"

"I don't like it, that's why," he told her.

"That's a stupid reason," she argued. She put her hands on her hips and frowned at him. Her wrapper opened, and he was given a healthy view of her full breasts pressed against the thin nightgown.

"Sara, when is this condition of yours going to be over?" he asked.

She didn't answer that question but nagged him back to the topic of his name. "Why don't you like being called Nathanial?"

He took a threatening step forward. "I see red whenever I hear it, Sara. It puts me in a fighting mood."

That wasn't really a suitable explanation, but she wasn't about to point that out to him. "When aren't you in a fighting mood, husband?" she asked.

"Don't bait me."

"Don't yell at me."

He took a deep breath. It didn't calm him one bit.

She smiled. "All right," she whispered in a bid to placate him. "I won't ever call you Nathanial . . . unless I want you in a fighting mood. You'll know to be on your guard, husband. Agreed?"

He thought those comments were too ignorant to answer. He'd backed her over to the side of the bed. "Now it's your turn to answer me, Sara. When is this damned woman's thing finished?"

She slowly removed her robe. She took her sweet time folding the garment. "You aren't going to do anything about Nora and Matthew, are you?" she asked.

"No, I'm not," he answered. "And neither are you. Leave them alone. Do you understand me?"

She nodded. "I'm going to have to think about this long and hard, husband."

Before he could make a stinging remark about her ability to think much at all she pulled her nightgown up over her head and tossed it on the bed. "I have finished this damned woman's thing," she whispered shyly.

She was trying to be bold, but the blush ruined that effect. Nathan was making her feel awkward because of the way he

231

was looking at her. His hot stare made her toes tingle. She let out a sigh and then moved forward into his arms.

He made her kiss him first. She was in an accommodating mood. She put her arms around his neck and tugged on his long hair to bring his mouth down to hers.

And Lord, did she kiss him. Her mouth was hot, her tongue wild, and it didn't take her any time at all to get the response she wanted.

Nathan took over then. He held her captive by making a fist in her hair, then slowly lowered his head again. His open mouth settled on hers, and his tongue thrust deep inside to mate with hers. Her breasts were pressed against his bare chest, and her arms were wrapped tightly around his waist.

He let out a low growl when she sucked on his tongue, so she did it again. The sound he made was as arousing to her as his kiss, and she couldn't seem to get close enough to him.

He pulled away to remove his clothes but stopped when she began to nibble on the side of his neck. He shuddered in reaction. His hands stroked her smooth shoulders. The feel of her silky skin against his rough, callused palms made him realize once again how very fragile she was. "You're so delicate," he whispered. "And I'm . . ."

He couldn't retain his thought, for she was making him forget everything but feeling. She kissed every inch of his chest. Her tongue tickled his sensitive nipples. When he gruffly ordered her to cease her torment she doubled her efforts to drive him beyond the brink of sanity.

She was forced to stop when he pulled on her hair and shoved the side of her face against his chest. He was taking deep, gulping breaths. Then her fingers circled his navel. He quit breathing. She smiled. "You make me feel so warm, so alive, so very strong. I want to show you how much I love you, Nathan. Will you let me?"

He understood her intent when she began to unbutton his pants. Her hands shook. Then she slowly disengaged herself from his embrace and knelt down. Nathan didn't remember much after that. His delicate little wife had turned into a blaze of sensuality. She was like the sun, scorching him with her soft mouth, her wet tongue, her incredibly arousing touch.

He couldn't take the sweet agony long. He wasn't very gentle when he pulled her up and lifted her high off the ground. He forced her legs around his waist as he captured her mouth for a long, intoxicating kiss.

"God, Sara, I hope you're ready for me," he whispered on a low groan. "I can't wait any longer. I have to be inside you. Now. Then I'll be able to slow down, I promise."

He tried to shift positions, but she pulled on his hair. "Nathan, tell me you love me," she demanded.

He answered her by kissing her again. Sara soon forgot all about wanting to hear his declaration of love. Her nails dug into his shoulder blades, and all she could think about was finding fulfillment.

His hands gripped the sides of her hips, and he began to ease slowly inside her.

Her head fell back. She let out a low whimper. "Please hurry, Nathan."

"I want to drive you crazy first," he ground out. "Like you drive me . . ."

She bit his neck. He thrust deep. He was shaking as much as she was. She squeezed him tight. He groaned with pleasure.

He braced their fall onto the bed with his knee, then covered her completely. His hands cupped the sides of her face, and he leaned up on his elbows and gently kissed her forehead, the bridge of her nose, her sweet lips.

"God, you always taste so good," he growled. He nibbled on the side of her neck, teased the lobe of her ear with his tongue, and the last thing he remembered saying to her was that he was going to set the pace this time.

But then she drew her knees up, taking even more of him inside her. She arched up against him. The provocation was too much for him to endure. He felt enveloped by her heat, her intoxicating scent . . . her love.

The bed squeaked with each deep thrust. He wanted their lovemaking to last forever. The fever of passion raged between them. Sara suddenly tightened even more around him. She cried out his name. Her surrender gave him his own. He poured his seed inside her with his last thrust. His deep, guttural growl drowned out their pounding heartbeats.

He collapsed on top of her, too weak to move, too content ever to want to move away from her. His head rested in the hollow of her neck. His breaths were still deep, shaky. So were hers. That fact made him smile inside.

As soon as she loosened her hold on him he rolled to his side. He took her with him for the simple reason that he couldn't seem to let go of her.

She couldn't quit crying.

It was a joyful interlude, but he knew it was just a matter of time before she started nagging him again to give her the words she longed to hear.

He didn't want to disappoint her, yet he wouldn't lie to her. And in the dark recesses of his mind fear took root. What if he wasn't capable of ever giving her what she wanted?

Nathan considered himself the master of the game when it came to hurting people. He'd had quite a lot of experience in that area. Yet when it came to loving someone he didn't have the faintest idea how. Just considering that problem scared the hell out of him. Damn if he'd allow himself to become so vulnerable, he thought. Damn if he would.

She felt him tense against her. She knew what would come next. He'd try to leave her. She wasn't going to let him this time, however, and she vowed that if she had to, she'd even follow him out the door.

How could her husband be so gentle, so giving, so wonderfully considerate when he made love to her and then turn into a statue of ice? What in God's name was going through his mind?

"Nathan?"

He didn't answer her. She expected that rudeness. "I love you," she whispered.

"I know you do," he muttered when she nudged him.

"And?" she persisted.

His sigh was long, drawn out. "Sara, you don't have to love me. It isn't a requirement in this marriage."

He thought he'd been very logical when he'd made that statement of fact. He'd skirted the true issue quite nicely, to his way of thinking.

Sara tried to shove him out of the bed. "You are the most impossible man I've ever known. Listen well, Nathan. I have something to say to you."

"How could I not listen, Sara?" he drawled. "You're screaming like a shrew again."

He did have a point there, she admitted to herself. She had been screaming. She rolled onto her back, pulled the light cover up over herself, and stared at the ceiling. "God's truth, you do frustrate me," she muttered.

He took exception to that remark. "The hell I do," he countered. He blew the candle flame out, then rolled onto his side and roughly pulled her into his arms. "I satisfy you every damned time I touch you."

That wasn't what she meant at all, but he sounded so arrogantly pleased with himself that she decided not to argue. "I still have something important to say to you, Nathan. Will you listen?"

"Will you promise to go to sleep directly after you've said this thing?"

"Yes."

He grunted. She guessed that sound meant he didn't really believe her. She was about to tell him what she thought about his rude behavior when he pulled her even closer to him and gently began to rub her back. His chin rested on the top of her head.

He was being extremely affectionate. Sara was astonished. She wondered if he even realized what he was doing.

She decided she didn't care if he realized or not. The

action was so telling, she couldn't contain the burst of joy that filled her heart.

Just to test him she tried to move away. He tightened his hold. "All right, Sara," he announced. "I'd like to get some sleep tonight. Tell me what's on your mind. Get it done so I can rest."

She couldn't quit smiling. That was quite all right, she told herself, because he couldn't see her expression. He'd pressed her face against the side of his neck. His fingers were gently stroking the hair away from her temple.

She had been quite determined to tell him that he loved her. She'd believed that once she'd told him, he'd realize she was right. Now she didn't want to say anything to ruin the moment. He wasn't ready to acknowledge the truth quite yet.

The revelation had finally settled in her mind. It stunned her a little. Nathan was afraid. She wasn't certain if he was afraid of loving anyone or just afraid of loving her . . . but he was afraid.

Lord, he'd go into a rage if she told him what she was thinking. Men didn't like to hear they were afraid of anything.

"Sara, damn it all, hurry up and get it said so I can go to sleep."

"Get what said?" she countered as her mind raced for a suitable topic to talk about.

"God, you make me daft. You said you had something important to tell me."

"I did," she agreed.

"Well?"

"Nathan, don't squeeze me so tight," she whispered. He immediately let up on his hold. "I seem to have forgotten whatever it was I wanted to tell you."

He kissed her forehead. "Then go to sleep," he instructed.

She snuggled up against him. "You're a fine man, Nathan." She whispered those words of praise and then let out a loud, thoroughly unladylike yawn. "You do please me most of the time."

His deep chuckle warmed her. It wasn't enough, though. "Now it's your turn," she instructed.

"My turn to do what?" he asked. He deliberately pretended not to understand just to prick her temper.

She was too tired to nag him any longer. She closed her eyes and yawned again. "Oh, never mind," she said. "You can have your turn tomorrow."

"You're a fine woman," he whispered. "You please me, too."

Her sigh of pleasure filled the room. "I know," she whispered back.

She fell asleep before he could give her a lecture on the merits of humility. Nathan closed his eyes. He needed rest, for God only knew what tomorrow would bring, with Lady Sara trying her damnedest to run things.

If Nathan had learned anything of value over the past weeks, it was never to expect the usual.

He had believed he would have to protect his wife from the world. Now he knew the truth. It had become his duty to protect the world from his wife.

It was an absurd revelation, of course, but the marquess still fell asleep with a grin on his face.

Chapter Eleven

The day they dropped anchor in the deeper waters surrounding Nora's Caribbean home Sara found out her husband had more than two titles. He wasn't just the Marquess of St. James and the Earl of Wakersfield.

He was also Pagan.

She was so stunned by that bit of news, she literally collapsed on the bed. She hadn't deliberately set out to eavesdrop, but the trap in the ceiling of her room was open and the two seamen were talking rather loudly. It was only when their voices dropped to whisper level that Sara began to pay attention to what they were talking about.

She refused to believe what she heard until Matthew entered the conversation and spoke matter-of-factly about the booty they'd divided from their last raid.

She had to sit down then.

In truth, she was more terrified than horrified by the revelation. Her fear was solely for Nathan, though, and every time she thought about the chances he took when he set out to pirate another ship she got sick to her stomach.

One black thought led to another. She pictured him walking toward the gallows, but only once would she allow herself to imagine that terrible possibility. When the bile rose in her throat and she knew she was about to lose her breakfast she forced herself to stop her black thoughts.

Sara would have been in complete despair if not for the last comment she overheard Chester make. The seaman admitted he was damned happy his pirating days were behind him. Most of the men, he added, were ready to take on family life, and their illegal savings would give them all a nice start.

She was so relieved she started to cry. She wasn't going to have to save Nathan from himself after all. He had apparently already seen the error of his ways. Lord, she prayed he had. She couldn't bear the thought of losing him. She'd loved him for so long, and life without him grunting at her and shouting at her—and loving her—was too devastating to think about.

Sara spent most of the morning worrying about Nathan. She couldn't seem to rid herself of her fear. What if one of his men betrayed her husband? The bounty on Pagan's head was enormous at last posting. No, no, don't think about that, she told herself. The men were a fiercely loyal lot. Yes, she'd noticed that right away. Why borrow trouble? What would happen would happen, no matter how much fretting she did beforehand.

No matter what, she would stand beside her husband and defend him any way that she could.

Had Matthew confided his dark past to Nora? And if so, had he also told her that Nathan was Pagan? Sara decided she would never find out one way or the other. She wasn't about to tell anyone, not even her dear aunt, what she'd learned. That secret was going to go to the grave with her.

When Nathan came down to the cabin to collect his wife he found her sitting on the side of the bed, staring off into space. It was as hot as the inside of a furnace, but Sara was

239

shivering. He thought she wasn't feeling well. Her face was pale, yet the more telling symptom was that she barely spoke a word to him.

His concern intensified when she sat quietly in the rowboat that took them to the pier. Her hands were folded in her lap, her gaze downcast, and she didn't seem to be at all interested in her surroundings.

Nora sat beside Sara and kept up a steady stream of conversation. The elderly woman mopped her brow with her handkerchief and used her fan to cool herself. "It will take a day or two to get used to the heat," she remarked. "By the way, Nathan," she added, "there's a lovely waterfall just a half mile or so from my house. The water comes from the mountain. It's as pure as a baby's smile. There's a gathering pool at the bottom, and you simply must make time to take Sara up there for a nice swim."

Nora turned to look at her niece. "Sara, perhaps now you can learn how to swim."

Sara didn't answer her. Nora nudged her to gain her attention.

"I'm sorry," Sara said. "What did you just say?"

"Sara, whatever are you daydreaming about?" Nora asked.

"I wasn't daydreaming." She stared at Nathan when she made that remark. She frowned, too.

Nathan didn't know what to make of that. "She doesn't feel well," he told Nora.

"I feel perfectly well," Sara countered.

Nora's concern was obvious in her expression. "You've been terribly preoccupied," she remarked. "Is the heat bothering you?"

"No," Sara answered. She let out a little sigh. "I was just thinking about . . . things."

"Any special thing in particular?" Nora prodded.

Sara continued to stare at Nathan. He raised an eyebrow when she didn't immediately answer her aunt.

Nora broke the staring contest when she asked her question once again. "I was suggesting that now would be an excellent time to learn how to swim."

"I'll teach you."

Nathan volunteered for that duty. Sara smiled at him. "Thank you for offering, but I don't believe I want to learn how. There isn't any need."

"Of course there is," he replied. "You'll learn before we leave for England."

"I don't wish to learn," she said again. "I don't need to know how."

"What do you mean, you don't need to know how?" Nathan asked. "You sure as hell do need to know how."

"Why?"

Because she looked so genuinely perplexed, he lost a little of his irritation. "Sara, you won't have to worry about drowning if you know how to swim."

"I don't worry about it now," she countered.

"Damn it all, you should."

She couldn't understand why he was getting so irritated. "Nathan, I won't drown."

That statement gave him pause. "Why not?"

"You wouldn't let me." She smiled.

Nathan braced his hands on his knees and leaned forward. "You're right," he began in a reasonable tone of voice. "I wouldn't let you drown."

Sara nodded. She turned to Nora. "There, do you see, Nora? There really isn't any need—"

Nathan interrupted her. "However," he announced in a louder voice, "what about those times when I'm not with you?"

She gave him an exasperated look. "Then I wouldn't go into the water."

He took a deep breath. "What if you fell into the water by accident?"

"Nathan, this is sounding very like the argument you gave me about defending myself," she said, her voice full of suspicion.

"It's exactly the same argument," he countered. "I don't want to have to worry about you. You're going to learn how to swim, and that's the end of this discussion."

"Nora, do you notice how he yells at me all the time?" Sara asked.

"Don't try to draw me into this discussion," her aunt said. "I won't take sides."

Husband and wife lapsed into silence. Not another word was exchanged until they reached the pier.

Sara finally took time to notice her surroundings. "Oh, Nora," she whispered. "Everything is even . . . greener and lusher than I remembered."

The tropical paradise was vibrant with every color in the rainbow. Sara stood on the pier and stared up at the rolling hills in the distance. The sun pierced the palm trees, shining bright upon the multitude of delicate red flowers sprinkling the way to the top of the mountain.

Clapboard houses painted in pastel shades of pink and green, with copper-colored tiled roofs, stood regal against the background of hills overlooking the harbor. Sara wished there was time to take her charcoals and paper in hand and try to capture the God-created canvas. She realized almost immediately that she couldn't possibly duplicate the masterpiece, and she let out a little sigh.

Nathan walked over to stand beside her. The innocent wonder on her face took his breath away.

"Sara?" he asked when he noticed the tears gathering in her eyes. "Is something the matter?"

She didn't take her gaze away from the hills when she answered him. "It's magnificent, isn't it, Nathan?"

"What's magnificent?"

"The painting God's given us," she whispered. "Look up at the hills. Do you see how the sun acts as the frame? Oh, Nathan, it truly is magnificent."

He never looked up. He stared down at his wife's face for what seemed an eternity. A slow heat seemed to permeate his heart, his soul. He couldn't stop himself from reaching out to touch her. The back of his finger slowly trailed a line down the side of her cheek.

"You are magnificent," he heard himself whisper. "You see only the beauty in life."

Sara was stunned by the emotional force in his voice. She turned to smile at him. "I do?" she whispered.

The unguarded moment was gone. Before she could so much as blink Nathan's manner changed. He became brisk when he ordered her to quit dallying.

She wondered if she was ever going to understand him. She walked by her aunt's side along the wooden planks that led to the street while she considered her husband's confusing personality.

"Sara dear, you're frowning. Is the heat beginning to bother you?"

"No," she answered. "I was just thinking what a confusing man my husband is," she explained. "Nora, he actually wants me to become thoroughly self-sufficient," she confessed. "Nathan has made me realize how dependent I try to make myself. I only thought I should," she added with a shrug. "I thought he was supposed to take care of me, but perhaps I was in error. I believe he would still cherish me even if I could defend myself."

"I believe he'd be very proud of your efforts," Nora answered. "Do you really want to be at a man's mercy? Consider your mother, Sara. She isn't married to a man as caring as Nathan."

Her aunt had given her something to think about. Sara hadn't considered the possibility that Nathan might have turned out to be a cruel man. But what if he had?

"I must think about what you've just said," she whispered.

Nora patted her hand. "You'll work it all out in your mind, my dear. Don't frown so. It will give you a headache. My, isn't it a lovely day?"

There were several men loitering along the pathway. They all stared at Sara when she strolled past. Nathan scowled at

their blatantly lustful looks, and when one overly appreciative man let out a low whistle Nathan's temper ignited.
When he walked past the man he casually slammed the back
of his fist into the bastard's face.

The blow toppled the man into the water. Sara glanced
back over her shoulder when she heard the splash. It was an
absentminded action, for she was also trying to concentrate
on what Nora was saying to her. She caught Nathan's eye.
He smiled at her. She smiled back before turning around
again.

All but one of the other men moved out of the way when
Nathan walked past. The less cautious individual had a
twiglike nose and a squint. "She's a fetching one, ain't she?"
he remarked.

"She's mine," Nathan announced in a low growl. Instead
of hitting the insolent man he simply shoved him off the
pier.

"Boy, you're getting a mite protective, don't you think?"
Jimbo drawled out. He grinned when he added, "She's just a
wife."

"The woman doesn't realize her own appeal," Nathan
muttered. "She sure as hell wouldn't walk like that if she
noticed how the bastards were leering at her."

"Exactly how is she walking?" Jimbo asked.

"You know damn well what I'm talking about. The way
her hips . . ." He didn't continue his explanation, but
turned his attention to Jimbo's last remark. "And she isn't
just a wife, Jimbo. She's my wife."

Jimbo decided he'd baited Nathan long enough. The boy
was working himself into a fury. "I can already see from the
looks of the place that we aren't going to be able to get the
supplies we need to repair the mast."

That glum prophecy turned out to be true. After sending
Sara with Nora and Matthew to get settled in Nora's house,
Nathan went with Jimbo to explore the tiny village.

It didn't take Nathan long to agree that they'd have to sail to a larger port. According to the charts, the nearest supply port was a good two days away.

Nathan knew his wife wouldn't like hearing about his departure. On his way up the hill, he made the decision to tell her at once and get the inevitable scene over and done.

He was a bit surprised when he reached Nora's house. He'd expected to find a small cottage, but Nora's residence was three times that size. It was a large, two-story structure. The exterior was a pale pink. The verandah that circled the front and sides was painted white.

Sara was sitting in a rocking chair near the front door. Nathan climbed the steps and announced, "I'm leaving with half the crew tomorrow."

"I see."

She tried to control her expression. She was suddenly filled with panic. Dear God, was he going away on another raid? Nora had mentioned that her island home was close to the pirates' nest located just a little further down the coast. Was Nathan going to meet up with past associates and go on one last adventure?

She took a deep, settling breath. She knew she was jumping to conclusions, but she couldn't seem to stop herself.

"We have to sail to a larger port, Sara, in order to get the supplies we need to repair the *Seahawk.*"

She didn't believe a word of that story. Nora lived in a fishing village, for God's sake, and the seamen would certainly have enough supplies on hand. She wasn't going to let Nathan know what she was guessing, though. When he was ready to tell her he was Pagan, he would. Until then she would pretend to believe him. "I see," she whispered again.

Nathan was surprised by her easy acceptance. He was used to arguing with her over every little matter. The change in her manner actually worried him. She had been acting peculiar all day long.

He leaned against the rail and waited for her to say

something more. Sara stood up and walked back into the house.

He caught up with her in the foyer. "I won't be gone long," he told her.

She kept right on going. She'd reached the second story when he grabbed hold of her shoulders. "Sara, what's gotten into you?"

"Nora has given us the second chamber on the left, Nathan. I only packed a few things, but perhaps you'd better have some of the men fetch my trunk."

"Sara, you aren't going to be staying here that long," Nathan countered.

"I see."

And if you're killed at sea, she wanted to scream at him. What then, Nathan? Would anyone even bother to come back here to tell me? Lord, it was too horrible to think about.

Sara shrugged off his hands and continued. Nathan once again followed her.

The bedchamber assigned to them faced the sea. Twin windows were open, and the lulling sound of the waves slapping against the rocks echoed throughout the spacious room. There was a large four-poster bed situated between the windows with a lovely multicolored quilt covering it. A large overstuffed green velvet chair sat at an angle near the wardrobe adjacent to the door. The color of the drapes matched the color of the chair exactly.

Sara hurried over to the wardrobe and began to hang her dresses inside.

Nathan leaned against the door and watched his wife for a minute. "All right, Sara. Something's the matter, and I want to know what it is."

"Nothing's the matter," she said, her voice shaking. She didn't turn around.

Damn, he thought, something was certainly wrong, and he wasn't going to leave the room until he found out what it was.

"Have a safe voyage, husband. Good-bye."

He felt like growling. "I'm not leaving until tomorrow."

"I see."

"Will you quit saying I see?" he bellowed. "Damn it, Sara, I want you to quit acting so damned cold with me. I don't like it."

She turned around so he could see her frown. "Nathan, I've asked you countless times to quit using blasphemies in my presence because I don't like it, but that doesn't stop you, does it?"

"That isn't the same," he muttered. He wasn't at all irritated with her near-shout. The fact that she was getting her temper back actually pleased him. She wasn't acting cold or uncaring.

Sara couldn't understand why he was smiling at her. He looked relieved. The man didn't make any sense to her at all. Nathan had obviously spent one too many days in the hot sun.

A plan formed in her mind. "Since you like using blasphemies so much, I shall have to assume that you gain immense satisfaction when you use such ignorant words." She paused to smile at him. "I've decided I'm going to use sinful words, too, just to test this theory. I'm also going to find out if you like hearing your spouse talk so commonly."

His laughter didn't bother her at all. "The only foul words you know are damn and hell, Sara, because those are the only blasphemies I've ever used in your presence. I was being considerate," he added with a nod.

She shook her head. "I've heard you use other words when you didn't know I was on deck. I've also heard the crew's colorful vocabulary."

He started laughing again. The thought of his delicate little wife using foul words was extremely amusing to him. She was such a feminine thing, such a soft, sweet lady, and he couldn't even begin to imagine her using a crude word. It just wasn't in her nature.

A shout from Matthew stopped their discussion. "Nora's

wanting both of you in the drawing room," he bellowed up the stairs.

"You go on down," Sara ordered. "I only have two more gowns to finish. Tell her I'll be right there."

Nathan hated the interruption. He had been thoroughly enjoying himself. He let out a sigh and started out the door.

Sara had the last word. Her voice was amazingly cheerful when she called out, "Nathan, it's a damned hot afternoon, isn't it?"

"Damned right it is," he called back over his shoulder.

He wasn't about to let her know he didn't like hearing her talk like a common wench. What Sara said to him in private was one thing, but he knew good and well she'd never use such blasphemies in public.

He was given a chance to put her to the test much sooner than he'd anticipated.

There was a visitor sitting beside Nora on the brocade settee in the drawing room. Matthew was standing in front of the windows. Nathan nodded to his friend, then strode over to Nora.

"Nathan, dear, I'd like to present the Reverend Oscar Pickering." She turned to her guest and added, "My nephew is the marquess of St. James."

It took all he had not to start laughing. The opportunity was simply too good to pass up. "You're a man of the cloth?" he asked with a wide smile.

Nora had never seen Nathan so accommodating. Why, he actually reached out and shook the vicar's hand. She'd thought he would be as ill at ease as Matthew. That poor dear looked as if he had a rash paining him.

Sara walked into the drawing room just as Nathan sprawled in one of the two chairs facing the settee. He stretched his long legs out in front of him and grinned like a simpleton.

"Oscar is the newly appointed regent for the village," Nora was telling Nathan.

"Have you known Oscar long?" Nathan asked before he spotted Sara standing in the doorway.

"No, we've only just met, but I did insist that your aunt call me by my given name."

Sara walked forward, then made a perfect curtsy in front of their guest. The new government official was a skinny man with rounded spectacles perched on the bridge of his nose. He wore a starched white cravat with his black jacket and breeches, and his manner was most austere. He seemed a little condescending to Sara, for his head was tilted back, and he was looking down through his spectacles at her.

He kept giving Nathan quick glances. There was a noticeable look of disdain on his face.

Sara didn't like the man one bit. "My dear," Nora began, "I would like to present—"

Nathan interrupted. "His name is Oscar, Sara, and he's the new regent for the village."

He'd deliberately left out mention that the man also happened to be the vicar.

"Oscar, this lovely young lady is my niece, and Nathan's wife, of course. Lady Sara."

Pickering nodded and motioned to the chair next to Nathan. "I'm pleased to meet you, Lady Sara."

Sara dutifully smiled. The man's spectacles must have been pinching his nose tight, she thought, as he had an unusually high, nasal voice.

"I should have sent a note requesting an audience," Pickering said, "but I happened to be out on my daily walk, and I couldn't restrain myself when I saw all the commotion going on up here. My curiosity, you see, got the better of me. There are several unsavory-looking men sitting on your verandah, Lady Nora, and I would advise you to have your servants chase them away. Mustn't mingle with the inferiors, you see. It isn't done."

Pickering frowned at Matthew when he made that last comment. Sara was quite astonished by the man's rudeness.

He wasn't as schooled as he'd have them believe, she knew, because he hadn't bothered to stand up when she'd walked into the room. The man was a fraud.

In her agitation she picked up a fan from the table, flipped it open with a flick of her wrist, and diligently began to wave it back and forth in front of her face.

"No one's chasing anyone away," Nathan announced.

"The men are part of the marquess's crew," Nora interjected.

Sara walked over to stand beside Matthew. It was a show of loyalty on her part, and Matthew's slow wink told her he knew what her game was. She smiled in reaction.

Then Nathan drew her attention. "My wife was just remarking on the heat," he drawled. His gaze was directed on Sara. His smile, she noticed, was devilish. "What was it you said, wife?" he innocently asked.

"I don't remember," she blurted out.

The look of satisfaction that came over her husband changed her mind. "Oh, yes, I do remember now. I said it was damned hot. Don't you agree, Mr. Pickering?"

The spectacles fell to the tip of the regent's nose. Matthew looked just as startled. Nathan, she noticed, had quit smiling.

Sara sweetened her smile. "The heat always gives me a hell of a headache," she announced.

She added up the reactions once again. Matthew was looking at her as though he'd only just noticed she had more than one nose on her face.

Her dear husband was glaring at her. That wasn't good enough. She was after total defeat, and with it the promise that he would never use foul words again.

She prayed Nora would be understanding when she explained her shameful conduct. Then she let out a loud sigh and leaned back against the window ledge. "Yes, it's a real pisser today."

Nathan bounded out of his chair. Like a man who'd just heard a foul suggestion and couldn't quite believe it, he demanded that she repeat herself. "What did you just say?" he roared.

She was happy to accommodate him. "I said it's a real pisser today."

"Enough!" Nathan shouted.

Matthew had to sit down. Nora started in coughing in a bid to cover her laughter. Mr. Pickering was out of his seat and hurrying across the room. He clutched a book in his hands.

"Must you leave so soon, Mr. Pickering?" Sara called out. Her face was hidden behind the fan so he wouldn't see her smile.

"I really must," their guest stammered.

"My, you're in a hurry," Sara said. She put the fan down and started for the foyer. "Why, you act as though someone just kicked you in the—"

She never got in the last word since Nathan's hand suddenly covered her mouth. She pushed his hand away. "I was only going to say backside."

"Oh, no you weren't," Nathan countered.

"Sara, whatever in heaven's name came over you?" Nora called out.

Sara hurried over to her aunt. "Do forgive me. I hope I didn't upset you overly much, Nora, but Nathan does like to use crude words, and I thought I'd give it a try. I didn't particularly care for this new government official anyway," she confessed. "But if you wish it, I will of course chase him down and apologize."

Nora shook her head. "I didn't like him either," she admitted.

Both ladies were pretending not to notice that Nathan was standing in front of them. Sara scooted a little closer to Nora. She felt as if she were going to be pounced on at any moment.

She didn't care for that feeling at all. She cleared her throat in a nervous action but valiantly held onto her smile when she said, "What was that book I noticed in Mr.

Pickering's hands? Did you lend him one of your novels, Aunt? I don't believe I'd trust him to return it to you. He doesn't seem the reliable sort at all."

"It wasn't a novel he was carrying," Nora said, her smile gentle. "It was his Bible. Oh, heavens, I really should have explained much sooner."

"Explained what?" Sara asked. "Do you mean to tell me that condescending man carries a Bible around with him? If that isn't hypocritical, I don't know what is."

"Sara, most of the clergy do carry Bibles."

She was slow to catch on. "Clergy? Nora, you told me he was the newly appointed regent."

"Yes, dear, he's a government official, but he also happens to be the pastor of the only church in the village. He stopped by to invite us to attend his Sunday services."

"Oh, my God." After wailing out those words Sara closed her eyes.

No one said a word for a minute. Nathan continued to glare at his wife. Sara continued to blush, and Nora continued to struggle not to laugh. Then Matthew's deep voice broke the silence. "Now that, Lady Sara, is a real pisser."

"Watch your mouth, Matthew," Nathan ordered. He grabbed hold of Sara's hand and pulled her from the settee.

"I can just imagine what the topic of his sermon is going to be come Sunday," Nora announced. She started laughing, and within a flash she needed to mop the tears from her cheeks. "Oh, Lord, I thought I'd die when you so casually remarked—"

"This isn't amusing," Nathan interjected.

"Did you know?" Sara demanded at the same time.

Nathan pretended ignorance. "Know what?"

"That Pickering was a man of the cloth?"

He slowly nodded.

"It's all your fault," Sara cried out. "I never would have disgraced myself if you hadn't prodded me. Now do you understand my point? Will you quit using blasphemies?"

Nathan threw his arm around his wife's shoulders and

hauled her up against his side. "Nora, I apologize for my wife's foul mouth. Now give me directions to this waterfall." He glanced down at Sara. "You're going to have your first swimming lesson, Sara, and if you use one more obscene word, I swear I'll let you drown."

Nora led them through the back of the house as she gave her directions. When she suggested she have the cook prepare a nice picnic luncheon for them, Nathan declined. He grabbed two apples, handed one to Sara, and dragged her in his wake out the back door.

"It's too hot for a swim," Sara argued.

Nathan said nothing.

"I'm not suitably attired for the water," she continued.

"Too bad."

"I'll get my hair wet."

"That you will."

She gave up. His mind was set on this course of action, she supposed, and it was wasted effort to try to reason with him.

The broken path was narrow. She held onto the back of Nathan's shirt when the climb became steep. She was just beginning to get weary of their hike when the sound of the waterfall caught her attention.

Eager to see a bit of paradise, as Nora had called it, she passed her husband and took the lead.

The foliage was dense around them, and the sweet scent of wildflowers filled the air. Sara felt as though she was in the center of a kaleidoscope of colors. The green of the leaves was the most vivid color she'd ever seen, save for Nathan's beautiful eyes, she told herself, and the pink, orange, and bright red flowers sprinkled about by Mother Nature's whim seemed to blossom before her eyes.

It really was a paradise. That admission carried with it the worry of a serpent.

Nathan had just lifted a fat branch out of the path and motioned for Sara to go ahead.

"Should I worry about snakes?" she asked him in a whisper.

"No."

"Why not?" she asked, hoping he'd tell her there weren't any of the horrid reptiles on the island.

"I'll worry for you," he said instead.

Her fear increased. "What will you do if a snake bites you?" she asked as she passed him.

"Bite him back," Nathan drawled.

That ludicrous remark made her laugh. "You would. wouldn't you?"

She came to an abrupt stop and let out a gasp of pleasure. "Oh, Nathan, it's so lovely here."

He silently agreed with her. The waterfall poured down over the smooth rocks and fell into a froth in the pool at the bottom.

Nathan took hold of Sara's hand again and led her to the ledge behind the waterfall. The area was very like a hidden cave, and when they'd reached the center the water became a curtain shielding them from the world.

"Take your clothes off, Sara, while I see how deep it is here."

He didn't give her time to argue with that command but turned to lean against the rock to take off his boots.

Sara took his apple, added her own, and placed both on the rock behind her. She put her hand out to touch the water flowing down and was surprised that it wasn't overly cold to the touch.

"I'll just sit here and dangle my feet in the water," she announced.

"Take your clothes off, Sara."

She turned to argue with her husband and found he'd stripped out of all his garments. Before she could even blush he'd disappeared through the curtain of water into the pool below.

Sara folded her husband's clothes and put them way back against the wall. She then removed her dress, her shoes, her stockings, and her petticoats. She left her chemise on.

Then she sat down close to the edge and let the water pour over her feet. She was just about to relax when Nathan caught hold of her feet and pulled her into the water. It felt too wonderful to protest. The sun was bright, and the drops of water seemed to glisten on Nathan's bronzed shoulders.

The water came to the middle of his chest. It was so clear, she could see to the bottom. Nathan's muscular thighs drew her immediate notice. He was such a fit man, she thought to herself. He was terribly gentle with her when he pulled her into his arms.

She wrapped herself around him and rested the side of her face on his shoulder.

"You're very trusting," he whispered. "Stand up. Let's see if the water covers your head."

She did as he requested. The water reached her mouth, but when she tilted her head all the way back she could breathe without difficulty.

"This is nice, isn't it?" she asked.

Nathan was trying to concentrate on the swimming lesson he was about to give, but her soft body kept getting in his way. The thinner-than-air chemise she wore clung to her breasts, and all he really wanted to do was make sweet love to her.

Hell, he thought, he had the discipline of a gnat when she was near. "All right, then," he began in a brisk, no-nonsense voice. "The first thing you're going to learn is how to float."

Sara wondered why Nathan was frowning so, then decided he was being brisk so she wouldn't try to argue with him. "If you say so, Nathan."

"You're going to have to let go of me, Sara."

She immediately did as he ordered. She slipped under the water when she lost her anchor and her balance, and she came up sputtering. Nathan lifted her up by holding her around the waist, then ordered her to stretch out on her back.

Sara was floating without his assistance in little time. He

was more pleased over her accomplishment than she appeared to be. "That's enough instruction for one day," she announced. She grabbed hold of his arm to balance herself and then tried to nag him into taking her back to the ledge

Nathan pulled her into his arms. His touch was gentle as he brushed her hair out of her face. Her soft breasts rubbed against his chest. He took his time lowering the straps. Sara didn't realize her husband's intent until her chemise was down around her waist.

She opened her mouth to protest. He silenced her with a long wet kiss. The sound of the waterfall drowned out his low growl of desire. Her knees went weak when his tongue moved inside her mouth. He swept her resistance completely away. She threw her arms around his neck and held him tight.

Nathan worked the chemise down her legs, then lifted her higher until he was pressed tight against the junction of her thighs. She felt so incredibly good to him. Kissing her wasn't enough anymore. He pulled back and looked into her eyes.

"I want you."

"I always want you, Nathan," she whispered.

"Now, Sara," he said. "I want you now."

Her eyes widened. "Here?"

He nodded. "Here," he said in a low groan. "And now, Sara. I don't want to wait."

Even as he told her his intent he was pulling her legs up around his waist. He was kissing her wildly, demanding her response.

Oh, how easily he could make her want him, she thought. Sara was trembling with raw need when he asked her if she was ready for him. She couldn't even speak. Her nails scraped his shoulders in answer, and she let out a little sigh of pleasure when he began to ease inside her.

Nathan captured her mouth for a long kiss, and when her tongue touched his he thrust deep inside. She tightened around him.

They both almost drowned. Neither minded. And when

they found their fulfillment they were both left spent from the bliss they'd just shared.

Sara didn't have the strength to walk to the ledge. Nathan carried her there and placed her on the rock next to the waterfall. The sun beat down on her, but Sara didn't mind the heat. She was still feeling happy and lethargic from their lovemaking.

Nathan lifted himself up on the ledge and sat beside Sara. He couldn't stop himself from touching her. He kissed the top of her head, then the ticklish spot behind her ear. She fell back against the rock and closed her eyes. "It's quite remarkable what happens when we make love, isn't it, Nathan?" she whispered.

He rolled to his side, propped himself on one elbow, and stared down at her. His fingers slowly circled her breasts, smiling when he saw the goosebumps his touch caused.

Sara had never felt so wonderful. The heat from the rock against her back warmed her, and her husband's touch made her shiver at the same time. She didn't think it was possible for her to want him again so soon, but when he began to nuzzle the valley between her breasts desire flared again.

She couldn't stop herself from arching up against him. He was driving her mad with his light, teasing caresses. He bathed each breast with his mouth, his tongue, and when he next looked into her eyes he saw the passion there, the need. His fingers tickled a path down her stomach. He teased her navel. She drew her stomach in. His hand moved down lower, and when his fingers slipped inside her she let out a low groan.

"You're wet for me, aren't you, Sara?"

She was too embarrassed to answer him. She tried to move his hand away. He wouldn't let her. And then he leaned down and began to make love to her with his mouth. His tongue made her lose her control. She writhed beneath him. She never wanted the sweet torture to end.

Her movements made him hard again. Just when he felt her tighten around him he moved between her legs and thrust deep inside her. Sara found her release then. The climax was so shattering, so consuming, she thought she'd died and gone to heaven.

Nathan was there with her. He let out a low groan and poured his seed into her.

Sara was too weak to move. Nathan thought his weight must be crushing her. With extreme effort he braced himself up with his elbows.

When he saw her bemused expression he smiled. "If we fall into the water now, we're going to drown."

She smiled up at him through her tears. She reached up and touched his mouth. "You wouldn't ever let anything happen to me. Do you have to go away tomorrow?"

He had started to turn away from her but her question stopped him. "Yes," he answered.

"I see."

God, she sounded forlorn. "What exactly do you see?" he asked. He nudged her chin up when she tried to turn her face away. "Sara?"

Because she couldn't come right out and ask him if he was going pirating, she decided not to say anything at all.

"Are you going to miss me, wife?" he asked.

She was nearly undone by the tenderness in his gaze. "Yes, Nathan," she whispered. "I will miss you."

"Then come with me."

Her eyes widened in astonishment. "You would let me come with you?" she stammered out. "But that means you aren't going . . . I did jump to conclusions. You have put it all behind you."

"Sara, what are you rambling about?"

She pulled his head down for a kiss. "I'm happy you would let me come with you, that's all," she explained. She sat up and leaned against his side. "I don't need to go with you now. It's quite enough to know you'd let me."

"Quit talking in circles," Nathan ordered. "And while I'm thinking about it, I want you to explain what was going on in your head earlier today. You were upset about something. Tell me what it was."

"I was afraid you wouldn't come back for me," Sara blurted out. It was a lie, of course, but her arrogant husband couldn't possibly know that. In fact, he looked quite pleased by her statement.

"I would never forget to come back for you," he countered. "But I'm talking about before, Sara."

"Before what?"

"Before you even knew I was leaving to get supplies. You were acting oddly then."

"I was feeling sorry for myself because my time with Nora was soon going to end. I shall miss her, Nathan."

He gave her a fierce look while he tried to make up his mind if she was telling the truth or not. Then she smiled at him and told him she was once again ready to go back into the water. "I haven't quite mastered this floating business yet," she said.

Husband and wife stayed in the pool most of the afternoon. They ate their apples as they made their way back down the mountain. Sara's delicate skin was already beginning to burn. Her face was as red as the sunset.

When Nathan put his arm around her shoulder she let out a squeal. He was immediately contrite.

Nora met them at the kitchen door. "Matthew and Jimbo and I held dinner so that . . . goodness, Sara, you're as red as a beet. Oh, child, you're going to suffer tonight. Whatever were you thinking of?"

"I didn't think about the sun," Sara replied. "I was having such a good time."

"What were you doing? Were you swimming all the while?" Nora asked.

"No," Nathan answered when his wife glanced up at him. He smiled at her and then turned back to Nora. "As a matter of fact, we were—"

"Floating," Sara blurted out. "I'll just be a minute, Aunt,

while I change my clothes and brush my hair. You really shouldn't have waited for us," she added over her shoulder as she rushed toward the stairs.

Nathan caught her at the bottom step. He slowly turned her around, then tilted her chin up and kissed her. It was a long, lingering kiss that made her feel she was going to swoon. It wasn't like him to show such affection in front of others, she realized, and he never kissed her unless he wanted to make love to her . . . or shut her up, she knew. Since he looked too exhausted to make love again, and since she hadn't been arguing with him, she could come to only one conclusion. Nathan was being affectionate just because he wanted to.

She was further confused when he leaned down and whispered into her ear, "I thought what we did all afternoon was called making love, wife, but if you prefer to call it floating, that's fine with me."

Her face was too sunburned for anyone to know if she was blushing or not. She smiled up at him even as she shook her head at him. He was teasing her. Good God, Nathan had a sense of humor, too. It was too much to take in all at once.

Then he gifted her with a slow wink. She knew she'd died and gone to heaven then. The sunburn didn't matter any longer, nor did her audience of Jimbo, Matthew, and Nora. Sara threw herself into Nathan's arms and kissed him soundly. "Oh, I do love you so," she cried out.

She wasn't even disappointed when he grunted in reply and didn't shout his love for her then and there. It was too soon for him to tell her what was in his heart, she decided. The feelings were too fresh, too new, and Nathan was quite stubborn. It might take him another six months before he could finally say the words she wanted to hear. She could wait, she told herself. She was, after all, patient and understanding. Besides, in her heart she already knew he loved her, and the fact that he wasn't ready to know it didn't bother her at all.

She didn't make it downstairs for dinner. Once Nathan

THE GIFT

had helped her remove her gown she seemed to swell up, and the thought of putting any clothing against her burning skin made her want to scream.

Nora provided a bottle of green paste. Sara carried on something fierce while Nathan gently applied the sticky lotion to her back and shoulders. Fortunately the front of her hadn't been burned. She slept on her stomach, and when she couldn't stand the shivers she slept on Nathan.

The next day Nathan didn't make a single rude remark when he kissed Sara good-bye. He pretended he didn't mind looking at the mask of green paste covering her face.

Sara spent the next two days with her aunt. The Reverend Mr. Pickering came back for a second visit. He was much more civil. Sara explained the reason she'd used such foul words in his presence. Pickering broke into a smile. He looked relieved by her confession, and his manner toward Aunt Nora warmed considerably.

During the course of their visitation the reverend mentioned that there was a ship leaving for England the following morning. Sara immediately went to her aunt's desk and penned a letter to her mother. She told all about her adventure, how happy she was, and boasted that Nathan had turned out to be a kind, considerate, loving husband. Reverend Mr. Pickering took the missive with him to give to the captain of the vessel.

When Nathan came back the following morning Sara was so happy to see him that she burst into tears. They spent a peaceful day together and fell asleep wrapped in each other's arms.

Sara couldn't believe it was possible to be so happy. Being married to Nathan was like living in paradise. Nothing could ever destroy their love. Nothing.

She wished everyone could be as happy and made that remark to Nora and Matthew late one evening. The three of them sat in wicker chairs on the verandah while they waited for Nathan to return from an errand.

"I believe Matthew and I know exactly what you're

261

talking about," Nora announced. "One doesn't have to be young to experience love, my dear. Matthew, are you ready for a brandy?"

"I'll fetch it," Sara volunteered.

"You'll stay put," Nora countered. She stood up and started for the door. "Your burn's still tender. Keep Matthew company. I'll be right back."

As soon as the door closed behind Nora Matthew whispered, "She's too good for me, Sara, but I'm not going to let that stand in my way. As soon as I put my affairs in order I'm coming back to live out my days with your aunt. How are you feeling about that?"

Sara clasped her hands together. "Oh, Matthew, I think that's wonderful news. We must have the wedding ceremony before we leave for England. I don't want to miss the celebration."

Matthew looked uncomfortable. "Well, now, Sara, I didn't exactly mention marriage, did I?"

She bounded out of her chair. "You'd best mention it now, Matthew, or you aren't ever coming back here. A single night of passion is one thing, sir, but a plan to live out the rest of your days in sin is quite another. Think of Nora's reputation!"

"I am thinking about Nora's reputation," Matthew defended. "She couldn't marry me. It wouldn't be right. I'm not worthy enough."

The seaman stood up and stared out toward the sea. Sara walked over and jabbed him in his stomach with her finger. "You bloody well are worthy enough. Don't you dare insult yourself to me, sir."

"Sara, I've led a . . . speckled life," Matthew stammered.

"And?" she asked.

"And I'm only a seaman," he said.

Sara shrugged. "Nora's first husband was a groom. He was probably just as speckled as you think you are," she added. "Nora was blissfully happy with her Johnny. She must like speckled men. Nora confessed to me that you are a dear, tenderhearted man, Matthew. I know you love her. She must love you, too, if she let you into her bed. As I said to Nathan not long ago, this would solve many problems. Uncle Henry wouldn't send anyone after Nora if he knew she had someone strong to protect her. You'll look after her interests. And I would be so very proud to call you Uncle."

Matthew was humbled by her faith in him. He let out a happy sigh. "All right," he said. "I'll ask Nora. But you have to promise me you'll accept it if Nora says no. All right?"

Sara threw her arms around Matthew's neck and hugged him tight. "She won't say no," she whispered.

"Wife, what the hell are you doing? Matthew, unhand her."

Both Sara and Matthew ignored Nathan's brisk order. Only after she'd placed a chaste kiss on Matthew's cheek did she move away from him. She walked over to the top step where Nathan stood and gave him a sassy grin. "We have to go upstairs now, husband. Matthew wants to be alone with Nora."

She had to pull him into the house and up the stairs. He wanted her to explain why he'd found her draped all over his seaman. "I'll explain everything when we're in our bedroom."

They passed Nora on their way across the foyer. Sara bid her aunt goodnight, then went upstairs. She paced while she waited to find out if Matthew had asked his question and if Nora had given him her answer. When Nathan grew weary of watching her wear out the carpet he captured her in mid-pace, tossed her on their bed, and made wild, passionate love to her. They fell asleep wrapped in each other's arms.

The announcement was made the following morning. Nora had agreed to become Matthew's wife. Sara guessed that much as soon as she saw her aunt's radiant smile.

Matthew explained that he would have to return to England for a short while, in order to straighten out his affairs and sell his cottage. He wouldn't take Nora with him, of course, for her life would be in jeopardy if the Winchesters sniffed out her presence in England. The older seaman wanted to get married before he left, and since Nathan was determined to set sail within a week, the wedding was scheduled for the following Saturday. It was a simple ceremony. Sara wept her way through the event and Nathan spent most of his time mopping at her tears.

He thought she was the most exasperating woman.

Nathan stood there watching his gentle little wife as she whispered and laughed with her aunt, and he realized then the joy she brought to others.

He heard her tell Matthew that her most fervent wish was that their marriage would be as perfect as hers was. He laughed then. Sara really was a hopeless romantic.

She was ridiculously tenderhearted.

She was outrageously innocent.

She was . . . perfect.

Chapter Twelve

There was more than one serpent slithering around in Sara's paradise, just waiting for her return to England.

The voyage back to London was uneventful, however. Ivan took Sara under his wing and tried to teach her how to make a proper soup. The woman couldn't seem to grasp the knack of using just a pinch of seasoning, but Ivan couldn't bring himself to tell her the truth. The rest of the men wouldn't tell her either. They praised her considerably, yet the minute she turned her back on them they tossed the soup overboard. Their empty stomachs weren't nearly as important to them as Sara's feelings.

Sara then wanted to try her hand at making biscuits. The ones stored in the wooden tins were filled with vile little creatures called weevils. The crew didn't mind the insects. They merely pounded the biscuits on the floor a couple of times to shake the weevils loose, then ate the biscuits whole.

Since Ivan had all the ingredients needed, he decided to let Sara make a batch. She worked all morning on the biscuits. The men pretended to be appreciative, but the things were as hard as stones, and they were afraid they'd break their teeth if they tried to take a bite out of one.

Chester had become Sara's greatest champion. He scoffed at the other men, then soaked his biscuit overnight in a full cup of grog. Come morning, even he had to whisper defeat. The biscuit was still too hard to chew.

Matthew suggested they use the leftovers for cannonballs. Nathan laughed at that remark. Sara happened to overhear the banter and took immediate exception. She retaliated that evening by eating the most disgusting meal ever put together by man. She made certain Nathan was watching her, too. The sour cucumbers soaked in strawberry jam did the trick. Nathan barely made it to the railing before he lost his supper.

Sara did seem to have an iron stomach and less than ordinary discrimination regarding food. Nathan watched her every move, and it wasn't long before he realized how enjoyable it was to have her around. He liked the sound of her laughter.

And then they reached London.

Nathan immediately took Sara to the Emerald Shipping office. He was eager for her to meet Colin.

It was midmorning when they walked down the crowded wharf. The sun was shining bright enough to make a person squint. It was warm, too. The door to the office was propped open to let the sweet breeze inside.

When they were just a half a block away from the entrance Nathan pulled Sara aside, leaned down, and whispered, "When you meet Colin, don't mention his limp. He's a little sensitive about his leg."

"He has a limp? What happened to the poor man?"

"A shark took a bite out of him," Nathan answered.

"Good Lord," she whispered in a rush. "He's fortunate to be alive."

"Yes, he is," he agreed. "Now promise me you won't say anything."

"Why would you think I'd mention his limp to him? What kind of woman do you think I am? Nathan, I do know what's proper and what isn't. Shame on you for thinking I'd say a word."

"You screamed when you saw my back," he reminded her.

He would have to bring that up. "For heaven's sake, that was different."

"How?" he asked, wondering what outrageous explanation she would give him.

She shrugged. "It was different because I love you," she said, blushing.

God, she was exasperating, he thought. Pleasing, too. He was becoming accustomed to hearing her tell him how much she loved him. Shaking that thought away, he continued. "And now that you know about Colin's leg you won't be surprised, and you therefore won't say anything to embarrass him. Isn't that right?"

Even as she nodded agreement she tried to get in the last word. "Lord, you're insulting."

He kissed her just to gain a moment's peace, but before he could stop himself he'd properly hauled her into his arms and let the kiss get completely out of hand. She opened her mouth before he would have forced her. His tongue swept inside to rub against hers. He didn't mind at all that they were standing in the center of the busy crosswalk, didn't care either that several passersby stopped to watch them.

Jimbo and Matthew came rushing down the walk but stopped when they saw the couple. Jimbo let out a snort of disgust. "For God's sake, boy, now isn't the time to be pawing your woman. We've got business to see to before the day's completely gone."

Nathan reluctantly pulled away from his wife. She sagged against him. He had to smile over that telling reaction. Then she noticed the group of strangers watching her. The mist of passion quickly evaporated.

"You forget yourself," she whispered to Nathan.

"I'm not the only one who forgot myself," he answered.

She ignored that truth. "I'm about to meet your business associate, and I would appreciate it if you wouldn't distract me so."

She turned her back on him before he could think of a suitable retort. While she smoothed her hair over her shoulders she smiled at Jimbo and Matthew. "Are you coming along with us?"

The two men nodded in unison. Sara took Jimbo's arm. "You may escort me, sir, and you as well, Matthew," she added when he offered his arm to her. "I'm most anxious to meet Nathan's friend. He must be quite a man to put up with my husband. Shall we go?"

Nathan had only enough time to get out of the trio's way as they continued down the walk. He trailed behind, frowning over the high-handed way his wife had taken charge.

"And by the way," he heard Sara say, "whatever you do, please don't mention Colin's limp to him. He's very sensitive about that topic, I can assure you."

"I thought you hadn't met him yet," Jimbo said.

"I haven't," Sara replied. "But Nathan has advised me. My husband is proving to be very tenderhearted when it comes to his friend's feelings. Now if I could only get him to show me like consideration, well, I assure you, I would be most grateful."

"Quit trying to provoke me," Nathan said from behind. He shoved Jimbo out of his way, grabbed hold of his wife's hand, and dragged her forward.

She was highly insulted by that command. She wasn't the ill-natured partner in the marriage. Since she was so sweet-natured, she decided not to take issue with Nathan. She'd wait until later to set him straight.

Besides, she was eager to meet his friend.

Colin was sitting behind his desk, sorting through a mound of papers. As soon as Sara and Nathan walked inside he stood up.

Nathan's friend was an extremely good-looking man, and it didn't take Sara long to realize his character was just as charming. He had a nice, genuine smile. There was a devilish sparkle in his hazel-colored eyes. He was handsome, though certainly not as handsome as Nathan. Colin didn't have the height, either, or the muscle. Sara did have to look up at him, of course, but she didn't get a crick in her neck as she always did when Nathan was standing close to her and nagging her to look him in the eye.

She guessed it was rude of her to stare at the man and immediately made a formal curtsy.

"At last I'm allowed to meet the bride," Colin said. "You're even more beautiful close up, Lady Sara, than from the distance at which I last saw you."

After giving her that compliment Colin walked over to stand directly in front of her. In a gallant action he formally bowed to her, then lifted her hand and kissed it.

She was quite impressed with his manners.

Nathan wasn't. "For God's sake, Colin, you don't have to put on a show. You won't impress her."

"Yes, he will," Sara announced.

"He's impressing me, too," Jimbo announced with a deep chuckle. "I've never seen the Dolphin act so fancy." He nudged Matthew in the ribs. "Have you?"

"Can't say that I have," Matthew replied.

Colin didn't let go of Sara's hand. She didn't mind. Nathan obviously did. "Unhand her, Colin," he muttered.

"Not until you've made a proper introduction," Colin announced. He winked at Sara and almost laughed when she blushed in reaction.

Not only was Nathan's wife exquisitely beautiful, she was also charming, Colin thought to himself. Had Nathan realized his good fortune yet?

Colin turned to his friend to ask just that question, then decided to find out for himself. "Well?" he said.

Nathan let out a long sigh. He leaned against the window

ledge, folded his arms in front of him, and then said, "Wife, meet Colin. Colin, meet my wife. Now let go of her, Colin, before I smash your face in."

Sara was appalled by the threat. Colin laughed. "I wonder why you don't like me holding your wife," he drawled.

He hadn't let go of Sara's hand but kept his gaze fully directed on his friend. Nathan, he decided, looked extremely uncomfortable.

Sara's comment turned his attention back to her. "Nathan doesn't like anything, sir," she announced with a smile.

"Does he like you?"

She nodded before Nathan could order Colin to quit his teasing. "Oh, yes, he likes me very much," she said matter-of-factly. She tried to extricate her hand from his grasp, but Colin held tight. "Sir, are you deliberately trying to provoke Nathan's temper?"

He slowly nodded. "Then I believe we have something in common," Sara said. "I always provoke his temper."

Colin threw back his head and laughed. Sara hadn't thought her remark was that amusing, and she wondered if he wasn't laughing about something else altogether.

He finally let go of her hand. She immediately clasped her hands behind her back to keep them safe from his grasp. Nathan noticed that action and found his first smile. Then Colin soured it. "You didn't need a reprieve after all," he told Nathan. "Sooner would have been better than later."

"Leave it alone," Nathan ordered. He knew Colin was referring to his past remark that he wanted to leave the chore of collecting his bride until the last possible minute.

"Sir, have we met before?" Sara asked. "You did mention that from a distance . . ."

When he shook his head at her she stopped her question. "I happened to see you one afternoon, but alas, I wasn't given the opportunity to make my presence known to you. I was on a mission, you see, to determine if a certain possession would fit through a window."

"I'm not amused, Colin," Nathan muttered.

Colin's grin indicated he was vastly amused. He decided that he'd prodded his friend enough for the moment. "Let me move those papers from the chair, Lady Sara, and you can sit down and tell me all about your voyage."

"It isn't a happy story, Dolphin," Jimbo interjected. Since there weren't any other chairs available, he leaned against the wall. His gaze was directed on Sara. "We met with one sorry disaster after another, didn't we?"

Sara gave him a dainty shrug. "I thought it was a lovely voyage," she announced. "Very uneventful, as a matter of fact. Jimbo," she added, "it's impolite to snort when you don't agree with someone."

"Uneventful, Sara?" Matthew asked. He grinned at Colin. "The enemy stalked us at every turn."

"What enemy stalked us?" Sara asked. "Oh, you must mean those horrid pirates."

"They were only a small part of the mischief," Matthew remarked.

Sara turned back to Colin. "Pirates attacked the ship, but we chased them away quick enough. As for the rest of the voyage, I declare it was quite peaceful. Don't you agree, Nathan?"

"No."

She frowned at him to let him know his rude denial wasn't appreciated.

"You're forgetting the parasols," he reminded her.

Colin thought he'd lost track of the conversation. "What are you talking about?"

"Sara's parasols turned out to be our greatest enemies," Matthew explained. "There were three of them . . . or was it four? I can't remember. I tend to block unpleasant memories. I get the shivers."

"Will someone explain?" Colin demanded.

"It isn't significant," Sara blurted out. She wasn't about to let her men drag out her venial sins like soiled linen to be

271

scrubbed clean in front of company. "Matthew's just jesting with you. Isn't he, Nathan?"

The worry in her gaze wasn't lost on her husband. "Yes," he agreed with a sigh. "He was just jesting."

Colin let the topic drop when he noticed how relieved Sara looked. He decided to wait until he and Nathan were alone to find out the story behind the parasols.

He lifted the stack of papers from the chair and hurried over to the far side of the office. After placing the stack on top of the cabinet he went back to his chair, sat down, and propped his feet up on the edge of the desk.

Sara watched him closely and couldn't help but notice that he hadn't limped at all. "Nathan, Colin doesn't have a—"

"Sara!"

"Please don't raise your voice to me in front of your associate," she ordered.

"What don't I have?" Colin asked.

Sara sat down, adjusted the folds in her gown, and then smiled at Colin. She could feel Nathan's frown. "A surly nature," she announced. "I can't imagine why you and Nathan are such good friends. You seem very different to my way of thinking, sir. Yes, you do."

Colin grinned. "I'm the civil one in the partnership," he told her. "Is that what you're thinking?"

"I dare not agree, of course, for it would make me disloyal to my husband," she replied. She paused to smile at Nathan, then added, "But you notice that I'm not disagreeing either."

Colin was noticing a whole lot more than that. Nathan couldn't seem to take his gaze off his wife. There was a warm glint in his eyes Colin had never seen before.

"You don't have to call me sir," Colin said to Sara. "Please call me Colin, or even Dolphin like the men do, if that will suit you." A mischievous look came into his eyes, and he glanced over at Nathan before asking, "And what might I call you, Lady Sara, that isn't quite so formal? After all, you are part of this enterprise now. Does Nathan have a special nickname for you that I might also use?"

Nathan thought the question was ridiculous. He didn't particularly like the way Colin was fawning over his wife. He trusted his friend completely, of course, and aside from that fact, Nathan would never allow himself to care too much about his wife, at least not to the point where he was actually jealous. Odd, though, he was still getting damned irritated. "Colin, I call her wife," he announced. "You can't."

Colin leaned further back in his chair. "No, I don't suppose I can," he drawled. "Pity you haven't given her any other nicknames."

"Like what?" Sara asked.

"Like sweetheart, or love, or even—"

"Hell, Colin," Nathan interrupted, "will you quit this game?"

Sara straightened her shoulders. She was frowning at her husband. Nathan thought it was because he'd accidentally slipped in a blasphemy. He almost apologized, then caught himself in time.

"No, Colin, he has never called me by any endearments," Sara announced. She sounded properly appalled. Nathan rolled his eyes heavenward.

"Even if I did," Nathan said, "you damned well couldn't. Partners or not, Colin, you aren't calling my wife sweetheart."

"Why would it bother you?" Colin innocently prodded.

So that was his game, Nathan thought. He's trying to find out just how much I care about Sara. He shook his head at his friend, then added a glare so that Colin would be sure to get his message to let the topic drop.

"Nathan does have a special nickname he uses when he addresses me," Sara announced then, drawing her husband's attention. "You have my permission to use it, too."

"Oh?" Colin asked. He caught the surprised look on Nathan's face and became all the more curious. "And what might that be?"

"Damn it, Sara."

Colin couldn't believe he'd heard correctly. "Did you say—"

"Nathan usually addresses me as Damn It Sara. Don't you, dear?" she asked her husband. "Colin, you may also—"

As if on cue, Nathan muttered, "Damn it, Sara, don't push me. I . . ."

Even he saw the humor then and joined in the laughter. Then Matthew once again reminded them that there was business to attend to and that they'd best get on with it.

The teasing banter ended. Sara sat quietly while she listened to Colin give Nathan a catch-up on the firm's activities. She smiled when Colin announced that they had five more contracts to ship supplies to the Indies.

"Nathan, does that mean we're . . ."

"No, we aren't rich yet."

She looked crestfallen.

"We'll all be rich when you—"

"I know what my duty is," she blurted out. "You don't have to explain it in front of my staff."

Nathan smiled. Colin shook his head. "I haven't followed any of that," he admitted. "What is the duty you have to perform that will make us rich?"

From the way Lady Sara blushed, Colin concluded the matter was of a personal nature. He remembered that Nathan had told him the king's treasure wouldn't be handed over until Sara gave her husband an heir. Because of Sara's obvious discomfort, however, Colin decided to let the topic drop.

"For the love of God," Matthew muttered, "quit this chitchat. I'm itching to get going, Colin. I've got some personal dealings to settle before the week's out."

"Are you going somewhere?" Colin asked.

"Oh, heavens, Matthew, you haven't told Colin about Nora," Sara interjected.

"Who is Nora?"

Sara was happy to explain. She hadn't realized the details she'd given until she was finishing up her explanation. "I cannot say more, Colin, about the quickness of the wedding, for to do so would damage my aunt's reputation."

"Sara, you already told him everything," Nathan interjected dryly.

From his position behind the desk Colin had a clear view of the street beyond the open doorway. Sara had just begun to explain why she hadn't truly revealed her aunt's unusual circumstances when a black carriage swayed to a stop across the street. There were five men on horseback escorting the vehicle.

Colin recognized the seal on the side door. It was the Earl of Winchester's family crest. He gave Nathan a barely perceptible nod, then returned his attention to Sara.

Nathan immediately moved away from the ledge, motioned to Jimbo and Matthew, and then casually walked outside.

Sara didn't pay any attention to the men. She was determined to convince Colin that her aunt was a decent woman and that she would never have become so passionately involved with Matthew if she hadn't loved him with all her heart. She also wanted his promise not to repeat a word of what she'd inadvertently blurted out about her aunt.

Just as soon as he gave her the promise she wanted she started to turn around to see what her husband was doing. Colin stopped her by asking another question.

"Sara, what do you think of our office?"

"I don't wish to injure your feelings, Colin, but I do believe it's rather drab. It could be very attractive, though. We need only paint the walls and add drapes. I'd be happy to supervise this task. Pink would be a lovely color, don't you think?"

"No," he said, in such a cheerful tone of voice that she wasn't at all offended. She became a little uneasy, however, when he opened the center drawer of the desk and took out a pistol. "Pink's a woman's color," Colin said then. "We're men. We like dark, ugly colors."

His grin indicated he was jesting with her. Besides, she reasoned, although she didn't know him at all well, she was certain he wouldn't shoot her just because he didn't care for the color she'd suggested. Nathan wouldn't let him.

As to that, where was her husband? Sara stood up and started for the doorway. She spotted Nathan standing between Jimbo and Matthew across the street. The trio was blocking the door of a black carriage. Sara couldn't see the seal. Jimbo's large bulk blocked it. "Who are they talking to, I wonder. Do you know, Colin?"

"Come and sit down, Sara. Wait for Nathan to come back inside."

She was about to do just that when Jimbo shifted positions and she saw the crest. "That's my father's carriage," she cried out in surprise. "How in heaven's name did he know so soon that we were back in London?"

Colin didn't answer her, for Sara had already rushed out the doorway. He shoved the pistol into his pocket and hurried after her.

She hesitated at the curb. Her stomach suddenly tightened up. Oh, God, she hoped her father and Nathan were getting along. And who were those other men?

"Don't borrow trouble," she whispered to herself. She took a deep breath, picked up her skirts, and rushed across the street just as her father climbed out of the carriage.

The earl of Winchester was considered by many to be a distinguished-looking gentleman. He still had a full head of hair, though most of it was silver-colored, and his belly was more firm than round. He stood two inches below six feet in height. He had the same shade of brown eyes Sara did, but that was the only resemblance they shared. Her father's nose was eagle-sized. When he frowned, or squinted against the sun, as he was doing at that moment, his eyes disappeared behind narrow slits. His lips, when pressed together, were as thin as a finely drawn line.

Sara wasn't afraid of her father, but he did worry her, for the simple reason that he wasn't at all predictable. She never knew what he was going to do. Sara hid her concern and rushed forward dutifully to embrace her father. Nathan noticed how the earl stiffened in response to Sara's touch.

"I'm so surprised to see you, Father," Sara began. She stepped back and took hold of Nathan's arm. "How did you know we were back in London so soon after our arrival? Why, our trunks haven't even left the ship yet."

Her father quit frowning at Nathan long enough to give her an answer. "I've had my men watching the water since the day you left, Sara. Now come along with me. I'm taking you home where you belong."

The anger in her father's voice alarmed her. She instinctively moved closer to her husband. "Home? But Father, I'm married to Nathan. I must go home with him. Surely you realize . . ."

She stopped trying to explain when the carriage door opened and her older sister Belinda climbed out.

God's truth, Sara was sorry to see her. Belinda was smiling. That wasn't a good sign. The only time Belinda ever appeared to be happy was when there was trouble brewing. She smiled a lot then.

Belinda had gained a considerable amount of weight since Sara had last seen her. The gold-colored walking dress she wore was straining at the seams. Her sister was heavy-boned and given to fat anyway, and the extra pounds she'd put on had settled around her midriff. She looked more pregnant than not. As a child Belinda had been the pretty sister. The men in the family doted on her. She had curly sun-yellowed hair, a dimple in each cheek, and adorable blue eyes. As she'd grown into womanhood, however, the dimples had been swallowed up in her overly rounded cheeks. Her glorious hair had turned into a mousy brown. The darling of the Winchester family wasn't the center of attention any longer. Belinda's answer to that change in status was to console herself with food.

Sara, on the other hand, had been a rather plain, lanky-legged child. She was terribly awkward, and her permanent teeth had seemed to take forever to come in straight. For almost a year she spit whenever she spoke. No one except her nanny and her mother ever doted on her.

It was a sin not to love her sister, and for that reason alone Sara loved Belinda. She thought she understood her sister's cruel streak. It had been born out of all the disappointments she'd suffered, and Sara always tried to be patient and understanding with her. When Belinda wasn't in a snit about something she could actually be quite pleasant.

Sara tried to concentrate on her sister's good qualities when she called out her greeting. Her grip on Nathan's arm was at great odds with her cheerful tone of voice. "Belinda, how nice it is to see you again."

Her sister rudely stared at Nathan while she returned her sister's greeting. "I'm happy you're finally home, Sara."

"Is Mother with you?" Sara asked.

The earl of Winchester answered her question. "Your mother's at home, where she belongs. Get into the carriage, daughter. I don't want trouble, but I'm prepared for it," he added. "You're coming with us. No one knows you've been with the marquess, and if we—"

"Oh, Papa," Belinda interrupted, "you know that isn't true. Everyone knows. Why, consider all the notes of sympathy we've received since Sara left."

"Silence!" the earl roared. "Dare you contradict me?"

Sara moved so quickly Nathan didn't have time to stop her. She pulled Belinda away from her father's side and positioned herself between them. "Belinda didn't mean to contradict you," Sara said.

Her father looked somewhat mollified. "I won't tolerate insolence," he muttered. "As to the few who do know about your disgraceful conduct, daughter," he continued, addressing his frown and his full attention to Sara, "they'll keep their mouths shut. If a scandal breaks before I've settled this matter, I'll face it."

Sara was more concerned than ever. When her father acted so sure of himself there was always mischief afoot. "What scandal, Father?" she asked. "Nathan and I haven't done anything to cause gossip. We're obeying all the conditions set down in the contract."

"Don't mention the contract to me, daughter. Now get into the carriage before I order my men to draw their weapons."

The ache in Sara's stomach intensified. She was going to have to defy her father. It was a first for her. Oh, she'd often stood up to him, but it was always in defense of her mother or her sister, never herself.

She slowly backed away until she was once again standing next to Nathan. "I'm sorry to disappoint you, Father, but I cannot go with you. My place is with my husband."

The earl was infuriated. To have his daughter openly defy him in front of witnesses was humiliating. He reached out to slap her. Nathan was quicker. He grabbed hold of the earl's wrist and started to squeeze. Hard. He wanted to break the bone in half.

Sara stopped him by merely touching him. When she sagged against his side he immediately let go of her father and put his arm around her shoulder. He could feel her trembling and became all the more furious.

"She isn't going anywhere, old man," Nathan announced in a low, controlled voice.

The denial was obviously the signal the earl's men needed. The pistols were drawn and pointed at Nathan.

Sara let out a gasp. She couldn't believe what was happening. She tried to put herself in front of Nathan to protect him. He wouldn't let her move. He tightened his hold and continued to stare at her father. He smiled. Sara didn't know what to make of that reaction.

Surely he understood the severity of the situation. "Nathanial?" she whispered. She used that name as a method to put him on his guard. She leaned up and then whispered, "You don't have a pistol. They do. Please take notice of the odds, husband."

Nathan quit his smile and looked down at her. He knew what she did not—that the odds were indeed on his side. At least eight of his loyal crew had come running at the sight of the carriage. They were lined up behind Sara, ready and armed for a fight.

There was also the fact that her father was bluffing. The look in his eyes indicated to Nathan that he didn't have the mind or the courage for a direct confrontation.

"This has gotten completely out of hand," Sara told her father. She was so upset, her voice shook. "Order your men to put their weapons away, Father. Nothing will be solved by hurting Nathan or me."

The earl of Winchester didn't give the order quickly enough. "I won't let you hurt my husband," Sara cried out. "I love him."

"He won't hurt him," Colin called out. "I'll put a hole through his forehead if he tries."

Sara turned to look at Nathan's friend. The transformation in Colin was so stunning to her, she caught her breath. Colin's stance looked relaxed, and there was a smile on his face, but the coldness in his eyes clearly indicated he'd carry out his threat without suffering a moment's qualm.

The earl immediately motioned for his men to quit their positions. When their weapons were back inside their waistbands he tried a different approach to gain victory. "Belinda, tell your sister about your mother. Since Sara refuses to come home, she might as well hear the truth now."

Belinda had moved back to her father's side. He gave her arm a little prod to get her started. "Sara, you really must come home with us," Belinda blurted. She glanced over at her father, received his nod, and then continued. "Mother's taken gravely ill. That's the reason she didn't come with us."

"She's longing to see you again," her father interjected. "Though after the way you've worried her, I can't understand why."

Sara shook her head. "Mother isn't ill," she said. "This is just trickery to get me to leave Nathan, isn't it?"

"I would never use your mother in such a manner," her father muttered with indignation.

He nudged Belinda again. Nathan noticed the action and knew the scene he was witnessing had been rehearsed. He hoped his wife was astute enough to notice, too.

Belinda took a step forward. "Mama took ill right after you left, Sara. Why, for all she knew, you could have been drowned at sea, or killed by . . . pirates."

"But Belinda, Mother . . ." Sara stopped. She wasn't certain her father knew she'd left a note explaining to her mother that she was going to help Nora get back home. Her mother might have hidden the letter from her father. "I mean to say, I sent a long letter to Mama when Nathan and I reached our destination. Mama should have received the missive by now."

Nathan was surprised by that news. "When did you write?"

"When you left to get supplies," Sara explained.

"Yes, we received both of your letters," the earl interjected.

Sara was about to argue that she'd only sent one letter, but she wasn't given a chance before her father continued. "And of course, I was pleased with the information you gave me. Still, daughter, the matter is not quite resolved, and for that reason we must continue to use discretion."

She didn't know what he was talking about. "What information?" she asked.

Her father shook his head at her. "Don't play the fool with me, Sara." He straightened his shoulders, then turned to pull the carriage door wide. "Your mother is waiting."

Sara looked up at Nathan. "Will you take me to see Mother? I'll worry until I've spoken to her."

"Later," Nathan replied.

Sara turned back to her father. "Please tell Mother we'll come to visit her as soon as Nathan finishes his business here."

The earl of Winchester had planned to wait until he'd gotten Sara away from the marquess before putting his plan into action. He didn't like direct conflicts. It was much more satisfying to have surprise on his side, and less dangerous as well. Yet when the marquess told him to take his leave, his rage exploded. "The prince regent has all the information before him now," he shouted. "It's only a matter of time till he decides you've violated the contract. Just you wait and see."

"What the hell are you rambling about?" Nathan demanded. "You're demented if you think I've violated any conditions. This marriage will not be invalidated. I've slept with my wife. It's too late."

The earl's face turned a blotchy red. Sara had never seen him in such a fury.

"Father, please calm yourself. You're going to make yourself ill."

"Sara, do you know what your father's talking about?" Nathan asked.

She shook her head. She and her husband both turned back to the earl again.

"This is a private conversation," Sara's father announced. He nodded to his men. "Wait at the corner."

He turned to Nathan again. "Dismiss your men," he ordered, "unless you wish for them to overhear what I'm about to say."

Nathan shrugged. "They stay."

"Father, I'll be happy to explain," Belinda volunteered. She smiled while she waited for their escort to leave. When the men were out of earshot she turned to Nathan. "Sara wrote to us. We never would have known if she hadn't told, you see."

"What wouldn't you have known?" Sara asked.

Belinda let out a mock sigh. "Oh, Sara, don't act so innocent. It isn't necessary now." She looked up at Nathan again and smiled. "She told us about your father. We know all about the earl of Wakersfield now. Yes, we do."

"No," Sara cried out. "Belinda, why—"

Her sister couldn't let her continue. "Of course, Sara only gave us the bare bones, but once we had that information— well, Papa had his important friend do a little investigating, and the rest was ferreted out. When Papa's finished, every-one in London will know that your husband's father was a traitor."

The earl let out a snort of disgust. "Did you think you could keep that filth swept under the carpet?" he asked Nathan. "My God, your father nearly toppled our govern-ment. Machiavelli was a saint in comparison to your father. Those sins are now on your shoulders," he added with a brisk nod. "When I'm finished you'll be destroyed."

"Father, quit these threats," Sara cried out. "You can't mean them."

Her father ignored her plea. His gaze was directed on Nathan. "Do you honestly believe the prince regent will force my daughter to spend her life tied to an infidel like you?"

Nathan was so astonished by the earl's comments that a fury he'd never felt before began to burn inside him. How had the bastard found out about his father? And God, when it was made public, how would his sister Jade react?

It was as if the earl had read Nathan's mind. "Think about your sister," he announced. "Lady Jade's married to the earl of Cainewood, isn't she? She and her husband have become the darlings of the set. That will soon change," he added with another snort. "The shame is going to make your sister a leper in society, I promise you."

Sara was terrified on Nathan's behalf. How had her father found out about the earl of Wakersfield? When Nora had confided that secret to her she'd told her no one would ever find out. The father's file was locked away inside the War Department's vault. No one could breach that sanctuary.

And then the full truth of what her father and her sister were trying to do settled in her mind. They wanted Nathan to believe she'd betrayed him.

She immediately shook her head. No, that didn't make sense, she told herself. How could they guess that she'd found out? "I don't understand how you learned about Nathan's father," she whispered. "But I—"

Belinda interrupted her. "You told us. You don't have to lie any longer. As soon as Papa read the shocking news he did as you instructed, Sara. For heaven's sake, you should be happy now. You're going to be free very soon. Then you can marry a gentleman worthy of you. Isn't that what you said, Papa?"

The earl of Winchester quickly nodded. "If the contract is set aside, the duke of Loughtonshire would still be willing to take you for his wife."

"But Belinda's pledged to him," Sara whispered.

"He prefers you," her father muttered.

The pain in Sara's stomach was so acute it almost doubled her over. "Is that why you're lying, Belinda? You don't want to marry the duke, and you've made a pact with Father, haven't you?"

"I'm not lying," Belinda countered. "You gave us the information we needed. Papa says he's going to demand that all the land the marquess inherited from his father be confiscated. When Papa's finished," she added with a sarcastic slur in her voice, "the marquess will be a pauper."

Sara shook her head. Tears streamed down her cheeks. She was so humiliated that her family would act in such a cruel, sadistic manner. "Oh, Belinda, please don't do this."

Nathan hadn't said a word. When his arm dropped away from Sara's shoulders the earl guessed that his gamble had paid off. He felt like gloating with victory. He'd heard what a cynical, hardheaded man the marquess of St. James was, and now he knew the rumors were true.

Sara needed to hear her husband tell her he believed her. She couldn't tell anything from his expression. "Nathan? Do you believe I wrote to my mother and told her about your father's sins?"

He answered her with a question of his own. "Did you know about my father?"

God save her, she almost lied to him. He looked so bored, so unconcerned. Yet his voice shook with anger.

He condemned her.

"Yes, I did know about your father," she admitted. "Nora told me."

He took a step away from her. She felt as though he'd just struck her. "Nathan? You cannot believe I would betray you. You cannot!"

Colin spoke up. "Why shouldn't he? It's damn telling evidence against you. That secret's been safe a long time. Then you find out, and—"

"So you find me guilty, Colin?" she interrupted.

He shrugged. "I don't know you well enough to judge if I can trust you or not," he said. He was being brutally honest with her. "But you are a Winchester," he added with a meaningful glance in her father's direction.

Colin looked at Nathan. He knew the anguish his friend must be going through yet doubted that anyone else was aware of that pain. Nathan had that uncaring look on his face. His friend had become a master at concealing his reactions. Ironically, it had been a woman who had first taught him how to protect his heart. Now another woman seemed to be proving Nathan's cynicism was more than justified.

Sara's anguish was apparent, however. She looked devastated, defeated. Colin began to have doubts about his quick judgment. Was Sara capable of such fakery? "Why don't you ask Nathan again?" he suggested in a softer tone of voice.

She shook her head. "He should have enough faith in me to know I'd never betray him."

"Get in the carriage," her father ordered again.

She whirled back to confront her father. "I've been such a fool about so many things, Father," she announced. "I actually made excuses for your sinful conduct, but Nora was right after all. You aren't any better than your brothers. You disgust me. You let your brother Henry dole out the punishment whenever you're displeased. Your hands stay clean that way, don't they? Oh, God, I never want to see you again." She took a deep breath, then added in a harsh whisper, "I'm no longer your daughter."

She turned her attention to Belinda next. "As for you, I hope you get down on your knees and pray God's forgiveness for all the lies you've told today. You may tell Mother I'm sorry she isn't feeling well. I'll come to see her when I'm certain neither one of you is home."

After making that speech Sara turned her back on her family and walked across the street. Colin tried to take hold of her arm. She pulled away.

Everyone watched her until she'd walked inside the office and shut the door behind her.

The earl of Winchester still wasn't ready to give up. The argument became fierce again and lasted several minutes before Nathan finally took a step forward.

Sara's father tried to go toward the office then. He shouted his daughter's name in such a booming voice that the veins in the side of his neck stood out. Nathan blocked his path. That action proved threatening enough.

No one said a word until the Winchester carriage rounded the corner. The men on horseback trailed after the vehicle. Then everyone started talking at once.

Jimbo and Matthew both argued in Sara's defense. "She might have told," Matthew said, "but only the way she told about Nora and me. Inadvertent like."

"I'm saying she didn't tell at all," Jimbo muttered. He folded his arms across his chest and glared at Colin when he made that emphatic statement. "You didn't help, Dolphin," he added. "You could have swayed the boy's mind if you'd argued in our Sara's defense."

"The last time I argued in a woman's defense Nathan damn near got killed," Colin replied.

"He was young and stupid back then," Matthew said.

"He still is," Jimbo stated. "You aren't at all surprised, are you?" he said then. "With your cynical heart, I imagine you expected our Sara to fail you. Isn't that right?"

Nathan wasn't listening to his friends. His gaze was centered on the corner where the carriage had last been seen. With a shake of his head he pulled himself out of his musings and turned to walk away.

"Where are you going?" Matthew called out.

"Maybe he came to his senses," Jimbo said when Nathan started across the street. "He might be going to apologize to Sara. Did you see the look on her face, Matthew? It tore me up to see such torment."

"Nathan wouldn't apologize," Colin said. "He doesn't know how. But he might be calm enough to listen to her now."

Sara had no idea Jimbo and Matthew had come to her defense. She believed everyone had damned her. She was so upset she couldn't stop pacing. She kept picturing the expression on Nathan's face when she'd admitted that she'd known the truth about his father.

He believed she had betrayed him.

Sara had never felt so alone. She didn't know where to go, whom to turn to, what to do. She couldn't think. Her fantasy of living in paradise with the man she'd always believed loved her was gone.

Nathan had never loved her. It was just as her relatives had told her. He was only after the king's gift. She'd thought those often-repeated reminders were lies meant to turn her heart against him. She knew better now.

God, what a fool she'd been.

The pain was simply too much, too overwhelming to

think about. Sara remembered the vile threat her father had made against Nathan's sister Jade. Her heart went out to the sister, and even though she'd never met the woman she knew it was her duty to try to warn her so she could prepare herself.

The plan gave her a mission, a reason to move. No one noticed when she walked outside. They were occupied shouting at each other. She walked to the corner, but as soon as she was out of sight she started running. She lost her way almost immediately, yet she kept on running until she was out of breath.

God took mercy on her, for when she couldn't go another step she spotted a hack in the middle of the street only half a block away. A passenger was getting out of the vehicle. While he sorted through his pockets for his coins Sara hurried forward.

She didn't have any shillings with her. She didn't know the address of her destination either. She couldn't worry about the lack of funds, though. She decided the coachman would have to be responsible for finding the address on his own.

"The earl of Cainewood's townhouse, if you please," she called out. She got inside the vehicle and pressed herself into the corner. Her fear was that Nathan might have sent one of his men to chase after her.

The coachman directed the hack to what he referred to as the fancy-pants section of town, yet he still had to ask directions from a passerby before he found the address his fare had requested.

Sara used the time to calm her queasy stomach. She took deep, gulping breaths and prayed she wouldn't be sick.

Nathan had no idea Sara wasn't waiting for him inside the office. He tried to rid himself of some of his anger before he spoke to her again. He didn't want to add to her upset. God help him, he couldn't imagine what her life must have been like living with such vile relatives.

Jimbo began to nag him in earnest. "I don't condemn her

for telling," Nathan said. "I understand her flaws. I wasn't surprised. Now, if you'll quit your hounding, I'll go and tell her I've forgiven her. Will that satisfy you?"

Jimbo nodded. Nathan strode across the street and went inside the office. It didn't take him any time at all to realize his wife wasn't there. He looked inside the back storage area just to make certain.

Panic filled him. He knew she hadn't left with her father, and that meant that she had literally walked away.

The picture of just what could happen to an unattended woman in that section of the city terrified Nathan. His roar echoed through the streets. He had to find her.

She needed him.

Chapter Thirteen

Sara cried her way to her destination. When the hack came to a stop in front of a brick-front townhouse she forced herself to gain a little control. Her voice barely cracked when she ordered the coachman to wait for her. "I won't be but a minute," she promised. "I have another destination after I've finished here, and I'll double your fare if you'll kindly be patient."

"I'll wait as long as it takes," the driver promised with a tip of his hat.

Sara rushed up the steps and knocked on the door. She wanted to get inside the townhouse before she was spotted by her relatives. She was also afraid her courage would desert her before she'd completed her mission.

The door was opened by a tall, arrogant-looking man with deep wrinkles at the corners of his eyes. He was quite homely in appearance, but the sparkle in his dark eyes indicated he had a kind nature.

"May I be of assistance, madam?" the butler inquired in a haughty tone of voice.

"I must see Lady Jade at once, sir," Sara answered. She

gave a quick look over her shoulder to make certain she wasn't being watched, then said, "Do let me in."

The butler only had enough time to get out of her way. Sara rushed past him, then demanded in a whisper that he shut the door and bolt it against intruders.

"I pray your mistress is here," she said. "I don't know what I will do if she isn't home."

That possibility was so distressing, her eyes filled with tears. "Lady Jade is home today," the butler told her.

"Thank God for that."

A smile softened the elderly man's expression. "Yes, madam, I often thank God for sending her to me. Now," he continued in a brisker tone of voice, "may I tell my mistress who has come calling?"

"Lady Sara," she blurted out. She suddenly grabbed hold of his hand. "And please hurry, sir. I'm growing more cowardly by the second."

The butler's curiosity was caught. The poor distressed woman was trying to squeeze the bones right out of his hand. "I shall be pleased to hurry, Lady Sara," he announced. "Just as soon as you let go of me."

She hadn't realized she was holding on to him until that moment, and she immediately pulled away. "I'm very upset, sir. Please forgive my boldness."

"Of course, m'lady," the butler returned. "Is there perchance a last name to go with the first?" he asked.

The question proved to be too much for her. Much to the servant's consternation, she burst into tears. "I used to be Lady Sara Winchester, but that changed, and I became Lady Sara St. James. Now that's going to change, too," she cried. "Come morning, I don't know what my name will be. Harlot, I would imagine. Everyone will believe I lived in sin, but I didn't, sir. I didn't," she whispered. "It wasn't sinful."

She paused in her explanation to mop the tears away from her eyes with the handkerchief the butler handed her. "Oh, you might as well call me harlot now and get it over with. I'll have to get used to it."

Sara realized she was making a complete fool of herself. The butler was slowly backing away from her. He probably thought he'd let a deranged woman into his employer's sanctuary.

The earl of Cainewood had just strolled into the foyer from the back of the house where his library was situated when he heard his man Sterns ask their guest what her full name was. Her bizarre answer had made him stop in his tracks.

Sara tried to skirt her way around the butler. She handed him the soggy handkerchief and said, "I shouldn't have come here. I realize that now. I'll send a note to your mistress. Lady Jade is certainly too busy to see me."

"Catch her, Sterns," the earl called out.

"As you wish," the butler replied. His hands settled on Sara's shoulders. "Now what, m'lord?" he inquired.

"Turn her around."

Sterns didn't have to force Sara. She moved without any prodding. "Are you Lady Jade's husband?" she asked when she saw the tall, handsome man leaning against the banister.

"May I present my employer, the earl of Cainewood?" the butler announced in a formal voice.

Her curtsy was instinctive, born from years of training. The butler made her stumble, though, when he added, "M'lord, may I present Lady Sara Harlot?"

She almost fell to her knees. Sterns reached out to steady her. "It was just a jest, m'lady. I couldn't restrain myself."

Jade's husband came forward. He was smiling at her. That helped. "You may call me Caine," he told her.

"I'm Nathan's wife," she blurted out.

His smile was so tender, so kind. "I guessed as much," he said, "as soon as I saw how upset you were. I also caught the part of your explanation about becoming a St. James," he added when she looked so bewildered. "Welcome to our family, Sara."

He took hold of her hand and gave it an affectionate squeeze. "My wife is most eager to meet you. Sterns, go and fetch Jade, will you? Sara, come along with me into the drawing room. We can get to know each other while we wait for my wife."

"But sir, this isn't a social call," Sara said. "When you learn the reason for my visit you'll both want to throw me out."

"Shame on you for thinking we'd be so inhospitable," he countered. He winked at her, then pulled her along by his side. "We're family now, Sara. Call me Caine, not sir."

"I won't be part of the family long," she whispered.

"Now, now, don't start crying again. It can't be as bad as all that. Have you come to tell on Nathan, then? What's he done, I wonder."

His smile indicated he was teasing her. The mere mention of her husband started the tears again. "He hasn't done anything," she said between sobs. "Besides, I would never tell on my husband if he displeased me. It wouldn't be loyal."

"So loyalty is important to you?" he asked.

She nodded. Then she frowned. "So is having faith in your spouse," she muttered. "Some do, others don't."

He wasn't certain he knew what she was talking about. "Do you?" he asked.

"Not anymore I don't," she announced. "I've learned my lesson."

Caine still didn't know what the conversation was about. "I haven't come here to talk about Nathan," she declared. "Our marriage will soon be over. You might as well understand that right away."

It took considerable effort for Caine to keep his smile contained. So it was a marital disagreement after all. "Nathan can be a bit difficult," he said.

"That he can, husband."

Both Caine and Sara turned toward the doorway just as Lady Jade came strolling into the room.

Sara thought Nathan's sister was the most beautiful

woman she'd ever seen. She had such glorious auburn hair. Her eyes were as green as Nathan's, and her complexion was porcelain-perfect. Sara felt completely inadequate by comparison.

She forced herself to put the matter of appearances aside and began to pray in earnest that Jade didn't share her brother's cranky disposition. "I've come with distressing news," she blurted out.

"We already know you're married to Nathan," Caine drawled. "There can't be anything more distressing to you than that, Sara. You have our sympathy."

"How very disloyal of you," Jade replied. Her smile indicated she wasn't at all irritated by her husband's remark, however. "Caine loves my brother," she told Sara. "He just hates to admit it."

She walked over and kissed Sara's cheek. "You aren't at all what I expected," she said. "That pleases me. Where are my manners? I'm so pleased to finally meet you, Sara. Where is Nathan? Will he be joining you soon?"

Sara shook her head. She suddenly had to sit down. She collapsed into the nearest chair. "I never want to see him again," she whispered. "Except to tell him that I never want to see him again, of course. Oh, I don't know where to begin."

Jade and Caine exchanged a look, then Caine mouthed the words "marriage problems" as his guess as to what the problem could be. Jade nodded before she sat down on the brocade settee and patted the cushion next to her. Caine immediately joined her.

"No matter what he's done, Sara, I'm certain the two of you will be able to work this out to your mutual satisfaction," Caine said.

"My husband and I fought all the time when we were first married," Jade added.

"No, love, we fought before we were married, not after," Caine said.

Jade was about to argue over that ridiculous remark when

Sara blurted out, "I haven't come to discuss my marriage. No, I've . . . why aren't I what you expected?"

Jade smiled. "I worried that you would be . . . restrained. Many of the ladies in our society tend to be superficial. They go to great lengths to pretend boredom. You, on the other hand, appear to be refreshingly honest in your reactions."

"You must be giving Nathan fits," Caine said before he could think better of it.

"I refuse to talk about Nathan," Sara said. "I've come here to warn you. You must prepare yourselves for the scandal."

Caine leaned forward. "What scandal?"

"I should start at the beginning so that you'll understand," Sara whispered. She folded her hands in her lap. "Do you happen to know about the conditions set down in the contract between Nathan and me?"

They both shook their heads. Sara let out a sigh. "King George, bless his broken mind, was determined to end the feud between the St. James family and the Winchesters. He forced a marriage between Nathan and me and then sweetened the vinegar in that action by setting aside a large fortune in gold and a tract of land that is situated between the two families' country estates. The feud dates back to the early middle ages," she added. "But that isn't important now. The land is actually more coveted than the gold, for it's fertile, and the mountain water that flows directly down the middle of the tract feeds the fields of both estates. Whoever owns the land could effectively ruin the other by withholding the water supply. According to the contract, the treasury goes to Nathan as soon as he collects me for his wife. After I give him an heir, the land will also come to us."

Caine looked incredulous. "How old were you when this contract was signed?"

"I was four years old. My father signed in my stead, of course. Nathan was fourteen years old."

"But that's . . . preposterous," Caine said. "It can't be at all legal."

"The king decreed it legal and binding. The bishop was with him, and he blessed the marriage."

Sara couldn't look at Caine or Jade. The easy part of her explanation was over, and it was time to get to the heart of the matter. She turned her gaze to her lap. "If I walk away from the contract, Nathan gets everything. And if he were to walk away, then I—or rather, my family—would receive everything. It was a very cunning game the king played with us."

"You and Nathan were his pawns, weren't you?" Caine said.

"Yes, I suppose we were," Sara agreed. "I think the king's motives were pure, though. He seemed obsessed with making everyone get along. I try to remember that he had our best interests at heart."

Caine didn't agree with that evaluation, but he kept his opinion to himself. "I've made you digress," he said. "Please continue with your explanation, Sara. I can see how upsetting this is for you."

She nodded. "Nathan came to get me over three months ago. We sailed away on his ship and only just returned to London. My father was waiting for us."

"What happened then?" Caine asked when she didn't continue.

"My father wanted me to come home with him."

"And?" he prodded again.

"Caine," Jade interjected, "it's obvious she didn't go home with her father. She's here with us, for heaven's sake. Sara, I'm having trouble understanding why your father would want you to return to his home. You'd be breaking the contract, wouldn't you? Why, Nathan would win it all, and I can't imagine the Winchesters allowing that to happen. Besides, I assume that you and Nathan have been living together as husband and wife. It's too late, isn't it—"

"Sweetheart, let Sara explain," Caine suggested. "Then we'll ask our questions."

"My father has found a way to break the contract and win the gift," Sara said.

"How?" Jade asked.

"He found out something terrible about your father," Sara whispered. She dared a quick look up and saw the alarm that came into Jade's eyes. "Did you know about your father's activities?"

Jade didn't answer her. "This is very difficult," Sara whispered.

Caine wasn't smiling. "Exactly what did your father find out?"

"That the earl of Wakersfield betrayed his country."

Neither husband nor wife said anything for a minute. Caine put his arm around his wife's shoulders in an attempt to comfort her.

"I'm so sorry to have to tell you about your father," Sara whispered. Her anguish was apparent. "But you must try not to condemn him. You can't possibly know the circumstances that led him toward the path he took."

Sara didn't know what else to say. The color had left Jade's face, and she looked as if she was going to be ill. Sara felt the same way.

"It was bound to come out sooner or later," Caine said.

"Then you knew?" Sara asked.

Jade nodded. "Nathan and I have known about our father for a long time." She turned to her husband. "You're wrong, Caine. That secret should never have had to come out." She turned back to Sara. "How did your father find out?"

"Yes, how did he find out?" Caine asked. "That file was locked away in the vault. I was assured that no one would ever find out."

"Nathan believes I found out and wrote the news to my family," Sara said.

"Did you know?" Jade asked.

"That was the very question your brother asked me," Sara said. The sadness in her voice indicated her pain. "I almost lied to Nathan because he was looking at me in such a frightening way."

"Did you know?" Jade asked again. "And if so, Sara, how did you find out?"

She straightened her shoulders. "Yes, I did know about your father, Jade. I can't tell you how I found out, though. It would be disloyal."

"Disloyal?" Jade would have bounded out of her seat if her husband hadn't restrained her. Her face was flushed pink. "Telling your family is what I call disloyal," she cried out. "How could you do such a thing, Sara? How could you?"

Sara didn't even try to defend herself. If her own husband didn't believe her, why should his sister?

She stood up and forced herself to look at Jade. "I felt it was my duty to come here to warn you," she said. Her voice was flat. "I would apologize for my family, but I've decided to disown them, and it wouldn't ease your torment anyway. Thank you for listening to me."

She walked to the foyer. "Where are you going now?" Caine called out. He tried to stand up, but his wife was pulling on his attention by tugging on his hand.

"I must make certain my mother is all right," Sara explained. "And then I'm going home." With that, Sara opened the door and left.

"So much for disowning her family," Jade muttered. "Caine, let her leave. I never want to see her again. Oh, God, we have to find Nathan. He must be terribly upset over this treachery."

Caine gave his wife a good scowl. "I can't believe what I'm hearing," he said. "If you're referring to the scandal about to break, Nathan won't be upset. Jade, the St. James men thrive on disgrace, remember? For God's sake, reason this through. You never used to give a damn what others thought. Why the sudden change?"

"I still don't care what anyone thinks, except you, husband. I was talking about Sara's treachery. She betrayed my brother, and that's why I believe Nathan must be very upset."

"So you've found her guilty, have you?"

That question gave her pause. She started to nod, then shook her head. "Nathan judged her," she said. "Sara told us he believed she betrayed him."

"No," Caine said. "She said he asked her if she knew about his father. Jade, you can't possibly know what he's thinking until you ask him. Your brother's one of the most cynical men I've ever known, but damn it, wife, I expect better from you."

Jade's eyes widened. "Oh, Caine, I did find her guilty, didn't I? I just assumed . . . and she didn't defend herself."

"Why should she?"

"She did tell us she was going home. For a woman who claims she just disowned her family . . . you think she's innocent, don't you?"

"I have only formed one conclusion thus far. Sara loves Nathan. All you have to do is look at the woman to know that. Would she have bothered to come to warn us if she didn't care about your brother, my sweet? Now unhand me, please. I'm going after her."

"You're too late, m'lord," Sterns called out from the foyer. "The hack has already left."

"Why didn't you stop her?" Caine asked as he rushed toward the door.

"I was occupied eavesdropping," the butler admitted. "I also didn't know you wanted me to stop her." He turned his gaze to his mistress. "I hope you don't mind that I gave your sister-in-law a few shillings. Lady Sara was without funds and needed to pay the fare to her next destination."

The pounding on the front door stopped the conversation. Before Sterns or Caine could open it the door was flung wide, and Nathan came striding into the foyer. There were few men who could intimidate Sterns, but the marquess of

St. James was one of them. The butler immediately got out of the big man's path.

Nathan acknowledged both men with a brisk nod. "Where's my sister?"

"It's good to see you again, too, Nathan," Caine drawled. "What brings you here today? Have you come to see your godchild? Olivia's sleeping, but I'm certain your bellowing will wake her in no time at all."

"I don't have time to be sociable," Nathan replied. "Olivia's all right, isn't she?"

As if in answer to that inquiry the sound of the infant's wailing came floating down the stairwell. Sterns frowned at the marquess before starting up the steps. "I'll see to the babe," he announced. "She'll be wanting me to rock her back to sleep."

Caine nodded agreement. The butler was far more family than servant and had taken over the care of little Olivia. The two got along extremely well, and Caine wasn't certain who was more firmly wrapped around the other's fingers.

Caine turned to give Nathan a proper set-down for disturbing his daughter's sleep, but when he saw the expression on his brother-in-law's face he changed his mind. It was a look Caine had never seen before on Jade's brother's face. Nathan looked afraid.

"Jade's in the drawing room," he told Nathan.

His sister stood up as soon as her brother came into the drawing room. "Oh, Nathan, thank heavens you're here."

Nathan walked over to stand directly in front of his sister. "Sit down," he ordered.

She immediately complied. Nathan clasped his hands behind his back, then said, "Brace yourself. The Winchesters found out all about our father, and it's only a matter of time before you're properly humiliated. Got that?"

As soon as she nodded he turned and tried to leave.

"Wait," Jade called out. "Nathan, I must talk to you."

"I don't have time," her brother called back.

"You always were a man of few words," Caine said. "Why the hurry?"

"I've got to find my wife," Nathan told him in a near bellow. "She's missing."

He was already out the front door before Caine's announcement caught him. "Your lovely wife was just here."

"Sara was here?"

"For God's sake, Nathan, must you roar every time you open your mouth? Come back inside."

The sound of little Olivia wailing again was followed by the loud slam of a door above the stairs. Sterns was obviously sending them a message to keep their voices down.

Nathan walked back into the foyer. "What was my wife doing here?"

"She wanted to talk to us."

"Why did you let her leave, man? Damn it, where did she go?"

Caine motioned his brother-in-law into the drawing room and pulled the doors closed before giving his answer. "Sara came to warn us. She wasn't quite as blunt as you were," he added dryly.

"Did she tell you where she was going?"

Jade hurried over and grabbed hold of Nathan's hand so he couldn't disappear on her. She started to answer his question, then caught herself when Caine shook his head at her.

"We'll tell you where Sara went after you sit down and talk to us," Caine announced. "For once, Nathan, you're going to be civil. Got that?"

"I don't have time for this. I've got to find Sara. Do I have to break your arm to get the information I need?"

"Sara's safe enough," Caine said. Unless wolves really do eat their young, he qualified to himself. He put his arm around Jade's shoulders and led her back to the settee.

He noticed Nathan wasn't following them. "Sit down," he ordered in a much firmer voice. "I've got a couple of questions to ask you, Nathan, and I'm not telling you where Sara went until I get some answers."

Nathan knew it was pointless to argue. Beating his brother-in-law into a bloody pulp wouldn't do him any good either. Caine would just bloody him up, too. Precious time would be wasted, and when the fight was over Caine would still remain stubborn.

It was just one of several reasons Nathan admired his sister's husband.

"Why the hell can't you be more like Colin?" he asked. He sat down and glared at Caine. "Jade, you married the wrong brother. Colin's a damn sight more agreeable."

His sister smiled. "I didn't fall in love with Colin, Nathan."

She looked up at her husband then. "I don't believe I've ever seen Nathan this upset. Have you?"

"All right," Nathan muttered. "Ask me your questions."

"Tell me how the Winchesters found out about your father."

Nathan shrugged. "It isn't important how the truth was found out."

"The hell it isn't," Caine interjected.

"Do you believe Sara told her family?"

"She probably did," Nathan said.

"Why?" Jade asked.

"Why did she tell or why do I believe she told?" Nathan asked.

"Why do you believe she told?" Jade qualified. "And quit fencing with me, Nathan. I can see you're uncomfortable with this topic. I'm not going to let it go, so you might as well answer directly."

"Sara's a woman," Nathan said.

He realized the foolishness in that statement almost as soon as his sister did.

"I'm a woman," Jade said. "What does that have to do with the issue under discussion?"

"Yes, of course you're a woman," Nathan answered. "But you're different, Jade. You don't behave like one."

She didn't know if she'd just been insulted or complimented. She looked at her husband to judge his reaction.

Caine's expression showed his exasperation. "Nathan, haven't you learned anything about women in all the time you spent with Sara?"

"Caine, I don't condemn her," Nathan argued. "I'm still a little angry with her, but only because she wouldn't admit to me that she had told them. She shouldn't have lied to me. Still," he added, "she probably—"

"Let me guess," Caine interrupted. "She probably couldn't help herself."

"Your views about women are appalling," Jade said. "I had no idea you'd become so misdirected." She realized she'd raised her voice and forced herself to calm down when she asked, "Is it because she's a Winchester that you have so little faith in her?"

Caine let out a snort. "Isn't that a little like the pot calling the kettle black? If Nathan doesn't have any faith in his wife because of her background, she sure as hell shouldn't have any faith in him."

Nathan was becoming more uncomfortable with each question. His family was forcing him to reevaluate beliefs he'd held for years.

"Of course Sara has faith in me," he muttered. "As I said before, I don't condemn her."

"If you say again that she probably couldn't help herself, I do believe I will try to strangle you, Nathan," Jade announced.

Nathan shook his head. "These questions are pointless."

Nathan started to stand up, but Caine's next question stopped him. "What if she's innocent? Nathan, don't you realize what that means?"

It was more the tone of voice than the question itself that caught Nathan's attention. "What are you suggesting?" he asked.

"I'm suggesting that if you happen to be wrong about Sara, then someone else got hold of your father's file. And that means that someone got into the War Department, breached the inner sanctuary, and got into the vault. We could damn well be dealing with another traitor. England's most carefully guarded secrets are kept inside that safe. Nathan, your file's there, and so are Colin's and mine. We're all at risk."

"You're jumping to conclusions," Nathan announced.

"No, brother, you've jumped to conclusions," Jade whispered. "Caine, you must find out the truth as soon as possible."

"Damned right I will," Caine announced. He looked at Nathan again. "Sara told us she was going home. It was a contradiction, though. She said she wanted to see her mother, and then she was going home."

"She also told us that she'd disowned her family. I got the feeling that you were included in that remark, Nathan," Jade said.

Her brother was already striding toward the foyer. "If I have to tear apart the Winchester's townhouse from rafter to cellar, by God I will," he bellowed.

"I'm coming with you," Caine announced. "There might be more than one Winchester waiting to greet you."

"I don't need your help," Nathan replied.

"I don't care if you need it or not," Caine argued. "You're getting it."

"Damn it, I don't need anyone to fight my battles."

Caine wasn't deterred. "I'll let you fight the bigger battle all on your own, brother, but I'm going with you to the Winchesters'."

Sterns had just started down the stairs when Nathan bellowed, "What the hell are you talking about, Caine?"

The infant's wail of distress echoed throughout the foyer. Without breaking his stride Sterns turned around again and started back up the stairs.

"What's the bigger battle?" Nathan demanded to know as he opened the front door and started out.

Caine was right on his heels. "The battle to win Sara back," he answered.

A tremor of worry nagged Nathan. He pushed the feeling aside immediately. "Damn it, Caine, lower your voice. You're upsetting my godchild."

Caine suddenly wanted to throttle his brother-in-law. "Nathan, I hope Sara makes you suffer. If there's any justice in this world, she'll bring you to your knees before she ever forgives you."

Nathan didn't tear down the rafters of the Winchester residence, but he did break through a couple of locked doors. While Caine kept watch from the foyer Nathan quite methodically searched every room from top to bottom. Luck was on his side. Both the earl and his daughter Belinda were away from the townhouse, no doubt searching for Sara, Nathan surmised, and at least he didn't have to put up with their interference. It wouldn't have stopped him, of course, but it might have slowed him down a little.

Sara's mother stayed out of his path, too. The fragile-looking gray-haired woman hovered next to the fireplace inside the drawing room and simply waited until the marquess had finished his task.

Lady Victoria Winchester could have saved Nathan considerable time by simply telling him that Sara had paid a brief visit and had already left, but the marquess of St. James overwhelmed the timid woman, and she couldn't seem to find her courage or her voice.

Caine and Nathan were leaving when Sara's mother called out to them. "Sara was here, but she left a good twenty minutes ago."

Nathan had forgotten the woman was in the drawing room. He walked toward her but stopped in the center of the room when she cringed away from him. "Did she tell you where she was going?" he asked softly. He took another step forward, then stopped again. "Madam, I'm not going to harm you. I'm worried about Sara, and I would like to find her as soon as possible."

His gentle voice helped her regain her composure. "Why do you want to find her? She told me you don't care for her, sir."

"She's been telling me these past weeks that I do," he countered.

Sara's mother slowly shook her head. The sadness in her eyes was apparent. Superficially, she looked like her sister Nora, but Nora had a zest for life, while Sara's mother looked like a frightened, defeated woman.

"Why do you want to find Sara?"

"Why? Because she's my wife," Nathan replied.

"Is it true you only want Sara back so that you can have the king's gift? My Sara's determined to find a way for you to have both the land and the treasure, sir. But she doesn't want anything from you."

Tears filled the elderly woman's eyes. "You've destroyed her innocence, m'lord. She had such faith in you all these years. We have both wronged my Sara."

"Sara has always had kind words for you, madam," Nathan said. "She doesn't believe you've ever wronged her."

"I used to call her my little peacemaker," she said. "When she was older she often took up my battles for me. It was so much easier, you see."

"I don't understand," Nathan said. "What battles?"

"Just family squabbles," she answered. "My husband Winston often dragged his brother Henry into our personal disagreements. Sara put herself in front of me to weight the odds more equally."

Nathan shook his head. He decided that Sara's mother had a little spirit left inside her when she suddenly straightened her shoulders and frowned at him. "Sara deserves to find peace and joy for herself. She won't settle the way I did. She won't be coming back here, either. She's very disappointed in all of us."

"Madam, I have to find her."

His anguish got through to her. "You are worried about her, then? You do care, if only just a little?"

Nathan nodded. "Of course I'm worried. Sara needs me."

Lady Victoria actually smiled. "Perhaps you also need her," she remarked. "She told me she was going home," she added. "I assumed she meant she was returning to you. She said there were several details she needed to see to before she left London again."

"She isn't leaving London." Nathan made that statement in a hard voice.

Caine walked forward. "Could Sara have gone to your townhouse?" he asked his brother-in-law.

Nathan frowned at him. "I don't have a townhouse, remember? It was burned to the ground by a few of my father's associates."

Caine nodded. "Hell, Nathan, where else could she have gone? Where is your home?"

Nathan turned back to Sara's mother. "Thank you for giving me your help. I'll send word to you as soon as I've found Sara."

The woman got teary-eyed again. She reminded Nathan of Sara, and he smiled at her. He knew where his wife had inherited her trait for weeping at the slightest provocation.

She put her hand on Nathan's arm and walked by his side to the front door. "Since my Sara was a little girl she's loved you. Oh, she would only admit it to me, of course. The rest of the family would have ridiculed her. She was always given to fantasy. You were her knight in shining armor."

"He's getting more tarnished by the minute," Caine said.

Nathan ignored that insult. "Thank you again, Lady Winchester."

Caine was astonished by the tenderness in Nathan's voice. When he bowed formally to the elderly woman Caine did the same.

They were both out the door and halfway down the steps when Sara's mother whispered from behind, "His name is Grant. Luther Grant."

Both Caine and Nathan turned around. "What did you say?" Nathan asked.

"The man who found out about your father," Sara's mother explained. "His name is Luther Grant. He works as a guard, and my husband paid him handsomely to look into the files. That's all I chanced to overhear," she added. "Will it help you?"

Nathan was speechless. Caine nodded. "Thank you. It saves considerable time, I assure you."

"Why did you tell us?" Nathan asked.

"Because it was wrong. Winston went too far this time. My husband gets caught up in his greed, and he doesn't consider what his plans will do to others. I cannot let Sara be his scapegoat again. Please don't let anyone know I told you. It would be difficult for me."

Sara's mother closed the door before either man could give her his promise.

"She's terrified of her husband," Caine whispered. "It sickens me to see such sadness in her eyes. No woman should have to live her life in fear."

Nathan nodded. His mind wasn't on Sara's mother, though, and when he turned to Caine he couldn't hide his fear. "Where do I look for her now, Caine? Where could she have gone? My God, if anything happens to her, I don't know what I'll do. I've grown accustomed to having her around."

It was as close as Nathan was going to come to admitting the truth, Caine realized. He wondered then if his stubborn-headed brother-in-law knew he loved Sara.

"We'll find her, Nathan," he promised. "I think we should go back to the wharf first. Colin might have some news for us. One of the men might have spotted her."

Nathan grabbed at that thread of hope. He didn't say another word until he and Caine had reached their destination. His fear was tearing at his nerves. He couldn't seem to think straight.

It was sunset when they reached the waterfront. The streets were cast in orange shadows. Candles burned bright inside the Emerald Shipping office. As soon as Nathan and Caine walked inside Colin bounded to his feet so quickly that shooting pains radiated up his injured leg.

"Did anyone find Sara yet?" Caine asked his brother.

Colin nodded. "She found us," he said. His forehead was beaded with perspiration, and he was taking deep breaths in an attempt to ease the pain. Neither Caine nor Nathan remarked upon his obvious distress, for they both knew their sympathy would only irritate the proud man.

Nathan waited until Colin lost some of his grimace, then asked, "What do you mean, she found us?"

"Sara came back here."

"Then where the hell is she now?" Caine asked.

"She demanded to be taken home. Jimbo and Matthew escorted her. Sara's back on board the *Seahawk*."

Caine's sigh of relief filled the room. "So she considers the *Seahawk* her home, does she?"

The tightness inside Nathan's chest began to loosen up. He was so relieved to know that Sara was safe, he literally broke out in a cold sweat. He snatched the linen handkerchief Colin had pulled from his vest pocket and wiped his brow. "It's the only home we've shared," Nathan muttered in a low, gruff voice.

"I guess that means Sara isn't holding a grudge," Caine

said. He leaned against the edge of the desk and grinned at his brother. "Pity, that. I was really looking forward to watching Nathan practice."

"Practice what?" Colin asked.

"Getting down on his knees."

Chapter Fourteen

Nathan couldn't stand the idle chitchat long. He had to get to Sara. He needed to see for himself that she was all right. It was the only way he would be able to calm his racing heartbeat. He had to know she was safe.

Without a word of farewell he left Colin and Caine and rowed out to the *Seahawk*. He was surprised to find that most of the crew had already boarded. The men traditionally spent the first night back in port getting drunk enough to fight anything that moved.

A portion of the crew stood guard on the three decks while the others took up their positions in the wardroom area. Some of the men had strung their hammocks up between the hooks in the ceiling and slept with their knives on their chests for the sake of readiness.

The hammocks were used only in foul weather or when it was too cold to sleep on deck. It was warm that day—exceedingly so, as a matter of fact—and Nathan knew the men were there solely for protective purposes. They were watching over their mistress.

As soon as they spotted him they rolled from their swinging cots and filed up the steps.

The door to the cabin was unlatched. When Nathan went inside he spotted Sara at once. She was sound asleep in the center of his bed. She was holding his pillow against her chest. She'd left two candles burning in their glass globes on the desk, and the soft glow from the light played against the angles of her face like dancing shadows.

He'd have to have another talk with her about the worries of fire, he thought to himself. The woman was forever forgetting to douse the candle flame.

Nathan quietly shut the door, then leaned against it. He was so hungry for the sight of her, he stood there for a long while just watching her sleep until his panic finally dissipated and it didn't hurt so much to breathe.

Every now and again she let out a little hiccup, and Nathan realized she must have cried herself to sleep.

The sound made him feel as guilty as hell.

He couldn't imagine living his life without her by his side. God help him, he cared for her.

That acknowledgment wasn't nearly as painful as he'd imagined it would be. He didn't feel as though his soul had just been snatched away from him. Just as amazing as the admission itself, he hadn't been struck by lightning.

Caine had been right after all. He had been a fool. How could he have been so blind, so indifferent? Sara would never try to manipulate him. Sara was his partner, not his enemy. The thought of spending the rest of his life without getting to shout at her again was simply too monstrous to think about.

Her love gave him renewed strength. Together they could face any challenge, he knew, be it from the St. James camp or the Winchester den. As long as he had Sara by his side Nathan didn't think he could ever be defeated.

His thoughts moved on to ways he could please his wife. He was never going to raise his voice to her again. He'd start calling her by those ridiculous endearments he'd heard other men call their wives. Sara would probably like that.

He finally took his gaze away from her and looked around the room. There was clutter everywhere. Sara's dresses were hanging between his shirts on the hooks.

She'd made the cabin her home. Her possessions were everywhere. Her ivory brush and comb, along with a multitude of colored hairpins, littered his desktop. She'd washed out some of her feminine undergarments and had hung them up to dry on a rope she'd hooked from wall to wall across the room.

He had to dodge the damp clothing when he took his shirt off. He could think of nothing but finding the right words to use when he told her he was sorry. God, it was going to be difficult. He'd never apologized to anyone before, but he was determined not to muck it up.

He bent over to take off his boots and knocked the makeshift clothesline. One of Sara's silk chemises was jarred free. Nathan reached out to catch the garment before it fell to the floor and only then realized just what his wife had used for her rope.

"You used my whip for your clothesline?"

He really hadn't meant to shout. It had just caught him off guard. His bellow of outrage didn't wake her up, though. Sara muttered in her sleep, then flipped over on her stomach.

It only took him a minute to calm down. Then he was actually able to see the humor in the situation. He couldn't quite smile, but he wasn't grimacing any longer. Tomorrow, he decided, right after he talked to her about fire hazards, he'd mention his special attachment to his whip and ask her not to use it for such demeaning chores.

He stripped out of the rest of his clothes and stretched out next to Sara. She was exhausted from the heartache both he and her Winchester relatives had put her through. She needed her rest. She didn't even stir when he put his arm around her.

He didn't dare pull her close to him, knowing full well that as soon as she cuddled up against him he wouldn't be able to stop himself from making love to her.

His intentions were honorable. His frustration, however, soon became damned painful. Nathan considered it due penance for the agony he'd caused her. The only thought that got him through the long dark night was the promise he made to himself that as soon as morning arrived and Sara was awake he'd show her how much he cared for her.

Nathan didn't fall asleep until the sun was starting to rise. He awoke with a start several hours later, then rolled over to take his wife into his arms.

She wasn't there. Her clothes were gone, too. Nathan pulled on his pants and went up on deck to look for her.

He found Matthew first. "Where's Sara?" he demanded. "God, she isn't in the galley, is she?"

The seaman motioned toward the wharf. "Colin rowed out earlier with some papers for you to sign. Sara and Jimbo went back with him to the office."

"Why the hell didn't you wake me?"

"Sara wouldn't let us disturb you," Matthew explained. "She said you were sleeping like the dead."

"She was being . . . considerate," Nathan muttered. "I appreciate that."

Matthew shook his head. "She was bent on avoiding you, if you want my opinion," he said. "And after the way we each took a turn lighting into her yesterday when she came back to the wharf, well, we were all feeling a little guilty, and so we let her have her way today."

"What are you talking about?"

"As soon as Jimbo saw Sara climbing out of that hack he started in lecturing her about the dangers of the city for an innocent woman traveling alone."

"So?"

"Then Colin had to have a turn," Matthew continued. "Next Chester gave her what for . . . or was it Ivan? I don't recall now. God's truth, Nathan, the men were all lined up waiting their turn to lecture her. It was a sight I thought I'd never see."

Nathan pictured the scene and couldn't help but smile. "The men are loyal to her," he announced. He started to turn back to the steps. He fully intended to go after his wife and bring her back. He paused suddenly and turned around. "Matthew? How was Sara feeling this morning?"

The seaman glared at Nathan. "She wasn't crying, if that's what you're wondering. Now, if you ask me how she was acting, I'd have to say she acted damned pitiful."

Nathan walked back over to his friend and stood by his side. "What the hell does that mean?"

"Defeated," Matthew muttered. "You've broken her heart, boy."

Nathan suddenly pictured Sara's mother in his mind. She was certainly a defeated woman, and Nathan knew that her husband, Winston, had been responsible for breaking her spirit. God help him, was he just as bad?

That thought terrified him. Matthew was watching Nathan's expression and was astonished to see the vulnerability there. "What the hell am I going to do?" Nathan muttered.

"You broke it," Matthew countered. "You fix it."

Nathan shook his head. "I doubt she'll believe anything I say. God, I can't blame her."

Matthew shook his head. "Do you still have so little faith in our Sara?"

That question gained a glare. "What are you saying?" Nathan asked.

"She's loved you for a heap of years, Nathan. I don't believe she can stop so suddenly, no matter what dastardly thing you've done to her. You've only got to let her know you have faith in her. If you stomp on a flower, you kill it. Our Sara's heart is like that flower, boy. You've hurt her, and that's a fact. Best find a way to show her you're caring. If you don't, you'll lose her for good. She asked me if she could accompany me back to Nora's island."

"She isn't leaving me."

"You don't need to shout, boy. I hear you fine." Matthew had to struggle to hide his smile. "She mentioned that you'd mind if she left."

"Then she realizes that I have begun to"—Nathan suddenly felt like an awkward schoolboy—"care."

Matthew snorted. "No, she hasn't recognized that," he said. "She's thinking you want the land and the treasure. She called herself the extra baggage that went along with the king's gift."

In the beginning that was all he'd been interested in, but it hadn't taken him long to realize that Sara was far more important to him.

And he was losing her. He had broken her heart, but God help him, he didn't know how to fix it.

He needed advice from an expert.

After ordering Matthew to take charge of the *Seahawk* for the day he finished dressing and went into London proper. He knew Sara would be safe with Jimbo and Colin looking after her, and so he went directly to his sister's house. He didn't want to see Sara until he knew exactly what he would say to her.

Jade answered the front door. "How did you find out so soon?" she asked her brother when he rushed past her.

"I've got to talk to Caine," Nathan announced. He looked inside the drawing room, saw that it was empty, and then turned back to his sister. "Where is he? Damn, he didn't go out, did he?"

"No, he's in the study," Jade answered. "Nathan, I've never seen you in such a state," she added. "Are you worried about Sara? She's all right. I just settled her in the guest chamber."

Nathan was halfway down the hallway before Jade had finished her explanation. He turned around then. "She's here? How did—"

"Colin dragged her back to us," Jade explained. "Nathan, please lower your voice. Olivia has just gone down for her afternoon rest, and I believe that if you wake her this time, Sterns will come after you with a hatchet."

That statement got a quick grin from Nathan. "Sorry," he whispered.

He started back toward Caine's study. Jade called out, "I've apologized to Sara because I shamelessly jumped to the wrong conclusion. Have you, Nathan?"

"Jumped to the wrong conclusion?" he asked.

She ran after him. "No," she snapped. "I want to know if you've apologized for finding her guilty of betrayal, brother. I know she couldn't have done it. She loves you, Nathan. She's set on leaving you, too."

"I'm not letting her go anywhere," Nathan bellowed.

Caine heard his brother-in-law's booming voice. He sat down behind his desk and pretended to be absorbed in reading the dailies.

Nathan didn't knock. He barged inside, then shut the door with a slam from the back of his boot. A baby's shrill cry followed that noise.

"I've got to talk to you."

Caine took his time folding his paper. He was trying to give Nathan a few moments to calm down. He motioned for him to sit. "Would you like some brandy?" he asked. "You look like you could use some."

Nathan declined the offer. He didn't sit down either. Caine leaned back in his chair and watched his brother-in-law pace until his patience ran out. "You said you wanted to talk to me?" he prodded.

"Yes."

Another good five minutes went by before Caine tried again. "Spit it out, Nathan."

"It's . . . difficult."

"I've already gathered that much," Caine returned.

Nathan nodded, then resumed his pacing.

"Damn it, will you sit down? I'm getting dizzy watching you."

Nathan suddenly stopped. He stood in front of Caine's

desk. His stance was rigid. Caine thought he looked ready to do battle.

"I need your help."

Caine wouldn't have been surprised if Nathan had lost his supper then and there. His brother-in-law's face had turned gray, and he looked like he was in acute pain.

"All right, Nathan," Caine said. "I'll help you any way I can. Tell me what you want."

Nathan looked incredulous. "You don't even know what I need, yet you immediately promise to help me. Why?"

Caine let out a long sigh. "You've never had to ask anyone for anything, have you, Nathan?"

"No."

"It's damned difficult for you, isn't it?"

Nathan shrugged. "I've learned not to depend on others, but I can't seem to think straight now."

"You've also learned never to trust anyone either, haven't you?"

"Meaning?"

"Sara says you expected her to betray you. Is she right?"

Nathan shrugged again.

"Look," Caine said. "When I married your sister, you became my brother. Of course I'll help you. It's what family's all about."

Nathan walked over to the window and stared outside. His hands were clasped behind his back. "I believe Sara might have lost some of her faith in me."

Caine thought that had to be the understatement of the year. "Then help her find it again," he suggested.

"How?"

"Do you love her, Nathan?"

"I care for her," he answered. "I've come to realize that she isn't my enemy. She's my partner," he added in a brisk tone of voice. "She has my best interests at heart, just as I have her best interests at heart."

Caine rolled his eyes heavenward. "Colin's your partner Nathan. Sara's your wife."

When Nathan didn't comment, Caine continued prodding him. "Do you want to spend the rest of your life with Sara? Or is she just a nuisance you have to put up with in order to receive the king's gift?"

"I cannot imagine living without her," Nathan said in a low, fervent voice.

"Sara's a little more than just a partner, then, isn't she?"

"Of course she is," Nathan muttered. "She's my wife, for God's sake. Colin's my partner."

The two men were silent for a moment.

"I had no idea this . . . caring thing could be so irritating. I've ruined everything, Caine. I've destroyed Sara's faith in me."

"Does she love you?"

"Of course she loves me," Nathan immediately answered. "Or at least she used to love me. She would tell me almost every day." He let out a sigh, then said, "Matthew was right. All this time Sara's given me her love without reservation. It's like a flower, and I've stomped on it."

Caine tried not to smile. "Like a flower, Nathan? God, you have taken a fall. You've become . . . eloquent."

Nathan wasn't paying him any attention. "She thinks of herself as extra baggage I have to put up with in order to get the land and the coins. That was true at first, but everything's changed now."

"Nathan, simply tell her how you feel."

"Sara's so delicate," Nathan announced. "She deserves better than me, but I'll be damned if I'll let anyone else touch her. I've got to fix this. I've stomped on her . . ."

Caine cut him off. "I know. I know. You've stomped on her flower."

"Her heart, damn it," Nathan muttered. "Get it right, for God's sake."

Since Nathan wasn't looking at him, Caine felt it was safe to smile. "So what are you going to do?" he asked.

Another five minutes passed in silence. Then Nathan

straightened his shoulders. He turned around to look at Caine. "I'm going to restore her faith in me."

Caine didn't think it would do him any good to remind Nathan that he'd suggested that very action not ten minutes earlier.

"That's a sound idea," he said instead. "Now tell me how you plan to achieve this—"

"I'm going to show her," Nathan interrupted. "Hell, why didn't I think of this before?"

"Since I don't know what you're thinking, I can't answer you."

"It's so simple, an imbecile could figure it out. I'll need your help to pull it off."

"I already said I'd help you."

"Now I need some advice, Caine. You are the expert or women," he added in a matter-of-fact tone of voice.

That announcement was news to Caine, and he was about to ask Nathan how he had come to that conclusion, but his brother-in-law answered him before the question was asked. "Jade never would have settled. If anything, my sister is discriminating."

Caine started to grin, then frowned instead when Nathan casually added, "I still can't figure it. You must have something only she can . . . appreciate."

Caine wasn't given a chance to respond to that barb. "I need your help with Luther Grant," Nathan announced.

"For God's sake, Nathan, will you quit jumping back and forth between issues? You just asked for advice concerning women, and now you're—"

"Grant's got to talk to us," Nathan insisted.

Caine leaned back in his chair. "I was going after the bastard anyway, Nathan. He'll get what's coming to him."

"He might be on the run," Nathan said.

"Don't borrow trouble," Caine said. "We'll find out soon enough."

"He has to admit his part in this scheme before

Farnmount's ball. If Grant has taken off, that only gives us two days to find him."

"We'll have his signed confession before then," Caine promised. "But why is Farnmount's ball your deadline, Nathan?"

"Everyone comes back to London to attend, that's why."

"You never attend."

"I will this year."

Caine nodded. "You know, Nathan, I always enjoy the affair. It's the only ball your friendly St. James relatives attend."

"It's the only ball they're ever invited to attend," Nathan drawled. He leaned against the window ledge and smiled at his brother-in-law.

Caine still didn't understand what Nathan was planning. He knew prodding wouldn't do him any good. Nathan would tell him when he was ready. "Everyone's afraid to go to the ball for worry that he will be your Uncle Dunnford's next victim," Caine remarked. He smiled when he added, "But they're also afraid to miss the fiasco. Dunnford does provide some refreshing entertainment. He reminds me of Attila the Hun dressed in formal attire. Now that I think about it, so do you, Nathan."

His brother-in-law barely heard what Caine was rambling on about. His mind was centered on his plans. Another minute or two passed before he said, "The prince regent always attends the party, too."

A sudden gleam came into Caine's eyes. He leaned forward in his chair. "Yes," he agreed. "And so do all the Winchesters, now that I think about it."

"I'm only interested in one Winchester," Nathan said. "Winston."

"Do you think that's when he plans to spring his scandal about your father? Hell, yes, it is," Caine continued. "What better opportunity?"

"Can you set up a meeting with Sir Richards? I want to fill him in on the facts as soon as possible."

JULIE GARWOOD

"The director of our War Section already knows about Grant. I spoke with him just this morning. He should be visiting with the bastard right about now."

"Unless he's gone into hiding," Nathan muttered.

"He doesn't have any reason to think we know about him. Quit worrying about Grant and tell me what you plan to do."

Nathan nodded. He then proceeded to explain what he wanted to do. When he finished Caine was smiling. "If luck is on our side, we should be able to set the meeting as early as tomorrow afternoon, Nathan."

"Yes," his brother-in-law answered. He straightened away from the window. "Now, about Sara. Someone has to keep a close watch on her until this has been resolved. I don't want the Winchesters to get hold of her while I'm seeing to the details. If anything happened to her, Caine, I don't know what . . ." He didn't go on.

"Jimbo's in the kitchen, eating the shelves dry. He already made it clear he's protecting Sara. He won't let her leave here. Jade and I will also keep a close watch. You don't think you'll make it back here before tonight?"

"I'll try," Nathan said. "Right now I've got to talk to Colin. It's only fair that my partner agree to my plan before I proceed."

"At the risk of sounding completely ignorant, why does Colin need to give his agreement about Grant?"

"I'm not talking about Grant now," Nathan explained. "I'm talking about Sara. God, Caine, pay attention."

Caine let out a long sigh. "I'm trying."

"I have one more favor to ask you."

"Yes?"

"You're always calling Jade by those ridiculous endearments."

"Jade likes hearing those ridiculous endearments," he muttered.

"Exactly my point," Nathan said with a quick nod. "Sara will like them, too."

322

Caine looked incredulous. "You want me to call Sara by the same endearments I call my wife?"

"Of course not," Nathan snapped. "I want you to write them down on a piece of paper for me."

"Why?"

"So I'll know what the hell they are," Nathan bellowed. "Damn, you're making this difficult. Just write them down, all right? Leave the paper on the desk for me."

Caine didn't dare laugh. He did smile, though. The picture of Nathan referring to notes while he tried to woo Sara was quite amusing. "Yes, I'll leave it on the desk for you," he said when Nathan glared at him.

Nathan started to leave. "Are you even going to look in on Sara before you go?" Caine asked.

Nathan shook his head. "I have to get everything ready first."

The worry in his voice wasn't lost on Caine. "The love words aren't necessary, Nathan, if you just tell her what's in your heart."

His brother-in-law didn't respond to that suggestion. Caine finally understood. "You're afraid to confront her, aren't you?"

"The hell I am," Nathan roared. "I just want it to be right."

Jade was just passing by the library door when she heard her husband's laughter. She paused to listen, but the only snatch of conversation she caught didn't make any sense to her.

Nathan had just announced that come hell or high water, he was going to fix his flower. He just needed time to find out how.

Now what in heaven's name did that mean, Jade wondered.

Chapter Fifteen

Sara spent the afternoon in the guest bedroom. She sat in a chair near the window and tried to read one of the leather-bound books Jade had brought up for her. She couldn't concentrate on the story, though, and ended up staring down at the small flower garden behind the townhouse. All Sara could think about was Nathan and what an ignorant country mouse she'd been to love him.

Why couldn't he love her?

She asked herself that painful question every ten minutes or so but never did come up with a proper answer. The future terrified her. She'd already made up her mind to break the contract so that her family couldn't have the king's gift; but once the scandal was made known about Nathan's father, wouldn't the prince regent be placed in the position of having to withhold the royal gift from Nathan as well?

Sara couldn't allow that. Her father had used trickery and deceit to gain the advantage over Nathan. Sara was determined to find a way to even the odds. She didn't want to live with a man who didn't love her, so she decided to strike a bargain with Nathan. In return for her signature giving up all rights to the gift Nathan would let Matthew take her with him when he returned to Nora's island.

Lord, there was so much to consider. The unfairness of what her father had done shamed her. She decided then that her only hope was to gain the prince regent's support. The thought of having to plead her case to him sent a shiver down her spine.

George, the future king of England once his father died or was, as the rumors were whispering, officially declared insane, was a handsome. well-educated man. Those were, unfortunately, his only good points. Sara disliked him immensely. He was a spoiled, pleasure-seeking fop who rarely placed his country's concerns above his own. His worst flaw, to Sara's way of thinking, was his trait of changing his mind on any matter. Sara knew she wasn't the only one who disliked the prince. He was extremely unpopular with the masses, and just a few months past she'd heard that the windows of his carriage had been broken by angry subjects. George was in the conveyance at the time, said to be on his way to Parliament.

Still, she didn't have anyone else to turn to, and so she penned a note to the prince requesting an audience the following afternoon. She sealed the envelope and was just about to go into the corridor to ask Sterns to send a messenger over to Carlton House when Caine intercepted her.

He'd come to fetch her for dinner. Sara was most polite when she refused his invitation, insisting that she really wasn't hungry. Caine was just as polite when he insisted that she eat something. The man wouldn't take no for an answer. He told her so as he coaxed her along the hallway.

Jimbo was waiting in the foyer. Sara handed him the envelope and asked him to deliver the letter for her. Caine reached over Sara's head and plucked the letter out of the seaman's hands before he could agree to undertake the errand.

"I'll have one of the servants take it over," Caine explained. "Jimbo, escort Lady Sara into the dining room. I won't be a minute."

As soon as Jimbo and Sara turned the corner Caine opened the envelope, read the letter, and put it in his pocket. He waited another minute or two and then strolled into the dining room.

Jimbo sat next to Sara at the long table. Jade was seated directly across from her. Caine took his place at the head of the table and then rang for the servants to begin.

"Though it was probably very rude of me to notice, I did see that the letter was addressed to our prince regent," Caine began.

"I don't know of anyone else living in Carlton House," Jimbo interjected.

Caine frowned at the seaman. "Yes, but I didn't realize Sara was on personal terms with the prince."

"Oh, I'm not on personal terms with the prince," she rushed out. "I don't even like . . ." She stopped in midexplanation, then blushed. She lowered her gaze to the table. "I apologize. I do tend to blurt out whatever's on my mind," she confessed. "As far as the note is concerned, I requested an audience. I hope that the prince will see me tomorrow afternoon."

"Why?" Jade asked. "Sara, the prince is certainly in your father's camp."

"I do hope you're wrong, Jade."

"I'm afraid my wife's correct in that evaluation, Sara," Caine said. "When the prince made it known he wanted to divorce his wife, Caroline, your father was one of a handful who supported him."

"But won't the prince put personal considerations aside and come to a loyal subject's aid?"

Her innocence was both refreshing and alarming. Caine didn't want her to be disappointed. "No," Caine said. "His own considerations always come first. The man changes his views as often as he changes his ministers, Sara. Anything he would promise you shouldn't be counted on. I'm sorry to sound disloyal, but I'm being completely honest with you. I don't want you to get your hopes up only to have them dashed. Let Nathan fight this battle, Sara. Stand by his side and let him handle your father."

She shook her head. "Do you know I refused to learn how to swim?" she blurted out. "I thought I shouldn't have to know how, you see, because it was Nathan's duty to make certain I didn't drown. I've been perfectly willing to take care of everyone but myself. Now you suggest I let Nathan fight my battles. It's wrong, Caine. I've been wrong. I don't want ever to cling to anyone. I should have enough strength to stand on my own. I want to be strong, damn it."

She turned bright pink after she'd finished her impassioned speech. "Please excuse my gutter language," she whispered.

An awkward silence followed that remark. Jimbo filled the space with a couple of spicy stories about his sea adventures.

The dessert tray was just being removed from the table when Jade asked, "Have you seen our beautiful daughter yet?" She'd blurted out that question in an attempt to keep Sara at the table awhile longer. She wanted to bring the conversation around to Nathan, of course. Jade was determined to interfere. It was such a heartache to see Sara looking so desolate and alone.

Sara actually smiled at the mention of the infant. "I've heard your daughter," she confessed. "But I've yet to see her. Sterns has promised me that this evening he'll let me hold Olivia."

"She's such a delightful baby," Jade announced. "She's smiling all the time now. She's very intelligent, too. Caine and I noticed that right away."

Jade continued to expound on her three-month-old's considerable accomplishments. Sara noticed that after each of Jade's boasts, Caine immediately nodded his agreement.

"Olivia's blessed to have such loving parents."

"Nathan will make a wonderful father," Jade interjected. Sara didn't comment.

"Don't you agree, husband?" Jade asked Caine.

"If he ever learns to lower his voice, he will."

Jade kicked her husband while she continued to smile at Sara. "Nathan has so many wonderful qualities," she announced.

Sara didn't want to talk about Nathan, but she felt it would be rude not to show some interest. "Oh? And what might those qualities be?" she asked.

Jade opened her mouth to answer, then stopped. She looked as if she'd forgotten the topic. She turned to Caine for assistance. "Explain Nathan's wonderful qualities to Sara."

"You explain them," Caine replied as he reached for another sweet biscuit.

That statement earned him another kick under the table. He glared at his wife, then said, "Nathan's trustworthy."

"He might be trustworthy, but he certainly doesn't trust anyone else," Sara said. She started to fold her napkin.

"The boy's got courage," Jimbo blurted out. He grinned, too, for he was inordinately pleased to have come up with something.

"He's remarkably . . . tidy," Jade said. Even as she gave that bit of praise she wondered if she was right.

Sara neither agreed nor disagreed. Caine decided they were taking the wrong approach. His hand covered Jade's, and when she looked over at him he gave her a conspiratorial wink. "Nathan's probably the most stubborn man I've ever known."

"He might be a little stubborn," Sara immediately countered, "but that certainly isn't a sin." She turned her gaze to Jade. "Your brother reminds me of a beautifully sculptured statue. On the outside he's so handsome, so perfect, but inside his heart is as cold as marble."

Jade smiled. "I never considered Nathan beautiful," she said.

"Sara can't possibly consider him beautiful." Caine squeezed his wife's hand before adding, "Nathan's an ugly bastard, and everyone knows it. His back is covered with scars, for God's sake."

Sara let out a loud gasp, but Caine held his grin. At last they were getting her to show a little emotion.

"It was a woman who scarred Nathan's back," Sara cried out. "And it was this same woman who scarred his heart." She tossed her napkin on the table and stood up. "Nathan isn't ugly, sir. He's incredibly handsome. I think it's dreadful that his own brother-in-law would say such insulting things about him. Now, if you'll excuse me, I'd like to go upstairs."

Jimbo frowned at Caine for upsetting Sara, then chased after her to make certain she did in fact go back above the stairs.

"Caine, you've upset her to the point where you're going to have to apologize," Jade told her husband.

Just then, Jimbo came rushing back into the dining room. "Sara's looking in on the little mite now," he said. "Tell me why you snatched her letter out of my hands. You weren't thinking I'd actually deliver the thing, were you?"

"The letter's in my pocket," Caine said. "I took it from you because I wanted to read it."

"Caine, that's an invasion . . . what did it say?" Jade asked.

"Just what Sara told us she'd written," Caine answered. "She requests an audience to discuss the contract."

"I'm assuming the boy's put together some sort of plan," Jimbo interjected.

"Yes," Caine answered.

"What did Sara mean when she said it was a woman who scarred Nathan's back? Who planted that misinformation in her mind? It was the fire that trapped him inside the prison."

"But wasn't Ariah responsible for having him locked up?"

"She was," Jimbo admitted. "It happened so many years ago, I doubt Nathan even holds a grudge. He came through it seasoned, to my way of thinking, and we didn't leave the island without a full booty to share amongst ourselves."

Caine stood up. "I've got a couple of details of my own to see about. I won't be home until late, Jade. Sir Richards and I have a little business to discuss."

"Why do you need to talk to the director of the War Department?" she asked. She couldn't hide her fear. "Caine, you haven't started back doing secret work for our government without discussing the matter with me first, have you? You promised—"

"Hush, love," Caine soothed. "I'm helping Nathan sort out a little matter, that's all. I'm fully retired and have no desire to return to the cloak-and-dagger days."

Jade looked relieved. Caine leaned down and kissed her. "I love you," he whispered before he started for the doorway.

"Just one minute," Jade called out. "You still haven't explained to me why you deliberately riled Sara up. Caine, we already know she loves him. All you have to do is look at her face to know that."

"Yes, we know she loves him," Caine said. "I just wanted to remind her," he continued. His grin turned devilish. "Now, if you'll excuse me, I've just thought of a few more endearments, and I want to write them down before I leave."

He left Jimbo and Jade staring after him.

For the first time that day Sara was able to stop thinking about Nathan. Little Olivia took her full attention. She was a beautiful infant. One minute she was smiling and drooling, and the next she was bellowing like an opera singer.

Olivia had her mother's green eyes. The sprinkle of dark hair on her crown looked like it might curl just like her father's. Sterns hovered by Sara's side the entire time she held the baby.

"I fear my little love has inherited her Uncle Nathan's inclination to bellow. She can be as loud as he is," Sterns confessed with a smile. "Olivia's wanting immediate gratification," he explained when the babe began to fret in earnest.

He took Olivia back into his arms and held her close. "Shall we go and find your mama, my little angel?" he crooned to the infant.

Sara was reluctant to go back to her room. It was lonely there, and she knew her problems would once again overpower her.

She went to bed early that night, and because she was so emotionally distraught she slept the full night through. She vaguely remembered cuddling up against her husband, knew he had slept next to her, for his side of the bed was still warm, and she came to the sorry conclusion that Nathan was still too angry with her to bother waking her up. He must still believe she'd betrayed him, she thought to herself.

Needless to say, that possibility infuriated her all over again. She worked herself into a rage by the time she'd finished her bath. Even though she'd rested long, uninterrupted hours she felt as refreshed as an old, wrung-out hag. She thought she looked like one, too.

There were dark half circles under her eyes, and her hair was as limp as her spirits. Sara wanted to look her best when she went to plead with the prince regent. She fretted over which gown to wear, just to take her mind off the real issue at hand, and finally settled on a conservative, high-necked pink walking dress.

Like a wallflower at a formal ball Sara sat in the corner of the bedroom all morning long, waiting for the invitation that never arrived.

She refused luncheon and spent a good portion of the afternoon pacing her room while she tried to figure out what her next step would be. It was terribly upsetting to her that the prince regent had ignored her urgent request. Caine had been right, she decided, when he'd said that the prince wasn't interested in the problems of his subjects.

Caine knocked on her door then, interrupting her thoughts. "Sara, we have a little errand to do," he said.

"Where are we going?" she asked. She started to put on her white gloves, then stopped. "I shouldn't go out," she explained. "The prince regent might still send word to me."

"You have to come with me," Caine ordered. "I don't have time to explain, Sara. Nathan wants you to meet him at the War Department offices in a half hour's time."

"Why?"

"I'll let your husband explain."

"Who else is going to be there? Why do we have to meet at the War Department?"

Caine was terribly smooth when it came to evading her questions. Jade was waiting in the foyer. Olivia was draped over her shoulder. "It's all going to turn out just fine," she told Sara. She was diligently patting her daughter's back.

The baby let out a loud belch. The sound made everyone smile. Caine kissed his wife and daughter good-bye, then gently nudged Sara out the front door.

"I'll have your gowns pressed and put in the wardrobe while you're doing this errand," Jade said.

"No," Sara blurted out. "I'll only be staying one more night."

"But where will you and Nathan be going?" Jade asked.

Sara didn't answer her. She turned around and walked down the three steps. Caine held the door to the carriage open. Sara sat across from her brother-in-law. He tried to engage her in casual conversation but quickly gave up when she gave him only whispered yes or no answers.

The War Department was situated in a tall, ugly, gray stone building. A musty smell permeated the stairwells. Caine took Sara up to the second floor. "The meeting's going to take place in Sir Richards's office. You'll like him, Sara. He's a good man."

"I'm certain I will," she said, just to be polite. "But who is he, Caine, and why does he want this meeting?"

"Richards is the director of the department." He opened the door to a large office area and motioned for Sara to go inside.

A short, heavy-bellied man was standing behind a desk. He had thin gray hair, a beak nose, and a ruddiness to his complexion. As soon as he looked up from the paper he was holding in his hand and spotted Sara and Caine he started forward.

"There you are now," he announced with a smile. "We're about ready. Lady Sara, what a pleasure it is to meet you."

He was such a nice gentleman, she thought. He formally bowed to Sara and then took her hand in his own. "You must be quite a lady to have captured our Nathan."

"She didn't capture him, Sir Richards," Caine interjected with a smile of his own. "He captured her."

"I fear you're both incorrect," Sara whispered. "King George captured the two of us. Nathan was never given a choice in the matter, but I would like to find a way to—"

Caine wouldn't let her go on. "Yes, yes," he interrupted. "You'd like to find Nathan, wouldn't you? Where is he?" he asked the director.

"Waiting for the papers," Sir Richards explained. "He'll be back in just a minute. My assistant is quite speedy. Don't worry, my dear, it will all be legal."

She didn't know what the director was talking about but didn't want to appear completely ignorant. "I'm not at all certain why I'm here," she admitted. "I—"

She quit speaking when the side door to the office opened and Nathan walked in. She couldn't remember what she was saying then, and when the pain in her chest started throbbing she realized she was holding her breath.

He didn't even acknowledge her but strode over to the desk and dropped two papers on top of a stack. Then he walked over to an elongated window seat and stood there staring at her.

She couldn't take her gaze off him. He was a rude,

impossible-to-understand, stubborn-headed man whose manners were no better than a hedgehog's, she thought.

A knock sounded at the door, and a young man dressed in a guard's black uniform looked inside. "Sir Richards, the prince regent's carriage is down front," he said.

Sara heard the announcement, but she still couldn't take her gaze away from Nathan. He didn't seem to be at all surprised that the prince was on his way up the steps. He didn't appear overly nervous either, for he leaned against the wall and continued to look at her.

If he wasn't going to speak to her, then by God, she wasn't . . .

He crooked his finger at her. She couldn't believe his arrogance. Both Sir Richards and Caine were in deep discussion over some topic or other. Their low voices were still quite close to her, and she wondered if she'd been included in the conversation. Then Nathan crooked his finger at her again. It would be a burning day in heaven before she obeyed that rude command, she told herself, even as she started walking toward him.

He wasn't smiling at her. He wasn't scowling either. Nathan looked so serious, so . . . intense. She stopped when she was facing her husband, just a foot or so away.

God help her, she thought, she couldn't start weeping. He wasn't making her torment any easier to bear. He looked so damned satisfied. And why shouldn't he? she asked herself. All the man had to do was crook his finger at her, and she came running.

She turned and tried to walk away from him. He reached out and pulled her back. He put his arm around her shoulder and leaned down to whisper in her ear. "You will have faith in me, wife. Do you understand me?"

She was so astonished by his command, she let out a little gasp. She looked up at him to make certain he wasn't jesting with her. Then she remembered that Nathan rarely jested about anything. Sara was immediately consumed with anger. How dare he demand anything from her? At least she had enough faith in him to lose some, she thought to herself. Her eyes filled with tears almost immediately, and all she could think about was getting out of the room before she completely disgraced herself.

Nathan suddenly grabbed hold of her chin and forced her to look up at him again. "You love me, damn it."

She couldn't deny it, and so she said nothing at all.

He stared at her for a minute. "And do you know why you love me?"

"No," she answered in a voice to match his. "Honest to God, Nathan, I haven't the faintest idea why I love you."

He wasn't at all irritated by the anger in her voice. "You love me, Sara, because I'm everything you could ever want in a husband."

A tear slipped out from the corner of her eye. He caught it with his thumb.

"Dare you mock me by turning my own words against me? I haven't forgotten that I said the very same words to you when we set sail for Nora's island. Love can be destroyed. It's fragile, and . . ."

She stopped trying to explain when he shook his head at her. "You aren't fragile," he told her. "And your love can't be destroyed." His fingers gently caressed her cheek. "It's what I've come to value most, Sara. I wasn't mocking you."

"It doesn't matter," she whispered. "I know you don't love me. I've accepted it, Nathan. Please don't look so concerned. I don't fault you. You were never given a choice."

He couldn't stand to see her anguish. God, how he wished they were alone so he could take her into his arms and show her how much he loved her. He was going to have to prove himself to her first. "We'll discuss this later," he announced. "For now I have but one order, Sara. Don't you dare give up on me."

She didn't understand what he was asking her.

Nathan turned his attention to the door when the prince

regent walked inside the office. Sara immediately moved away from her husband, bowed her head as any loyal subject should, and patiently waited for her leader to address her.

The prince was of medium height and had dark, handsome looks. He wore his arrogance like a cloak around his shoulders.

Each man bowed to the prince when he was greeted, and then it was Sara's turn. She made a low curtsy. "It's always a pleasure to see you, Lady Sara."

"Thank you, my lord," she replied. "And thank you, too, for granting me this audience."

The prince looked bewildered by that comment. He nodded, however, and took his place behind Sir Richards's desk. The two men accompanying him took up their positions as sentinels behind their leader.

Caine was concerned that Sara might make another comment about the letter she'd written to the prince. He strolled over to stand next to her. "Sara, I never sent your note to the prince. It's still in my pocket."

Sir Richards was discussing the meeting with the prince, and since neither man was paying them any attention Sara felt it wasn't overly rude to whisper back. "Why didn't you send the letter? Did you forget?"

"No, I didn't forget," Caine said. "The letter would have interfered with Nathan's plans."

"Then it was Nathan who requested this meeting?"

Caine nodded. "Sir Richards also put in his request," he said. "You'd better sit down, Sara. It's going to get a little rocky. Keep your fingers crossed."

Nathan was leaning against the wall, watching her. He heard Caine's suggestion that she sit down and waited to see what Sara would do. There was a wingback chair across the room and an empty window seat next to him.

Sara glanced over to the wingback chair, then turned and walked over to Nathan. He was arrogantly satisfied with her instinctive show of loyalty.

And then he realized he'd come to depend upon that quality.

Nathan sat and pulled her down beside him in the space of a second. He almost leaned down then and there to tell her how much he loved her. He stopped himself just in time. It had to be right, he told himself. In just a few more minutes he would show her how much he loved her.

Sara edged away from her husband so that she wouldn't be touching him. She didn't think it would be appropriate to sit so close in the presence of the prince.

Nathan thought otherwise. He wasn't at all gentle when he hauled her back up against his side.

"I'm ready to begin," the prince announced.

Sir Richards motioned to the guard standing by the front entrance. The man opened the door, and Sara's father came rushing into the office.

As soon as she saw her father she instinctively moved closer to her husband. Nathan put his arm around her waist and held her close.

The earl of Winchester bowed to the prince, then frowned when he spotted the others.

He was about to request that the office be cleared, for the matter to be discussed was a confidential one, but the prince spoke first. "Do sit down, Winston. I'm eager to get this matter settled."

The earl immediately took one of the chairs facing the prince. He sat down and leaned forward at the same time. "Have you looked over the evidence I sent to you?"

"I have," the prince answered. "Winston, have you met our esteemed director of War Operations?"

Winston turned to Sir Richards and gave a quick nod. "We met a time or two," he said. "May I ask why he's here? I don't see that the matter has any bearing on his department. It's a question of breaking a contract, nothing more."

"On the contrary," Sir Richards interjected. His voice was as pleasant, as smooth as sugared ice. "Both the prince and I are very interested in just how you came by this information about the earl of Wakersfield. Would you care to enlighten us?"

"I must protect the person who told me," Winston announced. He'd turned to look at Sara when he'd made that statement. His gaze deliberately lingered there a minute. Then he turned back to the prince. "How isn't important, my lord. Surely, after reading the facts, you've come to realize that my daughter can't live her life with the son of a traitor. She'd be shunned by society. The marquess's father didn't act in good faith toward the king or the Winchesters when he signed the contract binding his son to my daughter. I therefore demand that Sara be freed from this ludicrous commitment and that the gift be given over to her as payment for the embarrassment and humiliation she's had to suffer."

"I'm afraid I'm really going to have to insist that you tell us who gave you the information about Nathan's father," Sir Richards said again.

Winston turned to the prince for support. "I would rather not answer that demand."

"I believe you must answer," the prince said.

Winston's shoulders sagged. "My daughter," he blurted out. "Sara wrote to us. She gave us the information."

Sara didn't say a word. Nathan gave her a gentle squeeze. It was an awkward attempt to give her comfort. She didn't protest at all.

Don't give up on him, she thought. Those were his very words. Sara tried to concentrate on the important discussion underway, but Nathan's whispered command kept getting in the way.

Her father was giving one excuse after another as to why his daughter would share that damning information about Nathan's father. Sara didn't want to listen to those lies.

The prince caught her attention when he motioned to one of the men standing behind him. The guard immediately went over to the side entrance and pulled the door open. A short, thin man holding a dark cap in his hands came into the office.

Sara didn't recognize the man. It was obvious, though, that her father did. He couldn't quite hide his surprise. "Who is this man intruding upon our discussion?" he asked.

His paltry attempt to bluster his way through the ordeal didn't work. "He's Luther Grant," Sir Richards drawled. "Perhaps you've met him, Winchester. Luther used to work as a senior attendant in our department. He was so trustworthy, he was given charge of the vault. It was his sole duty to keep England's secrets safe."

The director's tone of voice had turned biting. "Luther's going to be protecting the walls of Newgate Prison from now on. He'll have his very own cell to watch over."

"The game's over," Caine interjected. "Grant told us you paid him to look at Nathan's file. When he couldn't find anything damning there, he looked at Nathan's father's file."

Winston's expression showed only disdain. "Who cares how the information was found out?" he muttered. "The only thing that matters is that—"

"Oh, but we do care," Sir Richards interrupted. "You've committed an act of treason."

"Isn't that a hanging crime?" the prince asked.

From his expression Sara couldn't tell if he was goading her father or if he really didn't know.

"Yes, it is a hanging crime," Sir Richards said.

Winston shook with fury. "I have never been disloyal to the crown," he announced. He stared at the prince regent. "When every other politician in this city has ridiculed you, I've stood firmly by your side. My God, I even argued in your defense when you wanted to rid yourself of your wife. Is this how I'm repaid for my loyalty?"

The prince's face turned red. It was obvious that he didn't like being reminded of his unpopularity or of his attempt to rid himself of his wife. He glared at Winston even as he shook his head. "How dare you speak to your prince regent with such insolence?"

Winston realized he'd gone too far. "I apologize, my lord," he blurted out, "but I am desperately trying to protect my daughter. The marquess of St. James isn't good enough for her."

The prince took a deep breath. His color remained high, but his voice was much calmer when he said, "I disagree with you. I've never taken an active interest in the War Department, for it bores me immensely, but once I read the facts about Nathan's father I asked Sir Richards to give me the son's file as well. Nathan isn't responsible for his father's sins. No man should have to be." His voice rose an octave when he added, "My subjects could blame me for my own father's weak condition if that was the case, isn't that so?"

"They don't hold you responsible for your father's illness," Winston assured him.

The prince nodded. "Exactly so," he muttered. "And I don't hold Nathan responsible for his father's errors. No, the marquess isn't responsible," he repeated in a weary voice. "But even if he were, he more than proved his loyalty by all the courageous deeds he accomplished on England's behalf. If the secrets could all be revealed, Nathan would be knighted for his heroic acts. As to that, I'm told that the earl of Cainewood would deserve like treatment. Reading the files took up most of my evening, Winston, and I now say that having all the facts before me, I feel honored to be in the same room with these loyal, distinguished men."

No one said a word for a minute. Nathan could feel Sara trembling. He noticed that she was watching her father, and he wanted to whisper to her that it was all going to be all right, that he'd never be able to frighten her again.

The prince spoke once more. "Sir Richards refuses to allow the information to be made public, however, and I have decided to bow to his superior wisdom in this matter. Suffice it to say that these men have my gratitude. I now have a bargain to put to you," he said. His gaze had turned to rest on the director. "If Winston assures us that he won't speak a word about Nathan's father, I suggest we don't lock him up."

Sir Richards pretended to mull over that suggestion. "I would rather see him hanged. However, the decision is up to you. I am but your humble servant."

The prince nodded. He looked at Winston again. "I know that certain members of your household are aware of the information about Nathan's father. It will be your duty to keep them silent. You'll be responsible for defending Nathan against any such scandal, for if a hint of a rumor reaches me, you'll be charged with treason. Do I make myself clear?"

Winston nodded. He was so furious he could barely speak. The prince's revulsion was apparent. The earl of Winchester knew he wouldn't be included in any of the more important functions in future. As soon as the prince gave him the cut direct everyone else would follow suit.

Sara could feel her father's rage. Her throat closed up, and she thought she was going to be sick. "May I have a glass of water, please?" she whispered to Nathan.

He immediately got up and left the room to fetch a drink for her. Caine also moved from his chair and took Luther Grant out the side door.

Winston turned to Sir Richards. "I could challenge this. It's still Grant's word against mine."

The director shook his head. "We have other evidence," he lied.

The earl of Winchester stood up. He obviously believed the director's bluff. "I see," he muttered. "How did you find out about Luther?" he asked the prince.

"Your wife told us," the prince answered. "She came to her daughter's aid, Winston, while you tried to destroy her. Leave, Winston. It pains me to look at you."

The earl of Winchester bowed to the prince, turned to stare at his daughter for the briefest of seconds, and then left the office.

Sara had never seen such black fury on her father's face. She was filled with terror. She knew her mother would soon bear the brunt of his anger.

Dear God, she thought, she had to get to her first.

"Will you please excuse me?" she cried out as she rushed toward the door.

Sara had barely received the prince's nod before she'd closed the front door behind her.

"Do you think she's ill?" Sir Richards asked.

"I can't imagine why she wouldn't be," the prince answered. "Richards," he added in a softer tone of voice, "I know how the various department heads whisper their contempt for me. Oh, I have my spies to keep me informed. I also know you've never said a word against me. Although I've incorrectly been judged as a ruler who changes his mind whenever the whim comes over me, I tell you now that it isn't so. I won't change my mind about this issue with Winston, I assure you."

Sir Richards walked to the door with the prince. "You do realize, my lord, that I lied when I told Winston we had other evidence against him. It really is Grant's word against his, and if he were to push this issue . . ."

The prince smiled. "He won't push anything," he assured the director.

Nathan walked in by way of the side entrance with a glass of water in his hand and Caine by his side. The prince had just taken his leave. "Where's Sara?" Nathan asked.

"She went to the washroom," Sir Richards explained. He went back to his desk and collapsed in the chair. "By God, that went smoothly. I couldn't be certain how the prince regent would behave. He was on the mark this time, wasn't he?"

"Will he stay on the mark?" Caine asked. "Or will Winston be back in his camp come tomorrow?"

The director shrugged. "I pray that he won't change his mind, and my feeling is that he'll keep his promise."

Caine leaned on the edge of the desk. "I cannot believe you let him read the files, Richards."

"Then don't believe it," his director answered, grinning. "I gave him only a brief summary of some of the lesser deeds accomplished. Quit your frown, Caine. Nathan, for God's sake, quit pacing with that glass in your hand. Most of the water's on the carpet now."

"What's taking Sara so long?"

"I believe she wasn't feeling well. Let her have a few more minutes of privacy."

Nathan let out a sigh. He went to refill the glass while Sir Richards caught Caine up on activities within the department.

Nathan tried to be patient, but when another ten minutes went by and Sara still hadn't returned to the office he decided to go after her. "Where the hell is the washroom? Sara might need me."

Sir Richards gave him directions to the floor above. "Are the papers ready for signatures?" Caine asked when Nathan turned to leave.

"They're on the desk," Nathan called over his shoulder. "As soon as I get my hands on Sara we can get this over and done with."

"He's quite a romantic," Caine drawled out.

"Actually, what he's about to do for his wife indicates to me that he really is a romantic at heart. Who would have thought Nathan would fall in love?"

Caine grinned. "Who would have thought anyone would have him? Sara's as much in love with him as he is with her. Nathan's determined to start over," he added with a nod toward the papers.

"Ah, love in bloom," Sir Richards said. "Sara will certainly be pleased with his thoughtfulness. God knows she's deserving of some happiness. It was hard on her today. Why, the look on her face when the prince made mention of her mother nearly broke my heart, Caine, and I'm certainly not given to emotion as you well know. Lady Sara looked so frightened. I wanted to reach out to her, to pat her and tell her it would all wash out. I'm not usually so demonstrative, but I tell you I had to restrain myself from going over to her."

Caine looked bewildered. "I don't recall the prince mentioning Sara's mother."

"I believe both you and Nathan were out of the room at the time," Richards said. "Yes, that's right," he added with a nod. "Sara sat all alone. Nathan had gone to fetch some water for her."

"Sara isn't in the washroom," Nathan bellowed from the doorway. "Damn it, Richards, where'd you send her? Down the street, for God's sake?"

Caine stood up. "Nathan, we might have a problem." His voice was harsh from worry. "Sir Richards, tell us exactly what the prince said about Sara's mother."

The director was already pushing his chair back so that he could stand up. He wasn't certain what the danger was, but the scent was there, permeating the air.

"Winston demanded to know who told us about Grant. The prince told him it was his wife who gave us the name."

Both Nathan and Caine were already running out the door. "Surely Winston wouldn't dare touch his wife or his daughter," Sir Richards muttered as he chased after the two men. "You're thinking that's where Sara went, aren't you? Charles," he shouted over his shoulder, "bring the carriage around."

Nathan reached the ground level with Caine right on his heels when Sir Richards turned the corner of the landing above. "Nathan, you don't believe Winston is capable of hurting either his wife or his daughter."

Nathan threw the door open and ran out onto the sidewalk. "No," he shouted over his shoulder. "Winston won't touch them. He'll leave it to his brother to mete out the punishment. That's how the bastard operates. Damn it,

Sara took your carriage, Caine. God, we've got to get to her before Henry does."

A hack was racing down the street. Nathan seized his opportunity. He wasn't about to wait for the director's carriage. He ran into the street, braced himself for the struggle, and grabbed the reins of the two horses.

He threw his shoulder into the side of the horse closer to him. Caine added his strength, and the vehicle came to a screeching stop.

The driver was thrown on top of the vehicle. He started shouting. The fare, a blond-headed young man with spectacles and a squint, stuck his head out the window to see what all the commotion was about just as Nathan pulled the door open. Before the man knew what had happened Nathan had tossed him to the pavement.

Caine shouted directions to the driver while Sir Richards helped the stranger to his feet. The director was being very solicitous until he realized he was about to be left behind. He rudely shoved the man back to the ground and jumped inside the hack before Caine could pull the door closed.

No one said a word on the ride over to the Winchesters' townhouse. Nathan was shaking with terror. For the first time in his life he rebelled against the isolation he'd always enforced upon himself. He needed her, and dear God, if something happened to her before he could prove to her that he could be worthy, could love her as much as she deserved to be loved, he didn't think he could go on.

In the space of those long, unbearable minutes Nathan learned how to pray. He felt as unskilled as an atheist, couldn't remember a single prayer from childhood days, and so ended up simply begging God's mercy.

How he needed her.

The ride over to her mother's residence wasn't quite as traumatic for Sara. She wasn't in a panic because she knew she had enough time to get to her mother first. Her father would have to go to his brother's townhouse. That ride would take him at least twenty minutes. Then he'd have to spend at least fifteen more minutes working his brother into a rage for the injustices dealt to him. Assuming that Henry would certainly be in the throes of his daily hangover, it would take him time to clear his head and get dressed.

There was also the oddly comforting fact that surely in that amount of time Nathan would put the pieces together and figure out she wasn't in the washroom. She knew he'd come after her.

Don't give up on me. His whispered command once again intruded upon her thoughts. She immediately tried to get angry over the insulting demand. How dare he think she'd given up on him. How dare he . . .

She couldn't work herself up into a proper fury, for in her heart she wasn't at all certain she had the right to be outraged. Had she given up on him? No, of course not, she told herself. The simple fact was that Nathan didn't love her.

He had shown her consideration, though. She'd give him that much. She remembered how he'd rubbed her back when she'd been in such embarrassing agony with her monthly cramps. His touch had been so gentle, so soothing.

He was a gentle lover, too. Not that he'd ever given her loving words when he was caressing her. But he'd shown her kindness, patience, and never once had she truly been afraid of him. Never once.

But he didn't love her.

He'd spent long hours teaching her so many little things he thought she needed to know to become self-sufficient. She thought it was because he didn't want to watch out for her. And while she did consider it her duty to protect those she loved, like her mother, she left the task of her own protection to her husband.

Like her mother . . .

Dear God, Nora had been right. Without realizing it Sara had been following in her mother's path. She had been determined to become dependent on her husband. If Nathan had turned out to be a cruel, selfish man like her father, would Sara have learned how to cringe whenever he raised his voice to her?

She shook her head. No, she would never allow any man to terrorize her. Nathan had made her realize her own strength. She could survive alone, and she certainly could stand up for herself.

He hadn't taught her how to defend herself because he didn't want to be bothered with the chore of watching out for her. He just didn't want anything to happen to her.

He was a kind man.

Sara burst into tears. Why couldn't he love her?

Don't give up on me. If he didn't love her, why did he care if she gave up on him or not?

Sara was so consumed with her thoughts, she didn't realize the carriage had stopped until Caine's driver shouted down to her.

She asked the driver to wait, then hurried up the steps.

The butler, a new man hired by her father, told her that both her mother and her sister had gone out for the afternoon.

Sara didn't believe him. She pushed her way past the servant and hurried up the stairs to the bedroom level to see for herself.

The butler sniffed at her lack of manners and retired to the back of the house.

The bedrooms were empty. Sara was at first relieved, then she realized she would have to find her mother before either of the Winchester men did. She went through the stack of invitations on top of her mother's writing table, but none gave her a clue as to the afternoon activities.

She decided to go back downstairs and force the information out of the servants. Surely one of them knew where her mother had gone.

Sara had just reached the landing when the front door opened. She thought it was her mother returning home and started down the steps. She stopped midway when Uncle Henry strutted into the foyer.

He saw her at once. The sneer on his face made her stomach lurch.

"Father went directly to you with his anger, didn't he?" she called out, contempt evident in her voice. "I knew he would," she added. "It's the only thing he's predictable about. He thinks he's so cunning to let his drunken brother dole out the punishment whenever he's upset. Father's waiting at White's, isn't he?"

Her uncle's eyes narrowed into slits. "Your mother should have her tongue cut out for turning against her husband. This isn't your business, Sara. Get out of my way. I'm going to have a word with your mother."

Sara shook her head. "I won't let you speak to her," she shouted. "Not now, not tomorrow, not ever. If I have to force Mother, I will, but she's going to leave London. A nice visit with her sister will be just the thing. She might even realize she doesn't want to come back here again. God, I hope so. Mother deserves a little joy in her life. I'm going to see that she gets it."

Henry kicked the door shut behind him. He knew better than to strike Sara, for he remembered the threat her husband had made when he'd walked into the tavern to get his bride.

"Go back to the cur you're married to," he shouted. "Victoria," he added in a screech. "Get down here. I'm wanting a word with you."

"Mother isn't here. Now *you* get out. The sight of you makes me ill."

Henry started toward the steps. He stopped when he

spotted the brass umbrella stand in the corner. He was too furious to consider the consequences. The chit needed to learn a lesson, he thought to himself. Just one good hit to rid her of her insolence.

He reached for the ivory-tipped walking stick. Just one good hit . .

Chapter Sixteen

She damn near killed him.

Tortured screams echoed into the street. The carriage hadn't come to a complete stop before Nathan jumped to the pavement and started up the steps. The god-awful screaming made him crazed with fear for his Sara—so crazed, in fact, that he didn't stop to notice it was a man's voice making all the noise. He didn't stop to open the door, either. He went through it. The frame bounded off his shoulder and landed with a thud on Henry Winchester's head. The heavy piece of wood muffled some of the louder cries.

Nathan wasn't at all prepared for the sight he came upon. He was so stunned, he stopped dead in his tracks. Caine and Sir Richards crashed into his back. Caine let out a low grunt. He felt as though he'd just run into a block of steel. Both he and Sir Richards recovered their balance and moved to the side to see what held Nathan transfixed.

It was difficult for the men to take in. Henry Winchester was shriveled up in a fetal position on the floor in the center of the large foyer. His hands were clutching his groin. The

man was literally writhing about in agony, and when he
rolled over their way Sir Richards and Caine immediately
noticed his bloody nose.

Nathan was staring at Sara. She was standing at the
bottom of the steps. She looked thoroughly composed,
absolutely beautiful, and completely unharmed.

She was all right. The bastard hadn't gotten to her. Yes,
she was all right. Nathan kept repeating that fact inside his
mind in an attempt to calm down.

It didn't work. His hands were shaking. He decided he
needed to hear her tell him she was all right before he could
start breathing normally again.

"Sara?" Nathan whispered her name in such a hoarse
whisper, he doubted she could hear him above the racket her
Uncle Henry was making. He tried again. "Sara? Are you all
right? He didn't hurt you, did he?"

The anguish in her husband's voice was almost her
undoing. Tears filled her eyes, and she realized that Nathan
was just as misty. The look on his face made her heart ache.
He looked so . . . scared, so vulnerable . . . so loving.

Dear God, he did love her. It was so apparent to her.

You love me, she wanted to shout. She didn't, of course,
because there were other people present. But he loved her.
She couldn't speak, couldn't quit smiling.

She started toward her husband, then remembered her
audience. She turned to Caine and Sir Richards and made a
perfect curtsy.

Caine grinned. Sir Richards was in the middle of an
acknowledging bow when he caught himself. "What happened here?" he demanded in a fluster of authority.

"Damn it, Sara, answer me," Nathan strangled out at the
same time. "Are you all right?"

She turned her gaze to her husband. "Yes, Nathan. I'm
quite all right. Thank you for inquiring."

She looked down at her uncle. "Uncle Henry had a little
mishap," she announced.

The director bent on one knee and lifted a remnant of the

door away from Henry's chest. "I surmised as much, my dear," he said to Sara. He tossed the piece of wood aside, then frowned at Henry. "For the love of God, man, quit that weeping. It isn't dignified. Did the door fell you when Nathan came charging through? Speak up, Winchester. I can't catch a word of your blubbering."

Caine had already put the pieces together. Sara was rubbing the back of her right hand in what appeared to be an attempt to work out the sting. Henry was clutching his groin.

"Uncle Henry had his mishap before the door fell on him," Sara explained. She sounded incredibly cheerful, and she was smiling at Nathan when she made that statement. Nathan still wasn't calm enough to reason it through. He couldn't understand why his wife looked so damned pleased with herself. Hadn't she realized the danger she'd been in? Hell, his nerves still felt as raw as a fresh wound.

Then she was slowly walking toward him, and all he could think about was taking her into his arms. He was never going to let go of her, not even when he lectured her on her sinful habit of taking off on her own.

Caine's smile proved catching. The director found himself smiling, too, though he still didn't know what was so amusing. He stood up and turned to Sara. "Please satisfy my curiosity and tell me what happened."

She wasn't about to explain. If she told him exactly what she'd done, the director would certainly be appalled by her unladylike behavior.

Nathan wouldn't be appalled. He'd be proud of her. Sara couldn't wait until they were alone and she could give him all the details, blow by satisfying blow.

"Uncle Henry tripped over a walking stick," she said, unable to stop smiling.

Nathan finally came out of his stupor and took a good look around him. Sara had just reached his side when he grabbed hold of her and stared intently at the red splotches on the back of her right hand.

That low growl she found adorable was working its way up Nathan's throat. She could also see the rage coming over him. She wasn't at all frightened, however, for she knew he would never turn his anger against her.

She didn't want him to get all worked up on her behalf. Sara wrapped her arms around her husband's waist and hugged him tight. "I'm really all right, Nathan," she whispered. "You mustn't worry so."

She rested the side of her face against his chest. The hammering of his heart indicated that her soothing words hadn't calmed him at all. Yet his voice was deceptively calm when he asked, "Did you have the walking stick, or did he?"

"He had the stick when he started up the steps to get me," she explained. "He grabbed it from the umbrella stand."

Nathan pictured it in his mind. He tried to peel her hands away. "Nathan? It's over now. He didn't strike me."

"Did he try?"

She felt as if she were clinging to a statue, so rigid had his stance become. She let out a little sigh, increased her hold on him, and then answered, "Yes, but I wouldn't let him hit me. I remembered your instructions, and I evened the odds, just as you promised I would in such a situation. As to that," she added, "I also had the element of surprise on my side. Uncle Henry isn't at all used to having women defend themselves. He looked . . . astonished when he fell backwards."

"Caine? Take Sara outside and wait for me. Richards, go with them."

All three of them told Nathan no at the same time. They all had different reasons. Caine didn't want the mess of getting rid of the body. Sara didn't want Nathan to go to the gallows. Sir Richards didn't want the paperwork.

Nathan was still rigid with fury when they'd finished giving him their arguments. He couldn't get Sara out of his arms long enough to rip the Winchester bastard apart. He found the situation extremely frustrating. "Damn it, Sara, if you'll just let me—"

"No, Nathan."

His sigh was long. She knew she'd won. She was suddenly in a hurry to get him alone so that she could win another victory. Come hell or his hide, she would get him to tell her he loved her.

"Nathan, we can't leave until I know Mama's going to be safe," she whispered. "But I want to go home with you now. What are you going to do about this problem?" She didn't give him time to answer. "I meant to say, Nathan, what are we going to do about this problem?"

Her husband wasn't one to give up easily. He still wanted to kill her uncle. He considered his plan a perfectly logical one. It would not only eliminate Sara's worry about her mother's safety, but it would also give him the tremendous satisfaction of putting his fist through the man's face. He kept staring at the walking stick and thinking of the damage a man could inflict with such a weapon. Henry could have killed her.

Caine came up with a nice solution. "You know, Nathan, Henry looks in need of a long rest. Perhaps a sea voyage to the colonies would be just the ticket to improve his health."

Nathan's mood immediately brightened. "See to it, Caine."

"I'll give him to Colin and let him arrange the details," Caine said. He lifted Henry up by the nape of his neck. "A few ropes and a gag are all the baggage he'll be needing."

Sir Richards nodded agreement. "I'll wait here until your mother returns, Sara. I'll explain that your uncle had a sudden desire to take a long trip. I'm also going to wait for your father. I want to have a few words with him, too. Why don't you and Nathan run along now? Take my carriage and have my driver return for me later."

Henry Winchester had regained enough of his sensibilities to make a doubled-over dash for the doorway. Caine deliberately shoved him toward his brother-in-law.

Nathan seized his opportunity. He slammed the back of his fist into Henry's stomach. The blow sent Sara's uncle back to the floor for another bout of writhing.

"Feel better, Nathan?" Caine asked.

"Immensely," Nathan answered.

"What about the papers you had drawn up?" Sir Richards asked Nathan.

"Bring them to Farnmount's ball tonight. We'll borrow Lester's library for a few minutes. Sara and I should get there around nine."

"I'll have to go back to the office to fetch them," the director said. "Set the meeting for ten, Nathan, just to be on the safe side."

"May I ask what it is you're discussing?" Sara interjected.

"No."

Her husband's abrupt answer irritated her. "I don't want to go out tonight," she announced. "I have something most important to discuss with you."

He shook his head. "You will have faith in me, woman," he muttered as he dragged her out the doorway.

She let out a gasp. "Of all the galling things to say to me . . ."

She stopped when he turned and lifted her into the carriage. His expression looked bleak. She noticed his hands were shaking, too.

He wouldn't let her sit next to him but took his place across from her. When he stretched out his long legs she was trapped between them.

As soon as the carriage started forward he turned and stared out the window.

"Nathan?"

"Yes?"

"Are you having . . . aftermath now?"

"No."

She was disappointed, for she hoped he'd need to vent his frustration the way she had when she'd experienced aftermath. The memory of just how her husband had helped her get over her tension made her face turn pink.

"Don't men have aftermath after they fight?"

"Some do. I shouldn't have hit Henry in front of you," he said. He still wouldn't look at her.

"Do you mean that if I hadn't been there, you wouldn't have hit him, or that you regret—"

"Hell, yes, I would have hit him," Nathan muttered. "I just shouldn't have struck the bastard in front of you."

"Why?"

"You're my wife," he explained. "You shouldn't be a witness to . . . violence. In future I will refrain from—"

"Nathan," she interrupted, "I didn't mind. Truly. There are times when it will happen again. I am opposed to violence," she added in a rush, "but I will admit that there are times when a sound punch is just the thing. It can be quite invigorating."

He shook his head. "You wouldn't let me kill the pirates, remember?"

"I let you hit them."

He shrugged. Then he let out a loud sigh. "You are a lady. You're delicate and feminine, and I will behave like a gentleman when I'm with you. That's the way it's going to be, Sara. Don't argue with me."

"You've always been a gentleman with me," she whispered.

"The hell I have," he countered. "I'll change, Sara. Now cease this talk. I'm trying to think."

"Nathan? Were you worried about me?"

"Hell, yes, I was worried."

He'd bellowed his answer. She held her smile. "I really would like you to kiss me."

He didn't even look at her when he responded, "No."

"Why not?"

"It has to be right, Sara."

What in heaven's name did that mean? "It's always right when you kiss me."

"I'll ruin everything if I kiss you."

"You aren't making any sense."

"Tell me what happened with Henry," he ordered.

She let out a little sigh. "I hit him . . . there."

A soft smile changed his frown. "Did you remember how to make a proper fist?"

She decided she wouldn't answer him until he looked at her. A long moment passed before he finally gave in.

He was fighting one hell of a battle to keep his hands off her. He thought he was winning the fight, too, until she smiled at him and whispered, "I knew you would be proud of me. Most gentlemen would have been appalled, though."

He roughly pulled her into his lap. His fingers were already twisting into her hair. "I'm not most," he said an instant before his mouth came down on hers. His tongue swept inside her mouth to taste, to caress, to tease. He couldn't get enough of her, couldn't get close enough, soon enough.

He kissed the side of her neck while he worked on the buttons at the back of her dress. "I knew if I touched you, I wouldn't be able to stop."

He'd lost all control. The carriage stopped, but only Sara realized that fact. She made him button her up again. It took him much longer, for his hands were shaking.

Nathan dragged her by her hand inside the townhouse. Jade smiled at the couple when they went flying up the stairs.

Nathan regained a little of his control by the time they reached their bedroom. He opened the door for her. Sara was already reaching behind her back to get the buttons undone again on her way over to the bed. She stopped when she heard the door slam.

She turned around to find that she was all alone. Nathan had left her. She was too astonished to react for several minutes. Then she let out an outraged scream. She pulled the door open and went running down the hallway.

Jade caught her at the landing. "Nathan just left. He said to tell you to be ready to leave by eight. He also suggested I lend you a gown, since your trunk is still on board the *Seahawk*."

"How could he have told you all that and have left already?"

Jade smiled. "My brother acted as though he had the devil on his tail," she said. "He finished his instructions from the walkway out front. He's going to meet us later, Sara. He must have some business to attend to—at least I think that's what he added when he jumped into Caine's carriage and took off."

Sara shook her head. "Your brother is rude, inconsiderate, arrogant, stubborn . . ."

"And you love him."

Her shoulders sagged. "Yes, I love him. I believe he might love me, too," she added in a mutter. "He might not truly realize it yet, or he might just be a little afraid. Oh, I don't know anymore. Yes, of course he loves me. How can you believe he doesn't?"

"I'm not arguing with you, Sara. I believe Nathan loves you, too," she added with a nod. "It's quite obvious to me, as a matter of fact. He's so . . . rattled. He's always been a man of few words, but now he doesn't even make sense when he mutters."

Sara's eyes filled with tears. "I want him to tell me he loves me," she whispered.

Jade was full of sympathy. She patted Sara's hand and led her to her bedroom.

"Do you know that I'm everything Nathan could ever want in a wife? No one could love him as much as I do. Please don't consider me inferior. I'm really not. I'm just very different from you, Jade."

Nathan's sister turned from the wardrobe to stare incredulously at Sara. "Why would you think I would ever consider you inferior?"

Sara stammered out her explanation of how the men on board the *Seahawk* had constantly compared her to Jade, and how she'd always lost the contest. "And then the pirates attacked, and I was able to redeem myself in their eyes."

"I would imagine so," Jade agreed.

"I also have courage," Sara said. "I'm not boasting, Jade. Nathan did convince me that I'm very courageous."

"We're both loyal to our husbands, too," Jade said. She turned back to her wardrobe and continued to sort through, looking for an appropriate gown.

"Nathan only likes me to wear high-necked gowns," Sara said.

"That's telling, isn't it?"

"I usually try to be accommodating."

Jade didn't dare let Sara see her expression. The anger in her sister-in-law's voice made her want to laugh. The poor love was getting all worked up again.

"Perhaps, Jade, that is the problem," Sara announced. "I've been too accommodating. I'm always telling Nathan how much I love him. And do you know what his answer always is?" She didn't give Jade time to guess. "He grunts. Honest to God, that's what he does. Well, no more, thank you."

"No more grunting?" Jade asked.

"No more accommodating. Find me the lowest-cut gown in your closet."

Jade did laugh then. "That should push Nathan right over the edge."

"I do hope so," Sara answered.

Five minutes later Sara held an ivory-colored gown in her arms.

"I only wore the dress once, and not out of the house, so no one's seen it. Caine wouldn't let me keep it on."

Sara loved the gown. She thanked Jade several times, then started out of the room. She suddenly stopped and turned around. "May I ask you something?"

"We're sisters now, Sara. You may ask me anything."

"Do you ever cry?"

Jade hadn't expected that question. "Yes," she answered. "All the time, as a matter of fact."

"Has Nathan ever seen you cry?"

"I don't know if he has or not."

From Sara's crestfallen expression Jade realized that wasn't the answer she was hoping for. "Now that I think about it, yes, he has seen me cry. Not as often as Caine, of course."

"Oh, thank you for sharing that confidence with me. You have no idea how happy you've just made me."

Sara's smile was radiant. Jade was pleased, though she admitted to herself she still didn't know exactly what Sara was so thrilled about.

Two hours later Jade and Caine patiently waited in the foyer for Sara to make her appearance. Jimbo paced back and forth by the front door.

Jade was dressed in a dark green silk gown with embroidered cap sleeves. The neckline showed only the barest hint of bosom. Caine still frowned over it before he muttered that she looked beautiful. He wore his formal attire, and she told him he was the most handsome devil in the world. Then Jimbo started nagging them about making certain someone stayed by Sara's side all evening.

"Don't let her out of your sight until Nathan shows up to take over," Jimbo ordered for the fifth time.

Sara drew everyone's attention when she started down the steps. Jimbo let out a low whistle. "Nathan's going to see red when he gets a look at our Sara."

Both Jade and Caine agreed. Sara looked magnificent. Her hair was unbound, and the soft curls swayed about her shoulders with each step she took.

The virginal-colored dress was extremely low-cut and ended in a deep V between her breasts. It was the most provocative gown Caine had ever seen. He remembered it, too. "I thought I tore that thing when I helped you get undressed," he whispered.

His wife blushed. "You were in a hurry, but you didn't tear it."

"Nathan's going to," Caine whispered back.

"Then you think my brother will like it?"

"Hell, no, he won't like it," Caine predicted.

"Good."

"Jade, sweet, I'm not so certain this is such a good idea. Every man at the ball is going to be lusting after Sara. Nathan's going to have a fit."

"Yes."

Sara reached the foyer and made a curtsy to her audience.

"You needn't be so formal with us," Caine said.

Sara smiled. "I wasn't," she said. "I was just making certain I wouldn't fall out of this dress when I do have to curtsy."

"What about when your husband has his hands around your neck and he's strangling you?" Jimbo asked. "Will the gown prove sturdy enough, do you suppose?"

"I'm going to find her a cloak," Caine said.

"Nonsense," Jade argued. "It's too warm for a cloak."

The argument continued even after they were on their way.

The duke and duchess of Farnmount lived a scant mile outside of London proper. Their home was gigantic in diameter, with impressive manicured lawns circling the terraces. Hired servants held torches along the side of the road, lighting the way.

"Rumor has it that the prince has tried to buy Farnmount's residence," Caine said. "He won't give it up, of course."

"Yes," Jade agreed, though she was barely paying attention to her husband's remarks. She was watching Sara. "You look flushed to me," she said. "Are you feeling well?"

"She's fine," Caine said.

Sara wasn't fine, though. Her mind raced with her worries. "The Winchesters will be there tonight," she suddenly blurted out. "None of the men would dare offend the duke and duchess. I don't understand, though, why this is the only affair the St. James family attends."

Caine grinned. "It's the only affair they're invited to attend," he explained.

"I worry about Nathan," Sara suddenly blurted out.

"Jimbo, I wish you could come inside, too. Caine may need your assistance watching out for my husband."

"The boy will be all right," Jimbo answered. He patted Sara's hand. "Quit your fretting."

No one said another word until the carriage drew to a stop in front of the mansion. Jimbo jumped down, then turned to assist Sara. "I'll be standing right beside this carriage. When you've had enough, just step outside the front door, and I'll spot you."

"She'll stay with us until Nathan arrives," Caine said.

Sara nodded. She took a deep breath, lifted the hem of her skirt, and went up the steps.

The ballroom was located on the top level of the four-story structure. The stairway leading up was a blaze of candles and fresh flowers.

A butler stood next to the entrance to the ballroom. There were three steps leading down to the dance area. Caine handed his invitation to the servant, then waited until the bell was dutifully rung. It was a signal to the other guests crowding the floor. Few paid attention, other than to give a quick look up toward the entrance, for a waltz was in progress, and they were busy concentrating on their foot-work.

"The earl of Cainewood and his wife, Lady Jade," the butler announced in a loud, booming voice.

It was Sara's turn next. She handed the man the invitation Caine had given her, then stood by his side until the introduction was made.

"Lady Sara St. James."

He might as well have shouted fire. The announcement had just the same force. A low murmur began in the middle of the crowd, and by the time everyone had added their whisper the sound had increased to earthquake proportions.

One couple actually bumped into another as the man and woman strained to get a better look at Sara.

She held her head high and stared down at the crowd. She prayed she looked composed. Then Caine took hold of her hand. Jade moved to Sara's other side and took hold of her other hand.

"Sara, dear, have you noticed that the Winchesters are all squeezed up together on the right side of the ballroom, and the St. James are all on the left? One might be led to conclude that the two families don't get along."

Jade had made those remarks. Sara broke into a smile. Her sister-in-law had sounded so perplexed. "Rumor has it they don't particularly like each other," Sara teased back.

"I think we'll take up the middle so as not to show partiality," Caine announced as he led the ladies down the steps.

"Nathan isn't here yet, is he?" Jade asked. "Sara, do keep smiling. Everyone's gawking at you. It's the dress, I imagine. You look positively stunning tonight."

The next hour was a trial. Sara's father was in attendance. He made quite a show of giving his daughter the cut direct. When she looked over to the Winchester side of the ballroom the guests turned their backs on her.

Everyone noticed the slight, of course. Caine was furious on Sara's behalf until he looked at her face and saw that she was smiling. He relaxed then.

Dunnford St. James hadn't missed the cut, either. The leader of the St. James clan let out a loud snort, then strolled over to speak to his nephew's wife.

Dunnford was a large, square-framed man with far more muscle than fat. His hair was gray, thinning, and cut as short as a squire's in olden days. He had a full beard, broad shoulders, and looked ill at ease in his formal black attire and crooked starched cravat.

Caine thought he was prettier than his wife.

"What do we have here?" he bellowed when he stopped directly in front of Sara. "This be Nathan's woman?"

"You know perfectly well who she is," Caine answered. "Lady Sara, have you met Dunnford St. James?"

Sara made a formal curtsy. "It is a pleasure to meet you," she said.

Dunnford looked bewildered. "Are you jesting with me?"
Now she looked confused. "I beg your pardon?"

"She has manners, Dunnford. Surprising in a St. James, isn't it?"

A sparkle entered the older man's eyes. "She just became a St. James. She'll have to prove herself before I'll welcome her."

Sara took a step toward Dunnford. That surprised him more than the curtsy had. He was used to having women back away from him. They never smiled, either. This one, he concluded bleakly, was different.

"How shall I prove myself to you?" Sara asked. "Should I shoot one of your brothers to gain your approval, do you suppose?"

She was jesting. He took her suggestion to heart. "Well, now, I suppose it would depend upon which brother you shot. Tom's always a good choice."

"For God's sake, Dunnford, Sara was teasing you."
Dunnford grunted. "Then why'd she offer?"

Caine shook his head. "It was a jest in reference to the time you shot your brother," he explained.

Dunnford rubbed his beard. His grin was devilish. "So you heard about that little misunderstanding, did you? Tom doesn't hold a grudge," he added. "Pity, that. A good feud livens up a family."

Before anyone could remark upon that outrageous remark Dunnford let out a low growl. "Where's your husband? I'm wanting a word with him."

"He should be here any minute," Caine said.

"Where is your wife?" Sara asked. "I would like to meet her."

"Whatever for?" Dunnford countered. "She's probably in the dining room seeing about my meal."

"Aren't you going to say hello to me?" Jade asked her uncle. "You're pretending I'm not even here. Are you still upset because I gave Caine a daughter and not a son?"

"You carrying again yet?" Dunnford asked.

Jade shook her head.

"Then I ain't speaking to you until I get a nephew." He turned to Caine. "You bedding her proper?" he demanded.

Caine grinned. "Every chance I get," he drawled out.

Sara turned red with embarrassment. She noticed that Jade was trying not to smile. Dunnford was giving Nathan's sister a hard glare. Then he turned to Sara again, and suddenly the older man reached out and clasped the sides of her hips with his big hands.

"What are you doing?" Caine demanded in a whisper. He tried to push Dunnford's hands away.

Sara was too astonished by the bold action to move. She simply stared down at his hands.

"I'm taking her measure," Dunnford announced. "She don't look wide enough to bring a babe into the world. The skirt could be deceiving," he added with a nod. "Aye, you might be wide enough."

He was now staring at her chest. Sara's hands immediately covered her bosom. She wasn't about to let him measure anything else.

"I can see you got yourself enough to feed the babe. Are you carrying yet?"

Her face couldn't possibly turn any hotter. She took a step forward. "You will behave yourself," she whispered. "If you touch me again, sir, I will strike you. Are you completely without manners?"

Dunnford guessed he was. When he said so, Sara took yet another step toward him. Caine was amazed by her boldness. Just as astonishing was the fact that Dunnford actually backed up. "I would like a cup of punch, Uncle Dunnford," Sara said then. "It would be proper for you to fetch it for me."

Dunnford shrugged. Sara let out a sigh. "I do suppose I could ask one of the Winchesters to fetch it for me," she said then.

"They'd spit on you first," Dunnford announced. "You're swaying toward our side of the family, aren't you?"

She nodded. He grinned. "I'll be happy to fetch a drink for you."

Sara watched her uncle force his way through the crowd. There was a line waiting for the servant to ladle out a portion of the pink punch. Dunnford pushed the line of guests aside with a hard shove.

"I wouldn't drink any of the punch if I were you," Caine drawled out after Dunnford picked up the giant punch bowl and took several long gulps. He put the bowl back on the table, then dunked a cup into the liquid and turned to walk back across the room.

He wiped his beard with the back of his hand when he presented the cup to Sara.

Caine noticed there was no longer a line in front of the punch bowl. He reached out and grabbed the punch so that Dunnford couldn't accidentally spill the pink liquid on Sara.

"Tell Nathan I'm wanting a word with him," Dunnford announced once again. He added a frown to his reminder, then turned his back and walked over to the far side of the room where his relatives were standing.

Sara noticed the other guests made a wide path for the man. She decided then that he was very like Nathan.

"The marquess of St. James."

The shouted announcement drew everyone's attention. Sara turned to look up at the entrance. Her heart started beating frantically at the sight of her husband. She'd never seen him dressed in formal attire before. It was a bit overwhelming. His hair was bound behind his neck, and he wore the black jacket and pants like a mighty king. The arrogance in both his stance and his expression made her knees weak.

She instinctively started to walk toward him.

It was easy for Nathan to find his wife in the crowd. As

soon as his name had been announced the guests had all moved toward the corners. Sara stood all alone in the center of the dance floor.

She looked magnificent to him. She was so delicate, so exquisite, so . . . damned naked.

Nathan bounded down the stairs toward his wife. He was already taking his jacket off.

As soon as Nathan came down the steps the Winchesters started forward. The St. James men immediately imitated that action.

Caine nudged Jade. "Go sit down," he whispered. "There could be trouble, and I don't want to have to worry about you."

Jade nodded. She wanted Caine's mind solely on protecting her brother. Then she spotted Colin coming down the steps. From the bulge under his jacket she surmised he was armed for any eventuality.

Nathan had his jacket off, but when he reached Sara he couldn't remember what he was supposed to do with it.

"Sara?"

"Yes, Nathan?"

She waited for him to say something more.

He seemed content to stand there and stare at her. Her love was so apparent in her gaze. Her smile was tender. Dear God, he thought, he was unworthy of her, and yet she loved him.

He broke out in a cold sweat. He started to reach for the handkerchief Colin had stuffed in his pocket, then realized he was holding the coat in his hands. He couldn't imagine why. He put it back on. He couldn't take his gaze off his beautiful wife, and his arm got all caught up in the sleeve, but he finally righted the thing.

Sara stepped forward and adjusted his cravat just so, then moved back again.

And still he couldn't speak to her. God, it had to be right, he told himself. She deserved that much. No, no, it had to be perfect for her, not just right, he decided once again. He'd take her down to the library, get the papers signed, and then he'd . . .

"I love you, Sara." His voice sounded as if he'd just had a taste of her soup.

She made him tell her again. Her eyes were filled with tears, and he knew she'd heard him the first time. "I wasn't supposed to say that—not yet, anyway," he muttered. "I love you."

Her expression didn't change. His did. He looked as though he was going to be sick.

She took pity on him. "I know you love me, Nathan. It took me a long while to realize it—almost as long as it took for you to come and fetch me—but I know now. You've loved me for a long time, haven't you?"

His relief was obvious. "Why didn't you tell me you knew?" he demanded in a whisper. "Damn it, Sara, I went through hell."

Her eyes widened, and her face turned pink. "You went through hell? You're the one who refused to have any faith in me. You're the one who would never tell me what was in your heart. I told you all the time, Nathan."

He shook his head. His grin was sheepish. "No, Sara, not all the time. You told me once a day. Some days you waited until after dinner. I'd find myself getting nervous."

She took a step toward him. "You waited each day for me to tell you I loved you?"

He could tell from her expression that she was pleased with his confession. "Will you marry me?" he asked her in a fervent whisper. He'd leaned down until he was almost touching her forehead. "I'll get down on one knee if you want me to, Sara. I won't like it," he added in a rush of honesty. "But I'll do it. Please marry me."

She had never seen her husband so rattled. Telling her what was in his heart was obvious torture for him. It made her love him all the more, of course. "Nathan, we're already married, remember?"

Their audience was enthralled. The couple staring so lovingly into each other's eyes was such a romantic spectacle. Women dabbed at their eyes with their husbands' handkerchiefs.

Nathan had forgotten all about the other guests. He was desperately trying to get his plan completed so he could take Sara home.

"We have to go down to the library," he announced. "I want you to sign a paper breaking the contract."

"All right, Nathan," she answered.

Her ready agreement didn't surprise him. She'd always had such trust in him. He was still humbled by her faith. "My God, Sara, I love you so much, it . . . hurts."

She solemnly nodded. "I can see that it does," she whispered. "Are you getting seasick?"

He shook his head. "After you sign your paper, I'll sign mine," he stated.

"Why are you signing papers?" she asked.

"I'm also going to break the contract. I don't want the inheritance. I already have the greatest gift of all," he whispered. "I have you." His smile was filled with tenderness when he added, "You're everything I could ever want."

She started crying. He couldn't stop himself from pulling her into his arms. He leaned down and kissed his wife. She kissed him back.

A collective sigh came from the women in the crowd.

Yet Nathan's hope that the evening would turn out to be perfect for his wife was not completely fulfilled. By the St. James family's standards it was a huge success. By everyone else's standards it was a nightmare.

No one, however, would ever forget the brawl.

It began innocently enough when Nathan turned to take Sara to the library. She tugged on his hand to make him stop.

"I believe you love me, Nathan," she said when she had his full attention again. "You don't have to give up the king's gift just to prove it."

"Yes, I do," he returned. "I want to show you how much I love you. It's the only way you're going to believe me. You've given me your love for so long, and I've given you nothing but aggravation. It's penance, Sara. I have to do this."

She shook her head. "No, you don't have to do this. Nathan, you will show me you have faith in me and my love by not giving up the gift. You waited long years for that inheritance, and you're going to keep it."

"My mind's made up, wife."

"Unmake it," she countered.

"No."

"Yes."

She could tell from the set look on his face that he was determined to make a noble sacrifice for her. She was just as determined not to let him.

"And if I don't sign my paper?" she asked.

She folded her arms in front of her and frowned up at him while she waited for his answer.

Dear heaven, how she loved him, she thought. And how he loved her, too. He looked like he wanted to throttle her. She felt like laughing.

"If you don't sign the paper, Sara, then your family can have the king's gift. I don't want it."

"I won't have it."

"Now, Sara . . ."

He didn't realize they were shouting. She did. She turned to look over the St. James section of the crowd until she found the man she wanted. "Uncle Dunnford?" she called out. "Nathan wants to give up the king's gift."

"Oh, hell, Sara, why'd you do that?"

She turned around and smiled at her husband. Nathan was already taking his jacket off. Then Sara noticed Caine and Colin were doing the same thing.

She started to laugh. God help her, she'd already turned into a St. James.

Nathan didn't look sick anymore. A sparkle had come

into his eyes. He was such a fit man. And she was just the woman to manage him. He was glaring at her chest. Then his jacket was around her shoulders, and he was demanding that she put her arms through the sleeves. "If you ever wear that gown again, I'll tear it off you," he whispered. "Hell, here they come."

The St. James men were moving forward like a troop of soldiers set on war. "I love you, Nathan. Do remember not to tuck your thumb under your fingers. You wouldn't want to break it."

Nathan raised an eyebrow over that suggestion. She retaliated by giving him a slow, sexy wink. He grabbed her by the lapels of his jacket, kissed her hard, and then pushed her behind his back.

It was, without a doubt, a night to remember. The duke and duchess of Farnmount, both surely in their late sixties, couldn't have been more pleased with the entertainment. Their little gathering would provide enough talk to keep everyone well fed in the gossip department for a good long while.

Sara remembered seeing the stately couple perched on the top step. They each held a goblet of wine, and after the first punch was landed the duke of Farnmount directed the orchestra to begin playing a waltz.

In truth, however, Sara liked the aftermath much better than the brawl. As soon as the fight was over Nathan dragged her out into the night. He didn't want to waste time taking her back to the ship, and so he took her back to Caine's and Jade's townhouse.

He was frantic to touch her. She was just as frantic to let him. Their lovemaking was passionate, wild, and filled with love.

Sara was sprawled on top of her husband in the center of the bed. Her chin was propped on top of her folded hands, and she was staring down into his beautiful eyes.

He looked thoroughly content. He was gently rubbing her backside in a haphazard way. Now that they were all alone

Nathan was able to tell her how much he loved her without turning gray at all. He was a bit of a romantic. He opened the drawer of the table next to the bed, pulled out a piece of paper, and handed it to her.

"Pick out the ones you like," he ordered.

She chose "sweetheart," "my love," and "my sweet" from the list of endearments on the sheet. Nathan promised to memorize them.

"I used to be a little envious of Jade," she told him. "I didn't think I could ever be like her, and my staff kept making comparisons."

"I don't want you to be like anyone else," he whispered. "Your love has given me such strength, Sara."

He leaned up to kiss her. "I have come to rely on your love. It became my anchor. It was the one certainty I had, and it took me a long while to realize it."

"How long will it take for you to have complete faith in me?" she asked.

"I already have complete faith in you," he argued.

"Will you tell me all about your past?"

He looked a little wary now. "In time," he finally agreed.

"Tell me now."

He shook his head. "It would only upset you, sweetheart. I've led a rather black life. I've done a few things you might consider . . . worrisome. I think it would be better if I just tell you one story at a time."

"Then it is only out of consideration for my tender feelings that you hesitate to tell me about your past?"

He nodded.

"Were some of these things . . . illegal?"

Her husband looked highly uncomfortable. "Some would say they were," he admitted.

It took all she had not to laugh. "I'm happy you're so concerned about my feelings, husband, and now I know you only hesitate to tell me about your past because I might worry, and *not* because you think I might accidentally blurt out anything of significance."

The sparkle that came into her eyes puzzled him. She was up to something, but he couldn't imagine what it could be. He wrapped his arms around her waist and let out a loud, satisfied yawn. He closed his eyes. "I know you love me," he whispered. "And in time—say five or ten years, my love—I'll tell you everything. By then you should have become accustomed to me."

She did laugh then. He was still a little scared. Oh, she knew he trusted her, knew he loved her, but it was all so new for Nathan, and it was going to take him time to rid himself of all his shields.

She didn't have any such problems, of course. She'd loved him for the longest time.

Nathan blew out the candle and nuzzled his wife's ear. "I love you, Sara."

"I love you too, Pagan."